Opprobrium

Book One of
The Lamentation's End Series

By Wade Lewellyn-Hughes

Publisher: Wisdom, Wonder & Whimsy Books
Front cover illustrator: Andrew Ryan
Developmental edit: F. Nicole Reynaud Peavey & Bryce Hughes
Copyeditor/Proofreader: Tammy Salyer, Inspired Ink Editing

ISBN-13: 978-0-9908175-4-3
ISBN-10: 0990817547
Version 2: 2017

WWWBOOKS
Wisdom, wonder, & whimsy books

This story is dedicated in loving memory to
Jessica Lee Phillips,

a friend who never required an explanation.

Free ebook!

When you sign up to join my newsletter, you'll receive a free ebook (pdf, mobi, or epub file) of *The Merchant's Son* novella as well as updates on current and future works on occassion.

Sign up for the newsletter at:

www.wadelewellyn.com

Contents

Fort Rodas

Peddleworth

Fort Calhoun

Rocksland

Conwy

Llandir

The Mint
Coast

Racine

Granville

THE GALLAIC CHANNEL

erith

Wycombe

Mindleton

Merith

"The King beheld his nightmare, his property made whole.
Choked in silence, his last breath sired the echoes of chaos."
—Sister Mariswell Ulthragar, the Chronicles of Cyr

Prologue

Few things drove Tadd to seek out Tinny Babcock. But when he heard Lissa's news, he marched straight to Tinny's stall and bartered more fish than he should have. Then he dashed off with the jug of moonshine all out in the open, only realizing his mistake once he reached the bay. He didn't care. Not today. The Judges could shove their flaming laws up their asses.

He lay there in his dory, staring at the waxing moon until the sky went dark around it and his blood slowed enough to let him think. Tadd took another swig and sucked in the sea air to relieve the burn in his throat.

Lissa would tear him to shreds later. His tunic had sopped up the fishy stench along with the puddle on the floor. At least it was cool. Little soothed this late in the Merithian summer.

South Thornton's port had grown quiet with the dark. The breaking waves and the tide bumping his starboard hull against the dock post made the only noise. Not even the gulls squawked a fuss down by the fishmongers' stalls. How late was it?

He should be home. It wasn't right of him to have left in such a flash, not when they'd just been told. One week. That was all he had left with his son. After the holiday, Ifan would leave the city gates and head off to his new home—Gower Port of all places, clear on the other side of the island!

They wouldn't see Ifan again until they were all in the Glades. Tadd blinked at the seven emerald lines crossing over the face of the pale moon. Only there, in the land of the dead, would his family reunite.

As he sat up, Tadd's blurred sight lowered to farther out in the bay, landing on the Great Barrier, a granite wall surrounding the island nation of Merith. He couldn't spot the archers patrolling the lantern-lit ramparts between its drum towers, but he knew they were there. His pulse quickened. Their lot, the Chancellor's army, would punish them if Ifan didn't go. "Bastards!" he yelled.

Shocked by the echo of his voice, Tadd sank against the floor of his boat and prayed to the Chancellor that they hadn't heard him. Footsteps creaked down the dock. Cold sweat beaded on his forehead.

"If I didn't know it was forbidden, Tadd Bowen," a young man's voice said, "I'd guess you were drunk." Judge Barret's frosty eyes sent Tadd scrambling back against the stern.

Respectfully, Tadd dropped his gaze to the three blue waves of the South Thornton crest on the man's tabard, then lower to the gauntlet squeezing the pommel at his waist. Tadd meant to splutter an apology but blurted, "They're sending my boy to Gower Port! You can't take a man's son and expect him to be happy about it."

Judge Barret hushed Tadd with a raised hand and glanced back down the dock. "But that's what the Seeding does, Tadd. By sending your boy north, the Tribunal gives Gower Port a skilled fisherman. It strengthens Merith and keeps its men from marrying their sisters." Tadd shook his head. "You knew this day would come the moment Lissa had a boy. It's been this way for generations. You have to make your peace with that."

"He doesn't turn eighteen for three more days! I should have another year. We thought we had another year!"

"He'll be nineteen by the next Seeding . . ."

Tadd bit his tongue. There was nothing more he could say to a Judge that wouldn't have him burned for blasphemy. If that happened, he'd never see Ifan again; souls burned by the Chancellor's Light never reached the Glades.

"I'm going to look away, Tadd. When I turn back, there won't be a jug of moonshine in your armpit. That way I don't have to ask where you got it." A rarity among the Judges, Barret was sometimes the kind sort, so long as he was alone. Tadd knew any of the others would've already strapped him up or, worse, sent him to the spider. Without rising, Tadd pitched the jug overboard. When the splash ended, Judge Barret offered him a hand, which Tadd accepted.

After Tadd's butt hit the dock, Judge Barret said, "Go spend the time you have left with Ifan. And don't pull this again."

"Yes, of course, my lord." Too shaky to trust his legs, Tadd said, "I'll rest for just a moment and be on my way home. By the Chancellor's Light, you have my word and my thanks."

Judge Barret nodded, then scanned the pier for onlookers. He made his way back down the dock without a word and disappeared between the stacks of crates lining the wharf below the Bay District's warehouses.

Tadd rested his feet on the boat's gunwale as he sobered up. He'd named the boat *Rachelle* after his ma. Her soft thumbs on his cheeks . . . the tears in her eyes . . . that's what he remembered from when he had entered the Seeding and left to make his home in South Thornton. Poor Lissa.

He prayed to the Chancellor for Ifan's safety during the long trip north and for a happy life full of children Tadd would never see. Ready to face Lissa's wrath for storming off, he kissed his fingers and tapped them to *Rachelle*. Tadd got his sandals under him and staggered from barrel to barrel as he followed Judge Barret's path to the wharf.

The lifelessness of the port sent goose bumps up his arms. But then, the holiday was coming and that slowed trade down a bit. Just one foreign sail rose above the docked ships. Vetskarrans.

Tadd had been fishing in the bay earlier when the chains blocking the Great Barrier's portal had lowered to let the gruesome ship through.

It wasn't rare to see foreign crafts pass under the two-hundred-foot arch, but Vetskarrans were another story.

"Slavers," he mumbled. They usually stuck to the northern ports where nobles gathered: in the capital, along the Mint Coast, and of course Gower Port.

The longer Tadd stared at the ship moored to the neighboring pier, the more the sight knotted his gut. Iron spikes stuck out from the beak of the ship, serving well enough as a warning to decent folk that brutes were aboard. *Brutes that had seen trouble,* he guessed by the condition of their ship. Their strange fanning sails were riddled with holes, scorch marks ran down the port hull, and most of the shrouds had been cut beneath a snapped mizzenmast. That ship had survived either a mighty thunderstorm or a battle with magi. Leave it to foreigners to bring their troubles to Merith's shores.

On the deck, a figure slinked into the shadows. Tadd's muscles stiffened. His eyes scampered, refusing to stop searching for the figure that had vanished.

His sensibility kicked in and jolted his legs into motion. Crawling along the barrels, he kept his eyes on the silent slave ship and the nearby shadows. He wished he'd followed Judge Barret.

When the soles of his sandals hit the planks of the wharf, Tadd tried to run but mostly wobbled through the crates stacked on either side of the path. Reaching the worn stones of his street, he glanced uphill past the warehouses. The crammed homes of his neighbors didn't block the candlelit window of his second-story room. Lissa was waiting for him.

Glancing back at the Vetskarran vessel, Tadd nearly shrieked. Small for a Vetskarran, a figure with a glowing golden gaze stood at the base of the stairs leading up to the scarred ship's pier.

Tadd closed his eyes and shook his head. Tinny's moonshine played tricks on your mind if it'd been awhile since you'd had it. When Tadd opened his eyes, the man leered at him with human eyes.

Keeping the foreigner in his sight, Tadd managed a stumbling gait toward his home. He heard steps ahead of him just before a burlap sack swept over his head.

Two men hauled him back toward the pier.

Tadd cried out, but a thick hand slapped tight over the burlap covering his mouth.

"Hurry!" a man whispered.

Tadd struggled as his captors lifted him. Stronger than any men should be, they didn't so much as shift their balance when he shoved against them. Flailing, Tadd screamed again before another set of hands clamped his jaws closed. He moaned louder, praying Judge Barret still patrolled the wharf.

"I'm telling you, I smelled one," the man holding Tadd's mouth whined.

Their footsteps thudded down the pier now.

Tadd struggled and yelled as loudly as he could through his teeth. If the slavers got him on their ship, the Judges would not—no one would—find him before they set sail! He prayed that the Ashwin would look down into the bay. Stupid archers! As his abductors hustled up the ramp to their deck, he put everything into his scream, not drawing a breath until they carried him belowdecks into the musty hold of the ship.

They hurled him.

He landed hard on his left shoulder. When he attempted to remove the sack over his head, his arms were twisted back.

Two of the men jerked him up to his knees and held him there.

"I'm not a slave!" Tadd yelled. "I'm Merithian! The Chancellor will burn you for this!"

No one moved.

"He thinks we're slavers," an amused man's voice said, calmly and quietly, not at all like a Vetskarran. "I admit I am wondering your intent by bringing this man aboard. I trust it wasn't for my entertainment."

Tadd's abductors shifted. "I smelled one, Lirus," the whining man answered. "But this was the only human on the docks." He quickly added, "The watchmen weren't there. No one saw us take him."

"And yet," Lirus said as his light-footed steps approached the man who had spoken, "he is not a magus." The whiner yelped. "You risked drawing attention to us for what? Can you not contain your appetite until Beez is ready?"

"Not food, Lirus," he cried. "We'll need numbers!" Something struck the whiner before he hit the floor. "But-but what about the magus I smelled?"

"I'll get it," a woman said from deeper in the hold.

"Stop!" Lirus yelled. "All of you, stop! We don't have the collars to hold more magi. When Beez wakes, he'll decide which he'll keep. Our task is to set the trap *without* creating suspicion. Is that clear?" Tadd didn't hear their responses. "Good."

"What about him?" the woman asked, nodding in Tadd's direction. "Is he food?"

The hunger in her question made Tadd's heart thunder louder. He felt it in his throat and shouted again. A meaty hand slapped over his mouth hard enough to burst his lip. Tasting the blood, Tadd bucked to no avail.

"He's not pretty enough to be a pet," the man holding his mouth said into his ear.

A silence hung for a moment before Lirus said, "We do require numbers. Grusk, bite him and his family and anyone else who might raise an alarm when they're missing for a few days. The High Guard cannot suspect a thing." The brute to Tadd's left released his mouth and stood.

With all of his strength, Tadd pressed against the man still holding him down but didn't budge him an inch. "Leave my family alone, demons!"

Strange popping noises, like branches snapping, came from the captor who had risen. The man grew against Tadd, pressing him into his other abductor. Bristles brushed against Tadd's forearm before a bestial panting lowered by his ear. A deep growl shook Tadd to his core.

He squirmed and shouted, "You'll never defeat the Tribunal! The Chancellor's Light will burn you all, Abandoned demons! Your filth will never enter the Glades to—"

A hot maw clamped over Tadd's shoulder, stabbing him deeply. Tadd lost control of his body. Warm spit and blood drained down his chest and back.

"When you wake, you will gladly tell us where to find your family," Lirus said. Tadd thought to fight back, but the beast bit deeper. "Welcome to the pack."

Chapter I: Bonds

Cord lay awake and fingered the word ASHWIN carved into the underside of Marlone's bunk. No crickets chirped, offering luck to his ascension as an archer of the Chancellor's army.

"I don't wanna be a slave, even for pretend, you know?" Marlone said from above.

Cord replied, "I don't wanna be burned alive, you know?"

Marlone leaned over the side of his mattress. His dusky face receded into a dimpled smile. "You'll be fine. I'll watch your back." He lay back. "I'll be branded because I can't hide my skin."

"You won't," Cord said. "You heard the headmaster. He saw a watchman with dark skin that time he went to Croathe. If they didn't brand that guy when he went through the testing, they're not gonna brand you."

"What if his skin was lighter than mine?" Marlone asked. "He coulda been lucky."

Propping himself up on his elbows, Cord said, "Nah. It'd raise too many questions, and we both know they don't want questions about the Catalyst rank."

With a sigh, Marlone sagged over the edge again and let his arm dangle. "Yeah, I hope so."

"I'll be there to watch your back too. The headmaster said that's why they're sending both of us to South Thornton."

Marlone's frown grew. Pretend slaves required pretend masters.

Cord shrugged an apology. They were both going to hate this rank, even if it meant they had finally ascended into the Chancellor's army. "You'll be back in Kenton before you know it."

Marlone grunted. "That's not much of a trade," he muttered, "not if you get to patrol the Great Barrier."

"*If* I survive the next three years *and* qualify."

Drawing his arm back up, Marlone propped his chin on his hand. "Is the army where we belong, Cord?" Cord pulled his blanket up and ignored the heresy. "South Thornton is a big city. If your . . . if *it* happens again, there are places we can hide."

Rolling away from him, Cord said, "I guess. Maybe I'll be your first catch. At least then this curse would serve a purpose."

Marlone slid down to the floor and sat next to Cord. He picked up Cord's belt and pulled out the knife.

Cord sat up.

Quick and sure, Marlone ran the blade down his right palm. He squeezed his hand into a fist. Blood dripped through his fingers as he offered Cord the blade. "Cord, I swear—magus or not—I won't mark you as Abandoned."

Cord took the knife and hesitated, not for the pain, but for the risk of touching another wound. He sliced his right palm. "Marlone, I swear I never made a deal with any demon, and I'll never mark you as Abandoned." He saw fear in Marlone's eyes too, but they clasped their bloody hands together.

Sure enough, the curse came; a shocking chill in Cord's elbow was the only warning he had. It jolted to his hand and into Marlone. A trance trapped Cord. As the chill filled them, Marlone shook. The skin on Marlone's hand re-formed, sealing his wound. Warmth washed down Cord when the trance broke. They both fell back panting.

A second cut appeared on Cord's palm, though smaller than it had been on Marlone's. His arm went limp. Exhaustion plunged him into sleep.

* * *

"Son of a bitch," Cord growled when he found himself in another nightmare. He reached for his belt knife, but the dream had swept him to these dark woods in his smallclothes.

Looming high above him, a giant oak dominated the sky, a storm cloud of branches and turbulent leaves, just as he'd seen last time. Like in that nightmare, snarls and barks sounded behind him. Racing away from the grunts, he glanced back but couldn't see his hunters through the trees. Praying that touching the strange oak would wake him this time too, Cord kept his path straight. In his bare feet, he leaped roots and branches.

Lightning struck the ground. The sudden quake stunned him. More lightning bolts penetrated the branches above and speared the woods.

Beyond the thunder, a nearby chortle snapped him out of his stupor. Cord darted ahead, bursting through undergrowth. He reached the oak's roots and scrambled up to the trunk. His hand slapped the bark. He spun to face his hunters. A flash of light filled the woods.

* * *

On the city of Brewing's Farrier Road, Scarlett studied Grary Jeth's window from below and tongued his handiwork, the gap in her smile next to her right eyetooth. The candlelight in his room had been snuffed out over an hour ago. Time for her revenge.

Leaving the cobblestones to the moonlight, she wrapped her shawl tightly around her neck and stalked through Master Jeth's smoke-scented blacksmith shop. Her bony fingers gingerly gripped the latch to the Jeths' home.

Dark and quiet, the Jeths' home had once felt welcoming, in a time when Scarlett would never have dreamed of stealing from them. But their son had poisoned that warmth and reduced his family to acceptable foes. Apples not falling far from trees and whatnot.

Scarlett slipped off her boots and tiptoed to the cupboard where Mrs. Jeth buried everything of importance to her in the potatoes. She knelt and carefully excavated an unassuming wooden box. After raising the cache's lid, she found various mementos of Grary's youth, a rare coin from the continent, and an emerald earring Lady Gwirion had lost a few months earlier. They all covered one slip of parchment. Scarlett sighed at the parchment: a merchant license. That wouldn't help. No, she needed a particular document, one certain to seal Grary's fate. She set everything back as she'd found it and closed the cupboard.

Softly stepping up the stairs, Scarlett tongued the gap from her missing tooth and stoked her anger for another fight. She pressed against his chamber door. It swayed quietly. There lay the brute on his bed beneath the window. Moonlight accentuated the scar Kylan had carved up Grary's cheek and over his nose.

Scarlett tugged on her bottom lip, contemplating how easily she could end him now without interruption. *If* she were certain she'd be joining Kylan and Rorry in their escape to the continent, she could. But if she decided to stay in Merith—to stay home—she'd have to play this smarter.

On the floor, rolled parchment stuck out of Grary's crumpled britches. Slipping the scroll free of his pocket, Scarlett smiled at the ingredient for Grary's passive murder. His Seeding papers.

With a blank decoy left in its place, she rose and twiddled the scroll in her fingers, silently gloating to the sleeping man who had depredated her friends. He deserved worse. Tit for tat in her opinion.

As her temptation rose and threatened to force her into fleeing with her friends, she backed away. Her victory felt shallow, but time would fix that. The desire to end him grew as she moved downstairs, coaxing her to do more. So, she did.

Sated with the Seeding papers and Lady Gwirion's emerald earring in her possession, Scarlett moved outside to don her boots.

Once she had put a few roads between her and the blacksmith's house, she unrolled the parchment and read it fully. Grary was supposed to go to Llandir in the Seeding too? Kylan would've hated that. The thought conjured memories of their fight. After what he'd done to Kylan—after what he'd done to Rorry . . .

Flames fluttered up the edges of the documents. Scarlett gasped and dropped them. She stomped out the fire and glanced around for witnesses to her accidental spell. After scooping up the singed papers, she ran home to plant them in her mum's garden.

Chapter 2: No Guarantees

A quiet conversation woke Cord. He rolled over to find his headmaster on a stool in the slanted morning light. The odor of burned sage told Cord that the headmaster had gotten up early to pray for them.

The twinkle left the headmaster's eyes when his gaze fell on the bags that Marlone had packed. Their elder's brown robes almost swallowed him as he leaned toward Marlone. "You know my thoughts on slavery," Headmaster Angsly said with whistling Ss. "I know they're heretical; may the Chancellor forgive me, I do. But I'll never understand how one man can disregard another's—"

The headmaster cut himself off with his hands raised. "At the rate the cities trade for foreign slaves, I doubt you were descended from the Abandoned tribes of Shallyghal." His cheeks purpled with anger. "The Chancellor himself saved you from the life of a slave so that you could serve in his army. Nevertheless, others beyond Kenton's palisade may not give you any more consideration than a branded slave."

Marlone said, "I'll be back before you know it."

"We both will," Cord added. He swung his legs over the side of his bunk and sat up. "You've trained us well. In a city, the testing can't be too hard. In three years—as soon as they let us, we'll come home."

Through the headmaster's unkempt cottony beard, his face wrinkled in a proud smile. That beard used to be as black as Cord's hair. "I'll pray for it every day," the headmaster replied. "Training you two boys is my greatest accomplishment in my devotion to the Chancellor. Yet I find my pride lies in the men you've become. I wish Nemma could see how you've grown."

Hearing his old nurse mother's name forced Cord to control his blinking. He tried to distract himself with the headmaster's whistling *Ss* but couldn't find the humor in it now.

Rising into the posture he assumed when addressing the village from the altar, the headmaster said, "You'll need to be careful, boys. The world you're entering isn't like this hamlet. Cities, like this South Thornton, are filled with greedy people who have no time for their neighbors. Enforcement spurs their devotion to the Light, instead of faith."

Headmaster Angsly put his hand to his back as he looked them over. Three tears trailed down the man's cheeks. "My boys . . . always look for the good in people but know the potential for evil in your own hearts. Stay in his Light and be the pride of Kenton and this academe."

Outside in the square, Widow Shinn shouted greetings of good morning to someone.

"If she's up," the headmaster grumbled, "the rest of the town will be soon. I'd better prepare for the sermon." He pulled out a pointed cap matching his robes in wear and color, wiped his face, and slipped the cap over his thinning hair. "Go say your prayers before the Idol. Rex will gather your bags." As he closed the door behind him, he said, "Do come home safe."

Marlone had forgotten to pack the aged vellum scroll swinging on the back of the door, tacked there ever since their first lesson. No, that needed to stay. Commoners and slaves wouldn't own drawings of battle stances. They couldn't even read the script.

Cord rubbed his right palm. It had already healed except for a thin scabbed line. A source of pride? Not with the curse of magic hiding in his bones.

At least he wasn't enduring the test alone. Yes, he had fair skin and a sharper nose than Marlone. But he had the same brown eyes and sense of humor. The world outside of Kenton might not see it, but they were brothers.

"I know I'm good lookin'," Marlone said with a dimpled grin, "but you don't have to stare."

Cord sniffed and got up. He dressed in plain clothes and led the way down the hallway's creaking floorboards to the nave's polished stone. Recessed into the wall, the Idol waited on its pillar. He and Marlone, the only cadets of Kenton, knelt before it.

Iconic red armor and a prominent nose identified the statue to all as the Chancellor. Though the paint had chipped and cracked, Cord already missed the Idol. However big and fancy, South Thornton's Idol would never feel as sacred to him.

Fixing his eyes on the flickering flame in the Idol's hand, Cord recited his morning prayers to the Light. Before he was halfway through, he felt Marlone watching him. "What?"

"Remember when we were kids and we'd pretend we were living in the wilds?" Marlone whispered.

"Yeah?"

Marlone gave a meaningful shrug.

"No, Marlone. We live in the Light."

The curved walnut doors of the academe creaked opened, returning the cadets to their prayers. Headmaster Angsly and skinny Ol' Rex came inside. On his way to the chapel, the headmaster released a heavy sigh.

When they were gone, Cord glanced over at Marlone, who watched the Idol's flame blankly. "You'll be fine."

Marlone murmured, "But what about you?"

Cord clenched his jaw and said through his teeth, "We're not talking about that in front of the Light." He sealed his lips when someone opened the doors again.

He glanced back to see Leila Moore sniffling and dabbing a moist kerchief to her swollen eyes. Her honeycomb-colored curls hung about her weary face as she came toward them with her full attention on Marlone's back.

Cord tilted his head to get Marlone to turn.

Upon seeing Leila, Marlone rose and held out his arms. Leila threw her weight against him.

Cord went about finishing his prayers.

"I don't know what I'm gonna do without y'all," she said in a voice muffled by Marlone's chest. "I wish I'd known that last Hansweighn's feast was our last together. I thought you wouldn't leave until the Seeding began."

"Hey," Marlone said softly. "I may be back in three years. Ol' Rex isn't getting any younger."

When the doors swung wide, she stepped back from his embrace. "That's true," Leila said in a suddenly lively voice, signaling her husband had followed her inside. "You're not choosing to patrol some silly wall on the coast."

Cord stood and returned Leila's teasing smile before he nodded to Tomlin, who was propping the entrance open with a stone. "And I'll be home as often as they allow."

Leila hugged Cord's neck. "You'd be home all the time if you'd give up your fascination with bows and stop flinging sticks like some Abandoned elf. Are you so awful with a sword that you can't be a Judge?"

"Sometimes I think it's the call of the forbidden that draws me to it," Cord said just above his breath. "You wouldn't understand something like that."

She made a face, warning him to tread lightly. After years of practice, his habit of teasing her had well-established limits, which had lessened since her marriage last winter.

Tomlin approached and waited a few feet behind his wife. Scrawny for a city fellow, the stretch of a man had looked downright sickly last year when he'd seen where the Seeding had sent him. If it were allowed, Cord suspected Tomlin would've run all the way back to Granville. Of course, that had only been until he'd spotted Leila. In that second, she'd owned Tomlin's heart.

"You'll be careful?" Leila asked, taking one of each of their hands in hers. "Leave the adventures for when you get home. I'm not gonna be there to save you."

Cord mocked her with a laugh. "You're the one who told your father we cut holes in the palisade to let the skunks outta town. You still think you're the better liar?"

Leila asked, "And whose idea was it to cut the holes in the first place?"

"Yours," Cord and Marlone answered in unison.

Her smile admitted nothing. Others meandered in and began filling the entryway.

Tomlin cleared his throat. "Leila," he said, "we should send them off appropriately."

Leila squeezed their hands and let go before curtsying to the Idol. She held Marlone's gaze as she dipped. With a shaky lip, she swept off to the chapel.

Tomlin wasn't a fool. With a bow to the Idol, Leila's husband said his polite farewells without extending his hand and stepped aside for the line of villagers waiting to wish them luck before moving on to the sermon.

Leila's mother, Mrs. Dunkel, took their hands the same way her daughter had. "I know it's a few days from Hansweighn," she said, "but I gave Rex some custards I made for you boys, anyhow. I don't know what they eat at their holiday feasts in South Thornton, but I couldn't bear you doing without this year." That custard had as much chance of surviving to midday as the summer morning dew.

After she kissed their cheeks, the entire village filed past in a blur, mostly offering hugs and some handshakes with their well-wishes. Even the ever-tardy Wynnes managed to arrive before the sermon began.

The villagers believed he and Marlone were off for more training before they received their post assignments.

Cord hated lying to them but revealing the true nature of the testing resulted in being listed as a deserter, labeled Abandoned, and burned alive. Few secrets in the army carried the weight of the spying rank of Catalyst.

When Ol' Rex impatiently waved for them to follow him outside, Cord smirked at Marlone. Rex had donned his finest watchman uniform for their send-off. The symbol over his heart, the embroidered green lines of the Glades, hadn't even begun to fray.

Marlone didn't notice. His eyes lingered on the door of the chapel, where the sermon had just begun.

Cord nudged Marlone and trailed Rex into the village square.

Surrounded by their neighbors' cottages, the square bid them farewell with a breeze swaying the wedding bell's broken clapper.

On the Barrows' porch, three rocking chairs huddled around a barrel with a Trinity game board. Simon Dunkel had been thrilled to take Cord's place in the game that had already lasted two days. Simon's father might ignore the wooden dragon tail Simon had moved out into the open, but Master Barrow's trefoil would take it in the next turn. Poor Simon wouldn't hear the end of that mistake for months.

Just as competitive, Mrs. Dunkel's rose mallows rivaled Mrs. Barrow's blue hydrangeas in an unspoken duel that had waged for years and had even spread to other yards down the main road. Their rivalry had nearly shifted into an alliance when it had become clear neither of the ladies brought life to the square like the Lloyds' green thumbs, ringing every tree in orange butterfly weed and purple starclusters.

Over the fragrance of the gardens, Cord smelled an unattended sweet potato pie cooling. Lucky for it, he had somewhere else to be. With his home securely painted in his mind, he moved away from the headmaster's voice coming through the chapel windows.

Down the main road, Ol' Rex flicked his hand at Cord's horse, Scute.

Bred and trained in Croathe, the black warhorse had a deeper chest and more intelligence in his eyes than any of the horses that had ever passed through Kenton's gate, possibly more than any watchman.

Running a hand down Scute's neck, Cord asked, "You're ready to go, aren't you, boy? Thank you, Rex."

Ol' Rex grunted something in response before he raised his upper lip in a disgusted manner, which meant he was about to say something nice. Instead, he turned about-face and marched back to the front of the academe.

"So, now we wait?" Marlone asked.

"I suppose so," Cord answered, still examining the watchman's work. Everything appeared in order, possibly even done with care.

Singing flooded from the chapel, signaling the end of the sermon. A scratchy voice joined in. Ol' Rex belted "Honored to Serve" while saluting them.

Cord chuckled before he could help it. Lost to the world again, Marlone didn't smile.

"I never . . . I'm real sorry," Cord said, "for the way things . . . for you and Leila."

Marlone shrugged. "Even if I weren't a cadet, they'd never let us be together."

Cord wasn't sure if he meant the Judges, who would uphold that law, or the Dunkels, who had swiftly paired Leila off with Tomlin. He didn't know what to say that wouldn't encourage something reckless. If Marlone and Leila acted on their feelings now, she'd be put into slavery for disappointing her husband or her father or both, and Marlone would be sent to the spider.

The townsfolk emerged from the academe with their song. Headmaster Angsly raised his arms, signaling Cord and Marlone to lead them to the gate.

With heavy feet, Cord brought Scute around and started the procession up the main road. When they topped the hill by Widow Shinn's cottage, the town gate came into view below. Cord took one last look.

Kenton's other two watchmen, Nat and Higgel, guarded the palisade's doors from their raised platforms on either side. Rounder with each passing year, Higgel joined in the song and saluted them. Nat leaped down and flung the gate open with a mumbled farewell.

Through the exit, a dirt path curved around a full magnolia in the woods. Those were the wilds of Merith, the land between towns where every young man who entered the Seeding knew his life depended on staying within ten feet of the road. This was where their test truly began. Once they stepped outside, there were no guarantees.

Cord stopped. He released Scute's lead and ran back to the shocked crowd, who stumbled over their lyrics. Grabbing his frail headmaster in a hug, Cord squeezed him tight. The small man laughed and hugged him back. As his neighbors' hands patted him farewell, Cord tried to regain control of his blinking and fixed the headmaster's askew hat.

"Live in his Light," the headmaster said.

When the villagers began awkwardly repeating the final verse of the song, Cord wiped his cheeks on his sleeve and made his way back to Marlone. He took up Scute's lead, prayed, and moved through the threshold into the land of witches and trolls.

The townsfolk swarmed the exit as their song came to an end. Leila waved one last time before Nat swung the gate closed. Higgel continued to salute them until they had walked out of sight beyond the magnolia.

Marlone threw his arm over Cord's shoulder as they set off for the Southern Road. When Marlone pulled his arm back, he said, "You know, this is as free as we'll ever be. Are you sure we shouldn't just make this home?"

The headmaster's last words still rang in Cord's ears. "We live in the Light, Marlone. As long as I can hide it, we'll be fine."

Marlone gave a half nod. "I'll be a slave and you'll hide the magic you can't control. Great plan."

"I won't desert," Cord said. "We'll pass the testing. Nah, better than that; we'll find so many Abandoned they'll let *you* choose your post."

Marlone just shook his head.

"We owe it to the headmaster to try."

"I guess so. But who is to say they deserve it any more than you do?"

Cord brought Scute to a stop and gestured up to the saddle. "Go on."

"I thought we lived in the Light?" Marlone asked.

"It's a stupid law. It doesn't go against the Light. We're not swearing allegiance to a demon and casting spells. Besides, I already swore I'd never turn you in."

Marlone dismissed it with a shrug. "And if we're seen by the Judges patrolling the roads?"

"Run," Cord answered. "Maybe a cricket heard your wish."

Grinning, Marlone mounted Scute.

Cord knew he shouldn't encourage the notion but carried on with a sharper watch on the road ahead and the comfort of having Marlone keep his questions to himself.

Chapter 3: Partial Peers

Two days into the wilds of Merith, they'd reached the delta, where every patch of woods within spitting distance of the road had too many places to hide. The sensation of eyes on Cord's back returned as he stood knee-deep in the bayou. "Probably thick with gators," he mumbled. Maybe it wasn't his best idea to leave Marlone at the road with Scute while he hunted. At least the mosquitoes had taken a break under the full bake of the midday sun.

Minnows scattered around his legs with each step that stirred the silt from the bottom of the refreshing lazy stream. It almost made the wilds bearable. If they did desert, it'd be easy to hide in this knotted marsh. Water. Plenty of food. They could do worse than gators for neighbors.

What was he thinking?

He scanned the shoreline around him. Witches and trolls would love this place too. And Hansweighn began at sundown. In a few hours, they'd be confined within South Thornton and officially rank as soldiers in the service of the Chancellor's army.

He rubbed the skin on his left thumb, where the first injury he'd taken from Marlone had healed. Maybe Marlone was right. Their arguments about deserting had filled Cord's dreams with childish adventures. But in reality, they'd be hunted by the army and unsheltered by the Chancellor's Light—not slaying dragons and bedding the witch Daughters of Sepholina.

Cord raised his makeshift spear and let the world move around him, waiting for another fish to swim near. Maybe a bass worth eating this time.

There was one thing Cord knew for certain; he'd lance that muskrat on the shore if it didn't stop its ruckus, digging in the reeds as if it'd made a deal with a demon for an impenetrable pelt.

A fat shadow slipped into view along the bottom of the stream. Cord drew slow, shallow breaths as the catfish lazily drifted into a clump of waterweed. He twisted to aim and stilled himself. His fingers tightened around his whittled stick. The wide head of the fish grew clear as it swam forward.

"Now!" Marlone shouted.

Cord screamed and lost his balance, falling chest-deep below the water. The catfish darted upstream before the billowing cloud of silt concealed its escape.

Marlone bent over in laughter against a cypress on the shore.

"Son of a . . . very funny," Cord said, betrayed by his own grin. He stood up. "Laugh all you like. That was your lunch."

Lifting the spindly bass Cord had caught earlier, Marlone said, "I already have mine."

"That little thing? Not with the way you eat. Now if you'll shut up, or maybe go watch Scute like you're supposed to be doing, I'll catch more. It's a shame you can't help. All that time flirting, and no time hunting."

Marlone picked up Cord's boot and held it over the water.

"Hey now!"

Marlone dropped the boot back on dry land. Making a face at the catch in his hand, he asked, "Fish again, though? That's all we'll eat in South Thornton. I saw a stag on my way to find you. If the army had let you bring your bow, we coulda had venison."

Closing his eyes, Cord pretended the too-thin shaft in his hand was his bow. With it, his resolve to stay in the wilds would be challenged. They probably could survive out here. "Even if I had it, we wouldn't have time to clean a deer."

"We *could* take all the time we wanted."

"This again." Cord groaned. "Stop making me repeat myself. We're a few hours from South Thornton. Can't you resist your temptation just a little longer?"

"We'd live as free men."

"Until they found us," Cord said. "The Judges would hunt us down like Abandoned! And we'd receive the same punishment as those demon worshippers. I don't wanna leave the Chancellor's Light, and I don't wanna be burned alive."

"You're already Abandoned," Marlone said with a grin. "You're a magus!"

"Why don't you just yell that shit!" Cord growled as he glanced around.

"Out here," Marlone said, "we don't have to worry about someone eavesdropping."

"No. We have to worry about witches and demons and trolls— never mind bears and wolves and gators." Cord tossed his spear aside, waded to the shore, and wrung out the bottom of his tunic.

"Aren't you gonna catch more?" Marlone asked as Cord picked up his boots.

"Let's just get outta here." Cord set off barefoot toward the road. "I'd rather go hungry than argue about this again."

"I'm arguing for your sake as much as mine."

"Don't," Cord said without turning. "I'm ready to ascend the ranks. I *am* worthy."

"Right. You can hide the magic," Marlone mocked. "Why didn't you before?"

Cord leaped puddles and sped across any grass he could find. Sticks tempted him to put on his boots, and the mud tried to slow him, but he powered through. He wouldn't let Marlone's muttering catch up to him. There was nothing left to say. Before long, Cord found the spot by the road where Marlone should have built a fire. He froze.

Scute glanced from Cord back to the rider on the road.

The sunburned stranger looked down on Cord from atop his cream-and-brown-dappled steed. He was Cord's age, too young to be in the army, and dressed as a commoner, even if his threads were finer than Cord's. Curly blond hair fluffed out about the sharp angles of his face. His pale blue eyes watched Cord expectantly from above his upturned nose.

Outside of the Seeding, which started tomorrow, only nobles and soldiers roamed the roads between towns; he had to be another cadet.

"Howdy," Cord said. The stranger squinted but said nothing. "Another cadet, I take it?"

"You should be careful what information you offer to strangers on the road," the rider said, then gave a friendly smirk. "In this case, you are correct." His words were slow and clear, like the northern soldiers forced to seek shelter in Kenton on their way south during the winter. "Julian Westcott, from Croathe."

Cord wondered if Julian's level stare was in anticipation that Cord would react with outright awe or an expectation that he would kiss the Croathite's boots for being from the Chancellor's own city. Regardless, Cord didn't twitch a muscle. "Cord Sullivan, from Kenton. Well met."

Julian nodded.

"This road leads to South Thornton. Is that where you're heading?"

"It seems we are set to be peers, wooder," Julian said.

Cord couldn't tell if he was teasing or just being a jackass. It wasn't the first time someone had called him a "wooder." During the Harvest Trade, the merchants in the nobles' caravans often called the villagers that. Some intended the insult to mean they were uneducated filth. Others thought that's what they called themselves, so where was the insult?

"Yes," Julian said. "It was meant as a joke. Testing got you nervous?

Do not be. If we work together, it will be easy. Stick with me; I never fail." He reached down to his saddlebag, pulled out a green apple, and lobbed it to Cord. "Here. I brought plenty." The apple's skin was shiny without a single brown spot.

Julian jerked his head southward. "There was a Judge from South Thornton visiting my academe before I left. He filled me in on some of the city's secrets. If you are finished playing in the mud, I will share what I know while we ride."

"Thanks," Cord said. "Can't hurt to have another ally. We were just about to have lunch. Why don't you join us?"

"We?" Julian asked. "I only see one horse. Do you mean him?" He laughed.

Marlone stepped out from the brush, carrying the bass that Cord really wished was larger now.

Julian sat up in his saddle and quickly hid a sneer before Marlone noticed him.

"We have company, Marlone," Cord said. "Julian Westcott. From Croathe. He'll be our peer for the testing."

Marlone swapped the fish to his left hand and wiped his right hand off on his tunic. "Marlone Ruff," he said, moving forward. He extended his hand for a shake.

Julian shook and asked Cord, "That is your lunch?"

"A snack," Marlone said. "You can have some if you'd like."

"Julian just gave me this apple," Cord said. "He brought plenty."

"Ah," Julian said, turning to search the saddlebag across from the one with the apples. "It seems I was more accurate in packing than I thought. I only have my lunch left."

Cord grabbed his belt knife and chucked his apple into the air. In one quick motion, he split it and managed to catch both pieces in one hand. "It's all right. I don't mind sharing."

"Care to join us?" Marlone asked the Croathite.

Julian studied the road ahead as he formed his response but finally nodded. "I suppose there is no rush to get to the city, now that we are so close. I could break for a short time. Something that small should not take long to cook."

Marlone laughed.

As he dismounted, Julian said to Cord, "I am thankful to see you are not eating squirrels or other rodents as they say your kind do."

Malone shot Cord a slight scowl as he bent to lay the fire.

If Julian hadn't said it with a full smile, Cord would've told him to ride on.

"Wooders," Julian added with a chuckle.

After wiping the mud from his bare feet, Cord pulled on his boots. Julian began advising them on the best way to lay the fire, to strike the flint, and to debone and cook the fish. Then he sat to eat his own meal of dried meat and grapes. The Croathite didn't pray before eating.

Cord would've expected someone from the capital, the seat of the Tribunal, to follow the path to the Light better. He loudly led a prayer when their fish finished cooking.

Before Cord and Marlone had picked the bones, Julian retrieved a green apple from the plumper saddlebag and mounted. Julian's fidgety steed sidled when his rider crunched into the fruit. "A High Guard will be expecting us, you know? It is not wise to keep a member of the Tribunal waiting." With that, his horse walked onto the road.

By the time Cord and Marlone had wiped their hands off, Julian had ridden a couple hundred feet farther, now watching and waiting. Cord unhitched Scute's reins and decided to walk alongside Marlone, which only encouraged Julian to ride back and spur them on.

After awhile, Cord and Marlone slowed again to speak.

"We don't trust him, right?" Marlone asked.

"No, we don't." Cord walked backward to hide his face as Julian stopped ahead to check on them again. "I'm sorry. This won't be easy, I know. But we'll make it through the testing. I promise."

Marlone nodded. "It would've been nice to have the afternoon though." He already sounded defeated.

"Yeah."

Chapter 4: Refusing Conformity

Perched on her windowsill, Rorry te Gwirion mentally rehearsed the lies she would serve at the feast that night. She lifted her golden-orange locks, allowing the breeze to cool her neck.

Sunlight gleamed along the cracks in the delicate stained-glass rose of the window swung out before her. The memory of a bluebird's broken little body interrupted her plotting.

Rorry let her hair fall and snatched a leaf off the aged persimmon tree next to her. Where was Kylan? She leaned into the branches for a better view.

The impending holiday left only the diligent servants trimming hedge walls in the gardens below. Beyond the Gwirion manor's enclosure of lilac stone, the high street bustled in Brewing's Market District.

Between the thoroughly brown river-rock buildings, mothers haggled over sugar and eggs with the same single-minded insanity as every year. Fish, berries, and linens were sacrificed in great quantities for the opportunity to spoil their sons with custard one last time. No matter the cost, they left with smiles on their faces, believing themselves prepared for the Hansweighn feast.

Master Wilson hobbled along with his youngest, Dannel. He proudly stacked a fishing rod onto the provisions in his son's arms. Rorry would have recommended a new pair of britches instead.

Tomorrow, Dannel, like all of the young men Rorry's age, would leave Brewing forever. While Dannel made his first impressions in threadbare britches that were inches too short for his legs, his father would actually have a reason to be a curmudgeon.

Rorry picked apart the leaf in her fingers as she imagined how the widower would spend months denying he had to lean on the community now. Luckily for him, Brewing was quite stubborn when it came to supporting its men.

Giggles trilled from the street. Doe-eyed girls skipped along the cobblestones after a boy, who teased them back with gestures worthy of correction. The girls pretended offense and chased him faster than before.

Her eyes followed the innocents until a tall figure sauntered past the watchmen at the gate. Under the keystone embellished with the ivory swan and enameled ivy of the Gwirion crest, Kylan's father's straw hat concealed his face. Butterflies swarmed in Rorry's belly. Finally!

She threw the leaf scraps out the window and brushed off her hands.

Kylan casually navigated the garden in his favorite cotton tunic with the sleeves rolled above his elbows and the turned-down boots he had spent the last week sewing pockets into. His spectacles reflected the sunlight when he risked a glance up at her, displaying the tightly held smirk she expected.

Rorry scanned the garden. No one paid him any mind. Even if they had, Kylan had visited the manor frequently enough to get away with loitering in the gardens. He liberated a honeysuckle blossom as he made his way to the persimmon tree, then nonchalantly rested against the trunk.

While he sucked out the flower's nectar, Rorry stood away from the window and appraised her possessions one last time. On her washstand, the collection of glossy rocks from the Endelweix River rekindled memories of her antics with her friends. Rorry dismissed the temptation to take her favorites; they would be creating new memories far away from her father's city.

A frosted, half-full bottle of scent, a gift from her mother, pulled her eyes to the vanity. The foolishness of traveling through the wilds of Merith wearing rose-petal perfume rivaled that of carrying river rocks.

In the last corner of her room, the sketched face of Her Grace hung above Rorry's writing desk. The drawing had always been a source of pride for Rorry. Yet now, in her last hours of seeing it, she noticed how sad her mother appeared.

No. She needed to travel light, and these memories should stay here. Kneeling at her bedside, Rorry swept the cloud of pink curtains away and reached under the bed, running her hands over the smooth floor planks. She seized the supple handle of her satchel and drew it close.

Everything she truly needed had already been packed, including the diamond earrings and necklace her father had given her. They could be sold for a decent start once she reached the continent.

About to signal Kylan with a tap of her nails, Rorry paused and bit her lip. She threw the bag on her bed and raced to her linen drawer. There, she freed a thin towel and slung it over the padded armchair at her vanity.

Rorry unstopped the slender bottle of scent and let the subtle aroma overtake her. In momentary solace, her mind swung back to the day she had spent with her mother in Croathe. A splendid day of social requirements that she wished she had repeated the next day. With quick upturns of the bottle, her fingertips wet her neck with the rose water and spread it through her hair.

A purposeful cough from outside snapped her back into the moment.

Rorry sealed the bottle and swaddled it in the towel. With a prayer that it would remain closed, she placed it in her satchel, which bulged a bit but latched without effort.

At the window, Rorry peered through the leaves at the gardeners' backs. She tapped twice on the glass and held out her only possessions. Kylan rounded the trunk. She released her grip and heard the catch.

Without acknowledgment, Rorry paced barefoot and silently recited their plan for the twentieth time that day. She put her hand over her stomach. They were really doing this!

If she handled her deceptions well at the feast that evening, not even her mother would suspect her flight until after the morning's first prayers.

That was when Grary had told her to expect him, when he believed his ploy would end in victory. Even a blacksmith's apprentice gets caught in the Seeding's current. Instead of using his strength to fight it, Grary had decided to use her.

Rorry sat on her bed and clasped her elbows to still her shaking. They had been friends once. Rorry struck her mattress with her fists. Burn him!

Grary would not find her successful in securing her father's acceptance of their marriage, securing his life in Brewing. No, the oaf would discover her empty chamber and finally be rewarded his just deserts. By then, his blackmail and threats and her father's wrath could not catch her. Lord Gwirion had already punished one disgraced daughter. Rorry would not wait about to share her sister's fate.

Massaging the tension in her shoulders, Rorry heard voices in the garden.

One of the servants, Terin, had stopped Kylan on his way to the secret exit by the alley, likely to share her tale of finding the missing emerald earring in the roses. The narrow-shouldered gossip could talk to anyone for hours without realizing her listener had died three topics past. Thankfully, Terin was equally oblivious to the fine leather satchel slung over Kylan's shoulder.

Kylan glanced about the garden as he feigned amusement and took a half step away.

Someone knocked at Rorry's door. Gripping the pull on the window, Rorry murmured, "Just be rude and go."

A second series of knocks prompted Rorry to close the window and move to her vanity.

"My lady?" Aribella called through the door. "May I come in?"

Rorry's handmaiden eased the door ajar. Blonde wisps of hair appeared before Ari's good eye peeked inside.

Sitting up in her armchair, Rorry said, "Merry Hansweighn, Ari! I will don all of the trimmings tonight. Even this." Rorry wound her sister's cerulean silk ribbon through her fingers as she flourished it.

Ari's tiny hand pressed the door closed. "You're in rather high spirits today," she said, her eyes narrowing on the scrap of silk. A nervous smile suggested she planned to coax Rorry out of wearing the ribbon, a ribbon that Ari had rescued from a dress Her Grace had stashed away.

Rorry had no intention of wearing it; she merely wanted Kylan gone before Ari—

"Oh! The heat upstairs is stifling! Let me open the window before your bones melt." As Rorry watched in the mirror, Ari's broad hips shuffled across the room. Built for breeding, Ari occasionally hinted at complaints that her husband had not employed the attribute. Obligatory marriages often had to overcome obstacles.

If Rorry were staying, she would have made Jero aware that ten years of marriage with no offspring reflected poorly on him too. She sniffed. No, she would not. Once upon a time perhaps.

A breeze filled the room, launching the frizz of blonde hair tied behind Ari's head. Recognition brought her gaze back to the garden. "Terin's caught another poor ear. Is that Kylan Nock?" Ari's face held an unspoken question when she looked to the mirror. "My lady . . ."

Rorry sighed when she saw her handmaiden's jaw tighten. "Ari, leave it be. All will be explained in time."

"It is your satchel, then?" Ari's face splotched with red as she pieced it together. "You'll be labeled Abandoned, as surely as if you could touch magic. You'll be burned!"

With her father's steely expression on her face, Rorry tossed her orange tresses over her shoulders. "I believe I will wear my hair up for the feast."

Muted, Aribella retrieved the ivory comb from the vanity.

At Ari's twelfth stroke, Rorry broke the silence. "I am going to find her."

In the mirror's reflection, her handmaiden's worried pout drooped into a patronizing frown.

"Your sister is the most important person in your life. Would you deprive me of the opportunity to know my own?"

"I would never wish to deny you that, my lady. Nor would I wish for the Judges to find you out of your township unescorted. Your father is a powerful man, but even he may not be able to—"

"Burn him," Rorry muttered.

Ari set the comb down and wrung her hands. The banal clothes of commoners usually washed out Ari's features, but now eggshells offered more color.

Rorry softened her tone. "You did nothing wrong by telling me, Ari."

"Didn't I? If I'd kept my mouth shut as instructed, you wouldn't be tracking down a girl who may honestly be dead. Your parents never wanted you to know."

"To know my father declassed my sister into slavery and sold her overseas?" Rorry asked. "I am not surprised."

Ari shook her head as she moved to the dresser. Fidgeting while she worked, she laid out a lavender linen gown and a pair of elegant white shoes.

Rorry had not considered Ari's burden, never being able to know whether Rorry will have succeeded in her flight to the continent or will have been burned at the Judges' hands, all the while believing it could have been prevented if she had kept quiet. "Ari."

The plump woman looked at the dress, the washstand, and finally into Rorry's eyes.

Rorry went to her and took her hands. "There is no guilt in this for you. My decisions are my own. If anything, you have given me something to hope for."

Ari lowered her eyes to her clammy hands. "Your father has a kind heart. He's a good man."

Rorry flung herself onto her bed.

Ari continued, "I was just a girl when Alis died. Everything I told you was gossip—you know that."

Rorry propped herself against her elbow. "Gossip carries more weight when one is directed not to share it, Ari."

"But, my lady, I only told you because in those days following our return from the capital, you seemed so fragile, lost. I simply thought the gossip would distract you—fascinate you with a rumor to correct. Now I've made things worse. How was I to know you were no longer your father's defender? You never explained what happened—"

"At first," Rorry interrupted, "things were worse." She outwardly ignored the phantom scent of charcoal tingeing the air. Remembering those days summoned it without fail. Rorry sat up, brought her hair forward, and breathed in the rose scent. "Now, thanks to you, I have hope, a pursuit beyond Merith, and that never has to haunt me again." Rorry could tell Ari was trying to work out what she did not want to say. As unintentional as they were, Rorry's teary eyes calmed Ari's fidgeting. "Please. I will not receive another opportunity."

Ari considered her words and, surprisingly, let her questions about Rorry's motive go, giving three small nods, as good as a promise. "You are going with Kylan Nock? Will he bring his sister? And I assume Scarlett Hywel?" She fixed one of her cautious stares on Rorry. "Mrs. Hywel will hunt her down no matter how far you run. Remember—she's not from here." That was the one thing everyone in Brewing said about Rorry's tutor, which made it impossible to forget Mrs. Hywel was a foreigner, as though her cooing Racinian accent would not remind them.

As Ari readied Rorry for the Hansweighn feast, Rorry divulged nearly their entire plan, omitting the parts involving magic. Those pieces were hypothetical and dependent on Scarlett's abilities anyway. Handmaiden though she was, Ari possessed one of the brightest minds in Brewing. Rorry poured her worry into her assessment, which aligned with Scarlett's. The plan was sound up to reaching Llandir, if adamantly adhered to.

Finished with her work, Ari stepped back. Her lazy eye tried to keep up as she looked Rorry over. "It is good to see you smile again." She squeezed Rorry tight. "I have your word you'll avoid the roads?"

Humming agreement, Rorry hugged her back. "You should be heading home! Jero will need help in the kitchen."

"He never lets me help! 'The kitchen's my realm,' he tells me. Hansweighn is a quiet holiday for us." She drifted in thought for a moment. "Maybe I will try to cook him a surprise." A meek smile said she would not.

They exchanged admiring glances, and tears welled in their eyes once more.

As Ari put her hand on the door latch, Rorry remembered an important instruction. "Ari, I will leave a letter for you in the linen drawer. Do not break the seal. Have them read it to you. It would not do for them to know I taught you how." That would be paramount to proving Ari's ignorance of their plan.

With one last appreciative smile, Aribella left.

"Goodbye, Ari," Rorry breathed.

Folding her hands in her lap as she sat, Rorry beheld a strange sight in the vanity mirror. A year had passed since she had last dressed to her station. She swore more freckles appeared on her oval face with each passing year. The murky blue of her topaz earrings paired well with her eyes and the token of her arsenal, the cerulean ribbon woven through her upswept braids.

Invigorated, Rorry decided to write. A more apt mood for farewells would not come and neither would the time. With a quick peek to make sure Kylan had moved on, she went to the neglected desk in the corner.

Her eyes rose to the doleful portrait of her mother. Could she pen enough love to garner Her Grace's forgiveness? Rorry readied the ink for the letter. Clearly and concisely, she would provide the only motive available, finding Alis. If she believed it, her eloquence would flow. Though potentially an affront, that reason to flee warranted a blindly noble quest and did not come with a call for discipline in disgrace. Gilt and paint might goad Brewing into respecting their wealthy councilmember, but Rorry's eyes were opened to her father's deceptions.

For the past year, Rorry had felt she'd lost at a game of Trinity, moving as her father desired and backed into a corner by Grary. Cheat if she must, she would neither share her sister's fate nor serve a quiet sentence to reward Grary's depravity.

She put the quill point to the parchment. Sanguine assurances of Rorry's safety were all Her Grace required. She would escape! Escape and find Alis.

At the hilly edge of town, Kylan stood on Mill Road and tried to interpret what Scarlett wasn't saying.

Downcast thoughts spawned behind her slate-blue eyes. Skin and bones, she wilted against the tall dry-stone wall bordering Mrs. Hywel's garden. When he held out Rorry's satchel, Scarlett released the tendril of dyed ruddy hair she'd been twiddling and took it.

Kylan raised his eyebrow.

"What?" she asked.

"You know what." He spied around the wall to the pathway leading through the garden to her house, searching for any sign of her parents. "You are coming with us? Don't back out now."

Rather than look at him, she studied the bag's decoration that made her commoner dress appear all that much simpler.

"Don't you want to study at the Tower of Trône d'Argent? Think of all the libraries and scholars on the continent." As she worked out her response, he crossed his arms.

A gentle hum from the path spared Scarlett from answering. Kylan glanced around the wall. An older version of Scarlett's owl-like face whipped around inspecting the garden as Mrs. Hywel bustled toward them with a basket hung over her thick forearm. Dressed identically to Scarlett, the woman had forgotten to remove her apron, which Scarlett claimed she often did on purpose because it was slimming or some nonsense.

"Your mother," he said, grabbing Scarlett's waist. Kylan quickly lifted her to sit on the wall. Scarlett slipped the satchel into the azaleas on the other side as Mrs. Hywel reached the road.

An itch ran up between Kylan's shoulder blades when his squat tutor saw him. "Out saying your farewells?" she cooed in her faded Racinian accent. "You poor dear." Gripping him in a hug, she said, "Now, you remember, there are things no one needs to know about. I feel I've served you well in your education and don't deserve the Judges beating down my door due to some slip from a drunken tongue."

Kylan laughed it off. "Drinking is illegal, Mrs. Hywel. So you have little to worry about."

She fixed him with a familiar warning stare.

"Where are you going, Mum?" Scarlett asked, drawing her mother's attention up the wall.

Mrs. Hywel stepped back. "What are you doing up there? Get down before you hurt yourself!" Kylan helped Scarlett back to the road. "Honestly, a lady climbing walls like that. You're a noble's friend; you should behave like it even when she's not around. You wouldn't catch Rorry doing something of the sort." Mrs. Hywel thumbed at Kylan. "Now this one . . . Perhaps I should be counting my blessings that you're out of my hair."

"Jean," Master Clienne called, "you forgot the—"

He halted his dash down the garden path upon seeing them. Rounder than his sister and hardly taller, the white-haired Racinian had still beaten Kylan to a pulp in their final training. "Niece. Boy."

If Kylan never saw another quarterstaff again, it'd be too soon—or those flaming wooden sais. Ashes, it hurt to breath around the man.

Mrs. Hywel snatched something out of Master Clienne's hand and whisked it into her basket.

Kylan flinched when Master Clienne leaned forward. "You remember: there are things you don't tell others."

"We've covered that, Barrey," Mrs. Hywel said. Grabbing Kylan by the nape, she bent him down and kissed his cheek. "Do take care, love. Llandir is a beautiful city and a fitting new home for someone who swims as much as you do."

"Say goodbye, pea," Mrs. Hywel said to Scarlett. "Then catch up to me. I'm heading to the Market District for more spice." She squeezed Kylan's wrist and left.

Master Clienne slapped him on the arm as he followed his sister. "Remember what I've taught you. Listen to the wind and live. Get caught up in your thoughts and die."

Kylan had first heard those words almost a year ago, when Master Clienne had come to yell at him as he lay in bed recovering from his fight with Grary. At the time, Master Clienne had been angrier about Scarlett's involvement in the brawl than Kylan's failure. The combat lesson that had followed had reopened a few wounds but seemed to soothe his mentor while he made Kylan relive every mistake until they were all countered successfully, including a few Master Clienne threw in for his own enjoyment.

Once Master Clienne turned onto South Cart Way, Kylan rubbed his arm and joked, "I think your uncle is going to miss me. That slap on the arm . . . He may as well have cried."

Scarlett smiled slightly. "He will miss you. Whom will he knock around now? If all three of us leave, he has no one left to teach."

Kylan shot her a sidelong glance. "We can't do this without you."

Her eyes disagreed.

"I will see you tonight? Where we planned?"

She nodded and folded her arms as she walked away from him. He started to shout after her, fishing for an assurance she would come but knowing better than to push too hard. Closing his mouth, he went in the opposite direction.

It was time to go home. Kit must be wondering where he was, especially if their father already had her cooking. At twelve years old, she couldn't reach the third shelf in the larder and, just to spite Kylan, refused to use the stepstool their dad had built for her.

Maneuvering through the alleys behind the detached river-rock homes on the outskirts of Brewing, Kylan made his way downhill toward Lake Cashelle. He avoided the streets filled with sympathetic faces on people who'd never really known him but were now suddenly sorry to see him entering the Seeding. He didn't have time for them or the stale remarks they dusted off every year.

In the town sermon that morning, the headmaster had bestowed upon Brewing's young men the only thing worse than false sympathy: forced responsibility. Kylan didn't have any intention of representing his hometown's virtues, or the infernal Chancellor's Light. They had never known him at all.

Taking the long way around the academe, he came upon the quiet

North Lake Road. Jagging uphill, Kylan spotted the cedar fence surrounding his yard. He snuck around to the back, hopped up, and straddled the planks for a moment to take in the view.

Beyond his father's woodshop, the rocky cliffs stood guard over the Endelweix River feeding Lake Cashelle. A few fishermen's boats still idled with their lines in the water.

The sound of sawteeth cutting inside the shed meant his father hadn't realized the time yet either.

Near the shop, three lifewood saplings caught the wind in their round clusters of teal leaves. Kylan had hoped to see their red bark begin to curl before he left. It would've been nice to see his father excited about something again—and to be rewarded for all the singing he'd had to do to grow the things over the years.

He dropped down and scudded past the shop and the saplings on his way to the cabin. Scaling up the pecan tree, Kylan threw his father's straw hat through his opened window and leaped down without hesitation. He caught a branch and swung inside, landing on his bed with as much ease as his brothers had in the years before they had left.

"About time," Kit said from across the room. Kylan made a face up at his little sister sitting on Ellick's bunk. Her long braid of brown hair rested in her lap where she had forgotten to hide one of his figures. "What? I need you to get the pot. The iron one. It's too heavy for me."

Kylan sighed, removed his spectacles, and wiped the sweat from his face. "Fine. I'll be down soon. Now get out of my room and put the figure back. Who did you take?"

She clutched it tight against her chest. "I didn't." Panicked by his approach, Kit began to kick wildly.

Kylan caught her ankle and tugged her off the bed. He slung her onto Seamus's bunk and tickled her.

Kit shouted, twisted, and giggled. "Stop!"

"I'm not stopping until you give it back," he said, seizing her leg just above her knee.

"All right!" she screamed.

Kylan sat back and snagged the walnut figure, one of his earliest, rough in detail and far too short to be accurate now. He must've been

Kit's age when he had carved himself. With his fingertip, Kylan wiped the dust off his childlike face.

Kit kicked his back and scowled as she regained control of her breathing.

He set it down in front of her. "You can have it. I'll make a new one someday."

She got up and whipped her braid over her shoulder. "I don't want it."

"Ah." Kylan wrapped his arms around her and stood. He spun faster and faster until she laughed and hugged him back.

When he slowed to a stop, she said, "Promise you'll wake me up when you're leaving."

He kissed her head. "You know I'm not supposed to."

"Kids?" their father called from downstairs. "You'd better start dinner. It's gonna be sundown soon enough."

"Coming!" Kit yelled. She glared up at Kylan. "Dad said 'kids.' You have to help."

"Kit, you need to learn to do it alone."

She punched him in the gut.

Kylan growled through his teeth, "Fine. Go!"

Satisfied, she grinned, raced out of the room, and stomped down the stairs.

Kylan picked up his figure and walked to the long table at the end of his bed. Most of the people he had ever known waited there for him, all smiling up in pine, elm, oak, or whatever scraps his father had let him keep. Through the years, Kylan had captured the townsfolk and those long gone. He set his figure down by his mother eternally holding an armful of fabric and a tiny needle in her fingers.

His hand swept over the table to the Koppels and took the only mahogany statue in the lot. Kylan walked to the window and sat on his bed. A breeze from the lake tousled his hair as he admired the carving of Crispin Koppel. He had been generous to Seamus's friend, endowing him with attributes that Kylan couldn't remember beyond fantasies. Crispin was probably married now.

Kylan placed the figure on the windowsill, lay on his side, and took in the view of the boats on Lake Cashelle. How long had he daydreamed of setting sail with Crispin over the oceans of Cyr, hunting the treasures of the lost races?

What would Crispin say about that? He'd probably beat him to a pulp.

Looking back on it, Seamus must've known how Kylan had felt but had never told. It was kind of him to spare his brother from being dragged down the streets behind a rampant horse. Burn Merith.

"Son?" his father called from downstairs. Three times out of four, "son" worked for him. Kylan suspected Kit would be called that for years. Every time, it'd sting a little. But Merith's Seeding would do that to them, not him.

Lifting Crispin, Kylan kissed the figure for the last time. He moved to the table and set him between the other Koppels. Kit could have them all.

He no longer had to live in dreams.

Chapter 5: Let the Testing Begin

For the final miles to South Thornton, the three cadets took a trail running along the southeastern shore beneath the granite Great Barrier. Cord kept his eyes peeled for an Ashwin patrolling the high ramparts but didn't spot a single archer before they reached South Thornton's wall. He figured they had a long stretch to patrol, but something still nagged at him.

According to their directions, the stout doors of wood and rusted iron in the city wall led to the academe's compound. Echoing clanks of practice swords told Cord they were where they were supposed to be, even if his gut didn't agree.

Julian rode up to the gate and pounded against the planks. A metal slot in the door scraped open. Whatever the dark-eyed person behind the gate asked, it sprung Julian's back straight. With a purple face, Julian unleashed his tongue. When his fit ended, the portal shut. "Dumb tarheads," Julian mumbled.

Cord glanced over his shoulder, relieved to see Marlone was too absorbed in his thoughts to hear the insult. He prayed this was the right choice. To keep them living within the Light, he didn't see an alternative.

Come sundown, they'd rank in the Chancellor's service. This was what they had trained for. Once the academe stable opened and they were sealed within, he'd have to face the test before them and could forget his fantasies of deserting.

"Can you feel it?" Julian asked Cord, staring up the wall. "We stand on the edge of greatness."

"You must be wise," Marlone said. "I see a barred gate."

Julian didn't respond.

The sounds of sparring faded from the other side of the compound wall before a stable-hand unbarred the gate. Cord winced at the wave-shaped scar branded on the stable-hand's bronze cheek.

Julian kicked his steed into motion. "You sure took your time."

Cord walked Scute into the long, narrow stable. "Sorry, it's been a long journey."

The branded man returned a bewildered stare for the apology, which widened when he saw Marlone's unmarked face.

Between a row of stalls and the tack room, a team of slaves in dingy brown robes bowed on the hay-strewn dirt. Without direction, the slaves gathered their bags and escorted the steeds away.

Cord followed Marlone's gaze to watch the gate close behind them, sealing them away from the wilds. Then he kept an eye on Scute until the soon-to-be Catalysts reached a door in the middle of the stable and exited to the academe's courtyard. Slaves shadowed them with their possessions.

Grit ground into the tiles with each step toward the behemoth of an academe, made of the same cold granite as the Great Barrier. This place of worship and learning had nothing in common with Cord's home. Pointed stained-glass windows taller than his academe filled a wall on the first level, which must have belonged to the chapel. Cord counted the floors above it. Six stories! How many cadets lived in an academe this size?

The academe blocked the view of the city but not the joyful roar of the people as they prepared for the holiday. What would a Hansweighn feast be like here? Platters of slimy okra, crawdads, and trout? Cord already missed Mrs. Dunkel.

A woman exited the academe's double oak doors with her hands raised for them to halt. Her gray linen robes hung crisply over her prim posture. Dangling from her silver-linked belt, a red star pendant identified her as a nurse mother. Grim as her academe, she sized them up without a smile. "I will show you to your quarters."

The nurse mother pointed to their left at an intriguing sight, a giant sandstone dome. Briskly turning, she led the slaves on. "Headmaster Baugh honors you with the use of the Reliquary as your barracks tonight. Repay that honor by staying out of sight."

Thin shadows covered the Reliquary's surface where centuries of sandy wind had smoothed down the etchings of gusts and waves. Four skinny towers squared out the base and held the same nature-worshipping designs, designs which dated the monument back to Shallyghal. After Merith's army had conquered the island, they had demolished everything connected to the tribes in the Purge. So why had this building been spared?

Wafts of smoke tainted the air. The courtyard tiles darkened underfoot. Dark smears led to a rusty, eight-armed horror nestled by the far wall between the Reliquary and the academe. Scorched gibbets dangled at the ends of its arms, eerily twisting over charred stone and freshly cut ricks. A spider!

Those cages had ended the souls of countless Abandoned, burned by the Chancellor's Light to prevent them from entering the afterlife. Human ashes coated the soles of his boots now. Each clink of the cages' chains sent a twinge worming through Cord's insides.

Marlone patted his shoulder and kept him moving.

Halting at the rounded entrance to the Reliquary, the nurse mother said, "Remain unseen. The Judges will come for you soon. Should you need assistance, your attendants will make themselves known." She had set off for the academe before she finished speaking.

Julian snapped at the slaves and strutted inside.

"You have our thanks," Cord called out to the nurse mother, a far cry from Nemma. With her chore done, she never looked back.

"She's the friendliest," Marlone said. "The other nurse mothers wouldn't dare deprive her of the thrill she gets from welcoming new arrivals."

Cord laughed as much in relief that Marlone was lightening up as for the jest.

As the shade of the Reliquary's entrance embraced Cord, a breeze from inside pressed his sweaty tunic against his skin, cascading shivers through him. Glancing up for the source of the breeze, he jumped back. "Bloody ashes!" White claws hung there, posed above the entrance.

The shiny skeleton of a four-legged snake guarded the round chamber under a small circle of open sky. Its wing bones fell just short of the opening in the domed ceiling. "A dragon," Cord breathed.

Headmaster Angsly had taught them about the winged beasts, deadlier than basilisk spit and a vital part of Shallyghal's defenses. But he hadn't mentioned they'd see the remains of one here.

"Now that's a relic!" Marlone said, his tone dangerous with awe. He wandered closer.

The eye sockets of the horned skull seemed to track Cord as he moved out of its reach. "That thing's got teeth bigger than you, Marlone."

"These must be the only dragon bones left in Merith. You remember the story Nemma told us?"

"'The Dragon and the Ferry Man'?" Cord asked. "How could I forget? Nemma had to recite it every night just to get you in your bunk."

The skeleton didn't bother Julian, who commanded the slaves to unpacked his bags around a cot in the center of the chamber. That left two cots for Cord and Marlone, on opposite sides of the dragon.

Cord's teeth gnashed as he moved down the curved wall to the cot on his left.

Mosaics of the Purge and Merith's victories over Shallyghal embellished the chamber, adding color to the sandstone walls. In the first mosaic, forked red banners helped Cord identify Merith's fleet in the sea. Waist-high piks and satyrs raised bows and slung stones at the fully armored troops of the army to protect a brown horse with a horn between its eyes. On the banks, the human tribes of Shallyghal resisted the front line. Their magi, humans painted black with no faces, danced under flames and lightning.

"These were us, then?" Cord asked, tapping the ships with his finger. "Before the Great Barrier, the first of the Chancellor's army?"

Julian snickered. "Only the first on the island. Merith ruled the continent before being isolated here."

Cord moved down the wall and made note of how well sound traveled under the dome. "I said the Chancellor's army, not Merith's army," he murmured.

A tower door tempted him to try it as he passed, but he ignored the instinct, promising himself to give it a go after Julian slept. As Cord neared his cot, the slaves swooped in to place a washstand and his bags. He hardly noticed, stunned by the mosaic before him.

The army's soldiers tugged on chains wrapped around a giant oak while others hacked at its base. The oak dominated the woods, just as they had in his nightmares.

Cord rubbed the healed skin on his thumb. He'd gladly endure those dreams every night to be rid of his curse. Magic had touched him. But how could he be a magus if he'd never offered up his soul to a demon? He pressed some of the chipped slate tiles against their fittings to reconnect the chain around the oak's trunk.

Marlone's steps scuffled off to the far side of the room. Aside from a slave blocking the entrance, the three cadets were alone. With the dragon.

Julian had stripped down to his smallclothes and unpeeled those when he said to Cord, "We will be summoned soon. Bathe before touching your uniform."

Cord spotted the treasure folded neatly on his cot and grinned. On top, a white cotton tunic had been embroidered with a golden feather, his first dye. Catalyst uniforms didn't have a lick of real armor, because they were only worn for ceremonies, but the sturdy kidney belt put his strip of hide to shame.

After a quick bath with a wet cloth, Cord tried to catch up with Julian, who had already laced one sandal around his ankle. The strange South Thornton uniform included shorts that ended just below the fall of his tunic. He traded uneasy smiles with Marlone as he tugged his tunic down over his crotch again.

The sandals were just as strange. "Lace it through the flap before you cross it over," Julian instructed Cord. "I could do it, if you want."

Cord declined the offer Julian hadn't extended to Marlone. With a sly study of Julian's feet, Cord finished lacing them correctly and went to help Marlone, who had already figured it out.

Clinking footsteps entered the Reliquary. The cadets snapped to attention. Two Judges wearing tabards with the three blue waves of the South Thornton troop came toward them. Oddly, only the younger Judge wore the full uniform with leather pauldrons and splint mail on his limbs.

The armored Judge scrutinized the cadets and shook his head. "Judge Barret," he said, then thumbed to his partner. "Judge Kline."

Judge Kline, who had thrown his tabard over loose commoner clothes, didn't even wear a bastard sword at his side.

"High Guard Horax sent us to prepare you for his audience," Judge Barret said. "Outside. Now."

They hustled into a lineup before the spider as directed. While they waited, Cord focused on the Judges' whispers instead of the grimy cages—a necessary evil but foul all the same.

Judge Barret's black hair and lean build made Cord wonder if they were kin. Not brothers—surely Cord didn't have a parent with curls and eyes of frost, never mind that Barret carried himself with the arrogance of a city dweller. Though, who could say where the Tribunal sent their orphans? Headmaster Angsly never could.

Judge Kline's bulging eyes jumped about like a wingless grasshopper, landing on anything that moved. His graying ginger-haired head jerked to follow a rat scurrying from the piles of logs beneath the spider. Hunkering his stocky frame, he took a step forward, as though he planned to chase the vermin. When Judge Barret turned to see what had distracted him, Kline leaned close to Barret and inhaled deeply. His hunting eyes shifted to Cord until Barret spoke again.

To Cord's left, Marlone didn't seem to have noticed the Judge's strange behavior.

Beyond him, Julian studied the spider from over his upturned nose.

The cage before Cord squeaked. He tensed. He was worthy! He'd never made a deal with a demon!

"Eyes forward," Judge Barret ordered.

Rubbing his thumb with his finger, Cord blinked away the spots the white uniforms had burned into his vision.

The back doors to the academe slammed open. Everyone stretched to full attention as a man exited, proudly holding out his chest with the emblazoned red hammer of the High Guard centered on his breastplate. From torque to toe, the dent-free plates of the warrior's armor gleamed. Far younger than Cord expected one of the Chancellor's personal Guards to be, the High Guard's clean-shaven skin held fewer wrinkles than Judge Kline's, and his cropped brown hair held no gray. He looked them over as his silver-covered fingers fondled the war hammer at his hip.

Two declassed slaves, fair-skinned men, who had either been purchased from foreign slavers or infuriated their fathers, followed closely. One of them carried a basket of scrolls. The other toted a small wooden chest secured by buckled straps of leather.

"Just three in a city this size?" the High Guard asked no one in particular. "Come forward, Judge Barret, Judge Kline." As Judge Kline approached, the High Guard narrowed his eyes at his uniform, or lack thereof.

Cord couldn't make out their whispers.

The High Guard's slaves kept their faces blank. Twice-branded, the hammer over their previous scars marked their current ownership by the Tribunal. Giving a final nod, the Judges headed toward the stable.

"You are in for a surprise, it seems," the High Guard said. His voice boomed as though he spoke to the dragon rather than the three cadets before him. "I am High Guard Horax of the Tribunal. My task here is to give you cadets your directives. My *choice* is to honor the Infallible Chancellor by fulfilling my duty to him and his Merith without question, without hesitation, and without mercy. Can you?"

Walking the line, Horax squinted as he met each man's eyes. "The Chancellor saved you castoffs," he said, his breath rich with sardines. "In a moment, we will see how prepared you are to repay that favor and serve in his army."

Sweat stuck Cord's tunic to his back.

Horax waved over the slave with the basket of scrolls. "While we wait, I may as well give you your orders." The Guard plucked out a scroll sealed with green wax. "Glyn Corey?" No one answered. "Is there a Glyn here?"

"No, sir," Julian said.

"City, then prime village," Horax hissed at the slave. He shoved the scroll into the basket and pulled one with a black seal. "Cord Sullivan?"

"Sir," Cord answered.

Horax picked out two more scrolls, then swatted the basket out of the slave's hands.

The slave scrambled to catch the scrolls.

"Two hit the ground," Horax said. "Two lashes."

Once the slave collected the papers, he bobbed and returned to stand with the other without expression. Was he so accustomed to lashings that they no longer scared him? Or did he receive more for showing fear?

"Your oath, boy," Horax said impatiently.

"By my name, Cord Sullivan, I vow to safeguard the Light of the Infallible Chancellor against the demons and their Abandoned followers. May he purge their magic from Merith today, Cyr tomorrow, and rise in the next life to burn the Abandoned who escaped to the Glades. Forever more, I will protect the secrets of the Catalyst rank and never waver in my devotion to the Chancellor's Light."

Horax threw the scroll.

Cord caught it next to his ear, garnering him a mysterious smile from the High Guard. The rough parchment teased him with the secrets held within. Fighting the temptation to tear it open, Cord tucked it into his belt.

"Marlone Ruff and Julian Westcott?" Judge Horax asked as he read the orders in his hands.

They recited their oaths and, in turn, caught their scrolls.

"Those papers detail your assignments, your living quarters, your contacts, and how to engage them. At sunset, you cease to be cadets of the academe and will be held to the same standard as every other Merithian unshielded by the Chancellor's generosity. Do I make myself clear?"

"Yes, sir!" they said in unison.

"Good." He squinted under his hand to check the location of the sun. "When the first man from the Seeding arrives tomorrow, the bells will ring. Pack your bags. Two Judges will escort you to Carno Bridge and back down the Southern Road to the city's main gate. Ask them your questions. Your Seeding papers are wrapped in the scrolls. Use them to enter.

"Establish yourselves in the community. Make friends with the questionable sort, and bring your concerns to your contacts. Three Abandoned a year, that's your goal." In a city this size, with only a handful of peers for competition, you'd have to be the village idiot's dumber cousin to fail. "If you achieve your targets, come here again at the close of the Seeding in your third year and receive your promotion. Which of you plan to test for the rank of Judge?"

Cord wasn't surprised to see Julian throw his hand up. Marlone wasn't allowed to test for anything higher than a watchman.

"Why not you?" Horax asked Cord.

"I'm gonna test for Ashwin, sir."

"Phah! Ashwin?" The High Guard glanced toward the Great Barrier, blocked from view by the compound wall. "Those lazy fools? They are only the front line to outsiders, boy. The rest of the world cares little about Merith. Until we cleanse our soil, how can we cleanse theirs? Consider that over the next three years and come back with a better answer."

Something scraped the ground behind Cord. It drew closer, freeing him from the High Guard's stare.

"Ah! Perfect timing," Horax said.

Barret and Kline returned ahead of a fully armored Judge with a dark beard waxed to a point at the end of his chin. He dragged an old man by the wrist. Red drained out of the accused man's nose and right ear. He croaked pleas between panted breaths as he settled on his knees in the ashes.

The High Guard gestured to the crumpled man. "This! This is what success looks like. One of your peers fulfilled his duty—and I daresay in the nick of time."

Putting his hands together, the old man cried, "You've made a mistake! I beg of you, my lord!"

Barret kicked the accused in his belly.

The act didn't tarnish Horax's glee. "Thank you, Judge Barret. Watch and witness a Judge at work," he said to Julian, then eyed Cord sharply.

The High Guard waved away the three Judges. Instead of joining the line with the cadets, they created a new one a few feet ahead of them.

Horax loomed over the captive and brandished his hammer, raising the man's chin with its steel head. "Stand."

The commoner wiped the blood from his nose as he obeyed.

Judge Kline leaned forward. Dribble ran from the corner of his mouth. This time Barret noticed it too. When Kline saw Barret's unspoken question, he wiped his mouth and stood at attention.

"Now, walk," Horax said, pointing his hammer at the nearest cage dangling from the spider's legs.

The townsman fell to his knees. "Please! I beg for mercy!"

A flick of Horax's hand brought the Judges to collect the man. Ignoring his mewling, they swung him into the coop. The accused yanked his hands away from the sun-heated iron of the door and pressed against the back of his swaying prison. With the clasp latched, the Judges returned to the front row.

Horax put away his hammer as he wandered over to the chest in his slave's hands. The slave opened the chest and held it out. "Now, what can you tell me about this?" Horax grabbed something from within and moved to hold the item inches from the prisoner's nose.

The man's shoulders rose and his head shook as he studied the shiny object. "My lord, I've never seen that before." His jaw trembled, mouthing unspoken pleas.

Passing by the cadets, Judge Horax presented a ring. A rounded watery-blue gem rested on the gold band.

Cord's shoulders relaxed when he didn't see anything magical about it.

"Oh," the High Guard said, "this is not yours?"

"No, my lord," the man whimpered.

Clicking his tongue, Horax pointed at the caged man.

His slaves set down the chest and basket, then ran out of view behind Cord.

"I see. Perhaps it belongs to a member of your family." He turned to the Judges. "Does he have family?"

The arresting Judge answered, "Yes, sir." His fingers tapped the handle of his sword impatiently, as though one word would send him running back to the man's home to fetch them.

Kline appeared lost in the tapping motion until he sniffed in the direction of the Judge.

"Please!" the caged man sobbed. "We were preparing for the feast. We're law-abiding, faithful citizens of Merith. May the Chancellor be praised!"

The slaves returned with arms full of logs. As they stacked them higher around the man's imprisoned legs, neither looked up from their task.

"We do have seven other cages here. Perhaps your family would be more forthcoming." Horax held the ring up to the old man's face again in a grand gesture. "Does this belong to anyone in your family?"

Sickness burned through Cord's insides.

The answer was garbled through sobs.

"What was that?"

"No, my lord," the accused managed. Tears streamed down from the corners of his eyes.

"Then it must be yours. We found it in your home, after all."

"Yes. Yes, my lord, it is mine."

"You see, there. He confessed!" The High Guard slapped the cage and raised his hands to the sky. Then he studied the cadets with hooded eyes. "Now, who believes him?" No one raised their hand. "Why?" he asked Julian.

Julian's grin broke. "He is lying, sir. He is covering for a member of his family."

"Wrong," Horax said and pointed to Marlone.

"He is trying to protect his family, sir," Marlone said. "But the ring doesn't belong to them either."

"Yes! Why?" Horax asked Cord.

The Judges twisted to stare at him.

"Why, sir?" Cord asked, his voice grainy.

"Why do they not know of the ring?"

The dust and ash in the air parched Cord's throat as he tried to think up a defense for the man that wouldn't send him to a neighboring gibbet. His freedom could come with Cord's answer. A drop of sweat trailed past Cord's temple to his chin. He swallowed. "They're innocent, sir."

Barret shook his head.

"Perhaps Ashwin is a wise choice," Horax said. "We are all in agreement the ring is not his. So, why is he here?"

Marlone cleared his throat. When Horax nodded permission to speak, he said, "The one who informed the Judges put the ring in his home, sir."

"Yes! Quite right! The Catalyst strived to fulfill his directives by framing this man. After all, why not send this wretch to death rather than burn as a failed Catalyst?"

Cord released a long breath, thankful that Marlone had a sound enough mind to save the innocent man.

"Such a pity," Horax muttered to Marlone. "A waste, really."

Marlone's face remained flat.

Julian's lips thinned.

The accused quieted as his breathing slowed. Logs were now stacked to the middle of his cage. One of the slaves retrieved Horax's chest and resumed his position. The other went inside the academe.

"You," Horax said to the slave and pointed to the tile next to him. Spinning the ring in his fingers, Horax waited for the slave to open the chest. He placed the ring inside. "Take my things to my chambers."

After gathering the basket, the slave all but ran inside.

"Shall we collect the Catalyst for you, sir?" the arresting Judge asked. "He shall burn for his lies!"

The High Guard checked the sky behind them and replied, "No, no. It is almost time for the feast. That is a shame. I would have liked to carry out the sentencing myself. Let him come to you on his own. He will believe he has succeeded and may as well be an example to his peers."

"Sir, no others remain to be promoted this year," Judge Barret said.

The wrenching returned to Cord's stomach. No Catalyst from that year had succeeded? They only had to discover three Abandoned each year.

Rolling his hand in the air, Horax said, "Well, let the older cadets watch him burn. You cannot ask for a better way to keep them in line."

Horax's slave, the one who had held the scrolls, exited the academe with a torch lit by the Idol's smiting flame. Poor fellow must not have been listening.

The man in the cage saw the torch. "Please, sir! You said I was innocent!"

"Ah," Horax said, noticing the fire. "Bring it here." The High Guard considered the three cadets. "Above all things, a Judge must be austere. He lied to me. If that were not enough, he has seen your faces. One life for the safety of the army? For the safety of Merith? I wish all decisions were this easy." Holding out the torch to Marlone, he said, "You can do the honors if you like."

Marlone shook his head.

"As you wish," Horax said disapprovingly. The High Guard handed the torch to Julian. "No mercy."

Julian's blond curls formed a halo in the sunlight as he brought the Light to the spider. He paused a few feet away from the caged innocent's protests. "By the word of the Chancellor," Julian recited at a shout, "you have chosen your path away from his teachings. By conspiring with demons, your soul is inimical and Abandoned!"

Cord rubbed his thumb as he stared daggers at Horax's back. There were no demons there! A provoked confession to protect his family had labeled the man Abandoned. Cord had more of a reason to burn. Yet his lips refused to part and argue against the ruling.

"You don't have to do this, son," the weeping man said to Julian. "I'm not a wicked man! I've never seen a demon! By the Light of the Chancellor's mercy, I am faithful!"

Julian ignited the pyre without looking the man in the eye.

Cord let his vision gloss over. He tried to think of anything besides the screams from the jolting figure within the gibbet. After a few logs blazed, the scent of burned hair and roasting pork reached them.

With a reverent nod, Julian handed the torch back to Horax and took his place in line.

"Well done," Horax said over the screams. "You are now Catalysts, the eyes and ears of the Chancellor." When he offered the torch to the slave, he said, "Do not drop *this*. Keep the fire going until he is ash and scatter him in the town square before dawn. We will settle your punishment later."

The slave bowed.

"I am famished," Horax said to the other Judges as he checked the sun again.

Judge Kline laughed deeply.

As Horax eyed the strange Judge, he absently addressed the Catalysts. "You three, go pray before the relic and study your directives. Commit them to memory and burn them. Ah, and do remember to bring your Seeding papers to the city gate." He pointed to the flailing fire to remind them what failure brought. "Dismissed."

The stink of burning flesh sent Cord to his knees. He emptied his stomach on the ash-smudged tiles. When he stopped heaving, he sat back on his heels.

Barret gave Cord a surprisingly sympathetic frown but only wore it briefly before Kline shoved him on.

As the Judges entered the academe, Horax grabbed the bearded Judge's arm and asked if the old man had a young wife or attractive daughters.

Cord retched again.

Marlone tried to get him to his feet, but Cord brushed him off.

"Ashes, Cord! Even Julian's better than this smell."

But it wasn't the stench keeping Cord low. Moments before the man's family would sing their praises and feast in celebration of the Chancellor's victory, he was burned in a display of power. Did they even know where he was?

Cord stared at what his silence, his cowardice, had begotten until the screams died behind the smoke. Then he recited the Rites of Passing. He didn't care who heard him praying for the Abandoned or if they believed the man's soul to be destroyed by the Light. The Chancellor was infallible; his Light would not burn a soul unjustly.

The slave bowed his head and said nothing.

When the prayer ended, Marlone helped Cord up. "Nothing coulda saved him, Cord. Horax wanted a show."

Cord didn't respond.

"That won't happen to you. I won't let it."

"How're you gonna stop it from your cage?" Cord asked. Not waiting for an answer, he staggered toward the Reliquary. "How'd you know the Catalyst lied?"

"It's what the headmaster told us," Marlone said. "Look for the good in people but know the potential for evil in your own heart."

Chapter 6: Brothers of a Feather

When they entered the Reliquary, Julian was bent in prayer beneath the dragon's skeleton in the center of the chamber.

Cord let his mind play; he imagined the horned skull snapping around Julian, shaking the shrieks out of its kill, and chewing him like a piece of fat.

Tonguing the front of his teeth, Cord moved down the wall of mosaics, running his fingertips along the tiny tiles. The more distance between him and Julian, the less likely he'd be to throttle the executioner.

If Horax had handed the torch to Cord, he would've brained the High Guard, or at least set the arresting Judge's beard on fire before getting thrown into a cage. No, wait. He was a coward. Cord pounded the wall, rattling a few of the looser tiles.

"The dragon said, 'The deed is done. Now, you must pay your debt,'" Marlone recited. His fingers stretched, falling just short of the bones in the dragon's barbed tail. "'I have saved the life of the daughter you loved most. In return, I take her as my servant. Come after us, and I shall devour you both.'"

In Cord's mind, their nurse mother's voice echoed the advice to never accept a dragon's favor. Then Nemma would tuck them in and lead the prayer before leaving the door cracked. She'd have known a reason, a pearl of wisdom in the Chancellor's teachings that would make the judgment easier to accept. "One life for the safety of the army, for the safety of Merith," Cord mumbled.

A familiar prominent nose lured Cord to the next mosaic. Red streaked the grout where the Chancellor's armor had received more coats of paint throughout the years. In the scene, the Chancellor, known as Prince Rhyn back then, oversaw a burning city full of colorful domed houses downhill on the coast.

Marlone gave up his fascination with the dragon bones and joined Cord.

"Is that South Thornton?" Cord whispered.

"I'd reckon so," Marlone answered, pointing to a sleek swamp dragon coiling in on itself high above the Chancellor.

Glancing up at the bones, Cord tried to imagine them covered with bumpy green flesh.

As he followed the mosaics, the agile dragon grew in size and sprouted more horns, ending in a menacing display. Black tiles of night sky surrounded the beast with the Chancellor—Prince Rhyn—standing in its maw under the Glades on the full moon. The prince's blazing spear had pierced the dragon's eye, defeating it and the nature-worshipping nation of Shallyghal. Without the elves and the dragons, the Abandoned tribes had refused to unify under a single race's leader. Fractured and scattered, they had no hope of fending off Merith's army.

On that night just over seven hundred years ago, word had reached Prince Rhyn of the revolts sweeping the continent. The demons had freed the magi slaves and birthed chaos. They had slain his father, King Vendral, and had marooned the last of Merith's army on Shallyghal.

Cord put his hand on the red tiles.

Prince Rhyn had refused his father's title. To him, there was only one king of Merith. In his first decree, the Chancellor had vowed revenge for the king and the innocent lives taken by the freed magi. Fearing his wrath for what their demons had done, the old gods had cursed him with immortality, forever protecting them from his reach in the Glades.

Julian cracked the wax seal on his scroll. He paced underneath the relic and read. "Odd," he said, flipping to the other side of the parchment. "I expected more. What does yours say?" he asked Cord.

Could the headmaster have been wrong?

Cord ripped the parchment around the black wax sealing his orders. His eyes skimmed the directives. Fishmonger, Bay District, contact protocols . . . No mention of a slave. He skimmed it again, then his Seeding papers. "Fishmonger," Cord said with a shrug to Marlone, who had let his Seeding papers fall to the floor as he read.

Julian moved to examine Marlone's orders himself.

Marlone paled and jerked them away from Julian's hands. "I'll be tested as Julian's slave," he said, glaring at Cord.

"Ah," Julian said with a satisfied grin.

"What?" Cord demanded, marching over.

"It makes perfect sense," Julian explained. "How many wooders have slaves? Would you even know what to do with one?"

An amused twinkle entered Julian's eyes when he saw Cord's unspoken apology to Marlone. "We all have our parts to play." He snapped his fingers at Marlone. "Pick up those papers. You need to be more careful."

Cord stepped between them. "Real quick now, you're gonna admit he's your equal," he growled. "The Chancellor chose him to serve! He's not a slave!"

That put Julian's shoulders back. "Ignore that," Julian said to Marlone. "We have our orders, and you will not bring about my failure by acting above your station."

Heat gathered on Cord's cheeks.

Marlone snorted and said, "Forgive me if I don't grovel."

"Oh calm down," Julian said. "They did you both a favor. How believable would you be as his master, wooder?"

"At least I'd pretend to obey him," Marlone said.

Julian shook his head. "Success can be easy or hard."

Thrusting his chest out against Cord's back, Marlone asked, "Is that a threat?"

Cord pressed him back. If Marlone started a fight, there'd be no explaining this to the Judges, and Julian certainly wouldn't let it go.

"You have the easy part," Julian teased. "Enjoy it. Be a subservient tarhead while we do the work."

Marlone lunged past Cord.

"No!" Cord shouted. He grabbed Marlone's arm, holding it back an inch from Julian's chin.

Julian sprang forward and struck Marlone's jaw, knocking him to the floor. Then he held his hand out to halt Cord and yelled, "Stop and think! If you injure me, you cannot deny his insubordination led to this altercation. End it now, and we can claim he injured himself. We can all three work together and pass this test."

"We should just trust you?" Cord asked. "When you've got the rights of a master, how do I know you won't take it out on him?"

The Croathite actually appeared offended by the notion.

The nagging voice in Cord's mind, the one that wanted to stay in the wilds with Marlone, egged him on. "No. We'll settle this now."

With his forearms raised, Julian fell into the Strong Tower stance. "Fine."

Marlone frowned when Cord's thumb directed him to keep watch at the entrance.

"Go, Marlone," Cord said. Once Marlone dashed under the dragon toward the entry, Cord relaxed into Stalking Panther. He smirked at Julian's confusion. The headmaster had trained them in every advantage he could find, never limiting them to the army's combat manual.

They circled. Explaining this to the Judges would be difficult, the penance probably painful, but Julian had to learn the consequences of treating Marlone poorly. "If I hear you've—"

Cord ducked Julian's swing and resumed his stance. He smirked at the red splotches darkening Julian's cheeks. "I am warning you, Cord. You do not want to be my foe."

"So you do know my name." Cord lazily threw a left hook, testing him. Julian easily dodged. They continued circling. Cord halfheartedly tried again.

This time, Julian drove his foot down Cord's shin, threw a punch to his chest, and gripped Cord's arm with both hands. Before Cord could brace, Julian heaved him over his shoulder.

Cord's back slammed into the mosaic of the Chancellor spearing the dragon. Black and red tiles scattered from the wall. On the floor, he tried to catch his breath. An ache crept from his spine to his shoulder blades.

Julian stood over him. "You should have seen that coming. Did they not teach you how to fight in your little backwoods academe? Instead of defending some tarhead, you should have been honing your own skills. You will regret declining my offer. No matter what, I would have made sure he succeeded." His voice was just above a whisper. "Why, you ask? Because if he failed, it would reflect poorly on me." He laughed under his breath, holding out Marlone's Seeding papers, ready to tear them.

"Don't!" Cord wheezed. His back cracked as he got to his knees.

The Croathite warned him to stay down with a slight rip to Marlone's papers. "How far will you go to keep him from being my slave? I see one way out of it." He awaited Cord's surrender with a raised nose, flaunting a victory he'd yet to secure. "If I must bleed that slave-born savage until he knows his place, I will. Interfere and you will burn first."

Marlone snuck close from behind Julian with something in his hands. A fresh log from the spider. His nostrils were flared. He'd heard every word.

"I could have made a Judge out of you," Julian said, releasing the parchment with one hand. Cord spit at him. Julian jumped back in disgust and landed within Marlone's reach.

"Wait! Don't!" Cord yelled.

Understanding sparked in Julian's eyes just as Marlone swung. The log smacked Julian behind the temple. He collapsed hard against the tiles.

Marlone said, "Now we've both got a reason to burn."

Chapter 7: Tumbling After

Cord rattled off prayers over his clamped fists, begging for the Chancellor's forgiveness and a way to keep them in the Light, while Marlone inspected Julian.

Leaning against the dragon's leg bone, Marlone said, "He's breathing."

"You won't be when he wakes up! They'll sure as shit burn you!" Too antsy to stay in one spot, Cord got off his knees and walked in a small circle until he heard the broken mosaic's tiles scratching against the floor. He stepped away from the debris and lowered his voice. "What were you thinking? You should've let me end it. The headmaster warned us about this, Marlone."

"Don't lecture me on the laws against my skin."

They exchanged glowers.

"Between being his slave and being hunted in the wilds, I choose the wilds."

Cord's face relaxed first. He wouldn't argue with that. However, by attacking Julian, Marlone had made himself even more of a target than a deserter would be. "You're never gonna get far enough away to hide before they come looking for you."

Staring in disbelief, Marlone asked, "You're not coming with me? They'll burn you too!"

"I don't know what happened," Cord said. "But I didn't make any deals with demons! I can keep it secret and stay here in the Chancellor's Light."

Marlone's eyes narrowed into a hard stare, calling Cord an idiot for even trying to believe that. "This isn't Kenton, Cord! They don't give a piss about you here." He raised his hand toward the rounded doorway and the spider. "That stench, that's the salvation they offer you. No bow, no glory, not even an afterlife."

Marlone threw the log aside. "Why'd you spit at him? If you're so vexed at me for defending myself, why'd you set him up for the swing?"

Cord shrugged and sucked the sweat from his bottom lip. He knew his words were hollow; he'd never really let Marlone go alone. That swing had set both of their fates.

"What will the headmaster think if we run?" Cord asked. Most headmasters of academes were the infirm cadets who couldn't take up a sword, but their headmaster had volunteered to leave a normal life behind because of his devotion to the Light. Their desertion would dishonor him.

A glint returned to Marlone's dark eyes. "We'll tell him together. Come on. We'll move faster if we go tonight and take horses. Judges can drink. They'll be too drunk to follow."

Glancing about the dragon's tomb of shame as he tried to calm his thoughts, Cord asked, "Do slaves attend the feast?"

Marlone regarded him flatly. "How would I know?"

"Dumb question," Cord mumbled. "Sorry. They'll probably bring us food soon. Where can we hide him? We can't just lay him on his cot, not with his bloody uniform."

Thinking as he spoke, Marlone said, "If they're still working, they'd find him in the stables." He smirked. "The spider's got some empty cages."

"In the Light," Cord repeated. "Let's try a tower, then." He retrieved the unconscious Catalyst's belt knife and papers. After slipping them behind his belt, he reached for Julian's wrists.

"Stop!" Marlone blocked Cord's hands. "Think about what you're doing! He's wounded."

Cord flinched away from Julian. If his curse kicked in again, Julian wouldn't rest until they were both scattering on the rising heat of a pyre.

Nodding to the nearest door, Marlone said, "Open it. I'll drag him over." Tucking his arms under Julian's shoulders, Marlone hauled him backward. Julian's sandals caught every lip in the floor.

The heavy tower door popped in protest as Cord swung it. Wind whistled through the cracks spilling the only light on the spiraling stairs.

Marlone climbed backward through cobwebs, lugging Julian up step-by-step.

"We can dump him here," Cord said at the base of the stairs.

"There's no way to lock the door," Marlone replied. "Besides, you know you wanted to see the view from the top."

It was nonsense, but Cord pulled the door closed and followed.

The higher they went, the stronger the wind whipped over Cord's fingers as he braced against the ancient sandstone. Where stone had given way, patchwork wood creaked underfoot. Five times, Cord had to stop himself from picking up Julian's ankles to help carry the load.

The boards threatened in louder snaps as they neared the top. Cord swallowed a complaint about his sore legs.

His face steely with determination, Marlone endured the same and carried Julian without bellyaching. A dozen steps later, Marlone shoved his back against a trapdoor. It splintered a hinge free as it crashed to the floor outside. Fresh salty air rushed in. Marlone finished his climb and dumped Julian on the sandstone beneath the twilit sky. "Asshole."

Already brilliant this early in the evening, the white orb of the moon presented a full view of the intersecting emerald streaks on its surface. Some curved, some straight, all seven verdant lines met in one valley, the Dales of Plenty. "You can almost see the trees in the Glades tonight," Cord said.

There, Merith's fallen waged war against the demons and awaited the Chancellor's arrival to burn them out of existence once and for all. Which side would they have to join now?

The high winds blasted Cord's ears and swayed the tower. Leaning against the short wall of the round platform, Cord glanced down. He snapped upright and stepped back. Being several limbs up in a pecan tree had nothing on this. He focused straight ahead to the east, on the distant Great Barrier. Still, no Ashwin patrolled the ramparts. That couldn't be right.

"You know," Marlone said, "I was thinking. If I can find it . . . Cord, what was that ring? The one Horax had?"

"How the blazes should I know?"

Dismissing it with a shrug, Marlone said, "Magic's new to me. I don't know how it works."

"Suddenly I feel much better about asking you whether the slaves have a feast."

The familiar, hardy laugh made Cord smile. Marlone wiped his face on his short sleeves and moved to Cord's side to take in the view. "Whew!" he shouted, then he cleared his throat and hawked his spit over the edge.

Cord leaned over the brim of the wall to see it splatter on the sandstone dome. In the round opening at the dome's center, the dragon's wing bones reflected the strengthening moonlight. As he watched the shimmer on the Abandoned defender, Cord said, "I'm sorry. I'm sorry I didn't listen sooner. For all of it." He took a deep breath of the muggy sea air.

"You're coming with me?" Marlone asked, as though he'd been waiting for Cord to figure that out.

"Of course I am," Cord said, "on one condition. We have to live in the Chancellor's Light, whenever possible."

With Marlone's solemn nod, it was decided.

Cord returned to his study of the sights around them. Could he find a way to fashion a bow and arrows down there in the woods, with access to any farmer's field at night and the whole of Merith to explore from the mountains to the delta? "This never really was an option for us, was it?"

"Maybe," Marlone answered, "if we were assigned together. But not like this."

Cord turned around to scowl at the unconscious Catalyst. "I thought if I just kept doing what everyone expected of me, that it'd work out. Now I've locked us both in the city."

"You know," Marlone said, "we could still try, if we made it look like he deserted for good." He let the suggestion linger. "They might assign me to you. If you wanna risk it, I will."

Wind-driven curls bounced around Julian's head where his blood hadn't matted them down. Shallow breaths promised an easy kill.

"No," Cord said. "We stay in the Light. We have to be worthy, Marlone."

Marlone snorted. "If High Guard Horax is worthy, I don't think we have to worry."

"I guess," Cord said. "You don't think the Chancellor knows how his High Guard behaves away from the Tribunal, do you?"

Across the emptiness above the courtyard, the academe bells pealed the beginning of Hansweighn. The feast was beginning.

"See if you can get this door to lock," Marlone said as he stepped into the tower. "I'll be back."

"Hey," Cord called. "Where're you going?"

"Inside. They gave the gate keys to the nurse mother. I'll find them while they're all at the feast."

If there was ever a time for stealing from the army, the Hansweighn feast was it. No one would want to miss that, especially if there was a High Guard to impress.

"I'm coming too."

"No," Marlone said. "It'll be easier for me to go alone. I'll find slave robes. They'll never look at me twice. Try to lock him up here and get the horses ready. I'll meet you at the stable. The sooner we ride, the better."

"Fine. But don't get caught! A newly weaned pup wouldn't believe your lies."

A rude gesture shot out of the hole to the stairwell. "I'm a better liar than you!" Marlone's laugh drowned in the wind.

The Reliquary's dome hid most of Marlone's path to the academe from Cord's view. He waited there, staring at the academe's back doors until Marlone snuck inside. Black smoke still soared from the spider.

Cord leaned back against the wall. Somewhere beyond the wooded hills to the north, Kenton called to him. Breaking from the army would cost everything Nemma and Headmaster Angsly had ever hoped for them, the pride of Kenton's academe. And his one dream of becoming an Ashwin. More than that, the army, the Chancellor, would smite them. Ashes, he might deserve it. Cord scowled at his palms.

In a few months maybe, they could contact Headmaster Angsly. Would he welcome them home with a scolding? "He oughta be impressed we weren't run off sooner," Cord told his nerves.

Lifting the door to seal the stairs behind him, Cord spared the Croathite bastard one last glance. Something blue shimmered in Julian's bloody hair. In a blink, it was gone. Cord stepped back up to the platform. It sparkled again. Somehow, it called to him, a slight tingle in his mind. Nearing the blue light, he knelt by the Catalyst. Cord's fingers used Julian's hair as a shield and pressed his head to the side.

A chill bolted through Cord and gushed through his fingertips.

Julian jerked and shook. The Catalyst's injuries, inside and out, lit in the blue light. Cracked bone, split skin, swollen flesh around blood clotting itself, all of it begged Cord to fix it.

Entranced, Cord worked the puzzle without thought, joining Julian's skull and tissue. With the skin sealed, the light extinguished. The trance broke.

Julian flailed his arm into him. "What—get off me!"

Cord fell back. His hand explored the wailing pain behind his temple and came away dark and wet. "No," he moaned. Maybe the demons didn't need an agreement for the pact.

Julian stared about in wonder, then shoved Cord aside. "I know what you are!" He got up and staggered toward the hole in the floor.

Cord tried to block him but couldn't straighten before the pain forced him back to his knees. He couldn't let Julian raise the alarm on

Marlone. Cord kicked wildly. His heel struck Julian's knee. It buckled, sending Julian headfirst into the opening to the stairs. Cord dove after him in vain. He listened as Julian tumbled down the spiral, coming to a stop with a smack.

Cursing under his breath, Cord felt his way down into the darkness. Burn the evil in his bones! Exhaustion crept in, drying his eyes and promising an escape from his throbbing headache. He fought the temptation back but nearly lost his balance on the stairs.

Midway down the neglected tower, Cord kicked Julian. The rasping wind covered any sounds from the Catalyst. Unwilling to risk another touch to see if he lived, Cord yawned, stretched, and stepped around him.

The pain in Cord's head had dulled by the time he reached the bottom and sealed the door behind him. Moonlight bathed the relic, reflecting the light's purity against the mosaics. Fatigue demanded control and kept drawing Cord's eyes to his cot. His clothes and boots were gone. Burn his luck! The slaves must have taken them to wash. He grabbed his empty saddlebag and sped to the exit.

Looking back to the horned skull, he wondered aloud, "Would you have defended us, dragon?" Doubtful, he searched the empty courtyard. The fire gnawed its meal, climbing the cage toward the spider's arm. Cord prayed the man's spirit had survived to be guided to the Glades.

Candlelight flickered through the academe chapel's stained-glass windows. Within, Headmaster Baugh led the cadets in the slowest rendition of "Sacrifice and Praise" Cord had ever heard. One more song and they would eat. Somewhere in that grim academe, Marlone lurked. And they wondered why city folk hated wooders. Cord grinned but wished he'd gone with Marlone.

He rushed past the spider, hugged the wall of the academe, and stayed tight against it, using the shadows to dull the moonlight on his uniform as he snuck toward the stable. Ready with a few excuses to tell any slaves inside, Cord held his breath and rushed through the light into the open stable door.

Horses snorted and nickered in the stalls, but no slaves worked the pens.

With a glance back to make sure he wasn't seen, Cord closed the door. Standing in the middle of the long barn, between the southern gate to the city and the northern gate to the wilds, only locks stood in the way of their freedom.

"Scute," Cord called. A solid black head peered over a stall door. Two months of mounted combat training wasn't much compared to what a Judge received, but he had bonded with his charger.

Cord slipped a halter onto Scute and brought his muscular steed forward. He hitched the lead around a rail by the northern gate before hunting down the saddle.

Even with the unavoidable stink of manure, the building boasted of the slaves' diligence. Oiled and tidy, saddles rested on their pads in rows of horizontal posts in the tack room.

After securing Scute's saddle bags, Cord removed the parchment from his belt and put it in a bag. Then he paused, recalling Julian's threat. Cord dipped his hand back in and removed Julian's set. He shredded the Seeding papers, letting the scraps fall on his sandaled feet.

Cord collected the gear for Julian's horse. CLAUSTRUM was stitched into the saddle. As he prepped the skittish steed, he wondered what Marlone would rename him.

With a bag of feed added to both horses' loads, they were ready. He patted Scute's neck before following the hay back to the entrance.

Inching the door open, Cord peered outside to the vacant courtyard. Marlone must still be searching for the keys, or with a cricket's luck, stealing food. Sitting to keep a lookout, Cord heard nothing over his own slowing breath. He finished two prayers before his dry eyes closed and sleep won.

* * *

"Another dream," Cord grumbled, as he took in the woods around him. Fabric brushed his legs. Under a green tunic, fancy by a councilmember's standards and tightened by a wide sheepskin belt, he wore britches and sturdy boots. Scrolled silver leaves decorated the trim of his tunic, and steel ones swept along his boots.

Mist swarmed in and smothered the forest in dampness. As quickly as it had come, it rushed away. A sapling in front of him twitched, swelled into a tree, and shrank to a stump. Within moments, the entire woods changed from seedlings to full growth to nubs. The cycle repeated.

Vines burdened with flowers as broad as his chest snaked their way around the forest bed, occasionally getting caught by a rising branch. The petals' hues were soft and varied at first and then, for only a second, became bright and uniformly as blue as Mrs. Barrow's hydrangeas.

An alder tree sank into its stump behind him, dropping a bloom the pink-orange of a sunset onto his shoulders. As Cord eased the flower off, shade swallowed the woods. The enormous oak from the mosaic dawned, stretching out over him. Cord's curiosity hooked him and set his wary pace toward it, listening for growls as he went.

Even the giant participated in the cycle, growing when the flowers turned blue. Then it shed its shield-sized leaves and disappeared into a stump as wide as the Reliquary. A dark spot appeared on the surface when the shaft vanished.

Cord climbed its unruly roots for a better view. After two more cycles, the blemish reappeared. Pieces of the oak's rings fell in, creating stairs into the darkness.

Resting his boot on the bark, Cord pressed against it and let his foot ride the growing tree. When the trunk vanished, his foot fell to the stump. Cord raced forward and slid into the opening.

Chapter 8: Honor Thyself

Every sprig of the hairy tickleleaf bush caught the moonlight, shielding Scarlett in its canopy as she spied over the rock wall dividing her mother's garden between the vegetables and the flowers. Rorry and Kylan had interrupted the debate in her mind that had been repeating louder and louder for days. Should she go with them and help her friends or stay and honor her parents? Either way, she couldn't face them until she decided. So she waited and watched them wait for her.

Wearing one of Scarlett's plain dresses, though a tad snug on her, Rorry took a step back between the row of tomatoes and the string beans. She reread the singed document Kylan had handed her.

Scarlett had wanted to surprise her together with Kylan. He never could keep a secret.

Though still wide-eyed, Rorry rolled up Grary's Seeding papers. She held them out to Kylan.

His eyebrow rose over the edge of his spectacles. "Uh-uh. Those are yours. Don't ask us to return them."

"We should—I should," Rorry said, failing to hide a grin. "It will mean his death."

Kylan snapped a tomato from the vine and bit into it. "He deserves it."

"I will never argue against that." The words hardened her freckled features. "Nor would I wish for either of you to murder for vengeance on my behalf."

"It's not the first time we've tried," Kylan said.

Scarlett tongued the gap in her teeth. Her victory over Grary still felt shallow.

Rorry flattened the papers and slid them into her satchel. "That does not ease my conscience."

After a glance over her shoulder to Scarlett's home, Rorry left the aisle in the direction of the provisions stashed behind the beans.

As they moved out of sight, Scarlett tightened her woolen shawl around her shoulders to combat a sudden chill in her bosom. How much longer would they wait for her decision?

Scarlett corked the bottle full of calendula petals in her hand and carefully slipped it into her poultice bag. She had been replenishing it in an effort to calm her nerves when her friends had arrived. With as little rustling as she could manage, she stepped up the dividing wall and crept behind the string-bean plants.

Being in her mum's haven only made Scarlett's decision more difficult. Despite the acres of fields outside the city wall, Lord Gwirion granted more land within the confines of Brewing to farmers than to any other profession. Scarlett's father had surprised her mum with half an acre of land next to their home, a shelter of wooden frames and stone walls devoted to nurturing her hobbies. After, they'd shared the longest kiss Scarlett had ever seen. Then her mum had set off planning, planting, and singing to herself. She had rarely stopped singing since while gathering components from the questionable herbs in the recesses.

Now, from within her refuge, Scarlett contemplated stealing her mum's glee.

Kylan whipped off the canvas Scarlett had thrown over their

supplies. "Yep," he said around the last bite of the tomato, "we'd have been fools to expect less. I guess it was too much to hope she'd only bring her poultice bag." Larger than the saddle and saddlebags combined, Scarlett's bedsheet bundled her possessions. "Who do you think'll wind up carrying that?"

That was easy for him to say. She didn't want to leave Brewing, her family, and her history—everything—to be forgotten in some mythical rebirth they seemed to believe would happen once their toes touched the continent's soil. She'd be the same person there as she was on Merith: a weak magus who would fail to be admitted to the Tower. Then what?

"The real question is how many books are in there," Rorry said.

None! Scarlett clicked her tongue then ducked. Thankfully they didn't hear.

"But look," Kylan said, pointing to the slender black crossbow and matching katana atop their bedrolls. "She did steal Master Clienne's weapons."

Scarlett prayed her uncle would forgive her for succumbing to Rorry's and Kylan's incessant requests to take the weapons from his hidden armory. In the end, she wanted to protect her friends, even if she didn't join them. Outright refusing to take the set's dirk for herself provided a small comfort.

Rorry ran her fingers along the body of the crossbow, over the indecipherable wavy script inlaid in silver, and said, "Please. We are borrowing them, not stealing. I feel guilty enough about taking them. This was surely not his intent when he trained us."

Snorting, Kylan said, "I have no guilt. You never had to endure his sparring lessons."

"Despite my requests."

"Trust me, you didn't want them."

"Yes, Kylan. I did."

Nodding slowly, he said, "Well, I had the training, and Grary still handed me my ass."

Rorry hugged his arm.

He gave her a wily grin. "Last laugh's on him."

He lifted the katana. Identical silver script decorated its black scabbard. Kylan tightened his belt around it.

After slipping a slim bolt case into her fine leather satchel, Rorry studied Scarlett's house again.

Scarlett did the same. Below the distant thatched roof, her parents' window was dark.

"She is tardier than normal," Rorry said. "Do you think she changed her mind?"

"Nah," Kylan said. "She'd never let us go without saying goodbye."

"She would if she thought we could talk her out of staying."

He conceded with a shrug and lightly kicked the bundle. "Maybe she went back for a quilt? The gods know she'll want to bundle up in this heat."

Already the teasing had begun and the journey hadn't even started. Any moment now he'd say something snide about her needing to eat more than a bird or being lucky to have thick skin to keep her bones warm. Honestly! Had he seen her mother? Scarlett had no intention of looking like an owl, as he so affectionately put it, before nature forced it on her. She preferred her hooked nose and broad chin on a thinner frame. The height she got from her Hywel blood wouldn't help that much.

"I do hope she comes," he said, "even if she doesn't get accepted to the flaming Tower of Trône d'Argent. That just means she can come with us to find Alis."

"Have you considered what we are asking of her?" Rorry asked. "She could be happy here."

Scarlett's heart chugged.

"Her family is here, Kylan. The Light knows her mother has my parents wrapped around her finger. Scarlett could stay, get married, and have kids. All she would have to sacrifice is magic."

"I know," Kylan replied. "I just can't see how that'd be enough for her. Who would want to sacrifice magic? We've seen what Mrs. Hywel can do. If Scarlett had the same training from the Tower, I bet she'd be even stronger. I wish she believed in herself enough to try."

Scarlett moved along the wall and out into view at the end of the aisle of beans. "Do you hear the locusts?" she asked timidly. It wasn't what she'd intended to say. But her eyes had gone to her parents' window again.

"There you are," Kylan said. "We thought you . . ." He set his arms akimbo. "You are coming with us?"

Blinking rapidly, Scarlett nodded. "Papa is going to have a tough year."

Rorry gave Kylan a guilt-ridden look, but he jokingly said, "They eat locusts in Taus. He may enjoy a good crunch in his food."

"You think Papa would eat a foreign delicacy? He'd starve first." Scarlett wrung her fingers. "He is not from a worldly stock."

"Yet," Rorry said, "you are your mother's daughter, the child of a wandering foreigner. She braved *quite literally* untold dangers to enter Merith, not to mention the forbidden roads to reach Brewing on the far side the island."

It wasn't the same. Scarlett wasn't leaving in a romantic gesture to find her true love. No, she'd flee to the continent just to hear from someone else in her mum's accent that her magic was minimal, far too minimal to become a mage. The Tower couldn't fix that. They didn't grow magic; they honed it.

Raising her chin, Rorry said, "Come with us. The Tower of Trône d'Argent will train you and declare you a mage, just as it did her. I refuse to allow them to turn you away."

Scarlett relented with a sigh as her eyes left the farmhouse's windows for good. "I placed their notes in the barn." Her parents knew she loved them. She hoped her mum wouldn't take it as personally as she would pretend to.

Offering his hand to assist her in stepping down from the divider, Kylan said, "Come. Let's see what mischief these mainland ports truly hold. Stalls with rare magic? Forgotten tomes? Treats to put some meat on your bones?"

Scarlett flapped her lips with a puff of air.

He shrugged. "Cocks for hire?"

"Kylan!" Rorry scolded. She caught the furtive glare he gave Scarlett. "Oh do not start. I will run my words together and swear foul oaths and whatever else you insist being common entails in more apropos moments, such as those to be found outside of Brewing. Until then, I suggest we wait to speak freely of men and what they have to offer."

Kylan made another face at Scarlett before he wrapped her in his arms and spun until her feet hit the ground.

Scarlett gave him a wide smile and reset her shawl around her neck. She tried not to peek at her home again as they gathered their belongings. Kylan chuckled when she picked up her bundle. It wasn't that heavy.

Through the humid night, Rorry led the way southeast toward the hills and the weak point in Brewing's defenses.

Midway there, Scarlett halted their uphill hike at the overlook in the hillside trails. Searching for her house, Scarlett released her bundle and stood on her tiptoes. But dense foliage blocked the edge of town. Beyond the empty streets of Brewing below, a moonlit current swept through Lake Cashelle, edged by the docks and the rugged cliffs on its far side.

"So long, Brewing," Kylan said.

Scarlett asked him, "Do you remember the time we found Dannel swimming around naked because your brothers had taken his clothes?"

Smiling, he said, "Those two were always more trouble than they were worth."

"I do not recall you complaining," Rorry teased.

"I could say the same," Kylan retorted, winning an indignant sigh. Hefting Scarlett's bundle, he winked at her. "Poor Dannel. Well, he'll make some woman very happy."

"Very happy," Scarlett repeated.

At arm's length, Rorry pointed the crossbow to the east. "If we must discuss vulgarities, let us at least travel as we do so."

"Speaking of vulgarities," Kylan said, taking off again. "I've been dying to tell you what I heard the other day. Cooter Reid came over and told my dad that he saw Master Farrow doing something I didn't think people actually did. I guess if you're really lonely . . ." Rorry should never have let Kylan's tongue off its lead. "You know how Master Farrow is always in his barn with all of those goats?"

"Kylan, may I tempt you to withhold this particular piece of gossip?" Rorry asked.

He agreed but didn't let her off the hook completely.

Scarlett giggled at his dockhand jokes, though he had shared them before, in exchange for his carrying her load. She noticed Rorry grinning a time or two too.

Kylan's wild grin said he was nearing another punch line. "'Yeah, I'm Clem the Dragon,' the hunter said and groped himself. 'Draggin' on the ground.'"

Rorry shook her queue, tied back by Alis's cerulean ribbon. "Well," she said. "You are clearly scraping the bottom of the barrel now. Let us turn our attention to discussing our plans, shall we? There is still the matter of sneaking us into Llandir after you get inside."

When they arrived at their first destination, the discussion ended with the same conclusion they'd been reaching for weeks: wait and see.

Burly Beechy, a tree every kid in Brewing had climbed on a dare at some point, swayed next to the boulders of Brewing's town wall.

Rorry bumped her shoulder into Kylan's arm and elbowed Scarlett. The sparkle had returned to her eyes. It'd been gone so long Scarlett had thought it might not come back. Rorry sprang forward and climbed up the limbs first. She spied over the wall before waving for them to follow close.

Scarlett's feet were light, no longer burdened with nostalgia.

Rorry dropped her satchel into the nightmarish land filled with mythical witches and trolls, curses and Judges, and lowered herself onto the mossy boulders.

With a nod from Rorry, Kylan threw her bundle, his bedroll, and his saddlebag over the wall. Then he hefted Spectre's saddle over. He ascended, offering to help Scarlett climb.

The cleanly shorn ring of grass surrounding Brewing was free of watchmen as far as the slope allowed her to see. Scarlett eased down to the town wall. At that height, nothing stood between them and the woods fifty feet beyond.

For a moment, Scarlett dangled her poultice bag over her bundle on the distant grass. Right or not, she had chosen this path. She released the bag.

"This is it," Rorry said. "Once our feet touch the soil of the wilds, there is no return." With crossbow in hand, she leaped in jubilation. Landing on her feet, she silenced her giggles behind an open-mouthed smile. Kylan landed beside her before she grabbed her satchel and dashed toward the shadows of the forest. Halfway there, Rorry spun to guard them.

Kylan gestured for Scarlett to jump.

Without thought, she fell into his arms. With a brisk sweep, he placed her next to her belongings.

Hefting the saddle over one shoulder and a saddlebag over the other, he followed Rorry.

Scarlett dragged her bundle after him as quickly and as quietly as she could manage.

Glancing over his shoulder, Kylan laughed at her. Only then did Scarlett realize she was smiling as broadly as Rorry.

Once secured within the woods, Kylan asked, "Spectre?"

Scarlett swiftly agreed, reaching to her bosom to untie the string binding Spectre's coin around her neck. If her mum did come after them, she'd be half as fast without him.

"No," Rorry said.

Scarlett whimpered.

"He is too easily seen at night. I believe only one glowing steed is required to send us all three to the pyre."

"Safe assumption," Kylan said. He offered Scarlett his saddlebag and bedroll. Gripping her bundle, he swung it over his shoulder again. "Which way?"

Rorry's finger set him eastward. "We should put some distance between us and the patrol route first."

"It shouldn't be far," Scarlett said. She reached into her poultice bag and retrieved an old folded map. "The mark is near the mouth of the Endelweix."

"Now we find out if you're right," Kylan said.

"This has to be the way Mum did it," Scarlett replied. "It makes too much sense."

"I know. I know," he said. "Why else would she have the map?"

"We are prepared either way," Rorry reminded them. "After all, even if we can access the tunnels, we cannot be sure they still connect."

For nearly a mile, they spoke in nervous whispers. More than one owl cried in the night. For all the stories Scarlett had heard to scare Merithian children away from the wilds, these dark woods seemed the same as those trapped within the city walls. She tried not to stare into the shadows for too long and certainly didn't mind when Rorry took her arm as they walked, not that she expected to happen upon a coven dancing naked in circles and feasting upon children who had eaten one too many puddings, or anything of that sort.

Roots grew denser across the forest floor as more branches blocked the moon. Then the moonlight flared in a patch as broad as a barn. They'd found it! The stump of a giant oak.

Climbing the roots to the flat surface of the stump, Scarlett said, "It's beautiful, even in death. They used to stretch out over the forest." Staring at the stars, she outstretched her arms to mimic the drawing of the tree in her mum's book. "All these centuries later, it still guards the secret of the elves."

Kylan let his cargo fall and stretched. "Let's hope so. You don't think we'll find the elves down there, do you?"

She and Rorry laughed off the question. Elves. No one had seen an elf in centuries. If they were in hiding, it surely wasn't beneath Merith.

Rorry put her hand on Scarlett's back and walked her forward to the stump's center. "Only you can make this work."

"I'm not sure," Scarlett said as she knelt.

"Do try," Rorry pleaded. "If you fail, then no harm has been done."

That wasn't what their hopeful faces said. Kylan nodded his encouragement.

Scarlett's success depended on how much magic the aged tree required; she had little to give. Her palms flattened on the wood. She heard her mum's voice telling her that strength in magic was random, and with her limited abilities she would be safer if she avoided using it altogether.

A minute passed and nothing happened. She heard Kylan sigh. Wrapping her arms around her chest, Scarlett said, "I can't." Unable to keep her eyes from watering, she didn't look up at them.

Her friends were quiet until Kylan said, "Try it again. Please."

"Yes," Rorry added. "The book said they opened with magic's touch. Perhaps if you tried . . . burning it?"

That was a stretch and more destructive than a key should be. Nevertheless, Scarlett did know how to trigger that spell, sort of. She put her palms against the stump again. Her mum would switch her until her bottom bled if she knew what she was up to. Yet if this worked, it could save them hours if not days of travel.

Closing her eyes, Scarlett located the spark in her mind, the stimulant hiding in the memory of their fight with Grary. The one that had taken her tooth. Not the hostility on his face before he'd struck her. Before that. The feeling rushing through her as she'd seen him trouncing Kylan.

A faint orange light brightened Scarlett's eyelids. She opened her eyes. The thinner rings shone under her touch. They brightened, blazing like a heatless flame. The light raced away and rippled outward beneath her, filling the rings with fiery light. Rorry leaped away from it as it ran under her feet to connect on the far side of the giant stump. Silently, sections of the surface broke apart, sinking into place to create a fissure on the surface. Scarlett pulled her hands back. The light was extinguished.

"You did it!" Rorry squealed. "The Starlight Tunnels." She raised Uncle Barrey's crossbow and led the way to the stairs.

Scarlett closed her mouth, thankful that the elves had set the enchantment for the touch of any magic user, even the weakest. What other wonders had they left within her reach? She and Kylan joined Rorry and peered inside. The moonlight only reached a few stairs down into the darkness, where the rings met stone.

Taking the first step, Kylan said, "Now for the real adventure."

Chapter 9: Losses Great and Small

Cord jerked awake against the stable door. He blinked at the hay. The evening's events came back to him in a string of stinging regrets. His hand rubbed the side of his head and brushed free flakes of dried blood. No tenderness remained. But where was Marlone? Yawning, he covered his mouth to keep out the taste of the horses and got up.

The door to the courtyard eased open with a soft whine. Moonlight glittered on glass shards scattered across the courtyard; the chapel's windows were jagged and broken. Firelight flickered inside the silent chapel.

A figure in bloody robes dragged himself out of the shadows and over the glass. He looked directly at Cord.

"Marlone!" Cord called, throwing open the door. He rushed to Marlone's side and rolled him over.

Marlone didn't answer, just grinned before his eyes closed.

Shredded, the slave robes clung to him in dark patches.

Cord easily tore them apart to see red swelling across the white uniform underneath. He grabbed Marlone's head with both hands. His skin blazed with fever. "Work, burn you!" Cord didn't care who saw. He'd burn before he'd let Marlone die.

His fingers tingled. Cord closed his eyes, forced a full breath into his lungs, and opened himself to the curse. A wave of cold crashed into them. He felt Marlone's back arch up off the ground.

When Cord opened his eyes, blue light gleamed in Marlone's wounds. A bite marred his shoulder; Cord saw it clearly now. Just below his ribcage, a smaller maw had dug into his flesh. The chill from Cord's touch forced muscle, tissue, and skin to mend. When the last gash closed, he released Marlone's head.

Abruptly aware of the cuts in his skin, Cord winced. His tunic lost its glow as the white spotted and soaked up his blood.

Marlone wheezed and shivered. "They killed them—you have to go. The keys . . ." He tried to remove a satchel from his shoulder.

"What? Who?" Cord asked, palming Marlone's head again. His fever had survived the mending.

Marlone knocked Cord's hand away and held out the satchel. "Listen!" Spittle clung to the corners of his mouth. "You have to run . . . they bit me . . . they can—"

He cut himself off and thrust his head up, searching the way he had come. His eyes darted.

Cord saw nothing. The fire had dwindled under the spider without finishing its meal.

"No! They're coming! They can smell you—" Gasps for air interrupted Marlone's words. He convulsed.

Cord held him down against the tiles. "No," he pleaded. "I can't do this alone. You hear me? I won't do it alone!" Why hadn't he gone with him? He should have been there to protect him!

When the shaking stopped, Cord hefted Marlone over his throbbing shoulder. The pain of his new injuries attacked him with each step, but he didn't surrender until he was inside the stable. After laying

Marlone on the straw-covered ground, Cord took his forearms and gently dragged him away from the door.

"Keys?" he asked, half hoping Marlone would respond. Cord whipped the strap of Marlone's satchel over his torso and rifled through the bag. When his fingers wrapped around a thick ring of iron, Cord silently thanked his friend.

"Where is he?" someone shouted from the courtyard. Cord rushed to the door and pressed it open a sliver. He didn't see anyone. Then a shadow stretched past the academe's corner. Cord nudged the door closed.

Marlone gurgled as Cord ran past.

"We're almost there," Cord whispered. "Don't give up, Marlone." Silencing the dangling keys, Cord dashed to the gate. He tried the first key in the lock. It didn't work. The second was too fat. The third failed to turn. Finally, the shortest key slipped into the hole and popped open the lock. Cord raised the latch, lifted the board barring the gate, and shoved the doors open. The wilds beckoned him, offering an unguarded path through the darkness.

Cord unhitched Claustrum's lead. The horse resisted every tug as Cord hauled him toward Marlone.

Prepared for the pain from his shoulder, Cord seized Marlone's arms. They felt wrong, limp. Cord put his fingers under Marlone's nostrils. He didn't breathe. Palming his head again, Cord said a prayer. Nothing happened. He relaxed his mind, but the curse wouldn't come.

The world went quiet; the shuffling horses, the wind from the opened gate, even the sharp jolts of pain from his shoulder faded away. Marlone was dead. Cord slumped. "Why didn't I listen to you? Why didn't I go with you?" He hugged Marlone against him and rocked. Shaking as his vision blurred, Cord said, "I'm sorry."

"What is this?" a voice said from the swaying courtyard door. Judge Kline, nude as a newborn, tilted his head. "We missed one." The horses battered their hooves against the stall doors, drowning the stable in noise.

Cord covered Marlone as Claustrum panicked and fled to the wilds.

Judge Kline froze his sneaking approach when Cord glanced back up.

Cord burst upright and growled, "This is your doing?"

The Judge responded with a slight grin.

"You son of a bitch! I'll quarter you with my bare hands!"

"Brave words for someone hiding his scent behind horse piss."

Blood pounded through Cord's veins. Unclenching his hands for a run at Kline's throat, Cord took one step. He froze.

In the dim light, Kline's eyes glimmered gold. He inhaled deeply. "Peppermint on ice. How did we forget you?" The Judge hunkered over, sending the horses into a renewed frenzy. As he groaned, his nose stretched into a snout. He shrieked in pain. Fangs erupted from his gums. Thick hair sprouted across his skin. Kline's bones popped and lengthened.

Cord backed away, unable to remove his eyes from the man. The Judge's scream soared into an earsplitting howl and broke Cord's stupor. He sprinted for Scute. Cries from the Judge fueled his speed. Cord plowed into the post holding Scute's lead and freed his horse.

A hand gripped Cord's wounded shoulder and flung him to the ground. Not a hand—a paw. A wolf's head topped the pelted, muscled body of a man. Its legs bent like an animal's. The beast snapped at Cord, flinging drool.

Cord scampered backward.

Snip by snip, the beast trapped him against the wall next to the open gate.

Without daring to look away from the golden eyes, Cord stood and groped for a weapon, for anything better than his belt knife. His hand brushed a wooden handle. He clasped it and swung; the filthy head of a spade clanged against the beast's skull.

It snarled and staggered back.

Cord readied another swing.

Thick black claws spread for a swipe.

Scute kicked, striking the beast's chest. The creature smacked against a stall door and whimpered.

Marlone's body lay motionless beyond. His friend wasn't in there anymore. He had died free of the Idol's flame, not as an Abandoned; his soul would survive to the Glades. The thoughts didn't comfort Cord but served their purpose. In a wrenching second, Cord made the decision to leave Marlone behind.

He snatched Scute's lead and hurled the spade at the beast. A sharp whine rewarded his aim. Cord ran his charger out of the stable. With a strained leap, he mounted.

The beast pursued with a limp at first, then galloped on all fours. It kept Scute's pace as they raced northward.

Cord broke away from the winding road and set their path straight for Kenton. Placing his head near his steed's neck, Cord pushed Scute harder. His heart fell into rhythm with the thunder of Scute's hooves.

Shortly after they breached the fields surrounding South Thornton, Cord lost sight of the beast in the tall grass. He didn't let Scute slow.

Cord's eyelids stayed closed longer with each blink. He began nodding off, giving in to the exhaustion that came with his curse. The image of Marlone's corpse flashed across Cord's mind. With gnashed teeth, he pushed away the desire to mourn.

A form leaped at them from the left, jolting Cord awake. He gasped and raised his arm to block a swipe. A tree—it was just a tree. The groves were connecting. Could he have reached the bayous already? How long had they been running?

Cord studied the dimming stars, refusing to see the Glades spread out over the full moon. Valor's Shield neared the horizon. It'd be dawn in a couple of hours. If he didn't let Scute rest soon, his steed wouldn't recover. He'd already pushed him too hard. With a glance behind them and at every other angle, he reined Scute in. There was no sign of their hunter. After swallowing to draw moisture back into his mouth, Cord said, "You did good."

The promise of daylight gave Cord courage. He'd make for Kenton. Headmaster Angsly wouldn't turn him away after hearing about the beast, and he might even know what that thing was. Was Judge Kline a demon?

Amid a steady flow of prayers, Cord eased Scute's burden by

alternating between leading him at a fast walk, trotting, and riding for short bursts at a gallop. Within the hour, he arrived at a shoal similar to one he and Marlone had camped near more than a day ago. Or was it two days now? He wished he'd stuck to the road.

Heading north, Cord hoped the water would lead him back out of the delta and up to the Andras River. He could find his way home with the Andras as his guide.

When the sun lit everything around him, Cord decided to risk a proper rest. Tugging Scute down to the bank of the stream they had shadowed for the past two hours, he tied Scute's reins around a thin ash tree. His young charger had been put to the test and only showed signs of thirst.

Cord slung Marlone's satchel around the pommel of his saddle and waded into the water. The blood on his hands had crusted. Furiously, he scoured his palms. He should've gone with Marlone! He could've saved him if he'd gotten to him faster! Cord didn't stop until his skin ached. He punched the water, then hit it again and again, pummeling as he unleashed a primal yell.

Sinking to his knees, Cord gave in to his mourning as the cool current passed around his shoulders. His breath ricocheted in his chest, refusing to calm as he wept. Why'd he have this power if he couldn't even save what mattered to him?

After reciting the Rites of Passing and a few prayers for Marlone, Cord wiped his face on his wet hands and rose out of the water.

Glints across the stream caught his eye. Something shone through the bushes not twenty feet away. He backed away to the rocky shore, never taking his eyes from the rustling thicket across the stream. Someone lurked there, watching him.

A heavy thump sounded behind Cord. He twisted in time to be flattened under the beast. Rocks and roots dug into Cord's back as he had the wind crushed out of him. Cord struggled to shift its weight enough to reach the knives in his belt but couldn't budge the arm pinning him down. His lungs filled with the stink of a wet dog.

The graying ginger wolf panted over him and nuzzled Cord's tunic up. The wolf's face sank behind its forearm.

Cord shouted as its hot breath hit his exposed skin. He squirmed, writhing as he uttered prayers.

It sniffed and groaned. The groan sharpened into a howl. Hot drool dripped onto the skin covering Cord's hip bone.

Kicking wildly, Scute whinnied and tugged against his binding. Focusing on his horse, Cord shut out the world around him as he continued to pray.

The beast shot upright and snarled, staring across the stream. Its whiskers curled. Yelping, it pawed at its face and leaned back. A thin shaft punctured the wolf's gut, spraying drops of hot liquid over Cord. The wolf fell off him and pawed frantically at the crossbow bolt.

A young commoner in spectacles trampled across the stream, bellowing a cry at the wolf. The long handle of a slender single-edged sword appeared at home in his hands.

Behind him, a girl reloaded a black crossbow. A shiny blue ribbon held back her golden-orange hair. A noble? At her side, a gaunt girl pointed at the creature with her bony fingers and whined.

Cord tried to stand, but his legs were jelly. He crawled away from his attacker as a second bolt struck its chest and brought it down.

The commoner positioned himself between the beast and Cord, assuming a stance he'd clearly been trained to use with the strange blade. "For what it's worth," the swordsman said to the wolf, "I'm sorry."

It growled from deep within.

Cord saw the silver arc of the blade in the sunlight.

The whimpering ceased. The beast's flesh wriggled as its joints crunched, a snapping of bone against bone. Paws turned to feet. Fur shed to reveal skin. The wolf shrank into a naked decapitated man. Judge Kline's head lay a few feet from his body, his irises still golden.

"Are you injured?" the swordsman asked. "Were you bitten?"

Cord tried to respond but relief washed through him. After a blink, his eyes wouldn't open. He heard his head hit the ground but didn't feel it.

Chapter 10: Fire and Nice

The rings of a great stump stretched out beneath Cord. Rolling hills pockmarked with dead trees surrounded him.

His every breath echoed in the dream. "What do you want from me?" he shouted. Magic had failed Marlone; it had failed him. Whatever this vision had in store for him, he wanted none of it. "Burn you, demons! And burn this useless curse!"

Howls exploded around him. The calls were close, just over the now bare hills. Cord held his breath and beat his heel against the stump, listening for a thunk identifying the entrance that had woken him last time. He put his ear to the rings and pounded with his fists but couldn't hear anything over the panting of the approaching wolves.

The growls of his unseen trackers drew closer. Their claws scratched the dirt as they ran.

As Cord flattened his palms and shoved himself upright, a tingling sensation ran from his elbows to his fingertips. Lying still, he let the curse take control. Waves of green-blue light coursed through the darker rings. The glow brightened. Light connected fully around the stump. A stairway lowered next to him.

Cord looked up in time to see the first wolf crest the hill. It wasn't a wolf at all. Amid all the howls and panting, a pack of gray-skinned men lumbered toward him. Shifting shadows curled about them but never hid their golden eyes and bared fangs. The distance was closing much faster than it should. Cord leaped down into the unknown.

The sunken rings met the stone steps of a staircase hugging the wall of a round chamber. He dashed down the curving stairs, past the lapis capping the ancient sanctuary, fifty feet down to a well-lit marble floor.

He stared up at the top of the stairs and the hole in the tree's stump. The blue light of his touch coated the roots, glistening across the chamber's carvings: leaves floating in water, suns, leaves caught in the wind, and phases of the moon.

Searching for an exit, Cord noticed the faceless alabaster statues frozen in a dance along the perimeter of the room. The sight set his skin crawling.

Between two of the statues, he found a way out, an archway. The stone frame had been cut to resemble bark. Cord peered into the darkness filling the corridor beyond.

As he crept forward, the roots flexed overhead, lifting the wood to reseal the rings. The chamber went dark.

* * *

Light flickered through Cord's eyelids. He opened them and blinked. Elm leaves blazed with sunlight, then dropped shade again as they whipped and rustled overhead. The distant rush of a river placed him in the wilds, killing his hope of Marlone's death having been a nightmare.

Cushioned against the flat ground by a bedroll, he tensed his muscles beneath a fine linen sheet. Scratchy twine bound his wrists and ankles. So his rescue might have been more of a dragon's favor than a cricket's wish.

To his right, the freckled noble sat on a blanket and tapped her fingernails on her knee as she watched something in the trees by the river.

A lump in the blanket gave away her crossbow's location.

Locks of flame cascaded down the pale, freckled skin over her collarbone. Where had her blue ribbon gone? Did she think he hadn't noticed? Even her eyelashes were fair. Her eyes met his.

Cord's cheeks flushed as his lips parted.

The corners of her mouth curled for a smile but straightened. "Kylan," she said.

The swordsman who had slain Judge Kline sat up next to her. He put his spectacles on over his ears and ran a hand through his brown hair. It fell back in place, mostly parting in the middle. Roughly Cord's age, this Kylan ought to be entering the Seeding this year. Kylan's deep-set blue eyes and broad shoulders made Cord ponder the relationship between the strangers.

A noble running off to wed a common suitor was something out of one of Mrs. Dunkel's stories. Cord imagined Leila swooning at the thought of it. Leila . . .

"Please untie me," Cord said as he sat up. "I have people to warn!" The sheet fell. Sunlight warmed his bare chest. Thankful to feel the confines of his shorts, Cord scanned about for his tunic.

"Right," Kylan said, picking up the bloody cloth next to him. "Sorry about that. We had to check for bites."

Cord's face flushed.

The girl's face pinked as well. She looked away downhill.

At the bottom of a knoll littered with the crumbling walls of ruins and patches of overgrown wildflowers, the other girl patted Scute by the river. Won over by an apple, the Croathite-trained charger nuzzled her. All the while, his owner suffered captivity.

Kylan ran his hand along the hilt of the sheathed sword that he hadn't bothered to hide and said, "Before we untie you—"

"If," the girl corrected.

"We need to ask you a few questions." Kylan stood to drop Cord's tunic on his lap. Then his sandals clunked against the ground. But it wasn't ground. Dark lines created large rings on the wooden surface.

The girl's focus narrowed on Cord until he smoothed his reaction to the giant stump beneath them.

"Never seen one this big," Cord mumbled.

Kylan snickered, which caused the noble to sigh.

This stump was smaller than the one in his dreams; did it hold the same secret?

Raising her arm, the noble waved for the other girl to join them. Too focused on rubbing down Scute, she didn't notice. There was something strange about the skinny girl, something more than her dark rust-colored hair. Bony and broad, she kept a brown woolen shawl folded over her chest and shoulders in the thick of summer.

"Is she sick?" Cord asked.

Kylan spoke as though Cord hadn't. "All of that blood stained your tunic, but you weren't injured. What happened?"

The image of Marlone's face flashed in Cord's mind. "It wasn't my blood." Some of it was, but he couldn't explain that to them. "That wolf killed my friend."

"Is that what brought you out here?" Kylan asked. "The wolfkin?"

"Wolfkin?" So, Judge Kline wasn't a demon? "Yes."

"And the thread?" Kylan asked, pointing at the tunic in his lap. "You're a noble?"

The noble's judgmental gaze briefly swept to her subject.

Even though he had deserted, Cord would never betray his vow to the Chancellor by revealing the secrets of his rank. These strangers had saved his life. They deserved his thanks, his honesty. But he couldn't trust them when they obviously hid their own secrets.

"Yes." Cord put on Julian's slow, proper accent and introduced himself as the councilmember of Weatherington's nephew. A gamble if the freckled girl was indeed a noble. Still, he reckoned he knew enough about Weatherington's nobility to pull it off, so long as he kept his drawl to himself.

"No province needed a councilmember and no lord's daughter required marriage," Cord explained, "so the Tribunal decreed my life be spent as a fishmonger. Headmaster Baugh graciously extended an invitation to his academe's Hansweighn feast as a welcome to the new nobles of South Thornton."

As they listened, the girl crossed her arms tighter over her breasts, watching him like a cat waiting for a fly to buzz into range.

The story got away from him for a moment, dragging him through his disappointment with High Guard Horax's judgment. When he relayed his slave's death, his voice cracked on Marlone's name. He hated painting Marlone as his slave, but his mind couldn't lie fast enough to keep up with his tongue. Cord had to slow his speech twice.

"That thing was Judge Kline," he said to the silence, meeting Kylan's cocked eyebrow without blinking. Leila might be right. He might be a horrible liar, but he had steered his words around everything to do with his curse, deserting, and even Julian just to be safe.

"Why would the nephew of a councilmember become a fishmonger?" the girl asked. "That is not a task befitting an educated child of nobility."

"Silver fish. I was to head the market on the ore harvested from their skulls. Besides, I am clearly not the heir of my line."

"Clearly," she repeated.

"Look, if it is all the same," Cord said, "I would like to get to my family as soon as possible. You have my word I will not cause trouble and will gladly be on my way if you release me."

Kylan unfolded his arms. "Kylan Nock," he said with a small smile. "Like nock an arrow, not knock on wood. I wouldn't bother to explain, but you can read. Should you feel compelled to report us, please spell it correctly."

That earned him a deep sigh from the noble.

"Naturally," Kylan said with a shrug to his friend, "we'd prefer it if you didn't."

So he could read? A forbidden trait for commoners. Or were they all nobles disguised for travel? Kylan sure didn't speak like one.

Standing for a curtsy, the girl said, "I am Rorry Pryce, Cord Sullivan. It is a pleasure to meet you." Her tone matched her flat expression. She settled on the blanket again, her hand falling on the hidden weapon.

Rorry's dress clung to the top of her boot, revealing the boot's ankle below the raised hem. Soft cloth folded over the ankle-high leather of the shoe. Above the fold, a brown ribbon had been twisted into a bow. The stout wooden heels were well made, not in the way a cordwainer would make a boot for travel, but the way one would make a boot for a noble.

The other girl noticed Rorry's summons. With a stiff posture and a flowing skirt, she resembled a small tree moving her roots to shuffle along the ground as she left Scute at the water's edge. Her straight hair didn't even bounce in the motion.

Cord held his wrists up to Kylan. "You have my word. I have to get home and warn them. Please."

"Well," Kylan said, "you're not sniffing wildly and drooling on yourself." He slid the sword's scabbard into his belt before, with a single tug, he undid the looped knots binding Cord's wrists.

"Scarlett, this is Cord Sullivan," Kylan said to the girl climbing the roots to join them. "He's the councilmember of Weatherington's nephew."

Cord ducked his head into his tunic and tugged it over his chest before reaching under the blanket to untie his ankles.

She dipped into a deep curtsy, pretending not to notice his struggle. "Scarlett Hywel," she said. "It is a pleasure to meet you." She flashed a sincere smile, but her hand rose to cover the gap from a missing tooth.

At Kylan's request, Cord repeated his story for Scarlett while he laced his sandals.

Rorry blatantly listened for inconsistencies.

This time, his tongue added more detail to Marlone's death. Cord had to stop and swallow to steady his voice.

When he finished the tale, Scarlett said, "We are honored to have been of service to you, my lord." She and Kylan gave him pitying looks mixed with curiosity.

After all, why would the death of a slave bother a noble, who probably collected slaves like silks? With Rorry's irritated expression, he could see her being that hard-hearted.

Cord stood to don his belt and realized just how tall Kylan was. He towered over all of them. Instinctively, Cord's hand patted his belt where his knife would've been. His and Julian's knives were gone.

"Is that why you are out of your township?" Cord asked. "Are they attacking elsewhere?"

"Yes," Rorry answered. "The wolfkin attacked Brewing yesterday."

"Oh, yes," Scarlett added. "Many losses. Extensive amounts of blood."

Kylan gave her a firm pat on the back.

"We were separated from our families and have been on the move since," Rorry said. "We only traveled this far south to avoid the hills. It seems that was in error."

"What are these wolfkin?" Cord asked.

"Cursed ones," Scarlett answered. "No one really knows how the curse began, but all date its origin prior to the fall of Shallyghal and the, um, Massacre of Merith. Most believe the curse to be cured. Well, eradicated. One wolfkin does not constitute an outbreak, but a Judge in Merith . . ." She bit her lip before she said to Rorry, "There will be more."

Scarlett's words sank in as Cord ground his teeth. Citizens would flee to the wilds to evade the wolfkin, only to face the wrath of the Judges—assuming they truly were Judges. That morning, the Seeding had sent young men out onto the roads all across Merith, walking straight to their deaths. There'd be no confining the beasts, just madness.

That was if what these strangers said was true. "How do you know all that?" Cord asked.

"How do you not?" Kylan replied. Before Cord answered, he said, "Will you be continuing on to Weatherington, then? A word of advice, I'd leave out the part of your story about the poor man being burned to death. It's plain as day that you disagreed with the verdict, and we all know what disagreeing with the Tribunal leads to."

Rorry cleared her throat.

Kylan went on. "I'm glad I've never seen a Judge's inquest. It probably nibbles at your soul just to be near that kind of cruelty."

Cord wished he'd not relayed the judgment to them. It didn't make sense for someone, especially a noble, to witness such a thing. Regardless, Kylan's question remained. Should he go back to South Thornton and fight this evil? Even as a deserter, he ought to protect the Light and the people of Merith. "How many more wolfkin could there be?"

Scarlett squeezed her bottom lip. "After one night in a city? If you started with one, which is unlikely. Fifty? Maybe more."

Kenton. He had to get to Kenton. "I must warn my family." He prayed Headmaster Angsly would believe him. "I will avoid everyone along the way, just to be safe."

"Correct spelling notwithstanding," Kylan said, "if you left us out of any reports, we'd appreciate it. Feel free to take credit for killing the Judge too."

"Very subtle, Kylan," Rorry said.

With a mischievous grin, he said, "It can't be helped, Rorry. There's something about him that prompts trust. I'm sure you know what I mean."

Cord tried to discern the meaning and shifted as Scarlett looked him over.

"We're out of our township due to circumstances beyond our control," Kylan explained. "After the story you shared, we can't be sure if a Judge would burn us for fleeing these beasts."

"Will you be safe?" Scarlett asked Cord. "Weatherington is not far from Brewing. Eighty miles?"

"Come now," Rorry said. "I am certain his city will welcome him home and send word to the Tribunal. After all, no roads connect Brewing to Weatherington through the hills."

"They may not be using those roads," Scarlett said.

Rorry rose without blinking.

Kylan adjusted his spectacles and joined Scarlett's stare back at the noble. He shook his head and said, "We're heading north ourselves, Cord. Would you like us to accompany you? It is our duty as common folk to see to your safety." He ignored Rorry's pursed lips. "We're several miles north of where we found you. I'd guess that puts us about two days from your province." He looked to Scarlett and received a nod. "Bear in mind, we'll move on once you're there."

With a tightly held smile, Rorry said, "Of course, you would move faster on your own."

They wouldn't travel that much slower with three on foot.

98

Unarmed, he didn't stand a chance against another wolfkin. "Where will you go?" Cord asked.

"Llandir," Kylan said. "The Seeding sends me there."

Kylan's papers would give him safety, but not the girls. Even an unescorted noblewoman would get stopped. The headmaster could see the Light better than the Judges. Maybe he'd grant them asylum. This chaos ought to allow for some leniency.

Cord offered his hand to Kylan for a shake. "You saved my life. I can request asylum for you at Kenton, a respectable hamlet in my province." When Rorry's head started shaking, he quickly added, "Or I can get you supplies if you insist on moving on. Regardless, parting at Kenton will save you from traveling north past Fort Warren with me."

While Kylan and Rorry had a silent battle of wills, Scarlett smiled at Cord. He tried not to stare at the gap in her teeth or the rift he seemed to be creating.

"We're interested in your safety, not repayment," Kylan said.

"I believe," Rorry said, "our best interest lies in advancing to a port at our earliest opportunity. However, before we alter any plans, perhaps you would like to freshen up, Cord? We can have a midday meal before we set out, together or separately."

Cord frowned. While he bathed, she'd coax her subjects out of joining him. Bloody nobles. Was his wooder smell too much for her delicate nose? "I would," he said, but only because Judge Kline's stench clung to him.

Scarlett opened a bag full of small bottles and removed a rolled cloth. She unfurled it, revealing several scented soaps molded into flat circles. He selected one that smelled of winter trees and thanked her.

Aiming for Scute, he strode through the thick silence and carried their heavy gazes on his back as he climbed over the broken walls of the Abandoned ruin hidden in the overgrowth. With a quick check on his merry steed, Cord moved on and uttered, "Traitor."

He glanced back as the three strangers started to argue. Scarlett pointed at what seemed to be a map in her hands as Kylan and Rorry exchanged whispers and hard faces. Cord prayed Kylan and Scarlett would talk Rorry into joining him. He didn't want to go alone, even if it meant putting up with the likes of her.

No matter what the haughty noble thought, asylum was their best chance for survival. If Llandir had received word of the attacks by the time they made it to the eastern coast, they'd find no quarter, just barricaded city gates.

Cord stepped into the line of trees shielding him from their view and began to undress. The cold water of the Andras ought to help cleanse his mind. As he loosened his sandal, his thoughts drifted to relaying the news of Marlone's passing to Headmaster Angsly. Reciting his prayers, he bathed.

* * *

"No!" Rorry said to Kylan's victorious grin. "We are leaving. Quickly! While he bathes." She stamped twice on the giant oak stump.

Scarlett lowered the map and worriedly said, "He has my soap."

"He is a—a flaming spy for the army!"

Kylan smirked. "And you're a *flaming* noble, Lady Gwirion. Oh, terribly sorry. It's Rorry 'Pryce' now, is it?"

She answered him with a scowl.

Ignoring it, Kylan asked, "Do you think he'll ever know he rambled on about his nobility in front of a councilmember's daughter? I could hardly look him in the eye without grinning. I'm rather impressed with myself actually."

"Pray tell, what will he do when he realizes we are fully aware of his ruse?" Rorry asked. "When he realizes we searched his belongings and understand very well what he is? The soldier's directives laid it out very clearly."

Kylan shrugged off her questions.

"If the wolfkin had taken the tunnels from Brewing," Scarlett mumbled, "they'd be at Kenton when we get there, assuming this line still connects. Wait. No. That one didn't."

Rorry put both hands on her stomach and squeezed her eyes shut. "Scarlett, please put the map away before Cord sees it."

"C'mon, Rorry," Kylan said. "He was shaking when he told us about his slave, the 'friend' whose blood stained his tunic. Right? He's not like the thralls we knew, even if he's a liar."

Too much admiration drenched that statement for her liking. "A terrible one," Rorry said, "whose deception you assisted, might I add."

He grinned. Grinned!

"You are letting his appearance influence you, Kylan. Control your quicksilver whims and consider our safety." Cord's square jaw and lean frame had failed to blind her. "Furthermore, you have no right to offer assistance before we are all three in agreement."

Kylan huffed. "He thinks we believe him." His hand stalled her interruption. "For now. I say that gives us the advantage. And we're armed. You do realize the army didn't command a wolfkin to attack him in order to lure us out? He's in just as much danger as we are."

She considered his statement and agreed the army would not have sent the wolfkin. "Our safety is my only concern."

Kylan hopped down between the roots and gathered an armful of the firewood they had collected earlier. "Now, Miss Pryce, what is this delicious meal you have planned?"

"We are not finished with this topic, Kylan."

The charming fool laughed to himself and squatted on what appeared to be the plinth of a broken column as he set to arranging the woodpile in a ring of rubble.

"Yes, Cord's loss is genuine," she admitted. "Yet I fail to see why that means we should alter our plans for a soldier in the very army we are attempting to avoid."

"You don't see it because you don't want to," Scarlett chimed in. She apologized with a wince when Rorry frowned at her.

Rorry took a deep breath. "We do not need him."

A tender expression overtook Kylan's face.

She could tell where his mouth was heading and spoke first. "He is not Grary, I know. May the gods never burden Cyr with two of him. Yet those papers prove Cord is not what he claims. You must know he believes demons dole out magic. That alone is enough reason to exercise caution and put distance between us."

"I can hide it," Scarlett said. She folded the map. "I have for years."

Attempting to lower the volume of their conversation, Rorry took Scarlett's arm and moved them through the blue thimbles and buttercups toward Kylan.

Scarlett paused to gather snippets of ironweed for her poultice bag. "As frightening as a wolfkin in Merith is, am I the only one who's relieved to have a more solid lie as to why we left Brewing?"

Walking on, Rorry answered, "It gives us more confidence in the telling. Whether a Judge cares to believe us is another challenge entirely. Cord may be credulous, but I doubt they will be."

Kylan scanned the trees upriver. "He's out of view, Scarlett. You can kindle it."

Without taking her focus from placing the ironweed in her bag, Scarlett waved her wrist. Flames sprang forth and swarmed the logs.

"You're getting better at this," he said.

Adding sticks to the pile, Rorry nursed the fire. "How foolish does he think we are? He did not even change out of his uniform."

"Survival may have interrupted his trip to the wardrobe," Kylan said. "Who hasn't been there?"

Scarlett giggled, encouraging his foolishness.

The humor faded from his expression when he saw Rorry's scowl. "Should we have let him die? Would you prefer that he had been turned into a wolfkin?"

Surrendering without a response, Rorry returned to the stump. She threw back Scarlett's blanket. It might have been silly to hide Master Clienne's crossbow, but there was no need to put Cord's guard up when he woke. Her tension eased as she ran her fingertips along the silver script.

The birch trees on the riverbank revealed nothing where the sad survivor had gone to bathe. Was she being too hard again? Cord's knives, now stowed in Kylan's boot, had not been requested. If anything, he seemed to be of a single mind in his desire to warn his family, whomever that entailed.

"I know it's not ideal," Kylan said, "but it feels important that we help him."

Given the sincerity in his voice, Rorry refrained from asking where those feelings had originated from, at the expense of a perfect opportunity to use one of his colorful innuendos. His warm smile melted her resolve. Perhaps it was unfair to assume Cord's face and muscles clouded Kylan's judgment any more than they did hers.

Scarlett lowered next to the fire and tapped her lips while studying the map again. "This oak must be the one in the Garden of the Gods."

Surveying the ruins, Rorry imagined how glorious something by that name must have been centuries ago. It had not survived the Purge any better than the tree. After rejoining the others at the fire, she spied over Scarlett's shoulder.

"There are several leading north," Scarlett said, "and more toward the core of the island. They should be fairly common on the way to Kenton, I believe." Scarlett's finger traced a line of faded red stars, each representing a giant oak stump. "We should stay close to these, just in case there are more wolfkin."

Translating some of the Old Tongue, Rorry determined a trip past Kenton meant sacrificing their cushion days. Their travels had already been delayed much of the morning to watch Cord sleep. Her friends were too kind, too quick to abandon their plan. Fools dallied as a hobby and died young.

Kylan sniffed and said, "Assuming we want to go back down there. Is it a coincidence we heard something following us and climbed up here to find a wolfkin attacking Cord?" With an unsettling amount of seriousness to come from him, he sat back on his heels and asked, "Should we consider Cord's offer of sanctuary, at least until a better opportunity presents itself? I hate to say it, but we faced enough danger escaping Merith under normal circumstances. With an invasion or an outbreak . . . we can't predict anything."

"Invasion?" Rorry asked. "It was just the one."

He shrugged. "That's how the ancient Dalians did it before the Cloud consumed them. They sent in wolfkin as scouts, right?" he asked Scarlett.

She hummed an agreement.

"See? They cursed the leaders and their opponents' defenses crumbled." Both looked at Rorry expectantly.

Rorry hung her head. She had been denying the impact the beast had made on their escape, playing it off as a hiccup, a coincidental monster to ponder once they reached the continent. "If we stay," she said, "they will send word and hold us in suspicion until our story is verified. We must keep going and hope we can outrun this—whatever it is."

Rubbing his chin, Kylan nodded. Then he snickered, foretelling something obnoxious. "Miss Pryce, you may want to figure out why we have this fire if you want that handsome lad to believe you're well-versed in the arts of wifery." He gave her that foolish Nock grin he used to make every joke acceptable.

"That's not a word," Scarlett murmured.

Without giving Kylan's comment the full attention it deserved, Rorry took a seat between them and laid the crossbow on the grass. "Very well. You can use the food we brought. If we are going to escort him, we may as well lighten your load. With a spy for the army traveling at our side, Spectre must stay in his coin." She meant for the comment to give Kylan pause, but it only spread his smile. "We will have to leave the saddle as well, to avoid raising further suspicion."

Scarlett never looked up from her plotting.

"Outstanding!" Kylan shouted. He threw the provisions bag to Rorry's side and sprang to his feet. "If you'll excuse me." He set off, hopping across stones toward the river.

"Wait!" Rorry called. "Where are you going?"

Topping a boulder, he gave her a wink. "In search of quicksilver whims."

Rorry watched him disappear behind the birches near where Cord bathed. Removing wrapped meat, cheese, and bread from the saddlebag, she said, "He had better keep his knife handy." She speared some salted hare with a stick and set it atop the fire.

"I'm sure he'll keep a sharp eye," Scarlett said.

Rorry laughed quietly and blushed, despite herself. She tried to draw her mind back from the sight Scarlett's comment conjured.

Scarlett lowered the map and asked, "Do you think our parents are safe? We could warn them."

The steely glare Rorry shot her was as unintentional as it was swift. She did consider the question, but would not abide another delay.

"No. I suppose we can't. The watchmen would detain us at the gate."

Rorry tried to lighten the mood by chuckling when she said, "Your mother could take on the Tribunal herself—without magic. There is no need to worry about Brewing. If this is an invasion, they would gain nothing by taking a town surrounded by hills on a river to nowhere."

Her Grace would scold her for saying that. She must be worried by now. Perhaps she had found her note and finally understood, even if Grary had held his tongue when they'd discovered Rorry missing that morning.

The sound of a large splash came from upstream. Not even the frigid waters of the Andras could dissuade Kylan. There was some wisdom in his approach—not of his obvious effort to interrupt Cord's bath, but of enjoying this freedom for which they had risked everything to obtain.

She slipped off her boots and stockings and ran her toes through the grass before sagging against Scarlett to breathe in her friend's apple blossom lotion.

"Should we tell Cord his friend isn't dead?" Scarlett asked.

"He may as well be. If Cord knew the truth, he might seek him out and either die at his hands or be cursed too."

Scarlett glanced over to Cord's belongings. "Maybe that ring of his can help us."

Chapter II: Seeds

By late afternoon, Kylan's temper had reached its brim. If it weren't for Scarlett's part in the plan, he would've insisted on her hefty possessions replacing her in Scute's saddle. He wiped the sweat from his spectacles in order to see Rorry's pout next to him.

"I do not loathe him," she said too loudly.

Whether he heard, Cord didn't turn back from leading Scute through the old Ysbrydoli Woods, or whatever their modern name was.

"Then why does your aim keep drifting toward his back?" Kylan asked.

"We may never know." With her eye on Cord, she unlatched her satchel and pulled out Mrs. Hywel's map.

Kylan walked ahead to block her from the soldier's view.

The bloodstains on Cord's uniform stirred Kylan's concern again. He hoped his dad and Kit were safe back in Brewing. If Mrs. Hywel came after them, it'd put Kit in danger and remove Brewing's greatest chance of survival at the same time. No, Rorry was right. Brewing would be fine.

Kylan heard her refold the map before she cleared her throat. He fell back to walk beside her. "Brewing will be fine," he repeated to himself.

"I have no doubts. As wicked as finding a silver lining in all of this is, we should be thankful the army has a distraction."

Like clockwork, Scarlett checked behind her to see Rorry point left. "May I let him run again?" Scarlett asked Cord, reaching for his coiled lead. "Thank you!" She set off with Scute, steering him in the direction Rorry pointed.

Not only did their plan have Kylan avoiding horse manure as he trailed behind, it had also taken them away from the cooler air of the river. His fantasies of tossing Scarlett's possessions behind a dead tree verged on irresistible.

Ahead, Scarlett gasped.

Kylan dropped the load and raced behind Cord toward her shouts. They broke through the foliage to find Scarlett alone, still in the saddle, at the edge of a cliff. Blocks of land had been cut away evenly beneath the cliff's edge. A small lake filled the bottom of the ancient granite quarry, one of dozens the army had harvested for the Great Barrier.

She had stopped the horse far enough back.

"Did the quarry jump out and scare you?" Kylan asked.

Scarlett shook her head and pointed across the pit.

"Oh," Cord breathed, "look at that."

At the far side, the giant oak Scarlett had been guiding them toward dangled over the quarry. A quarter of its roots were still buried, with no sign of anything having ever been beneath it but dirt. A flaw in the plan. That wouldn't sit well with Rorry.

Rorry palmed her satchel and said, "We are exposed here. I would like to be north of this quarry before we break next."

Siding with his polite self, Kylan gave up on letting the bundle be a casualty of the excitement. "Walk with me to get Scarlett's things?" he asked Rorry. As they left the others, he said, "If we have to use the tunnels, I can see how leaving a horse behind isn't a great cause for concern, but its owner may disagree—Oh hey, speaking of, what about its owner?"

"There is cause to be hasty here, Kylan. The next stump is over an hour to the northwest."

He stopped still, awaiting an answer.

"What do you want me to say? You and Scarlett are my responsibility, not him."

"Thanks, I think. We can't leave him to the wolves."

She carried on and said, "Should that circumstance arise, his decision is his own." Rorry seized Scarlett's belongings and dragged the bundle over the dead leaves. She released it in front of him. "Now, I am going to check on Scarlett. Do not tarry."

"I'm coming," Kylan said, throttling the tied sheet beneath the knot. "I just wanted to hear you say you'd let him make a decision before shooting him."

She splayed her arms as she walked away.

They were well beyond the quarry and another fully rooted stump before Rorry agreed to rest for a meal among more ruins. The late summer sky had just begun to pink over the boulder-strewn grass.

Sneaking away to be alone for a while, Kylan left Scarlett and Rorry speaking by the fire. Within sight of them, he happened upon a statue, well the large feet of one, half-buried in the tall grass. The statue must have been enormous before the army had destroyed it.

After climbing over the brush growing between its toes, he reclined on a foot and fished out the scrap of birch he had been trimming into Kit's figure. Her smile needed to be carved before his memory blurred.

From the hidden sheath in his right boot, he removed his father's fat-handled carving knife. With the point of the small blade poised on the figure's face, he set to work.

Before long, the grass crunched beneath more steps.

"Mind the toes!" Kylan said to Cord.

Cord flinched before he realized what Kylan was sitting on. He shook his head and climbed up to take a seat on the ankle behind Kylan. "I meant to thank you for saving me. In the midst of it all, I forgot."

"Binding someone does tend to make them forget their manners."

"Reckon it does."

"Reckon?" Kylan asked, unable to look Cord in the eye. The way his accent kept giving him away, it was a wonder he even tried to keep up his deception. "You sound like my dad. He's from Weatherington, one of the villages, Relman. But rumors say it burned shortly after he left."

"Are you a carver?"

"The son of a woodworker, though I suppose I should just say woodworker now. The Seeding claims that I am." He presented the figure. "This is Kit. I almost had one of everyone I knew in Brewing. I'd planned to take them to my new home as a way to remember them. In the end, I just have the one that was in my pocket."

"Did you love her?"

"She's my twelve-year-old sister, the youngest of the Nock kids. So, yes? Most days. Seamus and Ellick, our brothers, entered the Seeding years ago."

Kit had probably thundered swears throughout the house when she'd discovered he'd left without waking her. At least this winter she'd get all the cinnamon candies. After their mom had passed, Kylan and his brothers had insisted that their father make it every year at Winter Peak. Even though Kit never really knew their mother, she ate every last one she could find. Great, now he was craving candy.

"What about you?" Kylan asked. "Where are your siblings?"

The cadet's shoulders rose. Without much thought, Cord said, "I don't have—"

"I mean, the councilmember of Weatherington has a rather large family, doesn't he? Is that common for nobles?"

Kylan sucked back his grin as he pretended to listen to the tale Cord spun. He had to get Kit's nose just right, perfectly straight at the bottom. Once satisfied, he nodded to Cord, who had grown silent. There was a fractured innocence in the brown eyes watching Kylan's hands, not unlike the vacancy in his dad's eyes after his mom had died. He should've known better than to ask Cord about family. Cadets were orphans but were brought up like brothers. "Tell me about Marlone."

Cord clenched his jaw and eyed him. "There's not much to tell."

"He was a person, Cord. It's obvious he meant a lot to you—

there's no shame in a noble knowing his servants well."

Cord's eyes drifted toward the girls but didn't seem to land on anything in particular. He nodded and smiled slightly. "He was a lousy huntsman, too busy flirting to learn—with other slaves, of course, not with the girls in town. Flirting, not learning."

Kylan continued his work and listened without reacting.

"Marlone . . . he was fiercely loyal. He always watched out for me. I just wish I'd seen that sooner."

They sat in silence for a while, long enough for Kylan to detail Kit's apron. The figure resembled his mom a bit more than Kit while wearing that.

"She has your smirk," Cord said.

Kylan sniffed. "Yeah. Brat."

"Are you worried about her?"

"Nah," Kylan said easily. "My father would die protecting her. And, after all, we live in Merith. The Seeding would've removed them from my life today. Cruel fate either way, no?"

The question went unanswered. Let the Chancellor's thrall inside him mull it over. Kylan refused to dismiss Cord as a lost cause. Rorry had valid reasons for caution. Beyond valid. But Cord seemed so familiar, as though their friendship had existed before. A false bond, perhaps, but worth protecting as far as Kenton.

Cord ripped a few pieces of grass from the overgrowth and picked them apart.

"I'm sorry for your loss," Kylan said, pressing his spectacles up the bridge of his nose.

The girls sat up and searched about until they spotted them. Scarlett waved some skewered meat to signal dinner was ready.

They were at risk for the same end as Marlone. If Kylan hadn't agreed to Rorry's plan, if he hadn't felt he needed them with him for the courage to escape Merith, would they be safe at home in Brewing? He snorted at the thought of Rorry marrying Grary, especially after the beating he and Scarlett had taken.

Cord waited for an explanation for the sound.

"If this all goes to the stew," Kylan said, "I want to die first."

With a frown, Cord brushed off his hands.

Again, Kylan had stuck his foot in his mouth. He put the knife down. "It's not my place to suggest it, but you could leave with us, you know? The continent is safer than waiting out this wolfkin mess."

Cord's brow furrowed. "I can't leave. My people need someone to defend them."

"They have a whole army, *the* army. Not that it does a lot of good if the army is cursed, I'll admit. But think on it. We'd be glad for the company." Rorry would box his ears for planting that seed.

The soldier stood over him. "The army is protected by the Chancellor's Light. You oughta have more faith."

Arching his eyebrow, Kylan resumed his carving. "You must've forgotten your tale about the innocent who burned in South Thornton. That's not the first injustice I've heard carried out in the Chancellor's name." When he looked up, there wasn't enough fire in Cord's eyes to say he wasn't listening, but plenty of tension in his jaw telling Kylan that he was crushing the eggshells he should be walking on. "My mom used to tell us to inspect the larks we tie our hopes to. Have you?"

Mumbling, Cord set off for the food.

Kylan watched him leave. "I do love that uniform."

They finished their meal within minutes and set off again. It was over two hours later when they finally reached Carno Bridge, the point where Rorry said they would break for the night once settled on the other side of the Andras.

The covered bridge continuing the Southern Road arched with a gentle ease to the slim island in the middle of the river. Ornate bronze flames bordered both the sculpted cloudlike underside of the bridge's roof and the red jasper slabs of the floor. The bridge belonged to Shallyghal, not Merith. The army must've been too lazy to destroy it in the Purge and build their own. Maybe they liked the flames?

Kylan wasn't sure if they were in the South Thornton Province or if they'd passed back into Brewing. But he knew the bridge's twin on the far side of the island ended in the Weatherington Province.

It would've been an easy milestone to reach, if not for the obstacle smack-dab in the middle of the treeless island, the village named for the bridge. The brown stones of Carno Bridge's walls butted up against the shores and the road. The good news: there weren't any watchmen in sight. The bad news: there was nowhere to hide and no way to sneak by unseen, not with the brightness of the full moon.

Considering their options, Kylan rubbed his chin. While the papers kept him and Cord safe, the girls had no justification for wandering the wilds. If they had to, they could probably outrun any watchmen. Well, except Scarlett. She'd need to ride Scute, which was an even worse idea because the watchmen might pursue them on horseback and would definitely catch them all.

"You are a noble," Rorry said straight to Cord's face. "Could you not tell the watchmen we are your sisters?"

Cord studied the walls of the village as he thought of a way out of her trap.

"Funny," Kylan said to Rorry. "You don't look very noble. Servants, maybe?"

"How did you get past them before?" Scarlett asked Cord.

"I was not hiding three commoners," he answered.

Rorry nodded to herself. "You only need to hide two—"

"I say we run for it," Kylan said. "Put Scarlett in the saddle and just run." No. Something, a nagging in his chest, told him that wasn't right.

"Or," Rorry said with her hand around his belt, as though she meant to hold him back. "You two approach and signal when it is safe for us to sneak across. Villages with dense walls like those rarely have ramparts, which means the watchmen use spy holes in the doors to watch the road. If you block their view and distract the watchmen well enough, perhaps we can pass behind Scute."

"Distract them?" Cord asked.

She made an annoyed face at him and lifted her crossbow. "I could remove them, though that feels excessive."

Already moving to secure Scarlett's poultice bag to Scute's saddle, Kylan said, "Oh good. A conversation with strangers. My favorite thing."

Scarlett lifted the katana from his belt. "You should warn them, if you can."

"If they'll believe us," Kylan said.

"We should try," Cord agreed.

Rorry handed Kylan her satchel and said with sincerity, "Do not laugh."

"It's not a funeral. I'll be fine." Amused by Cord's confusion, Kylan didn't bother to explain.

After Cord secured the lumpy bundle to the pommel, they started over the river. The girls clung low to the walls of the bridge as he and Cord moved on. As soon as they stepped off the bridge, the horse's clops rang out in the night, hammering through the evening buzz and the gentle sloshing of the current behind them. Kylan took a deep breath when the town gate came into view.

As Rorry had predicted, eyes spied through barred holes that were large enough to see the watchmen's full heads and shoulders. Scute wouldn't be able to block their entire view without standing against the gate. That's when Kylan's nerves kicked in, uncorking his inappropriate mirth. He bit the inside of his cheek to keep from grinning. Rorry would slap him if he bungled this, even if it was her fault for bringing it up.

He was about to suggest that Cord do the talking when he realized the soldier walked on the opposite side of his horse, hiding the emblem on his uniform. Kylan hadn't considered the questions that might raise. Then what would Cord do? Act upon Rorry's fears and turn them in to save himself?

"I'll talk," Kylan grumbled, heading straight for the gate. Cord brought Scute close behind him.

He didn't get quite as near the gate as he wanted before a watchman with a saggy, wrinkled face like a rotten cantaloupe said, "Give me your papers or piss off. We don't trade with Seeders unless you belong here."

Inching forward, Kylan said, "Good evening." He hesitated, drawing out his reply until Scute blocked as much of the view as he could. "No, no. Not trade. We came with a warning, I'm afraid." The second watchman was uglier than the first. Unable to resist, Kylan snickered.

"Since when are warnings funny?" the watchman asked. His breath smelled just as rotten.

Rorry's wooden heels moved onto the road as loudly as Scute's shoes had and suddenly stopped.

"They're not," Kylan answered, shaking the amusement from his face. "I just never thought I'd say the words is all. We just came from the south. Wolfkin are attacking there."

"What are?" the guard asked. "Wolf-men?"

"Essentially."

"What are you saying, stranger?" the second watchmen asked in a high-pitched voice, not unlike the one his mom had used when voicing woodland critters in her bedtime stories. Kylan dug his fingernails into his palm, pleading for the pain to kill his curling grin.

He smelled Rorry's perfume. All he had to do was keep it together for a minute longer.

The watchmen squinted at each other. Then metal rattled behind the door. The lock squeaked.

A calming sensation rushed through his chest, like a blast of air squelching his laughter. He shoved the gate closed. "Don't open your doors!" Kylan yelled. "I'm talking about wolves! The wolfkin curse! Keep your gate closed and your town survives!" That seemed to offend the guards more than anything.

"Here," Kylan said. He opened Rorry's satchel and removed Grary's Seeding papers. "Proof." He passed them through the bars and stood against the gate.

The watchmen studied the documents.

Out of the corner of his eye, Kylan saw Cord waving the girls on. "If you don't believe me, tear them up. I can't read, so I dunno what those papers say. But I came from Brewing this morning and ran into my new friend, Cord, here. No sooner had we shaken hands than one of those beasts, a big ol' ugly thing . . ."

He wasn't sure why he suddenly had a bumpkin wooder's accent but ran with it. "Half man, half wolf. But a big fella, ya know? Bigger than one of us and ol' Rupert Magill. Well, you don't know Rupert, but he's huge. Anyhow, it just leaped outta the bushes with long, sharp fangs, snapping and biting like we were head to foot made of bacon. Ashes, we killed the thing and good, but it took both of us and a shitload of wish-rattling crickets."

The melon-face had stopped reading the papers and didn't blink as he watched Kylan. The other guard scrutinized every written word in the dim light.

Kylan put his right hand over his heart and held up his left. "May the Light burn those papers, right here and right now, if I'm lying."

While the guards read the papers again, Kylan checked beyond Cord's confusion for the girls' progress. Cowering and barefoot, they listened from the bridge to Weatherington.

"Well, anyway," Kylan said. "Cord thought we oughta warn you lot before we head on. The neighborly thing to do and all." Reaching his hand to the slot, Kylan waited for the guard to roll the papers and stick them back through. "Don't open the gate for anyone who's drooling all over himself now. The curse does that to them. It makes them hungry for flesh, the older the better. They like it aged."

Both pairs of eyes swept from Kylan to Cord and back.

"That goes for Judges too," Kylan added as he put Grary's papers back in the satchel.

"Now you just wait a moment," the second watchman shrilled.

And with that, Kylan's ill-timed humor returned. He barked a laugh.

"Are you telling us we're not supposed to open our gates for a Judge? You trying to get us burned, boy?"

Biting hard on his lip, Kylan couldn't respond without laughing. He pretended he didn't hear him and walked on. They could run for it now.

But Cord stepped around Scute and puffed out his chest behind the gold feather. "He speaks the truth."

Something about the display made Kylan queasy, probably the symbol of a vile tyrant's army being used to actually protect the people. Or maybe because it was defending his lie instead of the Chancellor's. "We're off, then," Kylan said, stomping after the girls.

"Pray to the Light that those beasts don't come this way," Cord said. "But be ready if they do. May the Chancellor's Light shield you, friends."

Pausing at the bridge for Cord to catch up, Kylan shrugged at him. "They're warned. Feel better?"

"I suppose." His worry disappeared with a chuckle. "'Shitload of wish-rattling crickets,' huh?"

Chapter 12: Proper Avoidance

Cord and Kylan had Scarlett laughing so hard Rorry had to shush them twice before she could force them off the road and deeper into the woods for the night. Invigorated by their victory, they did not seem to share Rorry's concerns for a safe place to camp. She had to suggest it three times over the retelling of Kylan's story at Carno Bridge before they stopped tripping over roots in the darkness and focused.

The white of Cord's smile disappeared when he saw her face. "I know a place to camp," he said. "I stayed there on my way south. It is near the road but out of view."

As the dark-haired stranger led the way, Rorry huddled against Scarlett and Kylan. "The three of us will need to take turns keeping watch," she whispered. They shared a tired expression but not with each other. "There are more dangers out here than him. I would prefer not to leave our well-being in his hands."

They agreed through their silence alone.

A half mile from the bridge, Cord led them up a stream to a pond filled by a waterfall from a rocky ledge. "This is it," he said. "I'll camp here. Y'all oughta be safe up there by the stream." After escorting them around the pond and up to the top of the hill, he made his excuses about washing the sweat from his clothes and left them for the night.

"It is foolish for him to separate from us," Rorry surprised herself by saying. She recovered with, "He could sneak back and turn us in."

Kylan sighed. "He didn't camp here alone last time, Rorry. We can give him time to himself."

They rolled out their bedding near the stream and lay there whispering for a while.

Scarlett was softly snoring when Kylan said, "I killed someone today. Why is that only bothering me now?"

"He was cursed," Rorry replied. "You did him a favor."

"Think he'd agree?"

"Is eating human flesh preferable?"

"I mean, as opposed to finding a cure, a way to break the curse?"

That curse had survived centuries. Centuries! The three of them would not find its cure traipsing across Merith and, were they willing, certainly could not haul a captive wolfkin with them. Unable to form a sensitive response, she let the question steep. She had already been too harsh today.

"Will you be sorry to see Cord go?" she asked.

Beneath the tree closest to the trail downhill, Kylan's chest rose and fell evenly beneath his crossed arms. In a way, she received her answer. His blanket now warmed the soldier down by the waterfall.

Aware she had volunteered for the first watch merely by staying awake, Rorry picked up the crossbow she had been carrying all day. The placid evening under the stars tasked her with recounting the day's events for entertainment. Remembering Kylan's success at the river earlier, she grinned and threw her blanket aside. Then she covered herself again. Scarlett lay completely swallowed in linens to her right. No one would know without Rorry telling them, which a lady would not. A lady would not peep like some criminal either. The excitement in her belly overruled her sensibilities. She got up.

Gingerly padding her way past Kylan and down alongside the stream, Rorry slowed near the rocky ledge. She removed her finger from the crossbow's trigger to avoid accidentally loosing a bolt due to jittery nerves and lay near the showering water to peer over.

The moonlight lit little for her. When she saw Scute, she ducked back. What was she doing? Contrary to what she wanted to be, she was the daughter of a councilmember. Raised to be a lady! Or should she embrace her new life as a common friend to a witch and a dandelion?

She rose up on her elbows to taste her rebellion. Cord stood waist-deep in the pool at the base of the waterfall as he wrung out his clothes and flattened them on the rocks to dry. A clump of shiny hair stuck to his temple, where it had curled. His wet torso glistened in the light off the ripples. Enough. She sat up with her back turned and listened to his splashing until his bath ended. Her lewdness had been rewarded. No need to make it an outright violation.

Quietly standing, Rorry froze when she heard a whimper from below. She eased her view back down. Wrapped in Kylan's blanket, Cord lay still beside his clothes. Was he weeping? That must have been what she'd heard.

For a moment, her concern challenged her perspective on the army's tool. A primal nurturing, surely. An innate trait in women. Empathetic foolishness. Yet she stood there willingly for the remainder of her watch, guarding her companions, all three of them.

Distracting herself, she dreamed of her plan, not the plan of Cord's deliverance or their planned trip to Llandir. No, she thought of the plan that brought a smile to her face and released her mind to a world drenched with possibilities, a place where encountering the unknown could be a happy event once more.

The spilling waterfall cast her thoughts to the waves and set her to imagining sailing on the ship Kylan would secure for their search for Alis. Would they find her before Scarlett received a mage's mantle from the Tower? What if Alis had already obtained her freedom? She might not remember she had a little sister, depending on the toll slavery had taken on her. Would Alis join them to aimlessly ride the waves across Cyr?

Would she want to stay with Alis?

The hours passed in a blur, occasionally interrupted by Cord talking loudly in his sleep and Kylan rolling over, unable to find comfort on the roots. When the woods felt safe to Rorry, she surrendered to the numbness in her cold feet. No one in their right mind should feel safe in the wilds. She woke Kylan with a gentle touch and wordlessly handed over Master Clienne's weapon. After sliding her stockings on, she sank against her bedroll, rubbed her feet together, and soothed the ache of her eyes.

The scent of a cooking fire woke her. The pallid sky, not yet blue, lazed above the trees. Her stomach grumbled for whatever that delicious aroma was. Fish? There wasn't a fire near her. Cord must have roused before the birds.

Moving to rub her eyes, her hand met something damp beneath her linen sheet. Unsure what to make of the wadded clothing at first, Rorry spread it out on her lap. She inhaled deeply through her nostrils.

Debating between the two rogues, she peered at Scarlett and Kylan. So far as she could tell, Kylan had fallen back asleep during his turn as guard, though the crossbow lay between her and Scarlett. Still fully tucked beneath her blanket, Scarlett might not wake from the impact; Rorry chose her target and slung the wadded smallclothes at Kylan, striking him in the face.

He woke in a daze.

"I am not amused," she said flatly. "I do not want to know how you got them; just take them back!"

Rorry could not tell if Kylan's confusion was genuine as he put on his spectacles.

He unwadded the undergarments. Laughter bent him over until it brought tears to his eyes.

Rorry's frown began to crack. "Honestly!" she said. "You choose odd times to ignore your sensitivity."

He took a breath and said, "I'm not gonna claim responsibility, but I'll take 'em back." He always sounded more like a villager, like his father, when he was tired. Kylan pulled his britches over his shorts and grabbed his boots. With the stolen prank in hand, he snickered loudly and shook with silent chuckles.

"Kylan," she scolded, sending more chuckles through him.

"I'll be right back."

Doubtful of his guilt, she watched him disappear behind the thicket. "Scarlett," Rorry said firmly.

Scarlett gasped awake, as usual. Her blanket fell as she sat up. Still draped in her dress and shawl, she looked at Rorry with concern.

"Would you happen to know how Cord's smallclothes pranced their way to my bedroll?"

Scarlett's large eyes wandered in a circle before she shook her head slowly. Even after a shared lifetime, Scarlett's tells evaded Rorry. It would take Kylan to figure this mystery out; Rorry could read him, and he did not mind in the least. If not for his laughter, she never would have known Scarlett to be guilty of half the scandals they perpetrated.

Sliding her right leg into her boot, Rorry let her accusation linger. She reached behind her knee to slip cloth loops over the three studs at the top and repeated the process with the left as Scarlett laced hers up. The road had been harder than Rorry had imagined. Already, her tender feet wanted to be free of their wood and leather mortars.

Eager to end this deviation, she forced her stiff muscles to lift her up. By nightfall, it would be over. She could tie her hair up off her neck with Alis's dyed ribbon, stop cringing each time Kylan opened his mouth, and most importantly, force Scarlett and Kylan back down into the tunnels. By this time tomorrow, they would be back on the path to freedom and she would be free of worry for what her friends' good intentions might bring.

Kylan returned as they folded their linens. He sneered before he said, "He was praying to the Holy Nose. I left them next to my blanket and snuck away."

"Ah," Rorry mocked. "You mean to say we should leave and reduce our complications, but we cannot heed such sage advice because our provisions are tucked neatly into his saddlebags?" Accurate or not, it felt good to get that off her chest.

"I do admire your restraint from self-righteousness," he said, knuckling his back.

Scarlett admitted, "I pray, sometimes. When I'm scared or sad."

"To the Chancellor?" Kylan asked, arching his eyebrow. "At least you have the sense to call on unseen mighty beings in the sky, as opposed to a man who believes death is a door to war. I'd sooner worship a horned toad." He began rolling Scarlett's bedroll. "You're welcome to join me, of course. We could start the Order of the Horny Toads, seclude ourselves off in the hills somewhere, and run amok in garments of offensively bright colors."

"I believe it takes more than seclusion and clothes to make a religion," Rorry teased.

"I defy your persecution. But you're right. We'll need an enemy. I appreciate your volunteering and accept."

A few moments later, Cord silenced their badinage by riding Scute uphill. Rorry kept her gaze off her friends' snickering faces. Though she had no real reason to feel guilty, she blushed.

He hopped down and passed a skewer of cooked fish to each of them. "I caught them this morning."

The cleaned, fluffy white meat stirred a ravenous appetite within Rorry, but could she trust it? Even if he had not possessed poison when they'd searched his bags, it grew in forests readily enough.

Scarlett secretly glanced to Rorry for a second, telling her the possibility of finding the ring was more appetizing to her than the meal.

After dinner last night, Cord had burned his directives when he'd thought no one was looking. She and Scarlett prayed he had not attempted to discard the ring in the same manner and had agreed one of them would check the ashes before they set out each time. It made Rorry angry to think of any advantage being lost to the wilds. Scarlett handed her breakfast to Kylan before excusing herself in order to wash her face down below.

Rorry's fingers began picking at the fish until she realized Cord was watching her. "Would you care to say the blessing for us?" she asked him.

"Of course," Cord said. As Cord bowed his head and prayed

aloud to the Light, Kylan made a face at her.

A twinge of vindication tempted her to smile. With any luck, one more "Almighty Chancellor" might convince Kylan to gag him. His flouting their plan to continue on had gained the soldier no favor with her.

By the end of the prayer, Kylan had already eaten half of his serving and was eyeing Scarlett's.

Cord began loading their belongings onto Scute, starting with Rorry's. When he bent to gather her bedding, she glanced down to see if he had donned the underclothes, merely out of curiosity. The lines under his shorts indicated he had.

Kylan smirked at her and received a proper scowl.

Once Scarlett had returned with a disappointed frown for Rorry, she let Kylan keep her fish. She should not have. Did she not realize how vital her energy was?

Cord brought his horse into a circle of light breaking through the forest's canopy and patted the saddle as an invitation to Scarlett. To Rorry's surprise, he had set Scute's direction to the north, not downhill and east to the Southern Road.

Taking up guard again, Rorry stayed closer to Cord and Scarlett this time. Scute carried most of Scarlett's belongings, dangling from twine, which eased Kylan's temper. Rorry hoped that freedom would not apply to his tongue.

Sparse of undergrowth, but not exactly a trail either, the old forest allowed a decent pace, albeit slower than the Starlight Tunnels.

Scarlett brushed Scute's mane with her fingers and occasionally smiled to herself. Rorry prayed she was not getting attached.

Cord sacrificed his break from walking for Scarlett's sake. He either believed her to be ill or wanted to speed her up, or both. In the end, it helped their strategy, so Rorry said nothing. Smiling up at Scarlett, Cord started yet another conversation about Scute.

Scute bounced Scarlett, and Scarlett groped her breast. Cord's head jerked forward, his ears blazing red. Rorry doubted he realized Scarlett held Spectre's coin in place on the string tied around her. No, the unlearned man would never dream such a thing as a spectral horse existed, not without hearing some fanciful tale of the Chancellor's conquest of one with an ear of corn and a tack, forcing the gods to curse Prince Rhyn with another five hundred years of uncontested rule. Regardless, she had meant to address the behavior with Scarlett last night.

With a sigh, Rorry considered letting Kylan finish his tale of interrupting Cord's bath, once the burdensome soldier was gone. It had taken miles to wipe the smirk from his face yesterday.

Cord glanced Rorry's way.

She jerked her aim to the shadows again and let the distraction hold her. Her face warmed. Burn Kylan for putting those thoughts in her mind!

Kylan cleared his throat by her ear and whispered, "Lady with the crossbow who is supposed to be safeguarding our lives, Cord asked you a question."

"Oh, pardon me," Rorry said, feeling the warmth returning to her cheeks.

"Where are we exactly?" Cord asked. "I am somewhat lost, since we didn't—did not stay with the road." To Rorry's feigned confusion, he said, "I thought I saw you with a map earlier?"

Resting her free hand on her satchel, she said, "Oh yes. Well, it is an older map and not very useful to gauge distance." Not on the surface. When Cord furrowed his brow, she had to force the crossbow to target the forest floor.

"We should be to Kenton by sundown," Kylan said with a stretch, "perhaps a tad before, as long as we keep moving."

Scarlett gave Scute a slight kick and clicked her tongue, prompting a trot with Cord still holding the lead. He stumbled before pulling Scute back.

Scarlett's giggle made Rorry momentarily glad for the turn of events. Perhaps her friends had not lost all reason when it came to the soldier. However, their distractions were typically less awkward. Anyone could have seen through that one.

Thankfully, Scarlett came to the rescue. She glanced back at Rorry with a knowing grin. "Cord, Kylan didn't explain why he declined to ride

Scute yesterday. We should tell you about the last time he tried to ride my father's horse."

Unable to help herself, Rorry laughed.

"The saddle *was* fastened!" Kylan said.

Rorry and Scarlett pressed on with their teasing. The heat lessened Kylan's good nature. But once Cord joined in the banter, he lightened up again.

As she'd feared, Kylan's mouth began to run freely. Rorry studied Cord's reactions to Kylan's lewd jokes, and even a few careless ones about the army. Cord did not preach against the minor heresy as much as gawk in wonder, perhaps bashfully grinning a time or two.

The morning went by without incident or the discovery of any ruins, besides a couple of stumps. Before long, their tactic backfired. Scute's jaunt led them to a dirt path. Contrary to common sense and Rorry's insistence, Cord convinced the others to take the seemingly disused trail to help him keep his bearings.

Not an hour had passed before Rorry wished she had fought harder. The dire consequences of roads, even this dirt path through the dark woods, now rode toward them.

To Cord's credit, he'd spotted the horsemen first and warned them into the darkness off the trail. Rorry helped Scarlett down from the saddle and moved her behind an old elm. Ten feet away, Kylan put his back to the thick, mossy bole of a long dead white oak splotched with lichen.

Rorry spied around the elm. "Judges," she said, as though this silliness had another possible outcome. Two Judges. They had not sped up, which meant they had not seen them.

When she turned back, Cord waited in Scute's saddle with a dangerous demeanor promising action.

Waving him off, Kylan insisted, "Take him deeper."

Cord shook his head and leaned down to whisper, "I'll lead them away."

"Are you mad?" Kylan asked.

"I have my Seeding papers," Cord said. "I'll be fine." They all knew that was an exaggeration at best.

"And if they're cursed?" Kylan asked.

Scarlett whined, verging on tears. Rorry took her hand and reconsidered Cord. If he would sacrifice himself for her friends, perhaps she had been too harsh. She squashed down the temptation to be rid of him and the Judges and said, "Never gamble with a Judge's tolerance! Do as Kylan says. Take refuge deeper in." Her words carried enough authority to stall any argument.

Nevertheless, his jaw set as though he planned to fight her on it.

They did not have time for a debate! She gave him the best condescending look she could muster.

The fight faded from his features. "I won't be far," he agreed, prodding Scute into the thick of the weald. They vanished behind the low arms of a stocky pine.

If Rorry had not seen where Scute hid, she would never have spotted him. Some semblance of security came with the knowledge that Cord watched over them, though she tried not to acknowledge it. She might owe her friends an apology if they survived this. For now, she just had to remain silent. Rorry fingered the spare bolt she had stuck behind her belt, checked the bolt on the bowstring, and assessed their situation.

The riders had not seen Scute and Cord, though they were close enough now. They wore ocher tabards over their hauberks. Polished armor reflected the sunlight off their limbs.

The clops of the horses' shoes grew louder. Kylan kept his back to the dead tree and his hand on the katana's hilt, waiting for Rorry's signal if things started going poorly.

Rorry glanced around the elm, only able to see their insignia, a multitude of intersecting green lines on their chests, before she stood back. Which fort used the Glades as their symbol? She took Scarlett's wrist as the Judges' conversation moved into earshot.

"He told them the Chancellor himself approved it!" a man shouted. "Can you believe that?" He sounded like the type of person who spit each time he spoke.

A deep voice answered, "It's just a hamlet. What if the disease had spread? The Seeding does that sometimes."

"I suppose," the other answered. "MacKinry said there was another one in the Faulkner Province."

"No one'll miss it. Faulkner should be absorbed by Weatherington. We defend half their outposts, and the councilmember has missed seven Summits!"

Rorry agreed with the baritone. Lord Tresdaine had not done Faulkner any favors. The man tried to seduce anyone under the age of twenty without enough sense to bring a chaperone. Worse, his economic plan involved creating problems that required solutions from elsewhere in his province.

"Now, there is a tale I need to share," the spitter said. "This wench in Ebas told me of Tresdaine's habit for bringing a certain pair of twins to his bedchamber. Not just any twins, but—"

A branch cracked, silencing the Judge. The hoofbeats stopped behind her.

Tightness seized Rorry's chest. She stared daggers at the trembling pine hiding Cord. Perhaps she had been right about him all along.

Chapter 13: Sins of Curiosity

Cord recognized the Judges' troop but not their faces. Weatherington, the largest province south of the Breslan Mountains, split its troops into four forts across its countryside. These Judges shared the symbol of the Glades with the watchmen in Kenton. That meant they hailed from the one closest to his home, Fort Warren. Whenever those yellow tabards entered Kenton's gate, people welcomed them, but the villagers' doors and window shutters proved they still worked so long as the guests were in town.

Leaning in the saddle, Cord forced down the pine branch next to him to see the others. The rustle caught Kylan's attention, but his eyes darted back to Rorry just as fast. Surely vexed at him for the delay and the danger, Rorry didn't look like a noble anymore, more like a copperhead waiting to strike. After brushing a spare bolt behind her belt, Rorry's hand touched Scarlett's wrist.

The Judges moved back into Cord's view. A tan horse carried the closest man, clean-shaven except for a thick brown mustache. He wore a standard Judge's patrol uniform, hauberk and all. His right hand rested by the hilt of his bastard sword while he searched the sides of the path and his companion gossiped.

On a copper gelding, the gossip had skipped his pauldrons today. His splint-mail greaves gaped at their closures around his legs. He sagged in his middle slightly more than his fuzzy double chin. More practice and less gabbing would have helped his armor serve its purpose.

Gemstones lined the leather baldric across the Judge's chest and the sheath at his waist. The sheath didn't house an issued bastard sword. His curved weapon fattened at the tip. The golden quillons of its hilt reached in opposite directions, one protecting the wielder's hand, the other reaching to the backside of the blade. Why would a Judge be allowed to use that?

Cord leaned into the pine for a better look at the foreign weapon. The branch cracked. Cord's stomach sank. He held the limb captive in his palm. Shifting his weight in the saddle, he braved a peek. The Judges had stopped between the trees hiding the others and were squinting at the pine.

Kylan tightened his grip on his strange sword. Scarlett bit her lip. Rorry glowered directly at Cord.

The first Judge dismounted and drew his sword as the gossip waited.

Rorry released Scarlett's wrist when she heard his step and nodded to Kylan.

Kylan slid his blade out of its wooden scabbard without a whisper.

Cord felt Scute readying to step aside, away from the awkward burden of his leaning. "Steady, boy," he breathed.

The Judge smashed a pine cone underfoot, prompting Kylan to begin inching his way around the far side of the decaying tree at his back.

Scarlett held her fists tight to her sides with her eyes closed, her face stuck in a sudden vexation.

Cord's muscles ached from the weight of the branch. It was his fault they'd come this way. He wouldn't make them burn for him. As he uncurled his fingers from the limb, he extended his legs to kick Scute.

"It was just a pine cone," the flabby Judge yelled. He heeled the copper's ribs, spurring it into motion. "But the important part of her story was that the twins were a boy and a girl. I can understand the desire to bring two girls to my bedchamber, but Tresdaine crossed a line that even nobility should not dare. I think we should inform the Tribunal. Wouldn't you agree?"

His partner scowled into the woods. With a long scan and a gruff exhale, the Judge finally sheathed his sword. He backed away to his mount, only looking away as he got in the saddle, and continued to watch in their direction until he was out of sight.

When the gossip had been out of range of Cord's earshot for a few minutes, Cord let the branch go and shuffle its needles to a halt. He dismounted and shook the tension out of his arm as he led Scute toward Rorry's heated frown. "Sorry."

* * *

Scarlett sat on the remnant of a giant oak as Rorry and Kylan debated deeper in the thickset Ysbrydoli Woods about how to handle the end of Cord's escort. She read their posture; they argued the same side, against common sense, denying the safety of the hamlet and exaggerating the urgency of reaching the continent.

Slowly the sun released its rule over the sky, casting a purple light over everything. The brighter stars were waking, piercing the veil overhead.

Scarlett raised the soft wool of her shawl to shield her neck from the cooling evening air, finding its way through the trees to make her eyes water. She dismissed Kylan's voice in her mind, which insisted she ate too little. This unseasonal chill was stronger, foreboding a shift, a warning.

Cord tapped the stump beneath her with his heel while trying not to draw attention to himself. Scarlett had already relayed her suspicion that he knew of the secret below. Neither Rorry nor Kylan believed it possible. If Scarlett turned to witness his examination, Cord would deny it. So she sat, ignoring the percussion and devising a plan to secure the trinket in his satchel.

Ever since she'd noticed the remains of his orders in their fire last night, she had searched the ashes of their campfires before departure. Unfortunately, he hadn't attempted to burn the ring yet. Was it second nature or part of cadets' training to burn the unknown? Had they never considered the fact that the "demons" they feared supposedly lived in an inferno before resurfacing in the Glades? Either way, the ring deserved better. "Such a waste," she said and blew air through her lips.

"What?" Cord asked, joining her at the edge. His feet came to light on the roots. He wrapped his midriff in his arms as he made one more check behind them, then squinted at Rorry and Kylan's hushed debate.

"Would you like a blanket?" she asked.

With a curious grin, he answered, "I'll survive." Out of the corner of her eye, a glow enveloped him. When she turned, it vanished for the third time. Cord offered more mystery than what they knew. Her mum would know what the pale blue shimmer meant. Any properly mantled mage would.

But that's why she was leaving, to receive the training her mother had forbidden her under the guise of safety. If Scarlett qualified, they would admit her to the Tower of Trône d'Argent in the Racinian capital.

Her friends insisted she could do it, but they'd never really witnessed how powerful her mum was. Might as well compare a pond to an ocean. She hadn't even been able to set that wolfkin's pelt on fire.

As Cord dragged a saddlebag close from behind her, he accidentally tipped over the satchel imprisoning the ring. His hand slipped inside the saddlebag and retrieved two of the out-of-season pecans he'd been collecting along the way. They cracked against each other in his grip and were offered with a smile.

She declined but felt warmer.

"Yeah," he said, frowning at his hand. "We should have a better meal in case it's our last together." He hopped down to collect debris for a fire.

Scarlett groaned under her breath at the idea of waiting for him to strike a fire with flint. However, it might present the opportunity she needed.

With the wood assembled and the kindling placed, Cord began clacking the stones. The sparks cooperated as well as they had during his last tedious attempt.

"Perhaps we should use your food because you are near your people?" she asked. Ignoring the impolite forwardness that made her cringe inside, she lifted his satchel. Before he could protest, she flipped open the lid, grabbed the largest obstruction in her view, and tossed the wrapped food to him.

The blood drained from his face.

"If you do not mind, that is?" Her prize greeted her, next to the black silk rectangle protecting a deck of cards. "Oh! What is this?" Success, though temporary, emboldened her. Her slender fingers held out the lightweight ring for his inspection as she moved closer to him. The aquamarine dome glimmered and teased Scarlett to discover its secrets.

Cord leaned away from it. "You shouldn't touch that!" he warned quietly. "That's why they burned that old man in South Thornton."

She feigned surprise. "You carry it with you?"

His eyes searched about for an answer as he wet his lips. "Marlone . . . it was in his satchel. He must've pinched it. The High Guard had it the last I saw. I wanted to give it to Headmaster Angsly—or my father—to have it destroyed."

That would not do. "I see. What does it do?" Scarlett asked, casually dropping it back into the satchel.

When it hit the lining, he relaxed and scooted closer to her. "I don't know." He reached for the satchel.

The kindling crackled.

As Cord pondered the blaze before him, she said, "Well done!" She scooped the insides of the satchel, brought the silk-covered cards out, and set down the closed bag as she lowered next to him. "This I do know." She removed the silk wrapping and handed it to him.

He released it and wiped his hands on his tunic.

"They are not magic, just myth, a game really." Scarlett sat back and arranged the deck of cards in her hand. Splaying the green-diamond pattern of their backs, she held the temptation out to him. "Pick one."

"Those aren't playthings," he said, busying his attention elsewhere by opening the wrappings on the food.

Holding them closer, Scarlett reassured him, "They are perfectly harmless, just a fortune teller's tool. A person takes a card, and you read their reaction to it. It's a trick, really."

The scent of rose petals preceded Rorry's approach. "Oh, we are playing a game?" she asked, lowering next to Scarlett. She plucked a card as Kylan continued on to the stump.

Cord stabbed something for the fire and set it over the flame. Salted meat that smelled like poultry hissed on its spit as he watched Rorry out of the corner of his eye.

"The Garden?" Rorry said skeptically. "A pensive purity and healing." Her dry tone mocked the card full of illustrated pansies and frost lily blossoms.

Scarlett swung her hands back to Cord. Rorry's participation countered his reluctance. Cord's fingers hovered over the cards and finally selected the third card from the left. His nose wrinkled as he tried to make sense of it. He held it up, displaying a table overflowing with oranges, grapes, roasted duck, and cheeses. The name of the card ran across the bottom in the Old Tongue script. Did the army not teach the Old Tongue?

"That is the Feast," Rorry said. "It means you will receive a bounty of cheer, friends, and fortune."

His fingers flicked the card into the fire.

Scarlett's smile melted with pity. Reforming the block of cards in her hand, she dropped the ring down her sleeve and selected her own. A pair of red eyes peered through a black square. "Death," she said, holding it out.

Cord's lips parted as though he were about to offer condolences.

Minutely shaking her head at Cord's frightened reaction, Rorry sighed. "It means an end, a change. This is why the army should not collect so-called magical items. In their ignorance, they may prove themselves correct and actually cause harm with them." Rorry pretended to lecture someone unseen but gazed at him as she finished.

She took the deck from Scarlett and reached for Death, but Scarlett emulated Cord's example. She whipped it into the flames with a whistle through her teeth. "Not to worry," Scarlett said to Cord. "I get that card a lot."

Cord leaned back and asked Rorry, "You own a set of these?"

Rorry cloaked the cards in silk. "Yes, we do—did. If you live in fear of something, how exactly do you learn to defend yourself from it?" She scoffed. "That is if it is even worth the consideration. Can you imagine? A game that has nothing to do with magic probably sent someone to the spider."

"Anything that would tempt a demon should be treated with caution," Cord quoted from the Rhynian Scroll. "Best to cast them away to the fires."

"Demons?" Rorry asked. "Do you really believe that?" She glanced Scarlett's way, clearly expecting a commiserating bitter smile.

Scarlett kept her features friendly, unsure why Rorry would need her agreement. She never had in the past.

Rising, Rorry appeared to be waiting for something. Then she said, "Allow me," and flung the deck into the flames. With her shoulders back, Rorry went to the stump and ascended the roots. She fell against Kylan, who had taken up whittling his figure of Kit again.

"I was just trying to warn her," Cord grumbled. "But she thinks I'm simple."

"And rigid and closed to considering new things," Scarlett said absently. She tugged on her lip. Rorry's reaction wasn't entirely Cord's fault. When Grary had initiated his plan to marry her and remain in Brewing, he'd turned Rorry, ever the optimist, into an untrusting and taciturn person. Scarlett suspected Cord challenged the wall Rorry had erected, or tempted her to challenge it, which perturbed Rorry all the more. At the same time, her mild tantrum might have been directed at the detour of the plan.

Turning the spit, Cord kept glancing back to Rorry with his mouth pressed into a thin line. His jaw muscles flexed.

Scarlett looked over to see Kylan give up on carving when Rorry wrapped her arm through his and laid her head on his shoulder. Did Cord believe Kylan and Rorry to be something more than friends?

Smiling at him through the blurry heat, Scarlett said, "I believe she wishes it were not so. Otherwise, she would not own such passion about it." That was true enough.

Cord sheepishly gazed into the fire and pulled his satchel to him. "Thanks, Scarlett. She'll be rid of me soon. But I can't imagine what she'd have me change." Blue shimmered around him again and vanished.

Scarlett removed the spit from the fire and offered it to him. "I suspect less than you might think."

He released his satchel to take it from her with nodded thanks and began his mealtime prayer.

"I wish we had more time," Scarlett mumbled.

Chapter 14: Cord's Homecoming

Night had come fully to the old forest before Rorry had finished eating. A chorus of owls and crickets had cloaked the final stretch of their trek to Kenton and the blessed end to this diversion. She should have been euphoric.

Waiting with Kylan and Scarlett inside a magnolia's tent, Rorry sank her heel into the damp soil as she peered out between the leaves.

Cord had not reached the gate yet. Whenever he stepped into a breach in the trees, the ungodly brightness of the moon reflected off his uniform and the sheen of his satchel.

Rorry wished the opportunity had arisen to take the mysterious aquamarine ring inside it. One more wonder lost to the army.

Earlier, they had reached an agreement that Cord would enter alone and bring them food at a secluded point on the eastern side of Kenton's palisade. Rorry planned to be miles away before Cord had the opportunity to deliver his end of the deal. She withheld that truth from her friends, knowing they wouldn't agree to go until they'd witnessed his acceptance at the gate.

"At any moment," Rorry said to Kylan, "Judges may come down this path."

He never looked away from Cord's back.

She pointedly sighed and parted the leaves again.

Cord had reached the weathered posts of the village palisade. He laid his hand on the gate. It swung, unlatched and unguarded.

"Something's wrong," Kylan murmured. Abruptly, he ripped through the leaves.

Rorry groped for his hand but missed. "This could be a trap!" she whispered.

He scudded down the trail away from her. Scarlett followed him, giving Rorry no choice. Kylan only halted when they reached the gate.

Holding his hand up for silence, Cord studied the road into the dark hamlet. Uncertainty brought the soldier to the surface, which didn't ease Rorry's concerns. "Even during a feast," he said, "it should've been guarded." He opened his hand between them. "Can I have my belt knives back now?"

Kylan ignored the urge for caution on Rorry's face and bent to remove the small blades from his left boot.

Cord took the knives and said, "Wait here."

"No," Rorry said and forced a laugh. "We are leaving. Thank you for the offer of hospitality and provisions." She tugged on Kylan's sleeve. He did not budge.

"Are the wolfkin here?" Scarlett asked Cord. "Is it worth the risk to go in?"

Cord spied back through the gate, down the quiet path inside.

"Nah," Kylan reassured him. "The watchman is probably appeasing nature. But we'll have a look around before we just abandon you to your fate." With a shaming expression directed at Rorry, Kylan entered the gate. If he had wanted them to believe what he'd said, he should not have drawn Master Clienne's katana.

Shoving her way past Cord, Rorry stepped onto the stone-free road of packed dirt. The drifting scent of honeysuckle reminded Rorry of her gran, not unlike the first cottage in view. Old, simple, and remarkably self-reliant. Worn by time, the curving wooden frame of the house was warped and split; yet it still held its charm. Its thatched bonnet stretched out over part of a robust garden.

Moving to Kylan's side, Rorry gave him an unsure but decidedly irritated glance.

Cord relinquished Scute's lead to Scarlett and hopped onto the porch of the cottage. He peeped into the unlit windows and, with a quick try of the door, entered without knocking. That sealed it; this hamlet was indeed his home.

Down a gentle hill, a handful of quaint cottages clustered around a town square that branched off on only three roads. Surprisingly few trees blocked the vibrant moon, considering a forest surrounded the town. What Rorry guessed was Cord's academe, a wooden hall running the length of the east side of the square, could hold a chapel and six rooms at best under its high thatched roof. Holiday or not, someone should have had a lamp lit.

Cord emerged and said, "It's empty." He pulled the door closed and thanked Scarlett before taking Scute's lead. His surefooted path led them toward the idle village's center.

She might have been wrong about Kenton's size. The deeper they delved, the larger it appeared. The palisade extended out of sight, likely encompassing a small farm or two beyond this cluster of a few dozen homes and a distant copse.

As they followed the main road down the slope into town, each dwelling only differed from the next by a straw wreath or a bed of rose mallows to compete with the neighbor's abundance of blue hydrangeas. Between rocking chairs on the porches, game boards were a common feature, most waiting for the players to finish their games. Nothing scuffled. No one sang in the dark windows. Only a hollow knell rang out.

A scent broke through to foul the air, as soft as a cheese breakfast on a gossiper's breath. Soon, the stench grew to a sickeningly sweet odor akin to a decaying deer. At the edge of the academe, they reached a parade of stepping stones paving the way to the town square. The bouquet of rot refused to be filtered through Rorry's sleeve.

Wide-eyed, Cord left Scute behind as they pressed on.

Rorry stuck close to him as he rounded the corner of the square. She bumped into his back when he abruptly stopped. He ambled forward, staring ahead.

A thickset woman in damp clothing lay on her side facing away from them. Her dark hair blew over the grass and stuck to a small rain puddle. Next to a motionless beagle, a man had slumped over the legs of a boy, who lay flat on his back, staring blankly to the heavens. The puffiness of his face turned Rorry's stomach. Then she noticed the rows beyond.

Bodies of men, women, and children lined the sides of the cultivated beds in the square, leaving room for a central aisle up to a dais with an ivy-gilded arch. No blood stained their clothes. Flowers were not trampled. Windows were whole. No signs of a struggle suggested what had befallen Kenton. They all appeared to have fallen over dead, turning the square into an open-air tomb.

Cord burst through the buzz of flies.

Rorry looked to her friends, both motionless as they took it in. Kylan put his hand on Scarlett's shoulder. Rorry swallowed before she tailed Cord down the aisle. Over her crossbow, she scanned the porches edging the square and tried to breathe as little as possible. Nothing moved.

Under the weak-clappered bell, Cord fell to his knees in the center of the dais.

When she reached him, she lowered her aim but kept searching for an explanation. She balked at the swollen faces around them and returned her gaze to Cord.

Pain crinkled his face. He sucked in air as his mouth quivered. Before him lay a corpse in black robes, formal dress for a headmaster. Above his white beard, the small headmaster's skin had turned waxy and dark, nearly as black as his robes and his askew pointed cap. Cord took the headmaster's hand in both of his. Then his back heaved as he let loose an angry wail, reducing him to sobs. This was his father, then, or as close to one as he would have had, the man who'd trained him.

Cord's hopeless mourning weighed Rorry down. She settled on her knees under the arch. His offer of sanctuary might have been genuine, after all. "I am sorry," she said and gently rubbed the warm fabric on his back. "Remember him as he was."

After a few minutes of silent tears, Cord managed, "This is Headmaster Angsly." Tears skipped Cord's cheek as they fell. "He would've liked you. He always liked people who speak their mind."

Rorry doubted he would have liked what she had to say, but understood the compliment.

"There are no bites," Scarlett said with a pinched nose. She tiptoed around the man and child by the beagle. "I don't see any wounds. I think they were kneeling when they died."

Kylan took Scarlett by the elbow and said, "Not now. We'll gather supplies and make ready to leave this place." He waited for a nod from Rorry and cautiously moved to the porch of the cottage behind him.

Rorry patted Cord's back as he seemingly forced himself to see the headmaster's body. Then she brought her sleeve back to her face.

When Cord's breathing slowed, he searched around and said, "The Rhynian Scroll is gone. They wouldn't have a sermon without it." He reached under the headmaster's beard and patted his chest. "Witches did this. Blighted magic!"

"Witches?" Rorry asked through her sleeve, unable to keep the mocking tone from her voice.

Cord set his jaw and nodded. "They hex people and offer their souls to demons."

She opened her mouth to explain the Daughters of Sepholina were a tale to keep children from climbing fences but sensed an opportunity to leave the courtyard. "If that is so, the stories say they would have defiled the altar. Let us have a look, shall we?" She rose.

Gently, Cord laid his headmaster on his back and folded his arms over his chest.

Then she escorted him, taking his wrist to gently pull him past the faces drowning him in sorrow. Rorry kept her sight on the academe's entrance, above the infestation of death and rings of flowers.

While most academes were constructed for intimidation, this one defied its brethren with the same curved charm that filled Kenton's homes. The builder had even rounded the tops of the windows. Through a door propped open by a stone, light flickered deep inside; the Idol's flame still burned. She let Cord enter alone, his face caught between emotions.

Twice now, Rorry had been confronted with horrors, situations she had no way of anticipating—and they were only one province from home. Their flight had become a game of luck, reducing strategy to the whims of fate.

Kylan left the cottage with a roll stuffed in his mouth and a harvest from the larder in his arms.

"Oh!" Scarlett said, looking up from beside a woman's corpse. "Maybe they were poisoned?" He spit out the roll and let the rest drop.

Through the doorway, Cord went down on his knees before the Idol. Prayer would not have been her first inclination, but she understood the desire for a higher power's clarity or intervention or both.

While Scarlett explained she was probably wrong about the poison, Rorry considered what role Cord could play in their escape, if he would accept it. He had nothing to keep him here. And yet, he believed magic had done this to his people. Perhaps it had. Would he hold such a bias against Scarlett, or potentially the blame? Surprisingly, she doubted it. He had offered himself for an escape from the Judges, fished for them, and helped them avoid the watchmen of Carno Bridge.

There was one way to be sure. "Prepare for the four of us to be away as quickly as possible," Rorry whispered. "I will check the armory."

The wind strengthened. Rorry's mouth soured. Determined not to sick up, she let the will fill her and entered the academe with her finger ready to pinch the crossbow's trigger, if necessary. The time for honesty had come.

* * *

Cord inhaled his home in ragged, shallow breaths. Spicy incense from the censer filled the sanctuary and warred with the scent of decay. Kenton's only light wept before him in the Idol's hand, starving for fuel. Kneeling, Cord took in the Chancellor's image over his joined fists.

Each crack in the Idol's painted red armor endured, right where he had left them days earlier. Kenton might not have been a chosen city, or even a thriving prime village, but the people . . . Cord recited an invocation, a plea. No price was too high, no object too sacred, that he wouldn't barter it in exchange for waking before the Idol as he'd done on countless mornings just to find it all had been a nightmare. "Where's the righteous truth in this?"

He licked the salt from his lips and prayed for Headmaster Angsly and for Marlone. His neighbors' faces and voices plagued his memories as he continued the Rites of Passing. In the middle of Leila's, he cut himself off and angrily swore into the Idol's eyes, "I will herald vengeance for Kenton. If it ends me—by the Light I swear it—I'll rise to finish it in the next life!" The flame flickered as he heard Rorry's wooden heels step into the nave behind him.

Without curtsying, she moved slowly down the hall to his left, toward the chapel.

Cord wiped his face on his hands. "Wait," he said, rising. After a bow of reverence to the Idol, Cord waved for her to follow him to the armory down the opposite hall.

Bars of moonlight from the barrack's doorway lit the hall. Even out of sight, his bunk called to him, offering a soft nest and a trove of memories carved into the underside of Marlone's bunk. Farther down the hall, the watchmen's rooms were as quiet as Nemma's. No swearing, no laughter. He ignored the tug in his chest and went to the armored door across from the barracks.

The key Headmaster Angsly had always worn around his neck now rested in the door's lock. Cord shoved the iron-plated door open to find the shelves barren in the windowless room. Scuffs marred the floorboards where the armor racks had been dragged out. Even his specially requisitioned bow and quiver were gone. Cord pounded his fist into the doorframe. "They robbed them!" He kicked the door. "When I find those witches, I'll snap every one of their necks!"

"This was a vault?" Rorry asked meekly.

"Every academe has an armory. I would've thought you'd know that."

She stepped away from the anger in his voice. He strutted back down the hall to the chapel, tensing as he heard Rorry's steps continue past the Idol, ignoring it again. The headmaster's chamber and the vestry flew past.

An odor of incense and oil welcomed him into the chapel. Cord swatted away flies that had entered from the windows facing the square, and inspected the room, resisting the urge to collapse on one of the plumped and centered cushions on the pews. Straight ahead, the long stone altar was orderly. None of the tomes lay stacked aside or closed around a kerchief or whatever the headmaster had handy. Dustless and tidy, neither how Cord remembered the chapel nor defiled by the witches with the blood of the innocent.

With concern, he said, "It's all in order."

The same superior glint in Julian's eyes found its way to Rorry's. She opened her mouth as Cord passed by but said nothing.

In the corridor, he hesitated before Headmaster Angsly's chamber, praying to find his headmaster propped against his writing table, muttering through whistles as he doggedly worked on a new training routine. But his cadets had left him. Cord opened the room.

The scent of old parchment reached out to him. In the corner, an empty stool sat under the writing desk, scratched and abused with ink dabs and tears of wax. An upturned crate spilled more books onto the floor next to the ratty bed, no larger than Cord's bunk. Drawers jutted out from the chest by the door, victims of a whimsical riffling.

Hanging on the wall above the desk, figures danced down a scroll of basic battle stances. The headmaster must have taken it from the barracks door after they had left. Cord palmed the yellowed vellum, tracing the black lines his headmaster had drawn for him ages ago.

Rorry stepped into the room behind him.

"Everything is as it should be here," he said. Stripping the threadbare blankets from the bed, a thud rewarded him. He fetched the black leather-bound tome from the floor. Holding the rough binding up to the window's light, Cord thumbed the stitched title, *Etiquette for Excellence*. He handed it to Rorry.

Parting the pages where a quill had been stuck, she read the content. "'When to dip and when to bow' . . . 'Touch only when a hand is offered.'" She bit her lip, clearly realizing she'd read it aloud; but Cord pretended not to notice. "He expected company. Important company."

"But who?" Cord asked. "He wouldn't welcome some magus into the village—clean the chapel and don his best robes, not for some Abandoned . . . unless he'd been enchanted." He stared at his hands. "Magic did this."

Rorry gave an irritated sigh. She closed the tome and tossed it onto the headmaster's bed. "You cannot always tell who is what."

"Well, I'm sure you'll wanna be on your way now." Cord headed to his old room, ignoring her calls. Slamming the door, he spun to put his back against it. The chest, the wardrobe, everything in the small barracks was open and bare. He'd never realized just how tiny it was.

He lunged onto his bed and rolled over. Unblinking, he let the tears come as he stared at the word ASHWIN carved into the underside of Marlone's bunk. He never should've left.

Blinking at what he would never become, he lay there with heavy limbs. All he could see now was the headmaster's face, barely recognizable after death's touch. Part of him didn't believe it. He needed to bury them before they decayed further, and take the time for proper rites and mourning. The others ought to go. They probably wouldn't wait for him, anyway. With his change in fortune, they'd be better off far away.

The door opened. Rorry stepped in with no fire in her eyes. Her newfound patience made her seem regal somehow.

Cord's own deception had fled him. He couldn't resume it and pretend to shrug off the death of a village as a loss of tithe. How many more ways would he fail before it ended?

Sniffling, Cord sat up and took a shaky breath. Though not as steady as he'd have liked, it stayed his tears. He wiped his cheeks on his sleeves and said, "I'll help Kylan. If there's anything you can use, they'd want you to have it. Mrs. Hender baked every day. The Dunkels have— had seven kids around our age." Leila . . . "They'll have clothes that'll fit you."

"You are not staying here," Rorry stated.

Cord looked up, ready for a fight.

But her eyes were kind, welcoming even. She closed the trunk across from him and sat on it, balancing her crossbow on her lap.

"They deserve a proper burial. This is my—my duty to see to these people."

"Cord." She said his name with a gentle familiarity. "The wolfkin did not do this, and those witches are a myth. I do not understand what happened. But if you stay here, you will likely die too, which means you have wasted our time." A subtle curve to her lips eased his anger. "Listen, we need to speak freely about something delicate."

A gasp came from outside, followed by a thwack and a thump. Cord shot to his feet.

"Scar—"

Cord smothered Rorry's call with his hand and jerked her away from the window, cocooning her in his arms at the end of the bunk beds. She struggled and lost her grip on the crossbow. They froze when it banged against the floorboards. He tightened his hold.

A horse trotted to the square.

"Scarlett!" Kylan yelled.

Rorry jerked against Cord but paused at the sound of metal striking metal. A hollow blow against wood preceded a series of crushing noises, like apples hurled into stone. She elbowed Cord in his side.

He held tight. After everything, he wouldn't let her die too.

"Well, well, two of them hiding out," a hoarse voice said.

"Do not be daft," another man grumbled. "How could they have hidden a horse?"

"Should we check the town?"

"Bah. If there are more, let them burn. Here, tie her hands tight." Another horse joined them. "For now, you two take these back to the fort. I will start the fire and watch the exit."

"Shame you killed the boy," the hoarse one said. "He would have sold well as a slave."

Rorry struggled harder.

"If I had not, you would be dead. Good enough trade for you?"

"Yes, sir."

The horses clopped away. Flint strikes sounded seconds before the light through the window blazed orange.

Cord relaxed his arm around Rorry's chest and spoke to her ear. "Hide here. I'm gonna—"

Her elbow smashed his bottom lip against his teeth. A quick knee to the groin sent him to the floor.

In three breaths, he pushed away the pain. Rorry and her crossbow were gone. "Rorry," he roared at a whisper. He got his feet under him. His tongue stung his bottom lip as it licked away the metallic-tasting blood.

The thatch across the square caught fire in a *whoosh* and lit every inch of the barracks. Cord darted into the hallway. Freeing his belt knife as he moved, he shied away from the Light of the Idol and went to the exit, ready to see who had slaughtered his neighbors. Craning his neck, he spied an armored arm lift the fiery crown of a torch, singeing the thatch on the Dunkels' cabin.

The porch's support beam blocked Cord's view of the man besides a head of thinning hair. As the man moved away from the burning cottage, the red hammer on his breastplate gleamed. A High Guard? In Kenton? They must know what had happened here.

Kylan lay prone several steps away from the Dunkels' porch. Blue shimmers ran under his tunic as his chest rose and fell, barely.

Maybe he could save him. With his hands raised, Cord ran to Kylan's side and called, "Sir!" The belt knife clasped in his fist didn't call for peace, but Cord refused to let it fall.

The High Guard turned. With one look, the warrior strode

toward Cord and hefted his hammer free of its leather holster. Drops of blood glistened on the head.

Confused, Cord whispered, "I am a Catalyst, sir."

The Guard didn't slow.

"We're under attack! There're wolfkin in Merith. I came home to warn them. Sir, what happened here?"

The High Guard ignored his question, approaching faster.

Cord held out the golden feather on his tunic. "You know what this means!"

The Guard flung his torch on the townsfolk, igniting a watchman's uniform. Rex. Cord tried not to give names to the other bodies. He stepped next to Kylan. Glass crunched under his soles. The wire of Kylan's spectacles jabbed his ankle, but Cord didn't take his eyes off the advancing soldier.

Joining his hands on the grip, the High Guard raised his hammer over his head.

Cord knew exactly how to counter the move and waited.

Before the Guard powered the swing, a crossbow bolt deflected off his armored thigh. Rorry pulled her crossbow in from the chapel window.

Surprise tightened into rage on the High Guard's face.

Releasing his knife, Cord leaped forward, grabbing the hammer with both hands. "Listen to me!"

"You listen to me, fledgling," the High Guard grunted. "You are insignificant." He swept a leg behind Cord's and pressed him back. Cord toppled over but clung to the hammer. The butt of it jabbed against his breastbone, knocking the strength from his lungs and arms. The handle was wrenched free of Cord's fingers.

A grim smile crossed the man's face. He readied his hammer above Cord and heaved for the blow.

Cord gripped Julian's knife in his belt.

"Halt!" Rorry called. She stood at the academe doors with her crossbow fixed on the High Guard. "I did not intend to kill you last time. If you proceed, I will not hesitate to send you to a disappointing afterlife."

"Ha!" The High Guard bellowed, repowering the swing. "Done in by a pretty piece of flesh? You have a seat and wait—"

A thunk sprayed blood over Cord. Red drained from the puncture in the High Guard's forehead. Cord scrambled back from the folding fountain.

Rorry stared blankly at her kill.

Intense heat burst forth from the blaze consuming the Dunkels' cottage. The Barrows' roof smoked. Soon the whole town would be in flames. They had to leave, now, before those other soldiers returned.

Cord scurried to pull Kylan back toward the gate.

Rorry stalked him as he tugged Kylan backward. She reset her crossbow and aimed it at Cord. She slid a bolt into the groove.

"He's alive," Cord said. "I can save him." He prayed he could. It hadn't saved Marlone. "But you have to help me."

Her voice icy, she said, "You had no right to hold me!"

The blue shimmers dulled beneath Kylan's shirt. Cord set Kylan's back to the ground and grabbed his head. "Stay with us," Cord breathed. Diving into the tingling sensation without effort, he examined Kylan's injuries. Both wrists were crushed. Freed blood filled his chest beneath cracked ribs. The chill rushed into the brightest lights, the broken bones and the wounds around the bleeding. Fighting against the trance to release before the mending was done, Cord jerked his hands away and fell back.

Kylan didn't stir, but his wounds were brighter. That'd have to do for now. He couldn't heal everything while they were in the fire's path.

"What did you do?" Rorry demanded.

"I don't know," Cord said, rising. His arms felt feverish and puffy. He tried to ignore it but released Kylan with a grunt at his second attempt to drag him toward the gate. Pain scattered through his ribs with each breath.

He needed help. Scute was gone. The High Guard's steed waited by the gate. Cord wouldn't dare drag Kylan near a skittish warhorse.

"You do not know? Answer me, soldier!"

Cord met Rorry's livid glare. "You want answers? I tell you what. Answer a question of mine first. Why would a noble pretend to be common?" That gave her pause. "Yeah, you're vexed with me for lying. That's fine. When we get somewhere safe, we *will* talk, Rorry Pryce." He scoffed. "More like Rorry te Gwirion."

She said nothing at the name of Brewing's nobility but lowered her crossbow.

He picked up Kylan's shoulders again, tempering the pain with his ire. "Where's the closest stump?"

Rorry shook her head.

"Don't lie to me! You're drawn to those things like flies to shit." Despite his anger, he wished he hadn't used that word in her presence.

"Not far. West of the gate," Rorry said. "But what about Scarlett? We cannot leave her!"

"She's gone," Cord barked. "You heard the horses as well as I did."

Rorry appeared torn, shaking her head. Without a word, she dashed toward the academe, vanishing into the square while Cord began shuffling up the slope to the gate.

"Ashes, Rorry! Come on!"

He dragged Kylan past Widow Shinn's cabin and watched his home char until the gate blocked his view. "Hold on just a little longer, pal," he said, lugging him without guidance over the knotty roots and undergrowth. He never should have brought them here. Marlone, Kenton, now Scarlett . . . There would be time to grieve later. "You're gonna be just fine. Then we'll find Scarlett together. I promise you that."

In less than five minutes of dragging Kylan beyond the end of the palisade, Cord found it. The enormous stump would've been harder to avoid than find. He hauled Kylan onto its surface and fell to his knees. His throbbing hands relaxed against the wood as he tried to catch his breath. "You have to work," Cord pleaded. The tingle came from his elbows to his fingers. The rings began to shine with blue light, though not as brightly as in his dream.

He heard Rorry trouncing the undergrowth in her approach. She gasped. "You are a magus?"

"Don't call me that!" Cord snapped. As the stairs fell, Cord gripped Kylan's tunic. "I swear to you, I'm not evil. I won't hurt him." He carefully pulled Kylan into the darkness.

Rorry raced to follow their backward descent.

Cord drank in the dank air as he rejected his body's sharp protests. After what felt like an hour, his sandal touched the level marble floor. But he tugged Kylan several feet away from the steps before giving in. As Cord's eyes adjusted to take in the round room he had dreamed of, roots shambled to close the stairs behind Rorry. Nothing else moved. They ought to be safe here, for now.

Rorry dropped the High Guard's hammer. She had been crying.

Before she had a chance to question him, Cord delved into Kylan again. This time, he'd salve every glow. He owed them. No matter the price, he'd pay it. From head to toe, he quenched the light marking Kylan's wounds.

When Cord finished, Kylan coughed. Rorry swooped onto her friend.

Now, they had to plan. Scarlett needed them.

Cord fell back flat against the dusty marble floor. His vision blurred as weariness conquered him. His mouth opened to tell them to wait, to promise to help find Scarlett. It was his fault; he'd make it right. And he didn't want to be left alone.

Chapter 15: Something Stolen, Something Blue

Metal clanged together, jolting Scarlett awake with a gasp. She brought her bound hands to her mouth to smother the sound. Hay poked into her back. A lock clicked, followed by clinking keys. Motionless, she listened until certain of her solitude.

A slight singe and a little wriggling bested the farcical bindings on Scarlett's wrists. Smothering her cries, she clutched her shoulders. Analogous to every abject nightmare she'd had leading up to Hansweighn, she found herself in a cell no larger than a stable stall. Blood smattered the mortared boulders sealing her in. The stench suggested a previous occupant had soiled a corner. Partially blocked by straw, flickers of light showed an opening at the base of the thick-planked door.

She expected her poultice bag to be gone, but why had they taken the shawl her mum had given her? Her tears warmed her cheeks as they trailed down by her ears.

"That one is occupied," a grizzled voice yelled.

Scarlett fell into the position she had woken in and bit her sniveling bottom lip.

"Over here." A door creaked on its hinges. "Who is that, then?"

"An acquisition from the Southern Road," a young man said. "He didn't have his papers, and there's something queer about his story. Judge Tyne wanted to question him later."

A grunt preceded a slam and the jingle of keys. "Tyne's soft this time of year. Stantz, go back to the village. Help Pellar." Their steps passed by her cell door.

When silence lingered, Scarlett groped her chest. Spectre's coin and the ring were still threaded on the string she had tied around herself.

She gingerly massaged the throbbing knot on the back of her head where the Judge had struck her and tried to remain thankful for not waking ablaze.

Above her, distant shouts came through the small, barred window. She stood on the hay, but it compressed under her weight, leaving her a foot shy of the opening. She couldn't make out the words, but the voice didn't belong to Kylan or Cord.

Scarlett stepped down off the hay. The heel of her boot thudded against the floorboards. She slid out her stocking-clad foot, placed her right boot to the side, and freed the other. Then she tiptoed forward, wincing at an unknown dampness, and eased to the floor.

A peek through the slit at the bottom of the door revealed nothing but rat pellets and a rock wall across the dimly lit hallway. No one patrolled.

Putting her back to the door, Scarlett vised her arms with her fingers and shivered. The Judges would return to check on her soon. Their inquisition would start after. Then she'd never be cold again.

She knew she shouldn't have come. Her abilities could never compensate for this burden. If her heart quieted, she could light a tabard on fire perhaps. Her friends had encouraged her, promising her acceptance to the Tower. But her mum knew better; a proper mage could weigh the power of those around her. On her best day, Scarlett was only a magus, barely worthy of being called a witch.

Could her mum save her here, if she even knew where to find her?

Scarlett would gladly listen to her guilt-wielding tongue for years.

Resting her elbows on her knees, Scarlett buried her head in them and wept. Her tears ran over her trembling lips, unwilling to open for fear of breaking the silence. Never had she truly thought such a steep sacrifice would be required for her friends to gain their freedom. She had already given up her family, her home. Now she would burn.

No. If they weren't here, they would come for her. Even Rorry would delay. Scarlett had to be ready to help from within. She wiped her nose on her sleeve, sat up, and slipped the string around herself to untie it. Spectre's coin emerged through the neck of her dress first. The brass token, with a raised depiction of a horse on each side, had a small square opening in the center where she had run the string. Saving him for a desperate measure, she tucked the coin behind her belt.

The dangling ring lowered onto her palm. Akin to dancing on fresh ice, poking at magical objects assured death. Scarlett glanced at the stars through the high window. At least it would be an entertaining distraction.

Maneuvering around the dampness to the hay pile, Scarlett donned her boots and resumed the pose she'd woken in. With a silent prayer for the others, she settled in and sucked in a deep breath as she rubbed the back of her head. "Be helpful," she whispered to the ring and set to work.

Chapter 16: Truth Be Told

When Cord woke, his ribs still stung with each breath. And no dream had disturbed his slumber.

He blinked and tried to take in his surroundings, unable to focus on the roots breaking through the lapis ceiling. Unlike those in his dream, these roots didn't hold even the slightest glint of light. But dim light seeped from somewhere, as though the stone itself lit the room just brightly enough to illuminate the shapes in the chamber. Under the edge of the lapis, the sculpted leaves that had sparkled in his dream now remained dark, riddled with cracks, and crumbling.

The fragrance of rose petals softened the damp air around him. He tongued his lower lip, flaked off a scab, and lifted his head from Marlone's stolen satchel.

Rorry sat beneath one of the dancing alabaster statues lining the round room. The shiny blue ribbon tied back her queue again. With the black crossbow readied on her lap, she sifted through her bag until she removed a slender bolt case. Her fingers opened it and counted the contents.

"Scarlett!" Cord said, sitting up. As he got his feet under him, the world shifted and forced him back to the dusty marble on all fours.

In a hard voice, Rorry asked, "Are you well?"

"Just give me a moment," he said softly enough to stave off the pain in his chest. "Where's Kylan?"

"Not far." She eyed him with a stony face, then pointed her chin to an arched opening. Chiseled to resemble bark, the stone arch framed the darkness of a passageway beyond.

"I see you found your ribbon, Lady Gwirion."

The bolt case clapped shut. "We have much to say, but first, I have agreed to apologize. Kylan is convinced you were protecting me—for which I am certain he will extend his appreciation. In gratitude for saving *him*, I shall do my best not to view it as though you held me against my will and prevented me from assisting my friends." Her tone certainly wasn't forgiving. "From this point forward, my years of training will protect me at *my* discretion."

"Training girls in combat is illegal," Cord said, "even for nobles."

Rorry rose to look down on him with her weapon in hand. "This *girl* saved your life. Be thankful some people see through the antiquated laws of Merith. Education should never be restricted to a wealthy man." She paced around him, running her free hand over the grooves in the robes of the statues stuck in their immortal dance. Their merry, slender faces seemed out of place in the forgotten chamber.

He had to stop following her with his eyes. The world spun enough on its own. "Is that how Kylan can read? You taught him?"

She tilted her head and donned a patronizing frown that would've made Julian proud. "I would teach a senile slave if he asked it of me. But no. Kylan learned at my side."

"At your side?" Cord repeated.

Rorry didn't elaborate, merely shook her head. "You should have told us you were a magus. All of this would have been much easier."

Unsure what she meant by that, Cord waited for an explanation but received none. "Hiding my curse makes more sense than you lying about your station."

"It was not a lie. I was a noble but am no longer."

Cord sniffed. "All right, fine. And what about Kylan and Scarlett? What are they to you, my lady?"

"My subjects," she admitted with a nod, "my peers, my friends."

"In that order?"

Her eyes narrowed on him. "What are you inferring?"

Drawing up to rest on his knees, Cord wavered a bit but balanced. "Provisions, sure. Quickly formed plans, fine. And how nice for you to come across bedrolls in your escape." He pointed at the crossbow. "But you'd have more luck finding a six-legged bullfrog dancing with a gator than weapons on the road. Y'all left Brewing before it was attacked—if it even was. Are your 'subjects' running away on your orders?"

"No," she answered defensively. "We are equals in this endeavor, with our own reasons to flee." Her eyes tried to bore through him for a moment, then softened. The dim light didn't hide her worried frown. "You are gentle." She made it sound like a compliment.

"A gentle soldier?" He sneered. "No room for those in the army." With a long inhale, he rolled his shoulders. "Ashes, maybe you're right. But why'd you flee? You're no magus; you're not even a commoner. The curse in my bones makes me Abandoned, but you—a noble, you have the protection of the Chancellor! Why shun it? Were the balls so grueling?"

"It is as simple as you are wrong." She resumed her walk. "My father has the Chancellor's protection so long as he stays in the Tribunal's favor. Believe me when I say he has no intention of deviating from it."

"Why should he?"

"Your ability lies bare, inherently marking you Abandoned, and you ask me to point out the faults in your doctrine?"

He turned his scowl to his hands.

"Did you make a deal with a demon? Have you ever seen a demon?"

He squinted at her. "We're talking about your reason to leave."

With a satisfied glint in her eye, she said, "Very well. All of my life I have believed my only sibling, my older sister, had died when I was an infant. Then a year ago, my handmaiden informed me of Alis's true fate. You see, Alis had fallen in love with one of the estate's slaves. My father, in his fury, declassed her into slavery and sold them both overseas." Reaching behind her head, she removed the shiny ribbon and let her hair fall. "My handmaiden gave me this strip of silk from a dress my mother had stashed away. It is all I have of Alis, not even a memory.

"My parents kept the truth from reaching me for years. They were ashamed, I suppose. And to think I used to find pride in Brewing being a province without slavery. Now I understand the real reason why." She turned her cold stare his way. "Whether the gossip is true in that my father branded her to exact his anger, he followed your laws."

Shaking his head, Cord said, "You won't find me championing slavery, Rorry. I live in the Light, as it should be." That seemed to confuse her. "So, you left to find Alis?"

Rorry faced the statue next to her. Only then did Cord notice the top of the ears on the statues, longer than a human's and tapered to a fine point instead of curving. Elves? She gently petted the long nose between its large eyes. "Yes . . . though I never would have agreed to trade the sister I have in Scarlett for the one who may have perished years ago."

Her voice cracked when she said, "We thought we were clever. Kylan would sneak us into Llandir after the Seeding. From there, we would hire a boat to smuggle us past the Great Barrier and on to Racine or to one of the other Bonded Nations." Rorry tucked her hair behind her ears and wiped her nose, leaving her attention on the lanky alabaster elf.

He shouldn't have questioned their friendship. Kylan and Scarlett fought with Rorry too often to be servants following her orders. His anger belonged to Kenton's murderer or murderers.

"We'll find her," he said. Rorry didn't respond. "Kylan is all right, though?"

"Yes. Why do you ask?"

"It doesn't always work," Cord answered. "It didn't for Marlone." She didn't change her curious expression. "I'm glad it did."

With a sweet smile, she said, "I hoped you would help us find Scarlett."

"She's one of the three people I know now," he said. Saying it aloud jarred him. He sat back on his heels. "Of course I'll help, as soon as I can. We'll get Scute back too."

Rorry put her focus on the statues as they waited in silence.

"Marlone knew what I could do, just him. We got into a scrap with an idiot in South Thornton, a bloody one. Marlone ended it with a blow to the rascal's head. He deserved it, but it should've come from me. Marlone would've burned if we'd stayed. So we deserted, or wanted to. We didn't have a plan, really, just to take off during the feast and live in the wilds. Then . . . the wolfkin."

"I never imagined I would actually see one," Rorry said. "You hear stories of monsters and curses but never expect to encounter them, especially on this island. I think the curse makes them pack animals." Her shoulders bowed. "Scarlett would know . . ."

"We will find her, Rorry," Cord said. "And the reason Kenton burned." He stood with the illusion of balance and brushed off his seat.

"You were lucky, you know?" she asked. "We heard something coming down the tunnels behind us and ran. We only surfaced moments before you arrived at the stream."

"I don't feel lucky." He waved off his comment. "What are these tunnels?"

Gesturing at the statues, she answered, "The Starlight Tunnels of the elves." Rorry opened her bag and presented the folded parchment they had been keeping from him. "This belonged to Mrs. Hywel, Scarlett's mother. We believe this is how she managed to cross Merith after leaving Racine." Rorry handed it over.

A black outline of Merith filled the map, soft with age. Gray lines webbed across the island. After a quick study of the hills to the west and the Andras running south, Cord placed them under a red star at the end of one of the lines. Pointing to the star, he asked, "Are these stumps?"

"Yes," Rorry said. "The lines are the tunnels. They date back to Shallyghal, which means many of them have collapsed over time. That is why Kylan is scouting ahead. That, and he is restless."

"Scarlett's mother is from Racine? Is she a witch? That's how you knew about the tunnels?" Cord rambled as he strained to study the map in the darkness.

"Yes, she is a *magus*. And no, she did not tell us. We gleaned what we could from her stories. The Hywels have many secrets, including a library concealed behind the hidden armory in their basement. Scarlett snuck books away to her room whenever she could and eventually found one that hinted at this place and scribbles in the margins about the giant oaks." She nodded toward the archway for Cord to follow.

He took a step and wobbled.

Rorry leaned back against a statue of an elven woman with hair flowing to her waist and waited. "Mrs. Hywel arrived in Brewing ages ago, claiming some ill-fortune had stranded her and her brother in Merith. My mother . . . must have been about my age back then. She took pity on the foreigners and offered sanctuary. To hear her tell it, she merely wanted the blessing of having another educated woman around.

"Fast friends, Her Grace and Mrs. Hywel reached an arrangement after my birth. Mrs. Hywel would tutor me with a more worldly education if Scarlett were permitted to attend the lessons as well. Not long after we began, Kylan's mother brought him along when she visited our manor to tailor new clothes for my family. We played whenever she came. After she passed, we convinced him it would be good for him to attend our lessons so we could still spend time together."

Rorry set the crossbow down and retied the ribbon behind her head. "I am certain Kylan regrets that request, though our mothers did not bat an eye when they heard we had told him our secret. You should have seen the look on Master Nock's face when Her Grace and the scandalous foreigner arrived at his door seeking his permission to illegally educate his child." Finished tying back her hair, she smiled at Cord, then glanced through the archway. "I know now they did it as much for Master Nock's sake as ours. With Mrs. Nock's passing, two older deviants, and an infant, he already had too much to contend with."

That answered quite a bit about his odd new friends but not everything. Cord glanced through the opening for Kylan. But darkness lurked a few feet beyond the arch.

Cord's finger followed the lines from the star and tapped the map. "She would've been taken to Fort Warren," he said, risking a step toward Rorry. He pointed to an empty space on the parchment to the northeast of them and passed the map to her. "Look . . ." Cord said, "I gotta ask. How'd y'all open them?" He pointed up to the roots.

Rorry debated something behind her eyes and finally said, "I hope this will not change your offer to help us. If it does, you are a fool." She struggled to say her next words. "Scarlett has a small talent with magic. Her mother always tried to suppress it, for Scarlett's safety. But you should see the things she can do! We hope she can study properly in the Tower in Trône d'Argent . . . well, if . . ." She rolled her hand in the air and let the silence hang.

After hearing admiration for magic coming out of someone so proper, Cord didn't know what to say. He started walking in a small circle to get used to moving. So Scarlett was a magus? She was nothing like the stories of the witch daughters. But then, neither was he.

As though she sensed his thoughts, Rorry mockingly said, "No. She never made a deal with a demon either." Suddenly, she looked up from the map. "How did you know about the stumps?"

Kylan stepped through the arch, startling Cord. He never would've expected Kylan to be stealthy. "This one goes as far as another junction."

"I owe you an apology," Cord said. "I stepped on your spectacles."

Kylan crushed him in a hug.

The pain from Cord's tender ribs sharpened and made him suck in air, which only made it worse.

"Not to worry; I don't need them," Kylan said and let go. "Whatever you did was fantastic! I can see better than ever. How do you feel?"

"Sore, hungry, mad," Cord answered. Now he understood why his vision was blurred. He prayed it'd pass like the other injuries had.

"Hold on to that last one," Kylan said. He looked to Rorry. "Did you ask him?"

She shook her head.

"Can you do anything else? Or just heal?"

"I don't think so," Cord answered. "I never tried to use the curse . . . it, for anything else. The magic just takes control."

They didn't seem to know what to make of that.

"I'd guess that's a no," Kylan said. "Is there an exit near this Fort Warren?"

"Yes," Rorry said, "a mile or two south of the fort. But, Kylan, I only have seven bolts."

Kylan slapped the head of the High Guard's hammer on his palm. "I have this. It's had a sad life and wants to deliver some actual justice."

"Do you know how to use it?" Cord asked.

Kylan fell into a Smashing Ogre stance. "Master Clienne—"

"Scarlett's uncle," Rorry said.

"He taught me well enough."

"As well as you would listen," she corrected.

"I listened," Kylan said. "To him. Culture and etiquette lessons don't bruise you for letting your mind wander." Kylan picked up Marlone's satchel and handed it to Cord. "Let's go. Night'll be our only advantage."

The more answers Cord got, the stranger his new friends seemed. "Scarlett's uncle gave you weapons?" he asked, following them under the arch.

"We stole them," Rorry said matter-of-factly. Then she added, "We will find a way to return them." She didn't sound sure of that.

Kylan groaned. "If we can even find the katana now."

On both sides of the tunnel, water babbled. Leaf-shaped spouts spilled down the walls into scalloped waist-high troughs. Above the waterspouts, the walls darkened to lapis and merged into a ceiling twinkling brighter than a noble's jewels.

Cord asked, "Are those stars?"

"Yes," Rorry answered. "Have you ever seen anything so lovely? The elves enchanted the ceiling to use the stars as guides in their travels. Those are the very stars above us now. If you watch long enough, they will move." She shot him a grin. "I envy you magi at times."

He wished she'd stop calling him that.

Training his eyes to the brightest stars, Cord drew out the summer constellations in the moonless cosmos. Valor's Shield shone brighter than the stained-glass window in the oratory ever had. The clarity in the purple clouds of Hylatia's hair revealed ringlets in her locks. Nepharni and Loathe, the dragons, blasted green and orange flames in their eternal battle. "How'd the tunnels survive the Purge? The army would've destroyed them."

"Come along," Kylan said, rapping his knuckles on the wet wall.

With Rorry and Kylan's acceptance of magic, Cord thought maybe he should give in to his curiosity. "This might help," he said, slipping his hand into the satchel. "Marlone took it from the High Guard." Holding the bag out, he jostled it. Besides his Seeding papers, it was empty. "The ring's gone!"

"Hmm," Kylan said. "Scarlett. She has fast hands."

Rorry's eyebrows rose. "Pray they do not find it on her, or Spectre's coin."

That doubled Kylan's speed. "I wish you'd have just told us you were a magus," he said over his shoulder.

Cord hurried behind them. "I wasn't sure that's what it—I was. May the Chancellor have mercy."

Rorry and Kylan shared a quick glance.

"Knowing what you do now, will you join us on the continent?" Kylan asked. Rorry didn't huff at the offer.

If they had listened to Rorry from the start, Scarlett wouldn't be in this mess. Cord's jaw clamped as he imagined Scarlett caged in a spider. She'd never been anything but sweet to him. Now she'd burn because he'd brought them to Kenton. "I'll do everything I can to help Scarlett. That's all I can promise until I avenge Kenton, but you have it."

"You're staying in Merith?" Kylan asked. "Knowing you're Abandoned?"

"*I* didn't choose to be Abandoned."

Kylan rounded on him. "We didn't choose! The rules the Tribunal has laid over its people only benefit the men who fit their ideals. Never mind if you use magic, or—who would choose to live like this? Leaving your family and home, never to return, even if you wanted to."

"Those are Mrs. Hywel's words," Rorry said.

Kylan shrugged it off. "There are always worse fates than burning to death. But by all means, delude yourself. It's probably easier for an orphan."

"Kylan," Rorry said, "you have had years to come to terms with this. It has been forced on Cord."

"No," Cord said. "It's more than that. I vowed to the Chancellor to avenge the people of Kenton. I can't do that from the continent."

Raising an eyebrow, Kylan asked, "You vowed to the Chancellor to avenge the very deaths the High Guard were concealing? Are you declaring war on the army?"

"The army defends the people of Merith!"

"Are you hearing yourself? The army is sworn to defend the Chancellor, not the people. How protected is Scarlett right now?"

Rorry stepped between them. "Walk and discuss it, or walk and be silent." She continued on.

Kylan spoke softly. "The High Guard burned your people like Abandoned, Cord. They deserved better." He stepped back and followed Rorry.

Cord's hand ran over the feather on his tunic as he walked. Staring at the ceiling until his neck began to cramp, he reflected on the changes his life had taken as they traveled the tunnels of the lost race, supposedly the strongest magi Cyr had ever known. From Marlone to Headmaster Angsly, from the wolfkin to the High Guard, he relived the past few days. All the while, his body recovered, even his vision, but his jaw and fingers ached from holding in his anger.

The High Guard had condemned the innocent in South Thornton, while the Judges had laughed. At the same time, these Judges had correctly apprehended Scarlett, a sweet girl with a bashful smile. She didn't invoke demons or drain the blood out of children, just held a dangerous curiosity. Evil didn't run in her blood. It didn't hide in his. The only evil he'd seen . . . "Did the High Guard kill my neighbors?"

When they paused, Kylan let Rorry answer. "I do not know."

"They didn't use the Chancellor's Light from the Idol," Cord said. "But they did burn them." He blinked to keep his eyes clear. "Good, decent people. Kids."

Kylan nodded and walked on.

Catching up to him, Cord said, "I'll help you flee, but I can't leave the province. Not yet." If there was corruption in the Tribunal, the Chancellor would correct it. If they were responsible for Kenton's massacre, Cord would take care of it himself. "After all, it's my fault Scarlett's in this mess."

"No," Rorry said, taking Kylan's arm. She turned them both to face her. "Blame is not helpful. We were right to escort you, Cord. Scarlett would not change that, even if she could. It is up to the three of us to ensure she does not become our sacrifice."

Kylan pulled Rorry close as he increased their pace.

Chapter 17: Solitary No More

Scarlett flicked away the blistering ring. It clinked against the wall and skipped across the hay on the floorboards of her cell. She sucked on her finger to soothe her skin. Fire was not the correct approach.

Searching for the ring, she wished for more light. The irony of wanting a fire made her sigh. Soon it'd be the last thing she wanted. Shivering at the thought, she tried to guess the bauble's trajectory and prodded the filthy straw.

Colors rushed into the gray room, causing the ring to sparkle. Shouts poured through the high window. Scarlett snatched the glimmering aquamarine ring and slipped it onto her forefinger, listening as the darkness returned.

"Seal the back gate!" a man yelled. "We are—"

A rumble silenced him before an explosion forced Scarlett to cover her ears.

More shouts relayed orders over the screams. Who was brash

enough to attack a fort of Judges?

She could wait a hundred years and never have another opportunity like this; she had to act. Focusing on the iron square backside of the door's lock, she held her hands out. Scarlett tried to ignore her shaking and focused on her frustrations of being separated from her friends. She needed ire. Fear mixed into her emotions as she imagined the possibility they'd continued on without her. She tried to force the fear out. Using the face of the Judge who'd struck her as the foundation, she built her anger. After running through each nuisance they'd encountered over the past few days, she checked her progress. The metal had warmed slightly.

Then she tried Grary again. She wasn't powerful enough!

Scarlett shoved against the door. It didn't budge. She put her back against it and sank to the floor. This required more strength. Another explosion shook the building. She squeaked. Motes of dust sprinkled down from the ceiling. She had to get out before it crushed her.

With Spectre's coin on her palm, she breathed, "Ride." The coin vanished as a cloud formed before her. She ran through it to the hay under the window.

As it filled in her path, the eerie glow brightened until the ghostly form of a horse stood before her. She greeted Spectre with a pat on his nose, smooth and firm, like a slab of marble.

Spectre whinnied without a sound and whisked his tail.

"We need to get out of here! That door will give if you kick it hard enough. Do you understand?"

Another quake struck the building and sent Spectre into a panic. His legs kicked the door with plenty of force. The lock didn't give, but the wood surrounding it did. Booms pelted the jail. Spectre flailed.

Scarlett dodged the phantom's hooves by falling back against the hay. "Hide," she gasped. The coin reappeared on the wooden planks. Scarlett collected it and crept to the demolished door.

Shorter than expected, the lantern-lit hallway ended in a barred door to the left. It only contained two other cells before ending in a mortared wall to the right.

Scarlett hurried toward the next cell to check for her friends. A blast flung her back, pelting her with pebbles of mortar. Her ears rang.

Spitting out a mouthful of her hair, she rose to her knees in the debris and peered into the resulting dust. The cloud dissipated, revealing a new opening at the end of the hall.

Through it, a small bald man in a sleeveless dark-leather jerkin noticed her. His ears stuck out, making him resemble a mouse studying a sleeping cat. He stared down the arrow of his drawn bow.

Her heart stopped.

The arrowhead lifted. He released.

Before Scarlett blinked, something fell behind her. She turned to find a Judge on the floor with the arrow's white spiral fletching protruding from the emblem of the Glades on his chest.

The bowman pulled a new arrow from his quiver.

Scarlett's hands trembled as she raised them.

He hopped the remnants of the wall and walked by. Tattooed whorls and points ran the length of his scarred, stalwart arms. "'Twas not a bother, my good woman," he said in a foreign accent. Dark stubble surrounded his crooked smile. "'Twill be over soon, yeah?" The short archer skulked through the barred door the Judge had left open and turned the corner.

A few deep breaths helped calm her. The attackers didn't wish her harm, only the Judges. Why was a foreigner in the heart of Merith?

With a quick glance through the fresh opening to make sure no one saw, Scarlett whipped her skirt above her boot and deposited Spectre's coin inside. She rose and ran to the next cell door. It was locked.

Settling to her knees, she peered through the slot at the bottom. Aside from two bales of crusted hay and a rat, the cell was empty. Scarlett moved to the last in the line, which gave her a view into the yard in the center of the fort. Judges lay scattered about. Seven chased after something beyond her sight.

The blast had torn rents in the final cell's wall and had removed half of the door. Inside, a young man lay prone on the floor, his blond halo of curls caked in dust. Slender, with almost as much height as Kylan, he wore drab garb too large for his frame.

Scarlett sidled past the splintered door and rolled the stranger onto his back. His wounds were sparse and far from fatal, though he could certainly do with a bath. She brushed back a few blond curls and wiped the hay from his angular face. The white-as-milk muscles of his torso didn't match his tanned arms. Her hand hesitated before pulling his tunic down.

With soap to kill the stench, he would have been a fitting suitor for Rorry. Yet he wasn't noble.

Scarlett ran a hand through her dyed hair, wishing she had taken the time to refresh the color before fleeing Brewing.

Outside, a man's call ended in a gurgle, breaking her daydream. Scarlett lifted her dress above her boot to retrieve her steed, then froze as a middle-aged woman entered the hallway by way of the yard.

She was plump. No, not plump—wide. There was little curve to her square frame. Her cranberry lips matched her fingernails clutching a sable cloak to her throat. Sprigs of black feathers framed her broad jaw and blonde hair, running the spectrum from tips of white to roots of ale. The style bordered impropriety with its manly cut.

With a jerk to free her cloak from the rubble, the woman surveyed the room with a confused expression, as though she'd taken a wrong turn. When she noticed Scarlett in the cell, she quickly bowed halfway over her wide belt of silver circles before grunting and correcting herself into a curtsy. Her midnight dress was slit to her upper thigh, revealing black boots tall enough to cover her knees. They were breathtaking, armored in their own way with a fanciful Racinian pattern of fleurs-de-lis layered in supple leathers. The thick heels were as long as Scarlett's hand.

"Good evening," the woman said in a husky voice. "Have you seen a—hmm, how shall I put this?—a crass woman clad in pelts that look to have fallen off diseased animals?"

Scarlett shook her head.

"No? Lucky you," she said with a mirthful grin. Her accent perplexed Scarlett. It fell somewhere between her mum's and the bald archer's. "Stay here. The fighting shall end soon."

As the woman turned to continue her search, she glanced back at Scarlett and halted with a curious expression.

Scarlett jabbed the ring on her finger under the unconscious stranger's side. His warmth felt blissful on her numb digits.

"It isn't my place to pry," the woman said. "But what do you use to color your hair?"

Pulling a strand forward with her free hand, Scarlett said, "Rose mallow and calendula petals. Sometimes marigolds, when I have them."

"Such resourcefulness! I've been rather astounded by the amount of innovation on this island." She stepped into the cell. "I-I am Maeverly Roux." The woman clenched her teeth behind her smile when she said her name.

Standing for a proper curtsy, Scarlett introduced herself.

"And who is this chap?"

Scarlett shrugged. "I don't know him." Would these foreigners aid their flight? If they had gotten onto the island, perhaps they could get them off it. A quick debate settled, Scarlett said, "I thought my friends might be in here. We were escaping to the mainland, but I was captured in Kenton. Where am I?"

Appearing at the opening, the archer said, "This building's clear."

Maeverly nodded to him. Turning back to Scarlett, she said, "You're in Fort Warren. This is where they bring people to put them to the question in these parts. We came here seeking a member of our band who went missing yesterday."

"Then there are others held here?" Scarlett asked.

The short man stepped forward and eyed the prisoner on the floor. Despite his thick-soled boots, he stood a head shorter than Maeverly. "Just you and your man, I'd wager," he said. "This fort's puny and those cages are still toasty, yeah?"

Scarlett blushed and was about to deny knowing the stranger again when Maeverly said, "Yes, thank you, Veen." Then she raised her hand to the half door behind him. An unseen force projected the remnants away.

Scarlett jumped.

"Perhaps you would look for their possessions, Veen?" Maeverly raised her eyebrows at Scarlett expectantly. She grinned at Scarlett's unblinking eyes. "Bah! You're in good company now, dear. No need to be bashful."

Scarlett swallowed, and said, "My shawl. It's brown. And my

poultice bag. I don't know what else they took. Perhaps a black katana and crossbow with inlays of silver writing?"

They looked at her as though she'd budded horns. Maeverly said, "'Katana' is an unexpected word to hear from a Merithian."

Three whistles came from the yard. "The siege is ended," Veen said. "C'mon, we'll find her legendary hoard together." He jumped the exterior wall.

"Come with me, Scarlett," Maeverly said. "Teague will want to explain this for himself."

Scarlett hesitated, still curious about the warm lad sleeping in the debris.

"He'll be fine," Maeverly assured her. She stepped down into the yard where the battle had ended.

The wall crumbled as Scarlett climbed over it.

Maeverly offered her calloused hand. "This ring is very old," she said, peering at Scarlett's finger. "Easily eight centuries." When Scarlett jerked her hand away, she grinned again. "Are you aware of what it does?"

Feeling foolish and a bit rude, she admitted, "No."

"It's quite harmless. Unless you're a hopeless drunk. In that case, it's the find of your lifetime." Maeverly strutted her way across the boulder-strewn ground.

Staring at the ring, Scarlett didn't see how the blue stone would affect alcohol.

"Later, we shall sample a glass," Maeverly said over her shoulder. "Now, I'm afraid we have work to do."

Logs with the girth of full tree trunks formed the stockade walls filling the gaps between the four buildings at Fort Warren's corners and the two gates on opposite sides. Only two of the stone buildings remained intact. The one to Scarlett's right had fared worse than the prison she had just left; now it sheltered a jagged view through to the woods.

Soldiers were scattered about, all dressed in tabards with the Glades on their chests or shining full suits of armor with the red hammer of the High Guard. The sight of that armor sent Scarlett's stomach spinning.

Most of the bodies had shafts protruding from their vitals. Some were missing entire limbs. A trio fanned out on the ground before them. Their singed, blood-smeared uniforms didn't distract Maeverly from her march. At least the grisly scene made sense to Scarlett, far more so than Kenton had.

Chains rattled in the middle of the yard where a peculiar device stood. Eight beams led out from a central post. Dangling from the beams, scorched cages hung awry in the wind over mounds of ash and dust. Scarlett slowed her pace. The academe boys used to tease the other kids in town about these horrors, these spiders.

Two men examined the ashes. One of them, a hulking mass larger than the spider's cages, prodded the piles with a plank-sized club.

The other, lean and of average height, noticed the movement of their approach. The slender man leaped up with a knife in hand. It disappeared when he recognized Maeverly. He began walking toward them.

Near one of the intact buildings, Veen embraced a lissome woman. Scarlett stared in awe at her silhouette, which suggested she wore britches, until it merged with Veen's. Using Veen to measure, the woman reached Maeverly's height.

Maeverly stumbled over the foot of a dead Judge. Feathers and arms flailed. She recovered with a modicum of grace and made an exasperated face, granting Scarlett permission to grin. Maeverly winked at her. "Teague," she said to the man who teased her with a tightly held smile as he joined them.

Finely tailored clothes clung to his confident stature in the most appealing places. His black leathery jerkin ended just above his trousers and held the pattern of rippling water in dark blue. She'd have to see it in the light to be sure, but it appeared natural, not dyed.

His foxlike features grew even more attractive with a disarming grin for Scarlett. "I see we've found a new friend, now have we?" he asked in a polished version of Veen's lilting accent. The brown archer's hat he wore was pointed more than her uncle's, which likely had fallen out of fashion decades ago. He bowed to Scarlett, flourishing his hat with its single white plume. Silver hair defied the lineless skin around his crystal-blue eyes. He could have been a generation older than Scarlett or three. "Teague Fuchs, my lady."

She dipped. "Scarlett Hywel. It's a pleasure."

"Hywel?" Teague asked, his eyebrows pinching together.

Scarlett nodded but received no explanation as his face smoothed.

"I lead this caravan of merchants from the continent, traversing Merith to barter our wares."

"You're merchants?" Scarlett asked. "I thought foreigners were not allowed off the docks."

"Aye," Teague said. "Most believe that. Merith has no coin to offer, so most do their trading from their ships, fill their hulls, and move on. We decided to explore the goods in the nooks and crannies, as it were."

Scarlett didn't believe him but wasn't in a position to weed out falsehoods just yet.

Giving Scarlett a look of admiration, Maeverly said, "No, Teague. I think the truth shall suffice." The woman ignored Teague's grimace. "We belong to a guild of mercenaries called the Hook. Have you heard of us?"

Scarlett had read mention of the Hook in one of her mum's texts but knew little beyond their involvement with the disappearance of the Shroud of Genplin.

"She's Merithian, J," Teague said to Maeverly. "I doubt Remy's hubris extends this far."

Scarlett wondered how Maeverly had earned that nickname.

"Not yet, no," Maeverly said with mock disappointment. "As far as mercenary guilds go, we're the largest. Our band is one of dozens. But before we give you the impression we enjoy rendering carnage against foreign armies while we're trapped within their formidable barriers, allow us to explain. We didn't come to Fort Warren looking for a fight, but rather in the hopes of finding Vega."

Teague gestured toward the ashes and said, "As it goes, we've changed that hope to not finding her."

"There's no one else here?" Scarlett asked. When he shook his head, her heart sank.

Maeverly put her arm around her. "Scarlett was in one of the cells. She was separated from her friends while they were fleeing from Merith."

Teague considered Scarlett with an amused twinkle in his eye.

"No!" the large man yelled from beneath the spider. He let go of his club and rescued something from the cinders. Clutching his find to his chest, he ducked and ran beneath the spider's arms. He must have been well over eight feet tall. Scarlett felt his stomps rumble through the ground as he neared.

Disheveled gray hair fluffed about the lower half of the giant's head where baldness had not triumphed. He ran his nose up his patchwork sleeve, darned haphazardly like the rest of his motley shirt. His begrimed hand extended, holding out a tiny, scorched knife with two finger holes in the hilt. The wrinkled, droopy features of his face watched Teague like a child waiting for an explanation from his parent.

Teague nodded his head slowly and pulled off his hat. "I'm sorry, Bevin," he said, patting the man's arm. "That is the knife Vega hid in her hair."

Cradling the knife, Bevin bawled as he walked it over to Veen and his companion.

"You have my sympathies," Scarlett said, suddenly dizzy as she considered the other deposits beneath the cages.

"Oh thank you," Maeverly said. "But there's no need for that. It's a loss surely. Bevin had developed quite the crush. But Vega was the challenging sort."

Teague said, "She was my responsibility, J." Facing the others, he stuck two fingers in the corners of his mouth and whistled. He waved them over.

"This isn't your fault, Teague," Maeverly said. "She disobeyed your orders."

As the others approached, Scarlett tried not to stare at the beautiful conundrum holding Veen's hand. She had never seen women wear leather, much less britches. Wavy brunette hair fell to the inked skin on her shoulders. As with Veen, no sleeves obscured her tattoos, vines and flowers winding down to the backs of her hands. Her plentiful lips grinned politely. Scarlett returned the gesture and looked at the blade Bevin displayed in his palm.

The five members of the Hook gathered around it, with Scarlett completing the circle. Teague put his hand over Bevin's. "Brothers and sisters of the Hook, we have lost a member. Her reasons for joining remain her own. The sacrifice Vega Durn has made garners our humility. May she find peace in order to start anew."

Most of the faces around Scarlett were bowed but devoid of mourning. Bevin wheezed, his droopy eyes glued to Teague's hand over the blade.

"Did anyone know her favorite song?" Teague asked. They didn't. "Well—"

Hoofbeats sounded behind Scarlett. She turned to see the man from the cell riding a black steed toward the gate. "Scute!" Scarlett called.

Scute slowed. The rider stared at her with consternation. After a hard jab from the stranger's ankles, Scute shunned his stubbornness and sped through the gate.

"Carolle," Teague said. "We'll drink to Vega later. Please bring the boy back with Scarlett's horse." Without a response, Veen's companion sprinted after them and out of sight beyond the gate.

Placing his other hand on Bevin's upper arm, Teague looked up at the sniveling mourner and said, "Bevin, please scatter Vega's ashes and make your peace. The fort burns within the hour, my friend."

Bevin moaned as he stomped away toward the spider.

Holding a finger up, Teague drew a circle in the air. Veen darted toward the back gate. "I'm sorry," Teague said to Scarlett, "but we need to leave this place. We can deliver you to the next town once your horse is returned."

"I-I need to find my friends," Scarlett said, her voice more panicked than she'd intended.

Teague donned his cap and nodded. "If there are any supplies to be found, you'll have all we can spare."

Maeverly harrumphed. "Teague, we should find them." He tilted his head in annoyance but waited for an explanation. She took Scarlett's elbow. "Do they know you're a magus?"

Scarlett blinked. "Kylan and Rorry do. Cord . . ." She shouldn't expose his lie. "Cord is someone we saved from a wolfkin. We thought it best not to tell him."

"A wolfkin?" Teague asked. "Here, you say? Gods, I didn't know the curse reached this far." He rubbed a pouch on his belt until he noticed Scarlett watching his finger.

"You see?" Maeverly asked before Scarlett could inform him that the curse was new to Merith. "I'd like to assist them in their escape and take Scarlett on as an apprentice, if she agrees."

Scarlett stepped back, her insides suddenly cold and her mind lost in questions around what that offer entailed. While she was seeking tutelage and felt kindly toward Maeverly, the woman was strange and, Scarlett suspected, a sorcerer.

Bevin roared and charged at the center of the spider, warping the iron post with his weight. The metal resisted with an unholy screech. He hefted his club and bashed it against the arms. Each strike broke cleanly through the metal and released sparks of lightning. The cages clattered to the ground.

"What of your folks, Scarlett?" Teague asked over the racket. "They must be worried, so they must."

"That's an odd argument," Maeverly said, "coming from you. I seem to recall a couple of lads running off for their own adventures not all that long ago."

Teague sighed at Maeverly. "What was it you called the woman looking for her daughter, 'the honey blonde'? We can't save them all, J, not even those who can color your roots. Think carefully before you exacerbate our problems." He started walking toward one of the undamaged buildings. "Send them through the Starlight Tunnels to the Mint Coast like the other magi we've found. 'Tis safer, if there are wolves about."

Scarlett couldn't move, aside from sliding her eyes from Maeverly to Teague. They knew of the tunnels?

"There are no assurances that way," Maeverly said, her voice deep.

Teague didn't slow his walk away from them.

"Teague, her abilities are inchoate; she's green, but she has the potential to surpass my sister's strength."

The Hook leader spun around. Maeverly moved closer to him and matched his masculine stance, crossing her arms over her shallow bosom.

Scarlett blushed as she timidly confessed over their whispers, "I am weak with magic. I can barely create a flame."

"Never limit yourself by what you have done," Maeverly said, without looking away from Teague's crystalline eyes. "With instruction, you'd soon surpass my abilities."

Teague wordlessly questioned the statement. When Maeverly nodded, he presented a charming smile and raised his hands in surrender. Then he asked Scarlett, "What say you then, Miss Hywel? Care to cross the water with the likes of us?"

Chapter 18: A Small Hiccup

Ever since Kylan had checked the tunnel behind them with a worried expression, Cord couldn't shake the feeling of being watched. He hurried through the Starlight Tunnels while pondering what he had said to Rorry earlier. As impossible as it seemed, they *were* the only living people he knew now. For the first time in his life, he felt the way people always assumed orphans felt: lonely. But he couldn't stay with them.

Once he helped Scarlett, these Starlight Tunnels could serve as his home. With plenty of fresh water and a magic touch required for access, they'd make a decent shelter from which to avenge Kenton. He'd find whoever had murdered his neighbors and make them suffer.

First Scarlett. None of it mattered if they failed at Fort Warren. And they'd be shit out of luck without a strategy. Seven bolts and a hammer wouldn't overwhelm the fort, not without a crate of generous crickets. "The fort won't have bows," he said, "just swords, hammers, halberds, and such. If we separate them, we can defeat them one by one."

"Is that possible?" Rorry asked, slowing to his side. "How many Judges live in Fort Warren?"

"No telling. Maybe a dozen or a full company? Most of them spend Hansweighn in the villages or go back to where they were raised." Cord avoided her sympathetic expression and ran his knuckles along the wet wall as he walked. Centuries of falling water had planed it smooth. "I wish I had my bow."

From up ahead, Kylan repeated, "We'll be able to plan once we're there and can see what we're up against."

Rorry's queue swayed as she shook her head. "You will not wait if you can rush in. Kylan, please," she begged, halting. "Can we rest for just a moment? We must discuss this!"

Kylan stopped with a huff. He pushed his sleeves up and joined them.

Cord splashed water onto his face and rubbed the sweat away. Following Rorry's example, he cupped his hand against the wall and took a drink. The chilled water tasted too pure to be from the river.

"If there are more than nine Judges," Kylan said, "we're in trouble. Rorry is deadly with a crossbow, but she can't make bolts out of air." Rorry held her head a little higher after that comment. "How do you fare unarmed?"

Removing Julian's belt knife, Cord said, "With this, well enough, I suppose."

"Against wolfkin?" Rorry asked.

Judging by Kylan's sudden jaunt away, he hadn't considered that either.

Pointing to the stars on the ceiling, Cord drew through the blue and white ones to connect a constellation. "That's Valor's Shield. When it reaches the horizon, the summer sun begins to rise. For what it's worth, we have a few hours of night left."

"If they give her that long," Kylan yelled back.

Cord left his hand in the cool water as he and Rorry trailed Kylan again. It tingled the same as when he mended. "Can Scarlett do what I do?"

"I have never heard of anyone doing that," Rorry answered. "But if someone does know more about it, they will not be found in Merith."

"Maybe I can seek them out," Cord said slowly, "after all of this. So long as they're not demons."

Rorry drew up to lecture. "Demons, Cord? Do you honestly believe in wicked creatures wandering Cyr to trade souls for favors or power? Shades, demons, carowan, blighters . . . each name applies to the same mythical creatures in countless religions and myths across Cyr dating much farther back than Merith, and certainly farther back than the Revolt of the Magi—sorry, the Massacre of Merith. Yet no one has ever claimed to see one. I find that odd." She sped up as Kylan neared the last turn in the tunnels. "Did you attain your power through some vile pact? Scarlett never did. Not everything in the Rhynian Scroll should be taken on faith."

"Says the woman instructed by a foreign magus," Cord said.

Rorry swatted his arm. "Look around you! There is so much beauty down here. Imagine how it would have been in the days of the elves. They were the most powerful magi in Cyr, and the most gracious. How can you believe a race capable of creating this—a race that harbored any and all refugees from the continental wars—would consort with demons?"

"Maybe we'll run into one," Kylan said. "Then you can ask it."

"What?" Cord asked. "Elves died out seven centuries ago. That's how Merith conquered Shallyghal. Everyone knows that."

"No," Rorry said. "Everyone knows they *disappeared*. Although, regardless of their immunity to aging, I doubt they would hide down here all that time, allowing their tunnels to fall into disrepair."

As merry as their statues at the entrance were, the thought of bumping into an elf sent Cord's eyes to the shadows at the edge of his sight again.

"My point is," Rorry said, "if you allow your beliefs to make things harder for us, I will not forgive you."

Ahead, Kylan brandished the hammer as he stepped around a corner.

Cord removed his hand from the scalloped trough and sprinted as much to escape the heretical lecture as to help. Rorry's steps stayed close behind.

Entering the crossway where four tunnels met, Kylan stood still, staring into the darkness ahead. "Does anyone else feel as though we are being watched?"

Rorry said, "Only you would say something unsettling like that."

"I'm serious," Kylan said. "It's stirring the hairs on the back of my neck."

Cord peered down the connecting halls as far as the starlight allowed but saw no one. "I feel it too."

Rorry prodded Kylan onward with a shove of her hand but held on to a fistful of his tunic as they went. The troughs ended as they came upon another arched doorway. She pulled out the map and retraced the turns they'd taken. "This is it."

After a quick glance at Valor's Shield, Cord entered the archway. A round room, nearly identical to the one he'd woken in, contained a curved staircase leading up the wall to the lapis and roots. The alabaster elven statues even appeared to be performing the same dance, though their faces were different.

Cord smelled smoke. A short stack of burned wood lay in the middle of the marble floor.

Kylan bent and said, "It's warm."

A soft step landed behind Cord before a high-pitched voice said, "Andion wasn't too late!"

"Bloody ashes!" Cord yelled. He grabbed the hammer from Kylan's hand and spun to see nothing there.

"Calm yourself," Rorry said, the corners of her mouth threatening a smile. "Please be at ease, little pik. We welcome your company."

Cord shuffled back a couple of steps when a man-sized hand reached out from behind one of the elven statues and grabbed its knee. Slowly, an eye peered around it before the pik moved fully out of hiding. Only as tall as Cord's thigh, the pik's slim body and broad head, feet, and hands made him resemble Leila's old stringed puppet. His ragged tunic and cloth shoes blended well with the darkness. His pale legs didn't.

Smudged with ash, the pik's forehead wrinkled as he took them in. Then a large grin split his square face over his cleft chin. "Andion's sorry and didn't mean to frighten you. Andion was late, but fortune smiles!

You're late too!" His voice squeaked like a child's.

"A pik?" Cord muttered. "Here? Ashes." The Tribunal would search every copse, hunt through every town, burn Weatherington to the ground, if they knew. "How?"

"Andion's my name."

"Surprising," said Kylan.

Cord edged behind Kylan as the pik moved closer.

Rorry leaned to Cord's ear. "He is just a wee creature of magic. You are a much larger one."

Cord's cheeks warmed, but he kept Kylan between him and Andion.

Rorry lowered and extended her hand, which Andion raised his eyebrows at until she placed it on her knee. "Well, are you not an adorable thing?" she asked. "I see no beard or even whiskers. You are very young to be out on your own in Merith."

"Andion is fifty-four years old," he said defensively.

"Fifty-four?" Cord breathed.

"You are nearly an adult, then," Rorry said, clearly for Cord's benefit. "Where are your parents?"

The pik hung his head and quietly answered, "They went up above our home. Andion waited five harvests, and one feast, and two nights." He counted his fingers as he spoke and presented them to Rorry. "Now Andion must go to the mainland as he was told."

His eyes ran over each of them in turn, stopping on Kylan, who stepped up to the bottom stair. Andion frowned and pointed back through the arch. "That's the way we go."

"No, it's not," Kylan said. "We're going this way and don't have time to waste."

Rorry looked at him, her face blank.

"What?"

"Who are you?" Andion asked.

"I'm Kylan." He put his hands on his hips. "Look, I don't mean to be rude, Andion. But we're on our way—"

"To the mainland," Andion finished. "That's why Andion waited."

Rorry rested her hand on the pik's shoulder. "It is not possible you were waiting for us, Andion. We came this way by chance."

The orphaned pik wrapped his arms around himself. "So, Andion was too late?" He wandered over to the center of the room by the charred wood and plopped down. Andion seemed more like a child to Cord than an Abandoned. Maybe a strong child with a large head but innocent all the same.

As Andion hid his face in his hands, Kylan stepped down and bumped Rorry with his elbow. He nodded to the stairs.

Rorry lifted her chin.

Cord could tell they were giving Andion the same consideration they'd given him, only with the argument reversed.

Kylan's eyes widened with a glower. He warned, "We have a dangerous path ahead of us."

"We can use all the help we can get," Cord said, just as surprised to hear his words. He shook his head to dismiss the comment. Bringing Andion into battle wouldn't help anything. He'd just get hurt.

"Andion can help!" The pik cartwheeled over to them. With a leap, he put his foot on Kylan's calf and scrambled up his tunic.

"Hey!" Kylan yelled, bucking to shake him off.

Andion tugged on two handfuls of his hair.

"Ouch!" Kylan slapped the pik's hand away.

When Andion's ankles locked around Kylan's neck, the pik hugged his head.

Kylan quit squirming. "You had better be wearing smallclothes," he grumbled. He gave Cord's grin a look that would've made an ornery old cat proud.

"Walk and Andion will sing," the pik said.

Kylan slapped the pik's hands from his hair again. "If no one else is going to say it, then I will. Use 'I' or 'me.' You shouldn't say 'Andion' unless you're introducing yourself, understand?"

Andion's eyes shrank to tiny beads. He tugged Kylan's head toward the archway.

In a somber tone, Rorry said, "Kylan is correct, Andion. We are not going that way. A friend of ours was taken by Judges to Fort Warren. We must free her."

"No," Andion said, hugging Kylan's head tighter. "The red Judges are there."

"Red Judges?" Kylan asked through the pik's hands.

"The High Guard," Cord answered. "How many?"

"Please," Andion said. "They do horrible things, not just to piks."

Kylan cleared his face. "Well we're not going to leave her. So unless you have any other useful tricks, I suggest you wait here for whomever you were waiting on. Maybe they are late."

"Andion can thief!" he said, his voice rising sharply. Abruptly, Andion leaped off Kylan's shoulders and flipped backward into the shadows between the statues. He disappeared.

Rorry took Kylan's arm as they stared with open mouths at the shadows.

"Where'd he go?" Cord asked.

"He—is it possible?" she asked. "He can ride the shadows?"

"It must be," Kylan said. "He's gone."

She moved to inspect the darkness closer. "But how? No pik alive can do that. They lost the ability ages ago."

As the minutes passed, Kylan's interest dwindled. He paced around the room with crossed arms and heavy sighs. "We're wasting time. Let's move on. Who knows how long it'll take him to return?"

Behind Cord, Andion whimpered and emerged from the darkness. The pik set a dagger and a wheel of cheese at Cord's feet. "These you can have if you do not leave And—me alone," he panted. "I only say my name to hear it. If you use it, I won't! I promise! No more alone, please." Over his hooked nose, his eyes scampered, blinking with each of his hiccups.

Maybe Cord did have more in common with this little pik than he realized. "Deal," he said, offering his hand. "Call me Cord." Andion beamed until Cord took his hand, nearly as large as his, and shook.

"Great," Kylan muttered.

Weighing down Marlone's satchel with the cheese wheel, Cord said, "Think about it. He can help you, even after I'm gone. And if not, he won't get in the way."

Kylan raised his eyebrow.

But Rorry approved. "Keep up this behavior, Cord, and I will no longer believe you a fool," she teased. "Where did you get those, Andion?"

"Wafer Bluff."

Cord barked a laugh. But the pik was serious. He had covered miles in a few minutes?

"Humans never notice missing food during feasts," Andion added. "They love their drink too much."

"Andion," Cord said as a plan started forming, "can you scout the fort for us?"

After chewing on his tongue for a few seconds, Andion reluctantly said, "If there is dark. Andi—I can only ride the shadows. Some rooms have lots of light."

"We just need to know how many Judges there are," Rorry said.

"Wait," Kylan said. "Could you find our friend? See if she's all right! Tell her we're coming!"

Andion shrugged.

"It would mean a lot to us," Rorry said. "Her name is Scarlett. She has darker hair than mine and a matching dress. Please tell her that Rorry—that we are on our way."

Cord picked up the stolen dagger by its blade, hardly larger than a belt knife. Offering the varnished rosewood handle to Andion, he said, "If you do this for us, you can keep this for protection." Faster than a lightning strike, the dagger was gone. Cord looked up in time to see Andion's feet disappear into the darkness.

"So we stand about some more?" Kylan asked, refolding his arms. "He can catch up to us if we keep going."

"Or he would believe we left him behind after asking him to take a risk for us," Rorry said. Her hand pressed into Cord's back, prodding him toward the bottom step up to the roots. "We will scout outside while you wait for him here." That was a good idea; Kylan might not stay put if he went up.

Rorry led the way upstairs and checked her crossbow.

As they climbed, Cord's lungs filled with rose perfume. From the abrupt edge of the top step, Kylan looked like an angry foot-tapping ant on the marble floor.

"Touch one," she said up to the roots.

Cord grabbed a spindly root in front of him. When it snapped away, he nearly lost his balance. Rorry gripped his tunic to keep him from falling. Another root pulled back. A few at a time, they whipped away as the stairs silently dropped.

Not waiting for them to lower fully, Rorry rushed up. On the last step, she raised her crossbow and spun in a circle before stepping out.

Coming out of the dimness of the tunnels, Cord was provided ample light by the night sky. The trunk of the giant oak rested at the edge of a grove. Beyond it, a meadow shimmered as a balmy wind stroked the knee-high grass. Crickets played the only noise in the dewy air. Luck might favor them after all.

The late summer constellations were dimmer behind the full moon that hadn't appeared in the elves' enchanted ceiling. Cord stared at the Glades, wondering what Marlone was up to. Had he found Leila and the headmaster yet?

From the meadow, Rorry called for him and kept her gaze on the northern horizon.

Cord walked into the itchy grass to see what held her attention. A black cloud touched the ground beyond the hill. Not a storm cloud, but what? Before Cord could ask, Kylan shouted from the stairs.

Andion's head popped through the opening, his face lined with worry.

Kylan emerged, holding the pik's legs tight on his shoulders. "Fort Warren is burning!"

Chapter 19: First Impressions

Rorry ran up the road toward the blaze consuming Scarlett's prison without concern for who saw her. For the third time in their mad dash, her boot caught on a half-buried rock. She kept her balance, but a whine betrayed her. Cord glanced back to her with the High Guard's hammer ready. Lifting her skirt higher, she outpaced him. The closer they got to the foot of the black cloud, the more her heart raced. In the back of her mind, she tried to find hope, to imagine a way Scarlett could have escaped.

Rubble was spread about a hole in one of the fort's corner buildings. Flames danced inside and fell from the ceiling. "Scarlett!" she shouted. Smoke coated her tongue.

Kylan slowly approached the smoking stronghold. He released Andion, whom he had slung over his shoulder.

A quick flip landed the pik on his feet. Andion snarled and tried to bite Kylan's leg.

Without taking his attention from the fort, Kylan shook the pik off.

Rorry released her dress, letting her modesty return, and aimed her crossbow at the ramparts before crying out again. No one answered. No one patrolled the ramparts. They would have been out of range regardless. She lowered her shaky aim and slumped against Kylan's side to catch her breath.

The fire crackled and spit. They would not be able to search the remnants of Fort Warren until the blaze subsided.

"Did the High Guard burn the fort, too?" Cord asked. Rorry barely heard the question, absorbed in searching for a way through the flames.

Kylan moved his hand to her back. His face struggled to grin for her. "Scarlett probably set the fire by accident." Nodding to the right of the fort, he said, "Search that way. Andion and I will go along this side and meet you two around back. We may yet find her." He gestured for Cord to pass him the hammer.

Andion's red face appeared by Cord's leg, his expression sour. "I go with him."

"After all we've been through?" Kylan asked, dropping his empty hand. He shrugged it off bitterly and strode into the woods.

For all of his supportive words, that told Rorry exactly what Kylan suspected to find. Her belly felt like solid ice and empty at the same time.

"Stick to the trees," she said to Cord.

"Andion'll protect me," he replied.

She managed a polite grin and slipped into the tree line after Kylan. A few yards in, she dallied to watch Cord follow Andion's scamper off the road and out of the clearing surrounding the fort.

As spry as he was, Kylan would require her to hurry to catch up. She stalked forward, pondering her role in Scarlett's fate.

Her arms fell limp as she came upon a hole through the trees to the charred palisade walls. The logs splintered into the fort's interior yard. A simple fire would not have created such destruction. Flames barred her entry, yet a closer view inside might tell her more about what had happened here. She decided to risk a look.

A stick crunched behind her. Rorry spun and aimed in reflex.

Kylan threw his hands up.

"Do not sneak up on me!"

He sniffed. "You walked right in front of me, though I suspect your mind was on the other side of the fort, possibly forgiving the army just a little because of that uniform."

She groaned. Scarlett was missing and he wanted to lighten the mood by teasing her about matters of insignificance. "This again? Give me enough credit to be concerned for our friend and not fantasizing about fluffing the pillows with a stranger." She continued on her course.

Kylan's arm pulled her back into a hug. "Someone attacked the fort, unless Scarlett was holding back on what she could really do with magic."

"I noticed," she said. "So focus on the task at hand. They may still be here. And if they harmed Scarlett—"

"She's fine," he said with a tone closed to alternatives.

With an exhale, she melted and laid her head back onto his chest. "I know." She exhaled a slight laugh at a sudden memory and pulled away from him. "Remember that summer when we ate all of the strawberries in Mrs. Hywel's garden and Scarlett told her mother she had done it?"

Kylan scoffed. "As though she ever ate more than a bird. It amazed me that she believed her."

"Her parents believed everything she told them! Do you think she ever lied to us?"

"Of course," he answered as though it was expected.

"Or," she said, smirking, "remember when we were eight and she and I decided to dress her for a ball?"

"Aww. Now you're just breaking my heart, Rorry."

"Why? She enjoyed herself!"

"Uh-huh," he grunted. "She did until my mom walked in to find her in your dyed dress and both of you with kerchiefs filling out your chests—straight out like a shelf!" He managed to say through his chuckle, "I'll never forget that, or the looks on your faces." Tears came easily to their laughter.

Rorry elbowed him. "You should not have been in the room."

He wiped his cheeks. "Mom was so flustered she agreed to make her a new dress just to get her out of your dyes." He hugged her close. "She'll be in good company, even . . ."

Rorry squeezed his wrist and brought him toward the heat of the blaze. "Your mother would never satisfy Scarlett's desire for more dresses. Let us not wish that on either of them."

Bright orange pockets flared in the wood and threw smoke, obscuring the courtyard, though Rorry made out several broken cages lying on the ground. What mess had she dragged Scarlett into?

Cord's accusation in the tunnels might have been more accurate than she had admitted. "Did we do this, Kylan? Is this our fault for talking Scarlett into coming?" Never would Rorry forgive herself for this.

He shook his head. "Not yours."

Rorry held his hand. "If she is dead, I will return to Brewing and put a bolt in Grary's head myself. And my father can do as he pleases."

* * *

Cord kept his distance from the roasting fort and examined the hammer in his hands. Although sturdy, with a well-balanced steel head and a reinforced handle no longer than his arm, it disappointed him. The only decoration amounted to one silver buckle on the leather strap crossing the head. This was the symbol of the High Guard, a weapon of the Tribunal? The reverence he had given these men . . . They were just men.

The leaves rustled above him before Andion whispered, "No." The pik flipped to the ground. "She isn't that way."

"Ashes," Cord grumbled. He had sent Andion deeper into the woods away from the fort, in part to speed up their search and partly to keep from quenching his curiosity. He opened his mouth to say they should move on but instead gave in and asked, "How did you do it? How did your parents hide from the army for so long?"

Andion frowned at the grass as he walked and thought. "They lived in woods and hills and old towns and searched for the elves. For sixty-two years."

"Wait. You're not descended from the tribes of Shallyghal?"

The pik shook his head. "Andion's from here, born here. My parents came from over the sea."

"And they thought the elves were still here?" Cord asked. "Why? What'd they want with them?"

A silent shrug answered him.

That only raised more questions for Cord. However, when he looked up at the fort, his concern for Scarlett overcame them. One of the gate doors leaned askew, revealing part of Fort Warren's interior yard. Cord set his satchel next to a tree and moved out into the well-lit clearing for a better view.

Andion danced his nervousness around Cord's legs.

"Maybe you oughta stay near the shadows," Cord said.

The pik agreed and ran back, keeping watch over his shoulder.

From the edge of the scorching air, Cord could see remnants of a spider scattered on the ground. He recited a silent prayer and moved closer. The heat reached through his flesh, deep to his bones. Using the hammer, he prodded the gate door. It groaned and cracked as it swung in and broke free. Sparks flurried out of the planks. He jumped back and waited for the view to clear.

Stacked armored bodies burned next to the flaming palisade. Deeper in, a stick ending in feathers stuck out of the ground. Cord blinked twice before he believed it was an arrow. Others protruded from the charnel heap.

"You!" a voice shouted. A gauntleted hand seized Cord's throat and tugged him back. Toppling onto the packed dirt, he landed at the feet of a man.

A black beard left the warrior's chin bare as it draped down the sides of his face to the red hammer on his breastplate. The High Guard's eyes clung to the feather on Cord's tunic and thinned to slits. "A Catalyst? Explain what I am seeing, boy. I—"

The Guard cut himself off with his eyes on the hammer in Cord's hand. Any hope to talk his way out of the situation vanished, which suited Cord just fine. He recognized that hoarse voice from Scarlett's abduction.

Cord rolled back and regained his footing, extending the hammer loosely in his right hand. This asshole might not have killed his neighbors, but he had taken Scarlett and Scute and had burned Kenton. No shiny armor was going to save him.

The High Guard assumed a defensive stance that put the haft of his hammer between them. "You think your training is a match for a High Guard? Fool."

If he believed him a novice, why not play along? Cord raised his hammer high, feigning Smite of Sparks, and exposed his side.

The High Guard aimed his weapon at Cord's ribs and lunged forward.

Cord gripped the thrusting hammer in his off hand and used the High Guard's swing to his advantage. With the man's arms extended, Cord released the hammer and jabbed two fingers into the base of the Guard's throat.

The High Guard dropped his weapon and fell to all fours. He gasped for air while his arm swiped at Cord's legs.

Cord kicked the man's war hammer into the cinders.

The veins in the Guard's forehead swelled. Cord had been on the receiving end of that move once by accident. The pain had blinded him; he hadn't trusted Marlone to spar fairly for weeks after. The effect would dwindle soon. Before it did, he needed to finish this.

"Why'd you burn Kenton? Tell me, you son of a bitch!"

The Guard reached for Cord's leg in another pitiful attempt. "I will . . . burn you too," he rasped.

Baring his teeth, Cord powered a swing with both arms.

The clanking impact dented the emblazoned symbol on the High Guard's breastplate. He splayed out on his back. The hairs under the Guard's nose moved in his breath.

Cord could question him when he woke. But what would that require? Where could he hold a prisoner? Not in the tunnels. Should he end him? The hammer felt heavier as Cord stood over his opponent.

"'Tis a grand night for a fire," a man said.

Turning, Cord strengthened his grip on the hammer.

Several feet away, the unarmed speaker lifted his brown hat. He ran a gloved hand over his silver hair before dropping the cap with its white feather back in place. His dyed britches marked him a foreigner, as did his hide tunic. "Please accept my apologies for interrupting. I'm Teague Fuchs." His accent glided, like he spoke a song he knew too well to remove the melody from it. "May I ask your business here?"

The foreigner carried no quiver to identify him as the fort's attacker but surely shared no alliance with the army.

"This man's evil," Cord said.

Teague's piercing eyes took in Cord's uniform as he approached at ease until Cord lowered the hammer and crossed an arm over the feather. The stranger nodded. "Out hunting evil, are you?"

"The Judges took a friend of mine." Cord pointed at the fort behind him with the hammer. "Did you do this?"

A bald man with black ink whorls on his arms appeared at the edge of the woods behind Teague. The shorter fellow's ears stuck out like a mouse. As he moved, the arrow he aimed from his black recurve bow held Cord's attention.

"Stay back!" Cord yelled. "I can use magic!" He awkwardly pointed two fingers at the archer.

The archer froze.

Slowly raising his hands, Teague said, "Perhaps I should have asked your name first."

"Cord."

"Ah," Teague said, relaxing. "We're good here, Veen. Retrieve the others and leave Master Sullivan and I to get acquainted, yes? I suggest caution. The girl has a crossbow."

Cord kept his fingers pointed at the archer as he wandered away.

Teague smirked at Cord's fingers, now pointed at him. "Veen's a chatty fellow when you get to know him."

"How do you know my name?"

"Scarlett Hywel," he said. "Big blue eyes. Dark red hair. You'd lose her in the long grass."

Cord's muscles relaxed. Though reluctant to believe it fully, he put his hand down.

"She's safe," Teague added with a smile. "However, she didn't mention a pik. When I saw ye four running up the road, I wanted to be sure ye were the ones we were waiting for. When Veen gets back with your friends, we'll head to camp where she's already enjoying Bevin's grand cooking."

As the news of Scarlett's safety sank in, Cord smiled. She hadn't died because of him, and these foreigners might help the others get out of Merith. "A cricket's wish, then," Cord said. "I wouldn't have forgiven myself if she'd burned." Scarlett had suspected he'd join Kylan and Rorry?

Teague went to the High Guard's side and asked, "What did ye plan to do here with one crossbow and a hammer?"

"Anything we could," Cord answered. "Die together, at worst, I reckon."

Teague knelt by the High Guard. His jerkin reflected the firelight. Cord had assumed the bumpy hide was gator leather, but dark blue filled the rippled grooves. What creature had a pattern like that? Something foreign.

Perhaps their luck really had changed. These outsiders wouldn't worry themselves with Merith's laws. "Do you have a bow to trade?" The hammer ought to be a fair swap, maybe for a few arrows even, if Rorry would agree to let it go.

"An archer?" Teague asked, quickly smoothing the surprise from his features. "You're in luck! We have three of the finest archers the Hook has to offer in our band. Veen's wife, Carolle, she's the real markswoman. Veen and I omit that fact in her presence. You understand." He winked.

"Bandits? Here?" Rorry yelled to Cord. Her crossbow hung empty in her grasp.

Kylan kept an eye on the bald man trailing them with his bowstring taut. "Merith is turning out to be more exciting than we had anticipated."

Blood darkened Veen's lip.

"Be at peace," Teague said. "We mean ye no harm." He cast a frustrated grin beyond them. "I was serious when I cautioned you, Veen."

Veen let his bowstring slacken and sucked on his lip. "Aye. You didn't say she was wound as tight as a clock."

Cord saw the fire in Rorry's eyes. "Scarlett's alive!" he blurted. "These foreigners—these men are gonna take us to her."

"Truly?" Kylan asked, glancing back to Veen.

Teague removed his hat and bowed into an introduction. "Miss Pryce, Master Nock, she'll be thrilled to see ye, if ye care to follow us to our camp."

Rorry's false name surprised Cord. If Rorry took any notice, she didn't show it. Maybe his excitement had fooled him into dropping his guard too soon.

"You should burn that hammer," Veen said.

"Why?" Cord asked. "Don't we need to be armed where we're going?"

"It may be superstition," Teague said, "but I must admit 'tis one

I agree with. Those hammers may be a risk, which is enough to make them unwelcome."

"It's not my decision to make," Cord said. "Rorry?"

She mulled it over until Kylan said, "Well, it did beat me to within an inch of death tonight. Burn it."

Rorry nodded.

As Teague and Veen tried to figure out what Kylan meant, Cord tossed the hammer into the fire behind him. When flames ran up the handle, he turned back to them. "It seemed plain to me."

Teague tugged on a leather cord around his neck. "Veen'll show ye the way. I'll catch up in a moment. There's one last thing I need to do."

The High Guard moaned and grabbed Teague's leg.

Cord didn't have time to look up before an arrow burst into the Guard's forehead. Kylan and Rorry gaped at Veen.

"I thought becoming a monk would make you less dramatic," Teague scolded.

"Really?" Veen asked with a wily grin.

Letting the leather cord fall back behind his jerkin, Teague waved eastward. "If you'd like to get the pik, we'll be off now."

Kylan ushered Rorry with his arm. "No need. He can keep up."

"I'll get him," Cord said. He returned to where he had left Marlone's satchel, but Andion wasn't anywhere to be found. With the satchel collected and a few more calls for Andion, Cord finally heard a rustle in the branches.

Above him, Andion held the rosewood-handled dagger and put a finger to his lips. The pik pointed to himself, to his eyes, and to Cord. Cord chuckled, imagining the pik coming to their rescue. Then he considered it seriously. What if these foreigners had visited Kenton before the fort? "All right," he said. "Good idea. Just stay close."

Andion nodded and shifted out of sight. With his questions ready, Cord hurried after the others, just as eager to see Scarlett's well-being for himself.

Chapter 20: Evil at Your Heels

Rorry listened to the men ahead of her, crunching the leaves on their way to the Hook's camp. The mercenary leader's clean scent of bath powder conjured memories of her father, which she promptly ignored. An intriguing mystery, Teague did not strike her as a hardened mercenary at all, despite his scaly jerkin. Compared to his grace, Rorry carried herself as well as a bumbling ogre; her aching feet were partly to blame.

Given the fine cut of Teague's britches, the silkiness of his shirt, and even his scent, he certainly enjoyed the softer side of life. That required wealth. The way he turned his conversation with Cord away from archery to the events in Kenton with a casual eloquence put him at home in a court, or at the very least, made him sound like a merchant. Or the son of one. Yes, that would make sense. His Lekelithian accent should have brought her to that conclusion sooner. That, and he winked far too often.

Veen kept an arrow fitted to his relaxed bowstring as he walked at Teague's side and answered most of Kylan's questions. Although his less refined accent sounded similar to Teague's, his dark leathers were practical. Tattoos like his were more common in the Dessrini tribes, people she had seen bartered as slaves by the Vetskarran savages on the docks in Croathe. Perhaps the bald monk's order, this Ukresti of the Mount, resided in the Dessrin Range. What kind of monastery spawned warriors?

"And are you also from Lekelith, Master Veen?" Rorry asked.

"Heart and soul," he answered. "Even if Teague's kind would call me a bogtrotter and be done with me."

"And, pray tell, what would ye lowlander bumpkins call me?" Teague asked.

"Nothing I'll be saying in front of a lady," Veen said. Both men laughed before Cord tactlessly brought the conversation back to Kenton.

These mercenaries knew of Scarlett and claimed her well-being but had received Rorry's false name. Did Scarlett not trust them fully, or was she merely respecting Rorry's identity?

Rorry groaned to herself upon realizing her ribbon still held back her hair. If it was enough to give her away to Cord, Teague already knew her station.

To the mercenaries' credit, they had allowed her to reload Master Clienne's crossbow and watched in silence when she tightened her belt and slid two bolts behind it. Her cheeks warmed at remembering the unintentional threat. Behind her excitement to see Scarlett, she must be exhausted. Everything seemed worse when she was tired. Even the trees appeared gnarled and ominous.

For the fifth time during their walk through the broken moonlight, a flicker caught Rorry's eye. When she looked, nothing remained. Andion must be assessing their situation. She smiled as she imagined the vivacious pik's attempted rescue, snarling and biting at these seasoned mercenaries of the Hook.

"They were all dead?" Teague asked. He exchanged a knowing look with Veen.

The monk bit off a profanity. "That makes four."

Addressing Cord, Teague said, "Since leaving Croathe, we've come upon three other towns that met a similar fate, though all were ashes when we arrived."

"Forgive my inquiry," Rorry said, "but would you not have been better served to keep the High Guard alive to answer why they burned the villages, Master Fuchs?"

"Again, please call me Teague. And, aye, that would have been my vote." He glared at Veen, who returned a toothy grin.

"What brought you to Merith?" Kylan asked.

"An investigation," Teague said with a charming smirk. The man had already figured out Kylan's secret. Or, perhaps he did not discriminate. Affluent Lekelithian merchants were rumored to use beds as bartering stalls. "Why don't we wait to have this discussion over a warm meal?" The flirt could keep his secrets as far as she was concerned, so long as they let them leave once they were reunited with Scarlett.

"An investigation that led you to attack the fort?" Cord asked.

"Nah, boy," Veen said. "We're kindred spirits in that effort. One of our own went missing after following some bad—"

"Aye," Teague cut in. "Sadly, we weren't as fortunate as ye. Vega's loss is a bad omen, if ye believe in such things. Gods rest her soul."

Cord slowed to walk at Rorry's side. "How was Scarlett when you found her?"

"Grand," Veen answered. "A little shocked. More concerned for youse and the wolfkin, so."

"I was surprised to hear Merith still had a problem with the curse," Teague added. "It left the continent ages ago."

"Outside of the Cloud," Veen said offhandedly. The comment caught Teague off guard, causing him to take a half step, practically a stumble for someone with his poise.

Cord said, "Judge Kline was the first wolfkin any of us had seen."

"Such a pity," a voice rasped behind them.

Rorry spun and aimed.

A Judge wearing the three waves of South Thornton on his tabard stood where they had just walked. His hand brushed a few black curls away from his vacant, wandering eyes. "They make excellent servants."

She stepped back from his stench, that of an unwashed builder.

"Judge Barret?" Cord asked.

"You know this one?" the Judge asked, wiping at the sallow skin around his cracked lips. "Then know he is weak. Two days and already he is an echo. But his pain soothes me." He tilted his head back and closed his eyes as though he were listening to something.

"No," Teague breathed.

The Judge's eyes shot open. "Teague?" he screeched. "My, what a celebration we will have!" A strange purr sounded in his throat. "So, the Hook breaks sanctions now? Whose power wields so much weight to bring you here, pretty?"

Teague did not budge, barely inhaling through his slackened mouth. His confidence crumbled before the Judge, or whatever it truly was.

Rorry's aim started to shake. She steeled herself and suspected Veen hadn't noticed Teague's reaction behind him. Otherwise, his posturing might have been more subdued.

"Hook business remains ours alone," the monk said. "We're going about it now. Don't be following."

Cord grabbed Rorry's elbow and pulled her a few steps back. Flames burst from the ground between them.

Rorry snatched her arm free.

"Do stay," the Judge said, never taking his eyes off Teague. The fire died, leaving smoke as a reminder.

When Veen saw Teague frozen in pale despair, he removed the slack from his bowstring.

A ghastly howl erupted, followed by two more. Something rustled behind the wild-eyed magus.

"Three wolves, Teague," Veen said. "Maybe four. Teague!"

Rorry held her breath and prayed her hands would quell their shaking.

"A deal," the Judge all but whispered, focused on Teague alone. "Give yourself and the one with the power to me. I will let the others keep their lives, minus a few digits, of course. Tidbits for the road!" He cackled, flinging a string of spit to his chin.

A glint caught Rorry's eye. Two black steel knives had appeared between Teague's fingers. His demeanor returned to stolid as he blinked and wet his lips.

"This one breaks and begs and breaks . . ." the lunatic whined. "Not a full day before he slips from me. You will not slip from me, will you, Teague?" The Judge's head rolled back, cracking the bones in his neck. With a slight step forward, he squinted and clicked his tongue. "I am not limited by the beggar's sight. Will you carve through him to get to me?"

Rorry's throat felt like a fist had formed in it. What was this thing?

"I'll slit my own throat before I let you touch me again, Beez," Teague said.

"Beez?" Veen asked. The monk drew his arrow's fletching to his cheek.

A wolfkin burst through the trees beside him. With a quick twist and release from Veen, the wolfkin fell, whining as it groped its chest.

"You are mine!" Beez's eyes burned like embers. "Give us the *tek'aran*, morsel!"

"*Tek'aran?*" Teague asked as the whimpering ceased. Veen had another arrow ready when Teague grabbed his arm to stop him from loosing it.

"Yes," Beez whispered. He closed his eyes and caressed the air with his finger. "The magic flows from within. My pets smell it, like peppermint on ice." He threw his head back again, releasing a crack. "We will have it!"

Rorry spied Cord out of the corner of her eye. He stood as still as Teague. Beez had to be referring to him.

Kylan leaped away and dashed between the trees. "You won't have me!" he yelled.

Hulking shadows converged on Kylan's path.

Rorry shot a bolt into the darkness where a shape pursued him. She scored a yelp.

Teague released Veen's arm and thumbed for him to follow. Veen chased after Kylan without question, only halting to let an arrow fly.

Rorry plucked a bolt free from her belt.

Teague raised his hand to stop her pursuit, never taking his eyes off Beez.

An inhuman smile split Beez's dry lips. Chattering, guttural noises issued from his throat. In a flash, he ripped through the air and pressed Teague to the ground, dragging him ten feet away to the base of a tree.

Both of Teague's blades plunged into Beez's side. Petting Teague's face with one hand, Beez choked him with the other. The Judge's mouth opened and lowered toward Teague's face.

Teague screamed.

The sound chilled the marrow in Rorry's bones. Her bolt flew true, digging into the middle of the Judge's back. Beez did not react.

Suddenly, Beez shrieked and flailed. He skittered sideways along the dirt and hissed at Teague. "You marred your pretty skin to deny me?" Blood trickled from his maniacal scowl. He stood. His armored legs rose from the ground. Hovering in place, he clutched his chest and said, "You have only slowed me down, pet. Deal or not, I will flay that ward and taste you soon." With a blink, he vanished.

Teague rubbed his forehead. "He's gone," he said to Cord, who was inching his way over to help him stand.

Rorry released the breath she had been holding. Beez's reek lingered.

Resting his hands on his knees, Teague spit. "Come," he ordered before turning heel to run after Kylan and Veen.

Rorry finished loading and matched his pace. Cord sprinted beside her, doubtlessly wishing he had that hammer now.

They passed a dead man with a bolt and an arrow in his back.

As Teague sped under an elm, a wolfkin dropped from the foliage ahead. Teague arced his arm out, releasing a knife with no sacrifice to his speed. The wolf fell. With the knife protruding from its neck, it convulsed and cracked as Rorry leaped over it.

Teague stopped.

Rorry was about to shout for Kylan when he raised his finger to his lips. No sound revealed their path.

After several heartbeats, Teague said, "'Tis in Veen's hands now. And I stood there like a tit in a trance." His expression darkened as he looked Cord in the eye. "If the wolves can smell you, magic boy, we need to get you to the caravan before Beez is the wiser."

"What the blazes was that thing? A demon?" Cord asked as Teague hurried on. "What about Kylan?"

"Our mission has changed," Teague kept repeating to himself.

Rorry put her hand on Cord's arm. "You heard him. Go." To the defiance in his brown eyes, she said, "If anyone will be fine, it is Kylan Nock. That boy has luck beyond reason." She tried to believe it.

Reluctantly, Cord followed Teague. What witch's oven had Cord trapped them in this time?

Rorry walked behind, guarding him and listening for clues as to where Kylan had run. Any snapping branch would send her running for it, but silence had resumed its reign over the old woods.

* * *

Dew slicked Kylan's erratic path. He threw his weight forward to ensure each step was planted, all the while the beast's huffs grew closer behind him. He cursed the darkness and the disadvantage it put him at. More than the darkness worked against him. Wolfkin could see, smell, and hear better. They were faster. They were stronger. Their swords hadn't been stolen.

Still, it wouldn't be long before they broke off their pursuit and went after Cord. Kylan upbraided himself; that was a horrible thing to hope for. And he would survive to see Scarlett again with his own eyes, not the eyes of glass normally sliding down his nose. Thank the gods for Cord.

Yawing again, he jumped between two pines, blocking him from the sight of his pursuer. A steep bluff saturated with black leaves and pine needles rose before him. "Shit!" he muttered. Kylan turned back.

The dark brown wolfkin cut off his escape. Standing two feet taller, the predator panted triumphantly. Its shiny black nostrils flared beneath its feral golden eyes, holding enough amusement that Kylan could practically hear the man inside the beast bragging. It swatted at him.

Kylan dodged and leaped up the bluff.

The wolfkin slapped his foot out from under him.

He struck the ground hard against his hip and slid down the damp leaves to the beast's feet.

Its hirsute chest heaved before releasing a deafening howl.

Kylan smashed his ears with his palms.

It quit its call and drooled, looking Kylan over with those gloating eyes. Then it sniffed. Growling, it squinted.

So much for his distraction. "Not the one you thought I was?" Kylan thrust his heel into the wolfkin's belly. Spit flung from its jowls as it reared back. Kylan's fingers dipped into his boot and met the handle of his father's knife. He plucked it out and drove the small blade into the wolfkin's foot.

The beast yelped and retracted its wounded paw.

Kylan pressed his elbows into the soft soil to get up. The wolfkin's bleeding foot pushed him back down. Its black nails dug into his skin as it added more of its weight to his chest.

Sniffing intently, the wolf lifted its muzzle. It twisted, churning a low growl as it searched the trees behind it.

Kylan struggled to breathe under its weight. He grabbed his father's knife and tore it free.

The wolfkin roared.

A *zip* sounded. White fletching vibrated in the bluff above Kylan.

Blood spurted from the side of the wolfkin's head. The wolf's seizing body collapsed onto him. Its rearranging bones crunched and snapped as the corpse shed its fur. Then the crushing waned.

Rolling the musky corpse off, Kylan inspected his attacker. The face had returned to a man's with a wax-pointed beard. He had the well-honed physique of a soldier, but the summer swelter couldn't be blamed for the shortcomings in the rest of his anatomy.

"How are ya?" Veen asked, occupying the limb of a mulberry tree. He lowered his black recurve bow.

"I wasn't bitten, if that's what you're asking."

He nocked another arrow. "On your feet then. We'll have to rejoin the others at camp quickly or be left behind."

After wiping his father's knife on his already bloody shirt, Kylan stood. "Thanks for the rescue."

Veen leaped down from the tree. His feet landed without a sound. He eyed the corpse. "There'll be a penance to pay. Doubt 'twill be severe. There's no cure for the curse that afflicts them. In killing wolfkin, you set them free."

"You could say that for any Merithian," Kylan joked.

Walking away, Veen said, "Follow me. If I stop, drop to the ground. I've got enough to contend with in these thick woods. I don't need your height in my way."

"Cheerful," Kylan mumbled, wiping his face. He spit out the bitter dirt his hands deposited on his lips and jogged to catch up.

"Why'd you run?" Veen asked. "We have weapons, don't we?"

"I'm not a coward. I just—I had to."

"You're not this *tek'aran?*"

"I don't know what you're talking about," Kylan lied. He might not know the title but knew to whom it applied.

"If 'tis one of your friends, you're in for a steep struggle. Much steeper than those other souls who fled Merith."

Kylan scoffed. "Others have left? How?"

Veen paused.

Kylan ducked.

"'Twas practice. Well done," the monk said before scurrying on.

Biting his tongue to avoid offending his defender, Kylan followed.

The monk's speed was impressive. Kylan matched it much easier than he had Rorry's and Cord's. They continued several hundred feet, nearing the sound of rushing water.

"I took down three wolves," the monk said. "There's at least one more and that demon, Beez. The river'll guide us back to camp. 'Tisn't far upstream, yeah?"

"Is he really a demon?" Kylan asked.

"Probably no," Veen answered. "Just pray you never see that face again or the one wearing it."

Kylan grimaced and scanned the forest around him. "You're a pint of sunshine, you know that?"

Again, Veen didn't respond. He seemed content with a silence that Kylan's nerves wouldn't let him enjoy.

"If it's against your creed to kill . . . you didn't seem bothered by killing the High Guard. Didn't you incur a penance for him too?"

"Nah. More likely gained favor."

"Why?"

Sighing, Veen extended his arms. "The gods know I strive to be

206

free of violence. In my youth, I killed many men. They deserved it, but the acts tainted my soul. After a decade with the Ukresti of the Mount, I'm mended and only take up arms to rid the world of deep corruption, like those self-important feckers you call the High Guard. Know I'd freely give part of my soul to stop that kind of evil. No one else should die by my hand if I can avoid it."

"You'd let a Judge live but not a High Guard?" Kylan asked skeptically.

"The gods don't always draw their lines clearly, boy. But any murder of a redeemable soul is abhorrent."

"What if a 'redeemable soul' attacks you?"

Veen halted at the edge of a cliff.

Kylan peeked over the side. Water reflected the moonlight at the bottom. Which river was it? The Staghorn, maybe. Its current was too strong for the Andras.

"There are ways to quell an attack without killing your opponent," Veen answered.

"Yes, I know." Kylan recited the list Master Clienne had instilled in his head. "Pressure points, incapacitation, and swift blows to the chin. If honor fails, kick them in the soft stones and gouge their eyes."

The monk seemed taken aback by the answer but didn't tarry long before sprinting atop the cliff, heading upriver.

Kylan looked back down to the water. Something felt wrong again, in his chest. He started to jog after Veen until a flicker in the brush caught his attention. The small shadow twitched again. "Andion?" Kylan asked, parting the branches.

A maw snapped at Kylan's arm.

Jerking back on reflex, Kylan barely saved his finger from the wolfkin's fangs. He started to shout for Veen, but the beast's arm struck him, knocking him back over the cliff. The air rushed through his clawing fingers until the shock of the brisk river water consumed him. Kylan righted himself and broke the water's surface, gasping for breath.

On the cliff above, the wolfkin quivered into human form beneath Veen's boot. Kylan felt the weight of Veen's frown as the monk shrank, and the frigid river rushed him downstream.

Chapter 21: Emotional Hazards

Mist had overrun the Hook's lowland camp around Scarlett. She clutched a bowl of soup to her chest, letting its fever thaw her fingers, though she remained skeptical of the creamy rosemary-and-potato concoction within.

Opposite her, Bevin stoked the cooking fire with a surprisingly gentle prodding for someone so robust.

One of the black pixie frogs filling the wilds with chirps landed on her knee. No larger than a pebble, her new pink-eyed friend seemed to have the confidence of a noble. Less certain of herself, Scarlett leaned back against a log shielding her from the river's cool breeze and observed the strangers around the campfire's ring of stones.

Bevin laid the poker aside and wiped his oversized hands on his tattered moleskin britches. Scarlett counted no less than five patches working themselves free from his colorful shirt as he reached into his cart, a white pantry on wheels really. He plucked out a spice shaker and tipped it over his cauldron with four cautious taps. The exaggerated shadows from the fire did his slackened face little favor.

The pantry cart sat horseless, the same as the three wagons lined up to face the road at the edge of the camp. Scarlett tried not to grin as she imagined the giant on his tiny cart. Then she noticed the single harness and sympathized for the horse chosen to lug it.

Beyond the curly-haired blond slumped against the log to her left, Scute grazed and mingled with the other horses, mostly beautiful and powerful Northpelts. The shaggy steeds made Scute appear small by comparison.

Her gaze fell to the silent stranger.

His eyes rolled dismissively and settled on the bowl he had been ignoring in his lap. The manacles around his wrists likely deterred his appetite.

Scarlett flipped some of her hair in front of her shawl and sat up straight.

Since Carolle had captured him, he hadn't made a peep, aside from squawking at the ring on Scarlett's finger. His features were quite agreeable, though the same couldn't be said for his sullen disposition.

Maeverly drew near, lowly humming a conversation she must have been rehearsing in her mind. She grabbed a curious bundle of wood and cloth from a pile leaning against the wheel of Bevin's cart. The magus loosened her grip, allowing the wooden legs to separate and tighten a band of fabric between them. As she sat, her boot-covered knees pressed together for decency, the price of wearing such a delicious dress.

Scarlett wished she'd recognized the stools for what they were and didn't have to contend with the knobby log at her back.

Bevin grunted and held out Maeverly's bowl.

A deep inhale of the soup's vapors challenged Scarlett's resolve to keep the heat on her digits.

At the rate Maeverly gulped from the bowl in her thick hands, it'd be emptied before everyone else had been served. Scarlett couldn't help but stare at the uncouth behavior.

Maeverly grinned and said in her husky voice, "Eat up. The warmth is even better in your middle."

Bevin gave the cauldron's vapors a few sniffs and nodded to himself. After ladling another bowl, he put his sausage-like fingers to his lips and copied a nightingale's song with surprising skill. When finished, he searched the trees until Carolle rounded the white cart.

Brunette waves framed Carolle's worried face. Bevin thrust the bowl into her tattooed arms. While the vines on her arms were identical, no two flowers were the same. Her wide lips pouted. "They've been gone too long."

Of all their accents, Scarlett enjoyed listening to Carolle's the most. The singsong of it made her smile, at least when it wasn't delivering concern for the others.

"You do not doubt their abilities, do you?" Maeverly asked.

Carolle shook her head. "No. I'm only saying I'm worried over my husband is all. When he and Teague are off on their own, they reminisce on the old times. Then they behave like they're twenty years younger. If they run into trouble . . . you know Veen's only dealt with wolfkin that once."

"That's all any of us have," Maeverly said.

"Behind the Cloud, wasn't it?" Carolle asked, causing Maeverly to shift. "I'm not being funny, but what if the same masters hold their leads by here? There's awful. I wouldn't dare suggest it to Teague."

"And right that you don't," Maeverly agreed. "Your husband's fine. The Cloud is thousands of miles away from here." She pointed to the stools. "Come, sit. Stop being an alarmist and help me convince Scarlett that while Bevin may not be appetizing to look at, he can make a delectable meal from any fallow field."

The ladle pealed against the cauldron's brim.

Scarlett jumped.

"It's a compliment, Bevin," Maeverly said with a twist of a smile behind her bowl.

Scarlett flinched again when Carolle let loose a thunderclap of a laugh. Somehow, it made the woman more likeable. The laugh came freely, as though from a little girl.

With a sweet sigh, Carolle thanked Bevin for the meal and took a seat next to Maeverly, opting for crossing her legs on the grass. Scarlett hadn't expected her snug leathers to allow such mobility.

Unable to resist the mouth-wetting aroma any longer, Scarlett lifted her bowl from her chest, which frightened away the pixie frog. A coward after all. The soup rushed over the curved rim and coated her lips. A staple at her home, her mum brewed potato soup whenever she had let the day flee by. Scarlett closed her eyes and let the memories wash over her. She imagined herself sitting at the rickety table in their kitchen as her mum added dish upon dish for her father and uncle to devour.

Her mum's soup didn't rival Bevin's. The rosemary balanced well with the cream. Other spices played there and perhaps a root of some sort. Her tongue mashed the potatoes as well as her teeth did. The combination of the scent, texture, and taste almost made her forget the comfort of the heat.

When she lowered her half-empty bowl, Maeverly winked. "You see?"

"This is delightful," Scarlett said to Bevin. What an endearing surprise.

Bevin blushed before he poured a large bowlful into his mouth and gobbled his serving.

Maeverly cleared her throat and leaned forward. "Dawn shall be here soon. We should discuss how accommodations are going to work if—when Teague and Veen are successful. We'll need to shelter five more bodies."

Scarlett did hope Cord had decided to come with them, even if it required her apology for taking the ring.

What if Teague and Veen couldn't find them? What if Kenton had held a worse fate for them than it had for her? Should she go back to check? If she didn't find them, she'd have to go home.

Carolle added, "And we didn't plan on the pri—new vardo housing a Merithian or four."

The stumble sparked Scarlett's intrigue. She had taken notice of the middle wagon in the line when they'd arrived. Plainly made and the only one likely originating in Merith, it mysteriously rocked now and then between the two ornate "vardos."

A large iron butterfly crowned the one Scarlett assumed to be

Maeverly's wagon. Light filtered through the stained-glass wings when the trees parted their shelter from the moon. It harbored more panache than she could imagine coming from Carolle, innocent girl or no.

"You shall stay in my vardo," Maeverly said to Scarlett. Carolle gave her a sidelong glance, which Maeverly readily dismissed with a wave. "There are a few rules we must discuss later, of course. It'll be like the old days in the Tower, staying up until all hours, practicing spells."

The shackled lad choked on his breath but avoided eye contact. The poor commoner must feel quite trapped between the exacting Judges and the heretical foreigners.

Scarlett raised her bowl again, only to find it empty. Embarrassed and a tad astonished, she let it fall back to her lap and pulled her shawl against her neck.

Bevin popped back up to the cauldron and ladled another bowlful before she could decline.

"As for you," Maeverly said to the young man. He gave her the same rude reaction he'd given Scarlett. "Precisely. I think you'd best remain under Bevin's care."

Bevin uttered disgusted moans from under the large bowl tilted over his mouth. The skin knotted between his bushy eyebrows as he gave the prisoner a look of disgust.

Scarlett suppressed a giggle, at least she'd intended to.

The young man's defiance diminished with a glint of fear in his eyes.

"Carolle," Maeverly continued, "if you'd be so kind as to see to our other guest before returning to the watch?"

"Of course," Carolle chimed.

Maeverly rose and tossed her bowl into a tub of water.

Again surprised to find an empty bowl in her hands, Scarlett mimicked Maeverly. Unsure what to do next, she lifted her poultice bag and stepped in Scute's direction.

"This way, dear," Maeverly said. "The vardo with the butterfly is where you'll be staying. We have a few things to discuss before we turn in."

At first Carolle seemed concerned but then flashed her pretty smile at Scarlett.

These vardos were more mismatched than Scarlett had initially realized. The first in line, a larger version of a noble's jewelry box, dribbled gold stripes from the roof to the chassis over its winter-tree-green paint. Large yellow wheels flanked its sleek sides. She ventured a guess by the sophisticated aesthetic that it belonged to Teague.

The plain vardo sat second in the lineup. Broadest of the three, it promoted function over splendor. The dark, planked exterior rested atop sturdy iron wheels. Four Northpelts would have to lead the hulking mass, which no longer rocked.

Who, or what, resided within its unassuming bulk? The suspicion didn't rest easy on her shoulders. Contrary to her instincts, Scarlett's trust in these strangers was short-sighted. She could already hear Rorry's patronizing remarks.

Scarlett and Maeverly reached the butterfly vardo. The sculptor of the gilded butterfly had favored anatomical accuracy, with grooves and notches detailing the finest segments. Something about the artwork called to her, something she couldn't quite place.

The whimsical façade of the vardo depicted waves meeting the wind, using a full rainbow of pastels. More paints colored the curved shutters of its round windows, leaving every surface vibrant. "You brought these from the continent?" Scarlett asked, tracing a slick whorl of pink.

"Yes, Racine," Maeverly answered. She let out a groan as she tapped up a curved staircase leading to the vardo's blue door. "My sister insisted that I take this one."

Scarlett pondered why Maeverly's sister would force the vardo upon her. A protection spell, perhaps? She had mentioned her sister was a magus. But why would that annoy her?

"What is your accent?" Scarlett asked.

Maeverly plucked a key from the plunging neckline of her dress. "Any Racinian would say I'm Lekelithian. Any Lekelithian would say I'm Patevian. The Patevians weren't sad to see me move to Racine as a child, so I'm guessing Racinian is what they'd say." Reading Scarlett's puzzled face, she said, "It's a bit muddled, more Racinian than anything, I think." Maeverly didn't sound much like her mum, though each class in Racine owned a different dialect. "That's where I lived in my formative years, until I ran away from the Tower of Trône d'Argent."

"How?" Scarlett breathed. Her mum had often compared the Tower to the world's finest prison. Of course, the comparison always finished with a compliment about the level of education they instilled.

The question went unanswered but wouldn't be forgotten. If she was from the Tower in Racine, did she know her mum? Scarlett held back her curiosity for fear Maeverly might send her back out of some form of loyalty.

Fighting the feathers of her cloak, Maeverly slid the key in and turned it. She pressed against the door. It didn't budge. Turning the key again, she rammed her shoulder into it. The rattling door bumped against the inside wall. "There. Shall we? There's a delicate matter we must discuss away from prying ears."

"The plain vardo?"

"What? No, not that. This is more pertinent to our sharing quarters."

Deceptively spacious, the wagon offered a horseshoe of drawers around the ceiling, identical in size to those in her mum's component cabinet, large enough for a pouch, little else. More stained-glass windows decorated the roof, secured by latticed ironwork. A series of clear panes allowed a view of the glittering butterfly.

Despite the available storage, Maeverly's wagon reminded Scarlett of Kylan's room when he'd shared it with both of his brothers. A jumbled assembly of red, orange, and pink pillows occupied two padded benches on the longer walls. Underneath the benches, trunks spilled clothes onto the varnished floorboards, leaving nary a clear space to step.

Maeverly kicked the clothing out of her way to the vanity at the end of the benches and slung her plumed cloak over a hook on the wall. Curious knickknacks and a dozen glass bottles covered the table. She pulled a wooden stool from underneath the vanity, sat, and flicked the wick of a lantern. It sparked to life. After Maeverly settled a red glass shade around the flame, giving the room a sense of warmth, she said, "Do come in."

Plotting her steps among the silks and lace, Scarlett discovered the vardo smelled more like her uncle's room than that of a lady. Taking a seat on the bench to her left, she set her bag next to her. The bottles clinked a reminder that the Judges had taken her willow bark. She would need to replace that.

Scarlett's eyes fixed on the opposite bench. A small brown tome peeked out from beneath a tousled blanket. "Oh! Which is it?"

Having followed her gaze, Maeverly asked, "You enjoy reading? I didn't believe there were any books outside of the army's control here, let alone literate commoners."

"I do very much!" Whether borrowed from the Gwirion manor or her mum's library, every book she'd found she'd read a dozen times each, including a few instructional texts from the Tower that her mum had hidden in a cubby beneath the stairs. They were far beyond Scarlett's abilities but had served well as fodder for daydreams.

Passing the book to Scarlett, Maeverly sighed. "It's not a very interesting read, I'm afraid. You're welcome to it when you have the time. However, I do request that you leave it in here."

Ivy or Silkshade: Where Magic Meets Botany by Trudinia Scott was embossed on the bumpy tome's front. Scarlett didn't remove her hands to cover the gap in her smile.

Maeverly picked up a slender stick from the vanity and twirled it between her fingers. "Tell me. Do you truly intend to study at the Tower when you reach Racine?"

Scarlett nodded, dividing her attention as appropriately as she could between Maeverly and the treat in her lap.

Maeverly tapped the tip of the stick to her fingernail. The lacquer changed from cranberry to midnight. "Are you aware there is an alternative?" Following down her hand, Maeverly tapped each nail, altering its hue in turn.

A breath escaped Scarlett. She ogled as the woman moved on to the other hand.

"Ah yes. A beauty, isn't it? After nearly two decades of searching and many meandering adventures, I finally got my hands on one." The stool squeaked as she turned to offer it to Scarlett. "I do have a tendency to show it off. Go on."

Scarlett let the tome close and took the silky featherweight stick.

She tried to memorize the characters running down it, which resembled hen scratch more than any derivative of the Old Tongue.

"In your hands, you hold a Wand of Shades. Only three are commonly known to exist today. It's nearly a thousand years old, not unlike that ring of yours. Gifts from the elves to the royals of their time. Since the magic of the elves never fades, they're priceless." A forlorn grimace curved Maeverly's mouth. "But most of the elven artifacts have been broken, melted down, or, typically, vaulted away in the various Towers for study.

"In fact, that is my speciality of sorts, or at least my hobby. I signed up with the Hook for several reasons but mostly to find artifacts like that one. No one expects a mercenary to hand over their spoils, even a guild as organized as the Hook. I wish I'd brought more to show you. Alas, Merith isn't the best place for that."

Maeverly watched her expectantly. "Think of a color and tap your nail."

Unsure what color to select, Scarlett wondered what Rorry would choose. With a firm image of Alis's cerulean ribbon, she tapped her thumbnail. Running away from the wand's touch, that exact shade of blue coated her nail. One touch to the others and they matched. "Astounding!" Scarlett breathed.

"It is. It is," Maeverly agreed. "Unfortunately, it doesn't color hair." She took the Wand of Shades from Scarlett and turned to her mirror. Placing it against her lips, she drew a new color as she moved it. The midnight shade, matching the woman's nails, made her resemble a corpse. Maeverly's frowning reflection seemed to agree with Scarlett's assessment, and she set about replacing it with a spiced-wine color.

Scarlett lifted the aquamarine ring. "And this?"

Holding a finger up, Maeverly answered, "Later. It's a bit early in the day to start that." She pressed Scarlett's hand back and hunched forward with her elbows on her knees. "Have you heard of sorcerers?"

"I've heard they're magi who are too lazy to learn the discipline that magic requires and put others in danger by allowing their emotions to fuel their abilities," Scarlett answered, nearly verbatim from her mum's mouth.

Maeverly leaned back. "That is a blunt yet common opinion." She halted Scarlett on the verge of apologizing. "In a sense it's true, though I daresay laziness factored less in my path than the ridiculous rules the Tower feels—"

She cut her words off with her hands raised. "That's neither here nor there. Suffice it to say, I feel I'd be doing your education a disservice if I didn't make you aware of your options. Contrary to the Tower's teachings, fancy words and ingredients aren't required for any spell."

Maeverly pulled a trunk forward and began piling its contents on the bench across from Scarlett. "It's the belief of sorcerers that mages use these techniques as a crutch, something to set their expectation toward success."

Scarlett tugged on her lips. "I'm afraid I don't follow."

Maeverly quit rifling. "The success of a spell is dependent on confidence—and the power of the magus, but greatly confidence. Sorcerers use their own confidence mixed with emotion to fuel the spell. Mages need an alternate way of ensuring the desired result, something more perfunctory. They believe counting out each gram of powder and the correct inflection of every syllable are what bring about success, be it a fireball or an enchantment. In short, sorcery is more efficient and less expensive. We leave the recipes to the cooks."

Watching Maeverly's back bob above the chest, Scarlett let a question slip past her judgment. "Sorcerers are less precise and more prone to accidents, aren't they?" Her mouth quirked askew during the asking.

"Ah, here we are." Maeverly sat up with a green tome in her hands. Setting the worn book next to Scarlett, she said, "You are correct. There are times when training your emotions to weave into your abilities can produce less desirable outcomes. Over time, I've learnt to control it. For the most part. Usually."

Scarlett flipped to the second page of the weighty green tome, having already decided to finish *Essential Focus* before the botany book in her lap.

"In any case," Maeverly said, "the choice is yours. I can set you up for success in joining the Tower or in learning sorcery."

Scarlett closed the tome. Her mum would lock her in her room for a week for even entertaining the notion of sorcery. Yet Scarlett had never read that the two approaches were mutually exclusive, and her mentor's experience with the more dangerous path might protect her. Once in the Tower, she'd be denied any experimentation along those lines.

She'd still go to the Tower, of course. Her heart did lean toward the "perfunctory" ways of the mage, just like her mum's had. However, stating it without offending her mentor would require eloquence.

"Think on it," Maeverly said. "It has to be what feels right to you. With magic, everything has to feel right if it's to be successful."

Scarlett didn't believe Maeverly to be unbiased but trusted her to give the best tutelage she could.

"Now that we've established that part of what I am," Maeverly said, "there's something else to explain."

"Hook, ready to strike off!" Teague's voice bellowed from outside.

Panic gripped Scarlett's chest. "My friends?"

Perturbed at the interruption, Maeverly rose and reassured Scarlett with a raised finger as she went outside. Unsure if she should wait, Scarlett stood just as the door reopened.

Rorry entered and flung Uncle Barrey's crossbow onto the bench before she tackled Scarlett in a hug. *Essential Focus* fell to the clothes on the floor. Smoke had overtaken the rose perfume. "We were so worried," Rorry said with genuine tears in her eyes.

Though touched, Scarlett didn't let it deter her curiosity. "What's happening? Where's Kylan? Did Cord come with you?" she let out in a barrage. She sidled around Rorry to peer out of the open door.

Cord waved.

She waved back.

"He did," Rorry said.

Maeverly's and Teague's arms were crossed again. The sorcerer called over Carolle and Bevin. When Bevin's stomps turned Cord's attention, the shackled lad ducked behind the log at his back. Was he hiding from Cord? Surely not.

Either way, Cord's wide eyes stuck to the giant until he stepped behind Bevin to eavesdrop on the Hook's argument. His face clenched as Teague spoke.

"Where's Kylan?" Scarlett asked.

"Scarlett," Rorry paused until she looked at her, "we ran into something horrible. A thing—a magus—I think, wearing another man's body. It was grotesque, dark magic . . . He is after the *tek'aran*, whom I believe is Cord."

She had Scarlett's full attention. "*Tek'aran?* That's not the Old Tongue. Why do you think it's Cord? And Kylan, Rorry? Where is he?" Her mouth didn't close after the question. Chills crept up her arms to her chest.

"Kylan pretended to be that, whatever it is, and dashed into the woods. Veen chased after him, but so did the wolfkin. The magus, 'Beez' is what Teague called him, disappeared right in front of us." Rorry shivered. "It was unnatural."

Rorry joined her at the door and took her hand. "I think Teague wants to leave us. He is terrified. There is some history between them, though I have yet to determine what."

Teague shook his head at his cohorts, who were clearly standing against him.

"Cord may require more assistance than he is willing to provide," Rorry explained.

"Maeverly is a sorcerer," Scarlett said. "She has offered to train me and won't allow us to be left behind." She hoped. "Maybe she knows a spell to use against this Beez?"

Was this what Carolle was afraid of? Were these things from the Cloud? The whole situation felt like a severe version of waiting for a switching. Kylan always lightened moods like this.

Scarlett returned to her seat and picked up *Essential Focus*. "Kylan would tell us to do the good we can. Right now, I believe that means we should pray for them and rest." In truth, her eyes would have to be forced closed when she had a manual to unlocking the power within her, however limited. She flipped open *Essential Focus*.

As Scarlett scanned the pages for something that hinted at dealing with possession, Rorry set aside her satchel, slipped her boots off, and deflated on the opposite bench. Rorry grabbed an orange pillow from behind her and reclined to her side. "Cord is a magus too."

Scarlett met her eyes.

Rorry nodded. "He opened one of the ancient oaks for us. That is how we escaped Kenton, after I killed a High Guard." She rolled over onto her back. "Then he healed Kylan. I did not know magic could heal people."

Neither had Scarlett. If he was a magus, it might explain the glow she had seen around him.

After several clarifying questions, Rorry surrendered and told the full story of what had transpired in their separation. She emphasized the urgency with which they sought Scarlett's rescue and the uncertainty they willingly faced when planning to attack Fort Warren. Scarlett's heart swelled, knowing they'd endured this peril for her sake.

"Bless him. Where is this pik now?" Scarlett asked.

Rorry answered with an uncertain frown. She moved to her side and intertwined their arms before resting her head against Scarlett's shawl.

Scarlett resumed her reading and finished a few pages. Then she closed the tome around her fingers and laid her cheek on Rorry's warm golden-orange crown. "The fates are quite fond of Kylan," she whispered. "We will see him again." Let the gods keep it true.

Chapter 22: Catalysts' Reunited

From behind the balding giant, Cord eavesdropped on the Hook's argument.

"What's there to vote about, good boy?" the pretty brunette asked Teague. Her grace defied the ink on her skin and her leather armor's deep neckline, which Cord struggled not to ogle. "Could you live with yourself if we blazed a yellow trail to Croathe and left Veen behind? What it is, Teague, we're pissing against the wind either way."

"Veen'll be fine without us," Teague said. "I want ye to consider our options. Ye know what the Dregs are capable of, the hash we're in. We've already lost Vega. I won't lose any more of ye, if I can help it."

"Come now, Teague," the broad blonde woman said. "We're loyal to you." The giant grunted and patted Teague on the back. "You gained that loyalty by making admirable decisions. Don't stop now. If this *tek'aran* brought the bloody Dregs out of the Cloud, they must need it. That's reason enough to ensure they fail."

Peppermint on ice. That's what Judge Kline had said before he'd turned into a wolf. Beez had used those words too. Cord clenched his fists.

After Kylan's sacrifice, Cord wouldn't let Rorry and Scarlett be left behind because of him. They'd be better off with the Hook. He stepped around the tattered shirt of the giant.

Teague spotted him and averted his gaze.

"Whatever it means, I think I'm the *tek'aran.*" As the others puzzled out what he meant, Cord said, "I can't ask for your protection. But take the others. Please. If I'm the one these things want, Rorry and Scarlett are safer far away from me."

An instant ally to his cause, the older woman with squared-off shoulders creased her face, almost forming a friendly grin for Cord amid her shaming sidelong glance at Teague. Cord tried not to leer at her appearance, both masculine and wildly foreign. She didn't seem concerned by the damage that had been done to her dress, torn high up on her leg. "Please give us a moment," she said, gesturing to the campfire behind him. "We shall *all* leave soon."

Scarlett no longer watched from the strange butterfly wagon. Tempted to check on her, Cord instead did as instructed. The last thing he wanted was to give the Hook another reason to leave them behind.

Despite the woman's words, the debate carried on as Cord moved away. If the Hook decided to help just Scarlett and Rorry, he'd be alone. And he wouldn't be fighting a rogue war to avenge Kenton from the tunnels but hiding from this demon, Beez, and his pack of wolves. Or were they responsible for Kenton?

Cord glanced down the path they had taken to the camp. Where was Kylan? If the Hook did leave Cord behind, he'd find Kylan first. He might still be alive; Teague had done something to Beez, though it was hard to say what since Judge Barret's body had already blazed with blue wounds. The thought of Barret's face put a bitter taste in Cord's mouth. Teague said he had no magic to feed Beez. Did that mean Barret had been a magus? How many hid in the army's ranks?

Chains rattled behind Cord seconds before something slammed into his back and knocked him flat against the mud. He rolled over.

The world slowed as Julian, the reason he and Marlone had been forced to desert, the reason he wasn't with Marlone now—climbed on top of him. Julian threw a left hook across Cord's cheek.

Cord's vision speckled. He roared and stretched for Julian's face, tearing at any part of him that he got his hands on.

Julian drove his knees into Cord's chest, forcing Cord to press against the weight on his ribs. He seized Cord's throat. "I know what you are," he whispered. "You ruined my life. I will see you burn!" Julian's eyes shot open wide as his body suddenly lifted, freeing Cord's breath. Julian released a shrill cry.

The giant dangled him by the scruff like a misbehaving kitten. The mercenary's face drooped in confusion as Julian swung his chained hands at him in vain.

Teague and the blonde woman gathered around them, obviously trying to work out the history between the Catalysts.

Cord growled, "You oughta be dead! How'd you escape the wolfkin?"

"Wolfkin? I saw no wolves, just the goat-seeder who knocked me down the stairs," Julian yelled. "When I woke from your assault . . ." A vacancy entered Julian's gaze before the fight left him. He addressed Teague. "Release me! I want nothing to do with this deviancy you foreigners are sowing."

Cord pulled himself upright out of the muck, forcing Bevin to swing Julian back from his reach. "He could be cursed!"

Julian exposed his canines in a snarl.

"He's a—cadet from South Thornton." The stumble saved Cord from breaking his vow but not from the Hook's scrutiny.

"So, ye're not friends, no?" Teague asked, glancing down at the feather on Cord's chest.

Cord swung for Julian again, but Teague's arm blocked him. "You oughta leave the son of a bitch!"

"Hold now," Teague said. "I don't believe he can betray us, himself coming from one of Fort Warren's cells."

The Catalyst slipped into his patronizing tone. "I had no papers. The Judges did what they were supposed to do."

"All very well," Teague said. "But I'd like to hear about the part where you said you woke and didn't find the wolves?"

"After this goat-seeder tripped me down a flight of stairs," Julian repeated, "I woke up the next morning. He and his friend were gone with my Seeding papers." Then he started to pale. "I went into the academe. You left me no choice. I noticed the shattered windows in the courtyard first. Inside . . ." He looked ready to sick up. "Those stupid sandals. Cold blood puddled around my feet when I stepped onto the carpet. Someone had strung up . . . there were not enough pieces to make a cadet." He shook his head. "I ran to the horses. They were slaughtered too. I am not sure how long I stood there before I saw the gate to the wilds was open. I ran and did not stop until my feet bled."

The fire returned to Julian's eyes. He said to Teague, "I have no reason beyond my treatment to betray you. Set me free and our paths will never cross again." He flexed against his chains.

Grabbing the handle of his belt knife, Cord said, "He could still be a wolf. Judge Kline was!"

A black steel blade appeared in Teague's hand. "A wolf wouldn't be taken captive, lad. They mercilessly avoid subservience to all but their alphas and masters. For now, 'tis safest to stay together. The lot of us."

"Don't," Cord said. "He's not worth—"

"You're not in a position to argue," Teague said firmly. "Bevin and I can handle this, Maeverly. Would you be so kind as to inform Rorry and Scarlett that we're heading out immediately?"

Maeverly narrowed her eyes.

"I'm in," Teague assured her.

Keeping a watchful eye, she marched toward the wagons.

Nodding at Cord's grip on his belt knife, Teague said, "Violence won't be tolerated here."

Cord released it. A tickling sensation ran through his hand as the skin corrected the grooves left by the knife's handle.

Teague withdrew his arm but kept the throwing knife ready. "If we're to help either of ye, ye'll abide by our rules."

"I never asked for your help," Julian spit.

"Then fortune smiles upon ye both," Teague said. "Are you

familiar with the Ukrestian monks—I'm sorry? Julian, was it?"

"Julian Westcott," Cord answered, nearly adding *from Croathe*.

"Are you familiar with them, Julian?"

The Catalyst shook his head.

Looking past the line of wagons, Teague raised a finger into the air. "No one knows how it happens. Broken souls enter the massive doors of the monastery and years later emerge, well, the most deadly opponents you could face." He held up a second finger. "Some say they spend all of their time training in combat. Others insist they imbibe magic or will their souls to wild gods long forgotten. Perhaps a whiff of all? Whatever the truth, the gods have blessed us with two in our party." Teague lowered his fingers to point at an elm near the plain wagon. "Carolle watches over us now."

Straining, Cord couldn't see her, just Maeverly harnessing the horses.

"I am not afraid of her!" Julian said.

"Oh, aye? Hasn't she already bested you once?"

Julian's face darkened.

Placing two fingers to his lips, Teague released a songbird's call. He removed a white kerchief from his belt pouch and flicked it into the air. It fluttered inches from his hand before an arrow drove it between Julian and Bevin, hammering it into a log by the fire.

Julian yipped.

Bevin grunted a laugh and set Julian down without releasing his tunic.

"Ye see, in our company, ye'll be well protected from each other. Challenge the peace, Carolle will stop ye, know what I mean?"

Teague patted Julian's shoulder and said, "I don't expect deference for saving your skin, but I won't welcome distractions. We have ground to cover, for all our sakes. Wouldn't you agree, Bevin? You'll have the honor of riding with Julian here. Keep him close and safe from Cord."

Bevin's mouth fell open, showing a cramming of yellow teeth as he mulled over Teague's words. After taking Julian by the scruff again, Bevin ignored the Catalyst's hurled insults and wild swings as he carried him over to a white cabinet on wheels.

"I should probably thank you, Cord," Teague said. "Julian's been so quiet I thought he was away with the fairies." He tapped his temple with his finger.

Teague removed his glove and fished around in a pouch on his belt. He pulled out a brass key, whistled, and tossed it to Bevin.

On his forefinger, Teague wore a silver signet ring crowned with a black oval. Why would he need one of those here? It reminded Cord of Scarlett's theft. Had she figured out the blue ring's enchantment?

The Hook's leader took Cord's arm in a firm grip and led him away. "That's him sorted. As for you, soldier, how well do you follow orders?"

"As well as I trust the person giving them," Cord answered.

"Ah," Teague said. "Then trust this. I know you're the good sort. And you know you're more important to protect than that bleeding bastard. But give me further reason to leave you to fend for yourself, and I'll leave the girls as well."

Cord ground his teeth. He didn't believe the threat, but nodded.

Thumbing over to the horses, Teague said, "Scarlett mentioned the black one is yours. Mount and wait there until we set out." As Teague sauntered by Maeverly, who was selecting one of the Northpelts and pretending not to watch them, he said, "My lady."

She frowned at him and brushed off her hands.

With another silent threat for Julian, Cord moved off to find Scute. Relieved to see his friend again, he leaned against him. "I'm sorry I lost you, pal. I promise those bastards got theirs." Scute nuzzled his hand without a grudge. Someone had readied his saddle. With a sandal in the stirrup, Cord swung his leg over and observed the Hook finishing their preparations.

Bevin packed everything down to the stones from the fire ring. Despite the din of clangs, clinks, and clatters, he was precise in his loading, setting his ladle just-so to allow the door to latch.

Carolle bound the last two horses loosely to a tree nearby. "This'll help my husband and your friend to catch up, proper fast," she said to Cord. Kylan wasn't going to like that. She smiled to herself as she tucked something under the speckled gray's saddle.

Once the shaggy Northpelts were bridled, Maeverly said something to the girls inside the butterfly wagon.

Rorry waved and closed the door. At least they were safe for now.

Cord patted Scute's neck again as he searched the shadows for Andion. The scuffle Julian had started must've kept him from coming out of the shadows. Or was it the wolves? Ashes.

When Carolle climbed onto the seat of the plain wagon, Teague whistled from the green. He started the caravan on its way. Carolle drove her team behind, followed by Maeverly with the girls in tow under the glass butterfly.

Fearing being stuck with Julian at the end of the line, Cord set Scute clopping toward them. He glanced back at the jackass and grinned.

The seat on Bevin's cart was too small for both riders. Julian pouted, perched on Bevin's right knee. The giant held the sour Catalyst in place with a handful of his loose shirt. Where had he stolen those clothes?

Maeverly beckoned Cord closer.

He clicked his tongue, prompting Scute to catch up.

"If you don't mind," she said, "I'd like for Carolle to use your horse until she's rejoined with her own. He's a proud destrier, ready for anything, I suspect."

"That's what he's trained for," Cord said. He winced. Talking about the army was dangerous. Already he had nearly revealed Julian as a spy for the army. Even if he hadn't given away the rank or its real purpose, he'd skirted close to breaking his vow. The farther he ventured from Kenton, the closer he got to breaking another.

"You must have a lot on your mind," she said. "Anything you wish to share?"

"I just said some things I shouldn't have is all."

"Hah! Welcome to the human race." There was something refreshingly candid about the strange woman. "While we ride, tell me what brought you out here, Cord Sullivan. Or, dare I say, *Tek'aran?*"

"I'd prefer it if you didn't. Should I call you J or Maeverly? I heard Teague use both."

She huffed. "Maeverly shall suffice."

Safeguarding his vow with embellishments, Cord shared his story. Lying was getting easier, especially with the liberty of adding Julian's despicable acts to his story. They were merely cadets that had fallen out over Marlone's treatment. He even included his decision to desert with Marlone rather than become an Ashwin and never mentioned the Catalyst rank, Marlone's assignment as Julian's slave, or magic.

Foreigners didn't have the same attitude toward magic, but Cord didn't want to talk about it. And they didn't seem to know what a *tek'aran* was any better than he did.

When he finished his tale, Maeverly wore a pitying expression. "I'm sorry, Cord. I know how difficult it is to want something for so long, only to have it ripped away from you. On top of it all, you lost a friend."

Cord let the comment go and kept Scute walking beside the colorful wagon. All the while, he tried to build up the courage to tell Maeverly what he suspected made him the *tek'aran*. He could tell she was disappointed he hadn't even mentioned the word.

When they reached a proper road heading east, Maeverly said, "Teague is a good man. What you overheard before—"

Cord raised his hand to stall her excuses. "I get it," he said. "He wants to protect y'all. But I saw the look in that thing's eyes, Maeverly." Cord didn't have the nerve to say he couldn't tell if Beez's lust or hunger was stronger, and didn't want to think about what either of those meant. "Beez isn't gonna let Teague go."

"No," she said, "I never thought he would." She put on a confident grin. "That's why sticking together provides our best chance."

They were already divided. Cord looked behind him for Kylan before scanning about for Andion. Should he be off searching for them? Could he defeat Beez to save them? Cord asked, "How do you fight demons without the Chancellor's Light?"

"No, no," she said. "They're not demons." Her laugh made him blush. "As odd as it is to say, they don't have an official name. They're a drifting evil, dark souls taking shelter in others until their hosts waste away. Teague said when Beez possessed him it felt like there was nothing beyond the vitriol of Beez's soul. Only the worst pieces of the man Beez had been remained. So we call them the Dregs—perhaps not entirely accurate; I suppose that's what happens when you discuss them over sleepless nights filled with tea and coffee. When we rest next, Teague can elaborate more."

She let out a breath. "This came as quite a shock to him. Regardless, you and your friends are safe with us. He won't do anything foolish. He's come too far for that."

"Protecting Julian is foolish enough," Cord grumbled.

Conceding with a head tilt, Maeverly said, "He'd save the world, if he could. That's how I know he was in fear's grasp when he called for that vote. Try not to let it taint your opinion of him too harshly. He knew what was right."

The white feather in Teague's cap whipped about as he kept an eye on their surroundings. Cord wasn't sure he'd understood half of what Maeverly had said, except that Teague had survived Beez's possession somehow. If he had secrets to share, Cord needed to know them, which meant gaining his confidence. "Well, we owe y'all. How can I help?"

Chapter 23: Bursting with Evil

Shivering behind Veen, Kylan squished along the sludge of small rocks and silt deposited at the river's edge. He had to hunch over to follow the mousy monk through the hollowed path the river had carved into the underside of the cliff. And that obnoxious summer sun had yet to rise and offer any help in spotting wolves on their trail. "Do you think they're still after us? This is making my back ache."

"*Whisht!*" Veen hissed.

"What?"

"Be quiet."

"Why didn't you just say that?"

"Your gob got us into this mess, yeah? Try listening."

"Forgive me," Kylan said. "The closer to death I get, the chattier I am. Who knew? If someone had told me, I wouldn't have believed it myself. Which I guess you are telling me. In a way."

Veen spared a glance over his shoulder. "Best to assume they're still hunting. Even if they've gone after the others, they'll be somewhere close. And your annoyance is a small price to pay for the concealment from the sky." He carried on with a flip of his hood over his bald head.

"The sky?" Kylan asked. "Where is that sun?"

"If you're intent on talking, tell me this," Veen said. "What grand lie did you have ready to spin when youse got to whatever port?"

Kylan concentrated on following Veen's steps over the firmer dirt. "Lie? I'm entering the Seeding like the other men my age. It's what Merithian men do, or hadn't you heard? We leave our homes and families and take our skills to new cities to forge new unwanted relationships and strengthen the imprisoned populations in distant towns, by ordinance of the godlike Chancellor and his wholesome and considerate army." Though relieved to speak freely, Kylan half expected Mrs. Hywel to appear out of nowhere and box his ears, while agreeing with the sentiment all the same.

"And the girls? They're not branded as slaves."

"We thought we'd get to Llandir and figure out the best way to sneak them in."

"Ah now, so you didn't think it through," the rodent squeaked. "The townsfolk wouldn't realize there were two strange women? How would you feed them? Did you plan to do so well at your trade that you could feed three in your first year? That's vain for a Merithian, no?"

Boring holes into the little man's back with his glare, Kylan asked, "Aren't monks supposed to instill peace? All you're inspiring me to do is toss you into the river when the opportunity arises."

Veen didn't respond.

The rocky shore had dried along a lip where their hillside cover backed away from the river for a span. Kylan braced against the water-smoothed bedrock and stretched his back. The sky held a little more color than when he'd last seen it.

Veen briefly studied the woods on the hill above them and carried on.

"We have Cord now," Kylan said. "If your band won't take us, he and I can do well enough to feed us all until we get through that flaming Great Barrier." That assumed Cord would forsake his vow of vengeance, which he should consider to be his only sensible option now.

Curling his lip in amusement, Veen looked back. "How exactly would you get him on the job registry?" He shook his head.

"I understand. Yes, we're simple, we slow-speaking Merithians. But we did plan. And every good plan allows for alterations. It wasn't intentional, but we have an easy solution to that problem. He can use Grary's Seeding papers."

Veen spun on Kylan with such imposition he felt his equal in size. "You mean you stole someone else's documents? You condemned an innocent to death for your own gain?"

"Hardly," Kylan said without blinking. "There's not an innocent bone in Grary Jeth's body. When he burns, the Judges will have finally gotten something right! If I could, I'd torch the jackass myself!"

The monk stood motionless, weighing Kylan's words.

Kylan lowered his voice. "Look, we didn't take his papers on the off chance we'd make friends on the road. And yes, we knew we'd probably die before getting through the Great Barrier, but reaching the continent is worth that risk. Life here, it's not what we want. It never could be. At least, not for me. Like I want to marry some woman and be—"

His lips sealed. Kylan's cheeks singed, but it was too late to reel the words back in. "They don't just burn us," he blurted. "Men like me, they drag us through the streets and let the cobblestones bludgeon us until they tire of it. Then they burn us, alive or dead. I want—I *deserve* better than that!"

Smirking as if he'd finally received the answer to a riddle he'd been working on, Veen said, "Too true. Well, let's get you out of here then." He slapped him on the arm and walked on.

Kylan waited for the warmth to leave his face. For years, he'd held that secret close, and to just blurt it out to a stranger had stunned him. This wasn't like telling Scarlett, who'd nodded along sympathetically, or even the drawn-out explanation with Rorry, who'd questioned him for what had felt like hours after she'd wrapped herself around his arm. Veen had just brushed it off. Was that really all of the consideration foreigners would give it?

When he felt close to normal again, Kylan caught up. "So, little monk, is it routine to rile the person you're protecting?"

"Anger is the quickest path to honesty," Veen said. "And I had hoped you'd sulk in silence."

"Alas," a scratchy voice said, "it does not make you invisible."

Beez hovered over the shore behind Kylan. The Judge's body dangled below his tensed, blood-spattered chest and arms. His palm thrust out; an unseen force propelled Veen into the air over the river. A flick of Beez's wrist smashed Kylan into the embankment.

Though he remained standing, Kylan couldn't get his petrified limbs to move. The stench of rotting flesh descended as the abomination glided down before him.

"If I could, I would wear you," Beez said to the center of the river where Veen had disappeared. One of the Judge's eyelids had swollen; the other didn't blink as he focused on Kylan. Strands of fluid connected a yellow stain on his tabard to his mouth. Blood filled the cracks between his teeth. "Monks feel like silk and last so much longer than most of you mortals, *Tek'aran*." Abruptly, his broken lips grimaced and parted. Beez cracked his neck. "You have no magic!" he spit.

Kylan threw his shoulder into the Judge's chest and struck a solid barrier. The pain forced him down to his hands and knees.

An invisible claw tugged Kylan back up by his collar. It dug into his nape as it closed his windpipe. Kylan pawed at the spell but couldn't grip it. His toes left the reach of the rocks.

"You do not wear such protective markings, plaything," Beez slurred. Every orifice in his head leaked. "You will know what it is like to die while I wear you—a fitting punishment for your deceit!" The fetid breath of the former Judge stung Kylan's eyes as his mouth came forward.

Kylan swung a fist for Beez's face.

The demon drifted out of reach and cackled at Kylan's anger. A spell jerked Kylan's arms to his sides and bound them. The world darkened and blurred around the edges of his vision.

In a blink, a brilliant light erupted from the Judge's ribs. Beez hissed.

Kylan collapsed beneath the shrieking puppet.

Beez's back arched as he twisted in the air and removed a small blade from his side. Light shone forth from the wound. The knife fell from Beez's hand.

Veen stood above them on the hillside. His finger dabbed blood from a wound in his arm and scribed something on a throwing knife. He flung the knife at the gurgling creature. It sliced into Beez's chest with little resistance, spraying forth more light.

"You will die for this!" Beez screeched. "We will have the *tek'aran!*"

"*Imeacht gan teacht ort!*" Veen shouted.

The light disappeared before another knife sank into the Judge's skull. Portions of the corpse splattered when it hit the rocks.

Kylan scrambled back. He covered his mouth and nose with his hand as he tried to catch his breath. His throat felt like it would never fully reopen.

Veen slid to the shore and pulled his knife free of the corpse.

"You did it," Kylan rasped, massaging his neck. "You killed him?"

"No. He left the body. 'Twill have to do."

Kylan searched the air. "He's still here?"

"No. He's gone." Veen rolled the body over and retrieved the last knife. Then he rolled it once more, giving the carcass and the stench to the water. "They return to their urns when their vessels die."

"Urns?"

Offering a hand, Veen helped him to his feet. "'Tis something you put ashes or pieces of the dead in, like a jar, canister, or the like." Correctly reading Kylan's face, he said, "Aye, that must seem odd to a Merithian."

The monk knelt at the water's edge and rinsed his weapons. "I lost my bow to the river, but we've bought ourselves some time."

Kylan looked downstream for any sign of the monk's bow and realized how easily he saw the leaves in the trees. "That means they didn't find Cord."

"He's the one you were protecting?" Veen asked.

"Yeah." Kylan fetched the cold steel blade Beez had dropped before him. Nothing special stood out, beyond the bloody pus covering it now. Kneeling beside Veen, he let the Staghorn cleanse the blade in its current. "What did you do to these knives?"

Veen stopped. His forehead wrinkled. "Em . . . the blood of the sacred is said to hold certain power," he said and continued scrubbing. "The truth is, the power is in the symbols. Any blood can do that. But the less centered the donor, the less predictable the outcome."

Grimacing, Kylan eyed the smeared wound on Veen's forearm. "How about you just give me a vial of yours then?"

Veen released a laugh. "'Tisn't something I'm willing to share, for your sake. There's darkness in that magic. 'Tis a last resort and can be fatal. So, whatever you say about it, say nothing."

"My last resort would be thrusting the blade into myself to keep Beez from wearing me, which is assuredly fatal."

"If you're meant to know it," Veen said, "you will in time."

"Now, that's the crock of shit I'd expect a monk to say."

Veen ignored him again. With his blades tucked into the folds in his belt, Veen gestured to their path on the shore.

A few purple martins chattered and clicked up the slope. "The sun decided to finally show its face," Kylan muttered. "Coward."

The monk walked backward while he watched Kylan. "I don't have the opinion of you that I did earlier, Kylan Nock. You're no poltroon, boy. In the moment when Beez was about to end you, you impressed me. You let go of the spell afflicting you and focused on your opponent. Many wouldn't have had the clarity in their panic to do that."

The compliment brought the heat back to Kylan's face. "I'd be dead if you hadn't come back."

"You weren't evenly matched, were you?"

Unsure how to respond, Kylan nodded. "Then show me how to defend myself against him."

Veen turned heel and led on with more speed than before. "Should you need to find yourself in the future, my order wouldn't be able to turn you away."

Kylan wheezed with laughter. "Find myself? What? Me, a monk?"

"We're not the celibate, sit-on-a-rock-for-days type of monks,

Kylan."

"No, I suspect you prefer a tree or a hole."

"'Twas just a suggestion," Veen said with a sigh. "The road you walk will have casualties. Should they be more than you can handle, the Mount may be a solution."

Chapter 24: Ink and Lacquer

"Disremember what you saw," Veen repeated.

Kylan groaned at the absurdity. If these Dregs were vulnerable to the symbols the monk had scribed on the throwing knives, they should be shouting it from the mountaintops. Nevertheless, Kylan let the stingy monk have his reprieve.

Veen was right about one thing. The Hook's caravan was gone, if this grassy field in the river's marsh was actually where they had camped. Kylan wasn't convinced. His heel stuck to the ground again. "Mud, mud, and more mud . . . You're sure we're not lost?" he asked over the squawking crows overhead.

Veen scratched the stubble on his chin as he replied, "I'm a bit experienced at this, amn't I? If you look hard enough, you'll find the signs they were here. 'Twasn't safe for them to stay. But they'll have left us a way to track them."

As they rounded a cluster of pin oaks and a black walnut tree,

Veen raised his arms in victory.

A snort greeted him just as the wafting scent of fresh manure stopped Kylan cold. "No," Kylan grumbled. Two equipped horses, a sandy mare and a speckled gray stallion, recognized Veen.

"You don't know how?" Veen asked. "Right, you'll ride with me then."

Refraining from making a comment about Veen not blocking his view either way, Kylan skewed his lips and said, "I can figure it out. I've ridden before, just prefer my own legs."

Veen ran his hands between the gray's saddle and padding. He removed two pieces of white parchment, one folded into a triangle, the other a heart.

As the little man opened the triangle, Kylan spied over his shoulder to see a series of scratches and dots. "What's that?"

"A message from Teague. They struck off on the same route we'd planned." He refolded the note and tucked it into his leather jerkin. "East to the pass, then north."

"I could've told you that," Kylan said. "The wolfkin are to the south, and there are no ports to the west, just hills." If they were taking the pass to the north, then Llandir wasn't their goal. "We're going to Croathe? It'll take us longer. If these Dregs have taken the southern ports, we should head straight on to Llandir. It's still north of the Breslan Mountains but nearly due east."

"'Tis Teague's call," Veen said as though that ended the conversation. The monk opened the heart. His ears flushed to crimson.

"What? What does it say?"

"Never you mind," he answered, shoving the note next to the other. "You'll lead the way. I'd hate for you to fall off without me seeing it." He held the mare's reins out to Kylan with a crooked grin. "Nightingale is yours for the trip. Be gentle. Carolle won't be happy if you harm her horse."

Reluctantly taking the reins, Kylan sighed. Nightingale looked as unsure as he did. "I'm sorry," he said to the tan mare.

"Come along," Veen said, already mounted on the gray. "Don't let the grass grow around your feet."

Kylan hefted himself into the saddle. He balanced and ran a hand over the bristly hair of Nightingale's shoulder as she adjusted her stance. It wouldn't take him long to tire of the warmth beneath him. Why did Scarlett enjoy this so much?

Lightly tugging the reins to the right, Kylan turned Nightingale east and started her walking. Allowing himself to get used to the shifting, he kept his legs spread to hold her pace.

Following closely behind, Veen said, "We could've walked this fast, yeah? The purpose is to catch up to them."

Gripping the pommel, Kylan glared back at him. "I need to get comfortable with it first."

"Ah, giddygo!" Veen blared.

Nightingale bolted. Kylan choked the pommel with both hands and curled over it. The horse's mane whipped his face. He meant to curse Veen, but only "ooooh" managed to come out.

Thudding along the ground behind him, Veen's gray closed the gap. "Sit up! Keep control of her reins, keep them slack and even."

Kylan did as instructed. Slowly, his shaking eased. He almost enjoyed the experience once they reached the mostly even road. After several minutes of avoiding eye contact, he said, "You will pay for that, mouse."

"Why does everyone keep calling me that?" Veen laughed. "Get in line, boy. Beez has claimed the first go. The Dregs never like it when you free their meat suits. Poor fellow."

A chill grasped Kylan's spine. "How can you jest about that? That face—that stench—will haunt me forever."

Riding up alongside him, Veen stared straight ahead. "My death'll come, be it today or when I'm wizened. The path I walk has me prepared for it at a moment's notice."

The rhythmic plodding of the horses carried them for a time. Eventually, they slowed to give their mounts a break.

Veen rode ahead to the crest of a hill to scout the road for patrolling Judges.

Pondering the tattoos on the monk's arms, Kylan asked when he reached him, "What do your tattoos mean? After you helplessly landed in the river, Beez mentioned something about your markings keeping him from wearing you."

"Helplessly?" he asked, feigning a pout.

Kylan smirked.

"He was referring to this." Unbuckling three straps on his black leather jerkin, Veen spread it apart. On the right side of his hairless abdomen, five interlocking rings covered his muscles. Four, the top, bottom, left, and right, were inked. A scarred circle of burned skin overlapped them in the center. Reading Kylan's twisted lips, Veen said, "Aye, with a branding iron. Not the worst injury I've had. But now, Carolle wouldn't want me showing that to everyone." He refastened the straps.

Kylan exhaled a laugh. "How'd you get it—the mark? Is that some elaborate monk ritual?"

Regressing to his silent self, Veen shook his head.

"Tell me, and I'll forgive you for what you did back there."

Picking a wayward leaf out of the gray's mane, Veen forced a smile. "Sometimes things just happen to you."

"Not to pry . . ." Kylan said.

Veen squinted at him in disbelief.

"Fine. To pry, what sent you to the Mount? You said the road I walk will have casualties. Is that what happened to you?"

"Sometimes even good deeds can hurt your soul, boy." Adrift in thought, Veen ran his left hand down the markings on his right arm. His fingertips danced along the points. Though he didn't watch, he touched each inked prong.

Kylan doubted Veen's suggestion that he could become a Ukrestian monk. Being burned to be free from Beez, which was more desirable than being free of the Chancellor's army, already required more will than he had. "Burned if you do, burned if you don't," he mumbled.

* * *

Rorry lay on her side and gazed through the curtained window above her padded bench, observing the shifting landscape as the vardo trundled on. The rolling hills and deep valleys had sprouted dry-stone walls before the road leveled out to the Flats of Merith. Trees grew scarce while verdant crops thrived, unguarded for the holiday. The caravan passed some of the wealthiest farm towns in the nation in the hours that put them halfway through the Weatherington Province.

Scarlett still slept on the bench across from her. The opened book on Scarlett's chest told Rorry that she had compromised between her curiosity and her exhaustion by reading herself to sleep.

As Rorry's thoughts dipped into worry for Kylan again, her nerves tasked her to control what she could: the messy vardo. When the road tilted, tiny bottles of various colors clattered and rolled across the floor to hide in the hurriedly produced, though beautiful, garments strewn about. Powders and herbs shook free of their open drawers with each bump.

Kylan and his brothers had a cleaner room, even if it did not smell better.

Thankful for a little vial of licorice root, Rorry opened it and planted it in the folds of a blanket on the bench. It refreshed the air better than an open window could. Well, nearly better. These windows did not budge.

Selecting a lightweight crimson linen dress from the floor, Rorry examined the inside. The stitching would tear too easily to last long, especially with this treatment. Perhaps Maeverly's wealth allowed her to breeze through clothing. Mrs. Hywel had said Racinian fashions changed by the year and only repeated after a few decades. Rorry hugged the neglected fabric and let herself get lost in daydreaming of garments she could have tailored in Trône d'Argent, a petty inspiration, but exciting. Racinians would not be caught dead in common makes, even in the brightest dyes. Though some, like Maeverly's tufted black cloak, appealed less to her imagination.

Unable to locate another hook to hang the dress on, she tucked the sleeves back and folded it. Sighing at her lack of options for laying it down, Rorry set it on the bench she had slept on.

The vardo hit a bump, rocking its insides. Rorry slapped her hands against the cabinets above her to steady herself. With a cricket's luck, she saved one of the drawers from falling on her. Rorry huffed and shoved it flush into the wooden frame. Then she flicked a brass tab to hold it in place. Doing the same to the plethora of other hazards above them, she had aching arms when she finished.

Lifting a dark blue dress by its sleeve, she accidentally set a bottle free to thud to the floor.

Scarlett bolted upright with a sharp inhale.

"The bump did not wake you, but that tap did?" Rorry teased.

The cork had come free of the bottle, dispensing a pestled green substance as it traveled. Rorry recognized the heavy, spicy scent. Tazzarian merchants wore it in their lockets while they traded goods on the docks in Croathe. The name eluded her, but she remembered they believed it protected them from the evils and diseases of foreigners.

Rorry released the sleeve and grabbed the glass pest. She firmly pressed the cork back in.

"How long did I sleep?" Scarlett asked.

"I am not sure." Rorry looked up but could only tell midday neared. "I only woke a short while ago myself."

Using three fluffy pillows next to the folded dress, Rorry made a prison on the bench. She dropped the first captive in. The bottle dared her to turn away as it rocked. "How does she live like this?"

"Hmm?" Scarlett said over the edge of her green tome.

Dismissing the questions with a shake of her head, Rorry picked up the blue dress from the floor and shook it. The shiny plush weighed more than the crimson linen. Perhaps this was velvet? The exquisite corseted top had a lighter blue overlay to emphasize the bosom and a slimming gold trim. Maeverly should be shamed for casting it to the floor.

When Rorry spread the dress over the bench, she noticed a wooden rod jutting out from underneath. She pulled the pole and freed the bristled end of a small broom. Finally, a lark of sanity in this wagon!

Rorry threw the remaining garments from the floor over Scarlett's legs. Quickly capturing the other rolling menaces, she slipped them into the pillow cell beneath the blue dress. In a flurry, she swept toward the door. A mound of dirt and dust mixed with the mustard, sienna, and sage deposits waiting to meet the road.

Braced against the interior, Rorry prepared for any jolts and unlatched the door. As she pulled it open, the fresh air rushed in and made her aware of just how stuffy the wagon had gotten while they'd slept. She tasted the threat of rain on the wind. It would be soon but not until the afternoon at least.

The outlandishly large man who had been cooking when she'd arrived at the Hook's camp waved, raising a patchwork sleeve of clashing colors. She noticed that a full red tunic had been added to cover a hole over his chest.

She returned a polite smile until her eyes fell to the young man laid across his lap.

The golden-haired boy met her eyes and floundered, causing the larger man to pin him down on his knees and rebalance.

Two quick strokes cleared the dust pile. She pressed the door closed and flipped the latch.

Rorry set the broom against the corner, intent on asking Scarlett about what she had seen, but her friend remained lost to the outside world.

Flinging the thick dress into the air, Rorry set about creating order again. Struggling to get the thicker material to cooperate, she sat on the vanity's stool and used her lap as a table. When she fetched the next garment from the mound on Scarlett, a silky orange coat with a damask pattern, she asked, "Are you learning anything useful?"

Scarlett put a finger to the page and halfheartedly answered, "Yes."

"That does not sound convincing."

Her friend scooted up to sit, freeing her legs. "This is more

243

aligned with sorcery than the kind of magic I had expected to learn."

Relishing the feel of the silk on her skin, Rorry stalled her work and ran the coat over her hands. "What do you mean? I assumed magic was magic?"

Hoisting the book in front of her face, Scarlett said, "It's more complicated than that. I fear it'll require me to choose between the two, if only for the sake of attuning my abilities. Only this isn't what I think would make sense to me."

Rorry folded the gentle shirt and put it atop the pile on her bench. She did hope it would stay free of ruin. "You are the smartest person I know, Scarlett. If you will it, you can learn it."

Scarlett smiled fully. It did Rorry's heart good to see that infectious grin. When Scarlett raised a hand to cover her mouth, it presented a strange sight. Above Cord's ring, her nails were blue, the same blue as Alis's ribbon.

Grabbing Scarlett's hand for a closer inspection, she asked, "How did you achieve this?"

"Oh. You must see." Stretching to the remaining mound of Maeverly's castoffs, Scarlett grabbed a stocking. She closed her book around it and set her reading aside. Picking up a thin stick from the vanity, she said, "This is a Wand of Shades. Watch." Tapping each finger, one by one, her nails turned a deep purple.

"Marvelous!" Rorry breathed. "Can you use it on me?"

Hesitating, Scarlett thought. She held the wand out for Rorry to take. "I'm not sure it requires magic. Test it. Think of a color and touch your nails."

Unsure what to choose, Rorry pictured the stained-glass rose on her bedroom window and tapped away. It worked. She held her hand out for Scarlett to examine. She finished her other hand before relinquishing the wand to Scarlett. The beautiful lacquer made her a little homesick.

Scarlett ran the stick along her bottom lip, turning it plum. Her concentration must have slipped as she progressed because her upper lip matched the pink on Rorry's fingers. She laughed at herself in the mirror.

The vardo stopped. Scarlett set the wand on the vanity. The door latch was sprung.

Opening the door, Maeverly said, "Mealtime, ladies." She smiled when she noticed their new colors and stared in awe when she saw her tidier abode. "One thing I've never been accused of is having a woman's touch. This is nice. Thank you very much. Oh, very nice," she said to the latched drawers near the ceiling. She pounded the walls to see if they jostled free. The broom rapped against the floor.

"F-fiddle," Maeverly said, standing it up only to knock it over again. She groaned and left it. Running her finger around her mouth, she said to Scarlett, "You'll want to fix that. Then come eat. Bevin shall not be kept waiting. Oh, and your friend just arrived with Veen." She gave them a wide smile and descended the stairs.

Chapter 25: Believe It or Not

The caravan pulled to the side of the road beneath a tree the likes of which Cord had never seen. The king of the lonely thicket held its own against the forceful breeze fighting to break the rounded shape of its branches and the blue-green leaves that had taken Maeverly's breath away. As massive as it was, its ruddy trunk would've only been a sapling compared to the elves' oaks, if his dreams could be trusted.

Muddy, Veen and Kylan rode past Cord and cheered their own arrival all the way to Teague's gold-and-green vardo at the front.

Cord clicked his tongue to get Scute to chase after.

The monk blew a kiss to his wife, who winked back from the seat of the plain wagon, before he convened with Teague inside the green.

Cord slipped out of Scute's saddle next to the horse Kylan had reined in by the thicket. He hitched Scute to a barren mulberry branch and reached into his saddlebag for two of the peaches Maeverly had had him "liberate" during their feast through the flats.

After lying across the saddle, Kylan dismounted with his belly rather than his legs. Blood speckled the shreds in his tunic. Hair showed through the ripped fabric.

Cord rubbed his own chest. A loose thread tickled his finger, bringing his attention to the fraying golden feather. Offering a peach, he said, "I'm not sure if I'm more thankful to see you or for what you did back there. I owe you."

Kylan took the peach and crushed Cord in a hug. "I returned a favor. Besides, we're both indebted to Veen for defeating Beez. Well, almost defeating him." He let go and chomped into the peach. "Where're the girls?"

While hitching the mare by Scute, Cord answered with a nod to the butterfly wagon near the roots of the tree. Then he hustled to catch up to Kylan. "We haven't seen hide nor hair of Andion since the fort."

"He'll turn up. I'd imagine he's a bit shy around strangers."

"He wasn't with us."

Dismissively, Kylan said, "Daylight, then. Give it until night before you worry too much. He'll find us when it's dark."

Taking in the strange tree above them, Kylan said, "Look at that thing! It's huge! Lifewood . . ." Its shaggy bark lifted off its trunk like a hickory but filled the area with the smell of cedar. "My dad would kill to have that much bark to work with."

Bevin's provisions cart had caught up to the caravan, coming to a rest farther back outside the lifewood's shade. Each time Cord had embarked on one of Maeverly's errands, he had seen Bevin lumbering through the fields to gather more. Thankfully, the mercenary hadn't pinched any of the livestock.

Pots and utensils clattered as Bevin rattled half-formed orders at Julian, who lifted a stone to reset it where Bevin pointed.

Kylan had already eaten half of his peach before Cord bit into his. The relief of having Kylan and Scarlett back alive let him relish the fresh, tangy juice. Most peaches were only fit for preserves or pies by the time they arrived at Kenton for the Harvest Trade.

As they rounded the brightly painted wagon, Kylan cast off his pit.

Maeverly stepped down the curved staircase. She extended her hand to Kylan. After wiping his hand off on his shirt, he shook hers. "Kylan? Maeverly, well met. Well met." She half stepped into a curtsy before grunting. "All right. I'd better help Bevin." As she walked off, Kylan arched his eyebrow at Cord.

Cord shrugged. "That one can spin a thousand salty tales in an hour. I think she's all right. She sure loves watermelon, and she offered to help me keep an eye on Julian."

"Who?"

"You'll see soon enough."

"Well she looks like a bulldog in a frock," Kylan whispered. He pointed at Veen emerging from the green. "And there's a mouse." He moved his finger to Carolle. "A duck." Carolle's lips weren't quite as large as Kylan made them out to be. Then he settled his finger on Teague. "And a fox. It's like some strange joke, probably ending with the mouse and duck being married."

Scarlett stepped out.

Kylan's arms pulled her from the stairs. "Miss me?" he asked, spinning her about.

"Oh!" she yelled and hugged him while her fingers clamped on to a thick green tome. "You're not a demon, are you?"

"No," Kylan answered. "But would I tell you?" He thinned his lips until she grinned.

Rorry leaped onto the huddle. Cord felt like a trespasser until Kylan yanked him forward.

"Listen," Kylan said. "Do we trust these mercenaries?"

In front of the yellow door to the green vardo, Teague appeared calm again, while Carolle and Veen ignored everything except each other, leaving no space between their leathers. Carolle had locked her arms around Veen as he stared up into her eyes.

"We have little choice," Rorry answered. "For now anyway."

Scarlett stopped nodding and asked, "But what about Brewing?" Her guilt was as evident as her hope someone would talk her out of returning. She hugged the book.

Rorry came to her rescue. "Absolutely not. No more talk of that kind. Should we return, what benefit could we provide? None of us could take on one of those things!" She ended by raising her chin at Cord.

"Don't look at me," he said. "I wanna know for sure if one of them killed my neighbors before I bring the *tek'aran* to them."

Red flooded beneath Rorry's freckles. She pouted, damming the words her expression relayed. She could call him a fool. Maybe he was, but he'd do what he'd sworn to do.

"There's sense in that," Kylan said.

Rorry disagreed and chose a new target. "Enough to fill a thimble, which is about the volume required to believe it is a good idea to run off into a pack of wolfkin while claiming to be their prized catch."

"I know," Kylan agreed. "If I keep heeding my own advice, I'm going to get myself killed."

She wasn't amused.

"It worked, didn't it?"

Preserving the harmony, Cord pointed to the ring on Scarlett's finger and asked, "Did you figure out what it does?"

"Oh," Scarlett said, slipping the ring off. "I didn't. Well, not exactly. Maeverly knows. It's elven in origin and affects or makes alcohol . . . I think." She placed it in her palm and offered it to him. "I'm sorry for taking it."

"No," Cord said. "That's all right. You can have it."

Her disbelieving eyes began to water before she hugged him. "I'll cherish it!" She put it on and admired the gem.

Tempered by Scarlett's glee, Rorry touched the tatters of Kylan's shirt. "You are not injured, are you?" Had her fingernails always been that pink?

"Never better. Why do you smell like licorice? I'm famished."

Teague cleared his throat behind them. "Then let's convene for a meal, yes?" He corralled them beneath the noisy wind rushing through the leaves.

Gathering for a shower, the clouds dotting the sky had already stretched the cool of morning into the midday.

The monks passed by hand in hand.

"May I have a word, Cord?" Teague asked. "I'll return the lad unharmed," he said to the curious faces around him. He didn't wait before heading back down the line of vardos. Why now? Couldn't he wait to say Kylan would be left behind too if Cord misbehaved?

Kylan pulled out the figure of his sister only to find a clean snap had broken it in two at her waist. Rorry rubbed his back as he held it in his palms.

Cord sighed and hurried to catch up with Teague.

"Everything seems clearer in daylight, so it does," Teague said. "I owe you an apology. I've embarrassed myself by even suggesting we leave you behind. Gods bless them, my friends are more honorable than I am. They've kept us within our guild's principles."

"Since when do mercenaries care about anything other than wealth?" Cord asked.

"A fair question. We're not mercenaries in the strictest sense. No matter how much coin you lay at the Hook's feet, hire a band, hire a hundred, we won't go against our creed—even if we take your coin and say we will. We've joined wars to subvert the greater of two evils. We've stolen artifacts of immense power just to keep them out of the hands of slavers. We—I have even manipulated kings and queens to avoid wars." He grinned broadly and added, "More fun than you'd suspect."

When they reached the gold-trimmed wagon, he unlocked the door and swung it open. Behind a simple cot sat a writing desk. Unlike Headmaster Angsly's, the wood held its sheen. A silver tray kept the inkwell, quill, and sealing wax tidy.

Climbing inside, Teague ran his hand along a tall black dresser across from the cot. "I'm sure you can imagine we're not always a popular lot. Either you love us or you hate us." He unlocked one of the shallow drawers of the top row with an iron key. "I cannot give you what I originally intended since Veen lost his. But you'll find more use for these than I ever did." He pulled out a pair of oiled leather gloves and handed them to Cord. "They're nothing special, but there you go now."

The weather hardly warranted gloves. Cord didn't lower his hand after receiving them and waited for Teague's full attention. "I appreciate the gesture, but if you wanna ease your guilt, don't give me gloves. Make me a promise. If you change your mind about me and hightail it, take the others to the continent. They shouldn't be punished 'cause I'm cursed and you're a coward."

Teague smoothed his reaction to the insult and said, "'Twon't come to that. We'll get you out of Merith too." Cord held his piercing stare. "Agreed." He closed the drawer and locked it. "The gloves guard against bow rash. If you want to be an archer, you need the proper gear, yes?"

After Cord heard that, the gloves made more sense. Cord slipped one onto his right hand. Snug cloth covered his palm and fingers. A stiff strip of hide ran up the inside of his forearm, secured by two buckled bands. "Thank you. I'm grateful."

"If we find a bow, 'tis yours, so long as you agree to defend everyone, including Julian, against our foes. You know yourself, that also means Merith's army. Don't suppose you'd accept one of my shirts, would you?"

Cord knew in his heart he had deserted the army his uniform belonged to. But he'd worked hard to get to that rank; so had Headmaster Angsly in training him for it. Cord's blood had stained it, but so had Marlone's. "This one fits just fine."

Teague ran his tongue over his teeth before he said, "So be it."

"If *anyone* tries to harm me or my friends," Cord said, "I'll put them down. Even the army. I'm a deserter anyway."

"I watched you defeat a High Guard, Cord. I'm more worried about you distracting us with your feud with young Master Westcott." After closing the door behind him, Teague started their walk back to the others.

"Master Westcott" had positioned himself far away from everyone else seated around the ring of stones.

"Also," Teague said, "I'm not a coward."

"You can understand my confusion," Cord said.

Teague gave him a hard smile. "You don't know what you're talking about."

"Then tell me. What are these Dregs exactly?"

"I'll save you the trouble of repeating it and answer with your friends present."

"All right. Do you think Beez came to Merith for me?"

With a brisk sigh, Teague leaned against the red-veined planks of the plain vardo, which Cord only now recognized as lifewood. "I don't know, lad. I can say our paths are shared for now. We're both prey. Separating us only delays the inevitable for the other." He gripped the wagon's iron wheel to still his trembling hand. "Beez has a fetish for me. I'm a plaything. You, he's given a title. I don't know what it means, but titles aren't doled out for pretty pets."

Cord's skin crawled.

"We'll keep you out of Beez's grasp, if for no other reason than we don't know what it'd mean for him to have you. And as for the threat earlier, ye two seemed determined to kill each other; I was merely trying to keep the peace. Consider what we're up against if more Dregs than Beez are leading packs of wolfkin across Merith. We need people on our side and have to trust whoever is guarding our backs. If Julian can't handle that, 'tis my call to set him loose. Understood?"

As much as Cord wanted to, he couldn't really argue against any of what Teague said, not without reinstating his threat on his friends. "He's not worth it, but fine. What brought you to Merith in the first place?"

Tapping the wheel with his thumb, Teague said, "So many questions and not an answer to share?" He stood up straight. "When you're ready to discuss what makes you so sure you're the *tek'aran*, I'll consider being more forthcoming. Until then, I won't reveal our mission or our sponsor, so I won't. Please pass that along to Rorry." Teague strode on.

At the circle around the unlit fire, Carolle sat between Veen's legs, leaning back against her husband. Both monks watched Teague with a look of warning in their eyes.

Cord put his back to the group as he walked. "Remember. You can't trust Julian."

Teague bit his words. "Not your problem, lad. He'll come around, or I'll deal with him."

"You are chattel!" Maeverly yelled. Flames roared through the logs in the fire pit as she rose.

Julian tumbled back off his stool. Cussing up a storm, the Catalyst righted himself. He bent to lunge at Maeverly.

Racing forward, Teague put a blade to Julian's collarbone. "Enough," he commanded. "While you're under our protection, you will be civil. Do you agree?"

Julian gave a curt nod.

Maeverly released a loud sigh but remained standing.

Oblivious, Bevin hobbled through the middle of the conflict, carrying a tarnished iron cauldron to its setting above the fire.

Cord sat on the grass between Kylan and Scarlett, who flipped a page to scratch it across the fabric over her chest and resumed her reading.

"Avoid mentioning how easily Fort Warren was conquered," Kylan whispered. "Where'd you go? Bartering for gloves?"

"Later," Cord said.

Rorry nodded from her stool next to Kylan.

"Thank you, J," Teague said. "That's an important point we should make. Magic is neither forbidden nor frowned upon while ye are in our company. There is no need to fear magic, only those who wield it to further their own ambitions, the same as any other weapon."

"You would say that," Julian muttered, as he righted his stool. "Lekelithians."

"Actually, only Teague and Veen are," Maeverly corrected. She dragged her stool closer to Scarlett and plopped down, creating a snap that most ignored.

Kylan snickered and chewed his bottom lip. Thanks to that, Cord averted his eyes and sucked back his grin.

"Right, introductions," Teague said and clapped once, gathering everyone's attention. He went around the circle and introduced them, including the Merithians. Cord wondered why Stille van Veen went by Veen until Teague ended with, "And our mountainy half-ogre cook here, Bevin Freidig."

Half-ogre? How does that happen? The brute didn't look up from his chopping block, where he split a cabbage.

"I see our first meal is to be a fragrant one," Teague said. "Let's hope that's not an omen."

Circling in the space between them and the fire, Teague delivered a summary of the Hook's purpose, as vaguely as it had been given to Cord. "For years, Oren Ko has lent his skills to our band. But we thought it best that he skipped this particular assignment, given that Merithians watch outsiders unless bribed. If said outsiders have skin darker than a walnut, Merithians scream murder when no act has been committed. Or worse, they commit the act and send an innocent to the spider.

"Furthermore, we had to claim citizenship to a slaver nation to receive our merchant licenses. None of us would ask Oren to take the brand of a slave."

Julian rolled his eyes at Cord's scowl.

"I thought foreigners were restricted to the docks," Kylan said.

"Most are," Rorry answered. "Dignitaries and merchants of slaver nations are not. Yet, considering that more luxurious trade is found in Croathe than elsewhere in Merith, few venture off the docks to brave our notorious wilds. Coupled with the fact that Merith offers no coin, merchants need only stay until their inventory is depleted." Her face tensed. "Or they have more slaves than they can hold."

As Julian's eyes wandered over Rorry, his expression lost its disdain.

"Precisely," Teague said. "Replacing Oren gave us the honor of accompanying Vega on her final mission. She disappeared early yesterday morning, following misinformation that we believe led her into a trap. We tracked her to Fort Warren and, sadly, discovered her untimely end."

Bevin wiped a tear from his cheek, but the stinging punch of freshly sliced onions might've been the real cause for his tears. He moved over to the cauldron, blocking Cord's view of the monks, and lowered his chopping block. A handful of yellow powder joined the vegetables before he stirred them, dragging the ladle around the bottom.

"Fort Warren was quickly defeated," Teague continued.

Kylan sucked air through his teeth.

Maeverly beamed. "Another example of the Merithian Tribunal's racism leading to their downfall. If they'd had a few archers in the ramparts, there may have been a challenge. But, alas, archery is of the elf. I'm not even sure how that belief came into being. I can explain the unfounded persecution of magic, originating from the crushing defeat of Merith during the Revolt of the Magi, which—"

"We have archers!" Julian spoke over her. "They are called Ashwin."

"Yes," she said. "They guard a wall on the coast of a tempestuous sea. It's a wonder they don't throw rocks instead. Or would that be of the ogre?"

White flashed through Julian's snarl. "We have trebuchets. If Merith is so easily conquered, why is your benefactor only now sending in mercenaries? I find it convenient your mission coincides with the invasion of these wolfkin. Admit it; evil arrived with you!"

Maeverly leaned forward and tapped her lip with a dark blue fingernail. "Evil beyond slavery? And aside from the persecution of those born with magical talents?" She raised a finger. "Has it ever occurred to you that if they didn't destroy all of the confiscated treasures, each magical trinket costing a person their life, your Chancellor would have a crimson dragon's hoard by now?"

Julian's eyes blazed. "That is sacrilege!"

Cord tensed and grabbed his knife's handle. Her blasphemy went too far.

Kylan elbowed him and shook his head.

"Perhaps you can explain to me why people who are merely suspected of magic are burned alive?" she asked. "Or why the color of skin determines the class of a man? Or why women are possessions, forced into slavery if they disappoint a cruel husband? Forgive me if I adulterate your beliefs with a little knowledge of the world beyond your instructed subservience."

Cord released the handle. While he didn't condone her heresy, he wouldn't argue against the rest of her speech. How much of it would the headmaster have agreed with?

Julian appeared ready to ignite. At this rate, Cord could hold his tongue; the bastard would doom himself.

Teague blatantly weighed the Merithians' stances on Julian and

Maeverly's argument. "Fort Warren. Where we met these two lovely young people, the boy who tried to run and the girl who insisted we wait for her friends."

Misinterpreting Teague's gesture toward Scarlett, Bevin ladled a pungent bowlful and handed it to her. She finally noticed the stool someone had placed in front of her. The book flopped onto the canvas seat, resting open as she ate.

Once everyone had received a bowl or small pot of the ogre's salty stew, Bevin began cutting into a flank of meat.

Teague continued, "Yet another fine meal, though poorly timed for this topic. The real source of the wolfkin infestation is Beez, the creature who wore your Judge Barret."

"A demon," Cord said, just to get another rile out of Julian.

Julian snorted. "Then have your demon worshippers ask him to leave us be," he said to Teague.

Maeverly laid her bowl aside. "I shall try but must sacrifice you in the attempt I'm afraid."

"He's not a demon," Teague said with a weary frown at Cord. "The Dregs have no magic of their own to speak of beyond possession. That's why they seek out magi as hosts."

"So leave the magi," Julian shouted, glaring at Cord not Maeverly.

Over Kylan's scowl at the Catalyst, Rorry looked to Cord, doubtlessly wondering how Julian knew about his curse, or knew him at all.

Teague's hand stopped Maeverly from rising. "Suggest that again, and we'll leave you for their chowder."

Cord tried not to look smug when Teague turned back around.

"What they are remains a mystery," Teague said. "Tales from the Dessrini tribes say they were human once, magi who feared their own mortality. Through pacts with demons, they learnt to jump from one body to the next, cheating death and robbing their vessels of life. Same as your beloved demons, they were believed to be the weavings of rumors and ghost lore, until ten years ago." Clamping his rattling spoon to the side of his bowl, Teague stared into the fire, captive to his own thoughts.

Veen got up and said, "They live behind the Cloud over the Saratial Sea, on the islands between the continent and Taus, and call themselves the Ancients. We refer to them as the Dregs, because that's all that remains, not even a sliver of their humanity."

"The Cloud?" Cord asked. "Wasn't the Cloud created by the ashes of Merith when the grand nation collapsed?" He didn't mention what else Headmaster Angsly had said, which rang true now. The dark clouds forever swirled around a nightmare where blood rituals governed the people trapped within, and the sins of magic defied nature.

"The timing is right. Though it sounds a fairy dream compared to the truth," Teague said to the fire.

Kylan said, "You've been inside—"

"Your man," Veen interrupted, "the Judge, has been laid to rest. And while they do seek hosts who can touch magic, the Dregs can take anyone."

Rorry started to ask a question, but Julian interrupted with a sniff. "Lies," he said. "I do not believe a word out of your foreign, fear-mongering mouths. Leave me here. I will risk facing these *Dregs* on my own."

"Beez is not a branch scraping against your window at night," Teague said. "He's the invisible wraith wearing your mother as she carves herself into a childless widow. All the while, she watches from behind her eyes and pleads with him to stop. He loves it when you scream."

"Teague," Carolle said.

Julian rolled his eyes, but his face had gone pale.

"I don't mean to be coarse but concise, so I do," Teague said with a frown. "We cannot claim to know what the Dregs want here, or if Beez is acting alone. The wolfkin follow his orders without question. This Seeding of yours is just going to give them snacks and recruits on the road."

Leaning closer to Kylan, Rorry asked, "Is Merith lost?"

"It's a matter of timing," Maeverly answered, smiling gently for Scarlett's worried face. "The sooner we reach the continent, the sooner we can send aid, assuming Merith accepts it."

Kylan asked, "And the tattoos? The circles, they can keep the

Dregs from possessing us?"

Veen's ears flushed. He rubbed his forehead at the Hook's questioning faces and answered, "They would, if we had the means to mark youse."

"That raises a good point," Maeverly said. "As estimable as their powers are, they do have their weaknesses."

Teague glowered at her, then the rest of his band. "Let me make myself very clear. If ye encounter Beez, in whatever skin, ye run. Do not engage him." He let the statement hang until each of them agreed, twice for Veen.

Then Teague placed his bowl on Bevin's table and spoke to Cord. "As for the other matter, the villages full of bodies, if there are answers on the road, we'll find them.

"Racine is our goal. We'll make haste for a port. Beez will track us from the south. Merith's army will stop us on the roads if we give them cause." He scanned the road. "May the gods stand between us and all harm."

"Kylan can take Vega's chores, yeah?" Veen said. "He'll enjoy it, I suspect."

Kylan cocked his eyebrow in suspicion of the monk's toothy grin.

Unsure, Teague let it go with a nod from the monk. "Julian, assist Bevin."

Bevin released a loud moan and let his shoulders go slack.

"No free rides," Teague said. "No malingering. The Dregs will catch us quickly if we don't work together to get off this fecking island."

"Do not bind me to this half-breed," Julian barked.

Squeezing Julian's arm, Teague said, "You'll have the opportunity to learn the culinary skills of a master, creating meals that have never been tasted away from the Bonded Nations. Does that not appeal to you? I only wish I had the time." He started traipsing back to the wagons. "Rorry, Cord, please come with me to see to the horses."

Scarlett sighed and puffed out her cheeks but flipped over another page.

"Teague," Carolle said. "If it's fine with her, I'd like to spend some time with Rorry."

Rorry stiffened but smiled and smoothed her dress over her knees.

Clapping Cord on the shoulder, Teague said, "Bevin, eat, get us stocked, then hitch the cart. We leave when he's ready. Many of us haven't slept. I promise we'll rest soon."

"Come then, dear," Maeverly said to Scarlett.

Scarlett hugged her book to her chest and rose while Rorry eyed Carolle, who received a second bowlful from Bevin.

They all stopped when Julian demanded, "Tell us why you are really here!"

Pulling Cord along with him, Teague walked away and answered, "Ah, the usual chicanery, of course! Finding lost lovers, stealing secret documents, running from dragons with their treasures in our pockets." Without turning back to Julian, he waved his hat in a flourish.

Quietly, he asked Cord, "Surprised I can spot an arsehole? I've been doing this longer than you've been drawing breath. You should have more faith. 'Tisn't that what your kind is supposed to be good at?"

Bevin wore a disapproving gaze and dropped a pail in front of the slumping Catalyst, splashing him with water.

"I'll always have more to learn," Cord quoted his headmaster. And he would learn Teague's secrets, even if he had to admit he was a magus out loud.

Chapter 26: The Hook's Unlikely Prisoner

Kylan watched Maeverly close the door of her gaudy wagon behind Scarlett. He hadn't expected Scarlett's studies to drive a wedge between them until her mandatory seclusion in the Tower. He wasn't the only one annoyed with being divided so soon after their reunion.

Rorry gave him an expressionless stare.

Kylan cleared his throat.

Slowly breaking away from the sensual kiss he shared with his wife, Veen brushed her cheeks with his knuckles. The bald monk jerked his head to the side, signaling for Kylan to join him away from the others.

When they were out of earshot of the fire ring, Veen whispered, "I have someone else to introduce you to."

"Who?"

"Get a bowl of stew and a waterskin," Veen said. He pointed to the lifewood wagon. "Then meet me there."

The cook had taken Teague's instructions rather literally. Red-faced, Julian sat on his lap while Bevin guided his hands to scrub the dishes. Bevin resembled a father with a small child in his lap. A grumpy, lumpy father. If it weren't for Julian's acidic attitude, Kylan might have pitied him.

Under the half-ogre's bushy-browed supervision, Kylan collected a maple bowl and filled it. But he didn't see any waterskins.

Bevin pointed Julian's arm at the cart and grunted.

The cart's white door chirped open, releasing an overwhelming garlic odor. Its shelves were crammed with food. Mounded leather canteens filled the bottom shelf beneath cucumbers, potatoes, and other finds from the flats. The water bulged away from Kylan's fingers when he seized a skin from the pile.

Carolle had moved to sit next to Rorry while finishing her meal.

Kylan groaned under his breath. Relaying the news of the symbols Veen had used to defeat Beez would have to wait. Chiding himself for sounding like Rorry when a plan fell apart, he carefully sped off to see whom Veen had been referring to.

As Kylan made his way down the caravan, Veen exited the green wagon with a yew longbow and a refreshed quiver of arrows.

Gesturing to the bow, Kylan said, "Longer than your last one."

"Too long," Veen said with a frown. "'Twill work for now." He examined what Kylan held. "Good. You could've brought him a spoon but never a knife. Make him give them back every time, understand?"

"No."

"You will, so."

Veen led him to the lifewood wagon, hopped up the steps, and fiddled with the lock.

Kylan breathed in the tree's scent as he waited. Red veins still shimmered in the wagon's weathered planks, as they did in the bark on the tree. Whichever tree had shed the bark used for the wagon must have been ancient; the core of the bark had to be over a foot thick for timber as dense as the side of the wagon.

In the grass nearby, Cord and Teague brushed down a pair of

horses. Whatever Teague was saying had Cord bent in fits of laughter; even Teague's smile appeared mostly genuine. Kylan didn't expect that, given their tense walk earlier.

Finally, Veen jostled the iron ring handle to the door. "This is where youse will travel."

Kylan stood aside as the monk swung it open. He peered over Veen's shoulder and strained to see into the dark interior.

Someone stared back. A man with olive-toned skin lay behind bars at the end of the otherwise empty room. A trimmed black beard surrounded his mouth and came to a point just beneath his chin. His bare, narrow torso ended where his hands disappeared behind a furry thigh. The black fur covered his leg all the way down to its cloven hooves.

Rolling toward the door, the prisoner stamped a hoof against the wall of his cell. "Do come in." His voice rumbled as he moved his hands up his body, revealing what they had held. "I'll show you where the differences begin."

Veen peered inside and slammed the door shut. "You've got until the count of ten to be decent, or your rations go to waste!" In an apologetic tone, he said, "You never know what to expect out of this one."

Kylan started the sentence three times before he managed to say, "That's a satyr!"

Hushing him, Veen whispered, "Keep this secret close, Kylan. Your friends accept things like magic, but that Julian doesn't. If Teague makes us endure that fool's company to the continent, this secret may be too great for him to hold."

"I thought they were extinct, like the dwarves."

"We all did, didn't we?" With sincerity, Veen warned, "Be on your guard. He's better at manipulating people than my Aunt Sheryl. 'Tis his mouth that led Vega into that trap." He took a deep breath and added, "I'm sorry about that display."

Kylan shrugged it off. This. This made an adventure.

"Ten!" Veen yelled.

"Wait," Kylan said, holding the door closed with his elbow. "That's what you thought I'd enjoy?"

"No? My mistake." Veen laughed at Kylan's flushing face. "He'll be your responsibility now. Treat him respectfully but keep your guard up."

When the door opened, unbuttoned leather britches, mostly comprising interwoven strips of black and red leather, now covered the legs of the satyr, who eyed them stoically. "You can hardly blame me for entertaining myself," the prisoner said as he ran a hand over his bare chest. "You're a monk for the gods' sake." He could have passed as human from the waist up, even if his ears stuck out a bit.

The satyr didn't appear to be much older than Kylan. Although, neither did Andion. Kylan didn't have a clue as to how long satyrs lived.

Stepping inside the wagon after Veen, Kylan discovered he could stand at his full height with some room to spare. He left the door open behind him to combat the tang in the air. Windows no taller than Kylan's hand lined the top of the longer sides of the wagon but provided little light.

The prisoner ogled Kylan through the iron bars. Each rod punctured the wood in the floor and ceiling, isolating the last few feet of the long room under the driver's bench. A sturdy lock secured the door in the middle of the bars. Iron links coiled through the rods, doubly securing the cell with a second lock.

Veen gave the satyr a disapproving look and pointed to a short opening at the bottom of the barred door. "Slide the food through there. He gets a meal when we do. Nothing more, nothing less."

Kylan slid the bowl and waterskin along the floorboards.

"He'll try to charm you. Keep your wits around him and make sure your possessions are out of his reach."

"Am I squirrely?" the satyr asked. He lifted the maple bowl and sniffed the stew. "Does that mean you're done with me, mouse?"

Kylan couldn't repress a snicker. "I'm Kylan. A pleasure to make your acquaintance."

"Pleasure," the prisoner said with a wry grin. The black toes of his hooves clacked together in a placid rhythm. "Ferix. The last satyr, I'm afraid."

"Don't bother, boy," Veen said. "This one's a bag of lies. We'll see what tale he weaves for the Towers and the Luminary when we're back in the Bonded Nations, so we will."

Bending to draw his waterskin closer, Ferix said, "Strange to see a native of Merith joining this laughable band of mercenaries."

"Laughable enough to catch the likes of you," Veen replied.

The satyr let it go. "Did they promise to save you from your backward island?"

"Not exactly," Kylan answered. "But I'll get to the continent, with or without their help."

Ferix's eyes strolled down Kylan's body. "I'm sure you will."

"Maybe this wasn't a good idea," Veen said, snagging Kylan's sleeve and nodding to the door.

"A little conversation with my meal is not out of the question," Ferix said before taking a long drink from his bowl. "And what waits for you there?"

"I'm not sure," Kylan admitted. "If I had my choice?" There was only one intersection between the adventures he had fantasized about and their needs in tracking Alis. "A ship. I'd buy a ship."

"Bah!" Ferix groaned. "A house to drown in? This is the guard you've chosen for me? Prettier than the last one but dumber."

"You don't like the sea, I take it?" Kylan asked, trying to decide whether he was insulted or flattered.

"You must know nothing of my kind, islander."

Veen patted the leather jerkin over his chest. "I'll keep the key to the cell. Only Teague can unlock the chain."

The satyr stamped his hoof against the wall, shaking the vardo.

Palming the sleek planks, Kylan said, "Lifewood won't give way, especially with this level of craftsmanship." He turned to Veen. "Where did you get it?"

"Some town on the way down. We traded a couple of his things to pay for it."

Ferix grimaced for a moment, then kept chewing. "I shall make note of it along with your larceny of my time."

"My father once told me that the only downside to lifewood is that it's too dense to float," Kylan said. "Aside from that, it should be impervious to anything a Judge could throw at it."

"Magic?" Ferix asked flatly. Kylan wasn't sure if he was joking, or if Ferix really thought the Judges were magi. Maybe he knew as little about Merithians as Kylan knew about satyrs. "I would prefer to die by magic over drowning. It's much faster."

The emptied bowl skidded out of the cell and into Kylan's foot.

Ferix reclined and moaned, "I'd like my pipe back."

"If your manners had been better, I might have felt there was a reason to reward you," Veen said. "No, actually, I wouldn't, seeing as you led a member of my guild to her death!"

"Believe as you wish," Ferix moaned. "Can you make your own judgments, Kylan? Tell me, in a word, what do you see when you inspect me?" He unabashedly leered.

"Guile."

"Insipid," Ferix retorted. "If you will not return my pipe, may I remove my pants now? You're welcome to stay, if you like."

Veen grumbled something under his breath as he turned Kylan toward the exit. His silent steps led the way. As Ferix watched them depart, Kylan got the feeling that the satyr was considering something more than a way to use him to escape.

The monk closed the door behind him. "You see what I mean? He tries to get in your head. Don't let him, or he'll be doing more than stroking his smig at you, so."

Kylan's face flushed again. "Smig?"

Veen went red and scratched his stubble. "Ack! His hairy chin, boy! Now you've got me blushing like a wee girleen."

Chapter 27: Societal Sensibilities

Thankful for the breeze that had grown scarce during their meal, Rorry considered waiting for Carolle in the shade of the teal tree rather than watching the monk finish her soup. The woman wore the clothing of a Vetskarran dockhand. Yet, unlike those slaver brutes who sweat on the coolest days in the capital, not a drop appeared on Carolle's creamy skin. The ventilation of her cleavage could not be that soothing.

The monk had not said much, which was rude, given that she had requested her audience. She certainly seemed to be a silly woman. From her seat on the grass, Carolle smiled around her chewing.

Rorry studied the smooth pink lacquer on her nails.

The others' dishes dried on a mat Julian had laid out before the half-ogre carried him into the fields to forage.

Julian's sniveling had embarrassed Rorry. Was that the impression these foreigners would hold of Merithians?

When Carolle tipped her dish to her wide mouth, the vines on her arms moved with the flexing of her muscles. Here and there, flowers bloomed along them. None were the same family or design, and only a few were recognizable to Rorry. One tulip near her elbow appeared as though a child had drawn it, whereas an intricate frost lily on her shoulder appeared to have been inked skillfully by an artist. "They're a memorial," Carolle said. "The flowers are loved ones who have fallen during my life's journey. In this way, I carry them with me."

Rorry adjusted her posture. "I am sorry that you have lost so many. Will you be adding one for Vega?"

Carolle guffawed abruptly. "No." Her voice was certainly suitable to the outdoors. "We didn't see eye to eye. Still, her loss cost us our sixth member. In the Hook, a bad omen that is."

She rose with surprising grace and placed her bowl on Bevin's preparation table. Her silhouette would send a Judge running for his hammer, or worse.

Rorry had not cleared the judgment from her features before Carolle saw.

"There's an answer," she said.

"An answer to what?" Rorry asked innocently.

"I was wondering why you don't like me very much. It shouldn't, but it always bothers me when someone thinks the worst of me. We hadn't spoken until now, so I have to assume it's because of the way I dress."

Rorry did not deny it.

"You know," Carolle trilled, "before 'virago' meant loud, ill-tempered shrew, it meant a woman with strength and spirit. Merith changed that definition for the world. So I'm curious as to how a woman in your position views herself. You posture like you've a crown on your head, nose in the air like, to compensate for the burden. What I can't decide is if the burden is Merithian propriety and hatred of sensuality or something else."

Stunned by her rudeness, Rorry said nothing aloud.

"Here, get that crossbow you were carrying. Let's teach you how to shoot better." Carolle walked off toward a grove of trees in the next field without waiting for Rorry's reply.

Rorry rose with indignation, knocking over her stool, and stewed as she hurried to the butterfly vardo to retrieve the weapon. This monk did not know her. Why did she assume that a woman demonstrating standards of propriety could not defend herself? If Master Clienne had taught her anything, it was that she could take an enemy down at range. On the other hand, she hoped Carolle's lesson wouldn't reveal his refusal to train her to use a sword or stave.

His rote argument played through Rorry's mind. "Girl, don't let them get that close!" That had done her no favors, as it turned out.

Rorry's heart chugged by the time she slung open the azure door to the butterfly vardo. With a rushed pardon to Maeverly and Scarlett, she snatched the weapon and skipped the stairs on her way out. Rorry closed the door more forcefully than she'd intended and shouted an apology. Both actions made her cringe before drawing herself up.

Already, Carolle had traipsed halfway through the field on the other side of the road.

Cord and Teague brushed down a pair of the coppery Northpelts at the end of the line. Rorry wished she could hear what had made Cord laugh so hard. Teague's sporadic smile was as convincing as his change of tune. Cord should keep his guard up around the charmer. Fear made people unpredictable, even to themselves.

The muck of the field slowed her progress, fanning her ire. "'Ere, let's tich you how to shoot bet-ter," Rorry mimicked in Carolle's singsong accent. Without the breeze, the heat kicked up the perfume of the dandelions and other wildflowers spotting the lea. She refused to let it improve her mood.

In the smattering of spindly pines, a mix of dogwoods, and some trees Rorry didn't recognize, Carolle moved farther in. No leaves crunched under the monk's feet as she stepped. No twigs snapped. She yelled, "Stay by there." Carolle drew her belt knife and carved a rough outline of a man in a dead tree's lichenous bark. She stood aside.

"I have limited ammunition," Rorry said. "Is it wise to waste a bolt on practice?"

Nodding, Carolle began walking back to her. "The green vardo is where we keep our munitions. If you need arrows or bolts or knives or whatever your poison—except poison, I suppose—Teague'll get them for you. Just ask. Here, I brought these. It takes the slimmer ones, doesn't it?" With an elaborate wave, she produced five bolts from thin air. The warm silver cylinders were just slim enough to fit the crossbow, which had a narrower groove than the one Rorry had trained on.

"How did you do that?" Rorry asked. "Teague pulled knives from where, his sleeve?"

"Yes, or his jerkin, or his belt. He has more hidden on him than any of us. We can alter your garments, if you like." Carolle frowned at the skirt. "A dress may be more challenging. In the hem, maybe?"

"I prefer my clothes as they are." Disdain coated Rorry's words. She pressed the lever to set the string and slipped a bolt into position. The weight and ease of reloading made this bow a luxury, which the monk appeared to admire.

"I don't do it for attention, you know?" Carolle asked. "My clothes allow me to run, to climb trees, and to defend myself without limiting my movement. The attention is just an advantage, Rorry." She winked.

Rorry turned away to raise her eyebrows and her weapon. She centered her aim on the outline's neck and squeezed the trigger. Without a sound, the bolt flew and made a knocking sound as it struck right on target.

Carolle showed no surprise or approval. Instead, she pointed to the chest and said, "In battle, aim for a sure shot. Tempting as the head and neck are, they're too small, doubly true if you're on horseback. Leave little to chance and take your enemy down. Try again."

Heat washed beneath Rorry's cheeks. She loaded another bolt and loosed it. It sank into the man's shoulder. How had she missed the heart?

Humiliated by Carolle's disappointed grunt, Rorry reloaded.

"Hold a moment," Carolle said. She went to the tree and drew an arc over the chest of the outline. "Below this line is a fatal shot. Outside, you'll bring him down temporarily. Not a bad shot, really, if your intent is to wound and gain a prisoner. We already have one, so let's aim to kill, all right?"

Did the woman think her an imbecile? Some flighty debutante who hadn't already killed a High Guard? Rorry did not wait for Carolle to move away before she pulled the trigger. Again, she missed. The bolt nailed the stomach.

Never flinching, Carolle pulled the bolts out of the tree. "Better!" she yelled. "Again."

"Wait," Rorry said. "What prisoner? Julian?" In her frustration, she had almost missed that statement.

"No. You'll see now after." She pointed to the tree and took a step back this time. "Focus. Again."

Rorry had learned her lesson; aim for the core of a man. A tall blade of grass flickered with a swish of leaves. Swinging the crossbow to her right, she shot. The noise stilled.

Sprinting, the monk went after the bolt. Carolle lifted a hare and brought it over. "Good on you."

"I thought the bolt should count for something."

"Ah," Carolle said. "I'm glad I was wrong about you being haughty. Your skills are honed to perfection? Willing to gamble your friends' lives on that?"

"You insult me, Mrs. van Veen. My friends knew of my abilities when we left Brewing. They have faith in them; why should I not?"

"As you wish," Carolle said. "I've dealt with nobles most of my life, Rorry. Most swoon, praise and prattle, or bathe you in proper scornful glances. Then there are those with passion in their souls, who aren't so buried in the shite and pettiness that they can see the truth, the importance of the world around them. They can see it in the people around them too. Like you, running off with your magi friends. But now, you act like a bloody-minded royal. Why for?" Rorry didn't look her in the eye. "What hurt you so deeply that my clothes are more important than you learning to survive a crisis?"

"You are *deeply* mistaken," Rorry said.

"No, I'm not." Carolle held the hare at arm's length. "Go clean this. If you don't know how, Bevin can show you."

"What?"

Disappointment curved Carolle's lips. "Tell me your intent was not to take a life to prove a point, good girl."

Rorry remained silent, unsure of what to say. She had never had to clean a kill.

"You're not wrong. We do need the meat. Now prepare it. When you're finished, wait with your friends." She dangled the bloody animal for Rorry to take.

Rorry grabbed the hare's soft fur and disconnected herself from its warmth. Raging inside, she could not decide if she was closer to screaming or crying. What was the monk's ploy? And why did she want to confess everything to the trollop? "Why?" Rorry asked. "Why did you spend your life around nobles?"

Carolle stretched and twirled. She stepped around Rorry in an elegant dance and soon beamed while she circled. "I traveled in the Patevian Royal Dance Troupe. Selected by Queen Ada, no less." Rorry nearly smiled at the brag. The monk slowed to a stop with her arms beautifully poised in the air. "My life once." A familiar pained expression crept over Carolle's face. "Before the Mount, before Stille, before the Hook. It feels very far away now."

That brief sadness told Rorry all she needed to know. She couldn't dismiss Carolle as a simpleton. Something had hurt the monk, hurt her deeply. Was that why she had joined the monastery? Is that how she recognized it in her? Yet Carolle laughed loudly and freely now, uninhibited by her past. Could Carolle show her the path back to the girl she used to be?

"It was wrong of me to dismiss your help," Rorry heard herself say. "I would be honored to learn from you, if you are willing to instruct me."

As friendly as before Rorry's insulting judgment, Carolle said, "The honor's mine. I never believed you a fool, Rorry. *Diolch*—thank you—for proving me right." She glided by with a grin.

When Rorry turned, Carolle leaped up the branches of a pine and leaned back on a limb midway up the tree. The monk lobbed a couple of bolts to Rorry's feet. "Keep them. You're quite skilled at range, *my lady*. How about next time we spar unarmed?"

Rorry smiled.

"I thought you might like that. And *diolch* for showing me what a Ghost Augur's crossbow can do. I'd been curious since we found the katana at the fort. What was the third in the set? Something small, I'd guess, if he was carrying those around."

Ghost Augur? Blinking at the crossbow, Rorry answered, "A dirk. Scarlett did not wish to deprive her uncle of it, even though we promised to find a way to return them."

Another blaring laugh came from the woman. "Tempting problem there. They're keen weapons, derived from an art nearly gone. You see those silver words running down the sides? The Ghost Augur's premier wish. If all else were false in the world, the Ghost Augur holds to that one desire to anchor him. As long as it was pure, he would not lament. Kind of romantic for deadly assassins, don't you think?"

"Romantic is not a word I would use to describe Master Clienne," Rorry replied. Neither was "assassin." But what did she truly know of him? Not the significance of the weapons. Shamed again, she realized her self-importance had deprived him of a sacred object. Although his tutelage had begun out of boredom, he had taught them well. A deeper apology for her trespasses would have to accompany their return. "I did not know any of this."

"It's all right," Carolle said. "Ignorance isn't bad or insulting. Any person can overcome it, if they accept it and are willing to learn."

Hooding her eyes from the sun, Rorry asked, "Why would someone refuse to learn?"

"Probably pride." She grinned down on Rorry, then looked out to the caravan. "Knowledge changes things, Freckles. Don't you feel different after our little chat?"

Taking the lack of eye contact as a dismissal, Rorry trod toward Bevin's preparation table. Perhaps Scarlett knew about Ghost Augurs. What was Master Clienne's premier wish? The weapon fell to her side. As she ignored the hare outstretched in her hand, Rorry opened herself to the influence of the flowers.

Chapter 28: Nurturing the Sparks Within

Sitting cross-legged on the floor of the butterfly vardo, Scarlett studied the intricate fleurs-de-lis on Maeverly's boots and neglected the jar in her hands, waiting for the sorcerer to return her attention from the vanity and declare another failure. The floorboards began to make Scarlett's bum sore as her mind wandered, running through the questions she'd compiled. Where did these Dregs originate from, and how? Who, or what, was rocking the lifewood vardo? And perhaps most importantly, what did *tek'aran* mean? It must be connected to the magic Cord had used to heal Kylan.

"Not quite, I'm afraid," Maeverly said at last, squeaking the stool as she turned to face her pupil. "Did you concentrate?"

Scarlett feigned a sheepish smile and offered up the jar. When Maeverly took it, Scarlett climbed to the padded bench, eventually acknowledging the skepticism on her mentor's face.

Maeverly exhaled. "This isn't working."

"I'm sorry."

"Oh, it's not you. Well, it's not entirely your fault. We're not being honest with each other, and I can't say I care for it." Rolling the jar in her thick hands, Maeverly thought. She swiveled her stool and nodded to herself in the mirror. "I promised the others I wouldn't, but I must tell you something. Mentors and pupils should have a relationship where no topic is restricted, nothing is forbidden."

Scarlett's mouth went dry.

As if answering her prayers, the door opened. Rorry rushed in and snatched Uncle Barrey's crossbow. "Pardon me, ladies," she said in a steely voice clearly not meant for them. Her cheeks were flushed, her shoulders back. Something was wrong. Without explanation, she leaped out of the door and slammed it shut. "Sorry!" she yelled.

Unconcerned, Maeverly leaned in. "As I mentioned before, with both methods of magic, confidence is the key. For example, I feel more confident in a dress and heels, and therefore, I am more powerful. In being true to myself in that manner for many years, I've developed a thick skin. So when people deride me for it, it impacts my abilities less."

Confused about how the woman's wardrobe affected her draw on her abilities and why the Hook would wish to hide it, Scarlett tilted her head.

"Really? You didn't suspect?" Maeverly asked. "I'm a man, Scarlett."

Suddenly the sorcerer made a lot more sense. Her face went slack.

"My real name is Joseb Roux. Maeverly is my twin sister. I'm sorry I lied to you. I had intended to confess this morning but was overruled."

Glimpsing his reflection, the sorcerer said, "Being a woman is a stretch, but I can't strut about in a dress as a man in the most intolerant nation in the world. Eh, second most. And I have less power outside of a frock than I do pretending to be Maeverly, so it's safer to be her on this mission. Does that make sense?"

Scarlett let her eyes wander as she thought it over. "But . . ." She swallowed. "Do you feel as confident when you are a woman? I mean, pretending to be something you're not . . . and do not . . . want to be?"

The sorcerer nodded emphatically. "I am a man and have never believed otherwise."

"Then, would pretending to be a woman not make you less powerful than a man in women's clothing?"

"Hah! Men's. Women's. They're just clothes in my opinion. I say what's sauce for the goose is sauce for the gander." He put a hand on her knee. "You are very delicate, you know? You're going to find it difficult to offend me; I've heard it all. I've been painting my face since I was a boy. As I said, better to be Maeverly than Joseb on this mission."

"Then does it hurt your feelings?" she asked.

Joseb squinted, not understanding her question.

"That your friends would ask you to hide who you are, I mean?"

"Ah. They mean well—and they are accepting. It's just a precaution—and only on Merith; you can understand that, right?" He seemed to be waiting for her to agree.

Scarlett slouched and rested her chin in her hands. "My friends don't want me to hide who I am anymore. Kylan says it's unfair. They get angry sometimes when my mum . . ." Her mouth drifted into areas she didn't want it to. Joseb didn't want to hear about that. Grinning broadly, she said, "Kylan and Rorry wouldn't care, if they knew you, the real you."

Joseb's face tightened.

"I won't tell them! I promise!"

"If they guess, so be it. It does feel good to have that off my chest." He smiled and ran a hand over his cheek. "I need to shave. Keep trying with that jar."

"I'm not sure what you want me to do."

His eyes didn't believe her. "We're being honest here, remember? Tell me what you're afraid of."

Scarlett braced herself and decided to just say it. "I've always been told sorcery is too dangerous. I would prefer to learn the ways of a mage."

"Didn't I mention you can do both?"

She grabbed the green tome beside her. "*Essential Focus* says a person's connection with magic bends, aligning itself to be most powerful in its common usage. If I learn your way, wouldn't I be inhibiting my entry to the Tower?"

Joseb laughed. "I appreciate your faith in my prowess as a mentor but know from experience that it takes years to create such an alignment. And when that's achieved, it merely makes the deepest reserves of your magic easier to access, through cold logic or emotions. In the days it'll take us to reach the continent, I'm more likely to talk you out of the Tower than affect your draw on your connection."

Feeling a bit silly, Scarlett said, "Then would you teach me both?"

He thought it over and nodded. "That's fair. I said I would anyway." Hunching over, he held up a finger. "*If* you cease your diffidence and genuinely try."

She agreed and meant it. She wouldn't allow her mum's words in her thoughts.

"So," Joseb said, picking up the jar. "With that sorted, let's try this again. Have you ever fancied someone to the extent that when they walked into a room, it brightened, as though all of your senses awoke and homed in on that person?"

Scarlett bashfully shrugged. There must be sorcerer spells that didn't require passion.

Joseb's eyes smiled at the container before he closed them, wrapping the glass in his hands. "I always think of my first kiss for this spell. My mother had remarried and moved us from Patevia to Racine, which stuck me in the Tower. Eventually, I became friends with a girl who had arrived shortly after me.

"Even at sixteen years, Daniella had a full bosom and a womanly walk. She was lovely. All of the older lads bullied each other to gain her affection. Little did they know she was interested in me, the jester that I was."

He tightened his hold. "I remember the time she snuck into the boys' dormitory. . . how velvety her lips were when they touched mine . . ." A green flame puffed to life, suspended in the center of the jar. Joseb rolled his head back. The ball of light swelled from the size of a button to that of a fist.

Opening his eyes, he said, "Ah, there." He set the jar in Scarlett's hands.

No warmth radiated from the fire.

"Creating something requires a great deal of your own power. When you are just learning, vivid memories and emotions can help you to master the basics. In this case, I imbue the glass, or perhaps the air within, with a touch of that emotion. Do you think you could mimic that spell with an experience? No need to be shy. We've shed our secrets."

Scarlett shook her head and watched her tutor mask his disappointment. "Perhaps if I learned how a mage would concoct it, I would be able to replicate the effect with the sorcerer's approach?"

Giving a noncommittal hum, Joseb squeaked his stool as he turned to the vanity. He rifled through a drawer.

Unintentional failure didn't sit well with Scarlett. Her temptation to think of Julian during an attempt fluttered away quickly. After their acrimonious debate around the fire ring, she'd prefer not to tell Joseb that Julian stirred those feelings. The thought idled as she recalled his lean torso. The flame pulsed.

She dropped the jar. The latch hit her foot and unbuckled, extinguishing the green light.

Joseb ignored the noise as he shuffled through another drawer. "The cinnamon . . . I thought," he said to himself and pulled forward one of the chests beneath the benches. He emptied out its contents. Unable to find what he sought, he grunted, refilled the chests, and began searching drawers in the horseshoe-shaped cabinet above. "Ah, here we are!"

He dug out three pouches and handed them to Scarlett. Cinnamon, a bundle of tiny sticks, and a red spice that smelled like pepper filled them. "Put these in the jar. The holly burrow sticks first, then add half of the cinnamon, and finally a quick dash of pepperflame. Clean your hands before touching anything—especially yourself—after handling that stuff. The burning takes hours to subside." He groaned. "I speak from experience."

Doing as instructed, Scarlett moved to the floor and filled the jar. Then she passed the pouches back to Joseb. As he flung them onto the clothes Rorry had folded, she latched the jar closed.

"You'll want to let it breathe for this method," he said. "We're going to create regular fire this time."

Scarlett reopened the jar.

"All spells can be accomplished through sorcery and," he strained to keep his face flat, "the ways of the mage. However, the basic lessons are not the same for each. That is why I can't supply you with the same spell. I'm afraid I'd need a spell book for that."

Scarlett tilted the jar toward her for another glance at the ingredients. "I have cast sorcerer spells then," she admitted. "I can start a campfire without words or pepperflame."

"Interesting," Joseb said. His face crinkled with concern. "That usually requires anger, focused anger."

Scarlett shifted as the man studied her. "Fire is easy," she confessed. "I thought it was menial, something everyone could do with magic."

A deep purple flickered about Joseb as he thought. A myriad of other colors blurred at the edges but disappeared too quickly for Scarlett to see them all.

"Well, you won't want to feel that while we're doing this. Now take a long breath. Clear your mind of everything. Purge emotion from your body. When you feel that you have, give me a nod."

Scarlett's muscles relaxed. In Joseb's presence, she felt safe allowing herself to feel hollow and still. The questions ceased their endless circling in her head. She nodded.

"Accept that a fire shall start when you lean over the jar and say, '*Ignolio fervente*,'" Joseb whispered. "When you believe it to be true, say it."

"*Ignolio fervente!*" A click heralded a flicker. As the smoke subsided, the flame roasted the sticks. She beamed up at Joseb, until heat registered near her right ear. The garments blazed where Joseb had set the pouches. Scarlett gasped.

With a determined glare, Joseb waved his hand at the engulfing fire. The flames turned to ice. Between the drawers overhead, mist swirled into a tiny cloud and began to drop snowflakes. He sighed. "That's not what I meant."

Scarlett tightened her shawl around her shoulders and asked, "Did I do something wrong?"

"No, no. I botched it. Shouldn't have laid the components near you. You did very well. It took me a month of study in the Tower to attune my abilities enough to cast that spell. When I did, it was only a spark." He grinned victoriously. "I said you were powerful."

Joseb blew out the flame in the jar. The cloud thinned. "Open the door, will you?" he asked as he fanned away the smoke. "If I'm to be of any service to you as a mentor, I'll need to brush up on the lessons of the Tower myself. It's been years, mind." He grimaced and admitted, "Decades."

Smoke wafted out as Scarlett opened the door.

Teague chuckled when he looked up from his conversation with Bevin. He tapped two fingers to his hunter's cap.

Scarlett waved back.

"Next time," Joseb said, "we practice outside." He examined the damaged clothing. "Help me clean this up. Then I'd better shave before we set out."

With the mess cleared, Scarlett took *Essential Focus* and managed to sneak away the remnants of the pouches as well. Unable to wipe the smile from her face, she tucked them into her poultice bag and left to find her friends.

Just as her feet hit the ground, Kylan grabbed her by the elbow. "You have to see this!"

Chapter 29: Out of the Shadows

When Rorry began washing her hands for the third time, Kylan tapped his thumb against his leg and grumbled from the lifewood's shadow. Scarlett read at his side. The breeze had disappeared but still rustled the teal leaves above him. He rolled his sleeves up tight as he tried to fathom why Rorry had skinned a hare. Probably some punishment for being haughty to Carolle. As though she'd never worn his britches after swimming in the lake.

"Come quickly," he said once Rorry had finished scrubbing and collected her crossbow. "You have to see what's in the lifewood wagon."

As casually as if out for an afternoon stroll, the girls hid their intrigue as they passed the mercenaries and Cord harnessing the horses to the caravan.

Kylan peeked inside the dim prison. Ferix was napping, with his britches on. Swinging the door open just enough to get inside, he motioned for Rorry and Scarlett to follow. Thankfully, the room smelled more like the cedar-scented lifewood than the captive.

Rorry took his arm as she peered around him.

"You see?" he whispered. "How old do you think he is?"

After gently closing the door, Scarlett set her poultice bag down. She moved up to the bars and gave her bottom lip a tug. "How did he get to Merith?"

Rorry stroked her crossbow and said, "I am more concerned with what he did to warrant confinement. Is he another descendant of Shallyghal in hiding, like Andion?"

"I don't think so," Kylan said. "He speaks quicker than a Merithian. I didn't recognize his accent. It's not Racinian. And besides, piks live off Merith. He's something else."

Scarlett stepped back beside them. "I've read of nomadic tribes seeing visions of satyrs in the dunes of the Yuht desert."

"Are they evil?" Rorry asked her and received an uncertain pout in response.

Kylan thought over the question. "I'm not sure I trust what I think of him." He blushed at Scarlett's teasing grin. "He's a tad foul, as the stories say satyrs are."

Scarlett slid her back down the wall to the floor and spread her book in her lap.

Suddenly, daylight filled the vardo. Under a mound of pillows and what now passed for their possessions, Cord shambled inside and said, "They've only got six merchant licenses, so Teague said we have to ride in here until our next break."

In unison, Kylan and the girls turned to the satyr. His shameless brown eyes sampled them.

"Maeverly had some blankets and pillows for us," Cord said. "They reek of smoke but win out over sitting on the floor." He released the pile and began sorting through it, throwing pillows over his shoulder. "Here."

Kylan's pillow hit his back and fell to the floor. He pulled Ferix's attention from Cord with a stare and shook his head as a warning. Cord didn't seem to handle newness well. And Ferix spoke freely of things Kylan didn't have any interest in sharing with Cord, at least not yet, probably not ever if he wanted to keep his friendship.

"More prisoners." Ferix sighed.

Cord cleared all the air from his lungs in one blaring yelp.

When the shout ended, Kylan said, "A fine, manly scream. Impressive." Ignoring Cord's gaping mouth, Kylan said, "Cord, Rorry, and Scarlett, I'd like to introduce you to Ferix . . . the last satyr." His hesitation made it sound more like a title.

Rorry curtsied. "I beg your pardon. Though I am not inclined to trust Teague," she said to Cord, "we are not prisoners. We are merely joining you for the trek."

Veen appeared at the base of the stairs. He smiled at Cord's attempt to pant his disbelief away. "Ah, good. All settled now, yeah? We'll break in a few hours. Enjoy the ride and stay away from Ferix. He lies and probably bites."

The door shut. Metal rattled.

"Wait!" Kylan shouted. "Are you locking us in?" He shoved on the unyielding door.

"'Tis for your own good, so," Veen yelled. "Just relax and get some rest."

Ferix repeated, "More prisoners."

Scarlett pressed her finger to a page. "If we were prisoners, I doubt they would have let us keep our weapons."

With one hand on her hip and the other ready to use her crossbow, Rorry addressed the door, "Master van Veen, there are two women in this vardo, and the prisoner has no option beyond his chamber pot—chamber pan. Certainly, you are not suggesting we be subjected to such a scene."

Killing a laugh, Veen answered, "Kylan will set Ferix straight, if need be."

"You're more than welcome to try," Ferix said with the same lewd expression he'd worn earlier during his entertainment.

Kylan glimpsed Cord snapping out of his shock. Cord's disgusted scowl said the comment had planted him firmly back in the prudish teachings of the Chancellor's army.

In the vague direction of the cell, Rorry said, "We have not given them cause to lock us up." She lowered next to Scarlett.

The vardo lurched into motion. Maintaining his balance, Kylan threw a quilt to the girls.

Ferix lay on his side facing away from them, opting to sleep rather than converse.

Stretching out between his friends and the prisoner, just beyond reach of the cell, Kylan folded his arms behind his head and glanced over to Cord.

Plumping a pillow with his fist, Cord kept a cautious eye on Ferix. He propped the cushion next to the door and leaned against it, only letting his gaze leave the satyr when Rorry was repositioned.

Before long, Rorry stopped reading over Scarlett's shoulder and began braiding Scarlett's hair. Kylan knew the presence of the satyr frustrated her. She'd be the first to want to clear the air. He wouldn't have rushed them inside if he'd known they'd be trapped.

Tempted to share how Veen had defeated Beez anyway, Kylan decided to wait. He didn't know this satyr and wouldn't start a discussion that might reveal Cord's secret, even if he doubted Ferix knew what *tek'aran* meant.

Taking the opportunity for what it was, Kylan put the Dregs out of his mind and slept.

* * *

The strangeness overtaking Cord's life had grown tiresome. It was one thing to walk the ruins of a lost race but a complete other to ride alongside a breathing member of one. Those bars Ferix slept behind gave Cord all the warning he needed. *Ashes, a flaming satyr!*

As they put distance between them and Beez's hunters, the swaying vardo lulled all of its passengers to sleep except Cord and Scarlett. Before giving in, Rorry had braided half of Scarlett's hair into thin stems branching out from her head, which made Cord grin every time she turned to face him.

Scarlett flipped the tome over in her lap, then clinked through her poultice bag. She flapped her lips in a huff and resumed reading, mumbling about the light.

Next to her, Rorry lay curled in a quilt matching Maeverly's pillows. She looked peaceful, nothing like an Abandoned on the run.

Green fluttered outside the high windows before a branch thudded and dragged along the side of the wagon. A few more trees brushed past. The small windows made tracking time difficult.

Scarlett thumbed over another page.

Cord wished he could talk to her. But the beast in the cage had taken his tongue. What might a satyr know of a *tek'aran*?

With the prisoner napping, it probably wouldn't hurt if he did the same, just for a bit. His eyelids lowered.

A crash jolted everyone upright. Between Kylan and the cell, a varnished walnut trunk bounced against the bars. If not so well cared for, it'd be identical to the one in his barracks.

The satyr tucked his beastly legs under him and crouched away from it. If he hadn't caused it to appear, what had?

Scarlett shielded herself with her book when Kylan reached for the trunk's lid.

"Kylan, no," Rorry said, lifting her crossbow.

"You think the Dregs possess furniture?" Kylan asked. The hinges creaked as he opened it. Sorting through the contents, he pulled out a commoner's tunic, a bread roll missing a large bite, and a black trinket box.

Something rolled and rattled inside the box as Kylan handed it over to Scarlett. Light reflected off the square lid, revealing embellishments carved into the surface.

"It came from the shadows," Kylan said. "I'd bet Ferix's freedom this is your little friend's work." After closing the lid, he flung the shirt to Cord. "You should see if this fits, soldier."

Cord felt the satyr eyeing him but flushed when Rorry's pink cheeks turned away. He threw the tunic back to Kylan. "Keep it. Yours looks like the hounds chewed it." He didn't mind the risk of a bloody uniform if it kept him from stripping in front of Ferix's waiting gaze. Besides, he wasn't ready to give his tunic over. Not yet.

A thump from inside the chest knocked the lid open. Fingers clutched the brim. Andion struggled to get his head to peep over the top. "Help!" he yelled.

Kylan grabbed the pik by the arm and stood, pulling him free of the chest. A bulging burlap sack lifted out with him.

"Not me!" Andion swung the sack into Kylan and let it fall with a clatter. Kylan did the same to the pik, though Andion landed gently on his feet. "Brute."

"Brat."

As wide-eyed as Scarlett, the satyr watched with neither twitch nor breath.

"Andion," Cord said. "This is our friend, Scarlett."

Andion gave a little wave, then shouted, "That's mine!" She offered the box freely to his clutching hands. Andion caressed the divots and grooves in the wood before he nodded his thanks.

"And this," Kylan said, "is our prisoner, Ferix."

"I preferred 'the last satyr,'" Ferix mocked. "Fate is strange."

The pik's eyes widened. He took a step toward the cell, but Kylan's arm brought him back.

"Probably best to keep your distance," Kylan said.

Lumbering over a bump in the road, the wagon sent a silver bowl rolling from the mouth of Andion's spilled sack to the door. Fabric edged out. Andion jerked a cloak free. "I thiefed clothes and food and weapons."

"Weapons?" Ferix asked.

"Andion," Cord said, scooting over to him. "Where've you been?"

Chewing his tongue, Andion stammered over his words. "Food, clothes . . . All the humans were dead. They didn't need it."

"Where?" Ferix demanded. Without a flinch, Andion pointed through Ferix's cell to the wall.

"We are heading right for it," Kylan said. "How far?"

The thief shrugged. "Andion cannot go far without jumping shadows. *I* didn't have to."

Another village had shared Kenton's fate? "What's happening to the villages?" Cord wondered aloud.

To the golden feather on Cord's uniform, Ferix said, "Your Chancellor, most likely."

"You know what I think?" Cord asked as he stood. "You oughta keep your filthy mouth shut."

Kylan positioned himself between them.

Rorry's fingers touched Cord's arm as her glare told him to hush. She gazed through the bars. "What do you mean?"

"What are you asking him for?" Cord asked.

Her grip tightened, but her expression didn't change as she waited on the prisoner's answer.

"Ask me when he isn't here," Ferix said.

Kylan shut the trunk and sat on it. "That's not going to happen today. Tell us if you know something. Or will it lead us into the same kind of trap you sprang on Vega?"

Annoyed, the satyr replied, "I had no more influence on that loose woman than a donkey, probably less. She seemed the type."

"Filth," Cord said. "That's all he knows. Nothing outta his mouth is worth a whoop."

Rorry removed her hand. "More pressingly, the High Guard may be on their way to burn that village. Cord, Kylan, move the chest to the corner. Andion's loot can wait until we warn the others." With the trunk filled, they hauled it away from the cell.

Kylan pounded on the ceiling and shouted, "Veen!"

The vardo eased to a stop. After jiggling the lock, Veen pulled the door ajar. "We're nearly there. Couldn't this wait?" The silver bowl chimed down the stairs. "What's going on in here?"

Teague appeared behind Veen with the bowl in his hand.

"We need to stop heading east," Kylan said. "Andion just came from there."

"Came from there?" Veen asked. The pik ducked behind Cord's leg when Veen squinted to see him.

"There's another village full of bodies," Cord said, "which means—"

"Glory be to the gods!" Teague said. "That's precisely where we're going."

"Is that safe?" Rorry asked.

"No," Ferix shouted.

"'Tis now," Teague answered.

Veen asked, "Faffing about, Teague? We'll be—"

"I'll explain on the way," Teague said to Veen. "Wake Carolle. Maeverly and Bevin can stay with the vardos. We'll scout ahead and see what remains."

The monk ran out of sight.

"I'm going too," Cord said.

Teague blocked his exit. "Have you slept, Cord?" Cord's face betrayed him. "Aye. We're not looking for liabilities. Get some rest, Cord. Ferix can't bite through the bars."

Rorry's expression warned Cord not to challenge Teague's decision; else she'd surely make him regret it. Cord fell to his pillow in defeat.

The satyr shook the vardo with a kick. "I don't bite! I'm not an animal."

"He does," Kylan said, pointing at Andion. He whisked away his finger when the pik bared his teeth at it.

"My dear ladies," Teague said, "if ye'd be more comfortable in Maeverly's vardo, please feel free to transfer." With that, he left.

Kylan started to follow.

"Where are you going?" Rorry asked.

"Just watering a tree," he said. With a hop down the stairs, he left too.

Rorry beckoned Scarlett to rise. "Do try to rest, Cord. If you would be so kind, please ask Kylan to visit Maeverly's vardo when he returns." She waited at the exit for his response. Cord agreed but didn't want them to leave him alone with the prisoner. To make matters worse, Rorry closed the door behind them.

When Cord stood to follow Kylan, Andion did as well. He couldn't let Julian see him and wouldn't let the satyr push him into causing harm for the orphan. With a low growl, Cord surrendered his curiosity. Teague would share what he found. He'd have to!

Cord settled to his knees by the trunk and flipped it open. As he started digging through the chest, he said, "Show me what you found, Andion. Anything good? More cheese? Is that all you eat?"

The thief clapped and jumped to his side.

Chapter 30: Bent by Chaos

As the door of the cedar-scented wagon creaked open, Cord rolled away from the light and buried his face in his elbow.

"Andion, no!" Kylan shouted.

Cord jerked upright, shielding his eyes against the blinding lantern in Kylan's hands.

Andion cast Kylan an annoyed scowl from the bars, where the satyr's fingers lingered inches from the rosewood handle above the pik's belt.

Snagging Andion's fraying collar, Cord dragged him back while the pik yipped. "What are you doing? Don't trust him!"

"He did no harm," Andion whined, wriggling free.

"That dagger in your belt could've changed that," Kylan said. "Where would his requests end, beyond his freedom, if he held it at your throat?"

"Better give it to me for now," Cord said.

The thief slouched. "He wouldn't do that."

"I would," Ferix admitted. Unashamed, he lay back.

Andion didn't seem to believe him but removed the blade and set it on Cord's palm.

Through the door Kylan had left open, the wings of the butterfly shimmered. Shadows moved across the glass roof of Maeverly's vardo, letting Cord know the girls were still up.

Cord slid the dagger behind his belt. "Are the others back?"

Shaking his head, Kylan said, "It's been hours. Bevin's getting antsy, but Maeverly won't let us check it out." He leaned in to whisper. "I say we go anyway." A dangerous excitement wove through his words.

Cord would've agreed, if it wouldn't have risked putting Kylan on Teague's bad side. "They just agreed to help you. We'll get the answer when they get back."

"Us," Kylan corrected suspiciously. "They're helping us."

Scattered about, Andion's loot reflected the lantern's light. Cord began clearing everything within reach of the cell, starting with some tarnished cutlery. "How would we help? And with what? A spoon and half a clove of garlic?" He offered the crinkly treasure to Kylan's flat stare. "Teague said to wait here."

"Teague said?" Kylan asked. "You trust him?"

Cord scooped up a knitting needle. "I need him to think I do. He's survived Beez before, Kylan. I wanna know how." He did trust in the promise Teague gave him, to keep his friends safe even if he left Cord behind.

"What if they were captured?" Kylan asked. "Or worse, we're just sitting here waiting for the Dregs to claim the prize Teague left for them?"

"He wouldn't leave Maeverly and Bevin behind."

"We're still just sitting here, Cord. Have been for half of the day. How long before we're discovered?"

"I have not received my meal," the satyr said.

Setting the lantern down by a cheese wheel, Kylan removed the knife from the pocket in his boot. He sliced a wedge loose, put it in a silver bowl, and slid it along the planks under the cell door.

"You cannot be serious!" the satyr protested.

"It's more than we've had," Kylan said. "There will be a meal later, but not until Teague and the others return. Bevin can't think clearly enough to focus on his duties."

Ferix examined the cheese, pinching off a nibble to sniff. He tasted it, then chewed contently.

Kylan dragged a stoneware jug to himself and unplugged the cork. He sniffed the contents and reeled away from the fermented odor filling the room. "Well, it's what we have." He placed the jug next to Ferix's cell. "You'll have to manage through the bars."

The satyr eyed the modest container. "What is it?"

"Wine." Kylan sighed.

Ferix gave him an impressed frown and reached for a sample. *He ought to enjoy himself*, Cord thought, which made Kylan's idea to leave all the more appealing. Loosening the scummy satyr's tongue couldn't help but lead to awkward questions and more leering.

"If Bevin's worried, maybe we oughta go," Cord said.

The wine glugged as Ferix lowered it from his lips. "This will surely be my final meal." A silent belch interrupted his laugh.

Kylan snipped off a smaller piece of cheese and served Andion, who had settled onto the quilt the girls had used earlier. He looked at the jug pressed against the satyr's lips again and said, "You'll have to find water."

Putting all of his attention on the black box in his lap, Andion didn't reply. The lid clicked with each touch of Andion's finger.

Cord moved for a better view. The box's engraving depicted a ship in rough waters. In the clouds above it, a string of strange symbols posed a question. Characters marked the waves, some repeating farther at sea.

Andion pressed one of the waves; it remained sunken. After selecting a few more, he held his finger over the dulled ship and pressed. The crests popped up, flush with the others. Andion released a frustrated sigh.

Offering Cord a small chunk of the cheese wheel, Kylan asked, "Shall we?"

Cord took the snack and said to Andion, "We'll be about it then." The cheese didn't have much flavor beyond salt. That didn't stop Kylan from cutting himself another serving before standing.

"While you're out," the satyr moaned, "fetch my pipe from the mouse. If he's dead, please take it from his corpse." Kylan rolled his eyes at the prisoner's innocent shrug.

A sudden gust battered the door against the wagon. Cord leaped out to silence it. When Kylan exited, he cut them off from the lantern light and the satyr's ogling, and latched it closed. Andion's obsession with his puzzle might keep him out of trouble; Cord prayed it would.

A flock of ducks pointed south overhead. Without a cloud to block it, the moonlight flared. To Cord's left, grass taller than mature cornstalks rippled along the length of the caravan.

They snuck beside the butterfly vardo. Metal chimed against glass behind the round windows. Concealed by curtains, the ladies giggled, Maeverly included.

Crouching next to the wheels, Kylan gripped a thick spoke and spied over it. "Do you think Bevin could lift a horse? I'd wager so. Julian's asleep and shackled."

Cord knelt beside Kylan. The horses ambled beyond the cart, where Bevin waited motionlessly as he stared into the distance. Cord thumbed to the whipping reeds away from the half-ogre.

They rounded the vardo and, with breath held, dashed into the tall grass, leaving wakes of swaying stalks behind them. Cord loped to avoid losing Kylan in the brush. After a few minutes, they broke free at the road's edge and paused to listen for Bevin's stomps. None came.

Never had Cord witnessed such an unhindered view. The exposure made him itch for cover, but the sight enthralled him. The valley below resembled a curved game board, squared off with fields walled in by rock, only interrupted by a grove butting up against the town.

Kylan kicked a pebble, sending it to ricochet down the rocky path dipping deep into the dale.

Spindly clouds of smoke rose from the village. The farmers' pride wouldn't be harvested this cycle.

With a glance up to the Glades, Cord held back his memories of Kenton and said, "We oughta leave the road."

They sprinted through the scarce cover, veering north to make sure they didn't run into Bevin's line of sight. When they reached a stretch of hardwoods in the grove next to the town, Cord surveyed the hilltop. Bevin wouldn't be able to see them through the thick canopy.

The rustling leaves above them masked the crunching under their feet as they snuck forward into the odor of burned wood. A few paces in, they found the weathered stone wall that hadn't safeguarded the town well enough. Mortared to a height above Cord's reach, it blocked their path.

Cord rapped his knuckles on it. "Now what?"

"Come on," a familiar voice said.

Cord turned to see Kylan squatting and cupping his hands together in order to boost him up.

"What?" Kylan asked.

"Did you say that?"

Kylan cocked his eyebrow.

"Forget it." Marlone had loved this kind of senseless adventure. Of course he'd be here with him in spirit.

Cord stepped into Kylan's hands and vaulted up. Securing his grip on the crumbling mortar, he pulled his chest up over the gritty surface. Near the main gate, sprigs of smoke escaped the branches above the charred homes reduced to piles of cinders around bricked chimneys. A few smoldered with sparks when the wind lashed them, releasing more smoke and flitters of light. But the fresh kill lay devoid of its predators.

Flecks of mortar scraped beneath Cord's weight as he topped the wall. With a glance down to the garden below, he reached back over to give Kylan a hand up. "Only the homes by the gate are burned. They must be farther in town. The—"

Four eyes stared back at him.

Kylan turned to see what Cord was gaping at just as Andion slapped his leg. Kylan hooted and clapped a hand over his mouth. A smile split the pik's square face.

"You're supposed to be in the vardo!" Kylan hissed. Andion shrugged. "Fine. Then come here," he growled, snatching Andion's tunic.

Squirming out of Kylan's grasp, Andion dove into a cluster of bushes. The same rustle sounded in the garden below Cord's foot. Andion waved him on excitedly.

"He's in," Cord said, offering Kylan his hand again. With a running leap, Kylan was up. Cord checked the ground beneath them before he dropped into the sweet perfume of the garden.

Kylan landed and uttered a curse for the holiday as he took in the freshly harvested patch. "Not even a green tomato."

Wind blasted them as they skulked down a dirt path to the homes untouched by the blaze. Closer to the middle of the hamlet, long planks of stacked stones formed chest-high walls, separating the land around each cabin. Their path crossed with another broad road, leaving them exposed as they scurried across.

Nearing another road crossing, Cord spotted light in the town square. Rather than risk the exposure, he tapped Kylan's shoulder and nodded to a break in the walls.

They entered a yard thick with flowers, bordering the lawn on all sides and the porch of a dark-windowed cabin. Its door stood eerily ajar. Cord kept an eye on it as they made their way to the corner, which would give them a view into the town square. Andion sprinted ahead, tumbling and cartwheeling as they hunkered over to follow.

In the corner between a pair of prickly rosebushes, they peered over the flat stones. The scratching of a shovel froze them. A cabin blocked part of Cord's view to the left side of the square, but he saw plenty.

Dogwoods and benches ringed the dais in the center, bricked up a few feet above the grass. There, torches blazed around three young Judges bound on their knees. The one farthest back bucked against his rope bindings. The others didn't budge. Blue shimmers ran under the tunic of the one closest to Cord, pleading to be healed. Not far from the Judges, fresh graves had supplied a mound of dirt.

Kylan directed Cord's attention to a neighboring garden. Green light bounced behind a veil of string beans.

"You will never get an answer out of me, Abandoned!" the bucking Judge yelled.

They ducked. Kylan recovered first and waved Cord and Andion up.

Veen walked into view from behind the cabin and speared the dirt mound with a shovel on his way to the dais.

Cuts on the Judge's face had darkened his beard with blood, but he stared defiantly at Veen.

The green light snuffed out before Teague hurdled the garden wall. "Ah, now," he said. The Judge struggled to keep his balance when he turned his head toward Teague. "We've already been through this Abandoned balderdash. So, for the last time, let's forget all of that." Rage held the captive's face as Teague hopped up next to him. "How do they do it? What is the Tribunal hiding from the rest of Cyr?"

Veen whispered something in Teague's ear, then retrieved his shovel.

Ducking, Kylan tugged on Cord's sleeve. He pointed through the wall and mouthed *Judges!* Andion crouched and put his back to the wall.

Two Judges and a High Guard deftly approached on the road. Oblivious, they passed by Cord and the others.

He rose in time to see them stop at the cabin by the square, not thirty feet from them, and spy around it. Cord whispered, "We have to warn Teague."

Making a face that called Cord everything from an idiot to a dog's favorite thing to lick, Kylan said, "They can handle three."

A battle cry erupted from the square. With their weapons raised, three more Judges scudded behind another High Guard toward Teague. Teague stumbled back in surprise.

The soldiers near Cord waited behind the cabin.

"What about now?" he asked Kylan.

Veen joined the fray before the soldiers reached the dais. The shovel clanged against a Judge's forearm, disarming him.

Teague rolled away from the arcing swing of the High Guard's attack and stabbed his throwing knife into the unarmored backside of the guard's knee.

Kylan nudged Cord. Following Kylan's horrified gaze to the roof above the waiting reinforcements, Cord saw Andion struggling to keep his balance as he squeezed a stone to his chest. As large as a sword on a human, the rosewood-handled dagger had found its way back to Andion's belt. "Shit," Cord muttered.

The pik's large, cloth-shoed feet stopped at the roof's edge as he peeped over to the High Guard and Judges below. He slipped and whined, releasing the stone and catching the lip of the roof. When a Judge looked up at the sound, the stone crashed into his face.

Andion fell.

Cord leaped over the wall and rushed forward to help. The conscious Judge kicked the bushes beneath the ledge where the pik would have fallen. He was gone. The High Guard glanced around in confusion until his eyes locked on Cord standing in the wide intersection of the road. Marred with a long scar from temple to chin, the Guard sneered before he knocked against the Judge's arm to get his attention.

Kylan landed next to Cord.

The wiry Judge moved away from the Guard, stepping onto the road ahead of Kylan. "What the blazes is a Catalyst doing here?" the Judge asked.

Cord cringed, hoping Kylan hadn't caught that.

His superior put himself between Cord and the square where Teague and Veen still fought. Readying his hammer, the Guard answered, "Dying."

As the Judge barked a laugh and drew his bastard sword, Kylan said, "I'm beginning to feel regret."

"Just stay calm," Cord said, slipping his belt knife free. "We'll get out of this."

"Oh, I know," Kylan agreed. "But why'd I have to get the scrawny one? It'll be like wrestling a worm."

Cord grinned, which stalled the Guard for a moment.

"Stay close," Kylan whispered. "I may need your curse." In a flash, he flung his father's knife at the Judge. The soldier cried out as it dug into his hip. Kylan leaped forward. Dodging swipes of the Judge's sword, he easily set him off-balance.

Raising his hammer, the High Guard charged at Cord.

Cord jumped to the side and ducked beneath a wild swing. It cracked against the stone wall behind him. Borrowing Teague's technique, he jabbed his knife into the back of the Guard's leg. The High Guard was faster than Cord expected; his hammer grazed Cord's crown before a solid punch landed on Cord's forehead, toppling him back.

Kylan had plucked his father's knife free from the fallen Judge and was running to tackle the Guard when Carolle yelled, "Hold!"

They all looked up to the roof above the garden where they had been spying.

Carolle squatted on the ledge with her longbow drawn, the arrow set for the Guard's head. "Drop the hammer."

Grunting with each breath, the Guard considered her words. His scar trembled in fury. Finally, he let it fall.

Andion appeared out of nowhere and grabbed it before disappearing again.

"*Diolch*, boys," Carolle said with a chuckle in her voice. "There's right entertaining. Really, my sides ache from holding it in. But enough is enough; time the Hook took over."

The High Guard slumped to the ground. "You will die for this," he said to Cord. "The Chancellor will burn your wicked bones to ash!"

Carolle whistled to the square where Teague had a blade at the other Guard's throat and Veen stood among the downed Judges on the lawn. They both perked up at the noise. Teague forced the Guard to limp forward.

The shovel spun in Veen's hands as he strode down the road toward them. "What's the root of this nonsense, boy?" he asked Kylan. "You wanted to be separated from your friends again? No, I know. You just wanted the pleasure of my company on another horseback ride. I'm flattered. I am. Too bad my wife snared you first." The monks laughed.

Kylan crossed his arms and huffed. "Ferix wanted his pipe."

Teague wasn't amused. "This is serious. Ye shouldn't be down here."

"Oh, give over," Kylan said. "Someone should have checked back in with us. Bevin is nervy." He gestured to the High Guard and over to the Judge. "And we helped."

It would have been more convincing without his glance up to Carolle. She let loose a shout of a laugh and kept giggling as she let her bowstring slacken. "You should have seen it, Stille!"

"Then go," Teague said in a somber tone. "Tell Bevin we're fine."

Abruptly, Veen shoved Cord into Kylan.

The High Guard's swing narrowly missed Cord's neck. Dripping with blood, the belt knife Cord had left in his leg went for Veen. Swipe after swipe, it missed.

Finally, Veen snatched the Guard's wrist. Spinning, the monk drove his heel under the scarred soldier's chin. The snap stopped Cord cold.

"Veen!" Teague yelled.

The Guard's armor clanged and scraped down the stone wall as his body fell.

With barely time to blink, Veen launched the belt knife toward Teague's prisoner.

Teague's hands clapped around the handle inches from the captive's throat.

The living Guard stumbled back, mouthing wordlessly until he managed, "Rodders!"

With a murderous glower for Veen, Teague kicked the Guard's injured knee. When the soldier collapsed with a shout, he punched him in the chin. Blue lights danced around his jaw and leg as the Guard fell back.

"You want us to fail, do you?" Teague shouted. "Is that your intent?"

Carolle dropped from the roof to the stone wall, then to the road. Her humor had left her.

"I'm protecting you!" Veen said. Hearing the monk raise his voice put Cord's hair on its end. "You shouldn't use it! You shouldn't even touch it! 'Tis that sort of thing we're on the run from."

"No," Teague said. "We need this, Veen. The Hook needs it!" Veen's bald head shook with chagrin. "If all goes well, 'twill be a day, maybe two."

"A day of what?" Cord asked.

They fell silent. The monks looked to Teague.

"Well, that answers that," Kylan said.

Teague removed his cap from his silver hair and plopped it onto the garden wall. "Veen, take these two back to the caravan, while I do what we were sent to this cursed forgotten island to do." His fingers dug into his collar and brought out a necklace dangling a black circle. He cupped the pendant to his chest and went back to the Guard he'd knocked out.

A tiny smile from his wife encouraged Veen to do as Teague asked. Veen snatched a handful of Kylan's tunic and hauled him down the main road.

Kylan ignored the small monk and twisted to see behind him as he was towed. Cord followed, watching behind them as well.

Teague crouched by the High Guard. Hanging the pendant over his palm, he set it spinning.

"What's he holding?" Kylan asked.

Now suspended by Teague's fist, the circle swung in the wind over the Guard's head. Teague's jaw moved, but Cord couldn't hear his words.

"What's he doing?"

Veen released Kylan and squared off, facing them. Pointing at Cord, he said, "This one should be tucked away in a vardo."

Angered by more secrets and questions, Cord stepped between them. "By virtue, I deserve to know who's killing the villagers!"

"By virtue, you don't belong to yourself anymore, boyo," Veen said. "You're our responsibility, us and your friends now. We've chosen to protect your arse against the Dregs, which could easily bring our end. You'd throw that in our faces and toss yourself in harm's way for your own curiosities, yeah? 'Tis shameful."

"I never asked for that. For any of it. Look, I need—"

"No," Veen said without sympathy. "You didn't ask for it. And yet we may be saving the world by putting something else before our wants.

You should look beyond yourself and do the same. Vengeance is never as urgent as it feels. If you can't see that clearly, we should shackle you in manacles like that lanky streak of piss."

Grinding his teeth, Cord tried to stare Veen down but knew he was right. Headmaster Angsly wouldn't have asked him to take risks for the sake of avenging him. Cord could retaliate in time, no matter how wrong it felt to put it aside.

"It was my idea," Kylan said. His voice held no regret, just ownership. "Tell us why Teague needs the High Guard. I assume that's why you bound the Judges, to ambush them?" Veen started shaking his head. "Don't deny it. Teague saved him! I doubt it was to show off his trinkets."

The High Guard shrieked in pain.

Veen winced as much as his steely face allowed. "Nasty business, this one, boys. Let us interfere while we can, yeah?" His tattooed arm rose toward the caravan with his forefinger extended.

Hooking his thumbs over his belt, Kylan appeared in a new light. He negotiated with the monk through a bond of respect, as an equal. And while Cord had failed to take down his High Guard, Kylan had brought down an armed Judge with just a knife. Ashes, even Andion had taken down one of the Judges.

With a low growl, Veen gave in and lowered his arm. "C'mere," he said. "I don't know why we're here, not fully. People are panicking on the continent. There's a shift happening, so. At first, 'twas just as if magic were fading. Fewer people have it these days, and they're all weaker than the last generation. Then the dragons vanished, except those crimson bastards. Silver, swamp, jade—all of them! Gone overnight, after eons in their lairs and temples. Countries that have been allies for centuries are now threatening to advance against one another for petty reasons.

"Not just on the continent, neither. The Cloud is swelling and sending out icebergs into the Saratial Sea. Do you know how fecking hot the Saratial Sea is?"

A repeating squeal from the High Guard ended Veen's rant. The wounded animal was silenced.

"All of Cyr is suffering these strange events," the monk said.

"Except Merith?" Kylan asked. "What does the High Guard have to do with it? Sure, they abhor magic; that doesn't mean they could affect the rest of the world."

Veen glanced through them toward Teague. "No, not exactly, boy. 'Tis complicated. I don't know the full connection. Not sure if Teague does. I'll just say this; Shallyghal may not be as dead as Merith believes. Now strike off."

Cord elbowed Kylan and jogged ahead a few steps. Then Kylan said, "You were supposed to escort us."

"Strike! Off!" Veen patted him on the arm and watched them climb the slope.

The High Guard's screamed pleas of mercy set their pace. Reluctant to use the main gate, they left town the way they'd come in and didn't stop running until they reached the lifewood vardo, and didn't speak until Kylan latched the door behind them.

Odors of overripe fruit and spice saturated the air. Ferix grinned and hoisted a pewter cup in cheers.

Cord groaned. He had forgotten what they had left behind.

With the High Guard's hammer on the quilt next to him, Andion raised his focus from his puzzle box and waited expectantly for clues on whether to smile at their adventure or sulk at the disappointing outcome.

Kylan fell to his knees and panted. "What was that medallion Teague wore?" he asked Cord. "And that green light?"

"I don't know," Cord said. "Whatever it is, Teague's using it to get answers about the Tribunal."

"There is something evil afoot with the High Guard," Kylan said, "beyond their usual torment."

"But how?" Cord asked. "They're not magi." The comment sparked a surly face from Kylan. "You know what I mean."

Lifting the hammer for a closer look, Kylan said, "They may know something about Shallyghal that we don't. Seems right, really. The Chancellor has been here since that time. And something that powerful may be what the Dregs are after, not just you. Or maybe not you at all."

Cord glanced over at the satyr, who appeared lost in his unheard song. "I'm not sure whether I should pray for that." Cord lifted the dagger from Andion's belt without any protest from the pik. "The Tribunal can't even purge magic from Merith. I don't think it makes sense to blame them for the rest. They are burning the villages, but how are the villagers dying?"

Clacking his hooves together, Ferix sang, "Clovers. Lots of clovers." He took another gulp.

Kylan grated out a sigh. "Veen is going to kill me. Did you drink the whole jug? Where did you get a cup?" Kylan's arched eyebrow darkened Andion's demeanor.

"He cannot use a cup as a weapon!"

Redirecting his reproach to Ferix, Kylan said, "He's not your squire and does not run errands for you."

The satyr tapped out a tune with his hooves and rolled the back of his head against the wall in rhythm to an unheard melody.

Andion pecked at the box again, shook his head as it reset itself, and pecked some more.

Cord tossed a pillow down and sat next to the untouched cheese Kylan had cut for the pik. "You should eat, Andion. We may need more of your help to get out of this."

"In that case," Kylan said, "pass the jug, Ferix."

Andion's lip curled in a silent threat. He tightened his belt around the dagger.

"Stop doing that!" Cord said, seizing the dagger again.

The satyr leaned his head against the iron bars before clinking his cup against them. "Never die sober."

Chapter 31: Trust in Titles

The next morning, the caravan still sat next to the celery-green grass swaying in the breeze that had calmed considerably overnight. Lured by the aroma of eggs cooking, Cord left the stairs of the lifewood vardo. If Bevin had resumed his chores, Teague had finished his torture. The hairs on Cord's neck stirred when he recalled the High Guard's screams. Who were these people he'd entrusted his friends to?

Gray clouds blocked the sun in their lazy crawl from one horizon to the other. Their dreary shadows were reflected on the faces around the campfire.

Rorry poked at the contents of her bowl with her spoon. Her sister's ribbon tied her hair back off her shoulders. The blue coating her nails matched.

Cord grinned, until he saw Julian spying on her from Bevin's worktable. After what had happened last night, Cord already wanted to hit something. That rascal's nose would work just fine.

Only Maeverly appeared lively, in a bright purple dress that could have been seen from Croathe and a belt made of a hundred silver medallions. Her hands emphasized her every word as she chatted quietly with Scarlett on their stools.

Bevin cracked eggs on the edge of an iron skillet. His brawny hands added sliced red and green vegetables before moving the skillet to the fire. After a dinner of cheese, the enchanting scent reeled Cord closer to the others, and to Teague, who now sat cross-legged on a fallen tree.

Even on this muggy morning, steam escaped the tea in the mercenary leader's cup. Deep in thought, Teague ran his finger in circles around the medallion hidden beneath his black-and-blue jerkin. His eyes had dark circles under them; the torture must have run late. "Let's make it quick, Bevin," Teague said as Cord sat next to Rorry. "I've already felt a few drops. That storm could catch us." Then he cleared his throat.

Maeverly perked up.

"Cord," Teague said, "come with us." The charmless invitation was not a request, though Maeverly smiled and directed Scarlett to keep reading.

Cord let the magus walk between him and Teague as they escorted him back to the wagons, away from breakfast and Rorry's curious watch.

Kylan stumbled down the stairs of the lifewood vardo as they walked by. His face sagged after a night of drinking with the satyr. The unusual spikes of his hair gave the others a quick laugh. He squinted his way toward the food. The fresh tunic helped him look slightly better than dead.

Cord prayed the harsh morning-after would deter Kylan from repeating the offense. Whispered debauchery from the drunken prisoner hadn't made for a restful night. In truth, he hadn't understood half of it and hoped Andion hadn't either.

Teague opened the yellow door to the green vardo and let Maeverly enter to light a lamp on the writing table and take a seat on its stool.

"You forgot this last night," Teague said, handing Cord the belt knife he'd left in the High Guard.

Cord hesitated before taking the cleaned blade. While his imagination played through a few possibilities of what had happened to the captive High Guard and the rest of the Judges, his stomach wrenched. Coaxed with a reassuring smile from Maeverly, Cord climbed inside.

Impossible as it seemed, the ornate wagon smelled cleaner than its owner, a mix of wood polish and bath powder. Cord sat on the cot under the window, scooting the neatly folded linens and pillow aside.

Cord studied the drawers across from him until he kicked something with his heel. A slender black scabbard with silver script lay underneath the cot. "That's Kylan's sword."

"Aye," Teague said, stepping inside to close the door. "Scarlett said as much." He crossed his legs to sit in the narrow space between the cot and the drawers.

Cord's knees were inches from the others'. He definitely preferred the lifewood vardo, maybe even with the scummy satyr.

"As we're all at risk for something none of us fully understands," Teague said, "I've asked Maeverly to assist in determining exactly what makes you the *tek'aran*."

So it was his turn to be interrogated, trapped between a mage and an inquisitor. Cord's hands started sweating. "I prayed for him. The man you tortured last night."

Teague's mouth straightened to a thin line.

"That man," Maeverly said, "he wasn't what you believe him to be."

Never taking his eyes off Teague, Cord asked, "Did he confess to killing the villagers?"

"Would it justify my actions, if he had?" Teague replied.

Unwilling to surrender the truth and admit it would, Cord shook his head.

"He didn't," Teague said and slid the sheathed sword onto Cord's lap. "Perhaps you'd be kind enough to give that to Kylan for me."

Running his fingers over the silver script as he had seen Rorry do a hundred times, Cord relaxed. It was oddly comforting. "You said you'd tell me more when I told you why I think I'm the *tek'aran*," Cord said. "Did someone pay you to find the source of these massacres?"

Teague's face gave nothing away. "I can't say for certain. That is to say, I haven't found answers to the questions we have."

Maeverly didn't seem convinced by her leader's response. "After we fiddled about for a full night, let's hope Beez stayed equally distracted long enough to keep his decaying breath off your necks."

"We'll keep a jackrabbit's pace, as best we can," Teague agreed with a warning frown. "You know yourself, there's no guarantee that seizing the northern ports is outside of the Dregs' plan."

Cord's chest tightened. "It's not just Beez? There are more of them?"

Teague shook his head apologetically. "We don't know any more about the Dregs' intentions now than we did yesterday."

"Well, let's get some answers," Maeverly said. Whatever the girls had done last night had left her voice raspy, but her eyes sparkled with excitement. "Now, Teague mentioned you can use magic?"

Putting his hands together, Cord said, "It's more of a healing curse, I guess."

Maeverly jerked her head back and asked, "Healing?" She shared a dumbfounded expression with Teague. Then the mage handed Cord a sealed jar from the desk. The glass fogged around his clammy hands. "Don't worry, lad. It won't hurt. Hold this and close your eyes. Good. Clear your mind and think only of Rorry."

Heat pricked Cord's cheeks. He opened his eyes, trying to determine what game she was playing at.

"Don't be bashful," Maeverly said. "Your eyes mine her for diamonds every time she swishes by."

Cord looked to the torturer for help. "I'm not comfortable with this."

"Aye. That makes two of us."

Maeverly seized the jar. "I was merely determining if he has other abilities."

Teague worked a leather glove off his left hand. Two signet rings adorned it now, the black stone in silver from before and a green stone in a gold band. They shared the symbol of a heron in flight. "Healing is a new magic to me and more likely what the Dregs want with you. A demonstration of your known abilities may be more appropriate." He slipped a knife from his sleeve.

"No!" Cord said—too late.

Teague's blade had already slid across the back of his hand, opening the skin. He extended his arm, shimmering blue where red trickled out to drip off his wrist.

"I receive the injury that I heal, just a smaller one."

"Ah," Teague said. "My apologies." He pulled his arm back and placed a black kerchief over the wound. It didn't hide the blue shimmers.

The grudge Cord held against Teague wasn't one he harbored fairly. They sought answers to the same questions. If he ever wanted to find out what had happened in Kenton, he had to accept that Teague was an ally. Cord removed Teague's cap; the silver-haired man watched him with amusement. "It's easier if I touch your head." His fingertips gripped Teague's temples.

They both jerked when the trance kicked in, presenting Teague's health to Cord.

An echo in the trance, Maeverly's voice asked, "Can you describe what you're experiencing?"

"The wound glows . . . and also . . ." Cord muttered, awash in the chilling flow. He examined the man from head to toe. Though he couldn't see it, he felt an old burn on Teague's back in the shape of a ring. "A circle is burned into your back." That must be what kept Beez out. Afraid of breaking the protection, Cord left it. With the cut mended, he released Teague.

Falling back against the door, Teague caught his breath. He wiped his hand with the black kerchief. The skin was whole. Cord showed them where a smaller cut had appeared on his hand. Blood dotted the injury, no more than a bad cat scratch.

Surrendering to a deep yawn, Cord fought the urge to lie down. "I usually sleep after," he mumbled. "When it takes hold of me, I can hardly stop myself until every wound is closed. Then, when it ends . . ." Another yawn escaped.

Maeverly grabbed his arm with a calloused hand, then took Teague's. "And they are always soporific? You sleep immediately after you go into this trance?"

Cord nodded. "I can barely stay awake, and if I do, I collapse at the first chance."

"That is perplexing, and extraordinary," Maeverly said. "This is nothing I've heard of! I honestly doubt anyone has. And yet, I sense no latent magical talents in you at all."

"Then I'm not a magus?" Cord asked, his voice more excited than he'd intended.

"I'm afraid that's not entirely true," she said. "Did you know there are different schools of magic? Sorcery, for example."

Teague sighed, staving off what appeared to be a lecture forming.

She waved her hand. "A lesson for another time. Suffice it to say, you use magic. Why that does not connect you to the arsenal most magi have is the question. I've never seen evidence to suggest there were different types of magic, just different approaches and spells, stronger talents, and the like. Except—no that wouldn't be possible—centuries ago perhaps. Or maybe?" Suddenly aware they were watching her ramble, she asked, "How was it for you, Teague?"

"Quite refreshing. I feel as though I slept through the night with a cool pillow and a warm blanket. If you can't feel it, J, this ability must be tied to the title. I wish we knew what it meant."

Maeverly agreed. "Which leads me to believe it's not something others can learn."

Cord's eyelids closed. When they opened and his eyes refocused, the others were watching him. He yawned again.

Rising, Teague said, "Rest here. I'll rouse you when next we stop. I'm afraid our curiosity has cost you your breakfast. We'll get fruit or bread, whatever Bevin will allow, and send it with someone, yes?"

With permission, Cord lay on his side. The down pillow lulled his senses away. "Not Julian," Cord managed. "Never him . . ."

* * *

Rorry smoothed down her dress over her legs, waiting for clues as to what had transpired with Cord.

Teague had more of a spring in his step when he and Maeverly returned.

In her violet linen dress, Maeverly squatted on her stool against the fallen tree and disturbed Scarlett's reading to resume their discussion of honeybees. The woman seemed quite wrapped up in grooming Scarlett for the Tower, contrary to the way she chewed the word each time she said it or "mage."

Kylan leaned against Rorry and let his empty bowl drop to the grass. He looked as well as she felt after an evening of sampling what the aquamarine ring had to offer. She could still taste the potent strawberry libation twisting her stomach to liberate her breakfast. It had not affected Maeverly or Scarlett as strongly, despite drinking five servings each. On second thought, that might have been why Scarlett had asked for willow bark this morning. She often did for headaches.

"I need a volunteer to deliver some food to Cord and to ride with him this morning," Teague said.

Rorry's curiosity won a flashed debate in her mind. Doing her best to maintain composure amid internal scrutiny, she rose next to Kylan's raised arm and said, "I would be glad to." Her tone trilled, even and innocent. Nothing suggested otherwise. That was, if you ignored the shock on her friends' faces.

"Lucky man," Maeverly teased.

Rorry let the comment pass without changing her demeanor.

"He is not worthy of it," Julian said. "I beg your pardon, my lady, but I can manage the task."

Careful to hide her surprise at his sudden manners, Rorry slowly turned to him and, relieved to see he was not ogling her, politely smiled.

"Besides," he said, "I would be grateful for the opportunity to ride in a more comfortable fashion."

She could not argue that point directly and cringed at her new tactic as it came out of her mouth. "I am afraid I must insist. Though I do appreciate your situation, I would cherish conversing with another noble. In our escape, we have yet to have a proper exchange or to discuss the capital even. It would do a world of good for my nerves." That was the best she could come up with? Be the silly councilmember's daughter that others always assumed she was? She could not even be certain Cord had relayed that particular lie to the Hook.

From Kylan's arched brow to the slight curve in Teague's lip, everyone recognized it for what it was, except Julian, who was confused, or perhaps conflicted. She blushed but held her head high. Cord had obviously filled in the Hook on his true identity. And now, so had she, even if she suspected they all knew. As embarrassing as it was, this served as proof that the four of them needed to be on the same page.

"Sounds reasonable," Kylan said.

She shot him a look of subtle irritation, nearly exaggerating it when his teeth stabbed his grin.

Regardless, Teague held out a waterskin and a couple of pears to her. "You are right to complain, Julian," he said. "Bevin can be a speck rank and cares as much as a dog rolling in manure. You can ride with me."

The giant's eyebrows drooped as he gave himself a deep sniff.

Julian pouted. "You should let me rest inside one of the wagons this time."

"Ah," Teague said. "Maeverly, do you mind if Julian—"

"Forget it," Julian snipped. He turned his back to them and folded the preparation table.

From over her book's binding, Scarlett stole a glance at his backside. Rorry felt affronted. When would Scarlett stop trying to sell herself short? She deserved better than that whiny pest.

With a curtsy, Rorry said, "I will be off."

She had not anticipated that Teague would escort her, eliciting memories of her father with his scent. As they passed the lifewood vardo, he whispered, "There's something I left at the end of the cot. Would you mind telling Cord 'tis his now?"

"Of course," she said. Did he believe the others would be jealous of his favor? He owed them nothing. In fact, it might ease the tension to exhibit his generosity toward Cord now, given his shameful display of cowardice after their encounter with Beez.

With the gentlemanly gesture of opening and closing the door for her, Teague left her alone. With Cord.

Hunched over in the doorway, she feared moving and waking him, despite her quest for answers.

The gold feather rose and fell in an even cadence beneath his charmed face.

She watched it until two thumps from above gave her a moment's warning that Teague had the reins. Rorry slid onto the stool at the writing desk just as the vardo jounced. It rocked until they reached the road. When the rumbling evened, the oblong fruit and waterskin joined an empty jar and unlit lamp on the desk.

Harnessed by its strap over Cord's sandaled foot, a simple yet well-made quiver struggled to remain upright. Burnished iron reinforced the felt-lined cache. The leather matched the gloves Cord had not removed since receiving them. What was Teague's game with these gifts? Were they rewards or attempts to buy Cord's trust?

Master Clienne's katana lay next to Cord on the cot. She tried squelching her guilt by adding urgency to her promise to return the weapons. Would he come after them? A premier wish didn't sound like the kind of thing someone would accept as lost.

Rorry busied herself with the other sights of Teague's vardo. The ebony dresser teased her briefly before she wrapped her fingers around one of the dimpled brass knobs. Should she? She most certainly should! Even if it yielded no discovery, the search would lend more justification to her volunteering.

Having successfully searched everything without a lock, which only applied to a drawer of assorted silk kerchiefs in every color of the rainbow and another full of munitions, she retook her seat.

The writing table offered less in its mahogany drawer, parchment covered in hen scratch, a bottle of ink, and two spare quills. She caressed her face with one of the feathers before replacing it and closing the drawer.

The green wagon plunged through a dip in the road, sending Rorry's stomach to her throat. Wood creaked around her but trundled on without further protest. Roads between towns were not commonly used and were oft in need of repair. She rolled her eyes at the realization that she had just thought what her father had said during every trip to Croathe.

Still, Cord slept. Would nothing wake him?

She watched the scenery change through the parted lace curtains of the three-paned window. The world sagged beneath the clouds. Rorry's gaze drifted downward for increasing stints. Each time she reset it to outside.

Tossing a pear between her hands, she inspected Cord again. He appeared gentle. At the same time, his training made him strong and quick, able to best an armed and armored High Guard. Yet her discomfort now dissipated around him, much the way it did around Kylan.

Since they had left Brewing, the previously ever-present phantom scent of coal rarely arose to bury her.

No! She would not gaze upon Cord and think of Grary! Cord had saved Kylan. He fought the army now. With a deep breath, Rorry cleared her mind.

She shouldn't have volunteered. Touching his lips with an imaginary finger, she let herself feel hope again, a desire she didn't need to fear. Silly girl. Even if Cord reciprocated the interest, which she suspected to be the case, it could not lead to marriage. He was Merithian and held the same standards any Merithian man did. Worse, he defended the Chancellor, as though corruption did not trickle down in a tyranny.

The last thing she wanted upon arrival to the continent was a suitor to cloud her decisions and bind her to his whims. "Still, a tryst would be fun," she could hear Kylan say. She blushed.

To increase her discomfort, the fates brought Carolle sitting astride Nightingale to the window. No matter how well Carolle feigned surprise and a smile when she acknowledged Rorry, she spied. Well, she would be disappointed if she wanted to see anything beyond a woman sitting in boredom and tossing fruit about.

Nightingale fell back out of sight as Rorry chastised herself and blamed the strawberry liquor for altering her judgment, though she knew its effects had worn off hours ago.

Cord appeared far more comfortable on a cot than anyone surely could be. *Tek'aran?* The handsome riddle drifted inside himself too; the devout follower of a religion that would burn him, betrayed by a source of love, by faith.

Only a few freckles ran across his nose. Their children would inherit them—if that were to happen. Again, she blushed. And, once more, Nightingale entered the view.

Carolle unabashedly winked at her. Did she have no decency?

No. Rorry had erred, being alone with a man, despite all of it. Well, better to face fears, else they will tear at your skin in your dreams. She groaned at thinking her father's words again.

Kylan was correct about one thing. The South Thornton garments gave reason to be thankful. Cord's legs were quite firm.

"Is that pear for me?"

Rorry stood, knocking her head into the ceiling. The pear fell from her hand. Cord caught it. Unable to look at him until the heat in her face subsided, she watched raindrops trail down the glass. When had it started raining?

"Please sit," he said. "I didn't realize Teague would ask you to ride with me. I figured it'd be Kylan."

After taking the stool again, she moved the waterskin to the cot. "If you are thirsty," she said, not connecting with his brown eyes. "Did you have pleasant dreams?"

He grunted, "No dreams."

"Is that disconcerting?"

"I'm not sure." The quiver strap fell from his foot. "What's this?"

"It is yours, a gift from Teague."

He picked it up and inspected it from every angle with less enthusiasm than she'd expected. "Quivers slow you down," he explained. "Maybe I can hook it to my belt somehow." After briefly studying the buckled strap, he laid the quiver next to him. "Did Kylan tell you about last night?"

Her back stiffened. Kylan had sat next to her through most of their breakfast without a proper greeting, much less conversation. "No. Judging by his disheveled appearance this morning, I did not believe he wanted to converse." He would speak with her about this when next she saw him. Surely he understood the importance of gossip at a time like this!

She was going to relay the same lesson to Cord about this leap of faith in revealing his past to the Hook until he said, "We snuck down to the village."

"What? Why?" Nock foolishness at its finest.

Cord debated answering after receiving her patronizing tone.

She tried to smooth it out. "You could have invited Scarlett and me."

He seemed to accept the statement as a reduction to her judgment of the idiocy. "Kylan—we," he said.

Kylan.

"We were concerned because they'd been gone for hours. We were just checking in on them."

Yes, as simple as peeking in on a sleeping child. Men could be bullheaded at times. *What is it about adventure that sponges up their reason?*

"They caught us," he admitted. "Well, Carolle did, after we took down a couple of Judges and a High Guard."

"One would assume scouts are skilled at that sort of thing," she said, only removing her scolding tone toward the end of the sentence with a less than hardy giggle. "And throwing yourself into harm's way, how was that received by our uncompensated mercenaries?"

"As well as you'd suspect, I suppose," he said with a sheepish grin. She shared no amusement, putting his shoulders back in defense. "Right. Well, we saw Teague use . . ." He contorted his face. "I mean, we saw Teague using something that created a green light."

Rorry sighed. Cord relayed news as well as her father. "Did you see what it was?"

"A black pendant, a circle. He wears it on his necklace." Cord studied the pear in his hands. "He tortured a High Guard with it."

She would not have expected that to worry Cord. Had he already forgotten his own story of High Guards' cruelty in South Thornton? No, perhaps Cord did not want to put Teague on the same level as the High Guard. That bothered him. This was a fortunate turn of events then. No matter how many assurances Teague and his companions laid at their feet, she could not trust the flirt, and neither should Cord.

Pear juice ran down the corners of Cord's mouth and dripped down his chin as he devoured the fruit, unleashing its sweet scent. He wiped his face on his sleeve. "Sorry, I'm always hungry after I mend."

"They had you heal one of them?"

He nodded as he chewed. When he swallowed, he said, "To see if it was magic. Teague cut his hand and asked me to heal it."

She furrowed her brow. "Is he disturbed? If not magic, what else could it be?"

Cord rubbed the back of his hand, though she did not see why. His hand seemed fine to her. "Maeverly said I'm not—well, I'm not exactly sure what she said. I use magic but not like most magi." He stopped chewing as his eyes glossed. "Do you think they'll make me visit one of the Towers when we get to the continent?"

"It will be your choice," she answered. That did not reassure him. "I will join you, if you wish—we all will."

Thunder rolled. Through the window, lightning created a dazzling display, eerily concentrated in one direction. Carolle was nowhere to be seen outside. Cord scooted over to give Rorry a better view, but she stayed seated on the stool.

Finished with his meal, Cord cast the stem next to the door. "Here we are, the noble pretending to be a commoner and the commoner pretending to be a noble." He laughed to himself.

"Only you are no longer pretending, are you, soldier?" she said heatedly. "You were forthright with the Hook. I could tell when I lied on your behalf."

He shrugged curtly.

"We need to get our stories together."

"Then let's just be honest! I'm tired of these lies, all of this manipulation to hide—I don't even know who is offended by what anymore, Rorry. I'm a magic-cursed cadet of the Kenton Academe. You're a noble trying to reach the continent to find her enslaved sister. Let those be our stories for a change!"

A clap of thunder loud enough to rattle the vardo silenced them. Rain tapped against the window harder now.

How long had it been since Rorry had been free to wear her own face, not a cheerful mask for propriety? Even now, in this inescapable crisis, she held back truths tied to her flight.

Staring out the window, Cord said, "I know you think it was reckless. But running down to that village, it felt like Marlone was there. I know it wasn't my fault, what happened to him, and I might not have been able to save him, but I'll always regret not sneaking into the academe with him."

Running her hand down the dresser, Rorry played with the knobs. "Perhaps you should not listen to me. I do not always feel what I am supposed to, not anymore. Trust, least of all." Taking a deep breath, she tried to summon the girl inside her, careless and open. "I was not entirely honest with you in the tunnels and would like your forgiveness for that."

She could feel his eyes on her. "Finding Alis was only part of my reason to leave Brewing. The blacksmith's apprentice attempted to blackmail me into marriage. He did not wish to enter the Seeding and saw me as a means to an end." Blinking, she tried to clear her eyes. If she could not control herself, she was not ready for this.

"Blackmail you with what?"

She released a halfhearted laugh. "The very nature of blackmail suggests it is not something you wish to share."

"You brought it up." The cot creaked as he leaned forward. "Rorry, you confessed to stealing Scarlett's uncle's weapons. I saw you kill that High Guard . . ."

She wiped her cheeks and glared at him.

He held his hands up consolingly. "I'm just saying, I didn't judge you for that. So what can't you tell me now?"

Her lips smacked when she opened her mouth to say, "Later." Drawing herself up, she met his warm eyes. "I promise to tell you once we reach the continent, if I am not compelled sooner. Can you respect my discretion on this?"

"Of course," he said earnestly.

Without standing, she opened the top drawer with the silk kerchiefs and pulled a silver one free to run over her face.

Cord snickered at her. "Already went through his drawers, huh?"

Unable to stop a giggle, Rorry let it take her over.

The vardo jolted. It shook violently as it raced down the road. Teague yelled something outside.

Rorry pressed against the dresser and the writing desk to keep her seat.

"The thunder must've spooked the horses!" Cord said. He caught the jar after it slid from the desk, and braced the lamp.

Each bump jostled the window. Much more of this and Rorry was certain the vardo's axles would break.

Carolle flew past the window on Nightingale. Slowly, they brought the horses back under control and eventually to a stop. Snippets of a conversation between Carolle and Teague reached them but little more than murmurs.

Next to Cord, Rorry put her face to the window. Maeverly passed by wearing a bizarre wide-brimmed black hat with a beryl-green scarf wrapped around it and under her chin.

"Perhaps we should join the others in the satyr's vardo?" Rorry asked, gaining a grimace from Cord. She did hope it had more to do with the satyr than the proclivities he shared with Kylan. Standing, she waited at the door for his answer and removed the silk ribbon from her hair.

"All right. Fine." He slung the quiver and waterskin over his shoulders and picked up the Ghost Augur's katana while she folded the ribbon and stored it in the top of her boot. "And thanks for the pears, Rorry."

She curtsied, unlatched the door, and exited into the warm summer downpour.

Veen smirked from his seat behind the four Northpelts hauling the bulky lifewood wagon but did not dare meet her eyes as she hurried by.

Now Kylan would give her a proper retelling of the night's events before she let him have the sharp side of her tongue. But first, she needed to collect Scarlett; she might know something about this talisman. Rorry shouted back for Cord to go in without her.

Hurrying to the end of the butterfly vardo, Rorry's hand pressed the latch of the azure door before she realized they had stopped in front of a cemented rock wall, a town wall.

Chapter 32: Spy and Cry

Scarlett kicked herself for not leaving when Veen retrieved Cord to help with the horses. Rorry's censure of Kylan filled the vardo, much to the amusement of Andion and the prisoner. Scarlett brought the book closer to her face.

Vision enchantments on mirrors, sending whispers over the wind, turning wood to porcelain . . . With as many recently rediscovered spells as *Essential Focus* detailed, Scarlett hadn't found one to assist with Beez. And as intriguing as they all were, they were years beyond her ability—assuming the core of her power was strong enough to conjure them once attuned. She flipped the pages to the Masters of Craft section in the back again. Those spells shouldn't be beyond Joseb, assuming he was strong enough.

Someone knocked on the door.

Andion ducked beneath the quilt next to her. His hand reached out to clench his puzzle box and dragged it under before the blanket flattened.

Rorry's frustration continued to vent at a volume just below a shout.

The rapping repeated. Did they expect her to answer it?

Scarlett closed *Essential Focus* with enough force to quiet Rorry. The tome fell onto her pillow as she rose.

Rorry concluded her argument with sharp eyes at Kylan. Bless him. He might not take it seriously, but he knew better than to smirk.

She firmly moved Rorry out of the way and opened the door to the downpour.

Drenched, and unbothered by it, Veen strolled inside. Cord ran in after him.

"We sure are taking a lot of breaks," Kylan said.

Veen ran his hand over the shoulder of his jerkin and flung the water at Kylan. "You get what you pay for, Merithian. If your company is all you've got to offer, don't expect the royal treatment." He glanced to the cell, where Ferix now pretended to sleep. "Gods willing, this'll be a quick one while we wait for the storm to pass. That's wetting rain, that is."

"The horses aren't taking kindly to the thunder," Cord put in.

Glancing into the opened trunk and the plethora of items Andion had stolen, the monk asked, "What's this?"

"Andion," Kylan answered. "He has a habit of picking up things that don't belong to him."

Hoisting a war hammer out from the clinking treasures, Veen said, "I'll dispose of this."

Rorry agreed, as though it emphasized her argument with Kylan. "What town is this?" she asked.

"Unless it uses the Shallyghal name," Veen answered, "I don't know. 'Tis abandoned, if you'll forgive the term. The inhabitants seem to have run off in the middle of the night, beds unmade, candles burned to nubs. Carolle and I ran through. Didn't find anything sinister. Disturbing, but as good a place as any to pen the horses until this ungodly storm passes." He pretended to sling more water and made Kylan flinch. "We even found some feed, not enough, but some. Youse are welcome to stretch your legs, yeah?"

"I would like to!" Ferix shouted, striking the wall with his hoof.

"I'd recommend staying nearby," Veen said over the prisoner. "If you find anything of interest, give a shout." He propped the hammer against his shoulder and turned to leave. "And, boys, keep out of mischief."

Scarlett knew Kylan would take the statement more as a challenge than a reprimand.

Rain hammered the road outside. Veen didn't even throw his hood up as he strolled out into it. Scarlett shivered just witnessing it.

"Yes," Rorry said, "you should share discoveries with your companions."

Thunder drowned out some of the heat in her tone.

Kylan groaned and picked up Uncle Barrey's katana.

Ferix shook the vardo again. "You could respect your kidnap victim's request and return his pipe!"

"I told you I already asked," Kylan said.

Cord huffed. "Y'all, come on. Let's find some privacy. I gotta tell you something." He leaped out into the rain and splashed into a puddle before sprinting off with Kylan.

The rain had chilled since Scarlett and Rorry had changed wagons. Scarlett stretched out her wool shawl as shelter for Rorry too. They left at a run to the town gate that had been swung open wide.

Over the entrance, script had been chiseled into the dark stone archway. Scarlett stopped to translate, sending Rorry running into the pelting rain without cover. Abernathy-on-the-Way? After Rorry's prompting, Scarlett chased after the others.

Abernathy-on-the-Way was a narrow corral of a village, smaller than a district in Brewing. The far end was visible from the entrance, straight down a cobblestone street flanked on both sides by continuous rows of settled stone buildings. Lightning flares didn't penetrate the darkness sheltered in the windows.

Freezing water soaked her dress as they ran into the empty farming village. Cord entered the first shelter in sight, a small shack of weathered planks only as large as a storage shed at the Gwirion manor.

Before they reached it, Joseb stepped out from behind the shack's splintering door. His oiled broad-brimmed hat never turned their way before he headed deeper into town. Something had mystified him. Scarlett wanted to follow to hear his thoughts but knew Rorry would insist she stay after Cord had admitted to harboring news.

Kylan held the door open as they dashed inside and let it clack shut behind him.

Scarlett's damp shawl fell to her shoulders. The wet chill sent a shiver from her neck through her chest to her waist. She whimpered and drew a slow breath through her teeth.

"You don't find it invigorating?" Kylan asked, unfazed by the trailing drips slicking his hair to his forehead. He always did prefer the cold.

She stuck her tongue out at his teasing smile.

Half-formed barrels helped her identify the musty workroom as a cooper's shop. Dodging the leaks from the roof, Cord examined the tools tacked to the walls. A thick layer of dust covered them and a worktable in the far corner. However, the sappy odor suggested the stack of lumber Rorry leaned against was freshly cut.

Scarlett wondered if something in particular had absorbed Joseb's attention as her friends discussed the town and Rorry lectured about not keeping secrets, satyr-be-burned, and not revealing more to the Hook than necessary.

"You know," Kylan said, "they hide their own secrets. When Veen vanquished Beez, he cut himself and used his blood to draw symbols on his knives. That's what did the deed. I wasn't close enough to make out what they were, and he wasn't inclined to share, no matter how hard I pressed."

"Why wouldn't he share something like that?" Cord asked. "Does Teague know?"

"I don't know," Kylan answered.

"If he did," Rorry said, "he would have used it in the woods when Beez attacked him. And, there is the talisman Teague wears." Her chin inched up as she faced Kylan.

Knowing what was coming, Scarlett sighed.

"What do you want me to say?" Kylan asked. "I'm not sorry we snuck down to the village. It felt like the thing to do."

"I am a little tired of your feelings causing trouble," Rorry said. "Next time, please tell your gut, 'Another time, perhaps.'"

Kylan drew in a deep breath. "It's not like that. It's . . . I don't know. A whiff of fresh air . . . a charge on the wind. But inside . . ."

Rorry gave him a glassy stare. But Scarlett listened with wonder. Was that the wind her uncle had told him to listen to? She wished she had some actual answers about Ghost Augurs. Had Uncle Barrey done something to Kylan during their training? Even if he hadn't, a Ghost Augur had trained him. What might that mean exactly?

"It felt like a thunderstorm in my veins telling me to go!" Kylan said. "How do you ignore that?"

No one said anything until Rorry looked Scarlett's way. "Have you ever heard of a black pendant used for torture, Scarlett? It creates a green light."

Intrigued, Scarlett released her lip to answer. "No. I have never read mention of any of this."

"Julian is a cadet from the academe in Croathe," Cord said. He shied away from Rorry's slackened jaw, correctly expecting to be backhanded. "I wanted to tell you, I did! I told Teague." That was a misstep he should have omitted.

"Why'd he agree to bring him along?" Kylan asked.

"He *wittingly* brought two cadets along," Rorry said.

Cord flinched. "Well my say-so doesn't carry much weight. After the clash Julian and Maeverly had, I can't imagine she's all right with him staying. And anyway, Teague's got Bevin watching him. It's not like he's gonna run off anywhere to bring the army back to us." Cord found no sympathy when he looked to Scarlett. He put his hands up. "Ashes! I'm sorry for not telling y'all sooner, but we didn't have the chance with that blazing satyr listening to everything we said."

Kylan crossed his arms and joined Rorry's glare. "Cord, tell us everything. We already know you were a spy. We saw your directives before you burned them."

Cord slumped against a worktable. Dejected, he slowly revealed his history with Julian. Kylan's and Rorry's faces wavered between anger and forgiveness as the news settled in.

His story nauseated Scarlett. It explained quite a bit, actually, about Marlone's death and the rude bigot. To think she'd used thoughts of him as fuel for a spell.

Rorry folded her arms over her chest and aimed her frustration at Scarlett. "Do you have any secrets you have been stowing away?"

Scarlett raised her shoulders and shook her head. She had promised not to reveal Joseb's identity, and it wasn't of urgency.

Kylan narrowed his eyes in suspicion and grinned slightly. How could he always tell?

Before Rorry and Cord saw his reaction, Scarlett eased open the door behind her. The rain beat the cobblestones in thick bands now.

"Where are you going?" Rorry asked.

"One of us should stay with the Hook," she answered. "If they discover what happened here, or make mention of these markings or the pendant, we should have our own witness."

"Good idea," Kylan said. Surprised he didn't force a confession, Scarlett stopped working on lies to cover Joseb's truth. "And while she does that, we can find Cord a new tunic."

While Cord defended his uniform, Scarlett nodded her appreciation to Kylan and set out in Joseb's direction. Moving briskly down the street, she didn't bother raising her shawl. Each raindrop felt like it fell fresh from an icicle, numbing her skull.

Veen strutted her way, away from Teague. Neither paid her any mind. The dripping brim of Joseb's hat ducked into a door on the right side of the street, in the middle of the clustered buildings. Frozen to the bone, Scarlett tried the next door she came to on her right. It opened to a drab sitting room and closed behind her. Without interest, Veen walked past the glassless window.

For all the simple pinewood furniture that very well may have been assembled by a child, the room held one treasure: a tall fireplace. Without a second thought, Scarlett moved to the threadbare oval rug in the center of the room and birthed a flame.

Kneeling to rub her hands together by the fire, she thawed and prepared to make another drenching run toward the sorcerer. By her knee, score marks peered out from under the rug. She flipped the rug's end aside. An arc of scratches led away from the hearth as though it swung out frequently.

Two sconces above the mantel provided more insight. Smoke smudged the underside of both, but fingers had smeared some of it away on one. More fingers had smudged the lintel, as though someone taller than she had grabbed it as they'd ducked under.

Scarlett reached up and pressed the sconce where its sheen remained. Nothing happened. Then she twisted it; the fireplace clicked, jutting away from the wall by a few inches. Now she wished she had asked Kylan to join her. Putting her shoulder into the task, she shoved with all of her strength. The fireplace slid forward easily, only resisting once it met the scars on the floor.

A portal nearly as wide as the fireplace offered passage under the flue. Scarlett waved away the smoke and surveyed the next room. Behind a highly polished bar, casks of ale and brandy had been racked. Spilled mugs of stale ale scented the eerily empty room. Some chairs were toppled. Others faced the fireplace entry from their ring-stained tables. A tavern in such a small town was a conundrum and definitely necessary to hide from the army.

Perhaps there were more entrances to this hideaway, possibly one leading to Joseb that didn't involve the frigid rain. She breezed between the tables and through the door behind the bar. The clean kitchen appeared to have been used within the past week, though Scarlett didn't see anything edible left behind.

Mice ran from the larder when she opened it. Plaster littered the floor. Shelves had been torn from the wall. But nothing of interest hid in the debris or on the remaining shelves, just some emptied bags of flour and rusting pots.

Ready to abandon the search, Scarlett noticed a light flicker on the wall inside. She traced it to a crack in the plaster ensconced behind a small sack of salt and a chipped ewer. Something moved on the other side of the aperture. She closed the larder door and cleared the obstructions. Setting her arm across the crumb-covered shelf, she spied.

In another sitting room, the flame of a candle smoked in Joseb's hand as he studied something out of her view.

Teague's voice turned him toward the street. "We have an empty town. No bodies, and 'tisn't burned. This only makes sense if the people were taken to grow the Dregs' packs."

"Or to feed them," Joseb added with a grimace. He used a huskier voice than Maeverly, at ease with his friend. "Do you believe this storm is of their doing?"

Lowering onto a rocking chair, Teague said, "I cannot tell. I told you before, Beez only had the power of any other magus, never something as strong as commanding the weather."

"They do live behind a giant storm cloud," Joseb replied.

Nodding, Teague dropped his hat onto the round table next to him and leaned back. "Give the horses a little longer. If we lose them, we're lost ourselves."

"What did you learn from the High Guard?"

Teague flipped a black disc out of his collar, removed his necklace, and offered it to Joseb.

Holding up a hand, Joseb said, "I'd rather not. You know, even I wish that had remained lost to the ages."

"I understand, so I do," Teague said, putting the talisman back around his neck. "'Tis a desperate measure, but necessary."

Joseb wrinkled his brow in doubt.

"The Guard's not forthcoming. Too busy praying to the gods for forgiveness. He seems to think I'm their servant, sent to punish him."

Scarlett barely breathed, reluctant to believe she'd heard correctly. Teague carried a High Guard inside the talisman?

Taking the chair next to Teague, Joseb set the candle on the table. "The rumors may be true. Those superstitious fools in the army may not be burning the towns to stop the curse."

Scarlett could have told them that. Even if the High Guard believed the dead villagers to be wolfkin, the bodies in Kenton had died more than a day before they'd burned them. The curse only required a few hours of death.

"Ach!" Teague began rocking. "You're sounding like Veen. I never thought I'd live to see the day."

The sorcerer's serious expression didn't change. "If the High Guard is pleading to the gods instead of the Chancellor, it answers some questions. Has he mentioned the Chancellor?"

"Nothing substantial. He calls him Prince Rhyn now. I suppose that's a start."

Light fell on them from the doorway. Veen walked in and removed a large, smashed scroll from inside his jerkin. Dragging another table over, he held up one end of the scroll and let it tumble open. Then he spread it across the table, obscuring it from Scarlett's view. "Here we are now, boys."

"If that map's worth a piss," Joseb said. "It's not even complete. We really are ill-prepared for this mission."

Leaning forward to study the map, Teague said, "Clarkson scouted what he could, which wasn't much. 'Tisn't his fault, or Remy's. They didn't know we'd leave Croathe. Is that a pass there, above Granville?" He hummed. "No, I suppose not."

"Veen," Joseb said, "I didn't get a chance to ask you. How did you defeat Beez?"

The monk rolled his shoulders. "Same way as before. Cut the vessel's head off, yeah?"

He lied. Why? Scarlett understood not teaching Kylan the symbols drawn in blood, just to keep him from doing something brash. But not telling his band, that was something else entirely.

"You're right, Teague," Veen said, directing their attention to the map again. "With reinforcements at sea, they could trap the Tribunal on the peninsula." Veen plucked out an arrow from his quiver to point. "The wolves come in through South Thornton, take some villages to grow along the way, and move up the Breslan Pass to hammer the Tribunal in Croathe against its own Great Barrier.

"The Dregs have the south by now. They've probably taken the northwest too. If we're not going after the spoiled prince ourselves, that leaves the one pass in the east, yeah? But with you boys, Beez might follow no matter which pass we use."

With more certainty than Scarlett had seen from him all day, Teague said, "We're not going back to Croathe. 'Tisn't worth the risk. Our boat is lost to us, so it is. The Mint Coast is our goal. With the lax defenses we saw in Croathe, pray the Chancellor is not there instead. Our task—our *main* objective—remains the same; we get back to Racine. The Dregs wouldn't dare attack one of the Bonded Nations. They don't have the numbers or the safety of their storm."

Joseb stood for a better view of the map. Pointing a lifewood-inspired teal nail, he said, "If Beez is not the sole Dreg here, let's hope another Dreg hasn't taken . . ." He squinted and moved the candle to read in the dim light. "Llandir."

The monk leaned closer to verify. "What? Really?"

"You've heard of it?" Teague asked.

"That's where the young ones were heading before meeting us. Kylan's papers are for Llandir. Fate guides them better than we do."

Rocking again, Teague said, "Thank the gods for that."

Humming as he thought, Joseb paced. "Let's say we're right about Beez's intent in invading Merith. What if they want the *tek'aran* for the same purpose?"

Teague regarded him flatly. "I think we can call him Cord at this point, J."

"Not in mixed company, no?" Veen said. "Not with that Julian fellow around."

"Yes," Joseb added. "About him, I seem to recall someone telling me recently that we couldn't save them all."

Teague split a hard look between them. "We cannot very well send his kind through the tunnels, can we?"

Joseb continued, "Anyway, the cut on Cord's hand is gone now, not even a blemish. If they're after the Chancellor's secret of immortality, Cord's ability may offer something close. Imagine if they used him to heal their vessels. Would he even decay the way the others do?"

With his face in his hands, Teague breathed, "Shite."

"Cord would make an easier target," Veen said. "They wouldn't need an army of wolfkin to drag him back to the Cloud. 'Tisn't like he burns at the touch."

Thunder boomed, quaking the building. Scarlett gasped and clapped her left hand over her mouth. She peeped through the crack and relaxed upon seeing they hadn't heard her.

"Fecking storm," Veen said. "I'd better help Carolle and Bevin."

Once the door closed behind him, Joseb retook his seat and asked, "What did you mean earlier? You said Remy didn't know we'd leave Croathe."

When they'd rescued Scarlett from Fort Warren, they had referred to this Remy as having hubris about the Hook, which likely meant he was one of their leaders, or maybe *the* leader.

"Our benefactor made a few requests to me personally."

The sorcerer crossed his arms. "Oh, such as the satyr? What does she want with him?"

"She?" Teague asked innocently.

"You know of whom I'm referring," Joseb said. "I don't see why you're keeping that a secret from us. We've always known our benefactors before."

"Aye. Then there must be a reason," Teague replied.

Joseb slouched with his elbows on his knees, something he could do in the violet dress that only slit on the sides as high as his calves.

After a short while, Teague asked the air, "But how? How does the Chancellor do it?"

"I doubt Remy can fault us for returning without an answer," Joseb said. "Not after hearing about the Dregs. Wouldn't you think?"

"Definitely maybe," Teague said. "There's more to consider than that, J. If we must turn and fight, the answer could be our salvation against Beez."

"That's why we tarried last night? You're asking that High Guard about a hypothetical weapon? I would've agreed to raid the bloody Sorrow Mines of Nelth to avoid that delay! What if we can't even use it?"

Teague sighed and said, "We cannot debate each disparate possibility, and you don't have to remind me what we face, J."

"You're right. Sorry."

Suddenly, the larder door swung wide. Scarlett, still covering her mouth, did not gasp but clutched her shawl over her heart with her right hand.

Bevin stood in the doorway examining the goods around her. When he bent to collect the sack of salt, he noticed the view of the meeting in the room beyond. The sack joined various containers lining his arm as he stood erect. With his forefinger to his lips, he smiled. A gentle shutting of the door left Scarlett in the dark again.

Bless him. In that moment, she didn't care if his oniony pungency dallied. The half-ogre had her thanks.

She resumed her watch.

"You've got time for a lesson, I think," Teague said. He fetched the map, rolling it as they departed.

More questions had been added to Scarlett's list. Pondering how to get answers from Joseb without giving away her eavesdropping, she grabbed the handle to the larder door. Her hand brushed something free. It tapped against the plaster on the floor. Scarlett picked it up and pulled the door open for more light.

Yellowed and split, the tiny disc only made sense to her when the light hit dried blood on the underside. A fingernail! She threw it away and wiped her hand on her skirt, scrubbing the memory of its texture from her fingers. But why would a fingernail . . . Pressing the door forward, Scarlett's heart stopped.

Bloody scratches were gouged deeply into the wood. She stood away from the horror she'd been hiding behind. At least two people had been clawing their way to be free of the larder, a man and a woman, judging by the size of the other nails embedded in the oak. Scarlett hummed a frightened cry and raced after Bevin.

* * *

Wringing out her hair, Rorry flung it behind her shoulders. This second floor was the same as in the last two homes, merely a large bedchamber. Only the nuances in the placement of furniture and the wear of the linens made the similarities less bizarre.

In the corner of the spacious room, four posts stood around an abused mattress. The bed snuggled dangerously close to the fireplace. On the opposite side of the chamber, open windows that had never held glass allowed the rain to pepper the stone floor. The shower did not deter Cord and Kylan from taking in the view of the village below.

"Freckles!" Carolle called from outside.

Rorry's shoulders fell with her jaw. "I will not answer to that." She scowled to kill Kylan's chuckle and remind him where he stood in her graces.

Pushing between the boys, Rorry spotted the monk. Beneath a balcony across the street, Carolle had wrapped herself around Veen like a tall blanket. The monks engaged in indecent, though thankfully married, affection.

Carolle saw Rorry immediately. "Come along now."

Descending the stairs in hopes of quieting the woman, Rorry hurried. Her ire warmed her as she slowly approached the orgy of leathers and ink on the road. Remembering the nature of the proposed lesson, her temper cooled before the water on her face sizzled. Her pride would not impede her this time.

After taking a breath, Veen said, "She's tossing me aside for you. I hope you learn something horribly wonderful."

Staring beyond them, Rorry wished the man would not address her while speaking into Carolle's mouth. She had braced herself for Carolle's laugh and did not jump when it arrived.

"You'll always be entwined with me, Stille van Veen."

When he stepped back, Carolle let his hands fall to his side. He made his way toward the caravan, turning twice to see if she watched before he stepped out of sight.

Relinquishing her gaze, Carolle frowned at Rorry's soaked dress. "I do wish you'd consider britches or pantaloons. Anything but a dress would make this easier."

"Forgive me," Rorry said, crossing her arms over her chest, "but those garments would not be easy to come by here." Last time she had been rude and, rightfully, had paid a penance for it. This time, she would absorb all she could learn from her self-appointed mentor. This lesson had taken years to arrive.

Throwing an arm over Rorry's shoulder, Carolle ushered her away from Kylan and Cord's view. "Let's find some privacy." As if the rain did not wish to inconvenience Carolle, the downpour suddenly quelled.

In the distance, Julian watched them. Teague must not consider him a risk with nowhere to run. That was foolish. He disappeared inside another of the identical homes. Rorry glanced up to see Cord pointing out Julian's location to Kylan. What few admirable qualities Julian had were inadequate to redeem him in her eyes, not after hearing of his treatment of Marlone. If Cord sought revenge and could do so without risk, she would not interfere.

She and Carolle passed through a weathered gate of gray planks and walked down a passage between two buildings into a well-appointed garden, robust with the scent of wet plants and soil. Near the back wall, moss grew up the side of a disused well surrounded by peonies and a few weeds. Two iron benches decorated the small grassy block of land, sheltered under the limbs of tulip trees. Several ripe black apples hung from the higher branches of the only other arbor.

Turning, Carolle gripped Rorry's arms and said, "You are never trapped until you stop trying. If you forget everything else I show you, remember that, yeah? Defend yourself. Be creative. Be forceful." Her gentle smile harbored sympathy. "First lesson, scream."

"I beg your pardon?"

"Don't beg my pardon. Scream!" Carolle shouted. "Strip off your pompous, dignified shell and let the gods hear you."

Rorry recoiled. The woman was mad! "Surely, I can under—"

Carolle pinched Rorry's nipple and twisted.

Rorry screeched and slapped her hand away. "That hurt!"

Letting loose a string of expletives that Rorry would have preferred not to hear, Carolle assaulted the courtyard. The woman ended her tirade with a childish smile.

Rorry squeezed her arms tighter around her bosom. Perhaps she should have been avoiding this lesson after all. "I think we should be off, yes? The storm seems to have passed, and this place does not make sense."

"It does not make sense!" Carolle shouted.

Rorry tried not to encourage the crazed monk with a smile. "Please be quiet."

"No!" She reached out to pinch her again.

"All right!" Rorry screamed as she doubled over to protect herself. "Stop shouting, you mad, foreign trollop!"

Reacting faster than her brain had, Rorry's hands covered her mouth. She uttered apologies over Carolle's laughter. Giving into the gaiety, Rorry yelled, "I am sorry!"

"You're what?"

"I am sorry! Sorry! Sorry!"

"At this moment," Maeverly said, standing before Bevin in the passage, "I believe we all are. Is there sense in this, or have you fallen under some obnoxious enchantment?"

Composing herself, Carolle waved them away. "We are learning to defend ourselves, my lady. Sometimes we forget all of the weapons nature has given us."

Bevin stomped away, groaning at no one. He accidentally dislodged the gate door and carried it away with him, which sent Rorry back into her fit of laughter.

Maeverly's mouth twisted toward a smile. She did seem to enjoy putting the half-ogre on edge.

Carolle raised her inked arms and stretched gracefully. "I promise we are done with the shouting," she said to Maeverly. "But we'll be sparring a bit. Would you mind asking the others not to wander by here? Rorry's going to lose the dress."

Rorry's laughter ceased.

Chapter 33: Ignoring Instinct

Tracking Julian's movements, Cord leaned over the ledge of the second-story window. "He's up to something."

Staring elsewhere, Kylan didn't reply.

Following Kylan's gaze to the distant western sky, Cord saw the worst of the storm. Lightning speared through the clouds to a point on the largest hill at the edge of the flats.

"That has to be a Dreg," Kylan said. "How far away do you think that is?"

"I'd rather not find out," Cord replied. "Half a day?" Far enough that the storm wasn't the immediate threat.

The distraction had let Julian disappear. Each time he popped out of a house, the Croathite glanced about for onlookers like a gopher on his way to a prized carrot. "This way," Cord said, leading downstairs and out to the drizzle.

"Let's tell Veen what we saw," Kylan said. "Maybe he'll light a fire under the others."

As they trod the rain-slicked cobblestones, Cord studied the two buildings Julian had vanished near, one on either side of a line of tall juniper shrubs. "In a minute," he said, deciding which of the homes they should check. Picking the first, Cord went to the door.

"Julian's not important," Kylan said.

"I thought you agreed with me?" Cord asked. "There's gotta be more to his story, Kylan. If he just ran after waking up, where'd he get those clothes?"

The shrubs fluttered between the homes. A breeze shook them from behind, away from a cracked stone wall.

Cord went to investigate. Prying the scratchy branches aside, he revealed a hidden passageway. Cord forced himself through to an arched tunnel through the wall.

Kylan hesitated until Cord urged him in.

At the open end of the passage, Cord spied around the corner. Instead of finding Julian, he discovered a small courtyard that appeared to have been an herb garden at one point. Even in this moist soil, it lay in ruins, browned and dry. A soaked wooden bench sat rotting between the herbs and a broken well. The well's pointed roof had collapsed, capping it from use.

Kylan grunted at the find but seemed relieved. "Come on." As they turned to leave, a loud splash sounded from inside the well.

Circling it, Cord whispered, "Help me open it."

Running a hand through his hair, Kylan thought for a moment, then said, "This doesn't . . . no. It doesn't feel right, Cord."

"I snuck away with you last night, didn't I? This is nothing compared to that."

"We shouldn't," Kylan said. He went back to the passage. "Let's go."

"Oh, right. What is it this time, a drizzle of doubt? Snowy hesitation? Maybe the wind between your ears?"

Kylan's glower told him where to shove his teasing, but he came back and grabbed the edges of the fallen roof. "Mark my words. It won't be good, whatever we find. So enjoy this before you realize it's a mistake." In a roaring shove, Kylan heaved the lid off without Cord's help. It cracked loudly against the ground.

Splashes of someone running echoed up the well. Cord peered down. Footholds grooved the inside. At the bottom, a cask floated in the shallow water at the mouth of a tunnel. "There's a passage," Cord said, hoisting his leg over the side.

Kylan backed away. "We tell Veen. Now."

"Let's just take a quick look," Cord bargained. "It's probably Julian."

Raising his eyebrow, Kylan asked, "Who also sealed the well above himself? No. Something's telling me to leave it be, Cord. Let's go."

Lowering himself inside, Cord said, "I gotta tell ya, you pick strange times to be yellow. You'll charge at a wolfkin but won't climb into a well?"

"I already told you—"

"Yeah, yeah. Sleeting cramps. Got it." Cord heard Kylan's growl as he scaled down the bricked-in ladder into the moldy air. At the bottom, Cord eased into thick water. Slime coated his sandaled feet and calves.

Chalky boulders created a path over the waterline as far as he could see down the dark tunnel, which wasn't much farther than ten feet. Waving Kylan down, he hopped onto one of the boulders.

More pale stones and a floating barrel were ahead in the tight tunnel. Leaping to the next boulder, Cord nearly fell when it crumbled beneath his weight. He regained his balance against the fuzzy brick wall as it settled.

From behind him, Kylan breathed, "Cord, stop moving." His wide eyes stuck to Cord's feet. "Look."

The water had bubbled and darkened where the stone had broken.

"What kind of rock is this?" The next sunken boulder held a shape. Above the waterline, a man's face sprouted a snout. Frozen in stone, claws erupted from the statue's fingers. Someone had chiseled the transformation of a wolfkin into the weak stone?

"We need to leave," Kylan whispered.

"Because of some statues?" Cord hopped off the back of what appeared to be another work of the crazed sculptor.

His splash ended just before a hiss filled the tunnel. Something clacked against the brick walls.

Kylan shoved Cord behind him and drew his sword. "Go!"

Cord stumbled over a statue's leg before he located the source of the hissing. As large as a bear, a six-legged, black-skinned lizard clung to the shadows on the ceiling. Its beady green eyes reflected an unseen light from Kylan's sword. The creature swung its clubbed tail from side to side, chipping away at the bricks.

Kylan stepped forward, waving the sword and forcing it back. He took another step.

The lizard's tail beat a rapid warning. Its mouth opened.

Cord flinched.

With an abrupt hiss, it released its grip and plunged into the water, sinking out of view.

Blood. That's what darkened the rippling water around his legs. Cord swallowed to clear his throat. "Was that—"

Kylan pressed him back and kept waving the sword with his left arm. "A blazing, carrion-eating basilisk? Yes. Get up the well! Now! We're going to find Veen."

Chapter 34: Lizards and Lessons

Scarlett stepped back out of the drizzle into the doorway of the sitting room with the hidden entrance to the tavern. She accidentally bumped into Cord. He too had ignored Joseb's instruction to wait inside.

"Kill it," Teague said to Veen and Joseb in the huddle Kylan was trying to force himself into. "Basilisk skin can buy us passage out of the port without questions."

"What about the Dreg we saw?" Kylan asked.

"*Thought* you saw, boy," Veen corrected.

"Make it fast, Veen," Teague said.

Veen bowed. "Fast as a gurrier with a freshly cut purse."

Joseb closed his eyes. "Right." He pressed his hands together. After a moment, brilliant yellow light spilled out from between them.

Kylan eased over behind Veen.

The light solidified and began to gather at the edges of the sorcerer's fingers, jabbing upward. Joseb's spell stretched and dimmed to solid metal, whiter than silver. Taking a shaky breath, Joseb inspected what he had created. Although simple, with only a tiny yellow orb of stone decorating the hilt, the short sword befitted a noble.

Scarlett memorized every groove of the weapon, determined to learn the ability herself. Her curiosity tempted her to head back to the vardos to scour *Essential Focus* for the spell.

"That's all I can conjure for now," Joseb said. "It won't last for long, I'm afraid."

Cord's breathing resumed in Scarlett's ear.

Veen took the enchanted sword. "Not necessary," he said, turning on Kylan. "We have another blade that can cut through that hide, yeah?"

Pulling Uncle Barrey's katana out of his belt, Kylan asked, "Can I at least watch?"

Veen grabbed the weapon by the scabbard and sprinted off without answering. Kylan darted after him.

Joseb noticed Scarlett and Cord in the doorway. "Go on into the tavern. Get yourselves a drink—"

Lost to a coughing fit, Joseb bent over. His hoarse barks obviously came from a man.

Kylan paused at the overgrown juniper shrubs across the road. Recognition dawned in his eyes. When he looked to Scarlett, she slowly shook her head. Confused, he ran after Veen.

He knew Joseb's secret now, which meant Rorry would know within a day. Scarlett turned for Cord's reaction, but he'd already gone through the secret entrance. She did hope Kylan had sense enough not to tell him.

Teague comforted Joseb with a few hard pats on the back. "The poisoned ones get me every time," Joseb said hoarsely.

Scarlett entered the tavern.

"Ashes, did you see that?" Cord asked. "She made a flaming sword out of nothing!"

Smiling, Scarlett took a seat at Cord's table. At last, he'd found an interest in magic. "Yes. Imagine if the sword actually flamed. I've read mages can do that."

That set his mind wandering. A small grin gave away his thoughts. It disappeared when his finger began twiddling the gold thread on his chest.

"I'm sorry," Scarlett said. "Being raised to believe your magic is a curse, that must have been hard."

He pulled his hands to his lap. "I didn't know. It only showed itself a few weeks ago. Before that, life was good." His brown eyes lifted to her. "Real good."

Bless him.

"So," Joseb said, ducking into the room. He untied the scarf under his chin and flopped his hat onto the table next to theirs. "These poor souls were taken by the wolves." Brushing droplets of water from the medallions of his belt, he went behind the bar. He helped himself to the kegs, filled two mugs, and uncorked a bottle.

"Beez's wolves?" Cord asked.

"It's possible," the sorcerer answered. He returned to the table with his hands full and placed a cup of spiced wine in front of Scarlett and a draft of ale before Cord. "If so, they advanced without his immediate guidance. Veen bought us at least a day's lead on Beez. It all depends on where his urn was."

Raising his own mug of ale, Joseb said, "A toast to loosen us up a bit. To new friends. Cheers!" He took a drink and drew up the chair beneath him. His lips twisted as he uttered a mildly disappointed hum at his mug.

Cord's mouth puckered as he put his down.

They should have had the spiced wine. Scarlett took another sip.

Joseb slapped their table with a clack. Lifting his hand, he left a Racinian gold coin amid the water-stained rings. Untarnished and unmarred, the regal profile on the coin's surface had to be that of Queen Ameera of Racine, the only ruler who had assumed the silver throne after Scarlett's mum had left the continent.

"We'll need every advantage to leave Merith," he said to Cord. "That means, if there is even the slightest possibility you can learn other spells, we must try."

To her surprise, Cord simply nodded. Joseb must have appealed to the soldier in him with that short sword.

Sweeping his eyes from one side of the table to the other, Joseb considered his pupils. "Who wants to go first?"

Scarlett shifted in her seat as Cord stared at the coin.

"Very well, we'll toss for it." Joseb balanced the gold piece on his lacquered teal thumbnail. "Heads or scales?"

Cord looked to Scarlett for an explanation. "Heads," Scarlett offered. She knew this game.

The coin churned the air and clattered on the table, wobbling to a stop. PROTECTING THE PEOPLE circled the depiction of a wingless water dragon.

Cord waited for her reaction. She winced an apology.

The sorcerer slid the coin to rest beneath the golden feather. "Let me start by saying, you are in a safe place. Now close your eyes. Good. I imagine this won't be difficult; focus on wanting to go unnoticed. If you have trouble, I always imagine Vetskarran slavers are hunting me. I've taken shelter behind a tree and am doing my best to be silent."

Cord's eyelids wrinkled.

Joseb lowered his voice. "The tricky part is intensifying that desire and removing fear from it. This particular spell is very susceptible to fear. Do you feel the need to be invisible?"

Swallowing, Cord nodded.

"I want you to follow that feeling from your head down to your chest, where it's thick. Now, without fear, imagine pulling a wisp of that emotion free and touching it to the coin."

Scarlett held her breath in anticipation. The light blue aura flashed around Cord again. This time, the edges were tinged a sickly green.

After a minute, Joseb pressed his lips together and patted Cord on the shoulder.

Cord opened his eyes. When he saw the coin, his face was unreadable.

A teal nail slid the coin before Scarlett. "Your turn," Joseb said.

Multiple colors flickered around Joseb's purple aura. Certain it somehow related to magic, Scarlett felt emboldened to ask. "You said you could sense I was strong with magic. How?"

"When you're more experienced, you'll connect to magic on a deeper level, sensing it around you, in others and in objects. It develops as you pull the core of your ability closer to the surface."

"Oh," Scarlett said. "Then why do I see colors around magi?"

Joseb gawked before a wild grin crossed his face. Giddy as a child, he asked, "What color am I?"

"Purple," she said. "There are others but mainly purple."

"Hmm. Purple? Not orange. Huh. Not a dark blue?"

Scarlett shook her head. "Like an aubergine."

"Huh," Joseb grunted. "I'm not familiar with that one. And him?"

Cord shrank back in his chair.

"Blue," she said. "A bright blue, like the summer sky."

"I shouldn't be surprised that I don't know that one, I suppose," Joseb said.

"What does it mean?" Cord asked.

"It's a rare talent," Joseb answered, "but some can see the strengths of other magic users. For example, if Scarlett saw dark red, almost black, around you, it would mean you naturally excel at mind control and the like."

Cord sneered.

"Bad example. Sorry." He turned back to Scarlett. "Do you only see blue around Cord? Nothing more? Often a swirl of colors announces other natural talents, weaker than the primary."

She tried not to look at Cord, who sank deeper into his chair. "Just blue, really. A little green around the edges."

"Dark green?" Joseb asked hopefully.

"Yellowish." After scouring through a list of yellowish-brown items in her mind, she gave up. "I am not sure how to describe it. Mustard seed . . . but greener?"

"Does that mean I can do something other than heal?" Cord

asked Joseb.

Tapping his nails on the table as he thought, Joseb said, "You know, I believe it might. There was a book on the spectrum in the Tower. But I didn't commit it to memory beyond what I was interested in: conjuration, illusions, and the like. Scarlett would have to identify the color, regardless. Each hue varies." He held a finger up. "You could show us with the Wand of Shades. Although without the book, it wouldn't do any good." Joseb frowned to himself and repeated, "More than one . . . Well, it was a silly theory anyway."

"What was?" Scarlett asked.

The sorcerer sighed. "I thought Cord might be an elf."

"What?" Cord shouted.

"It was a valid theory!" Joseb held his palms up as he explained. "While humans and the other races have multiple manipulations for magic, the elves had only one each. However, that singular ability was as powerful as a force of nature. And just as varied, mind you. We're not talking fireballs and illusions. One of them grew those oaks that cap the tunnels. Supposedly another even flew on the wind."

"Could any of them heal?" Scarlett asked.

Cord appeared to have stopped breathing altogether.

Humming as he thought, Joseb answered, "I don't know. They didn't overlap much of the history we know today. The elves were a reclusive lot—friendly and helpful but isolated for the majority of the time they were here."

After gulping from his mug, Cord slammed it back down and stared at the table. "You can't just say something like that! Not to someone who doesn't know where he came from. Ashes, Maeverly! You thought I was an elf? I don't have pointed ears."

"Bevin doesn't have warts covering his forehead," Joseb said with a shrug. "If a human and an elf had an offspring, who is to say what their child would look like? Elves couldn't reproduce themselves; if it were possible between an elf and a human magus, you would have more abilities than the two. Or so I would assume. *Tek'aran* must mean something else."

Cord examined his empty mug.

"The beast is dead," Teague shouted into the adjoining sitting room.

After taking a long swig, Joseb rasped, "We won't be here much longer. Invisibility is white. I do remember that." He pointed to the golden image of Queen Ameera and got up to refresh his and Cord's mugs.

With her eyes closed, Scarlett recalled sitting in her bed at night, reading by moonlight, and hearing her mum's footsteps coming up the stairs. Altering the fear of being caught into purely a desire for her mum not to interrupt her reading, she imagined stretching a tendril of that feeling to the coin. Something happened; she felt it and opened her eyes.

A hole larger than the coin appeared in the table, revealing her dress beneath. Scarlett's finger flattened against the invisible coin.

Joseb beamed with pride as he set down the refilled mugs.

"Gore me on a slit's horn!" Cord murmured.

The pride disappeared from the sorcerer's face as his posture shifted to that of a Judge. "Never use that ignorant word again!"

The innocent stumble put some color back in Cord's cheeks.

"Mirokar is the polite name," Scarlett said with a gentle smile, "even if it means 'demonkin' in the Old Tongue. And they don't all have horns. Some have scales, or fangs, or claws, or tails . . ."

Joseb squinted at her, then realized his folly. "I apologize, Cord. My reaction was sharp. I didn't consider that was something you needed to learn. Of course you haven't been exposed to them."

"You know one?" Cord asked.

"Everyone knows one, an aunt, a cousin, a buxom tavern wench who makes the sweetest peach pies south of the Asdales. The last time a mirokar would have set foot here, they would have been referred to by that pejorative. Do you know why they were called that?"

Scarlett shook her head as well. Her mum had never spent much time on the topic, aside from the endless list of revolts mirokar had started.

"The mirokar are a relatively new race, only appearing in the Chronicles of Cyr within the past thousand years. When they appeared, Merith spanned the continent. Humans who could touch magic were enslaved, controlled by the most powerful amongst them, called Speakers. Did you ever hear the tale of Benny the Spark?" Joseb asked with a grin of admiration. "No? Oh well. Remind me to tell you later."

Silence lingered for a moment. Scarlett exchanged a confused glance with Cord.

"They are all magi, then?" Cord asked. "The mirokar?"

Pulled out of what Scarlett assumed was a mental rendition of Benny's story, Joseb blinked and answered, "Just as often as humans, it seems. Back then, there was little distinction between a man with horns and a—well, one of us, in regard to oppression. I suppose the binding collars fit us all."

Scarlett had expected Cord to react to the statement lumping him in with the magi. Instead, he listened intently.

"When a Speaker was upset at one of their herd—or if they felt particularly cruel, they would set a pyre and make an example of the offender. Merith has been burning people since long before it smothered Shallyghal. The problem they encountered is mirokar don't burn well. We know now that it's because they're immune to fire.

"However, in that time, the Speakers believed the only way to torch one was first to cover the poor soul with a thousand tiny cuts, or slits. It would have been a slow death. Most say they suffocated rather than bled out." His eyes drifted to stare through the hole in the table. "Those are the broad strokes of it, anyway." He muttered, "The knowledge of tomorrow is born out of the ignorance of today."

The queen's profile reappeared on the table. Joseb slid it to Cord. "Now humor me. Try again."

* * *

Kylan gave Bevin space as the half-ogre busted apart the well's mortared stones with his club. Lightning sparkled down the plank with each strike.

When it was cleared away, Veen tossed up a rope to the half-ogre. With little effort, Bevin hefted out the six-limbed basilisk and dragged it into the herb garden. Distracted by the smells around him, he released his grip and began plucking herbs.

For all of Seamus's and Ellick's efforts to find a basilisk when they'd been younger, Kylan had succeeded. If he ever spoke to his brothers again, it'd be the first thing he'd tell them.

Drenched, Veen popped out of the well with a toothy grin.

Kylan rolled his eyes.

The monk handed him the katana and said, "Excellent distraction. The bleeding beasty didn't take its eyes off it to see me swimming up behind."

"I'll keep that in mind," Kylan said. He slid the scabbard behind his belt.

Up close, Kylan recognized the basilisk skin's rippling blue pattern as the same in Teague's jerkin. Everyone knew the value of basilisk venom. But what immunities did the hide offer? Whatever it was, Teague believed it a fair exchange for smuggling them through the Great Barrier.

Kylan helped Veen untie the rope. "What does the skin do?"

"Didn't you hear me? You can't cut it without an enchanted weapon," Veen answered. "That's why most clobber basilisks, especially when they're young. Any peat cutter in Lekelith will tell you that. The adults are feckin' near impossible for Jack Boggytrotter to kill."

With the corpse laid out, Veen set to work with the blade Maeverly—if that was the correct name to use—had created.

The basilisk's body jiggled with every cut as Veen carved out the panels of its bumpy skin. When he peeled a large section of the beast's abdomen free, exposing the poisonous meat and intestines, thick liquid strands stretched from the mottled pink of the innards to the skin.

Kylan swallowed hard and remembered something else he should be doing. "Where is Teague?"

Directions received, Kylan set off to retrieve the Seeding papers from Rorry's satchel. She had assembled them all before suggesting Teague might have experience with forgery. Deciding against three light-hearted pranks and a slightly dangerous one, Kylan took the papers and left the butterfly vardo as is.

Back in town, he opened the door to the fourth house on the left and froze. In a chair propped against the wall, Teague slept with his cap over his face and his heels on the table before him. A marmalade cat stretched in his lap and melted as it lazily closed its eyes.

Kylan debated whether he should disturb Teague's slumber. Unnervingly handsome when they'd met, Teague had begun to look haggard.

"Do come in," Teague said, without moving.

With the door closed, Kylan went to the table and laid the Seeding papers next to the man's boots. "Sorry to bother you. This isn't urgent. I wanted to ask if you, perhaps, can forge documents."

Teague slid his hat back with his mouth puckered on the verge of asking a question. The chair legs knocked against the floorboards as he sat up.

"Mine don't need it. But I brought them as a guide."

"Why? Maeverly can conceal ye within the vardos."

Rather than admit Rorry didn't trust the mercs and wanted an alternative, Kylan said, "Plans fail. We've already been separated once."

Scratching the cat's head with one hand, Teague spread the pages out with the other. A murmuring purr built to a steady pace. "Three?"

"One extra, in case, well, everyone makes mistakes."

"Aye. What was Grary Jeth's?"

Kylan felt his expression sour but staid his tongue when the latch clinked behind him.

Julian's wet head poked in. The cadet halted upon seeing them.

A brisk hiss erupted from the cat. The bristled critter growled a warning at Julian before it leaped away and scurried into a dark hole in the floor.

Sneering, Julian left and pulled the door closed behind him.

"I love cats," Kylan said.

Teague stared at the door as he considered something. Returning to reading Grary's papers, he nodded. "'Twill take some time, but I can do it."

Kylan took a seat opposite Teague and asked, "Can I return Ferix's pipe to him?" The fox's crystal-blue eyes whipped to him as his chest bucked with a silent chuckle. "I'm serious."

His lips curled at the edges. "Why?"

"It'd give him something to do other than disrobe for entertainment."

Teague's laugh was quiet but genuine. "He's a prisoner, Kylan."

"And you have been very vague as to why. Is it just because he's a satyr? Is that fair?"

Teague took a deep breath, the mirth gone. "Didn't Veen tell you Ferix is responsible for the trap that ended Vega?"

"Yes. *After* he was a prisoner, she burned as an Abandoned. Does the army consort with satyrs? That might make them more interesting."

"A smart killer lets others do his work for him," Teague said, nonchalantly tapping his fingers on Grary's singed Seeding papers.

Kylan kept his reaction flat, refraining from casting suspicion on Scarlett as the thief. He wished he'd been clever enough to doom the bastard at the army's hands.

"You have a point regarding Ferix's desire to perform," Teague said with a smirk. "You do. Walk with me; I'll fetch his pipe for you." He rolled the papers as they stood.

They exited to find the rain had returned in a heavy drizzle, pattering on the puddles between the cobblestones. "A moment," Teague said. He ducked into the passageway to the basilisk, laid bare by Bevin's bulk.

Kylan waited by the uprooted junipers while Veen and Teague spoke quietly.

Veen quit his skinning and stabbed the white sword into the basilisk's shoulder. Approaching Kylan, he removed his necklace. Only half of a finger's length and slimmer, the key to Ferix's cell dangled on the string. "Take this."

"Why?" Kylan asked.

Teague moved to oversee the exchange. He held up the Seeding papers and said, "A token of trust."

Under his breath, Veen said, "Listen to what Teague says. Promise me you won't do something rash, yeah?" Kylan nodded. Veen lowered his brow. "Say it, boy."

"I promise."

"You're sure?" Veen asked Teague. With a nod from his leader, the monk settled the warm key onto Kylan's palm.

Julian left the house across the street. When he spotted them, he adopted an air of innocence no one would have believed and walked farther into town.

Teague gestured to Veen, which sent the monk after Julian. For a minute, Teague waited. Then he gave Kylan a halfhearted grin and led the way out of town.

They walked in silence until Teague unlocked the yellow door to his wagon. "You're a soul of decency, Kylan."

Kylan scoffed.

"You don't think so? Ferix doesn't deserve much kindness, beyond what we would afford any prisoner. He's been pulling strings that run across nations. Worse, they run through men."

Teague opened the door and took a seat on his cot. Petting the oak floorboards with his right hand, Teague found what he was searching for. His fist pounded the board, popping up the other end. Reaching under the plank, he retrieved a brass key as ornate as the wagon.

The key slipped into one of the knobless bottom drawers of his ebony dresser. Teague pulled the drawer forward. After propping up a black leather bag inside, he jingled the contents as he groped within.

Kylan leaned against the doorframe in order to get a better view of the satyr's belongings. Matte-black leather filled the drawer beneath the bag.

Teague lobbed a white pouch to Kylan. "The grass." It didn't smell like the grass Rorry's father used. The cotton pouch gave off a heavy odor of cloves and spices.

After dipping into the bag again, Teague said, "Here we are now." His hand brought out a white horn pipe. Blackened wood lined its mouthpiece. Kylan reached for a closer inspection, but Teague pulled it back. "If 'tis all the same, I'd prefer for Maeverly to examine it for any hidden tricks." He pressed the drawer closed, locked it, and concealed the key in its nook.

"Teague, I was thinking. If Beez winds up in his urn after his vessel is killed, can't we just destroy the urn?"

"A good theory, lad. But no. Saw one smashed to pebbles. Beez just got another. There's nothing special about the urns, just a house for all that evil to gather and reform."

"Oh. Nasty bastards."

"Too true. Too true."

Kylan tucked the white pouch in his pocket and set about knotting Veen's cord around his neck. Unsure why Teague watched the process, Kylan eyed him.

The older man climbed out of the vardo and appeared on the verge of saying something serious, unsettlingly serious. Then Julian stumbled out of the town gate.

Veen exited behind Julian and thumbed at the idiot before displaying a set of knives in his other hand, including a gold-handled dagger. He shoved Julian toward Bevin's cart and, most likely, his manacles. After pretending to kick Julian in the rump, the monk shook his head and followed the cadet.

"Is it really a good idea to bring him along?" Kylan asked.

"Cord is a soldier too," Teague said.

"Oh yes. They're exactly the same. Behind that pissy demeanor of his, Julian's probably hiding some ability that'll save us all. He just needs to trust us before he can tell us about it. Did you ask to braid his hair? He won't let me."

With a weary face, Teague said, "We all make mistakes."

Kylan crinkled his nose at him. "Most of us don't admit they are mistakes while we're making them. Why don't we just leave him at the next village?"

Teague's face darkened as he stared at nothing.

Uncomfortable with the silence, Kylan pointed at the pipe protruding from Teague's belt pouch. "You'll ask Maeverly to inspect it?"

"I will, yes. Guard the key. We are running out of room for regrets, my friend." Teague's eyes warmed when he donned his happy mask. He checked the clouds. "Seems as though 'twill be a soft day from here on. Let's head off." Sparing Kylan a charming wink, he strolled toward the gate.

Veen reappeared as Teague went into town to release a series of whistles.

Bevin wandered out with a cask under each arm. Veen waved the half-ogre over. Kylan followed. "Your man has been harvesting," Veen said, holding up the golden dagger with three rubies in a straight line down its handle. Bevin grunted and stamped toward the end of the line, where his cart and Julian waited. "Like I said, boyo's a lanky streak of piss. I didn't know he had the brains of a sparrow too."

Veen slipped the dagger into his belt. "I guess I'll see if this has any magic to it." After glancing around, the monk whispered, "I got you something." With a flourish, he presented a glass vial. A pink blob rolled about in its juices inside.

"An organ? How kind."

"That's a venom gland," Veen said. "They have four, but I'll tell Teague I accidentally cut through that one. You get that to Trône d'Argent and someone can extract the venom safely. One drop is all it takes to turn a man's skin to stone. So, 'twill fetch an awful grand price. May even get you that boat, yeah?"

Kylan took the vial and beamed at the bit of flesh. "Thank you, Veen."

"No bother. Thank you for lending me your sword. I slew a basilisk today," he boasted. "Oh, you should have been there!"

Kylan barely tolerated the toothy grin.

Veen strutted toward the gate. "Now, you can watch me walk away. For this, you're welcome."

"The view is better from behind," Kylan joked. He ignored the warming of his cheeks as he rolled the blob around in the glass and decided to check in on Ferix.

Chapter 35: Stille van Veen

Kylan's eyes returned to the dark windows set in the lifewood. He listened to the rain as he lay awake, unable to shake the feeling that something was wrong—the same way he had felt at the basilisk's well, only far worse.

After they had left Abernathy-on-the-Way, bouts of rain had surged through the afternoon and well into the late of night, forcing the Hook to take a reprieve from their travels and seek shelter inside the vardos. The thunderstorm hadn't returned, at least not the one in the sky.

While the guys slept without any problems, he had noticed more than once that Rorry lay awake as well. That was Andion's fault. He's the one who'd agreed to steal the candles for Scarlett's incessant practice, lighting and relighting the things every time she finished a page in her book. Now that Scarlett had given in to sleep, Rorry lay curled up next to her.

Kylan's heart now boomed with each beat. He rolled his eyes at the inexplicable sense of urgency, the uncomfortable static in his veins, and sat up. No one stirred when he slid on his boots and rose. With the katana in his belt, Kylan gently stepped over Rorry on his way to the door. Just as he straddled her, her eyes opened.

Blinking, she rose on her elbows and whispered, "Where are you going?"

Kylan looked to the door and back at her. "I don't know," he answered, unwilling to open himself to more ridicule. Concern on her face, she patted the floor next to her. He hesitated but surrendered and lay back on the floor.

"What in the world would you do out there?" she asked.

Unable to answer, he laid his head next to hers but didn't remove his boots or the sword. His heart, the very blood pumping in his veins, put him on edge. Something told him to leave, to go outside. Maybe he just needed some fresh air. With the four of them, Andion, and Ferix sleeping in the vardo, it was warmer than Kylan could tolerate.

Rorry tucked her fingers in the rolled cuff of his sleeve and closed her eyes.

When he was certain she had dozed off, Kylan slowly pulled his sleeve away until her hand rested on the floorboards. With steady breaths, he methodically got himself upright. Hoping to move without creaking the wood beneath him, he stepped over Rorry and Scarlett, and Cord's arm. Then came the real test.

Laying a finger on the door latch, Kylan lightly pressed it. The metal whined and, with a clunk as quiet as a mallet striking a bell, he unbarred the door. If that wasn't enough to wake everyone, the rain pelted the ground so hard it sounded like Kylan had opened the door to a room full of applause. After hearing Scarlett's waking gasp, he turned and muttered, "Gotta piss, sorry."

Before Rorry could question it, he leaped down into the refreshing chill of the rain and shut the door behind him. His pulse slowed as the water weighed down his hair and streamed over his cheeks. Maybe he had been too warm, being pent up with the others.

The Hook hadn't bothered to move the caravan off the road before they took shelter inside. Fields surrounded them with nothing of interest. Most were fallow, settling beneath wild grasses.

Nevertheless, Kylan's legs moved, taking him southeast toward a thick band of trees two fields over. He couldn't explain the pull in his chest, but the closer he got, the faster he ran. Mounting the dry-stone walls to avoid the mud, he dashed along the wet rocks. His eyes never left those woods on his steady course. He hopped the gaps in the stones and finally leaped into the grass edging the trees.

A dozen steps into the forest, he stopped and listened. Rain pattered on the canopy. A reinvigorating burst hit him, sending him deeper. For what must have been five hundred feet, he ran. Then the wind left his sails; the energy vanished. Panting through the water running down his face, he scanned the woods around him. He didn't see anything strange. What would have brought him here?

Something moved. He eased forward until he saw a hulking shadow. Sliding the katana free, Kylan gingerly crept on and hoped he'd happened upon Bevin. The smacking, chortling sounds of a wolf eating suggested otherwise. Cursing the foolish notion that had led him this way, Kylan told himself it couldn't be a wolfkin. No, it was much too large, easily twice the size of the one they had rescued Cord from.

The shadow twitched and growled quietly. Steeling himself, Kylan stepped into form with his blade readied over his thigh. Golden eyes flickered his way before the shadow vanished. Quicker than Kylan's eyes could follow, the massive wolfkin left a wake in the branches where it fled. Stunned, Kylan stood still and listened for its return, for it to leap at him from behind.

In that moment, there was no force pulling him, no reinvigorating sensation, no thunderous pulse. It'd been replaced by a sinking sensation in his gut. Kylan saw what the wolf had been dining on, an opened corpse. Looking away from the carcass, he maintained his form. He watched the wind hammer the woods around him as he inched closer.

His lips shook as his mind began to accept what he would find. The only people out here were those who traveled with him—unless maybe someone from the Seeding had fallen prey. Forcing his eyes from the wolf's path, he glanced down. Half of the person's skull was exposed and gnawed on. Beneath the blood coating the body's arm, ink decorated the skin. Whorls and prongs. Kylan fell to his knees.

Gasping, Kylan blinked away his furious tears and stood. He raised Master Clienne's katana but couldn't lift his foot to chase after the beast. A half growl, half moan came from his throat. Sinking down, he held out the sword with one arm. "I won't leave you," he said, taking Veen's hand in his. "I'm sorry. I didn't know. I didn't know what it meant."

* * *

Rorry opened her eyes, amazed she had managed to fall asleep at all. The windows were gray enough with morning light for her to rise without guilt for waking the others. She stretched her back. The hard lifewood floor put the thin mats in Maeverly's vardo into perspective.

Remembering the worry on Kylan's face, she searched for him. He had not returned from his blatant, and crude, lie.

The satyr nodded a greeting to her. Then he squatted, repositioned, and sank to the floor. A curious thing, seeing a man standing on hooves. It would take some getting used to. She recognized her bias, but something about him, a darkness in his eyes, warranted caution.

Someone banged on the door. Scarlett gasped at the rude awakening. Andion leaped into the trunk and closed it.

Teague flung the door open, his face taut. "Is Julian in here?" His stony blue eyes ran over the disheveled passengers. Without explanation, he left. The door drifted in the breeze.

"What's he done now?" Cord asked, grabbing his sandals.

"I do not know," Rorry answered. "But I can tell you I would not refuse a warm meal."

Scarlett agreed and draped her shawl around her neck. She had benefited the most from Bevin's cooking, already losing some of the gauntness in her cheeks.

Finished lacing up his sandals, Cord led the way outside.

The rain had passed, leaving the air fresh and cool. Rorry appreciated the rare mercy in the late summer, though the clouds loitered overhead and had left a soppy mess to trudge through.

The Hook had positioned them in quite the exposed location, with the wheels still on the road and a green field on either side of the caravan. Woods offered ample cover beyond. Perhaps they feared damage from falling branches or getting stuck in mud. Untended, the horses meandered on either side.

"Something's wrong," Scarlett mumbled. Rorry followed her

gaze to see Kylan standing in the road at the end of the line of wagons, staring off into the woods. Scarlett exchanged a concerned glance with her as they started to walk in his direction.

To Rorry's dismay, Bevin's table and the stools remained packed, and the half-ogre was nowhere to be seen. Bevin's makeshift lean-to, a soaked cloth stretched between the cart and stakes in the ground, was empty. Half of Julian's manacles peered out from one of the muddy bedrolls underneath.

Drenched and motionless, Kylan jumped when she touched his arm. His exhausted blue eyes filled with regret before they returned to watching the southeastern woods. "I knew I should have gone last night," he said.

Wrapping herself around his damp arm, Rorry felt him shiver.

Two figures approached on the road. Carolle traipsed behind Julian, whose wet curls adhered to his head. She appeared to be laughing, which grew louder when she saw them. Julian struggled to maintain his decency in a nude stroll, carrying a wad of clothing in front of him and shielding his backside with a hand.

"Oh," Rorry said. "Scarlett, look away."

Scarlett did not even pretend to cover her eyes. "If I had a jar," she murmured.

Rorry let the comment go as some strange magi saying she had picked up from Maeverly. However, Cord gave her a furtive glance.

Upon seeing them, Julian sprung upright. "Can I not be trusted to bathe alone?" He redirected himself to the tent. "I have been doing so since I was a child."

Teague lunged between Rorry and Scarlett. He gripped Julian by the throat and forced him down to the sludge of the road.

Julian tried to fight him off and hold his clothes over himself. "I was taking a bath!" Julian shouted.

A knife flipped into Teague's hand. Rorry squeezed Kylan's arm harder. "When did you leave?" Teague roared. The blade dented Julian's neck. "When?"

Julian gawked. "It was dark. I was just bathing; I swear it! I was not going to run!"

Confused, Carolle gently said, "Teague, he speaks the truth. He was having a bath when I found him on my rounds."

The mercenary snatched Julian's clothes out of his hands.

Rorry turned her back. Upon realizing her friends had not, she inched her gaze forward. One eye observed plenty from beyond Kylan's sleeve. Julian's hands were not exactly proper covering but worked well enough for her to pretend to not be scandalized.

Frisking Julian's clothes, Teague checked every lining down to the smallest hem. He slung the tunic aside.

"I just washed that!"

Whatever Teague sought, he found in Julian's belt. His fingers pinched two slivers of metal.

Without as much backbone, Julian said, "If you had to lounge in the mud with that foul ogre, you would want to sneak away for a bath."

Carolle tried again. "Teague, what are you on about?"

Rorry heard stomping behind her. Next to Bevin, Maeverly drooped but nothing compared to the whimpering giant. Bevin cradled something in a green blanket against his shoulder.

"No," Carolle breathed, swaying slightly before she ran for them. Maeverly intercepted and embraced her. Carolle moaned and clawed for what was in Bevin's arms.

"J!" Teague shouted. "I need a little truth."

Maeverly gently released Carolle.

Bevin laid the bundle down as Maeverly went inside her wagon. Defending the wrapping from Carolle's hands, he swallowed her in his mighty arms. She pounded him with her fists until he hugged her tighter. Surrendering, she wept into his patchwork shirt.

"Veen?" Cord asked.

Teague diminished his anger long enough to nod a sorrowful response.

Kylan sniffled and began breathing rapidly. Rorry did not dare look at him. The sight of Carolle in pain urged her tears enough. It would be akin to seeing a parent cry; she would have no choice but to join in.

Caught between the grieving widow and an interrogation, Rorry wasn't sure where she should go. So she laid her face back on Kylan's arm and supported the friend before her.

"Cord, fetch me his manacles," Teague ordered.

Cord obliged without question and fastened them on Julian himself. When the chains stopped rattling, Cord returned and put a comforting hand on Rorry's shoulder.

Maeverly broke the silence as she bustled past. "Manacles, Teague? Do you honestly think he—"

"The bottle, J."

Rorry braved the view in time to see Maeverly uncork a stubby green bottle. She pressed it against Julian's chest. "Get away from me, witch!"

"*Bresolle amacda*," Maeverly breathed. A lavender vapor whirled from the bottle. It lingered in the air before abruptly jamming itself into Julian's nostrils.

He screamed, until the gas choked him.

Cord's grip tightened.

When Julian's coughing stopped, Teague sat him up and held the blade to his throat. Julian's eyes fogged, as though he were waiting for something to break his ennui.

Teague asked, "Where were you last night?"

"I slept." Blue fog wafted from Julian's mouth.

"Did you see Veen?"

Red fog answered, "No."

The blade pressed forward into Julian's skin. Teague snarled. "Lie to me again and I will finish you, understood?"

"Yes." Blue.

Tears dripped off the interrogator's nose. Teague's voice quavered. "Did you have anything to do with Veen's death?"

Rorry relaxed when blue air answered, "No, I slept. Then I went to bathe."

"Why did you lie about seeing him?"

"I did not mean to," Julian said, with blue vapors escaping his mouth. "I did not know I had." Even with his glazed eyes, Julian started sniveling. "End me now if you wish. I am a doomed man. The army turned its back on me. They will never take me back now. So I am stuck with you foreigners, spitting on our ways. Unless I am working, you bind me. You drag me across Merith, but you have offered me no salvation." If Rorry understood the spell correctly, his blue breath meant he spoke truthfully. "Unbind me or leave me to my fate."

Cord removed his hand from her shoulder. His sad eyes watched Carolle now.

Rorry had nothing further to learn from the truth spell. Instead, she concerned herself with what had taken Veen. "How did it happen?" she asked.

Maeverly put her arms out. "Let's give Teague and Julian some privacy. I think we've all seen enough of this display." She corked the bottle in her hand.

"A moment, J."

She nodded to Teague and gestured for them to go on to the wagons. "I shan't be long."

Rorry tugged Kylan into motion. He ambled on ahead of them, wearing a trembling grimace.

Scarlett stuck close to Kylan when Rorry knelt to embrace Carolle. Veen had only brushed her life, beyond the time she'd split his lip, but she had begun to care for his wife . . . his widow. She joined in the monk's mourning and remained even after Maeverly went to the others.

* * *

Bleak-faced and lost in their thoughts and the broken flickers of the lamplight, his friends filled the prison wagon around Cord. Next to him, Scarlett absentmindedly picked at a loose thread in the hem of her sleeve. Her book stayed closed in her lap.

Cord answered a knock at the door.

"It is time," Rorry said from outside. Scarlett left after Rorry.

Kylan sat on the trunk, alone in his thoughts. Not wanting to abandon him, Cord waited for a dismissal. "Are you sure?" Cord asked.

Kylan's gaze didn't lift from his boots. "I laugh at funerals; always have. I refuse to laugh at his." Tears betrayed his argument, but Cord let it go. "We should stay." Kylan looked to him. "We should stay and kill every one of those cursed bastards!"

Cord didn't have to speak before Kylan released the idea. Their only hope of surviving was finding shelter in the Bonded Nations. He wasn't even sure if Racine would be far enough away.

"We'll see him again," Cord said, "in the Glades."

"I knew something was wrong last night," Kylan said. "But I acted like a scared child, waiting. I should've gone sooner." He pounded the plank next to him with his fist. "That feeling—the one you were teasing me about—it could have saved him. If I'd gone faster . . . Never again."

Even though the satyr pretended to ignore the conversation, Cord saw concern for Kylan on his face. Cord spared a weak smile for Andion, who had given up his puzzle to provide silence for their mourning.

Slumping forward, Kylan wiped his face just before Cord closed the door.

The knee-high grass made Cord's skin itch as he waded to the Hook, assembled a short distance away in the field. The placid trees beyond them defied the wind that had been picking up steadily. A shovel scraped against dirt, adding to a pile next to the grave.

The girls stood between Carolle and the sorcerer. Maeverly cocked her head to the side, surprised to see Cord alone.

"Kylan?" Teague asked. Cord shook his head, unsure what to say.

Rorry understood. "He is not in a state to join us but will make his peace separately."

Carolle didn't seem to hear any of it, lost to the world outside of the green bundle Bevin held.

Julian climbed out of the grave, dropped the shovel, and wiped his grime-covered hands on his britches. Teague had forced him to dig Veen's grave, even though he'd been proven innocent.

It would've been nice to force Julian to dig Marlone's grave. Marlone would have laughed.

"Now you may bathe," Teague said, his tone still hard. "Make it quick and keep an eye out for the beast that did this." Julian kept his gaze low. No one watched him depart. "Bevin?"

Gently cradling the blankets around Veen's body, Bevin wept and stepped into the deep hole, still only chest high to the giant. He laid the bundle on the damp soil, patted it a few times, and climbed out.

Carolle sniffled, squeezing her fist to her mouth.

Teague tried to speak. He dabbed a few tears away with a green kerchief. With a deep breath, he began again. "Brothers and sisters of the Hook, we have lost a member. His reasons for joining remain his own. The sacrifice Stille van Veen has made garners our humility. May he find peace in order to start anew."

Rorry pulled Scarlett close when the rain began to fall in large drops. They stared at the shroud in silence for some time.

Veen didn't follow the Chancellor's Light, and might have been offended by it, so Cord didn't pray, just relayed his sorrow and well-wishes for Veen in thought.

"In Lekelith, they say 'happy is the corpse the rain falls on,'" Teague said. "If only that were true for those left behind." He glanced over to Carolle and asked, "Do you mind if we sing his favorite song?"

She forced a brief smile and shook her head.

"The 'Song of the Fallen Mercs,'" Teague said. "The shorter

version."

With a weak chuckle, Maeverly said, "Leave it to Veen to make me feel irreverent one last time." She and Teague began to clap. Bevin's hands drowned out the sound of the others joining in.

Teague and Maeverly chanted together:

So ye want to be a merc
Then sit and try not to smirk
Be brave and be bold
And do as you're told
To survive in this kind of work

Many have come before ye
Who found the bad kind of glory
When you risk your loin
For fame or for coin
Be sure ye leave a good story

Don't forget the tale of Jack
His senses were a wee bit slack
With an oracle's blessing
He sought dragons nesting
And changed his fate from saint to snack

And recall Donnie Malone
The best captain the seas had known
During one stormy drench
He bedded a fast wench
Disease killed the man through his bone

Wade Lewellyn-Hughes

Remember Boastful Clara
And her twin, Beautiful Sara
While counting their gold
In a tavern, not hold
They brought about the end of their era

Behold Great Maxim the Brave
Who was hired by an unknown knave
When the treasure was found
The Great Maxim was bound
And left with a cave for a grave

Then there was swasher Glen Fyfe
Who fondled an ax man's fine wife
Oh that maritime clock
Put his brains in his cock
And brought a sharp end to his life

These verses, true and morbid
Are told to help ye get sorted
Keep your cocks in your jocks
And your gold behind locks
In health, ye shall be rewarded

Carolle had joined in for the last verse, but her smile faded fast.

Maeverly went to the mound of fresh dirt, grabbed a fistful, and released it over the bundle. She rubbed Carolle's arm with her clean hand and departed with her head low. Cord followed Rorry to do the same and grabbed a handful for Kylan as well. The moist soil stuck to his skin and crumbled over the grave, like flour over dough. Rorry deposited the broken figure Kylan had been carving of his sister next to Veen as he had requested.

A pop turned everyone's head toward Scarlett. With a cork in her left hand, she shook a bottle above the open grave, releasing dried pink and orange petals that twirled down to the body. She curtsied to Veen and to Carolle before joining her friends for the walk back.

Cord let the girls go inside alone and watched the rest of the funeral from the lifewood's steps. Bevin dropped a mound of dirt before he picked up Carolle in another hug. The poor widow observed the grave with the same expression from the beginning of the funeral through to Teague replacing the last shovelful. Teague brushed off his gloves and held her close.

Cord gave them their privacy and went inside. Too much death surrounded him. He prayed there wouldn't be more.

* * *

Scarlett released the latch to Joseb's wagon, then forced herself to grab it again and press.

Joseb sat on his stool with his face in his hands. Straightening, he said, "I'm not sure now is the best time for a lesson."

Possibly the hardest thing she'd ever had to do, she entered, sat on the bench, and said, "I know. And I'm sorry to insist." Lowering *Essential Focus* from her chest, she revealed the three beeswax candle nubs that had been pressed between her shawl and the tome.

Handing them to Joseb, she said, "I read that using magic is the best way to draw your core to you. Then I read three different references in the Lost Novice Spells section that said the practice of specific spells is what makes them more potent, so I've been lighting those candles with sorcery each time I finished reading a page, but . . . I only know the two spells to practice and neither seems like it'd be strong enough to use against wolfkin."

Hugging the book to her chest, she said, "I'm not strong enough to burn a wolf. Not yet. And those novice spells are ridiculous: making coins shinier, refreshing stale air to smell like fruit, cracking nuts." She shrugged. "So, please, teach me something to protect my friends."

The sorcerer closed his eyes and lowered his chin. "You're better served with those two spells. Veen was a dear friend and a great warrior, Scarlett. I don't know if any of us could have fared better." He put his focus on the mirror at the vanity and began redrawing the dark lines around his eyes with the Wand of Shades.

Trying to find her patience for the man's mourning, Scarlett rose. "Then I will keep practicing on my own."

"Don't leave," he said, turning. "Those spells are all you need— the one really, invisibility. Fire is extremely dangerous to entwine with your emotions. What I need to teach you is how to extrapolate the invisibility for something larger than a coin. It's a challenging trick at first and shall take time, but do sit. The exercises can be done on your own later."

After she sat, he took her hand. "Hide first. No matter what, hide yourself first. Then hide the others. Gods blind me if we aren't going to need you and your friends before this is all over."

Chapter 36: Mad Monk

Cord thought repeating the song from Veen's funeral might cheer Kylan up but doubted he could recall it with any real accuracy and didn't want to bother Scarlett for help. Since she'd returned from Maeverly's wagon, she had been busy reading and flicking the candlesticks in and out of sight.

Rorry had gone back to the grave for Carolle but only at Kylan's insistence. He wanted isolation. They could only afford silence, aside from the clicks of Andion's mysterious riddle. Now and then, Andion glanced over at Kylan, who sat alone with his head buried in his knees. Ferix watched little else.

The black puzzle box slid away from Andion. With a sigh, he cleared the space around him. "Piks do not mourn long," he said to Kylan. "Our lives are longer than yours, and they're still too short for it."

Kylan's irritation shot to the surface.

Andion raised his hands and said, "You are sad for your friend.

And yet, his life must be celebrated. I can dance for him. I do it every night for my parents, just in case . . . to know someone has."

The pik's cloth shoes slapped the floor. Bobbing his oversized head, he began to dance in a circle and clap. A backward flip landed Andion on his hands, where he continued to cavort to the rhythm, slapping the floor.

Scarlett started clapping, then Cord. Kylan's lips managed a weak grin. It strengthened when Ferix clopped along.

With a shove, Andion flipped back to his feet. From hands to feet to hands to feet, he switched, then to one hand to one foot. Kylan joined in by the time Andion took a final spin and bowed deeply. "And now," Andion panted, "his dance has ended."

The salty merc song might have worked a little better, but Kylan said, "That was kind of you, Andion."

While Scarlett gave encouraging condolences for Andion's parents, Cord wondered how many more times the orphan would dance. For Kylan? For Scarlett? For Rorry? Each one put in harm's way by him.

Every wolfkin would smell this *peppermint on ice* cursing his bones. As much as the others were afraid to say it, Beez wouldn't be the only Dreg dogging him. They'd all be safer if he left, even Teague.

Three small knocks hushed them. Teague's gloomy face leaned inside. "Cord, Kylan, we'll need ye to take turns driving this vardo."

Cord's hand stalled Kylan's rising. "I'll go first," he said, summoning the courage to do what he should've done days ago.

Outside, the clouds had thinned since the funeral, letting through a white circle where the midday sun hung. Still standing over Veen's grave, Rorry held Carolle's hand.

Closing the door behind him, Cord called, "Teague, can I have a word?" The man huffed in response, clearly expecting to defend Julian. His polite patience had run out, which made Cord's request all the more urgent. "Listen, I thought about it. If you want me to head off in another direction, I will." Teague's blank features gave nothing away. "Y'all have got a better chance of making it without me."

"Hear me!" Teague commanded. The words pinned Cord against the vardo. Teague put his face inches from Cord's. "You haven't had a

Dreg inside you. I have. My skin knows the feel of things it shouldn't. Beez used my body to kill, to rape, and to butcher innocents, all for desire and power. And if I refused to play into his schemes—screamed that I didn't want it, then I got what they did."

"Then turn around and fight him!" Cord yelled. "He can't touch you! I saw him try. We oughta both get marked, send the others on to Racine, and hunt *him* down."

A fleeting glint in Teague's gaze agreed, but there was no digging the man out of his fear. "If I were mad, I would. What if we lost? What would Beez do with you?" He tapped his temple and said, "My guess is he'd kill your friends and worse while you writhed for control of your body. What then? Then he's gained the power to keep his vessels in rude health. Do you wish to extend their torment? You want him poking around in your thoughts? Giving you nightmares for the rest of your days?"

Jabbing Cord's breastbone with a finger, Teague pressed him back. "Consider what I'm saying. The people of Kenton are dead, Cord. So is Veen. If you insist on remaining in Merith as some form of vengeance, you'll fight me to the death." Teague didn't blink. "Don't fret, lad. I make my mercy kills swift."

Cord snarled. "I'm not your prisoner!"

The merc threw his hands up. "'Tis your choice. A limited one, but yours. I'd hate to think you'd dishonor Veen by giving up now." When Teague turned away, Carolle and Rorry were standing behind him in the road.

Whatever they'd heard was enough. The fire in Carolle's wounded glare shamed him. "Survive," she demanded and followed Teague to the green vardo.

He tried to apologize but couldn't face the accusation of betrayal in Rorry's eyes. She went inside and slammed the door.

* * *

Under the full afternoon sun, Cord urged on the sixteen hooves beating the masoned road as loud as thunder. They traveled faster now that longer stretches of the road remained intact. Cord wasn't surprised to find the road well-kept at the border of Granville and Weatherington, two of Merith's wealthiest provinces and frequent rivals if the stories were true.

In the hours that had distanced them from Veen's grave, the clouds had broken to reveal the snow-covered Breslan Mountains bumping up the northern horizon of the plains.

Born and raised in one of the villages near the Northern Pass, Headmaster Angsly had often reminisced on the mountains' beauty, complaining that his description didn't do them justice. Cord reckoned he was right. Seeing them, he felt the headmaster watching over him.

His headmaster had clung to the memories of his childhood village and had done his best to shape Kenton into the same community. Cord wondered if he'd ever be able to think about Kenton without the pain. The village belonged solely to his memory now, full of ghosts and regrets.

They'd ridden past a few wide-eyed young men traveling to their new homes for the Seeding. Cord figured more had hidden off the side of the road until the strange caravan had gone by.

Aside from cautiously eyeing the Merithians, Teague hadn't looked back since they'd left. Julian slouched against the opposite edge of the green vardo's seat. Shackled again, he probably wished he was back on Bevin's lap.

Behind the vardo's yellow door, Carolle rested. Or more likely, she sharpened her blades to exact vengeance, wetting the whet stone with her tears. Her shift in demeanor had been quick and brutal, and Cord's fault. She'd given him a basilisk's glare with her command to survive, as if the horrific ideas Teague had planted weren't enough to keep him in line.

Cord owed them both an apology; his offer had dishonored Veen. If Rorry's face had meant what he suspected it did, he'd have more apologies to dole out during their next break.

Since they had crossed over the last bridge hours ago, Cord hadn't seen the Staghorn River but suspected the snaking forest hid it from his sight on his left. The trees had grown denser, and hills rolled on the eastern horizon. If those hills indicated the edge of the flats, then this was definitely the Granville Province. He had left Weatherington. He wondered for how long.

Whistling, Teague waved for them to leave the road.

Four riders were coming their way, just close enough for Cord to make out the colors of their horses. They wore tabards. Judges. Cord's stomach cramped. He steered his team to follow the jostling gilded wagon into the brush and brought them to a stop.

Dragging Julian down from the seat, Teague still looked vexed. Hauling Julian to the yellow door, Teague knocked along the side of the vardo. Then he shoved Julian inside with a fast apology to Carolle.

As he made his way back to Maeverly, Teague stared daggers at Cord. "Sit tight, stay quiet, and lose that fecking uniform!"

Dropping down from his seat, Cord hid behind the horses as he jerked his tunic free of his belt and over his head. He folded over the gold embroidery and climbed back to his seat. Without a better place to stow it, the tunic cushioned the lifewood bench for him as he tried to calm his breathing, knowing a fight was coming.

The Judges slowed to a halt on the road between the green vardo and Cord as they took in the caravan. None of them reached for their swords. Younger than any Judges Cord had seen, three of the four wore tabards with the green flags of Granville stitched on their chests. The helmeted Judge in the front, their leader, ran his fingers down a mustache that curved to his jaw.

The man without a tabard, a toad with sloping shoulders and uneven eyes, had several years on them. Though he wore the pride of a Judge, his threads were common, and his limbs had neither armor nor the muscles to suggest they ever had.

Cord's curse brought his eyes to the largest Judge in the back. The soldier hunkered over his pommel, holding the reins loosely in his right hand. Blue shimmers danced about on his left forearm. Sweat dripped from the injured Judge's chin, but he shivered.

"I greet ye, my good sirs," Teague shouted as he and Maeverly came forward. In midstep, she stopped, then sauntered with more sway in her hips. Both members of the Hook were as confident as the first day Cord had met them. The Judges had no idea of the danger coming their way.

"Explain yourselves," the man in commoner clothes said, earning him tolerant looks from the Judges.

A whisker wider than the neck of his steed, the third Judge reached over and steadied the wounded Judge in his saddle.

Their leader removed his helmet from his smashed, sweaty brown hair. "We've seen some trouble in these parts and wouldn't wish for you to add to them."

"We are merchants," Teague said, extending the licenses to the Judge. "Not the trouble-brewing sort."

Flipping through the documents, the Judge said, "There are six licenses, but I only see three of you. Where are the others?"

Maeverly exhaled loudly. "It was terrible! He was—"

"You speak when you are spoken to," the toad croaked. His hand ran down his tunic, seeking an absent emblem. "The men are talking."

To Cord's surprise, Maeverly dipped with an apologetic nod before Teague spoke. "As she was saying, one of our members died when a wolfkin caught him unaware. We buried his remains several miles down the road if ye require proof."

The Judge turned back to face the others.

"Did ye know Merith is under attack?"

"That's our business, meddler," the old toad said. "We should take your goods just for asking! And where do you get the audacity to taint our land with your dead?"

"Silas," the lead Judge reprimanded. "Be quiet."

The yellow door flung open. As Carolle's foot hit the grass, the wooden limbs of her longbow flexed. Swinging her aim to Silas, she said, "Were you the one who said my husband was unworthy of your dirt?"

Crackling sounds brought Cord's attention to the wiry Judge. Sparks of lightning leaped between his fingers, waiting for a target. Cord's jaw fell. Another magus hiding in the army?

Julian jumped out of the wagon; his mouth opened to shout something, but he gaped at the purple bolts dancing along the Judge's hand.

The leader's expression hardened when he saw Julian's manacles.

Teague raised his hands between the Judges and Carolle. "Seems we all have some answers to provide, yes?"

"Yuris," the sickly Judge moaned to the leader. His bay sidled when he touched its neck to steady himself.

The leader nodded back to him. "My lady," Yuris said to Carolle, "Silas is a silly little man." He scowled at Silas, who hadn't removed his eyes from the lightning. "He's not a Judge but a homeless Merithian and has no right to spout his opinions and endanger those who are trying to help him."

If Silas heard a word the Judge said, he didn't so much as blink.

Relaxing her bowstring, Carolle stared without kindness. The lightning disappeared from the slim Judge's hand.

"Judge Yuris Mason," the leader introduced himself. "Judge Tyre and I were seeking aid for Judge Feln when we came across this fool."

Now Silas looked ready to spit fire but held his tongue.

Yuris pointed his chin at Julian. "So, what's your story?"

"I took more than my share of rations," Julian answered. "These merchants saved me and are taking me to safety. Yet I broke their rules all the same. I have told you I am sorry," he said to Teague, who took the bizarre lie in stride.

Yuris squinted at them.

"Foreigners would be better than magi," Silas grumbled.

The magus, Judge Tyre, said, "If that's how you feel, then go on, Silas. Good luck surviving those beasts on your own."

Maeverly tapped her chin with a green nail as she studied them. Cord would've given a custard for her thoughts.

"Bevin?" Teague shouted down the line of wagons. Booming steps sounded immediately. Cord couldn't figure what Teague hoped to accomplish by bringing out the half-ogre.

The Judges' faces slackened as they saw what was coming. Cord held his breath as Bevin thudded by. Bevin met the riders' eyes evenly with his feet firmly on the ground.

"And what magic is this?" Silas hissed.

Bevin grunted at the toad's disapproval. The horses snorted and sidled.

"Aye," Teague said. "A big wind wouldn't stir him." He frowned thoughtfully at Julian. "I'm afraid I'll need you to take over custody of Julian for a while. He has apologized and should behave himself, yes?"

Yuris lowered Teague's documents to him.

The wounded Judge moaned again.

"Judge Feln is injured?" Teague asked.

"Barlin," Judge Feln replied. He wiped his forehead with his sleeve. "Call me Barlin. And it's just a bite." That silenced everyone until Bevin rattled Julian's manacles.

Yuris nodded to their pitying faces. "Those beasts took Fort Trent while we were in Granville for Hansweighn. When we returned, they attacked us. If Barlin hadn't thought it strange that the High Guard received orders from a Catalyst, they would've caught us. Fortunately, we survived the attack, mostly."

Then he pointed at Silas. "This idiot rode out of a village when we passed. He said the wolves attacked there too. We didn't deviate to verify his tale but couldn't bring ourselves to leave him."

Yuris and Barlin hadn't flinched when Judge Tyre lit up his hand with sparks. And they broke the law in order to protect a commoner. They deserved any support this mismatched caravan could provide, if for no other reason than they were the first Judges Cord had seen with any sense of honor.

"I can heal him," Cord said, dropping to the road.

Raising a finger at Cord, Maeverly said, "Hold on. Given your ability's trait of transferring the wound to you, I would advise against it. The curse may transfer as well."

"I've healed a wolfkin bite before," Cord, unintentionally putting hope on their faces. "But he still died."

Letting the hope go, Barlin nodded. "The curse does that." Then he spoke to the back of Yuris's head. "That's when I want you to end me, Yuris, when I die. Don't let me come back from the dead as one of those things."

Cord's insides chilled. Dying was part of the curse?

"My lady," he continued, "if it pleases you, may I rest next to your husband? I'd prefer not to be buried alone in the wilds somewhere."

Carolle agreed wordlessly, though her expression had softened.

Placing a hand on Barlin's back, Judge Tyre said, "Then we shouldn't tarry longer. How far?"

"Less than a half day's ride," Teague answered. "Now what village was it that met the same fate as Fort Trent?"

"What business is it—"

An arrow struck Silas's chest. His horse pranced about knocking his body from the saddle.

Carolle lowered her bow.

Teague put his hands up and muttered an apology about dramatic monks to the shocked Judges. He went to Silas's body and opened his eyes. The irises were golden. "Forgive Carolle's efficiency. If the horde had taken a village, someone in his shape wouldn't have survived. I'd guess he was keeping track of Judge Tyre. The wolves can smell magi and are well rewarded for bringing them back to the Dregs." Teague glanced up to Maeverly. "There's no denying an invasion now."

"The what?" Judge Tyre asked.

Teague calmed Silas's horse and went on to explain the Dregs while Cord's mind ran through the events of the night Marlone had died. Was he a wolfkin now? Ashes, he'd be in Beez's pack. The others, Scarlett at least, must have known. Why hadn't they told him?

"And Granville, the city?" Teague asked.

"Unknown," Yuris answered. "There were so many at the fort we assumed Granville already had some in hiding. If you're determined, a bridge will take you over the river just beyond Silas's village, Scalebrush, another fifteen miles down, but I wouldn't recommend it."

"Coward," Cord said, stoking a fire in Yuris's eyes. "You are meant to protect the people of Merith."

"Our directives in this situation are to inform the councilmember in Brewing of what befell Granville," Yuris said. "When Lord and Lady Gwirion know of the attack, we'll return."

They were off to see Rorry's parents then. What would she think of this?

"Granville is not without its allies, even with its looser interpretation of the Tribunal's restrictions."

"Looser?" Cord asked.

Yuris thumbed at Judge Tyre, as though it explained everything.

Teague wore a proud grin for the Judges. "South Thornton is a loss. I would suspect any town south of here would be. Farther down this road, beyond . . . beyond Veen's grave, an empty village remains standing. It may serve ye as a safe place to camp. The pack that took the town cleared out days ago. Best ye avoid any storms too."

Yuris extended his hand to Teague. They shook before Teague handed over the reins to Silas's horse.

"And avoid the High Guard if you see them," Cord added. They grinned at him, as though that was common sense.

"Do ye have a map?" Teague asked.

"We're Judges, my good sir," Yuris said. "We don't need a map when we're within the Great Barrier."

"Safe travels then. Remember, keep a northern trajectory and avoid the villages."

They nodded. Judge Tyre waved farewell before replacing his hand on Barlin's back. Then they reined their horses west.

Maeverly clicked her tongue. "Lambs to the slaughter. We should have told them of the tunnels."

Teague cleared his throat. Cord followed his glance to see Julian's curious expression.

"Oh, I don't know," Teague said, running a finger over the black pendant under his jerkin. "I have a feeling they'll make it. The good news is we were right. We're not the goal of this slaughter. Beez's obsession is our main obstacle. The bad news is another Dreg's wolfkin have crossed our path ahead and in large numbers. Until we know more about Llandir's fate, our plan remains unchanged. We'll just alter our tactics."

"Tactics, Teague Fuchs?" Carolle asked. "Is that something you want to share with the rest of us, good boy? Or are you playing this close to your vest too?"

As interested as Cord was in the answers, his stomach was working itself into knots, a rancid stew of anger and nerves. He wanted to know what his *friends* knew. Why would they let him think Marlone was dead? He snatched his tunic from the bench, shoved it over his head and arms, and thudded down to the grass. Ready to pick a fight, he flung open the door to the vardo and said, "Hey! Y'all wanna—"

Rorry and Kylan had their weapons in hand, poised to take down whoever opened the door. Scarlett stood behind them. They relaxed, waiting for an explanation for why they'd stopped.

"'Twasn't!" Teague shouted angrily.

They brushed past Cord to see why the man had yelled. Maeverly raised her eyebrows at them as Cord chased after.

Teague glowered at Carolle. "You know yourself."

"Speak the truth, charmer," she said. "What it is, Teague, I don't think you know anymore." When she saw them gathering around, the monk shoved Teague inside the green vardo and sealed the door behind them. Then Carolle let loose a mouthful of Ferix's favorite words.

"Bevin," Maeverly said over the argument, to which Bevin wiped his nose on his sleeve. "We know what we're heading into. Let's break now. Unshackle Julian and take the young ones for a walk in the spinney. Then prepare dinner. Shout if you run into trouble."

The half-ogre groaned at her and waved off the request. Freezing, his eyes bulged. He sniffed the air. His jaw slackened. He sniffed deeper, faster, spinning as he searched about.

Causing the ground to quake, he raced to the provisions cart and returned seconds later with his club and a few burlap sacks slung over his shoulder. He unbound Julian, grabbed his arm, and took off for the woods. Julian had to run to keep up.

Maeverly gestured for Cord and the others to go along.

Cord urged the others to come away from the intensifying argument. He wasn't sure what Bevin was after, but this would give him the opportunity he needed to get some answers.

Chapter 37: Sparking Regrets

As the group trailed Bevin through the thickets leading north to the Staghorn River, Cord bit his tongue and distracted himself by counting the outline of twenty faded patches that had been darned together to make the backside of the half-ogre's colorful tunic. Bevin hunted something, slowing only to inhale deeply and smack his lips, but Cord didn't care about that.

His sense of betrayal swelled with each minute he had to wait to ask about Marlone, away from Julian. One comment from that jackass and Cord would return his belt knife, hilt deep.

Scampering between more broken dry-stone walls, Bevin brought them to a meadow sloping down to the river. He paused to snort the air beneath an old pear tree, then threw a burlap sack at Kylan. Grunting, the half-ogre pointed at Kylan and Cord, then the tree. Bevin flung another sack at Julian's face and pushed the Catalyst next to Scarlett. He pointed at them and to a patch of woods. Neither of them seemed to understand what his grunts were telling them to retrieve. But he didn't elaborate before waving on Rorry and, unexpectedly, squealing with excitement. The half-ogre practically loped away from them.

"I will follow Bevin then?" Rorry shouted back as she hurried after.

Uneasy about Scarlett going off alone with Julian, Cord squinted a silent threat at the Croathite.

Julian curled his upper lip. "I meant what I said. There is no salvation for me here. So do not worry for your witch friend, wooder, even if I refuse to become a heathen." He cut away at the word, labeling Cord.

"Honestly!" Scarlett shouted at Julian. "Why should they take you to the continent? At every opportunity, you express your disgust for their ways and for their culture. If you want help, you should start by being nice. Magic is not something someone like you can touch."

With a patronizing sniff, Julian said, "Just because I need their help to get out of here does not mean I will absorb every word out of those iconoclasts' mouths like you magi." He sneered at Kylan. "And what is your excuse?"

After seeing the evasive shrug from Kylan, Cord had to admit to himself that he didn't know Kylan's original reason for leaving Merith either.

Scarlett's shoulders climbed to her ears. "Cord prays to the Chancellor before every meal, before every nap! And yet he recognizes the corruption in the army. He hasn't lost his religion, just his religion's intolerance, which is the only side we've seen from you."

For the first time Cord had seen, Scarlett lowered her shawl to hang from her elbows and put her hands on her hips. "Do you think we are all out to get you? We are a bit preoccupied with surviving, something we have to depend on each other to do. If you want to debate dogmas, do it over tea, not in the midst of being hunted by the Dregs." Ripping the sack from his hands, she set off for the woods. "If you've learned nothing from today, allow me to relay the lesson blatantly laid at our feet. Grow up!"

Not just pink from his sunburn, Julian followed her without looking Cord's way. When Scarlett disappeared in the thick, Cord broke his stare.

Wide-eyed, Kylan said, "I'd guess she's apologizing right about now, but I don't know who that was." He continued to watch the woods.

"I swear, Kylan; if he harms her, I'll behead him myself."

Hooding his eyes with a hand, Kylan surveyed the fruit tree above them. "Who knows? Maybe she'll set him on fire and save us a heap of trouble. Dare to dream. Dare to dream."

Even through his anger, Cord felt pride from Scarlett's defense. After everything that had happened with Veen that morning, he knew Kylan wasn't in the right state for an argument. Why had Bevin taken Rorry? She'd have no problem yelling the truth at him.

Swinging himself onto one of the old pear tree's lower branches, Kylan started to climb. When he had tossed down enough pears to fill most of their sack, Cord couldn't hold back any longer. He had to have answers.

"After all, someone's gotta use that sword," Cord said.

That woke Kylan's eyebrow. "There's a challenge in that somewhere." He chuckled. "A basilisk is a bit much for me. But if you want practice, I can thrash you soundly."

"No," Cord said. "But I would like to know when y'all were gonna tell me about Marlone."

Kylan closed his eyes and took a deep breath. Then he kept working, as though Cord hadn't said anything.

"You knew? Y'all knew he wasn't dead!" Cord shouted. "Why didn't y'all tell me?"

"The longer we've known you, the less reason we've had to send you to your death," Kylan answered, dropping another pear. It hit the ground. "Cord, the creature he's become has Marlone's memories, but he's not your friend. Marlone's gone."

Cord kicked a dried mound of mud, one of the crawdad towers dotting the area. The mud burst in a satisfying cloud of destruction, encouraging him to take down three more.

"It's not like we wanted to lie to you." Kylan swung down from the tree. "Tell me you haven't already thought about running back to find him? Tell me honestly, and I'll apologize."

Clenching his jaw, Cord glowered. Part of him understood, but that didn't take away the sting. They thought so little of his control that it made sense for them to lie to him, to let him think his closest friend had died because he'd been too slow to heal him. "No, y'all just keep your secrets, don't you?"

"What does that mean?" Kylan asked, setting a few more pears in the bulging sack.

"Why are you leaving Merith, Kylan?" Cord wished he could take the question back as soon as he asked it. His suspicions told him it wasn't something he wanted to know.

Kylan's face reddened from his chin to his eyebrows. Ignoring Cord's question, he said, "Let me rinse off my hands, and we'll head back." He rubbed his palms together, grabbed a pear, and bit into it on his way to the river.

Too wound up to let it go, Cord left the bag and trailed him to the water's edge.

Lily pads and cattails lined a cove of calm water where the river turned north, rippling slightly in its current. Their approach frightened a few sunbathing turtles from the driftwood.

"With this many crawfish around, there may be another basilisk," Kylan teased, tossing the flimsy stem of the pear into the river. As he scrubbed his hands, his eyes glossed over. He suddenly jerked upright, focused on something in the water. "Do you see that?"

"Whatever it is, it can wait till I have my answer."

Tugging his shirt off, Kylan didn't pay him any mind. He laid the sword on his tunic and stripped to his smallclothes. Then he tiptoed around the edge of the water.

"What are you doing?" Cord asked.

"Looking for a corpse." He did have a strange sense of humor.

Cool water splashed Cord's legs as Kylan plunged in. Not far out into the reeds of the cove, Kylan lifted a stick barely visible above the water. "I knew it!" He tried to lift it higher, but something had ensnared it below the surface. "Throw me my knife."

Retrieving the blade from Kylan's boot pocket, Cord lobbed it to him.

Dipping under, Kylan cut the stick loose. He swam back to the bank and sloshed out of the river with his prize held high. Notches and symbols marred the curving shaft. Black by nature, the wood had somehow staved off saturation. Two beveled troughs were dug into the ends.

"A bow?"

"Veen's," Kylan said. "He lost it when Beez threw him into the river. It must've washed all the way down here." He dressed as Cord studied the weapon. "Carolle should have it."

"What are the chances we'd find it?" Cord asked.

"It's proof we're on the right path. The world, the gods, someone is giving us a sign that we're meant to be here."

Cord found the sentiment as unusual as the bow. "I hope it's not a sign we'll share Veen's fate if we stay on this path."

"Less vinegar, Cord. I refuse to believe the fates are so cruel as to take Veen without a just cause."

With a huff, Cord said, "You wanna answer my question now?"

"Why do you want to know?"

"Maybe I don't," Cord answered. "Maybe y'all oughta just go with the Hook, and I'll go find Marlone. He didn't keep secrets from me."

"Oh," Kylan said mockingly. "You feel betrayed because we thought you'd run to your friend and get killed? Only now we know it'd be much worse than that, don't we?" He grabbed the bow from Cord's hand. "You know nothing of betrayal." He shook his head apologetically before he said, "Or maybe you do. The Tribunal doesn't really take a shine to your kind either."

"What does that mean?" Cord asked, crossing his arms.

"Look, we have to get along to get out of here. It didn't make sense for me to tell you that your Chancellor would have me dragged behind the horses. Wait, did you take a vow to do that too? To tie up the men who didn't want to marry women and have them bludgeoned to death on the cobblestones, to smear them out across the streets as an example to others? And burn their remains? I know how you love your vows."

Cord took a step back. "Are you . . . are you saying—"

"I'm a dandelion?" Kylan asked. "Should I have used the Tribunal's words? I desire to lie with a man, maybe more than one. And how am I supposed to do that here, where I have to marry a woman by my twenty-fifth year or be slathered across the streets?" Kylan's body tensed as though he expected a fight. He focused on the bow in his hands as tears welled in his eyes. "Are you going to tie me to one of the vardos now?" he asked with less heat.

Cord felt hollow inside. He didn't know what to say, so he said nothing, just backed away and walked up the slope to collect their sack of pears.

Kylan scoffed, but followed.

Beyond the wall, something moved. Cord froze. A figure in a brown hood walked with a misshapen man as tall as Bevin. They were heading east toward Rorry and the others.

Marbled in ruddy colors, the misshapen man's features didn't make sense. Sprigs of grass protruded from the lumps of clay covering his body. "What is that?" Cord whispered.

The strange man halted. As it turned toward them, rocks bubbled up to the surface of its skin. It charged. Passing through the wall, it added some of the dry stones to the cluster on its chest. Its legs stretched and compressed with each step, booming toward them. Rocks slid to its knuckles. Muddy skin dried to set them in place.

"Bevin!" Kylan shouted. "Someone!"

The hooded figure watched from behind the wall without moving.

"Run!" Cord said and sprinted back to the river.

The ground protested against the heavy steps of the clay colossus behind them.

At the water's edge, Kylan said, "If it's mud, maybe it'll avoid the water."

"I can't swim!" Cord growled.

Judgment entered Kylan's eyes, but he said nothing. Instead, he drew his sword. "I doubt a katana will stop something like that."

Its steps shook the pear tree as it passed underneath.

Scarlett popped out of the tree line behind the shambling mound. Julian appeared behind her. Upon seeing the monster, he ran in the opposite direction.

Throttling the burlap sack's nape, Cord shouted, "Go!" He slung the bag with all his might, toppling over in the effort. It struck a solid blow, knocking the muck man off-balance.

Kylan ran left toward Scarlett and the woods.

Trying to distract their attacker, Cord darted to the right.

The mud man recovered in time to stretch one of its massive hands and clip Kylan. He fell and stayed down. A small boulder slid to the end of its mucky arm as it rose, ready to pummel Kylan.

Cord dashed toward them and prepared to leap. Heat forced him to stop and cover his face. A ring of flames encased the muddy limb.

Scarlett held her hands out, her face unnervingly vexed. The arm cracked as it dried and broke off completely, crumbling when it hit the ground. Scarlett gasped when the face caked with straw and leaves focused on her. She closed her eyes.

The clay monster left Kylan, charging toward its new target.

Cord stayed on its heels and leaped onto its back, trying to grip its head. An arm, uninhibited by bone and tendons, grabbed Cord's torso and flung him to the side. When he stopped rolling, he wheezed, "Run!" Cord got to his knees in time to see Scarlett disappear, from the waist up. The skirt of her dress shifted as she took in her error.

The hooded figure jumped between Scarlett and the muck man. Her hood fell, allowing a mass of brown and gray curls to whip in the breeze. "Hold!" she ordered.

The monster stopped. Its knees hit the ground. Though their attacker now resembled a lifeless mound, Cord felt it watching him.

Kylan stood, holding his arm. "I'm fine," he said coolly to Cord and picked up the katana.

With a watchful eye, they passed the mound and approached the common woman inquiring about Scarlett's well-being. Wearing a friendly smile, she seemed old enough to be their mother. "You can't see it," she said, "but she is well. I'm sorry about that. He was ordered to protect me. I didn't know you were sympathetic until I saw the fire."

"Are you a witch—a Daughter of Sepholina?" Cord asked. "Is that a troll?"

Scarlett giggled.

"No," the woman said, amused. "Is that what you three are doing out here? Seeking witches and trolls?"

"Laughter, the sure sign of a battle," Maeverly's voice said. Footsteps followed. The sorcerer moved into view first, tilting her head as she took in half of Scarlett, the strange woman, and the mound. "A golem?"

"See?" Julian asked Teague.

"What happened here?" Teague asked. "Where is Bevin?"

The stranger held up a hand. "I'm afraid I am to blame for this commotion. Though I do have some questions of my own." Following Teague's focus on the golem, she explained, "That's not mine, actually. I'm no magus. I'm Laurel Parin."

After removing his cap, Teague introduced everyone, with a pause for Scarlett's dress that curtsied. Laurel's attention stuck to Teague, as though the rest of them weren't there. He gestured to the golem. "Where did that come from?"

"It belongs to someone in my town. Come," she said over her shoulder. The golem walked to her side.

Kylan stepped behind Scarlett.

"He's only here to protect me. Please don't be afraid."

Rubbing his arm, Kylan said, "I think it's a little late for that."

Maeverly tapped her nails on her chin. "How does someone here know how to create one of these? I've only seen one other myself, and he wasn't very forthcoming in conversation."

Caution crept into Laurel's eyes as she looked over Maeverly's purple dress. "Are you all foreigners, then?"

Julian snorted. Teague's glare cut him off. "Maeverly and I are from overseas. These four came to be in our company as we've been trying to escape this lovely nation of yours."

Laurel's smile hinted at attraction beyond her amusement. "Then you're aware of the strange happenings?"

"Aye, though we have little evidence to prove the source."

She released a long breath. "I'm returning from investigating one such event. A boy arrived at the West Granville gate last night and claimed to have witnessed the slaughter of his village. It's only a couple of miles from here and thoroughly burned."

"Are we that close?" Teague asked. "Granville's across the river, yes?"

"Almost directly." She turned to point. "You could see the walls if not for the trees on the opposite bank." She debated something when she met Teague's eyes. Finally, she said, "There are faster ways to travel that don't require bridges."

Teague studied the obstructed view of Granville. "Ah, the tunnels." She certainly smiled with more than approval. "Unfortunately, they cannot assist us with our caravan."

Or the prisoner they plan to take to Racine, Cord thought.

"My good woman," Teague said, "could I speak with this boy from the village?"

Laurel's lips parted for what appeared to be a polite decline.

"'Twould be a great help to know what we're running from, and I am excellent with children."

Maeverly rolled her eyes.

With a small laugh, Laurel smiled. "Go get a new arm," she said to the golem. "It wouldn't do for us to have one more thing to explain to Katrin when we get home."

Shadowing the golem, Maeverly watched it absorb the moist dirt from the ground and re-form its limb. "Is Katrin the one who created this? I'd love to know how it's done."

"I'm afraid it's not my place to say," Laurel answered. With the golem complete, she entered the woods, prompting the others to follow.

Teague rounded on Maeverly. "It may be best if you wait here. I'll have enough to mitigate as it is." He squinted at the space above Scarlett's skirt. "See them back with you. And find Bevin. There had better be truffles for dinner to explain his absence."

Maeverly lowered her brow. "Don't deny me this, Teague! A golem!

Even you can't disavow its usefulness in our immediate circumstances."

"Gods speak reason . . . How long did it take you to learn to conjure a knife, J? Two weeks. Two more than we had planned to spend in Taus, putting us on Remy's list of—the point is we don't have the time." He secured her agreement, though not her approval. "Once I've inquired on the happenings at that village, we'll depart. Let the others know we'll be back before dark."

Oddly, Cord found himself agreeing with Maeverly. If the sorcerer could create a golem or two, it made sense for her to learn how, even at the risk of her saying something ornery.

"You need rest, Teague," Maeverly said. "No one would expect you to put yourself through this torment."

Fondling the talisman through his jerkin, he shook his head. "We've dragged our heels enough. I'll be free when we get some real answers."

"I will go with you," Julian offered.

As confused as the others, Teague started to shake his head.

"I have been trained as a soldier. You should not go alone. Let me prove I want to help! I will earn my passage to Racine."

Teague gave in. "You are not to leave my sight."

Cord squeezed his fists. He only had to look at Kylan to see he wanted to continue their conversation. "I'm coming too," he said to Teague and was waved along.

"You improvised very well," Maeverly said to Scarlett. "Did you turn your nervous energy into excitement? Let's practice that trick a bit more, shall we? We can make Bevin's arms disappear. That's always fun."

Following Laurel and the golem, Cord glanced back to see Kylan watching them. Did the girls know Kylan's reason? Of course they did. Did the satyr? He didn't want to think about that.

He turned his thoughts to how Laurel would open the Starlight Tunnel's entry if she couldn't use magic. Cord's insides chilled when he realized Julian was about to witness the Starlight Tunnels. If he informed the army, they would never be safe. Neither would Laurel and this Granville magus. Why would Teague allow this? Was he really buying *Master Westcott's* act?

They reached the base of the once majestic tree, the largest stump Cord had seen yet, stretching out farther than Kenton's town square.

On the side near the river, Laurel said, "Go on."

The golem dropped a fist on the stump, then another. He pounded it with boulders until the stairs began to drop.

A lanky brunette woman, younger than Laurel, waited inside. When she saw them, she turned her pinched nose and sped back down the stairs.

"It's all right, Mivvy. They are friends," Laurel shouted after her. She sighed and stepped inside.

The golem insisted on following first.

Cord's jaw ached from the day's irritations. He let Julian, his face stunned, enter the stump before him. Only one solution would keep the tunnels safe now. The fates had decided; Julian had to die.

Chapter 38: That Immortal Man in Red

As everyone descended to the marble floor and the golem fled under the archway after Mivvy, Cord kept a close eye on Julian.

The roots startled Julian when they lifted the steps to seal the entrance of the Starlight Tunnels. He warily scanned the alabaster elven statues, as though they were only pretending to dance, just waiting for him to turn his back so they could snatch him.

More magic might loosen his tongue and put an end to this ruse fooling Teague into trusting him. But how much would Teague require to silence the jackass?

"That's an elf," Cord said, pointing to the statue behind Julian.

After Julian spun, Teague said, "Aye, what's in these corridors is all that's left of them."

"You sure about that?" Cord asked. "Maeverly seems to think they still exist. Kylan said they disappeared but might be down here somewhere."

"Well, I have not seen any," Laurel said, unhelpfully reassuring him.

Julian's eyes settled on the dark corridor where the golem had fled.

"Wait till you see the ceiling," Cord said to him. "You can see the stars without the sky getting in the way."

"Yes," Laurel murmured, smothering Teague in attention. "They are lovely." She was definitely not helping Cord set the right mood.

"Overseas, these tunnels are said to be haunted," Teague said.

Cord perked up, but Laurel laughed it off. Teague offered his arm and escorted her into the corridor.

With only a glance at the field of stars above them, Julian kept checking behind them as they walked.

Cord cupped a handful of the chilled water from one of the troughs. "Do you think this comes from the river?" When Julian looked, he drank. "It tastes too clean; is it magical?"

Teague's eyes narrowed. "'Tis water, lad."

Laurel asked Teague, "Have you been in these tunnels before?"

"Where have I not been? Though not for many years, feels like a lifetime ago."

Considering how to get Teague back on the topic of the haunting, Cord mentally connected the vibrant stars above them, first forming the floating swan of Iridienne's constellation.

Before he had a plan, the golem came into view ahead of them. Behind it, four women waited with varying degrees of caution. Mivvy, the tallest, peeped from behind the golem's arm.

A plump dark-haired woman folded her arms across her full bosom and moved in front of the clay guardian. If her proud demeanor didn't give it away, the lapis-blue dye and four-inch embroidered hems of her dress boasted of her nobility. Matching eyeshade colored the lids of her eyes, full of censure for Laurel.

From the opposite side of the golem, an older woman with a severe cut to her boy-length white hair mirrored the noble's stance.

The last of the four, a half twig with short wavy hair and bulging eyes, bobbed her head around the noble's shoulder. It would have been a stretch to call her attractive, even without the spiteful clench of her face.

Laurel removed her arm from Teague's. "Her Grace, Lady Katrin te Sungspear. Katrin, I have seen the village. It's as we suspected." She didn't receive a response. "And there were bodies. Some were far enough away from the buildings that they were not turned to ash."

A thick hand rose to silence Laurel. The noble's eyes burned like coals. "Fine," Her Grace said. "What did you hope to mitigate by bringing these outsiders here, Laurel? I see no philanthropy they can offer. You have only increased our woes."

Laurel nodded for Teague to answer. He removed his hat and bowed. "Teague Fuchs, Your Grace. I'm leading a caravan of merchants—"

"You are early. We trade our slaves after the Seeding, not before."

"We're not slavers, Your Grace."

"You have a Catalyst with you," she said, raising her chin at Cord.

When Cord's hand jerked to cover the feather, Julian sniffed an I-told-you-so.

"Two then," Lady Sungspear said. "Did you come to spy? To see if we are still worthy of the Tribunal's favor?" A finger wearing a hefty emerald ring jabbed into Teague's jerkin as Lady Katrin forced him back. "If you want to survive this introduction, you will tell me the truth!"

Maintaining his charming smile, Teague slowly raised his hands. "You have my word that we are not here on behalf of any Merithian force. I merely wish to speak with you, in part about the tunnels you've stumbled upon."

Lady Katrin's grimace deepened.

"They have magi in their company, Katrin," Laurel said. "Equals. I wouldn't have brought them otherwise."

That cooled the noble's coals. Her posture remained sharp, however. "We did not 'stumble upon them.' It took us months to excavate a tunnel to them. Where are you from then? Fair warning: do not lie to me again about this merchant drivel. I have never seen one without his purse, even if there was no coin for a hundred miles."

"Lekelith," Teague said. Given the opportunity to speak, he put his hat on. "'Tis important that ye do not allow these tunnels to be discovered. They serve a vital function—"

"Do not lecture me about the tunnels!" Her Grace said. "Do you know how dangerous it is to sneak people out of the city to one of those stumps? This way, we do not have to concern ourselves with the inconvenience, or whether a magus is willing to assist." She glared back at the wavy-haired woman, who rolled her eyes, and Mivvy cowered behind her.

For the first time Cord had witnessed, Teague blundered over his words. "You know? That's good, so it is. But ye trade slaves?"

"Criminals," the noble answered. "Every Seeding sends us a handful. We declass them. It is a cruel justice, I know. Yet they provide more benefit than the goods we acquire in exchange. The Tribunal sees the records and believes we do our part to keep Merith trading."

With a deep breath, Her Grace said, "We are the Ladies Council of Granville, most of them. These clandestine escape routes have been operated by us for well over a decade, nearly two."

Escape routes?

"Granville is not a place where we tolerate injustice. The men of our great city change, so the women safeguard that trait."

"I see," Teague said. "Then please allow me to expand my introduction. I lead a band of the Hook. Not a week past, we landed in Croathe under the guise of Tazzarian merchants and have made our way down south. Given the troubles that have befallen Merith, we're rapidly trying to reach Llandir, or any port still in operation."

Lady Katrin pursed her lips and nodded.

"Are you aware Merith is under attack?" Teague asked.

The white-haired woman came forward. "What do you mean?"

He gestured back to Cord and Julian. "These two came from South Thornton, where they narrowly escaped a pack of wolfkin. We encountered three Judges earlier today who relayed the news that Fort Trent is now a den. Have ye seen evidence of it?"

The small one snorted. "What Judges would tell foreigners anything of the sort?"

"Yuris Mason did most of the talking."

The ladies spoke in glances.

"We let them know to avoid the villages."

"Why should they?" the ugly sprig snapped. "They are Judges."

Patiently, Teague said, "We have encountered several reduced to ash along our path. Though I suspect they're unrelated to the attack; the wolfkin use villages to recruit and to feed before swarming a city."

Lady Katrin raised her thumb at the feisty eyesore. "Nella," she said as both a reprimand and introduction. "Her sister, Mivvy." Mivvy stepped behind the golem again. "And Beatrice." The eldest woman curtsied, revealing her bare feet below the hem of her dress. Without waiting for Teague to introduce Cord and Julian, Lady Katrin said, "Follow me. Mivvy, leave your friend here."

The meek witch held her hand up. The golem sank into a mound.

Then the ladies swarmed about Lady Katrin like a charm of hummingbirds on a morning glory, chattering as they swept deeper into the tunnels. Lady Katrin shouted through their whispers, "A boy came to the West Granville gate last night. He has been too spooked to speak."

Their words broke when Lady Katrin stopped at a jarring hole in the corridor wall. Barred with a simple plank door, the opening had broken the trough and cracked the wall upward toward the stars.

She knocked twice rapidly, then three more times slowly. "If you are charismatic enough to muddle Laurel, perhaps you can retrieve his story." The door opened as Laurel gave Lady Katrin a sidelong glance. The noble returned it threefold, halting the procession.

A man wearing the livery of a watchman stood at the entrance, with a green flag over his heart and a short broadsword at his side. No member of the army would keep the tunnels secret!

"Not the army you are used to, I suspect," Lady Katrin said to Cord and Julian. She pressed on into a crudely carved passage, lit only by oil lanterns hung on brackets every twenty feet. Water from the broken trough wet the uneven floor.

"I must admit I'm surprised as well," Teague said. "Rumors of Merith's intolerance to magic and nonhumans are known the world over, Your Grace."

Laurel returned to his side. "Granville has been working toward a better Merith for some time now. Our mothers' grans started this process."

"It has taken us a little over a century," Lady Katrin said, "but the city is of like mind. In the past decade, we have secured two of the villages as well. The Seeding sends us more challenges each year, but we have learned to deal with those." She executed an about-face. "In fact, I am disappointed in Yuris. He should have known to come here."

"His directives sent them to inform Brewing, Your Grace," Teague said.

Heaving her bosom with a sigh, she nodded. "Good. That was smart. Darren and Lizbeth should know what is happening here." She contemplated Teague's attire, and squinted when she raised her chin. "And call me Katrin. My father had a bitch named Grace. I believe the insult was intended for my gran, but I still prefer my name, or Lady Sungspear, if you must."

"I would be honored," Teague said, bowing his head. "If I may ask, was Scalebrush one of the villages you had brought about?"

"No, why?"

"It also fell to the wolves."

"Sacred shit," she muttered.

Cord snickered at Julian before he remembered who was standing next to him.

Lady Katrin turned on her heel and led on. Her charm shuffled to surround her once more.

"They will be making their move on Granville soon, Katrin," Teague said.

"Already have," Lady Katrin replied. "My husband is meeting with four Judges from Fort Trent right now. Let's make haste, shall we?"

Shouted orders and a merry song reached them before they exited the cavern into a black-stone chamber. Scaffolding lined the walls, packed with workers polishing embedded golden daggers and apples. Every surface reflected the light, even the ceiling, which was as high as the Reliquary's towers. Several commoners chanted as they tugged on a rope in unison, hauling an immense golden sconce higher up the wall to Cord's right. Centered between the already attached sconces, two figures outlined in gold identified the chamber's purpose for them.

The first was a female pik wearing a diamond-patterned mask over the top half of her face, and pointy shoes. She resembled Andion, with the same broad head but longer hair. A round belly protruded from the second pik's robe. Bearded and bald, he held a bitten apple in his hand. Old gods—they were restoring a temple. In recessed alcoves on the opposite wall, pedestals awaited their idols.

"The twins," Teague said to Cord. "Most piks now worship Pencer, the god of feasts. Lore suggests Merith killed his sister, Panette, the goddess of shadows. They say that's why piks can no longer shadow walk." He leaned to speak in Cord's ear. "I suppose your friend counters that notion, yes?"

The ladies crossed the floor tiles, whose designs alternated between two golden daggers behind a mask and a loaf of bread with a frothy mug.

Snapping as he walked on, Teague broke Cord and Julian out of their awe. Katrin and the ladies ascended a winding flight of stairs hewn long ago. They zigzagged up to another doorway. The guard saluted Lady Sungspear, earning him a quick smile of approval.

There was no shortage of oil lamps along the bricked walls of the cellar they entered beneath a ceiling of floorboards. Given the size of the cellar, Cord figured the manor of Granville ought to be upstairs.

"How do ye do it?" Teague asked. "Garnering the trust of the army."

"They are the easy ones," Lady Katrin said. "A strong sense of community and mentorships usually do the trick, though we do have to keep a watchful eye and open ears. For commoners, we protect their families who reside both within and outside our city, offering shelter to all who arrive and accept our ways. When the temple is complete, we can afford to use the tunnels to extend our reach." She shrugged. "Family for the army, family for the townsfolk. Never underestimate the power of roots."

If it weren't for the invasion, Granville would've offered everything they needed to stay in Merith. No, he couldn't vouch for Kylan's desires, and Lady Sungspear would probably recognize Rorry on sight.

As the procession walked by another flight of stairs, the savory aroma of beef stew floated down from the kitchen.

"We work to preserve the history of this island," Beatrice said without turning her white bristles to look at them. "But at the moment, our greatest need is current information."

In an area full of brandy casks and crates of wine, Lady Katrin halted before a cellar door and gripped the handle with her emerald-encrusted fingers. "We have some. Beatrice, let my husband know the Judges he let into the gate this morning are wolfkin. Calmly. And take the manor's guards with you."

The older woman's bare feet flew up the stairs. Peeking out from under her dress with each step, brilliant green stone ringed both of her ankles.

"What are wolfkin?" Mivvy whispered to Nella.

The shorter woman waved off her sister's question.

"You and I agree," Lady Katrin said to Teague. "The wolfkin are not killing the villagers, not the burned ones. Get his story and I will share what we know."

Cord nodded before Teague moved through the women and agreed.

"I plan to use you, Teague. Before you leave, you will promise to take what you have witnessed to the highest authority on the continent. I love my province. We are getting things right here, and I do not appreciate some foreigners mucking about in our progress."

He grinned. "I will offer the humble services—"

"Hogwash!" she belted. "Someone tasked you to investigate this country, mercenary. Someone with a vault of coin. I aim to have them as an ally."

Teague didn't relent, a statue of certainty.

The heavy door swung in to reveal a wash of lamplight in a room as large as the chapel in Kenton. Rich dyes in pale red, sky-blue, and the winter-tree green of Granville wove through thick rugs and tapestries. To their right, a dozen chairs framed a lengthy, well-oiled table. At the head, a tall-backed, cushioned seat waited. Cord didn't have to guess who sat there.

"Welcome to our council room," Laurel said, waving them to the chairs at the table.

A pile of green pillows sniffled in the corner.

Katrin gestured for Mivvy to come forward. The tall magus settled on her knees by the pillows and spoke softly to the pile.

Lady Katrin assumed her throne, prompting the others to sit. "He will not talk," she whispered, "but he will respond to Mivvy."

A pair of eyes peered through the plush barrier. Cord only made out "Two games, I promise," from Mivvy before the pillows started to move. A brown-haired boy, no older than six, dug himself out. He rose next to Mivvy and tried to hide behind her.

"You've no need to fear me, lad," Teague said, grinning while he straddled his chair. He sat and rapped on the seat next to him. "Would you care to join me? I was just about to have a snack."

The boy ignored him as he beheld the others.

"I have jerky." Teague removed a blue kerchief from his belt pouch and unfolded it, presenting the treat.

"Ooh," Mivvy cooed. "It does look tasty, doesn't it?"

With a few encouraging nods from Mivvy, the boy crept forward.

Teague laughed as the kid swiped the whole of it in one quick grab. "You have a hearty appetite. That's good. Have we any beverages?"

Laurel scooted back from the table and walked over to a wheeled cart. Two pitchers, copper cups, and glasses were placed neatly on top. As she tipped a sweating pitcher, a block of ice slipped out and toppled a glass. It shattered on the floor. "Mivvy." Laurel sighed.

Mivvy apologized and helped Laurel clean it up.

Chomping into the jerky like a grasshopper into spring growth, the boy hardly noticed.

"Do you like it?" Teague asked. "My friend, Bevin, is an excellent cook. He stands as tall as we would if you stood on my shoulders. I speak the truth! If I get the chance, I'll bring him by."

The boy smiled. "You talk funny."

"Aye, they tell me that. I'm from Lekelith. 'Tis a small country on an island like yours. Over there, everybody talks a little strangely." He put his hand to his face and whispered loudly, "'Tis all the drink." He stood and walked drunkenly in a circle until the boy laughed. Cord noticed a quick grin from Lady Katrin also.

While amused, Cord wished Teague would get on with it. Who'd killed the villagers?

Laurel served half-filled cups of water and retook her seat, eager to watch Teague's performance.

A joyful glint entered Teague's eyes as he bent next to the boy. "But you know what else we have in Lekelith? Tumblers!" Teague stood and leaped forward. In three swift flips, he narrowly avoided the serving cart. Andion couldn't have done it better. Laurel and Mivvy clapped as Teague gave a proud flourish.

"Again!" Julian called. The boy nodded in agreement.

Teague made a face at Julian through his smile, which caused Cord to chuckle. He surely wished he'd made Master Westcott remain with the caravan now. Tumbling forward, Teague plopped his hat onto the boy's head.

Teague fell onto his chair. "Do you like my hat? Aye, a very fetching look for you." He drummed the chair with his knuckles. "'Tis settled. 'Tis yours—I'm sorry. What is your name, lad?"

"Mortin," the boy managed around the jerky. "Can I have it?" he asked Lady Katrin.

She should have said no, in accordance with the law on dyes. However, things were different here. Lady Katrin slowly smiled and nodded. Perhaps not that different.

"Mortin?" Teague repeated. "That's a strong name. Now, Mortin, these ladies said you flew down from the sky last night. Is that right?"

Confused, Mortin shook his head.

"Did you swim?"

Again, Mortin's head shook.

"I think they are liars then. Would you like to call them liars with me?"

Nella's eyes threatened to burst in fury. Katrin and Laurel grinned; Laurel's wasn't forced.

Hanging his head, Mortin leaned against Teague's leg and said, "The red man. He hurt my family."

Lady Katrin nodded, as though that's all the explanation she needed.

Cord tried to work out what meaning she got from it. Only the Chancellor wore red, unless some councilmember boldly overstepped his bounds. Maybe Mortin meant the red hammers of the High Guard?

"Be at ease," Teague said. He put his hand on Mortin's shoulder and held him against him. "Calmly tell me what you saw, lad. You're safe here."

Mortin spoke to the floor. "I was hidin' some sweets in my chamber. After the feast. That's when they came. My da told me to hide. I thought they was gonna switch me."

"Who came?" Teague asked.

"The Judges with the hammers."

The High Guard had arrived before the villagers were dead? Cord leaned against his elbows on the table.

"I saw out the window. The headmaster led a prayer. Then the Judges took Cellie's baby 'cause it was crying. Then the man . . .'"

"The man in red?"

Mortin nodded. "He raised a flower—it was shining like it had fire in it. He raised it up over his head and they fell over."

Nella exhaled her disbelief.

"What kind of flower?" Teague asked.

"Glass. It wasn't real or nothin'." Mortin held his fist against his belly. "They took Cellie's baby. I ran to Momma, but she didn't see me anymore."

Teague hugged the boy and patted him on the back. "I think I know the rest, Mortin. You were very brave to escape the way you did. Your parents would be proud." When Teague's arm pulled away, a knife came out of the hat. It was gone from his hand when he stood. "Thank you. Enjoy the hat, my friend."

But who was the man in red? Surely Lady Katrin didn't think the Chancellor killed them. There had to be another explanation.

"Lads," Teague said, nodding to the door. In the cellar, he moved midway to the temple entrance before he waited for the ladies to gather. "Now we know," he said to Lady Katrin.

"You're gullible, you are!" Nella said to Teague. "The Chancellor killed them all with a flower?"

Cord agreed with the shrew. "The Chancellor would never slay his own people!"

"Many men do great evil under the guise of piety," Teague said. "Doesn't your doctrine state the Chancellor is above all of ye?"

"This is nonsense!" Nella said as Mivvy winced apologetically. "What would the High Guard want with a baby?"

"The next generation of the army," Lady Katrin answered. "Or, if it is a girl, she will be either a heifer to repopulate the villages or a nurse mother."

Teague nodded, impressed.

"Like I said, Teague, I have my suspicions. Yet that is fact. They take little care to hide how they populate the academes."

Julian and Cord spoke over each other. "What do you mean?"

"Yes," Katrin said, "that would appeal to you two. Every twenty years, the Tribunal comes through and a village burns at Hansweighn, though we only see the High Guard. They take the babes to Croathe, where the Tribunal's scribes disperse them back out to the academes on the opposite side of the island, the same as with the Abandoneds' babes. The scribes are very particular about each child's placement and keep meticulous records to avoid placing them where a close relative lives."

A tightness seized Cord's chest. Was that how he'd come to be in the Tribunal's care? There was a record somewhere in Croathe that could tell him. Still, he wouldn't believe their blasphemy about the Chancellor unless he saw it with his own eyes!

Katrin held up her round hand and counted fingers. "The same is true in Brewing, Weatherington, Llandir, Faulkner, Deyell, and South Thornton. I would wager my life that it is true of the other provinces. If they took a village a year, one from a different province each time, it would align with what Lady Gwirion and Lady Ffyddian have shared with me. Mortin's home, Kettlebree, burned exactly twenty years after

Dwindlebury did. But you mentioned others? They have not ruined this many before."

If Rorry's mother knew what they were up to, maybe Rorry knew more than she was letting on again.

"Why would they do such a thing?" Laurel asked.

"Immortality," Teague said, as though he had suspected it all along.

Katrin clicked her tongue and nodded in agreement. "He's taking the life force of the villagers—"

"That's blasphemy!" Cord yelled. "Your gods did that to him out of fear! Now you're saying he stole his sacred longevity by killing villagers with a glass flower? He abhors magic! The Chancellor leads the army against the Abandoned—to protect the people of Merith!"

A sickness built up inside of Cord as they, with both the defiant and sympathetic faces, remained quiet. Nella took Mivvy's hand. Even Julian seemed to accept the suspicions of a foreigner and a noble over his upbringing. Cord opened his mouth to denounce the High Guard and blame them for the villagers' deaths, but crashing metal interrupted.

On the stairs to the kitchen, a scullery maid covered her mouth with her hands as her tray rattled to a halt on the cellar floor. "Cord?" a familiar voice asked. "Cord Sullivan!"

"Leila?"

Chapter 39: Lost Friends

Leila lunged for Cord and wrapped her arms around his neck. Her honeycomb-colored curls buried his face in the scent of freshly baked bread.

He squeezed her, shocked by the warmth of the ghost in his arms.

She pulled back and ran a hand over his cheek as he stared in awe. With a smile as wide as his, she asked, "What are you doing here?"

"Me?"

The gathering in the cellar watched the exchange without so much as a loud exhale. Leila made a face for his eyes alone but failed to remove the disdain from her words. "This is Tomlin's hometown."

As Cord tried to piece together what had brought Tomlin back to Granville, Leila curtsied to the others. "Please pardon my clumsiness, Your Grace." She beamed at Cord again.

He knew her well enough to tell she didn't mean the apology or the reverence.

"Nonsense, Leila," Lady Katrin said with a scheme obviously building. "Might I suggest a quick meal to give them time to visit?" Her painted eyes vaulted the question to Teague.

Teague rolled his tongue in his mouth as he thought.

Cord was a bit torn. On one hand, he couldn't remove his arm from Leila's shoulder, afraid that she'd disappear back into the daydream she'd come from. On the other, conversation here flowed freely around things he didn't want Leila knowing, at least not about him or this misguided sacrilege.

"I believe we can spare a short tarry for a proper goodbye between friends," Teague said.

"Yes," Katrin agreed. "Nella, please let Larissa and Hindby know there will be four for bread and honey in the library. And jam. Everyone else should receive the same in the council room. Oh, and wine, I think."

Upset by the dismissal, Nella split a glare between Leila and Katrin, verging on a tantrum. When the bulging-eyed scold didn't get a reaction from Katrin, she stormed toward the stairs to the kitchen, kicking a pot to clamor across the floor.

"Do ask them to clear this mess as well," Lady Katrin added.

Julian followed Mivvy into the council room without question. He never looked away from her, not ogling the way he did at Rorry; this look was far more curious. Teague showed more concern about letting the Catalyst out of his sight than for Laurel's disappointment as she joined the others.

Leila's warm hand dragged Cord away to the stairs. "Tomlin insisted that we come here," she said under her breath.

On reflex, Cord thinned his lips.

"I'm his wife. He told me to go. I had to. If I had refused, I'd be branded a slave." Cord knew better than to believe that. Marlone held Leila's interest, but she'd owned Tomlin's from the moment he had laid eyes on her. "We left Kenton after the Hansweighn feast."

They went up the stairs to the kitchen, where an exposed oven belched flames and dried the savory air. Barrels and crates of potatoes, pears, and apples sat beneath the counters and tables. Rich lifewood planks covered the duller floor he'd seen on the ceiling in the cellar. Purple tinged the stones in the walls.

At a prep table mounded with rashers of bacon, a lone cook idly chopped a crookneck squash. Upon seeing Katrin, she whipped up to full height. Katrin hummed her approval.

Coming down the hall, a few slave girls giggled and whispered behind their hands as Leila and Cord went by. "This place lacks discipline," Leila groaned, pulling him faster down the hallway.

After the exhausting events of the day, Cord couldn't help but grin at his friend. Leila's short supply of discipline had brought about countless switchings. His mouth opened to remind her but then closed. Harking back to their youth might lead to questions. If he could avoid breaking her heart for even a moment longer, he would.

Nella's voice echoed down the hallway, which was filled with oil paintings, as she flexed her anger. Before they reached the harpy's full screech, Leila hooked left. Worn floorboards interlocked with those retaining their luster inside the reading room.

Beneath the high ceiling, shelves of tomes rose up the walls like ladder rungs. The books, fat to slender and squat to three hands tall, were sorted true to Headmaster Angsly's method of idle selection and easiest return. A good portion of the lower shelves had books lying atop others, while higher shelves had bare gaps. Cord imagined his headmaster and Scarlett sitting in the two cushy Granville-green thrones before the black marble fireplace. They'd be lost to the world, reading for hours.

In a portrait above the mantle, Katrin appeared regal and youthful; her rosy-cheeked husband, just as stout, had been tucked to the side behind her.

Teague pulled out Lady Katrin's chair at the varnished walnut table in the center of the room. He took a seat next to her.

"Your friend refuses reading lessons," Katrin said to Cord.

Leila dug her nails into Cord's hand.

As Leila sat across from her new noble, she stated, "It's above my station, Your Grace. I have no need for such a thing." Naturally, she dragged Cord into it by asking him, "Isn't that the way of the Chancellor's Light?"

"As your noble, I will insist. Every person within these town walls can read for a reason. Education prevents thorns in my side and makes for a stronger community." Katrin's tone suggested she might beat an education into Leila, who feigned a smile.

Halting further protest, Teague said, "Your home is even lovelier than I had anticipated, Katrin. 'Tis far more welcoming than the hard marble of Croathe."

"You're foreign?" Leila asked with a wrinkled nose. Without waiting for a response, she questioned Cord. "Who is this? I thought you were guarding a noble."

"No," Teague said. "Merely a merchant from the continent. Cord has been assisting my caravan through some difficulties, though I suspect more before we're through."

Leila didn't acknowledge Teague. Instead she asked the question Cord had prayed wouldn't come. "Where is Marlone?"

Searching for the right words, Cord suddenly understood all too well the reason the others had lied to him.

"If you're not allowed to say, just tell me."

A brown-skinned girl, one of the branded gossipers, entered with a tray bearing Katrin's request. She meekly set out a bounty that the four of them couldn't possibly eat in one day, let alone in one sitting; honey, jam, butter, and bread enough to serve Bevin as a meal. As soon as she finished pouring the spiced wine, she set a silver bell before Katrin and left.

"You do use slaves?" Teague asked. "That seems a wee bit beneath you."

"A wee bit?" Katrin snapped. "She is not a slave here. That is the sickle brand of Mayo on her cheek, not the flag of Granville. When the Seeding sends us more thick skulls than normal, we are able to trade for others' freedom. Cameya works in the manor, and her husband paints." She raised her goblet to the portrait over the mantel. "We provide for them the same as we do for all of our artisans, and Laurel. She keeps the book trade flowing through town. Besides, they make beautiful babies, and Granville can always use more beauty."

Leila's mind was clearly drifting back to Marlone, sending her questioning gaze to Cord. She twiddled with a lock of her long hair as she eyed the filth and bloodstains on his tunic. "Cord, whose blood is that?"

"Mine," he answered, sipping his wine. He nearly choked. Having never tasted wine before, he hadn't expected it to be so bitter.

When he lowered his cup, Leila waited for an explanation.

"If they've sent a few in already, the other wolfkin will be here at nightfall," Teague said to Katrin, starting the conversation down another path Cord had wanted to avoid. "Given the size and wealth of your city, at least one disciple of foul magic will lead the attack. He, she, or they will be more interested in someone like Mivvy than your troops. If I may suggest it, we could take her, or any of your magi, to the Bonded Nations for safety." Before Katrin stopped shaking her head, he continued, "Then I recommend you keep her hidden away and command her golems, yes?"

"Do not worry for Granville," Katrin said. "We will be ready."

Leila's eyes wandered over them and came back to focus on Cord.

He took another sip of wine and a deep breath. "Creatures from behind the Cloud are invading Merith," Cord said. "They attacked South Thornton the day Marlone and I arrived. One of the Judges was a wolfkin, a man cursed by magic to change into a wolf that stands on two legs, taller than a man."

Her eyes squinted at him as her lips curled at the edges. Ashes, she thought he was pulling a prank.

"I don't know if it was him, but one of the beasts . . ." He struggled to say it. Locking eyes with Teague, he managed, "Killed Marlone."

Her chair scooted back as she rose. "That's not funny!" Her face slackened. Slowly, reality set in to wet Leila's eyes.

Cord took her wrist until she floated back down to her seat. Holding her against his chest, he forgave his friends. They had been right not to tell him. Two days ago, he would've gone back for Marlone.

Before Cord explained Kenton's fall, Leila pressed back from him. Her eyes blazed with scorn for Cord. Tears skipped down her cheek as they fell. "How could you let that happen? You were supposed to take care of him!"

"I wasn't there when it happened, Leila. And I tried to save him. You don't gotta jump down my throat about it."

She jerked her wrist away from his touch and turned to Katrin. "This is what magic does! You let the Abandoned run around free to feed the demons and spread curses. The Chancellor should burn this city!"

The noblewoman's face flushed with anger. After a few deep breaths cutting the quiet, her pity renewed. More patient than Cord would've expected, Katrin must have been used to defiance from her new subjects.

Teague spoke. "I'm sorry for your loss but can assure you these dark creatures have no commonality with Granville."

"A foreigner is trying to console me," Leila said bitterly. "If your kind stayed in your country—"

"He's a good man, Leila," Cord said, more heatedly than he'd intended. Surprised at his own words, Cord admitted, "At least I think he's trying to be."

Putting the heels of her hands to her eyes, Leila sobbed. "Take me home, Cord. Tomlin can join if he wishes, but I . . . I can't stay here."

"Leila," Cord said gently.

"No! I want to go home! You can take me. This Abandoned hole can rot!"

"Kenton is gone," Cord said quietly. Her mouth hung open. "The High Guard burned it."

"My parents?"

"Everyone."

"Why?"

Casting a warning look at Katrin and Teague, Cord said, "I don't know." He didn't believe the lies about the Chancellor and wouldn't repeat them. Leila was the only one who knew exactly how he felt. But she had someone to live for. Squeezing her hands, he said, "Tomlin saved you."

She blinked. "I need to lie down. We can speak later."

"I can't stay," Cord said. "These Dregs, these things are hunting me. They think I'm—"

"That's enough!" Teague said. "Granville will face the Dregs soon. Don't give them a reason to suspect they can find answers here."

"There are a dozen potent magi in this city and a well-trained guard," Katrin said. "Fear not for us. We will keep her safe."

A correction lingered behind Teague's thinned lips; the magi needed to hide, but he didn't repeat himself.

Morale would be their only chance if the Dregs came and his stories were true. It'd be a test of endurance against suffering while they awaited support from armies overseas. Leila should come with him. Maybe Tomlin, too.

"Were you not listening?" Leila asked. "Magic is the cause of all of this! Demon worshippers! Each one of—"

"Leila!" Cord shouted.

She pulled her hands free of his. "How can you defend them? Their kind, they're the reason he's dead!"

"Leila, I'm a magus," Cord said.

She turned to him, curious at first, then hot with fury. Dampness surrounded the blame in her eyes. She stood away from him. "That's what Marlone wouldn't tell me. That was his secret." Bracing herself against the table, she swayed as she took it all in.

"Look," Cord said, "I'm sorry. I shouldn't have told you that on top of everything else. But I'm not a demon worshipper. You know me; you know that!"

Hatred showered down on him when she looked over. "It should've been you. You filthy witch." The last person who knew him walked away in silence.

Cord wanted to call out, to correct her, but let her go.

The day had rubbed him raw, dragging him through torments he'd never have believed yesterday. Anger started to give way to tears as he stared at her empty chair. So he closed his eyes and corked the sadness welling up. Flexing his jaw, he braved a glare at Teague. He knew it wasn't

Teague's fault. None of this was. He needed something to distract him. The sympathy on Teague's face didn't help.

"She does not mean it," Katrin shouted at the hallway as she moved around the table. Sliding into the seat next to him, she rubbed the back of his hand with her plump fingers. "She is in pain. We all say things we regret when we receive unwelcome news. In time, she will come around to understanding. Until then, we will take good care of her. She may even learn to enjoy it here."

As Cord fought to control his breathing, Katrin broke the bread and slathered her serving with butter and jam. "Please eat," she said to Teague. "We all know our fates rest on your shoulders. I will not have you fainting before you deliver the pleas of my people."

"The Bonded Nations will aid the people of Merith," Teague said. With a sigh for Cord, he continued, "Even still, I'll be challenged to find a sympathizer for your dictator and his murderous Tribunal. Can I assure them ye won't stand in the way if they take the advantage and end Merith?"

She dismissed the blasphemy with a groan. "We will not put a foreigner on our throne, if that is what you are implying. There are plenty of Merithians who would make fine rulers and possess a willingness to follow the laws and treaties of the Bonded Nations." Her unblinking stare removed any doubt that she was referring to herself, or perhaps her husband.

Teague smiled. "I see. Katrin, if you wish me to speak your husband's name into familiarity, I'd better know it in full."

"Alland te Sungspear." She raised her chalice to her lips and added, "Husband of Katrin."

Katrin rang the silver bell and asked Cameya to fetch a basket. "You will take all of this with you. I insist, Teague. And you," she said to Cord, "will eat this right now." Honey drizzled over the buttered plank in her hand.

Leaning away from the plate she put before him, Cord shook his foot against the table leg something fierce. A week ago he never would've sided with them over Leila.

"Now," she commanded.

Cord chomped into the fluffy and sweet distraction, but it failed to soothe him. Shame, sorrow, and anger puddled into a numbness in his chest. It burrowed through his ribs and deep into his gut, running all the way back up to his cheekbones. The noble forced another hunk of bread on him before he finished the first.

Cord rubbed his hands together to remove the stickiness from the honey as he chewed the last bite. He stood and said, "I think I've done enough harm here."

Teague still hadn't masked his sympathy. "Cord, I would offer to take her with us, but she is safer here."

"Everyone's safer away from me."

He was behaving like a child, not a soldier. He didn't care. He couldn't care about anything right then, just getting away from their accusations against his faith. His world was a darker place than it had been yesterday.

Katrin's bosom heaved with a heavy breath. "And I should see to my husband. We have much to do."

"See to me?" the portly man from the portrait roared as he entered the room. A leather oval adorned the front of his wide belt, cinching his knee-length green tunic around his largest feature. His black cap resembled a flattened cushion sliding off his round head. Fiery eyes watched his wife rise from the table. "Wolfkin? They were wolfkin!" He pointed behind him at Beatrice. "And you sent this one to tell me while I sat across from them?"

Beatrice leaned against the doorframe with her arms folded. "The guards stopped the lot of them," she reported to Katrin. "Killed two, trapped two."

"Go on," Lord Sungspear said to Beatrice. "Tell her how you told me they were wolfkin. She stabbed me, she did!" He held up the back of his hand where a red dot didn't even hold a blue glimmer.

"Prick," the older woman said curtly. "It was just a prick with a silver knife. It didn't swell."

Katrin's approving nod caused her husband to exhale through his opened mouth.

"The effect of silver is a myth best left to ogres," Teague said.

Lord Sungspear asked, "And who is this?"

"Visitors, just on their way out, dear," Katrin said. "Would you like Mivvy to assist the guard? Nella is primed for a fight."

The councilmember ground his teeth. "They are secured."

Teague reached for his hat out of habit, then bowed with his empty hand outstretched. "I am Teague Fuchs, Lord Sungspear. If my experience with these creatures is worth its weight, ye should kill the ones ye've captured immediately, along with anyone who is drooling uncontrollably or sniffing wildly. Freshly cursed bodies will do that." Katrin nodded to her husband as though she had said it. "The main force is likely to attack at nightfall, but others may have already entered. Best to check anyone new to town in the past few days, yes?"

Alland te Sungspear seemed a patient man, despite the quiet trail of profanity he unleashed. "Someone tell me what is going on here."

Katrin shuffled to her husband and centered the thick emerald pendant on the gold chain around his neck. "Beatrice, please see our guests safely escorted to the tunnels. Lord Sungspear and I must plan our defenses." The inclusion seemed to lower the councilmember's temperature.

"Teague," Beatrice said, "Granville is just the beginning. We can turn this country around with more help. You must find us allies from beyond the Great Barrier."

"To reiterate," Katrin said to Beatrice more than Teague. "We need allies to save Granville and Merith from this invasion. The provinces will see to Merith's woes without appointing a foreigner as our ruler. We have no need for more debt than we can repay."

Cameya kept her eyes on the floor as she delivered the basket, then left the reading room faster than a frightened salamander.

Teague bowed again. "I promise to tell all that I have learnt when I reach the continent. A queen's palace will be my first stop. We're old friends; she will not treat me as an apocryphal source."

Katrin released her husband to bid them farewell and, with sincerity, promised Leila's safety to Cord. "She will be more secure than she ever desired to be. Do not fret."

With the basket in hand, Teague put his arm over Cord's shoulders and led him away.

"She is safer here?" Cord muttered.

"That she is, lad," Teague answered. "We have our own battle ahead."

Chapter 40: A Gruesome Gift

Barely aware Teague was guiding him, Cord moved, lost in the motion and the clacking of the cook's knife echoing down the hallway of the Granville manor. Leila was nowhere to be seen. Cord considered pulling free of Teague's arm and tracking her down. But his leaden steps trailed Beatrice's bare feet along the red floorboards.

The old woman glanced back toward the library. "The world laments," she said to Teague. "Evil holds more hearts than good. Someone needs to spark a cleansing fire."

"Am I in the presence of a clairvoyant now?" Teague asked, mocking her.

"No," she said, eyeing the cook, who pretended not to listen. "I'm merely a part of Cyr, as are we all. On occasion, I may hear or see meaning in things that others simply find curious."

"A Nashin, then?"

Beatrice's wrinkles deepened as she mulled over the question. "If you need something to call me beyond my name, I suppose it would do. Their beliefs are close to those that have consoled me as I prepare for the end of my journey."

"And you believe war is the solution to the world's woes?"

She blocked the stairwell to the cellar. "Don't look at me that way, young man. I'm not defying Katrin's wishes, simply suggesting our aid enter from the north."

"To what end?" Teague asked. "Fighting the Chancellor's army and the Dregs in the north would delay your aid by weeks or months. Proximity alone makes a southern port or Llandir a better choice, so it does. And who's to say the slaver nations won't assemble to defend the north and provide more resistance? They'll not want to lose their bountiful supply." He fashioned a smug grin. "Level with me, Beatrice. Are you asking me to seek the destruction of Merith?"

Beatrice formed a small smile and said, "Merith bleeds each time sensibility breaks through the fear the Tribunal has nurtured. If defeating the Tribunal doesn't shine the light of truth in the villages, Merith is already lost."

Anger singed the numbness in Cord's chest.

Teague withdrew his arm from Cord. "There's a great risk in removing the Chancellor, risk to Merith's independence and to your leadership here."

"Katrin would never have control over the fanatics. It'd take more time and honey than all of Cyr could offer."

Running his tongue over his teeth, Teague didn't seem to be taking her seriously. "And now how would you propose the Bonded Nations deal with the Merithians who revolt against them?"

With her head tilted back, she said to his eyes, "You kill a god by killing its followers. Although the Chancellor is just a man—a magus, I suspect—the wise will see him as the selfish—"

A coughing fit overtook her. She bent against the railing and wheezed, creating an opening to the stairs that Cord didn't hesitate to use. As he descended, he cleared his throat to rid it of a tickle.

The ladies' council chamber was open, allowing him to see the insincere smiles and chewing filling the silence. Mivvy comforted the brat who had started these rumors as he held Teague's hat on his head. Julian smirked at them. Why wasn't he defending the Chancellor? Where was his passion for all things proper?

The Catalyst spotted Cord and abruptly stood.

Cord moved on toward the cavern. He had to get away from this place, these people. Power hid in the waves of irritation crashing inside Cord's chest, a wholeness, a calloused certainty burning inside him.

The watchman at the door to the temple snapped to attention when Teague yelled, "Cord, wait!"

With the basket in hand, Teague assisted Beatrice to the bottom of the stairs. When Beatrice waved him off to stand on her own, Laurel wrapped her arm around his and joined the procession back to the tunnels. Julian brought up the rear, snickering at Mortin as the kid watched them leave.

Beatrice stopped Mivvy and Nella and forced them back into the room with Mortin. Through a dry throat, she said, "Wait here, Alland and Katrin wish to speak with you."

"You oughta stay too," Cord said to Julian. "I seem to recall you boasting about your skills in combat at some point. Defend them."

"No," Julian replied. "Merith turned its back on me, as you know," he said to Teague. "You saved me at Fort Warren. If you take me with you, I will follow your orders without question."

Teague seemed pleased. Was this change in Julian's tune what he'd been waiting for? Why he was dragging the son of a bitch along with them?

A sickening sensation rushed through Cord, jumbling his insides. His head felt light. Julian collapsed to the floor. Bitterness filled Cord's mouth; Julian vomited. The others stepped back from the stench. His heaving continued to splash the floor as Cord relished the pain on Julian's purpling face.

Teague watched Cord with deliberative caution.

Shame cooled Cord's temper. Julian hacked as Cord relaxed and examined what he had done. He tried to deny it—there wasn't a trance, no exhaustion—but the taste of bile remained, and with it a sense of power. His curse had grown, turning his emotions against him.

Teague helped Julian back to his knees. Beatrice went into the council chamber and came back with a water pitcher and a cloth. Laurel started cleaning the Catalyst's face as he moaned, too weak to fight them off.

Dumbfounded, the watchman walked closer to the display.

Cord left without a word. Down the steps of the temple, he raced to avoid the lot of them. They ought to leave him alone, for their own good. Another curse, a harmful one, hid inside him. Was this the other ability Scarlett had seen?

As expected, quick feet padded on the stairs behind him.

Cord dodged workers in the old gods' temple and refused to see the piks' cheery faces. He strode into the rough-hewn passage and hurried to put more distance between him and Teague. Sprinting while unseen, Cord soon reached the next watchman, another hypocrite in a uniform.

A chummy smile greeted him. "Safe travels," the guard said, opening the door.

Staring at the embroidered green flag on his chest, Cord passed in silence. His gold feather felt cumbersome and restrictive. If he could bring himself to do so, he'd burn it when he reached the caravan.

That was, if he returned. Suddenly aware he was alone, Cord considered his surroundings. The Starlight Tunnels offered their corridors to him. How long could he hide down here? How long before the Dregs found the tunnels and sent their packs to hunt under the stars? "Fucking Dregs," he grumbled.

Anxious not to lose his headway, he sped on but only made it a few steps before the door opened again. He heard Teague's voice speaking to the guard. After the door closed, a single pair of boots pursued him. Cord skirted around Mivvy's pet, clumped in the middle of the tunnel. He didn't flinch when the top of the mound turned to watch him go by. The steps behind him slowed until they were beyond the golem. "Keep away from me," Cord demanded.

"Forgive my assumption," Teague said, "but I suspect you hold me in a higher regard than that horse's arse."

"It doesn't matter. I can't control this curse!"

Teague's footsteps stopped. "Always a curse, never a gift? That curse saved Kylan's life, did it not?"

Cord turned to yell, "A life that I put in danger!"

"You cannot claim that, lad. Your friends put themselves in harm's way when they left Brewing. Ask any of them and they'll say the same."

"Is that what you tell yourself to make Veen's death easier?" Cord asked.

Shocked at the unexpected prodding of his fresh wound, Teague's face twitched as the fury flooded his eyes.

"Just . . ." Cord shook his head and continued on. "Leave me alone." He went through the archway and ran up the stairs.

Teague caught up to him as he snagged a root. The rings slid apart, opening up to the pink sky of the late afternoon. "Cord, we'll give our lives to see that you and your curse make it out of here." His face seemed sincere.

"What's this, then?" Kylan asked from above. "Did we lose the bastard?"

Cord shoved past Kylan. Maybe Maeverly could stop this spell. Or would she laugh and think him foolish for believing in the Chancellor? They weren't always fast enough to hide it; Cord had seen their snide glances, their secret grins when he prayed.

Topping the stairs, Teague spoke with Kylan.

Cord didn't listen, too busy shouting his prayers in his mind. They felt hollow. He didn't hear anything else until Kylan's boots thudded beside him.

"Out with it," Kylan said. "What'd he do?"

Pausing in the thick of the woods, Cord realized they were alone. "You don't wanna be here right now," he threatened.

"Can't control your 'curse,' right?" Kylan shrugged. "Teague told me. I don't care. Believe it or not, I know what it's like to hide something about yourself from other people. It's not—"

"Don't! Don't you compare it to your sins!" He spat the words in disgust. "The way I see it, you can control who you bed. It's your choice! I can't even get angry now without making someone sick up, so don't!"

Kylan snorted. "You're right. It's not the same. You'd be perfectly happy never using magic, whereas I don't want to go through life—"

Cord growled and stalked off. "Just shut up!"

"I'd know something was missing," Kylan finished, racing to his side. "Hey!" he yelled, grabbing Cord's arm. "Listen to me."

"Back off!" Cord jerked his arm free and huffed through his nostrils, staring Kylan down.

"Yeah, you look pretty pissed off to me. If you can't control it, why am I not sick?"

The curse remained charged in his chest, but Kylan was right. It didn't reach out for him.

A smug grin curved Kylan's lips.

"Shut up," Cord said.

Kylan obviously wasn't going to give him any peace. Surrendering, Cord took a deep breath and sat on the ground. He brought his knees to his chest and tried to calm down.

Milling about, Kylan kept watch in the quiet of the late afternoon.

"It was Leila, not Julian." Cord's anger cut in half when he said it. Talking Kylan through it, he rushed the parts that threatened tears. When he finished, the anger charred again.

"Teague's right," Kylan said and clicked his tongue. "If you want to wallow in pity and shame, use what you are entitled to. Your zealous devotion to a murderer, for example. Your fear of what you can do—"

"Don't press your luck."

"Oh, but I am a lucky one," Kylan said with a foolish grin. "A human cricket, just also a village idiot." He laughed alone. "You know, I always find there are more important things to do with my time than counting woes. Like protecting those I care about. Speaking of, I should warn you that dashing off alone isn't the best way to stay on Teague's good side."

Cord ignored the advice and the advisor until Kylan said, "You know, you have new friends now."

"Who? You? You think you're a replacement for Marlone and Leila?" Cord scoffed. "Could Rorry and Scarlett be replaced?"

"No," Kylan said, more patiently than expected, "but you're not alone. You're one of us. And if what you've told me is true, Marlone would want you to keep going, to get off this prison of an island." Kylan bent and punched Cord's arm. "*Tek'aran.*"

"Don't call me that," Cord said, rubbing the soon-to-be bruise. "Ass bandit."

Kylan grinned at the trees and threw up his hands. "I am what I am."

Until then, Cord hadn't noticed Kylan still carried Veen's bow. "I thought you were gonna give that to Carolle?"

"I didn't go back. I wanted to finish the conversation that the golem so rudely interrupted, which I realize is strange since I didn't want to have it in the first place. But, look, I don't want any bad blood between us. You don't get your smallclothes in a bunch over my fondness for men, and I won't judge your religion, specifically as it relates to you, anyway."

Cord didn't know what to say.

"The ladies of Granville give their regards," Teague yelled from the surface of the stump. Julian's arm was draped over Teague for support, but his legs carried most of his weight. "That was an odd way to repay their hospitality."

The Catalyst snatched his arm back when he saw them and hobbled alongside. His eyes bore no fire, no accusation. He didn't know what had happened.

A figure emerged behind them. The watchman from the cavern slowed when he reached Teague, handing over a note. Julian shambled forward without interest. "Tonight," Teague shouted after the guard. "Maris and the gods, help us all," he muttered to the darkening sky.

Teague and Julian kept going when Kylan and Cord went to collect what remained of the pears by the river. Kylan cradled Veen's bow like a relic. Cord understood the affection; Veen had saved his life. However, a little more assistance with the sack would've been appreciated.

Maeverly, the girls, and Bevin were putting the horses in their bridles when they got to the caravan. On the outskirts of camp, the grieving monk sat cross-legged beneath a pine as she stared at the sunset.

"Carolle," Kylan called, breaking her concentration. He presented the bow. "I'm sorry for interrupting."

She rose with a disappointed smile for Veen's weapon and reluctantly took it.

Kylan said, "This is the bow Veen lost when he saved me from Beez. We found it caught in some reeds in the river. I thought you might like it back."

After rolling the weapon on her palms, Carolle tossed it back to Kylan. "No offense to you, Kylan, I'll avenge him with my own bow. You keep it. Stille would find that amusing." Dismissively, she sauntered toward the caravan, clamping the fingers of her left hand as though she was running through a list in her mind. With a sudden pause and a polite smile over her shoulder, she said, "Thank you, Kylan Nock. If we have the chance later, we'll toast Stille with a dark drink. 'Red or darker,' he always said."

When she was out of earshot, Cord said, "That was less heartfelt than I expected. What do you think she's planning?"

"Grief can send someone in a thousand directions at once," Kylan answered. "My dad was distant for nearly four years after my mom died. There was a . . . I don't know, an awareness in his eyes that never came back. He took care of us, my siblings and me, but life never interested him again beyond getting through the day."

"Think that'll happen to Carolle?"

Kylan shrugged. "My mom died giving birth to Kit. Dad didn't have anyone to exact revenge upon. And Carolle is a Ukrestian monk. I get the feeling there isn't one with a simple past." He elbowed Cord. "But who am I lecturing about grief?"

"You're such a jackass," Cord said.

Kylan laughed and thumbed a strange symbol carved into Veen's bow. "Can you restring this?"

Cord did have new friends—who accepted his flaws. It didn't remove the hurt or the desire to mend his friendship with Leila or to find Marlone; but, right then, he'd take what he could get. Someday, he'd set things right. For now, they had to keep going.

"If Teague has a string." As they walked toward the lifewood vardo, ready to depart, Cord asked, "You're not encouraging that satyr, are you?"

"Bloody ashes," Kylan groaned, and shoved him aside. "Go away. I'll take the first stretch." He climbed onto the driver's bench.

"Keep your sword handy," Cord said. "The wolves will be out tonight."

Chapter 41: No Time for Magpies

Halfway through the night, Kylan had finally received the signal to stop the lifewood wagon for their first break since Granville. The hours had put them well into the pass running through the foothills to the Mint Coast.

With the caravan sheltered between the rocky hillsides near the apex of the pass, Bevin had set to work. Kylan's fellow Merithians had perked up a little after their second helping of pear-glazed venison and truffle potatoes.

Granted, as Kylan ate, he had to forget the gifts Carolle had left beside the road along the way as she had scouted ahead of them. Seventeen fellows would have appeared to have been sleeping in the nude were it not for the blood. From what Kylan could tell, their deaths had been merciful. So many wolves . . .

Though now, his anxiety was roused for another reason, one burning a hole in his pocket ever since the sorcerer had handed it to him before dinner. Kylan shifted from foot to foot with the heat of the fire at his back, waiting on Bevin to fix Ferix's plate.

Rorry and Scarlett relaxed at the crackling fire, its sound challenged by the random hums from cicadas in the dales and valleys below. Wholly visible again, Scarlett had draped a blanket over her lap. Even if he tried, Kylan couldn't stop snickering at her errant spell. When she saw him do it again, she blew air through her lips in a failed attempt to pfft.

Rorry rested her head on Scarlett's shoulder and whispered something. She had complained about missing the opportunity to see the Ladies Council but had soon realized Lady Sungspear would have held her captive for her parents. Rorry had laughed off the idea of Lady Gwirion's involvement in such a group, claiming her father governed Brewing. However, she had confessed that her mother spent most of her free time in Lady Sungspear's company while in Croathe for the annual summits.

From the preparations table, Julian favored Kylan with an unexpected nod. He cut up his meal but didn't eat, likely still queasy.

Kylan tried not to think about Cord's new ability. He had taken a risk earlier, goading him on; but Cord had started the uncomfortable conversation, and Kylan would be burned if they didn't finish it. If not talked through, that kind of awkwardness festered. Rorry had complained about missing out on that conversation, too. It surely had to have been more interesting than Bevin's hunt for truffles.

Bevin forced another plate into Kylan's hands. Much to Julian's curiosity, Kylan snatched an unblemished pear for Andion and set off to deliver the meal to Ferix.

On the way, he glanced down to the next curve in the pass where Cord had gone to ask Teague for a bowstring. Teague appeared to be sleeping on the tall boulder where he was supposed to be keeping watch. Although curious, Kylan walked on; he had a treat in his pocket and expected one in return.

Entering the prison-on-wheels, he found the lamp sitting in the middle of the wagon, shining upon the usual display. Ferix reclined against the wall, groping his chest. Andion clicked away at the ebony box, issuing the noise that had been chipping away at Kylan's patience. It woke him each morning and several times throughout the night.

Whatever the riddle was, Andion wasn't sharing. Kylan tried to see around the pik's head as he set the extra pear by him. "Hey, Andion. I'm pretty good at riddles. Let me give it a try."

The pik's nostrils flared.

"Fine," Kylan groaned. "Then tell me this, because I couldn't figure it out. Why'd you even need us? Couldn't you have taken the shadows to the continent?"

Andion spread his hands over the lid of the box and gave him an agonized look. "That is too far," he squeaked. "Shadows don't work in water."

"But you could've caught up with the person you were waiting for."

Snarling, Andion stood with the box and climbed into the trunk. The lid smacked shut, leaving them alone.

"Yes, it was something you said," Ferix joked. When Kylan slid the plate under the cell door and leaned against the bars, the satyr asked, "Venison, again?"

"Here," Kylan said, holding out a pear. "I found Veen's bow in the river."

Ferix flattened his stare to silently threaten Kylan against more teasing about rickety bridges or flooded roads.

Kylan smirked. "You're safe now. We already crossed the last bridge over the Staghorn."

Unamused, Ferix took the pear and set it aside.

"Anyway, I had hoped the bow would cheer Carolle up a little. All it seemed to do was piss her off."

"I avoid women," Ferix said. "They catch whiff of a secret and hunt it without consideration of the outcome."

"You could say the same for Cord." Kylan shrugged off the satyr's interest. "Are there female satyrs?"

"What kind of question is that? You think we're made by trees?"

"Goats, maybe?" Kylan asked and received a dark scowl. "It was a joke!"

"My mother was no goat." He picked up one of the steaks from his plate. "We're as much animals as you beasts. Humans, you believe yourselves above nature. You put rules around everything anyone may want to possess, even magic. Just because your kind can touch magic, that doesn't mean you're made of it."

"Sorry," Kylan said, lowering to the floor. He lay on his side and cushioned his elbow with a pillow while the satyr ate. "At this point, my ignorance of satyrs is as much your fault as Merith's. You pin your lips closed at any personal question that doesn't pertain to your body."

After swallowing a bite, Ferix replied, "I am the prodigal man I claim to be. Is that hard to believe? Why must my tale be more complicated?"

"Because we both know it is." Kylan fished the satyr's pipe from his pocket, sat up, and casually ran his thumbs over it as he gave it a good study.

Ferix stopped chewing.

"I managed to get my hands on this. Having held it, I must wonder the value." Kylan tapped it to his chin, feigning deep thought. "An answer, I'd wager."

Ferix snatched for the pipe.

With a flick of his wrist, Kylan chucked it into the air and caught it behind his back. "Tell me something, without being evasive. You have scars on your back, your side, and on both arms. Your britches are boiled leather where it counts, which means you intend for them to serve as protection. And your horns are growing through your hair. You must file them down for a reason. And that fails to mention your presence in Merith. Why?" Kylan stuck the pipe in his lips. "Take your pick."

The satyr put his plate down and ran a hand through his dark hair, fingering the brown nubs beginning to protrude. The surprise on his face turned into a wry smile. "You have examined my body well enough to know where my scars are."

Kylan's face betrayed him with a blush. "Nothing provocative."

"The mouse called me a connoisseur of deceit. How would you know what was truthful?"

"I'll give you time," Kylan said. He scooted back and went to the door. "This pipe grass sure makes me hungry. It smells like warm harvest pie."

The prisoner stamped the wall. "I'm an assassin."

Kylan considered the answer, not sure whether to believe it. "Who was your target?"

The satyr frowned at his scrutiny. "I fulfilled my end of the deal. Deliver my pipe," he demanded. "And the grass."

The temptation to get another answer for the pestled leaf and spice subsided when he realized it wouldn't gain him any trust; and angering an assassin might not bode well. Kylan neared the cell and held the pipe through the bars. Freeing the pouch from his pocket, Kylan said, "Thank you for telling me." He dropped it through the bars.

Ferix wasted no time packing the pipe. He flicked the bowl with his nail, igniting the contents.

Kylan sat on Andion's trunk and tried to come up with another way to bribe the satyr for more answers to his questions. Assassin? An assassin with hooves?

After sucking a deep breath from the stem, Ferix melted against the wall with a delayed exhale. "Are you not worried Cord will be angry when his clothes smell like this?"

"At the pace we're going, I doubt he'll be awake enough to notice."

Offering his pipe, Ferix said, "Puff?"

"No, thank you." He opted to try his luck. "Your mark wasn't Vega, was it?"

After exhaling through his nose, Ferix said flatly, "For the last time, I had nothing to do with that woman's death, though I would have. She wouldn't keep her filthy paws out of my cage."

"So, who were you supposed—"

"You'll get no more from me tonight," Ferix interrupted.

Cocking his eyebrow at Ferix's sudden rudeness, Kylan stood. "Likewise." As he closed the door behind him, the satyr wore a shit-eating grin with his pipe clenched in his teeth.

* * *

After spending the hours of their eastward journey rigging his new quiver to hang at his hip, Cord had cooled down. He was ready to clear the air. That was, if Teague would wake.

Cross-legged on a high boulder at the eastern curve in the pass, the silver-haired leader of the Hook ought to have been watching the road.

At the base of the boulder, Cord cleared his throat and asked, "We left them to the slaughter, didn't we?"

Teague's sad eyes opened. "Not all. Cord, greater goods rarely feel good. You had better get used to that. I don't predict a lot of lazy holidays in your future."

He dropped down to Cord's side and sighed at the bow in his hands. "Let's cease to dissemble. As you heard from Lady Katrin, the Tribunal is suspected of abusing their power and using the lives of your people to prolong their existence. In the Bonded Nations, those rumors have spread to the extent that sons beg their mothers to let them go to war when their rulers haven't declared one. Our mission here was to pick the bones out of those rumors." He pointed a gloved finger at Cord's tunic. "You claim to be done with the army, to no longer be a Catalyst, was it? Yet you wear the uniform. It seems to agree with you, yes?"

Resisting the urge to run a hand over the feather, Cord said, "No. I don't belong to the army, Teague. But my faith is my own." That didn't appease the mercenary. "Look, I know you think I'm simple for believing in the Chancellor, given what Katrin said. But he's my god. I was raised to hold him above all others, to serve him and to lay down my life in his defense. You have my word I won't put anyone in danger with my devotion, no matter their blasphemy. And while I won't risk any of you for it, I can't—I won't turn away from his Light over the word of a kid half-scared outta his mind."

Teague nodded and said, "When people have made up their minds about something, they harbor little patience for those who haven't and even less for those who disagree. As long as your beliefs don't put us on the rack, who am I to judge?"

"Well, that's a polite load of horseshit."

"Most of what I say is, lad." Teague winked and laughed. "Difficult religions, I can work with at least. I hope you won't be offended if I insist you adopt less morbid attire. Blood is fine for the road, but city folk tend to frown on it." He didn't seem fully convinced by Cord's nod, but gestured for him to hand over Veen's bow.

Exhaling, Teague rested the end of the bow against his forehead. "Wherever did you find this? Veen said he lost it to the river."

"Kylan found it. He tried to give it to Carolle, but she told him to keep it. I was gonna ask if Veen had a spare string."

"Knowing Veen, a few. I was the one who had this bow enchanted, as much as I could afford at the time anyway. My gift to Veen's brother. For all the defensive magic laced into it, it doesn't keep its owners alive very well." Teague shook his head. "I'll have to get his key from Carolle." With a glance down the road to the east, Teague gestured for Cord to join him in returning to the caravan.

"All right," Cord said. "And while we're being honest, which king sent you to find a reason to invade Merith?"

"No king," Teague answered. "Simply a wealthy benefactor whose heart's in the right place, for all the good that does us. Without witnessing the event, we have no evidence, no? As you mentioned, a scared boy who says someone in red raised a flower and slaughtered his village won't be viewed as a reliable source." He flicked his finger against the basilisk hide over the pendant. "Even if I delivered the High Guard, who refuses to speak at the moment, the testimony may be seen as coerced."

"The High Guard?" Cord's stomach churned. "So, Scarlett was right? He's in your necklace?"

Teague tugged on the leather strap around his neck and removed it. The black-stone pendant dangled from his fist. Thin and delicate, it resembled the top of a whirlpool. Ridges had been cut into the edge of the whorl.

"What is it?" Cord asked.

"Something I stole from the Dregs. A prison." He slung the necklace up into his fist. "Yes, the High Guard Ludmire is trapped in here. Sadly, a mountain of patience and aggravation has only gotten his name. The secret of his longevity will take much longer, so long as he's rambling on about his torturous acts in Shallyghal."

Cord balked at the statement. "Wait, you're saying the High Guard lived when Shallyghal fell?"

"Aye, them too," Teague said. "They're the same High Guard who came over with Prince Rhyn seven hundred and two years ago. Not that he's admitted as such yet. You see why the rumors warranted investigating?"

"Ashes," Cord muttered. If the High Guard had the Chancellor's immortality, then the old gods would've had to have cursed them too. Cord's insides began to stew. When they reached the green vardo, he asked, "If you can't use him as proof, what will you do with him once he answers your questions?"

Teague grimaced and put the necklace back on. "I don't wish to deceive you, lad. The process is irreversible. His soul will be freed, but the body is long dead. We burned it."

"Good. They deserve to burn."

A thud came from the brown vardo. Sighing at the prison, Teague slapped the bow on his palm. "Shall we continue our discussion with a little practice?" He went inside the green.

Giggles bounced off the walls of the pass. Scarlett and Rorry hid their faces in embarrassment at whatever had set them off. Julian smiled at Rorry, an unnatural expression for his face.

"What's your plan for Julian?" Cord asked. "You don't actually believe he wants your help, do you?"

"Patience," Teague said.

Kylan had finished his delivery of Ferix's meal and started walking toward the girls, who were still laughing by the fire. Julian even greeted Kylan, which put Cord's hair on end.

He started to join them just to ferret out what Julian was up to, but Teague waved an arrow in front of his face. "Come. Let's talk away from the others." In his gloved hands, Teague held a clutch of spiral-fletched arrows and a finely formed longbow. "To have these, you must promise me you'll leave that one alone unless he is a direct threat."

"I don't trust him. I never will."

"That's your right," Teague said. "I know your history runs deeper, and believe me, I get it, so I do. For now, he's pulling his weight and has directly asked for our help. The Hook's creed keeps us from denying it."

"That's the dumbest—"

Teague moved the bow out of Cord's reach. "In Racine," he said. "Once we arrive, ye can work this out yourselves. We won't interfere."

The Seeding touched two more sunsets. They'd be in Llandir before then, and in Racine shortly after they secured passage over the Gallaic Channel. Cord took a deep breath and caught Rorry's eye. She smiled and resumed braiding Scarlett's hair. He agreed.

"Is that bow enchanted?"

"Just expensive, I'm afraid," Teague answered, depositing the arrows into Cord's quiver. "You keep these. We can use mine for practice." He thumbed over his shoulder to the full quiver at his back before handing over his end of the deal.

Cord expected the longbow to border on cumbersome. Instead, it balanced on his finger. The smoky gray shaft ended in golden curls beyond the string. "Thank you."

"We have an agreement, Cord," Teague reminded him. "Let's walk."

Past the boulder where Teague had kept his vigil, a thrill overtook Cord as he gazed into the forested valley below. Moonlight coated the swaying branches of the persistent winter trees on the slopes. The scent on the wind invigorated him.

As he took in the surrounding snowy peaks, he had to wonder what watched them back. Kylan had said Carolle had killed several wolfkin in the pass already.

At the road's edge, Teague extended an arrow to him. "If you need more, Rorry can show you where to find them."

Chuckling, Cord took the arrow. Aware he stood before an expert marksman, Cord aimed at the nearest target he trusted, a small tree on the slope about twenty yards down. He picked a leaf, imagined Julian's ornery head of curls, and released.

"You're no tyro," Teague said. "Where did you learn to shoot like that?"

"My headmaster requisitioned a bow for me. I ran the stream for years, hunting shadows mostly." He shrugged with his right shoulder. "I might have been aiming for the tree next to it."

Teague laughed. "'Tis rather windy up here. Perhaps I can offer a few pointers."

As they shot their way through Teague's quiver, the mercenary offered his tips and relayed tales just as salty as Maeverly's. Oddly, she didn't feature in any of them.

Cord's favorite was the origin of Teague's jerkin, a story involving Veen, Bevin, Teague, and their friends, Joseb, Oren, and Elanis. After overhearing whispers while in a Gorovi prison, the band had completed their assignment and set off hunting a rod of compulsion. Their directions hadn't led them to a thought-altering rod. Instead, they'd found themselves lost in a frigid swamp full of basilisks and, if Teague were to be believed, a cult that had raised a few score of the undead just to breed more of the beasts.

In the end, Cord took it for a good story and didn't dwell on the bits that were surely exaggerated, especially the garments Teague said his friends had turned their share of the hides into. Not that he thought armored smallclothes were a bad idea.

Teague took his turn and clipped a branch from a small tree he had been picking away at. "'Tisn't easy to lose faith, no matter the scale. Your world has turned over, but I suspect it has only done so to right itself."

"I'm trying not to think about it," Cord said. He took the bow. Eager to change the subject, he asked, "What was it like behind the Cloud?"

"Pain and torment. The deeds that send most men to swing from the hangman's noose pale in comparison to what happens behind that shell of wind, fog, and lightning. 'Tis just a shell, you know? Inside, humans and wolfkin alike bow and scrape for the Dregs' approval, often proving themselves with the heinous acts I mentioned before. The only fortunate event I recall during my captivity was the relief of not dining with their wolves. Cannibals, the lot. They prefer their meals rare and young."

Cord curled his lip. "People want to serve them?"

"More than that. They want to be worn. The taint of their upbringing. I try not to dwell on it."

After pulling the string to his cheek, Cord released it. The arrow struck with less speed than it should have. "How'd you escape?" He passed the bow over.

"Beez kept me secluded, like a prized mare. Luck, the help of friends, and some very difficult choices got me out of his clutches. I can promise you this, we won't succeed with Beez on our trail. He has to be dealt with." Teague swept his aim out toward the valley and loosed a wild shot into the sky. "Your turn."

"My brother is one of those beasts," Cord said without looking Teague in the eye. He nocked an arrow. "Every time I take aim at one, I'll be wondering if it's Marlone."

Teague's hand gripped his shoulder. "That kind of hesitation will kill you, lad."

"Is there any way to save him?" For all the encouragement Teague tried to wear on his face, the words didn't follow. Cord resumed his practice.

"If anywhere," Teague said, "you won't find a cure here. The best advice I can give you is to count your magpies when we get to Racine. Know what's important for tomorrow and what will have to come later. Try to sort it all out now, and you'll be standing still."

Before long, Teague left him to his practice with a warning to keep a close watch and the instruction to refill his quiver when he finished. The man lied, claiming he was off to sleep. It didn't take his incessant fingering of the medallion for Cord to know what truly occupied him.

Cord wasn't ready to surrender this awful day yet. One more clutch. Then he'd go.

"You must be exhausted, Cord," Rorry said. He jumped. "We were a little worried when you did not return with Teague."

"I'm fine. Just clearin' my head is all." He nocked an arrow and brought it to his cheek. The longbow's string relaxed, flinging the arrow off the cliff side at nothing in particular.

Her eyes followed its flight into the puddle of darkness between the limbs below. "It is peaceful out here."

"Can I ask you something, Rorry? You don't believe in demons; do you believe in the Chancellor's Light?"

She didn't have to answer; he knew from the way her posture tensed. "For my family, attending chapel was more of a social requirement than a spiritual one. Appearances were important. Vital, really. We never discussed the doctrine at home outside of mealtime prayers. Even those seemed to fall into tradition more than faith."

The embarrassment he'd been feeling for days grew. It was one thing to suspect how they saw him, but another to know. To them, he must seem like a simple wooder believing whatever he was told. "It must be easier for you," he said. "If you don't believe in the dark, why do you need his Light?"

"You are wrong again," she said, returning his sass. "Did you forget I was standing at your side when Beez came for you? This morning, when we buried Veen, I was there. I have seen the dark." Her lips squeezed together, holding something in. She broke her gaze and directed it up to the Glades. "I have a light, but it was never his."

"Well, he is mine."

"Freckles," Carolle called.

Rorry lingered behind Cord for a moment before she sighed. He listened to her steps fade into the wind before releasing his draw.

"He is mine."

The longer Cord practiced, the less he focused on it. His head swam through the day's challenges, what Teague had said about the High Guard being as immortal as the Chancellor, about Mortin's tale. His certainties had been reduced to his faith, and the feather on his chest was making it hard to breathe.

After wasting two more arrows on wild shots, Cord set his bow aside and removed the Catalyst tunic. He gathered the quivers and his new bow before heading back to the campfire.

Only Julian remained in its glow. The half-ogre was setting up his lean-to behind his cart. Cord didn't see Kylan and Scarlett anywhere, but Rorry and Carolle sparred in the distance.

Julian sat up on his stool when he saw Cord approaching.

Dropping the bow and quivers, Cord didn't slow. He went straight to the stones around the fire and flung the uniform onto the flames. Watching the frayed embroidery writhe and burn, Cord felt an invigorating sensation of clarity and weightlessness. That tunic meant nothing to him. It wasn't a mark of his failure to save Marlone. It didn't represent what Headmaster Angsly wanted Cord to be. There was no Light in it at all.

"I buried mine," Julian said, watching the fire. "It was too dangerous to carry. It might have saved me from the Judges though."

For Julian, that was oddly close to admitting a mistake. Cord kept his voice hard and asked, "Where did you get your clothes?"

"I am not proud of it," he answered, rubbing his hands. "I thought if I got rid of my uniform and had someone else's Seeding papers, no one would ever be the wiser."

Cord shook his head. "You took them from an innocent?"

Turning up his nose, Julian barked, "I said I am not proud of it! What was I supposed to do? No, I did not kill him, if that is what you are thinking. His clothes did not fit, but yes, I stole them and buried my uniform in a pasture wall. I left his papers. They were for South Thornton; a fat lot of good that would have done me.

"When the Judges found me on the Southern Road, they laughed at my story and told me to run." He shrugged. "Then I woke up in Fort Warren and found your horse." An unspoken question lingered on Julian's lips before he splayed his hands.

Relaxing his jaw, Cord said, "I don't trust you, Julian. Make no mistake about that. But I told Teague I'd set our differences aside till we got to Racine. Until then, we're allies." His words stirred Julian's haughty posturing, but the Croathite nodded.

Cord knew what was important, more important than his vengeance. He'd save Marlone first. Then they'd avenge Kenton together. If that meant he had to play nice with Julian and get to the continent to find the cure, so be it.

After picking up his bow and the quivers, Cord turned back to say, "The army is our enemy now. If we get into battle and you see a High Guard, he's mine." He set off for the lifewood. "He is mine."

Rorry drove her boot into Carolle's hand. "Again," the monk ordered. "Strike with your heel like I taught you. That's where the force is, not in your toe." She forcefully kicked Carolle's palm. "Good. Again."

Though it felt quite irreverent, Rorry was thankful Carolle's mourning hadn't ended her lessons. After five more successful blows, Carolle caught her ankle. For the sake of decency, Rorry lost her balance and fell to the grass.

"I'm not being funny, it really would be easier if you'd lose the dress."

This argument again. "We are exposed." The faces around the orange beacon of their campfire were easily seen. Where had Cord's tunic gone?

Carolle let her eyes close with her shrug. Losing herself in the wind, she took longer than normal to return to the situation before her. The circles around her eyes resembled bruises now more than weariness. "I told you before that I have clothing you can borrow."

"What made you want to become a monk?" Rorry asked, spreading her dress around her.

Carolle's brow furrowed at the unexpected question. "Is this really how you want to spend our time?"

Rorry did not blink. With a visible summoning of patience, the monk relented and joined her on the grass.

Propping up her knee, Carolle laid her chin against it. "As I told you before, I traveled as a member of the Patevian Royal Dance Troupe. The tour had just arrived in Trône d'Argent to open *Elysant on the Glass* when some men I barely knew made me a proposition. They offered me coin to spy on one of the nobles who owned a High House in the Tenth ring." Her breathing slowed. "Rodinger was a kind man. Proper gentle and all. When I accepted I had expected someone who abused his power and influence, or at the very least solved his problems with coin. Yet his morals were never for sale, even with the coercion of the men who had hired me."

Her finger caressed the outline of the frost lily on her shoulder as she stared into the stars for some time. "I loved him and betrayed him all the same. In the end, he died. I tried to stop it and was left for dead myself. Ever since then, if I'm in a fight and someone has a mace, I take them down first. I used to think they were stupid weapons."

Rorry pulled a leaf out of Carolle's hair and laid a hand on her back. "Is that when you went to the monastery?"

"No. I killed them, first. Then I went to the Mount because the pain didn't stop." A tear rolled down Carolle's cheek. "I know what it feels to be hollow like, and I know the joy that comes with filling that emptiness with yourself again." She nodded to herself. "There will come a time when Stille's death is bearable, but I'm not ready to accept that. Not yet."

Letting the silence speak for her, Rorry laid her head on Carolle's shoulder and hugged her. She had not realized what a blessing Carolle's laughter had been.

"Someday," the monk said, "Stille'll sing. Bevin'll prepare the meal. And I'll dance while the others cheat at cards. We'll do it all again in the Glades."

Resting her head on Rorry's, Carolle said, "The hardest thing you have to do in life is open yourself to the hurt, bach. Only then can you air out the wound and truly heal. Feel it and let it breathe. Stille taught me that." She sat up and lifted Rorry's chin with her finger. "Promise me you'll never give up on yourself, Rorry. No man, no coin is worth compromising your truth."

Rorry looked at Carolle's extended pinky finger and said, "I promise." She was not sure she meant it. But she said the words.

"Proper swear it," Carolle said. She grabbed Rorry's hand and wrapped her little finger in hers. "Now say it."

Grinning, Rorry said, "I swear I will not give up on myself."

"Good girl. Now get up. Let's start again. You won't always have me at your back in more than spirit."

Chapter 42: Notes Left Behind

The morning vista through the pass rewarded Rorry for rising early and stole her breath. To the east, a purple haze soared over the mossy-green edges of the famous Mint Coast. That haze was the eastern end of the Breslan Mountains breaking through the clouds. In that moment, it meant everything to her. The coast lay on the other side, and a little farther north was Llandir, their port to freedom. It would not be long now.

The scent of warm potatoes teased her stomach. Rorry returned to the fire ring and opted for one of the folding stools because the mist, or perhaps a cloud at this height, had slicked the ground. Pleased to see Bevin had let Julian sleep in, she smiled as the jovial cook danced to a song he hummed while balancing a pan, a knife, and potatoes. He even took a step back from the table in rhythm. A series of ochre snaggleteeth greeted her when his thin lips split with a smile. Bevin practically floated. What had put him in such a good mood?

Feeling a bit useless, Rorry distracted herself by watching the horses near the grass patch where she and Carolle had sparred only hours earlier. Scute and all of the Northpelts were accounted for. However, Nightingale and two of the other horses were missing. Assuming Carolle had taken hers to scout ahead, Rorry scanned the area for the others.

Her eyes went back to the satyr's vardo. She knew Cord had been exhausted, that yesterday had beaten him to a pulp. The isolation she had interrupted last night was his way of coping with more unwelcome news. She hoped sleep had eased his mind.

Hoofbeats approached from downhill and slowed as they neared the camp. Bevin didn't react, so Rorry remained seated.

Teague and Maeverly rode into view on the two missing horses. That strange feathered cloak draped Maeverly's shoulders again. She wore the same velvety midnight dress that she had worn last night when she had finally emerged to dine. While she appeared exhausted, Teague looked haggard.

They dismounted and let the horses roam with the others. Maeverly clutched her cloak to her neck, concealing her face in black plumes, and sprinted for the butterfly vardo. Teague passed by Rorry with a simple nod. The azure door closed behind Maeverly just as the canary-yellow one opened for Teague. He pulled out a brown leather sack.

"Ahh!" Bevin yelled, scaring Rorry to her feet. She nearly jumped out of her skin. He bowed his head in an apology and pointed to the food.

His shout woke Julian. When he saw her receiving her plate, his hands flurried to correct his disarrayed appearance.

Teague called to Rorry from his vardo and waved good morning to Scarlett, who had just left Maeverly alone.

Trying to ignore the prickly sensation of Julian watching her, Rorry passed Scarlett her untouched meal and moved on to Teague. She wanted to ask Teague what they'd been doing that had kept them up all evening, and would have if the company had not become complicated by Julian.

Teague handed over the sack from his wagon. "Let me start by saying she's safe," he said, which set Rorry's nerves on edge. "Carolle had some affairs to settle and won't be joining us to Llandir but wanted you to have this." Hugging the bag to her chest, Rorry curtsied. Expecting more of an explanation, she stood there awkwardly while Teague walked away toward the others, who had been joined by Kylan now.

What could Carolle have hoped to achieve by going off alone in this madness? Rorry tried not to be offended by the improper farewell. "Be safe," she said under her breath.

Kylan had left the door to the lifewood vardo open. Inside, Andion hung from the black wool tunic Cord was wearing, stretching it to fit. Until then, she hadn't realized how much smaller Veen was. She looked away before Cord caught her watching the process.

When Cord stepped out of the vardo, an apologetic frown crossed his lips. She let him off the hook with a grin. The light behind his brown eyes was sturdy. He would get past this, the Chancellor be burned.

With her appetite faded, Rorry decided to retire inside the whimsical wagon to examine her gift, likely something lewd that would just embarrass her in front of the others and subject her to endless teasing from Kylan. She smiled over her worry as she opened the door.

Maeverly gasped and scattered the bottles on her vanity as she jerked around. She held a straight razor in her hand. Why would—

Stubble covered half of her face! Rorry's eyes widened and swung to her friends. Scarlett bit her lip and hid behind her book. Kylan smiled through a cringe. Rorry's jaw snapped shut as she scowled at them. "Why am I always the last to find out?" she asked over Maeverly's stumbled explanation.

Rorry climbed the stairs and pulled the door closed behind her, which dumbfounded the sorcerer. "Sorry to intrude. Give me a moment," Rorry said, taking a seat on the unburned bench cushion. "Then please explain."

* * *

Rorry held her cerulean nail against the round window above her bench. She regretted the decision to skip breakfast. The morning had passed in a blur while she'd absorbed Joseb's story. Her friends should know she could handle the truth. She was not Cord! A smile erupted through her frustration. She hoped she would see his reaction to learning Maeverly's truth.

Scarlett's lesson dragged on, encouraging Rorry to imagine what busied Cord. She grinned when she realized he might be driving the vardo with the shimmering butterfly, and giggled when she realized the only alternatives were Kylan or Bevin. A snort caused her to cover her mouth.

The other passengers did not notice. Rolling over, Rorry turned her attention back to the inside of the vardo. The middle-aged man peered into a brass hand mirror as Scarlett read a chapter she had probably read nights ago. Her fingers divided the pages at several points within the book.

Rorry tried to peek around Joseb's shoulder to see the mirror in his hands. "How exactly does a half-ogre come about?" she asked. Joseb appeared shocked at the question and cocked his head as he searched for the right words. Rorry felt her blush all the way back to her ears. "I mean, was his father human?"

"No, his mother." Though never truly feminine, Joseb's real voice seemed errant. "Her name is Brutia, if that gives you any insight into her character." He laughed to himself. "In hindsight, he and Vega may have been a good pairing, in a quip on humanity and true love."

"Do you not believe it brings ill-fortune to speak poorly of the dead?" Rorry asked.

The man's gaze fell back on the mirror. "Quite the contrary. A healthy animosity does wonders for grief."

Rorry decided to try her luck while he gabbed. "Why has Teague been looking so . . . ill? Does it have to do with the amulet he wears?"

"It certainly does," he said, earning Scarlett's attention. "Someone should smash that unholy thing."

"Unholy?" Scarlett asked. "Is it from behind the Cloud?"

Joseb turned to her. "Not everything that's unholy is neatly confined. But, yes, Teague stole the amulet when we freed him." He set the mirror facedown and sullenly folded his arms. "One of my biggest regrets is not being able to find him sooner. It took us nearly a year, and five members of the Hook died before we found Beez's den off on one of the remote islands. I can't imagine we would've succeeded without Remy offering a high estate's wealth for information from the local tribes."

"Teague is a close friend?" Rorry asked.

He nodded, grinning suddenly. "We've been friends since we were younger than you two. His father was a merchant from Lekelith who sold fire opals to the High Houses and the Tower of Trône d'Argent." His grin widened. "You know, I can take him in a sword fight, even in Racinian high-fashion gowns." He waited for Rorry's smile. "And it was he who convinced me to leave the Tower, believe it or not. Even then, he was always caught in the tow of some adventure. I used to think they'd swallow him whole. He's more formidable than I gave him credit for. Or has been."

"Like Kylan," Scarlett mumbled. "You were younger than us when you left the Tower?"

"No, though I certainly wish I had been. I had a few years on you. By that time, my younger sister had caught up to my tier. I believe she was raised and mantled a year later; I can't quite recall. She's always had a knack for thriving within false complacency, and her natural talents put mine to shame." He began to say something but closed his mouth when the mirror caught his attention.

"You keep checking your mirror. Is it a vision spell?" Rorry asked.

He turned the mirror over and laughed. "That would be a great feat."

"They are covered in detail in the Masters of Craft chapters," Scarlett said, flipping the pages.

Sitting up, Rorry eyed the mirror.

"Therein lies the problem," Joseb said. "It's a challenge for someone with my limitations. I am trying, but I've not managed it yet." He held the mirror out to them. It showed only their reflections, which did not look as tired as Rorry had expected.

He examined his own reflection and grimaced. "Merith demands that my appearance hold a certain foreign quality about it at all times. While I've found shock and awe to be great allies in the past, this is a bit avant-garde for me."

Rorry suspected shock and awe were easily achieved.

"Did Carolle leave us to avenge Veen?" Scarlett asked, likely eager to change the subject before Rorry mentioned something awkward.

Rorry shot her a surreptitious pout to let her know she was onto her ploy, but waited for the answer.

"Yes," he said. "It's her right to find her balance. I don't have all of the answers when it comes to the monks, and we're expressly forbidden to ask." The lecturing finger Mrs. Hywel used to emphasize a point relocated to his hand. "I'm sorry. That is, *I'm* forbidden to ask. They tend to grow tired of my questions."

Rorry's eyes drifted to the bag behind her feet. Why had Carolle not delivered it herself? Rorry had initially seen the pretty monk as a tart and a termagant. Now she worried about her like a sister. She understood Carolle's decision to go; Rorry would do the same in her shoes. "Should we help her?"

Concern wrinkled the corners of Joseb's eyes. "No. As Teague has reminded us, the window for our escape is small. They'll be closing the ports as soon as they realize there's an invasion. I'd be surprised if they haven't by now with all this frittering of time over the Tribunal. It's best if we arrive at Llandir and assess our strategy. Her safety depends on her training and intrepid reasoning." He pulled a beeswax candle close. Flicking the wick, he created a small flame. "We can hope for the best for her."

Rorry knew of another way to honor Carolle. She lifted the bag to the bench beside her and removed the small note inside. Between the vines Carolle had drawn, she had written: *You're still the flower you were before the frost. Now you are even stronger. Make me proud, Freckles!*

"Do you have a sharp sewing needle and thread?" Rorry asked.

Joseb squeaked open a drawer and presented the items. "I never leave home without them. I'm a bit of a dilettante tailor. In my youth, I always made my own clothes. Even today, it's quicker and less complicated."

"Good," Rorry said. "I may need your help with this."

* * *

When Joseb chose to drive after lunch, Scarlett decided to ride in the vardo with Kylan, Andion, and Ferix. Rorry's project consumed her attention; Scarlett doubted she would mind the solitude.

After taking advantage of each moderately quiet moment to bring about this triumph, Scarlett removed her fingers and closed *Essential Focus* with a broad grin. Sadly, Kylan slept, or seemed to be sleeping amid the clicks from Andion's puzzle box. She decided not to wake him just to share in her victory of finishing the tome.

The satyr had noticed. If there were a king of secrets, Scarlett believed the crown to be his. She didn't have a legitimate example of his perfidious nature, but her intuition demanded caution. Kylan's interactions with him made it doubly true.

"Is it a proud thing to limit your mind?" Ferix asked. "You humans and your approach to magic . . ."

"Sorry?" Scarlett asked. "Do satyrs use it differently?"

He scooted to the end of his cage and whispered, "Give me a spell. Name any spell in that book, and I'll explain what I mean."

Without removing her skepticism, Scarlett flipped the pages. Her fingertip pressed to a random page in the Novice chapters. Curious to see what he'd make of this one, she said, "Refreshing the air with scents of citrus."

Stroking his beard, Ferix thought for a moment. Then he said, "Perfect example. How would you use that?"

"The function is in the title," Scarlett said. "You refresh stale air or cover odors."

"Yes, if you cannot think for yourself. Don't assume the author or the discoverer of that spell is the authority on its use. You humans love to stake claims, so take the claim out of it. What might you do with a spell that scents the air? Is it limited to citrus? Would it remove all scent from the air if dispelled? That'd be useful for an assassin. Or could you flood the air with a scent and overwhelm those wolves that hunt you?"

Scarlett's mind began racing with new possibilities, though she didn't want to admit her creativity had let her down.

Ferix's grin said he already knew. He lay on his side and closed his eyes. "Even a simple bottle can kill a man. Just break it."

Scarlett flipped through the spells in her lap. What a strange gift for Ferix to bestow upon her. The Novice section had seemed like a waste of time before. "Thank you," she said.

The prisoner didn't respond.

She'd wager her mum's adventure across Merith hadn't included receiving spell-casting advice from a satyr. Come to think of it, her mum wouldn't even know of these resurfaced spells, having closed herself to sorcery. Scarlett daydreamed for minutes on each entry, reconsidering new ways to use them, and giggled over what could be cracked, other than nuts. Having burned through the last of her candles, she earmarked the spells that she wanted to commit to memory first and decided to give her eyes a break.

Andion kept pecking the script of his box. He was quite diligent himself, though outright petulant in Kylan's presence. The pik hadn't let her study the script on the lid to know the riddle, a fact that made her wish she'd found adequate lighting when she had held it days earlier. Perhaps time had changed that. "May I help?"

A muffled reply dismissed the idea.

The satyr opened his eyes and rolled over to continue his slumber.

Pounding his fist into his thigh, Andion growled. "What did the convict awaiting execution possess that spurred envy from the soldier, the scribe, and the serf?"

Elated that he'd shared, Scarlett didn't want to disappoint. Giving the answer the prudent consideration it deserved, she said, "He would be idle. Time? No, not time. Leisure?" She scooted close to observe the nautical carving's response.

Andion entered her answer into the waves and pressed the smoothed ship. He frowned as the surface evened with a click. "Family, friends, love . . ." he muttered. "Nothing works."

"Courage?" Scarlett guessed. The characters compressed and popped back up.

He shook his head with a quick whine.

"Freedom," Kylan said, half-asleep.

Skewing his mouth at the uninvited answer, Andion pressed the script.

"I'm not sure that makes sense," Scarlett said.

"Why?" Kylan asked. "The convict has nothing to lose. He can tell the king to shove his royal scepter up his—"

The lid popped open. They gasped.

Kylan covered his head with his arm. "Now can I sleep?" he mumbled.

Andion raised the lid. He and Scarlett stared in wonder at the red cloth lining. Inside the box, a small scroll had been rolled and slipped through a thick silver ring. The yellow vellum appeared quite old. Andion picked it up and slid off the ring. He placed the trinket on his leg and unrolled the note. Deciphering the clean lines of script in the Old Tongue, Scarlett read:

To my dearest son,

> *When this riddle is solved, you must give the reward to the one who supplied the answer. If you came to it yourself, then keep it. Please understand if I doubt that will be the case. This ring is an item of chaos. You, my beloved son, are not. Give it away freely, for it knows where it belongs.*

> *Our time was too short. Know you are the pride of our people and your parents, my spritely prince. Live and show others the way.*

Love,

Papa

Wheezing, Andion clutched the message to his chest and shielded it from his tears. The ring fell off his lap and thudded to the floor.

Scarlett cautiously lifted the shiny bauble. Beautiful and heavier than expected, the silver band was etched with seven feathers, a series of mismatched plumes avoiding a pattern. Next to where a peacock feather stood, a curled duck tail feather lay askew. Somehow, it felt significant to her.

Sniffling, Andion wiped his eyes. He gently furled the note and set it in the box. The dense lid snapped as it closed.

Scarlett held the ring out to him and placed it in his palm as he rose. To her surprise, Andion didn't repudiate Kylan's claim. With the ring outstretched, he kicked Kylan in his side.

"Ow! What do you want?" When Kylan saw Andion's tear-streaked face, he sat up. "Are you hurt? What's wrong?"

The pik shook his large head. "You have solved the riddle and are entitled to your claim, my good sir."

The formality of his words raised Kylan's brow. He blinked several times before seeing the ring in Andion's fingers. "Oh, Andion, you can have it."

Andion dropped the ring on Kylan's lap. "No. It is your right. I have what I want."

Scarlett nodded to Kylan.

When Kylan picked the ring up, Andion returned to the box and entered the answer again. He read the note once more.

Sliding the ring onto his right forefinger, Kylan examined it. He shrugged to her and lay back down.

Andion sealed away the note. Then he opened the trunk, carried the puzzle inside, and disappeared.

Though she dared not guess what, Scarlett knew something had changed.

Chapter 43: Strength to Change

At the end of dinner, Cord listened as Teague gathered their attention around the campfire to review directives. For in the morning, they would finally reach Llandir.

"Take only what you must," Teague said to Bevin. "When you're ready, squeeze yourself into the larger vardo and keep our guest quiet."

"Who?" Julian asked.

Teague ignored the question. "Julian can ride in my vardo. Maeverly'll conceal the rest of ye with Bevin. 'Twill be a tight fit, but we'll reach the docks before you know it." Crouching next to Scarlett, he put two fingers on her book to get her attention. "If you have anything in Maeverly's vardo, be sure you get it out before we leave. It stays behind."

Cord had wondered why Bevin had parked the wagon in the middle of the grassy clearing, breaking the line-up of the caravan for the first time. In the dwindling light of the evening, the glass ceiling of the wagon shimmered. Rorry had holed herself up inside for the entire day.

Maeverly had brought her meal to her and had not come back.

"Kylan, lad," Teague said. "You'll be our scout until we set out. Meet me at the horses."

Though they hadn't seen any wolfkin as they'd traveled through the lush fern-filled forest of the Mint Coast, that was a risk. Kylan's sneer agreed as he followed Teague.

Cord got up and tailed them between the butterfly wagon's door and the vardos next to the road. "I'll do it," Cord said. "Llandir's half a day away, maybe less. We shouldn't be reckless now."

"Thanks?" Kylan replied.

Teague disagreed and kept walking toward the horses.

Kylan reclined against the butterfly vardo's wheel. "But Cord's right. I won't do it." If it weren't for Kylan's chummy grin, Cord would've expected Teague to retaliate beyond shaking his head in frustration. Kylan wasn't perturbed. "It's not right. The last time I ignored this feeling, Veen died. I promised myself I wouldn't do it again."

Without listening, Teague tried to drag the argument along to where the horses grazed.

"Kylan can't ride," Cord said. He struggled to keep his tone even, aggravated by Teague and Veen's itchy tunic. He tugged it down again. "I can!"

"I know the sore I pick at when I remind you what you are, Cord," Teague said. "Try not to force me. Kylan has been trained by a Ghost Augur. He can handle it. There is no happy medium here."

"No," Maeverly said, descending the stairs of her wagon. "I've never met a happy medium. They are obsessed with death and deception. 'Your gran has hidden her pearls. She wants you to bring them to me because you do not have the strength to do with them what must be done!' I'd much rather scam a child than a mourner." She saw Cord's confusion. "Despicable either way, I suppose."

"Yes, thank you," Teague said. "That's not what I meant."

"I think speaking to the dead should be a quick event if it were to happen," the sorcerer continued. "It's not exactly the natural order of things."

Cord understood that remark, aimed at the medallion around Teague's neck.

"We need a scout, don't we?" Teague asked her. "Kylan doesn't want the task. Cord is chomping at the bit for it."

Maeverly tilted her head. "And you are too busy yourself? Or have you finally succumbed to reason and decided to take a night off?"

"Aye. I'll get some rest while you take watch here, so I will. Cord needs to remain in the caravan, under supervision." That almost sounded like "under lock and key."

The butterfly vardo door closed. "Then let me go," Rorry said, tossing her queue over her shoulder.

Her plain dress had been given over for a ruddy version of Carolle's leather armor, which hugged her legs. The deep neckline had been filled in with white frills. Otherwise, it would've sunk much lower on her fair skin. Along the shoulders of her short jacket, boiled leather padding caught the light, slim enough to go unnoticed unless someone ogled her silhouette. Cord lost himself somewhere between joy and concern.

Rorry pulled her cropped jacket tighter around her chest. "We need a scout, do we not? Here I am." She ran a gloved hand over the pockets on her belt, worn low around her waist. Her fingertips protruded from her gloves. Had she cut them? Carolle had never worn gloves or a jacket that Cord had seen.

Teague glanced Cord's way, then shook his head.

But Maeverly spoke first. "You can't deny Carolle's endorsement."

Cord glowered at Kylan, who appeared to be on the verge of surrender when Teague said, "Aye. I suppose you're right. Get your crossbow, Rorry. We'll set your boundaries."

* * *

Night had fully developed by the time Rorry rode out with Teague. Scute's height required some adjustment. Rorry's palfrey back in Brewing had spoiled her by being short for her breed. Yet the mare could not compete with Scute's calmness. His black eyes calculated every movement that caught his attention, as though he wanted to seek it out rather than run from it.

Teague's coppery bay brought him forward. "He cares for you."

She looked past him to see Cord overseeing their departure. His face remained flushed from his failure to argue his way into taking her place. Rorry had had to run a hand down his arm and gaze into his eyes until he'd agreed, though her first impulse had said to shove him for insinuating she was not up to the task. Carolle's garments were oddly invigorating.

Waving as Kylan hauled Cord aside, she replied, "He is very kind to lend me Scute."

Teague frowned at the boys. He should not worry about those two. Besides, they were half a day from their destination. It would all be over soon.

"Did you complete the alterations to the Seeding papers?" Rorry asked.

He nodded. "I'll disperse them before we arrive, as a precaution only. You know yourself, Maeverly can conceal ye in the vardo with Ferix. I'm still not sure why I needed to alter Cord's papers rather than giving him the set already scribed for Llandir."

As silly as it seemed, Rorry had been the one to make the request. At the time, her motivation had been to keep anything related to Grary from assisting them. Now, it felt like too much of an insult to Cord. "Cord does not resemble a blacksmith."

The Mint Coast lived up to its reputation for misty, crisp air and vibrant vegetation. Lush environs spread over the hills surrounding their camp. She had never been to Llandir but knew from the stories of her youth that Her Grace loved the neighboring hills.

Teague focused on their whereabouts while Rorry studied him. She had been waiting to question him alone, and now that the opportunity had presented itself, she had lost the words.

"This is far enough," he said. "We'll circle the camp from here." Leading the way, he brought his horse to a trot, which Scute matched. "There's no reason to engage anything you encounter. Given the slightest hint that you're being watched, you race back, yes? Go directly now. Don't try to lose them; get back to camp." He winced and held his hand to his forehead.

"Are you well?"

He shook his head but did not explain.

"You are going to make me ask?"

He blinked, trying to focus on her. "The terror I feel when I think upon the fact that Beez is tracking us shall end soon. With it, the headaches." His voice stayed flat, no pitch suggesting victory or pleasure at the outcome.

She had not anticipated a direct answer of that sort. "Maev— Joseb mentioned you had a lengthy imprisonment with them."

He sniffed a laugh upon hearing Joseb's name.

Scute stopped and looked about, prompting Teague and Rorry to do the same. Before she finished, the horse continued on their path.

Still eyeing the woods, Teague said, "I was held for a little over a year." He ran a hand over his chest. "When they enter you, you live for days, sometimes more than a week, and witness the horrors they do with your body. If they tire of secular evils, they attack your mind, listening to your every thought and feeding you theirs."

Rorry's insides melted. "That sounds—'dreadful' seems inadequate."

"Each time I had verged on death, Beez found another host and nursed me back to health just to do it all over again." His frown aged him. "I've been struggling with that fear, selfishly so. Now I'll lay all of our lives on the line to keep Cord out of their hands. If they took him, I think they could wear him indefinitely and heal the others. Death would never end their torture."

A new respect for the Hook's flirtatious leader arose. How had he endured a year of that treatment?

He massaged the muscles in his neck. "Determination that makes your own friends expendable can be exhausting. To be honest, I wasn't sure I should agree to let you patrol. I trust your judgment, but Cord's . . ."

"Cord will do what any of us would do in his position, I suspect," she finished. She knew what he was alluding to, that Cord would leave the safety of camp to protect her. Worse, Kylan would encourage him to do something that ludicrous. Teague should have positioned Cord into a false sense of security rather than providing transparent, dire facts. Men could be quite irrational.

"'Tisn't going to end until Beez is dealt with. Now that he's out of the Cloud, he'll hunt me—us—even on the continent."

"Did he love you?" Rorry asked. Embarrassed, she upbraided herself for sounding like a little girl. "Is that why he will not let you go?"

"Love is beyond them," Teague said. "Ownership, control, lust. That's all they are capable of, so it is."

Rorry decided to quote His Grace one last time. "My father used to tell me that if you do not face your fears, they will tear at your skin in your dreams. It is not a comforting thing to tell a child, but I understand his meaning."

"Never truer words spoken," Teague said.

"Perhaps Beez is doing you a favor in his relentless pursuit. Have you considered setting a trap?"

He smirked at her. "I should head back."

"No. Not yet." Rorry balanced her crossbow in her lap and held out her gloved hand. When Teague laughed it off, she raised her chin. "You just informed me that my friends are expendable for this cause. That trinket around your neck creates a malediction making you vulnerable. If you want me to let Scarlett and Kylan fall in order to save Cord, you will end your own foolishness, Fox." She had not meant to slip into Kylan's vernacular but held Teague's stare all the same.

"I see ye have been sharing information," he said with a half chuckle. "Ye could have been your own band in the Hook, you know? Still can."

She did not smile.

He took the amulet off. "This . . . 'tis a dark thing, Rorry."

Precisely how the boys had described it, a black stone whorl with notches along the rim. "You can rip the soul out of a person. I know." She kept her steeliness, but her insides writhed. Her fingers wiggled.

"I'll end it."

"Allow me."

He grinned, again. "You don't know how." With her brow raised in impatience, he gave in. "All right. You shall see double for a moment, and hear the High Guard's voice." Teague held it against her gloved palm.

The world swayed. As she blinked, her vision settled in two different places, on the woods with Teague and on an eerie gray haze. Within the haze, a man's form darted about.

"More of these tricks!" the man yelled. "I saw their faces for hundreds of years. Show me no more! End this!" Sniveling, he curled into a ball one second and leaped up to run in a circle the next.

"Whose faces?" Rorry heard her thoughts.

"The people he killed," Teague said without his mouth moving. "He thinks I'm torturing him by showing you. You must resemble one of his victims." He removed his fingertips and said aloud, "Blow on the medallion in the direction of the crests on its surface to release him."

Rorry tried not to tremble as the figure darted about. "Speak, High Guard, and I will set you free."

His shadow stretched into the air. "Prince Rhyn wanted some toys. Who would miss an elf here or there? They said Shallyghal had hundreds. Gone! They were all gone! For years, we tortured the goats and pumpkin heads they had left behind. I got good at chopping the hooves from the satyrs. One whack!" The shadow rushed at Rorry and released a wicked laugh. "We cooked their dead and fed them back to the prisoners. Yet they never broke. Except one. The unicorn's lover."

Out of the corner of her eye, Rorry saw Teague growing concerned. Her stomach wrenched, but she thought, "Go on."

"He squealed! Told us where the staff was. The fool saved us. They would have quartered us on the continent, but with the staff, we conquered the last of Shallyghal. Immortality was ours! We killed the satyrs first. Then the little pumpkins. When there were only humans left, we trapped them in camps. In time, the prisoners' offspring grew loyal. They worshipped us in their fear. Prince Rhyn put his bastards over the provinces, bloody nobles." He moaned. "They should have been kings!"

Her brow furrowed.

Teague tilted his head forward.

"Tell me of the staff," she commanded.

"I cut his fingers off, one at a time. Do you know what I did with them, pretty girl?"

Sitting up straight, Rorry decided she had heard enough and blew across one side of the medallion. A wisp of wind and static came and went before she could react. No green light shone, like the boys had mentioned.

With a deep breath, Teague relaxed. "'Tis done." A genuine smile emerged beneath his closed eyes. "You have my thanks. In freeing him, you freed a part of me. Did he confess?"

Shaking her head, she said, "I am not certain what he said."

Teague reined his steed back toward camp. "I'm sorry you had to hear any of it." His face already appeared less weary. "If you'll excuse me, I must rest. I'll catch up to you in a short while when we're ready to strike off." He reached for the necklace.

Rorry tucked the unholy talisman into a pocket on her belt. "Get us inside Llandir. You achieve your goal, you collect your prize." She smiled at the renewed sparkle in his eyes.

With a bow, he said, "Fair enough," and was off.

The last thing she wanted was to be left alone after listening to the demonic ramblings of the High Guard. They fed them their dead? When Teague was out of sight, Rorry spit the bitterness from her mouth and resisted the temptation to call out to him. No, she had volunteered for this and would not rescind that offer. Rorry set Scute to a trot.

The possibilities of the strange pendant in her belt distracted her. She recognized Teague's intent, to use it as a weapon against Beez. His bravery in parting with it was admirable.

If she had to use it on one of her friends amid possession, what guaranteed it would remove the correct soul? Was she brave enough to do so if it came to that? Either way, Teague's behavior demonstrated there was danger for the user as well as the captive. Her sensibility, or perhaps her upbringing, said to destroy it.

Scute had circled the camp three times before she decided to keep the medallion. She closed the pocket and scanned the forest around her. Directing her attention to memorizing the path, she tried to enjoy the solitude and deny the despair of isolation.

Several bats swooped overhead through the branches. Imagining Carolle's company emboldened her. Rorry had to learn to be a protector. If they survived Beez, she and Kylan would seek out Alis to the corners of the continent, even out to the Charlen Isles, if necessary.

She would not mind if Cord joined them. Rorry daydreamed and planned that journey, drowning out the High Guard's voice repeating his words in her memory.

When Scute brought her over the road to the southern side and past a small pine curving over a mossy felled log for the seventh time, he halted. Rorry's pulse reacted, thudding in her ears. A single set of hoofbeats approached from ahead. That eliminated wolfkin and the Dregs. Taking shallow breaths, she prayed for it to be Teague, not Judges, and certainly not the High Guard. Aiming the Ghost Augur's crossbow, she caressed the trigger.

A speckled gray steed came into view. Kylan shifted awkwardly on its back. He had Master Clienne's katana tucked in his belt and an arrow extending the string on Veen's bow.

Rorry let her arms fall and heaved her breath in annoyance.

"Finally," Kylan said, relaxing the bowstring. "I've been riding for nearly an hour looking for you." His finger shimmered.

She leaned over and snatched his hand. "Where did you get a ring?" It was difficult to see the detail, beyond the way it labeled the ring expensive.

"Andion."

Releasing her hold, she said, "You should not encourage his thievery. It will lead him into trouble."

Kylan grunted. "What other purpose does he serve then?"

She cast him a shaming look and received a grin. "Did you remember to buckle the saddle girth?"

"Very well. You're fine. I'll be on my way."

"No, stay. I am grateful for the company. Come." Rorry kicked Scute into motion. "Is Teague sleeping? Does he even know you are here, Kylan?"

He gripped the pommel as he slowly turned the steed around. "I didn't see him. Cord equipped the horse for me." A smirk crossed his lips. "When I left, he and Julian were arguing that they should be joining you. It was getting rather heated and loud. They were probably discovered soon after I left."

She rolled her eyes but enjoyed the burst of pride that came from the comment. "He should be resting."

Kylan cocked an eyebrow. "Which one?"

She slapped his arm.

"Hey now," he said, righting his posture after his flinch. He dug his heels into the gray's side to catch back up to Scute. "Scarlett distracted 'Maeverly' with questions. Bevin was asleep. We were surprised that Julian was even awake. He's probably vomiting by now."

Unable to resist a cringe, she put Cord's new ability out of her mind. What Kylan had taken in stride had upset her. "Then it is good if they were discovered. You realize Teague plans to rejoin me soon?" She studied the sky. Valor's Shield hadn't reached the apex. The night was young.

Kylan laughed. "Do you think he'll be disappointed that I did as he asked?"

"No, not anymore," she said, which puzzled him. Rorry opened her pocket and displayed the medallion. "It is empty now." She slapped his hand away. "I will hold on to it."

He pouted. "Don't hold out on me."

As they continued to circle the camp, she filled Kylan in on Teague's tale and that of the High Guard. He asked her the same questions she had been wondering.

"It makes you feel a bit small, doesn't it?" he asked. "To know Cord's so important that for the sake of the races, we should die to protect him?"

"You tried before we knew the full story."

"We still don't." He pulled his reins to stop the gray. "I want to know what Teague knows."

In her sternest voice, she said, "Be careful, Kylan."

"You misunderstand me. Whatever Veen did to his knives, it made Beez leave the corpse he was floating around in."

"You have told us this, and Veen forbade it."

Kylan looked through her. "If they're willing to sacrifice us, then we should know all of the weapons at our disposal." He did not wait for her response before he heeled his horse toward the camp.

Rorry reined Scute to follow. "Kylan, Teague was petrified by what he witnessed. The price—"

"Is better than death."

"I disagree. The price is steep, Kylan. Steeper than we know."

At the entrance to a break in the trees, he stared her down. "No more secrets, Rorry. I'm tired of them! It's time we start trusting each other."

A chestnut mound glistened in the clearing. Rorry strained to make out what it was until she saw the black hair leading up its neck. Dark liquid shone in several splotches and puddles over the expanse, the loss of more blood than would have killed a man and a horse. Rorry pulled Scute to a stop and drew a quick breath.

"Obviously, we'd keep our personal secrets," Kylan joked.

She scanned the clearing for a sign of Teague. A severed hand lay several feet from the eviscerated horse. Three nude figures lay motionless on the grass. "Teague?" she yelled.

Kylan beheld the gore before them. "Go! Go to camp!"

She kept searching for Teague.

"Go, Scute!"

The faithful horse kicked into motion without a prompt from

Rorry. When they left the opposite side of the clearing, she ducked close to his neck and watched for wolfkin.

Kylan rode past. There was nothing ungraceful about his demeanor now. "Giddygo!" he yelled. He led the way into the dark camp and rode the gray straight to the butterfly vardo.

Continuing past, Rorry pulled Scute to a stop outside the lifewood. She dismounted onto the steps and poked her head inside. "Cord?" she cried, startling Ferix and Andion with an interruption to their conversation. Cord shot upright. Confused, he blinked to focus on her. "Stay!" She slammed the door and stepped back into the saddle. After freeing a bolt from her sleeve, she laid it on her lap for a quick reload.

Her thoughts circled back to the prison in her pocket. She would be strong enough! Even if it grabbed the wrong soul, she would not let her friends suffer.

Chapter 44: Boiling Over

Kylan leaped down the butterfly vardo's steps, while Joseb scurried out behind him and off toward Bevin's lean-to. "I'm taking them to where we found Teague's horse," Kylan said up to Rorry. "Shout if you see anything."

Sitting stiff-backed on Scute, she guarded the lifewood's door with the crossbow poised to fire. Her blue ribbon bobbed. "Hurry back."

The door next to her creaked open. "What's going on?" Cord asked.

Rorry kicked it shut. "Open this door again and I will lock you in the cell with Ferix!"

"Rorry." Kylan sighed.

Scarlett stepped out behind him with a book in her hands and her poultice bag in tow.

"Scarlett," Kylan said, "how about some tea for these two? Rorry can protect him just as easily by the campfire." An argument died on Rorry's

461

lips when he moved to release Cord. Waving to Andion and Ferix, he said, "All is well."

Cord stepped out with his bow and quiver, wary of Rorry's temper. "Are we under attack?"

"NAHW!" Bevin boomed, causing them all to jump. Bevin twisted his plank-of-a-club in his grip, ready to beat anything that got in his way, possibly everything.

Kylan rushed to Veen's steed.

Joseb mounted and hoisted a pole dangling a jar from twine. At his touch, green fire blazed inside the glass.

In the saddle, Kylan kicked them into motion. Bevin's footsteps rumbled behind as loudly as the hoofbeats and kept their pace.

Advancing to the lead, Joseb extended the green light before them. His plumed cloak flapped over the end of his horse.

In minutes, they arrived at the blood-splotched clearing. Joseb slipped his boot out of the stirrup and landed on the ground before his mount stopped.

Kylan put his fist under his nose to hold back the odor of the horse's innards. Flies already buzzed around its carcass, attracting bats overhead.

Spotting the severed hand, the sorcerer bent over to examine it as Bevin trod into the clearing. His muscular chest panted, issuing clouds of steam with each breath. Adjusting his grip on the grooved black steel handle of his club, Bevin searched about with a murderous glare.

Kylan moved his horse farther away.

"Eh?" Bevin grunted.

Joseb kicked the hand over with the pointed toe of his boot. "Age spots. It's not his."

Two of the corpses lay together. Kylan tried to avoid the death stare in their eyes. A girl's body, a little older than Kit, lay draped over a feeble man. The severed stub at the end of the man's arm forced Kylan to swallow as he backed away. "This man is missing his hand."

"An elder? And a girl?" Joseb asked, rolling over the third corpse, a spindly man with a sickle-shaped brand. He bent to retrieve a dark blade from the corpse's gut. "Black steel. These were Teague's kills." Joseb pointed to Teague's horse. "The bite marks on Shepherd's throat and their nudity . . ." He dangled the light near the elder's face. "Golden irises. Yes, wolfkin. They are already massing an army beyond Merith's soldiers in this region."

"What?" Kylan asked.

"These are stragglers," Joseb said. "Not the warriors Beez would have sent after Teague."

Bevin sucked air through his cavernous nostrils and repeated the process as he stomped about the perimeter.

"Teague's not here," Kylan said. "Maybe they weren't alone."

Joseb's vision stuck to something behind Kylan. "I believe they were." He hustled past and swung the lantern too close to a tree. The jar broke against a limb. The darkness jolted, almost as much as Joseb's shout of "Shite!" He threw the pole to the ground before freeing another of Teague's knives from the bark.

"Then where is he?" Kylan asked.

Wind whistled through Bevin's nose as he took several deep breaths. He wandered past Joseb and pointed his club southward. "Arr."

Dropping his head, Joseb said, "Bevin, wait. Look."

The same hen scratch Kylan had seen on Veen's note marred the tree's bark. "What does it say?"

"Keep going," Joseb answered. "Hells." The half-ogre raised his club to squash Joseb until a lecturing finger stopped him. "What did Teague say was our priority—if this very thing happened? Gods know how long he's been planning this!" He shouted to the south, "Bastard! As though we needed a sacrifice! After the price we paid to free him . . ."

Bevin growled but lowered his weapon.

"A sacrifice?" Kylan asked.

"A distraction," Joseb answered. "He's trying to bait them away from us." That struck a little too close to the heart for Kylan.

"In case there are more stragglers," Joseb said, "we should get back to camp." He raised his hands when Bevin glowered his way. "We can't go after him, Bevin. I don't like it any more than you do, but we are bound to this task."

Bevin bared his teeth.

"It's dangerous to piss me off! You know that." Joseb slapped his hand on the trunk's carvings to draw Bevin's attention to them. "He does not want us to follow. If he's already made up his mind, we'd be wasting our time going after him."

Without concern for grace, Joseb hiked his skirt and swung a leg over his saddle. "We head to Llandir now."

* * *

When she blinked, Rorry still saw the woods burned into her vision. "Have a seat," Cord said.

"No, thank you." She refused to let her guard down while she stood vigil over him and Scarlett.

The fire Scarlett had built was a comfort. She seemed pleased with the results of her practice, now setting the components of her spell next to her poultice bag.

Julian had woken during the commotion and joined them in time to witness the casting. To Rorry's surprise, he had not squinted with his usual disdain.

That did not alter Cord's disapproval of him. His bowstring remained relaxed on his lap, but the nocked arrow was aimed in Julian's direction.

Scarlett began preparing the tea, which she had liberated from Joseb's stores while retrieving Rorry's satchel. The tea's potency would enable them to stay awake for hours more. Rorry yearned for the assistance, even if it might make her twitch.

Leaving the water to boil, Scarlett rose. "I'll be back soon. Will you watch the water?"

Rorry pursed her lips but nodded, knowing full well that her friend was sneaking off to practice her spells. She watched Scarlett's straight-backed walk until she heard the azure door latch with her safely inside.

"We should leave," Julian said. "Now that the monks and Teague are gone, I doubt those other two fools can get us into the city. If anything, they will hinder us."

"And go where?" Cord asked. "Llandir isn't gonna welcome the girls, or you. Not without Seeding papers. Our closest shelter is Granville. And you heard Teague; they were probably attacked last night."

To Rorry, Julian said, "You are a noble. The Llandir watchmen might believe you."

"They'd jail her and summon her father!" Cord said. "You know

465

the army doesn't care about saving the people. If you wanna take your chances without Bevin and Maeverly, go on and go. We won't tell them." Cord's words were sharp to the point that they threatened violence.

Julian waited expectantly for Rorry's reply, as though Cord did not exist.

The muscles in Cord's legs tensed, preparing to leap at Julian.

Lowering next to Cord, Rorry placed her hand on his forearm, sending Julian's disgusted glare to the fire. She laid her head on Cord's shoulder.

It felt natural, almost like leaning against Kylan. Only her pulse quickened, and his never slowed. He released his bow to put his arm around her.

Sitting upright, she let the tension dwindle in silence for some time. Then she asked, "How could they have gotten past me? He did not make it back to camp, which means I was nearby when it happened. I should have heard it." She did not ask the question that had been repeating in her mind. Had she taken the one weapon Teague needed only moments before he was attacked?

"You might've been farther away than you think," Cord answered.

Shouts from the woods propelled Rorry to her feet. Joseb rode into sight, followed by Bevin. They bickered. Except for Scute, the horses whickered and sidled at the shouted insults. A few sprinted forward.

Kylan shrugged from behind Joseb and hurriedly waved Cord over before they disappeared behind the butterfly vardo.

"I'll find out what happened," Cord said, picking up his bow.

Rorry cracked a smile when Cord tugged down his tight tunic again. As her grin faded, she admitted to herself that, yes, she would have the strength to use the medallion on him. It was a risk, but she would not let him live through the torture Teague had endured. She wished on a cricket for Teague's survival, if it was not too late.

The arguing grew louder behind the vardo. Vulgar taunts flowed out of Joseb's mouth as often as sound logic.

Cord vanished around the stairs.

Water sputtered onto the flames. Rorry turned to retrieve the boiling pot and found Julian standing over her with a log in his hands. He swung.

Chapter 45: Shattered Butterfly

Beneath the butterfly, Scarlett read the same sentence three times before accepting there'd be no reading done within the vicinity, not with Joseb and Bevin's tantrum escalating outside. Bevin's grunts rattled the stained-glass panes. With "*spacebo*" memorized as the next word, she pressed *Essential Focus* to her chest and collected Joseb's botany tome to deposit it safely in the other vardo.

She yawned and realized she'd forgotten about the tea. If it didn't wake her, the chilly night air would work. Affixing her shawl, she exited. Tempted to plug her ears, she settled for a wide-eyed stare as she passed the bickering adults at the bottom of the steps. Then she set her path back toward the fire and resumed her reading.

Scarlett sucked air in through her teeth when she heard hissing. Water brimmed over into the flames. She dropped *Essential Focus* open on her poultice bag and reached for the pot's handle. Something crunched under her boot. Her bottles were spread about.

"Rorry?" Scarlett asked, placing the pot on the ground. "Did you need something?"

Julian flinched when she spoke. He tucked something into a saddlebag on one of the Northpelts, Hexel, which normally pulled Bevin's cart. He let the flap fall closed and said, "That was me. I had a terrible headache earlier and wanted to find that willow bark you prattle on about."

"Prattle?"

Rorry had slumped forward. Scarlett went to her. A shine in her hair reflected the firelight. Blood.

Scarlett screamed for Joseb, but an explosion erupted. Half of the butterfly vardo spewed across the camp in pieces, scattering the horses in bedlam. Flames roared and engulfed the vardo's doorway. She gasped.

Julian cursed at Hexel as the horse disappeared between the trees.

Clenching her fists, Scarlett tried to picture Grary as Julian approached her.

He grabbed her shawl and shoved her toward the fire.

* * *

As Scarlett descended the vardo's stairs and crept past Maeverly and Bevin, Cord grinned at her reaction to the bickering and waited for the other two to behave like adults.

Bevin stomped before Cord and shouted louder than the sorcerer.

With her heel on the first step, Maeverly continued the fight. "Teague's directions were not ambiguous, Bevin! We continue to Racine, no matter the consequence. So help me, if you raise that club at me again, it shall be cinders, Bevin Freidig! I don't care who gave it to you!"

Cord decided he'd rather wait with Kylan and the horses but paused when he believed the argument had ended.

Then the cook said, "No strong enuf be Maevlee."

Maeverly's expression soured, and she stepped inside her vardo. "You are an intractable toad!" She slammed the door.

An explosion flung Bevin into Cord, sprawling him across the ground. Cord's ears rang. His legs were pinned under Bevin's back. Splinters and shards of glass covered the area, projected away from where the sorcerer had stood. Black smoke began to rise from the flames now swarming the remnants of the wagon. Cord wriggled his legs free.

In place of the glass butterfly, a ball of yellow light whirled in the thin smoke. The light shattered. Flakes of it fluttered. Glowing butterflies caught air beneath their wings and spread out. Flittering, they flew in each direction, filling the camp with light.

Cord got his knees under him. Half of his bow came free with a tug. It had broken under the half-ogre's weight. He heard labored breath above the ringing in his ears. The blast had cast chunks of the vardo's frame into Bevin's chest. Darkness spread across his patchwork shirt in three spots, getting larger still. Could he heal a half-ogre?

As Cord reached to try, Kylan shouted, "Cord, help me!" Kylan stood amid the growing flames on the burning chassis, hauling Maeverly out of the fire.

Her body blazed with blue lights.

Cord sprinted to his side and helped the limp sorcerer to the ground.

"She lives? How?" Cord asked.

"I don't know," Kylan said. "But she's burned bad, Cord." Soot spread over her glossy red skin. Charred hair only remained in patches. "You have to heal her."

Cord teetered on the soles of his sandals. "Bevin's injured too. He'll die if I don't mend him."

"She goes first." Kylan's eyes left no room for debate.

"Right." Cord lowered to his knees on the opposite side of the sorcerer. With a quickly dismissed concern for what the burns would do to him and a prayer that he could save Bevin afterward, Cord leaned forward. His hands embraced her slick and sticky face. He didn't intend to pervade Maeverly's body; it happened naturally. What he found shocked him out of the trance.

Cord scrambled backward. "Ho! Whoa! She—that's a man!"

Glaring impatiently, Kylan asked, "Does it matter? You can sate your curiosities if he lives to answer."

"You knew?"

Kylan jumped over the sorcerer, put an arm around Cord's shoulders, and pressed him forward. "We need his magic to get us into Llandir. Don't let us die because of something you don't understand." Cord met Kylan's eyes, ready to defy him. "Please, Cord. We'll never beat Beez without him."

Was this the path he walked now? Cord shook his head but gripped the temples of the person before him and let the trance come. The damage was extensive but only burns. Still, the man had barely survived and wouldn't much longer. Cord heaved more energy than he ever had. It poured into the brilliant scene before him. Tissue cooled and began to rebuild. Gaps of missing skin filled. The heat of the transferred burn ran up Cord's arm before he was finished. His face felt dry from within the trance.

Maeverly didn't stir when he released him.

Cord stood, determined to heal Bevin as the burning pricked his skin. He shivered and stifled a groan from the pain.

Kylan walked next to him, offering support.

More butterflies broke away from the ball of light. Cord watched one flutter past and felt dazed. The desire to mend Bevin drowned as his body went limp.

* * *

Julian grabbed and shoved Scarlett back. Her shawl unfurled in his grip, spinning her atop *Essential Focus* and her poultice bag.

Glass broke under her weight.

Her brown wrap came away in his hands, as did *Ivy or Silkshade: Where Magic Meets Botany*. He opened the book and slapped it closed to taunt her. His sudden smile cruel, he released them both over the fire.

"No!" Scarlett pleaded. But the flames had their feast.

Malevolence held Julian's features. He reached behind him and brought out a golden dagger. As he twirled the hilt in his hands, he said, "This night just keeps getting better."

She scrabbled back.

"By the word of the Chancellor, you have chosen your path away from his teachings. Your soul is inimical and Abandoned!"

Stretching for magic, Scarlett couldn't touch it beyond her fear. She reached to the components beneath her and identified her weapon. When he stepped over her and raised the dagger in both hands, she held her breath and flung the pouch of pepperflame.

It struck Julian's chest. A red cloud billowed up to his face. It wasn't much more than dust, but he reeled as it coated his eyes and gasped when it sucked into his nostrils.

Scarlett crawled away from him. She rose and tried to plot a way around him to Rorry.

Julian shrieked as he inhaled again. Through his tears, his eyes were determined.

She lunged forward, then jumped back from the dagger.

He swung the blade wildly in wide arcs.

A flicker of yellow appeared behind him. Small butterflies of solid light shimmered past them in all directions. At first, it was a dozen. Then dozens more filled the area, brightening the woods. Julian stepped back from one gliding between them. He swung the dagger again to keep her back. More butterflies came. Frightened and snarling, Julian released the dagger and grabbed Rorry.

"Leave her!" Scarlett yelled.

He hefted Rorry over his shoulder. The manacles clanked as her arms fell over his back. Releasing a growl of pain, he glared at Scarlett when she retrieved the dagger. Reflective gold replaced his blue irises and froze her solid. He bounded into the woods.

Chapter 46: Ready the Hunter

Scarlett raced toward the blazing vardo. Splinters and torn fabric arched out around it. "Kylan?" she yelled. Rounding the fire, she spotted him cradling Cord and lowering him to the ground.

He waved her close. "He lives. So does Joseb." Her mentor slept on the ground behind them.

She followed Kylan's gaze to Bevin. The protrusions in his chest didn't lift; he didn't breathe.

"Where's Rorry?"

Her heart ached. Bevin had been so kind. Bless him.

"Scarlett!"

"Julian took her," she said, dropping beside him. Cord's skin had darkened to a deep pink. She could feel the heat coming off it from inches away.

"What?"

"She was unconscious. He attacked me too, but the butterflies scared him off."

Kylan stared into the woods but didn't release Cord's head. She had seen that look on his face before. He'd nearly died from the beating it had led to, though Grary had permanent scars.

"Kylan, he's a wolfkin."

He watched her stand as the news sank in.

"I have a salve that will help Cord," she said. Actually, she wasn't sure what remained of her poultices. "I think."

"Why do you think he's a wolfkin?"

"His irises were gold for a flash before he ran away with Rorry." She bit her lip.

Kylan slouched but didn't lose the clarity in his eyes. "Get the salve."

Rushing to the scene of her skirmish, Scarlett gathered what she could find and threw it in her bag. Luckily, the green bottle of sun salve remained whole. The pot of water misted over the flames. Their fate had changed too swiftly.

Uncle Barrey's crossbow protruded from the other items Julian had stacked to pack in Hexel's saddlebags. She grabbed it and Rorry's satchel.

The camp sat eerily empty. None of the strange butterflies remained in view. Only Scute watched from where the other horses had fled. They would need to address the fire soon, as its smoke would surely draw attention.

When she returned to Kylan, he was cutting the black woolen tunic away with his father's knife. Cord's skin stuck to the wool in spots, clear liquid stringing from him to the fabric. Bright pink skin extended down the right side of his torso. "Did you find it?" he asked.

Scarlett nodded and knelt to place the crossbow and satchel next to Kylan. She removed the bag from her shoulder and sifted through it.

Kylan held his hand out. "I'd better do this. He's not going to care for me much when I wake him." She wasn't sure what that meant, but she shook the green bottle and handed it to him. "Please ask Andion to come here."

She blinked at the odd request but set about it as Kylan slapped the white salve onto his palm. After glancing over her shoulder, Scarlett took a brief moment to lay her hand on Bevin's cheek. He had been such a kind soul. "You deserved better than this." With a deep inhale, she agreed to mourn him later.

Opening the lifewood's door awkwardly from the ground, she called out, "Andion?"

Ferix crouched behind the bars. "Are you yourself, witch?"

"Yes," Scarlett said. "I believe we are safe for the moment." The top of the chest thudded into the wall of the vardo as Andion climbed out. "There you are. Kylan needs your help."

Rephrasing that would have been wiser, as it yielded the exact reaction she'd anticipated. The pik puffed out his chest. "Andion will not help Brute."

"I'm afraid we are a bit beyond this, Andion. Teague is missing. Julian is a wolfkin and has taken Rorry. As best I can tell, Joseb's temper ruined one of the wagons and killed poor Bevin. Cord healed him and is now sleeping while Kylan tends to his burns." Andion's eyes had grown larger with each sentence. "Will you help us?"

Andion glanced over to Ferix and nodded. He peered around outside before he stepped down and sped toward Kylan.

"You will release me," Ferix commanded.

Something about the demand spiked her ire. "We are trying to reduce our complications at the moment."

He didn't protest as she shut the door.

Wringing his hands, Andion nodded to Kylan and watched him coat Cord's skin with the salve. She hoped it would help. The pik ran past her to Teague's vardo.

"What will he find there?" she asked.

"With any luck, a new tunic, our Seeding papers, and a magic solution to our woes." Kylan tapped the last of the salve out onto his fingers. With a final spread over Cord's chest, he rubbed his hands together and brushed back his sleeves. "I asked him to see if he can pick the locks to the drawers or empty them through the shadows, whatever he does."

Cord looked peaceful. His skin already appeared closer to its normal shade.

"Should we wake him?"

Kylan shook his head. "We'll let him heal as long as we can. If Rorry's hurt . . . Ready Scute. I'll get Joseb onto Teague's cot. Once we get Cord equipped for travel, we'll wake him and bless the arrow he puts in that bastard's eye."

* * *

Darkness obscured everything around Cord except for the bare rock wall before him and an arc of torchlight on the strangely even natural-stone floor. Dank air filled his lungs, but he didn't hear any water. The potency of this dream surpassed the others.

A simple iron ring held the steel torch, molded into a squared handle with a wide bowl for the flame. It could have been a mace just as easily. Cord hefted the fiery weapon out of its bracket and forced back the darkness. The circle of light fell to the floor around him. Each minute felt like an hour as he explored the nothingness. Finally, a faint light appeared in the distance, guiding him to the entrance of a cavern.

Brilliant crystal clusters grew out of stone pillars around the room and filled the space with a rainbow of light. Strangely, none of the crystals shone with their own color; the blues cast orange onto the walls, the yellows spread green, purples shimmered red.

Spotting another tunnel, Cord left the strange gems and discovered a small cavern, this one empty. He moved through the only exit from there and soon walked atop green and blue tiles in a chamber larger than the twins' temple in Granville. Ample white light poured out of a squared column of clear crystal in the center of the room, connecting the floor to the ceiling hundreds of feet above him.

At the back of the ancient chamber, colorful lights ran up a wall where a three-story depiction of a dwarf began to glow. First in red light, then yellow, and then blue. Cord neared. The light intensified and illuminated handprints at the base, one in each of the colors. Before Cord touched the blue one, all three lit in unison. The colors merged in the middle of the wall. It split and spread apart.

* * *

A chill knocked Cord out of the dream. Kylan knelt over him, emptying a waterskin on his face. "What are you doing?" Cord coughed. His throat was scratchy and dry. His skin burned. It felt brittle, like it'd crack if he moved too quickly. He grabbed the waterskin from Kylan's hand and gulped what remained.

When it was empty, he wiped the water off his face with a dark green sleeve. Black string loosely laced the neckline of the tunic he now wore. Where was his belt? Why did he smell like flowers?

"I'm sorry, Cord," Kylan said. "We let you rest as long as we could. Now you need to ride."

Scarlett led Scute into view.

"Where are we going? Whose is this?" He tugged on the shirt.

"Andion found it," the pik answered. "It was in there." He pointed to Teague's vardo.

Cord squinted at him. What had happened while he'd slept to bring Andion outside? "Where's Rorry?"

"Julian took her," Kylan answered.

"What?" Cord shot to his feet faster than he should have. Scarlett and Kylan supported him for a moment while his head caught up.

"Listen," Kylan said. "She's injured. He knocked her out and fled with her into the woods to the north. And, Cord, he's a wolfkin."

"What?" He couldn't have heard him correctly.

Veen's black recurve bow and Cord's belt with the quiver still attached rose in Kylan's hand. He held on to them until Cord mounted Scute. "Take these and this," he said, sliding the scabbard of the Ghost Augur's sword out of his belt. "You need to find her quickly."

Wincing at his stinging skin, Cord strapped the belt around himself.

"We'll wait here to watch over Ferix and the others."

Bevin still lay on the ground, but Maeverly had vanished. Cord's teeth gnashed when he realized he had failed the half-ogre. "Julian will pay."

"Andion will help," the pik said.

"No," Kylan said. "It's too dangerous, Andion. And we need your help finding the horses. We'll have to ride as soon as you get back, Cord. Today's the last day of the Seeding." His worried friends watched him from the ground as though they were ushering him into battle. Kylan removed any doubt to the contrary when he commanded, "Find her!"

Cord nodded. His friends were formidable, even without the Hook protecting them. Taking in one last look at Bevin, he slung the bow over his shoulder.

Scarlett pointed north.

Digging his heels into Scute's side, Cord glanced to the stars and hunted.

Chapter 47: Bindings Unseen

Swaying. Rorry swayed. Upside down. Someone carried her. A throbbing pain rang against the left side of her skull. She moaned. The world halted and touched the bottom of her boots. Her back arched to stand her upright. Blood rushed from her head. Metal clinked as she brought her restrained hand toward the ache above her temple. Rings connected one of her wrists to the other with twin cuffs.

Hands grabbed her shoulders. Julian's hands.

Jolted to her senses, she flinched away. "You kidnapped me?" she asked, testing the strength of the bindings. Her arms could not spread beyond the width of her shoulders.

Puffiness surrounded his eyes. Wiping a bit of drool from his mouth, he said, "I had to get you away from there. I knew you would not come willingly."

"You had no right!"

Julian shook his head. "It is my right, as a member of the army, to safeguard the Merithian nobility. You have strayed from the Chancellor's Light, but you have not done anything I could not forgive." His eyes lingered on her leathers as he finished the statement. The lustful gaze made her want to disappear and to scream at the same time. He read the disgust on her face. "Have it your way." Snatching the manacles, he hauled her away from her friends. Her arms flopped before her, too weak to resist, though she tried.

The army had become a distant concern in the past few days. Now one of the Chancellor's thralls barred her chance at escape. Snatched along by the fool, she stared daggers at his back and planned.

The high canopy of the Mint Coast's forest blocked the stars. Little moonlight trickled through, just enough to view large obstacles as they trod through the fern-covered hillocks.

Tension against Rorry's right forearm provided her some comfort. He had not searched her thoroughly enough to find the throwing knife in her leather vambrace. Removing it would require careful maneuvering to avoid alarming him with her clanking bindings, if she could get it past the tight metal cuff.

She needed to hurry. If she took too long, her friends would come for her and miss their chance to leave with the Hook and Cord, never mind the headache Cord would give his saviors. Rorry's mind turned to another reason—perhaps the most important—that she must return; she carried the talisman. Her belt pockets were closed, revealing nothing. She would not flee without knowing she possessed it.

The councilmembers of the northern provinces spent most of their time here on the Mint Coast, though they usually spent it coddled in the havens built upon the ancient hot springs in Llandir, far away from the landscape she now traversed. They boasted about that fact over their gem-encrusted chalices.

Rorry's parents had not visited in her lifetime but knew it well enough to detail the winter-tree-scented woods that rivaled the cliffs of Lake Cashelle for beauty. At the moment, she could not decide if the darkness revealed the truth of that beauty or distorted her appreciation for the natural retreat. Dead trees lined their way as other plants fed off the remains. Fuzzy moss covered everything, whether a dusting on a boulder or a second skin over bark. Silence kindled the ambiance of a god's tomb.

She needed to act. "I must rest for a moment." Her plea went unacknowledged. Perhaps he harbored more feelings than lust. "If you had not injured me, I would be able to keep up."

Julian eyed her as he tried to uncover the hoax, but he paused. Stepping closer, he let her arms slacken without relinquishing the chain. He panted, his breath wet on her face. The proximity sent shivers through her. She steadied herself. "What is your plan?" she asked. "You cannot expect the army here to welcome you any more than they did at Fort Warren."

He looked down his nose. "That is becoming less of a concern."

"Where are you taking me then?"

The chains tightened as he jerked her against him. She crossed her arms as best she could.

He sniffed the wound on her head. "I could take you here," he moaned.

In a flash of panic, she shoved her palm against his chest with enough force to propel them both. "You will keep your distance!" she commanded.

Bucking his shoulders in silent laughter, he said, "You will grow to love me."

The statement turned her insides acidic. "I will not continue this conversation, to avoid the certain illness that would follow." Suspending his hand as she raised hers, she said, "Lead on. I will welcome death to be free of your arrogance."

Julian sneered, which pleased her, though she did not show it. He usually saved that look for Cord. They were a pair if Julian's contempt had any say in it.

When she had imagined how she might die, it had involved a romantic gesture in the arms of the would-be archer. Although this ending was more fitting for an adult, she had been happy to entertain the fantasies of a girl.

If she failed, at least she would remove this pompous barrier from their path. She hoped the others continued on. Light, why had she insisted on taking Teague's necklace?

Plodding over the vegetation, Julian used his free arm to knock limbs and leaves out of his way. His commotion frightened the skittering creatures of the forest.

A memory sparked of Carolle and Rorry laughing at their mad shouting in Abernathy-on-the-Way. She had not considered the silence as an advantage. When he released a branch, grazing her head, she screamed, faking the pain.

"Silence!" he snarled.

Rorry met his anger with her own. "You should consider my injuries before you release the branches!"

Sneering again, he continued.

For several minutes, Rorry wobbled behind him as they crunched along. Anticipating any opportunity to yell, she began to abandon the requirement of a reason beyond want.

Julian grunted to a halt. A felled tree with a girth as high as her ribs blocked the path. They would have to cross it, for the density of the woods offered no easier alternative.

Moonlight poured through the vacancy that the forest had yet to reclaim. However, Rorry could not see enough of the sky to determine the time.

"You go first," he said, dragging her closer to it. He grabbed her throat and invaded her air with his humid breath. "Run and I will make sure you cannot do it again." He flung her forward.

Loosing a loud screech and whine, she felt foolish, but it might help her friends find her if they were coming. Rorry shifted her weight forward, slung a leg over the moss, and scooted to straddle the tree.

When an owl's cry turned Julian's attention back down the trail, she slipped her fingers into the talisman's pocket. It was empty.

Julian's breath caught the moonlight as he laughed. "Searching for this?" He spun the black medallion's leather cord in the air, twirling it around his fingers.

"That is not something to be played with!"

Gripping the manacles, he tugged her free of the tree. Sticks cut into her fingers as she cushioned her fall. "It should not exist!" he roared at her back.

Wincing at the realization she had forgotten to scream, she righted herself to view her captor.

He must have mistaken her regret for docility. Backing off, he nodded to the log.

As she crossed the fallen tree this time, something poked through the leather of her glove. The fall had jostled the knife free. Gauging by the ease of its slide, Rorry determined it would come loose at a moment's notice. She smiled to herself.

Julian put the necklace over his curls and let it dangle freely outside his tunic. He scrutinized her slightest movement as he climbed to her side.

Appeased by the blade, she played along and plotted as they marched. The terrain became rockier as they neared a hillside. North. He was hauling her north toward the foothills.

A wheeze escaped him. His arm slackened when his other hand went to his face. Wiping his eyes on his sleeve, he whined. His injuries might be the key to her escape. She inched forward for a better view. Drool ran down his chin. A blue eye registered her. He struck her chest and flung her off her feet. A fern flattened beneath her as others shifted their fronds to fill the opening. Thankfully, the armor cushioned most of the blow.

Moving to her side, he seemed surprised at the sight. "What is this? So eager to get started?"

Memories of Grary's weight stirred Rorry's panic. She forced them back, mollifying herself with the prick of the blade. Her wrist itched to be free of its splint. Curling into a ball, she sat and radiated with indignation.

"Cast your shaming gaze elsewhere. If you did not want it, you would not have put on the trappings of a harlot. They were meant for Cord, but I will be better. Trust me."

"You would not dare." Her voice shook.

Julian considered her words with a wry smile. "Do not tempt me. Get up!" Seizing the leash between her hands, he dragged her once more.

When she made her escape, the fern fronds would shelter her from view. With distance, he would never search thoroughly enough to find her before moving on in fear she had kept running. Rorry tacked it to the end of her plan.

The desire to reveal her blade nagged at her the farther into the woods they traveled. They scaled a hillside where the forest took a reprieve. Finally, the shining veil of the night sky came into view. Hours had passed since she had raced to camp with Kylan.

A cliff loomed high above them on their left as they marched down a wide grassy knoll toward a valley. The trees swayed in the dale as a breeze whipped past. She recognized nothing of the terrain.

Julian huffed. Erupting with laughter, he shook. The lids of his eyes twitched.

Rorry let her apprehensive posture ask her question.

"I just remembered something, something delicious," he said. "Then your dumb friend interrupted." His right arm trembled. He stared at it until it stopped.

At the promise he was not in complete control of his actions, she formed a new strategy, one that turned her stomach. Imagining Carolle's approval, Rorry reassured herself. "Julian, I am very warm. May I remove my jacket? My shoulders would like to breathe."

"No. You will not be free of your restraints."

She inhaled to expand herself. "Can I at least pull it down some?"

Ogling her, he nodded and let go of the chain. His mouth dribbled. Working against the phantom scent of coal, she revealed the thick leather straps over her clavicle as her skin cooled against the night air. As he thoroughly examined her, she considered the medallion. Her timing would have to be precise. Dwelling on the hope that the directions were reversed for entrapping someone, she took a deep breath under the guise of relishing the chill.

Gripping the links, he tugged. She feigned a stumble and planted her face against his chest. The crests on the amulet received her gust. Nothing happened.

Julian kneed her in the gut and shoved her away as he scrambled to remove the pendant. The cord snapped. He spun it and released, hurling it toward the rock underbelly of the cliff.

Rorry lunged for it but fell when his elbow bashed into her back.

The medallion clacked into the stone and shattered.

Rolling over and rising onto her feet, she tried to kill him with her stare. "Do you have any idea what you have done?"

"Yes, as a matter of fact. I have destroyed an artifact of magic," he gloated. Circling her with a bestial lust in his eyes, he uncoiled his belt. He removed his tunic and threw it at her.

Rorry kicked her heel at his groin.

He hopped aside and swung his fist.

Dodging the brunt of the blow, she threw her elbow into his throat. Julian stumbled. Unleashing her knife, Rorry jabbed it deep into his belly and released.

Julian swatted her away. The inhuman force sent her sailing back and sliding along the grass. Rising over her, he laughed. His skin leaked around the knife. No pain registered in his expression.

"I began to remember things in Granville," he said, "when your peppermint suitor started to smell like elderberry and the citrus boy clung to the apple magus. She smelled delicious!" His irises glowed gold.

Rorry gasped.

"Could you not tell? I am special. I am an alpha."

Chapter 48: Familiar Demons

The chilled air burned Cord's lungs but never tempted him to slow his pace away from Scute. Only the rare noise gave him pause. He hunted with his bow in his left hand and a few arrows in his right. Shielded by the trees, he made his path with care. A cry froze him. Rorry fought again. He sniffed the air but couldn't smell her perfume. "One more time, Rorry," he muttered. "Yell one more time."

An unnatural silence sent tremors through the muscles of his bare legs. Afraid to lose ground, he guessed the direction and deftly snuck forward.

Scaling a small hill, Cord identified their wake. Trampled ferns, scuffed patches devoid of moss, and broken branches pointed him toward a clearing beneath the cliff high above the trees. Julian was taking her north, but not northeast toward the towns on the coast. A rock ledge jutted out, forcing Cord's path around it.

Quieter than before, he darted atop bare ground and stone. Using the ends of the arrowheads, he parted the leaves of a bush at the edge of the clearing. His breath caught.

Rorry lay on the grass fifty feet ahead of him. Julian lorded over her, blood dripping from a knife in his gut. She screamed.

"It was I who ate the monk," Julian said. "I was ordered to change him, enlist his services." He unsheathed the knife from his skin without a whimper. Blood gushed from the wound. He threw the blade aside. "But he refused to grovel. Will you do the same?" His arm began to bulk, building his bicep to the size of his chest.

Drawing the string of the bow to his cheek, Cord aimed the arrowhead. His arms trembled, making the target an impossible guarantee. Fear put his new ability out of reach. Cord quelled his thoughts as he directed the arrow at Julian's face. He centered his aim.

Julian was focused on Rorry and hadn't noticed the motion of Cord's arrowhead piercing the foliage.

As often as he'd fantasized about being free of the jackass, none of his past reasons entered his mind. Rorry's safety was his sole concern. Cord released half of an exhale and opened his grip. The bow relaxed and launched the arrow on target.

A furry hand seized it inches from Julian's face. He laughed and flung the arrow aside. "Always too slow, wooder. I could smell you coming." His other arm twitched. Thick tufts of fur spiked out from his skin. "I hoped you would try this. So pathetic."

When Rorry saw Cord's face, her expression changed from worried to determined. She crawled to her feet.

Cord ran forward, fitting another arrow to the string as he closed the distance. He aimed and released.

Julian dodged the arrow and landed on Rorry. His wolfkin legs split his britches. When he rose, she squirmed before him, clutched against his body behind a massive paw.

Cord stopped.

"She needs a real man, Cord," Julian chortled. "Look at her. She craves a man's attention." He cupped her chest with his paw and pulled her head back by her queue. "Do not worry, I will give it to you. We will keep these clothes for special occasions." Fangs burst through his gums.

Veen's bow arched, ready to sling an arrow through Julian's eye.

The target ducked behind Rorry's head.

"It is good you came," Julian shouted. "When I turn her, we will want to feed." His eye peeked from behind her. This time, nothing human remained. Julian swung Rorry around before him as his size increased, keeping Cord from taking the shot.

Flailing with every free limb she had, Rorry fought against the wolfkin. She pummeled and kicked. The effort didn't set her free, but it moved her far enough to one side to give Cord an opening.

When Julian's eyes disappeared behind her, Cord released. The spiraled feathers zipped through the air and sank into Julian's forearm. He howled.

Rorry stopped flailing to cover her ears.

Julian bellowed again.

Grunts preceded three, then five wolfkin galloping uphill toward Cord. They were smaller than what Julian had swollen into. Cord felled the first one easily in its direct path. He snatched another handful of arrows from his quiver and targeted the wolfkin now in the lead.

Calling once more, Julian brought three out of the woods in the valley to scale the hill behind the others.

Cord aimed for Julian's throat and released.

His free paw shielded him, taking the arrow in his palm. Julian bit the arrow in half. It came free as Cord nocked another.

The wolfkin were too fast to ignore longer. Four shared the lead now, with three at their heels. They bucked and yawed as Cord's aim fell on them. Targeting a brown coat, he let the arrow fly. The wolf leaped but still took the shot in its thigh. It whimpered as the others raced over it.

Julian clutched Rorry with his wounded arm and sped down the hill.

"Rorry!" Cord called. His string unleashed a wild shot at her abductor. It missed.

The other six wolves Julian had called were upon him now. The white fletching of Cord's new arrow brushed his face as he aimed for a golden eye. His next missile was nocked while the gray became a crackling, writing lump on the ground.

Something zipped past him—and burst the eye he targeted. "Are you going to let him take her?" Carolle asked. She threw her bow down and sped past him toward the two wolfkin at the front. Two inwardly curved blades left their black scabbards at her thighs. No larger than a forearm, each shimmered with magic.

First, the red blade seared through a shaggy throat. Then Carolle rolled over the back of her next attacker and drove the blue blade into its skull, unleashing a *clink* like broken glass. The metal dimmed as she pulled it free. "Go get our girl!" she ordered and drew the wolves' attention away from Cord.

Rushing down the incline, he trailed Julian, who had paused to watch Cord's demise.

Steeped in pride, the wolf waited for him. Rorry's struggle had managed to free her arm. Rorry struck, squeezing the wound in Julian's forearm. He yipped and threw her at Cord. The impact sent them both to the ground.

Cord recovered first, picking up an arrow.

Compared to Julian, the other wolfkin were like cats to a hound. It would've taken three to equal this beast's size. The wolf arched forward, his hackles rising a foot above his snarling maw. When he saw Cord's arrow, Julian lowered his tail and charged.

Cord released. The beast didn't attempt to avoid the arrow that sank into his shoulder. Dropping Veen's bow, Cord unsheathed Kylan's sword.

As Julian raised his claws to strike, Rorry rolled out of the way. The first swipe missed. The second struck the blade, flicking sparks. Julian's thick black nails gleamed in the light.

Walking backward, Cord kept the behemoth at bay with quick slashes of the sword, always returning to first position with the single-edged blade raised above his thigh. Somewhere beyond them, he knew Rorry had run for shelter. He had to hold Julian's focus.

In a circle, Julian stalked him, testing him, waiting for a break from Headmaster Angsly's instruction. His claw swiped again, showering sparks when Cord blocked it.

"Is it the sword you fear, or me?" Cord asked. "I know you understand me."

With a snarl, Julian lunged.

Cord whisked the blade up. A spurt of blood flung free as the sword sliced through the beast's forearm. Though thin, the wound was deep. "If I gotta whittle you to pieces, I will." Tilting the edge of the sword, he kept his form and continued to follow the circling wolf.

Snipping at the blade, Julian attempted to throw him off-balance.

"You'll have to try harder than that. Come on now, what are you afraid of? A wooder?" Cord teased. "No, as usual, you're right, Julian. I'm a Catalyst. It's my duty to smite evil, such as you, Abandoned."

In a blur, Julian's arm slapped the blade. It tore through the meat of his paw cleanly but knocked the sword out of Cord's grip. Julian howled in pain as Cord lunged for the sword. The coarse fur of a warm paw landed on Cord's leg. It snatched him back toward his adversary, flinging the arrows from his quiver. Cord's calf burned as the claws tore his skin free. Julian pinned him to the ground with a paw on his chest, taking Cord's breath. Through the growls, he heard Julian gloat. He had bested him, and it would mean his doom.

A glint appeared behind Julian. Rorry stepped into view next to the wolf. She jabbed a knife into Julian's side, thrust it up, and sliced it out.

His swipe spun her to the ground but freed Cord from the wolf's weight.

Cord pounced. He didn't have a weapon. He didn't have a plan, but he wouldn't let Rorry die for him. With two fistfuls of the fur around Julian's mouth, Cord held the chomping teeth at bay.

Hair on Julian's functioning arm matted with blood as he clutched the wound in his side. Then, narrowing his eyes, he punched Cord free.

The solid blow struck Cord's chin. Cord collapsed to the grass. Dazed, he began to make peace with his end. Between Cord and the Glades, Julian's red-soaked mass hunkered over him. Cord closed his eyes.

A rattle of chains snapped them open. Something landed next to him on the grass, the sword. Rorry leaped onto Julian's back, wrapping the chain of her manacles around the beast's neck. The wolf groped for her, swinging Rorry as he bucked.

Cord wouldn't give up; Rorry needed him.

His knee bent, bringing Julian's attention back. Julian roared and splayed his claws.

"No!" Rorry yelled. She groaned and pulled the chain tighter.

Julian arched his chest out. A zip heralded hope before Cord saw the arrow clutched in the beast's paw. Julian looked up the hill to see where it had come from.

Cord didn't let the distraction pass. He forced his mind to disconnect from the shrills of pain coming from his leg. "Duck!" Cord shouted. In a solid motion, he grabbed the hilt of the sword and rolled. The arc of the blade glided through the wolf's neck.

Julian's body quivered and crunched as it shrank, and sent Rorry to the ground atop it. Cord swayed a bit. His injuries wailed for him to stop, but he had to make sure Rorry was safe. If he'd hurt her, he wouldn't forgive himself.

A smile greeted him from the ground. "Who?" Rorry asked, wiping Julian's blood from her cheek.

In the darkness, a lithe and graceful form lowered her bow as she meandered downhill.

"Carolle," he answered.

Slamming herself into his chest, Rorry squeezed. He winced at his leg's protest. The scent of rose petals filled his nose. He breathed her in and wrapped his arms around her.

Rorry shoved him back. "What are you doing here?"

She was angry? Of course, she was. He ought to let them all die for him. His jaw tensed as he composed a polite yet stern response.

Darkness matted her hair and sparkled for his eyes alone. "Let me heal you."

She stepped back, wide-eyed. "You will not. You have your own injuries to tend to."

"They'll be echoes of what you have. Don't worry." He lifted his hand toward her.

She slapped it away. "It is my body. I can choose whether I want to be healed."

Chastising himself, he nodded. Mending Rorry would reveal her full body to him, which was desirable but wholly invasive. "Of course. I'm sorry."

Searching for the right words to break the silence, he glanced toward Carolle, who cleaned her strange blades on the grass. She obviously spied on them through the corner of her eye.

Unsure what to say, he opened his mouth to tell her that Bevin had passed, but Rorry grabbed his face and pulled him into a kiss. He held his hands away from her.

Carolle cleared her throat. Pinching a brass key, her fingers opened the manacles. "Unless you'd prefer to leave them on? I make no judgments. Lady's choice, of course."

Rorry scoffed.

Cord's face blazed.

Chapter 49: A Generous Satyr

Even if it wasn't the guiding wind he had hoped for, Kylan welcomed the cool breeze on his sweaty forehead over the top of Bevin's grave, several feet away from the half-ogre's body. At first, he had fought Scarlett on spending their preparation time digging a grave, but it gave him time to think. And Bevin deserved it. Dawn purpled the sky; the dimming stars confirmed to him that his new plan was right. They had waited too long for Cord and Rorry.

Tossing the shovel aside, Kylan climbed out. Scarlett had removed the chunks of wood from Bevin's wounds and draped a blanket over his chest. With a nod, she stopped petting Bevin's balding head and grabbed his shoulder. Kylan gripped the other. Andion snorted as he approached the oniony scent of the half-ogre but tried to help by grabbing the moleskin on Bevin's calf. They heaved him toward the grave. Kylan managed a little progress before a cloth square ripped off in his hand.

"Wait," Scarlett whined. She whistled and clicked her tongue a few times. The horses they had gathered gave Spectre a wide berth as he pranced from the trees. The ghost was enamored with Scarlett. Kylan would've gone as far as to call him downright jealous when she paid attention to the others Andion had found.

"Ah yes," Kylan said. "Thinking. That's why nature trusted you with magic and not me. I saw some rope in Bevin's cart when I got the shovel."

After they harnessed Spectre, the relocation went smoothly, if one discounted the dropping of the half-ogre into his grave. At least he was lying on his back. Kylan sighed at the irreverence and said, "May he be at peace now." He hopped in and retrieved the rope.

Fleeing to the lifewood vardo, Andion didn't seem bothered to join in the rites.

When Kylan climbed out, Scarlett gathered a handful of soil and sprinkled it over the body. "Brothers and sisters of the Hook, we have lost a member. His reasons for joining remain his own. The sacrifice Bevin Freidig has made garners our humility. May he find peace in order to start anew."

Struggling under the weight of Bevin's club, Kylan lost control of the plank. It tumbled in and clunked against Bevin's head. Kylan chewed his lip, noted Scarlett was not amused, and busied himself with a handful of dirt.

"I don't know his favorite song, so I wrote him an elegy," Scarlett said. Kylan's lips pressed together to maintain sincerity. "Filling our bowls—"

A snicker escaped. He waved for her to continue. Poor Bevin. He really didn't want to laugh.

"With pear-shaped hopes—"

"Heh—" Kylan clapped his hand to his lips.

Scarlett's shoulders fell in annoyance until she snickered. Then her frustration doubled. "Go!"

Throwing his arms up, he let out a chuckle. "I'm sorry! I'll leave you to it," he said, unable to look at her. Sucking in a deep breath, Kylan tried to let the mirth roll off. This was a serious situation, *a grave one.* He groaned at his own joke. Bevin deserved much better than having him oversee his funeral. With a mournful breath, Kylan made his peace.

Browsing the goods from Teague's vardo that Andion had laid out, Kylan picked up the Seeding papers and collected the black leather vest he believed was Ferix's. Steel studs affixed jagged segments of hardened hide to the plush-lined leather. All in all, the sleeveless menace befit an assassin. His wrist scooped up a strap of the matching clove-scented bag.

Shaking his head one more time to rid himself of delirium, Kylan entered the vardo. No humor lay in this decision, but he knew it was right.

Lantern light flickered around inside. Ferix filed his horns in the corner. Andion stood at the bars, watching the process.

Kylan set the armor and the bag by the trunk. "Andion," he said, "despite the fact that you gave the prisoner a file, I have to trust you to do something else." Even with the predictable grimace forming on the pik's face, Kylan struggled to say the words.

"What?" Andion squeaked. "I won't make your soup, Brute." Then his chin lowered. "Oh, you want me to dance?"

"Sure. Later," Kylan said. He extended two black steel throwing knives and Cord's and Grary's Seeding papers. Teague had done well with Cord's papers. They were nearly identical to Kylan's. "Take these. Go, help Cord."

Andion's eyes grew to the size of biscuits. He reached for them slowly, keeping a check on Kylan's face for the catch. "Take them! Go. That way." He pointed north.

The pik slipped the papers behind his belt. With a knife in each hand, Andion danced in a circle. He hopped over the side of the trunk.

Kylan held the lid open. "Tell them to meet us in Llandir. And be careful, brat." Afraid he might stop himself, Kylan slammed the lid down. Shuffling from within the trunk announced Andion's departure.

The satyr crouched behind the bars. "You are covered in filth. Did you come to bathe?"

Mud and blood smeared Kylan's hands where his blisters had broken. "I had to dig a grave." This decision wouldn't be easy to explain to the others. Perhaps he should lie and blame it on that mysterious "wind" that kept making decisions for him.

Ferix's eyes lowered to Julian's golden dagger at Kylan's hip. The prisoner backed against the wall as Kylan slowly moved to the cell. "You have forgotten the water," he joked.

Seeking conviction, Kylan spoke with a slow cadence. "It gave me time to think. Our chances are slim. And I refuse to let Scarlett be taken again. To that end, I have to eliminate as many threats to our success as I can."

Kylan slipped his hand to his hip and pulled a key from behind his belt. The lock snapped loose. Untwisting the chain, Kylan slung the metal to the floor. Veen's key came out from underneath his shirt. With a twist of his fingers and a swing of the bars, Kylan stepped back.

The disbelief on the satyr's face almost made Kylan smirk. "It wouldn't do to have you die with us, would it? Go on. Let your luck determine your fate, not the misguided wanderings of common folk looking to find a way . . . a way to be themselves."

Ferix studied Kylan as he stepped out of the cage. "Why? What compels this compassion?"

Ashes, he was tall! Hunched over, Ferix stood taller than Kylan.

"I guess it's the good I can do," Kylan answered. "Besides, it'll be easier to deceive the watchmen without my vardo rocking itself." He pointed to the corner by the chest. "Is that bag yours? Teague got your pipe out of it."

The sentence hadn't finished before Ferix stomped to the loot. The satyr examined his armor before setting it aside. His arm shifted the contents of the bag as he removed one item at a time.

Something twitched in the back of his britches.

"Do you have a tail?"

"Not a very big one," the satyr answered. "And, no, it does not wag when I'm happy."

Moving for a better view of Ferix's possessions, Kylan pondered the hoof-shaped black pads attached to the end of some leather straps in Ferix's hands. "What are those?"

Ferix wrapped them around his ankles. He buckled three sets of clasps on each leg and kicked the side of the vardo. It shook but lacked the normal *clop*. "The gift of a plant half a world away. As an assassin, it pays to be silent." As if to accentuate the title, a small sheathed blade slipped free of the bag. Ferix slid it into a fold in his vest.

"'Assassin.' That word again," Kylan said as he leaned against the opposite wall. "For an assassin, you're awfully easy to smell." He stammered when he saw Ferix's insulted reaction. "Your smoke—the cloves, I mean." Thankfully, the satyr let it go. "I suppose you could tell me how you got to Merith, if you were feeling generous."

Apparently, he wasn't. Ferix donned his vest next with a wink to his audience. "They traded my kukris. Curse them. I'll have to track those down first."

Kylan crossed his arms. "Before you do what?"

Digging to the bottom, Ferix jostled the contents. He pulled his hand free and frowned at his palm. Six signet rings slipped onto his fingers.

Kylan stepped closer but could only see Ferix's left hand. They were identical to Teague's, with a large bird in flight on each face; only the colors varied. The glint of gold surrounded the orange and red; silver held the blue.

With his right hand, Ferix freed a black cloak from the sack. He flicked it in the air and let it fall as though he were laying it across a bed. He shook the bag again. His hands prodded every inch of the lining.

Standing, Ferix moved in close. "Did you take anything?" he demanded.

"Yes. I thought it might be exciting to let an assassin loose after I stole from him."

"Where are the other two rings?" A growl remained in his voice, cloves thick on his breath.

"Black and green?" The intensity of Ferix's stare assured him they were the ones. "Teague had them. He's worn them since before we left Abernathy-on-the-Way. What are they?"

Ferix wrapped a hand around the handle of his knife. "Was he wearing them when he disappeared?" His hand released the handle of his blade when Kylan cocked his eyebrow at it.

"He always wore them." Breaking the connection with Ferix's eyes, Kylan picked up the cloak and brushed it off.

"That fool. No wonder he was taken."

"Taken?" Kylan asked, holding the cloak out to Ferix. "He practically handed himself to them. Do you think we could save him?"

The satyr took the cloak and wrapped it over his shoulders. Full of mystery and more darkness than Kylan wanted to dwell on, Ferix kept his hands out of the light, making him a fearful sight. The armed, stealthy assassin could take advantage of being freed at any moment. "It's no matter to you."

"No matter? If we can save him—"

"You cannot save yourselves. If you could, you wouldn't be so inclined to separate our paths and undo their great find. We're extinct, remember?"

Kylan would attempt a rescue, but he wouldn't put Scarlett at risk. That didn't make it easier to stomach leaving Teague to his fate. "These decisions weigh heavily," he mumbled.

At the door, Ferix inhaled the dewy air. "You have done well. You're setting things in motion. The pik is not a child, contrary to his behavior. Save your concern for Teague for your friends and get off this cursed island." Ferix descended the stairs.

Kylan followed.

The dimmed stars were under careful study from the lanky satyr, who stood easily a foot taller than Kylan at full height. "My path is laid out before me." He packed a pinch of grass into his pipe and looked over the debris of the camp. Puffing out a long sigh, he winked at Kylan and trod toward the woods to the south. "When I find the fool, you have my word that I won't kill him for stealing from me."

"Wait," Kylan said. The satyr didn't stop. "Ferix!"

Ferix turned with a smirk. "You desire a kiss farewell?"

"What?" Kylan asked, blushing. "I want an answer. The full answer—the truth. You owe me that much."

"I could owe you more, my handsome savior," Ferix said, stepping closer and running his eyes over him. "It is rejuvenating to be under the stars again. Yes, I do feel suddenly generous."

Kylan put his hands up. "Listen. I'm serious. You're terrified of water. How did you get to Merith? You're not like Andion. Your accent, your, um, shoes, they're not from here."

Ferix sucked deep from his pipe again. "I flew." Kylan held his gaze. Amused, Ferix thought for a moment and said, "I won't give away my secrets. But I do like you. How about a riddle then, if you're so good at them?"

He took Kylan's right hand and examined the silver ring on his forefinger. Ferix twisted the ring twice, then let Kylan's hand fall without an explanation. "In Llandir, a crooked man passing gas will open a new world to you."

"What?"

"You will know it. It'll smell as it sounds. Though, it may help if you bring one of the magi. They tend to be more observant than the rest of your kind. And don't forget some radishes. That's very important now that you've let your sword wander off." His mouth opened as he glanced down at the ring again. Kylan was going to ask about it, but Ferix smiled. "Another time," he whispered. The assassin flipped his hood forward and bowed. "My lady," Ferix said over Kylan's shoulder.

Scarlett curtsied from a few steps behind. When Kylan turned back, Ferix was gone. The scent of cloves hung in the air. Studying the woods, Kylan knew the assassin watched back.

"Joseb hasn't woken," Scarlett said. "Would you like some tea?" She rubbed her hands together. "I'm sorry. Did I interrupt?"

"No." Kylan threw his arms up. "Pick one." He held a grimy hand toward the lifewood vardo and the other toward Teague's.

"For what purpose?"

He put his hand over his mouth, until he tasted the bitter dirt on his finger. "The lifewood is more convincing, something a commoner might own. Although I can say I bartered a wardrobe or something large and expensive for the green one. Perhaps a cottage?"

"Why do we have to choose?"

"Because I can only drive one, while you'll be using that illusion spell to hide yourself and your frock-loving mentor inside."

Fear entered her large eyes. "No, I mean why do we have to choose now? Shouldn't we wait for Rorry and Cord?"

Kylan had hoped she wouldn't ask. "We can't," he said with a crack in his voice. He cleared his throat. "The sooner we're away from this wreckage and secure within the walls of my 'new home,' the better off we will be. Besides, I'm not exactly sure how long it'll take us to get there. And the sun will rise soon."

She wilted upon hearing the words.

He supported her with his hands on her shoulders. "I sent Andion to tell them to meet us inside the city. He has the other Seeding papers. We have to trust Cord and hope for the best."

"That is a good plan," she said politely.

He let his hands fall with an apologetic wince for the stains they left on her dress. "Now we need to decide what to take and what to leave."

The smoke from the remnants of the butterfly vardo thinned as the pieces cooled. Kylan kicked a few planks over to see what was salvageable. The fire hadn't burned all of the contents of the vardo. Most of the back half had been projected out across the camp.

"I don't think sorcery is a good path for me," Scarlett said to the flames. "It's too dangerous. His temper did this."

"Well," Kylan said, "in that case, it may be perfect for you. I've only seen you lose your temper once. Twice now." She seemed prouder when he looked up at her. "Go get Joseb ready. We'll need to move him to Ferix's cell."

She grinned. "That vardo is larger and more likely to belong to you."

"Yeah."

Digging through the debris, he heard the door close behind Scarlett. The dark woods didn't reveal Ferix. A glass vial broke beneath Kylan's heel. "If a farting hunchback is to be our salvation, we had better not tempt the fates."

His hands ached in protest at the thought of sealing Bevin's grave as he walked between it and the mound of dirt. "Um, Scarlett?" he called. She peered around the yellow door. "Have you seen Bevin?"

The grave lay empty, club and all.

Chapter 50: Betrayed and Blackmailed

Periwinkle crept through the branches above Rorry. Green slowly seeped into the sea of gray as they searched the forest for Scute. Despite the humidity, the notorious fog of the Mint Coast had not made an appearance this far inland.

Carolle walked ahead with an arrow nocked and her elusive answers at the ready. Speaking mostly in smiles and shrugs, she revealed she had left to keep an eye on the caravan from a distance. "A vital reclaiming of her actions," as she put it. Did she not trust Teague any longer?

When Cord asked how the steel in the strange blades sheathed at her thighs had been imbued with magic, Carolle told him he would have to ask Ferix.

He groaned.

In another attempt to change the subject, Carolle teased him, "Even with your upwind approach, good boy, it shouldn't have taken three of us to slay one wolfkin."

Rorry hugged Cord against her side in support as he hobbled. Only a dull headache remained of her injuries, but his leg had been shredded. It was a wonder he could walk, even with assistance. "An alpha," Rorry corrected. "I shudder to imagine how many of his kind exist or even how they are made."

"Speaking of being made," Carolle sang with a mischievous grin. "I don't recall my armor having curtains." She glanced at Rorry's chest.

Cord's eyes flickered down.

Heat rushed to Rorry's cheeks. "You have delivered your vengeance, Carolle. Did it help this time?" Rorry bit her tongue. She had intended to distract them, not to remind the widow of her loss.

"No," she answered pensively. "Don't think Julian knew he was cursed."

"He knew," Cord said with certainty clearly rooted in hatred.

Letting it go, Rorry peeked at his wounded leg, surprised to see the skin over his calf had nearly healed. How long had he been carrying his full weight?

Down her arrow's head, Carolle examined the cedars and spruces ahead of them. "I'm only saying I'm not finished." She lowered her aim.

"Why?" Cord asked.

"Julian obeyed orders," Rorry answered. "He was told to curse Veen, but Veen refused to grovel." Again, Rorry winced at how exhaustion had removed her delicate eloquence.

Proud tears filled Carolle's eyes. "There's my Stille." Anger soon mixed in with each blink. "Once Teague is safe, Stille'll receive the memorial he is due."

Wondering what kind of flower Veen would receive, Rorry searched Carolle's arm for a location large enough for it and missed the obvious question Cord caught.

"Wait, Teague is alive?" he asked.

"Yes," the monk answered. "I think so. He has the basilisk's venom, whatever Stille didn't give to Kylan."

Carolle knelt and put her hand to the ground, then brushed her hair over her shoulder and pointed north. "Scute should be over by there."

Rorry embraced Cord's warm torso and breathed in the invigorating perfume of the woods. Her fingertips felt Cord's heart pounding.

"Then you're not coming with us?" Cord asked. "You're going to save him."

"You cannot stay!" Rorry shouted, setting a small flock of chickadees to flight from the underbrush.

Filling her cleavage with a deep sigh, Carolle nodded. "I must find my balance. Teague, Beez . . . whatever gets in my way. I won't return home . . ." She beat her bow against her leg as she thought. "What it is, after I helped Teague defeat the wolfkin who killed Shepherd, we had a forthright conversation. He knows I'm coming for him."

"You knew he left to seek out Beez?" Cord asked. "Why didn't you stop him?"

"Maybe I should have." Carolle rubbed her neck. "Maybe I was selfish. But there was something noble in his plan. I'd only heard tale of that Teague in Stille's stories. A reawakening of sorts. I wouldn't dare talk him out of that."

She smiled at Cord. "In the end, he did right by you, Cord Sullivan. When I asked why for, he said he was done with terror and wandered off on his own to find the Dregs, heading south to face his fear or it would tear at his skin or some shite."

Upon hearing her words, Rorry examined the ferns.

The monk took the lead again. "I trailed him for a while, but you take precedence. Otherwise, what's this all for?" Cord's breathing slowed. "Grateful, I am. Glad that you two sent that bastard to a blistering afterlife. *Diolch.*" The widow let her hair shield her face as they pressed on.

Though Cord balanced on his own feet, Rorry kept her side against his. His distant gaze moved over the trees while his jaw flexed. She knew what he was thinking. As stubborn as his horse, he wanted to seek out the danger.

Carolle held up a fist, and drew her bowstring, targeting a rustling fir. She whispered, "Is the pik following you?"

Cord grumbled, "He better not be."

After a few seconds of silence, Carolle relaxed the string and swatted the ferns out of her way.

"Why didn't Beez just come for us?" Cord asked. "We could have settled this as a group."

"Even horrific leeches take orders from someone," Carolle answered. "Don't worry yourselves. We'll get you to the caravan before Beez finishes his directives, or Teague. Maeverly and Bevin can get you out of Merith. Teague and I can end Beez and any other Dregs at his hive, assuming Teague is in the right state for it."

"Ash-licking Dregs," Rorry mumbled.

Carolle smiled proudly. "Almost what I'd say." She gestured over the ferns to Cord's warhorse. Scute returned to his grazing. Andion stood on his saddle, examining all directions except theirs.

"What are you doing here?" Cord called out.

The pik flipped and landed in the ferns. With his hands in front of his smiling face, he blazed a trail through the fronds. When Andion reached them, his hand raised two rolled parchments for Cord. "Brute sent Andion. We are to meet them in Llandir."

"Sod it all!" Carolle said. "Maeverly has to conceal Rorry in a vardo. She knows to wait, even if Bevin wouldn't!" She asked Andion, "Is she out searching for these two? Is that why for Bevin is giving orders?"

"Brute is Kylan, not Bevin," Cord said. He started to say something, closed his mouth, and started again. "Maeverly was unconscious when I left. Didn't you see the explosion?"

"Explosion?" Rorry asked.

"Her vardo," he said. "Bevin . . . Well, they were fighting over Teague. Maeverly lost her temper, I guess?" His mouth lingered open, but he waited for Carolle's response.

Carolle glanced south toward the caravan. With a growl, she let loose words that Rorry had never heard from a woman, which was not surprising considering women do not have the anatomy required for that particular act. Andion stared at his thumbs as he twiddled them. "I saw smoke but only had two things on my mind. Guess which one trotted by on his black horse when I got back from stalking Teague."

Kneeling next to Cord, Carolle examined his leg. "You're healing well already, but you had better rest by here while I fetch Nightingale. Let's see if we can catch them before they get to the city." She sprinted off and shouted back, "If not, say farewell to your hair, Freckles."

Rorry's chin rose. She could never pass as a man, especially Grary!

Stretching his back, Cord expanded his ribs amid a few crackling noises. Rorry stepped away from him to witness Carolle blending into the shadows of winter trees.

"Would you mind giving us some privacy, Andion?" Cord asked. The request stirred a discomfort in Rorry's belly. "Watch Scute for me, will you?"

Andion huffed and punched a frond out of his way. Mouthing to himself, he climbed onto the saddle and took a backward seat to resume his isolation with the horse.

Folding her arms, Rorry asked, "What did you not say? You were holding something back."

Cord shook his head. "It'll keep. I want to apologize for the other night when we were talking about the Chancellor."

"There is no need to apologize."

"Yes, there is. I was rude to you, and you didn't deserve that, even if we don't agree." He reached for her shoulder, but she moved away. His touch was becoming familiar. They were losing focus of what mattered. Why had she kissed him? It never should have gone that far. "What'd I miss?"

"Nothing." She smiled. "We are friends, Cord. Perhaps we should leave it at that until we reach Racine."

He resembled a scolded puppy. "Why?"

"Distracting ourselves by complicating things now . . . Waiting will give us something to look forward to." No one would have believed that excuse. Avoiding his eyes, she tried to absorb the solace of her surroundings and slid atop a felled tree. "You are Merithian—let us leave it for now."

Lowering onto the moss next to her, he breathed, "All right. But I reckon I'm not going anywhere without you. This has to do with the blacksmith's apprentice, doesn't it?"

"Yes," she said to a trembling fern. Confessing was the last thing she wanted. But Carolle had said she had to be open, open to the hurt, open to heal. She yearned for that, for the girl inside her to be free. At least he would know, and they could move on. "I will come clean about my reasons for leaving Merith. As I said—while my full intention is to find my sister, escaping a marriage arranged by blackmail was a strong motivation."

Rorry pulled her legs together and joined her hands in her lap.

The fog of Cord's breath shrank as he listened.

She would say it aloud. "Last year, my family took our caravan to Croathe for the annual summit. For the first time, our blacksmith brought his apprentice, a boy from Brewing. We were friends—well, I thought we were friends." She blinked and swallowed to calm her voice.

Cord scooted next to her. She flinched at his hand and rose.

Taking a few steps forward, she spoke to the dewy ferns around her. "I agreed to show him around the market on the docks. We met at the end away from the slavers, near the Tazzarian metalwork stands." She moved through the memories as though she ran through water. "He dragged me down an alley. Then . . ." She didn't smell the trees anymore, just the coal dust on Grary's hands. "He would not let me up. I thought he was playing at first. When he covered my mouth . . ."

Warm tears coursed over her lips that were no longer under her control. "Some dockhands cheered him on as they passed by. He made me feel powerless and ruined," she said, remembering the red bananas and jackfruit in the stall behind them. "When he was done, he told me I was pathetic and threatened to tell my father if I did not convince him to allow our marriage."

She licked the wet salt from her lips and scanned the woods. They did not reveal Carolle and Nightingale yet.

Cord's hand caressed her shoulder before his wet cheeks pressed against her head. Tears ran over his tensed face.

Shaking her head, she stepped forward. "They say I am not a befitting interest for a righteous Merithian man," she croaked. "And if my father knew, he would do the same to me as he did to Alis. I am an embarrassment to be publicly disowned, declassed, and sold."

"This bastard," Cord fumed, "he's that Grary, right? The one Kylan hates?"

Yes, she failed to say aloud, but nodded. The tears drummed on her leather jacket.

"I'm sorry, Rorry. I don't know what to say other than I want to kill him for hurting you. But that's your fight, isn't it?"

She lifted her chin, and when she saw the tears on Cord's cheeks, she smiled. He opened his arms to her. She stepped inside. He kissed her forehead and nodded to the log. After they sat, he held her close and rocked until her weeping slowed.

"You know," he said, "we defeated an alpha wolfkin together—I know Carolle helped—but we coulda done it without her." She grinned against his chest. "You stabbed him with a knife—twice—got knocked down, and jumped on top of him to strangle the flaming mongrel with the manacles he put you in!"

They laughed against each other.

"Powerless and ruined? The Chancellor's ass. A copperhead's what you are."

She sat up straight. "I know that now. I just had to get away to prove it to myself." Carolle had been right. The hurt lingered, but some of the sting had been removed with her fear.

"Rorry," he said softly, "take all the time you need. Like I said, I'm not going anywhere without you."

Moving away to watch for Carolle's return, Rorry hugged herself and smiled at Andion's curious face. Her mother had been right. The Mint Coast was beautiful.

Ripping sounds turned her back. Cord flung a fistful of shredded white parchment over the ferns. "And we don't need anything from him."

Her jaw dropped. She suddenly felt very foolish about hesitating to use Grary's papers. Doubly so when she realized he had torn up more than one set. "Cord! Are you mad? Carolle is going to thrash you!"

Chapter 51: Out of the Frying Pan

Kylan's heart slowed when Llandir didn't present itself around the curve in the road. When the prevalent lifewood grew tame, lining either side of the road like an orchard, he knew they were close. Making the most of his potential last moments, he sifted out the stink of the horses from the sea air mixed with winter trees and lifewood. His father would've been inspired for weeks by all of the shaggy red bark already working itself loose.

The harnessed team of horses drew them toward the top of another incline, teasing Kylan's nerves. On both sides of him, the white-tipped Breslan Mountains crested over the teal leaves of the Mint Coast. Yes, this would be a nice place to die.

No more than a quarter of a mile down the folding road, Llandir's lavender walls appeared beneath the brilliant summer sky. Sentry towers flanked the arched lifewood gate, taller than anything a man would transport through them. But then, the walls shielding the city weren't originally man-made.

The storm in Kylan's blood didn't stir, but his concern for the occupants of the cell beneath his seat blasted a flurry in his belly. While his papers tasked him to report to Llandir, they didn't say anything about a skinny magus and an unconscious lace lover. If they had found the merchant licenses, this would've been much easier. Swallowing the bitter taste of his nerves, Kylan uttered, "Maris, help us." Then he wrinkled his nose at Teague's words. "Or something."

A relief of the Tribunal decorated the gate's arch above the doors. Archers manned the ramparts and towers. One targeted the vardo while the others oversaw the young men queued for entry. If Ashwin watched over the Seeding, perhaps the army had reinforced the Mint Coast. If they'd closed the port, Ferix's riddle was their only chance.

Like all townships, a trimmed lawn encompassed Llandir. When the forest north of the road abruptly ended on his left, it presented a marvel. Smoothed into the mountainside chaperoning the coast, the sleek ancient towers and lilac dwellings of the dwarves had endured the ages. Contrary to the claims that they had been spared from the Purge for the hot springs within, Kylan suspected the architecture's survival had more to do with the invulnerability of the dwarves' work.

The poor dwarves might have been lucky to die out from disease rather than see their halls converted into the havens of the wealthy, the descendants of those who had crushed their allies in Shallyghal. Though he couldn't read them at this distance, Kylan guessed the gaudy yellow banners covering the mighty halls welcomed the sons of privilege to their new home.

Ahead on the road, the left door of the gate stood open. Three vulturine watchmen idly inspected the new arrivals as three more dealt with the registration. Uncertain of how to join the queue with a team of horses, Kylan inched the wagon forward onto the grass beneath the Ashwins' aim.

Pulling the reins, Kylan positioned the vardo away from the gate. His butt had gone numb from riding on the solid bench. Hobbling down, he made his way around to the back of the vardo and knocked twice on the wall to warn Scarlett. Needles ran through his legs as he did his best to maintain a casual approach.

The guards observed each painful step with their hands on their short swords. Their domed iron helmets looked like dinner plates festooned with trefoils smashed over their heads and started Kylan's snicker. He squashed the humor down and increased his painful pace.

Each of the watchmen greeting the new arrivals had a slender pouch slung opposite the teal trefoils over their hearts. A black-haired Seeder stood first in line. The watchman assisting him smiled and laughed kindly at the newcomer's confusion before pointing to something in the distance. They walked farther inside, disappearing behind the closed right gate, effectively vanquishing any sense of welcome from the lawn. The townsfolk ogled the newcomer, then succinctly ended their loud discussion of him and hungrily awaited another morsel.

Next in line, a pigeon-toed lad rambled while the handsome slave-born watchman assisting him feigned interest.

When Kylan reached the queue, the final greeter, a glossy-eyed man sporting a downy white mustache and equally bushy eyebrows, held up his hand and pointed to a spot on the road behind the human tree he was yelling at.

Rarely did events make Kylan feel short; this was the second one today. The fellow in front of him must have come from the south, given that he wore shorts and sandals. "But why do I have to go to an inn?" the sapling asked, curling a piece of parchment the guard had given him.

"Because people don't die as quickly as they used to!" the mustached guard yelled. Tomato-red blobs splotched the cheeks of the birch—he would definitely be a birch if he were a tree. "You'll get a house when one opens up. Be thankful you get a shelter at all. Now get outta my sight!"

The birch hustled through the gate, sowing chuckles through the watchmen and the crowd.

Snatching the papers from Kylan's hand, the curmudgeon asked, "Why is it all of you show up at once? It happens every year." Liquid patience had washed down the guard's breakfast, if his breath was any indication. "Kylan Nock, son of a woodworker, Northern District. Woodworker?" He eyed the vardo. "I guess that makes sense."

"Yes, sir. We built that two years ago. My father let me take it. He thought I might be able to barter for something more useful."

The guard eyed him. "And four horses, no less."

"Our family's in favor with our councilmember, His Grace, Lord Gwirion."

"Not anymore," the watchman corrected. "Lord Ffyddian is your liege now." He stowed Kylan's Seeding papers in his pouch and set off toward the wagon, escalating the thunderclaps in Kylan's chest, still not the rushing wind telling him to act. "Open it."

Turning back, the watchman yelled, "Cothi, aid me with this search."

The tawny-skinned guard nodded and directed the pigeon-toed fellow to the gate. Riotous laughter followed.

Kylan inhaled deeply. At worst, Joseb would wake up, get angry that he was wearing britches, and reduce everyone to chunks and slime. Parts of them might land on the continent. He grinned to himself until he saw the guard's impatient glare.

Freeing the key from his pocket, Kylan moved to unlock the door. With a quick peek, he discovered the entire cell was gone, bars and all. He stepped aside. The guard entered and pounded a fist into the planks as he inspected the craftsmanship. He opened Andion's trunk. Everything else was concealed in the cell with the magi.

"Right," the older guard said, letting the trunk's lid fall back into place. "There's nothing interesting here." Even still, he stomped on the floorboards a few times.

The second watchman climbed the stairs and froze, staring directly at the invisible cell. Kylan blocked his view and pointed at the trunk near the doorway. "Yes, a trunk and a few silver dishes. Like I said, my father gave me things to barter."

Cothi brushed past him.

The older watchman removed a scrap of parchment from his pouch and gave it to Kylan. "The Gilded Lavender in the Northern District is where you'll live."

"I can give him directions, Stotter," Cothi said. "I saw another one coming up the road, and Jameson is still in town."

Grumbling his true feelings for the Seeding and Jameson, Stotter blew out his mustache. The wagon shifted as he stamped on each step.

Cothi lowered his chin and said, "Explain yourself before I reveal what's going on here."

"Oh, right," Kylan said, hoping against hope that this was a simple misunderstanding. "You didn't hear me tell the other watchman where the horses came from. Our councilmem—"

The guard unsheathed his sword, cutting him off and trapping him against the wall. "Forget the horses. Who are the people in the cell?"

Kylan cursed. "Filthy, filth-soaked ashes," he finished. "They're friends of mine."

Cothi stuck the blade under Kylan's chin. "You cage your friends?"

"To keep you out, yes!"

"Give me the key," Cothi ordered.

"I don't have the key."

"That's unfortunate," the watchman said.

Kylan had trained for this situation. In three moves, he could incapacitate the watchman. But then what? Kill him? Kidnap him and run back to the wilds?

The spell faded, revealing the entire cell. "I have the key," Scarlett said, curling her bony fingers around it. In her other hand, Master Clienne's crossbow rested against the bars, steadying her aim at the guard's chest. She fit the key into the lock. After a click, the door swung open.

The watchman lowered his sword as Scarlett braced the crossbow with her other hand. "We're not enemies," he declared, sheathing his blade. "I apologize for the misunderstanding. The wealthy are often the worst at sneaking in magi as slaves." He sorted through the pouch at his side. Cothi handed Kylan a thin piece of parchment. Black ink formed lines within an egg shape.

Cothi traced a snaking line in the center of the city and said, "That's the Seles River. Don't cross it." Unlike the map Stotter had given him, an X marking the location of the inn was in the southern half of the egg.

"All of the obligatory pairings have been settled," Cothi said. "No need to worry about a bride." Relief washed over Kylan like a bucket of icy water. He hadn't even considered that. Otherwise, he would have delayed a couple more hours.

Tapping the southern X, Cothi said, "The Ale and Pumpkin in the Southern District will serve as your home until you depart. This map will gain you access to lodging and food. You'll receive further instructions when the time is right. Don't fear the slaves there; they'll help you."

"I don't understand," Kylan said. "That guard said—my Seeding papers said—I'm supposed to go to the Northern District."

"You wish to escape Merith?"

Exchanging a questioning glance with Scarlett, Kylan nodded.

"Ale and Pumpkin. There's no time to explain. Be off, and good luck." With a final curious glance at Joseb, Cothi stepped out.

Her eyes on the doorway, Scarlett asked, "How did he see me?"

Kylan shrugged. "If it helps, I didn't." This could be the answer they needed. However, Cord's papers would send him to the Northern District. Kylan's curiosity won out. They would check out the Ale and Pumpkin first. "Stay put. We're not out of the fire yet."

When he exited, watchman Stotter was berating another poor soul. Kylan climbed onto the hardwood bench and picked up the reins. As the wagon passed, Stotter pelted out answers about why the fellow had to go to an inn. With Cothi's signal, the right gate's bolts unlatched. It creaked under the strain of the inward motion. Map in hand, Kylan drove the team into Llandir's maw.

The roar of the crowd had deceived him. Only a gaggle of nags and a herd of village idiots shouted beyond the gate. Kylan kept his eyes above their calls and shaking heads. Engravings of flowers and reliefs of shields decorated every awning, cornerstone, and door. Naturally, all heraldry represented the Chancellor's line with a vertical white stripe through a sea of red.

Blue-and-yellow pinwheels spun from any place they would stand. Kylan guessed they were special to the holidays because they weren't sun faded. Matching tapered flags whisked along the roofs.

The streets were more level than Brewing's but provided the same sounds as townsfolk moved about in the excitement of the lingering holiday. Plots of land were set aside for gardens, where children played while their mothers gossiped in the same plain clothes as the commoners in the west. It would have been rather welcoming if not for the faces holding suspicion, returning an upturned nose or a squint each time Kylan's eyes lowered.

Turning the map upright, he set their direction south. Lumber became more abundant in the construction, though houses never dipped to a single story. The closer they got to the inn, the more women gathered to gawk at the newcomers. Their decency lessened by location as well. The differences between the ladies near the gate and this ravenous pack were that of pups and wolves. A few forward yells spurred the horses on.

Kylan searched for a sign above the crowd and kept his gaze on the seagulls. A dozen floral-scented kerchiefs had landed on him and his seat by the time he spotted his target, blocked by a crowd at the end of the street.

More cedar than stone and twice the size of the Gwirion manor, the inn occupied the full block. The top floor must easily provide a view into the Northern District and out to the Great Barrier, if not beyond to the Gallaic Channel.

Four slaves waved Kylan toward the inn as six more kept the horde parted by their presence alone. The shouts from the throng of outright hussies blended into incomprehensible noise. Little girls giggled, old crones picked him apart with their eyes, and those his age pretended to be coy as they shoved toward the front of the line. Even with the ounce of flattery he could find in it, Kylan wished the horses would charge.

He took a deep breath as they passed through the wrought-iron gate securing the inn's grounds. The slaves guided him around a wing of the inn to the stables. Next to a tiny courtyard lined with small cherry trees, Kylan brought the wagon to a stop. His guides began disconnecting the harnesses.

Brushing off the perfumed rags, Kylan hopped down to warn Scarlett not to poke her head out. Much to his chagrin, slaves were already unloading their possessions and carrying them to the inn.

Kylan mounted the stairs to see Scarlett receiving a curtsy from a stout woman with fawn skin and a bright smile. Her flaxen hair formed a bun at her nape. "We welcome you to Llandir."

Scarlett curtsied to the slave and said, "We appreciate your hospitality but do not plan to stay long."

"Of course, madam. We will avoid the eyes of the city as we bring you inside." She gestured to Joseb. "The men can carry him, if it pleases you."

"No need to bother yourselves," Kylan said. She curtsied to him. "We intend to cause you as little work as possible."

"As you wish, sir. Please know discretion will be shown by each slave you encounter here. If you need any assistance, please ask for Phaedra." When she put a hand on her chest, Kylan realized her brand was the swan of Brewing. "Breccan and I oversee the northern wing of the inn."

"Thank you," Kylan said. "Would you mind showing me to our new quarters before I bring my companions up?"

A man with a trefoil-branded cheek entered behind Kylan. He slapped the back of his right hand against his left palm twice before he raced to the inn.

"I do apologize," Phaedra said, moving to follow. "An urgent matter requires my immediate attention. Directions will be provided tonight, when the Seeding is complete." Then she chased after the slave at a full run.

Kylan cocked his eyebrow at Scarlett.

She laughed. "You did say we didn't wish to be a burden."

"I meant it. But did you see her brand?"

Scarlett dismissed it with a wave. Brewing did have slaves once, before Alis. Kylan wasn't sure if Phaedra was old enough for that to explain it. And why hadn't the swan been branded over?

"Third floor, seventh room," Scarlett said and presented a brass key in her hand. A string through the eye of the key dangled a wooden tag with three engraved circles and seven lines marring the backside.

He leaned out of the doorway and scanned the courtyard. No one remained besides the slaves he heard unbridling the horses. "I suppose it's safe to move him now."

Joining Scarlett in the cell, Kylan lugged Joseb forward and noticed his pale scalp. "You shaved his head?"

"Mm-hmm," Scarlett hummed. She tucked Rorry's crossbow

behind her belt. "His hair had burned. It needed to be evened."

They draped Joseb's arms over their shoulders and hefted the sorcerer. By the time they reached the bottom stair, Scarlett whimpered with each step. Midway to the inn, she stopped to catch her breath.

"I don't mean to push you," Kylan said, "but maybe now isn't the best time to rest." He barely finished the statement before four trefoil-branded men rushed to their side and pulled Joseb free.

"Thank you very much," Scarlett said, before Kylan could protest. "Third floor, room seven."

With a destination, the slaves whisked the sorcerer away. As guilty as Kylan felt for using their assistance, he couldn't deny their efficiency. He had to jog to keep up.

Inside, the scent of freshly baked bread and something fruity, a pie maybe, teased his appetite. All day, a feast would be laid out for his new neighbors to celebrate the end of their journey and build unity for a promising community. Instead of partaking, Kylan was sneaking a couple of Abandoned up the back stairs. He was disappointed to miss out on the food.

Before he had finished taking in the foyer, the slaves had carried Joseb up to the first landing of a wide staircase. The colors of their robes changed as they passed under a stained-glass window depicting ships at sea, the dark Great Barrier, and Llandir's purple retreats for the wealthy.

Scarlett tugged on his sleeve and started their climb.

Guilt, or perhaps his appetite, brought his mind back to the question he'd pondered for most of the morning. What had happened to Bevin? They hadn't spent much time searching for him before Kylan had insisted upon moving on, which he would've delayed if he'd known how close to Llandir they were.

After climbing the three steep flights, Kylan was thankful the slaves hadn't let them carry Joseb. "We can certainly take him from here," he said when he saw the ten iron marks on the first oak door.

Scarlett whimpered.

"We are very thankful to you," Kylan said, offering his hand to each. The men set Joseb's arms over his and Scarlett's shoulders and were off.

Passing chamber nine on their right, Kylan grumbled when Scarlett began to whine again. Seizing a firmer grip on the waist of Joseb's trousers, Kylan assumed most of the man's weight against his side.

All was going splendidly until a woman's voice exploded behind them. "You have no idea the stew you're in! March into the next room on your left this instant!" Mrs. Hywel shouted.

Chapter 52: Shadows and Sorcery

Peeking over Carolle's shoulder at Llandir's majestic lilac bulwark, Rorry frowned at the gate. Kylan and Scarlett must have already passed through the red wooden doors.

Carolle rolled back against the lifewood trunk and glowered at Cord. "Make your peace with it, for it's a reality," she said to him. "You have as much foresight as a cat on heat, Cord Sullivan. Boneheaded, tearing up those papers was."

Putting his back up, Cord said, "I told you—"

"And I get it!" The monk turned him around and shoved him away from the tree's far-reaching roots, prompting them to skulk deeper into the woods to avoid the Ashwin's sight. "I repeatedly have to remind myself that I do, but I do. Doesn't mean I can't spit on the inconvenience, good boy."

Fiercer than a crimson dragon finding someone knee-deep in its hoard, Carolle's persistent scowl needed to break.

Rorry ran a hand through Andion's hair at her side and said, "Neither of us could have passed as a blacksmith's apprentice anyway." When she saw Cord's wilted reaction, she realized the insult buried in her words. "There is no offense in it. They are brutes."

"All right, Cord," Carolle said. "Redeem yourself. Impress me with a new plan."

Before he could, an off-pitch whistle drew closer. Chomping into an apple, a carefree young man strolled down the road to Llandir. Studying the passerby, Carolle ducked behind a gnarling of red bark and roots and unsheathed Ferix's blades. "Well?" she asked, gesturing toward the unsuspecting walker.

Robbing an innocent for his papers was an idea, but not one without ample reason for guilt. They might as well kill him if they did, for the army certainly would. "No," Rorry said, "it would be cruel."

The monk gave her a flat glare. "Do you think he's just a boy? Any of these lads could be wolfkin, Beez's or any other Dreg's." As the potential wolfkin walked out of sight, Carolle kicked the tree and released another blush-inducing swear. "We don't even know if they're in the city!"

"Then that is where we start," Rorry said. "We have a way to find them." The pik stopped chewing his tongue when Rorry lowered to his side.

"Llandir isn't a village, Rorry," Carolle said. "It may take days to search the thousands of places they could be."

"And we'd need darkness," Cord added. "It's not like we have his trunk."

"We can make shade," Rorry said. "The trunk . . . wait, Andion, can you take people—"

"No!" he said sternly. "Taking humans is dangerous! If you fall, you fall forever." His voice lacked any shielding of innocence now.

That didn't dissuade Rorry. "But you can take others with you?" He emphatically shook his square face. "What if we were inside of something else, like a trunk that had a handle? You have taken heavy objects on your shadow walks before."

Bending before Andion, Cord put his hands on the pik's shoulders. "Why would we fall?"

"That is how you travel but not just down!" Andion stamped the dirt. "You fall up, this way, that way, down, and any way the path takes you. It's no place for humans!"

"And if we hold on to you?" Cord asked. "Will it harm you?"

Watery-blue eyes begged them to forget the idea. The pik bowed his shoulders and shook his head.

"Then we must ask you to let us take that risk," Cord said.

Fret wrinkled Andion's brow, but he gave a nod.

"That'll have to do," Carolle said. "Let's find some darkness for you to begin your search." Then she moaned sadly. "But, Cord, I doubt horses travel well through shadows. Say your farewells while you have the chance."

Rorry giggled at the image of Andion riding a horse out of the shadows but felt horrible when she saw Cord's face.

"Can you take him?" he asked Carolle.

"Of course," she said without hesitation.

As Cord set off with leaden feet, Rorry snagged Andion's sleeve and pointed at a clump of short spruces a little farther downhill. He glanced back at Cord before running to them.

Laying his head on Scute's shoulder, Cord whispered something Rorry couldn't hear. His steed was the last connection he had to his old life, now that her satchel had become a casualty of their separation. Burn that Julian! This had better work.

* * *

Kylan and Scarlett laid Joseb atop the beige quilt on Mrs. Hywel's bed. A twinge of pain in Kylan's back forced him to lean against a walnut bedpost as he avoided looking at the doorway and the guilt Mrs. Hywel heaped upon them. She began walking in circles in the middle of the large inn room, establishing her dominance over the mismatched furniture spread to the walls and Kylan and Scarlett, separated by the bed.

The frumpy owl of a woman reset the twin of Scarlett's shawl around her shoulders and gave her apricot-dyed bonnet a ready-to-murder tug. "You impetuous, ungrateful children! What witless notion sent you running for the Great Barrier? And who in the blazes is this?" Fidgeting between clasping her hips and splaying her hands in disbelief, Mrs. Hywel flapped her draping sleeves around the component pouches hanging from her belt.

Wary of which spells she had prepared, Kylan said, "I'm not sure what you mean. This is where I'm supposed to be."

"In the Ale and Pumpkin?" she retorted.

"That's where the guard told us to go," he answered.

Mrs. Hywel fixed her gaze on her daughter. "And your excuse?" Scarlett backed away, past the cherry wardrobe and closer to the dirty mortared fireplace at her back. "You just had to be away from me? Am I that awful?"

Verging on tears, Scarlett shook her head.

Kylan bared his fangs. "We are leaving Merith. What's wrong with that?"

"Your family is in Merith, boy! I know you didn't want to be here, but you shouldn't have hauled my daughter along. And where is Rorry?"

That question took the wind out of his sails. "She'll be fine."

"What does that mean?" Threat poisoned her tone.

Scarlett chewed her lip and looked away.

He was alone in this. "She's with another friend of ours. They're on their way here." He hoped.

Mrs. Hywel shook her head and quickened her dominant strutting, blocking the door.

"We're not children. Your brother trained us to fight. Why else did you teach us the ways of the world outside of Merith?"

"That argument alone proves how naïve you are."

Scarlett uttered, "But—"

The Ghost Augur crossbow freed itself from her belt. Butting the floor, it shot. The bolt sailed past Mrs. Hywel's ear and nailed the doorframe.

Unleashing a roar, Mrs. Hywel snatched the crossbow. "That settles it! You are all coming home with me tomorrow." She rounded on Kylan. "Clearly you can't be trusted to make sensible decisions."

Kylan stepped into the bear's den with a shrug and addressed the dyed bonnet. "It's an odd argument that puts the army on my side, but legally, they are, so long as I don't dress above my station."

Staring daggers at him, Mrs. Hywel set the crossbow on the vanity. Eventually, she broke eye contact. "Fine, *if* you go to the Gilded Lavender in the Northern District, where you should be. *And* you apologize to Lord Gwirion. He didn't pull strings for you to cut them."

Before he could ask what that meant, she trapped Scarlett. "You, young lady, shall need to make your peace with saying goodbye. What were you thinking, pea?"

Scarlett met Kylan's eyes. "I want to study in the Tower of Trône d'Argent."

Laughter erupted from Mrs. Hywel. She waved her hands about and leaned onto the washstand to catch her breath.

"It's not funny," Kylan said. "You should see what she can do."

She pointed a plump finger at him. "You mind your own business! I shall have you know that my daughter is not strong enough to enter the Tower." She put her hands on her hips and gave Scarlett her best patronizing frown. "That was your plan? You three would get to the continent, and then what? What would you do when the Tower rejected you?"

"She has an advocate," a voice said. Joseb took long blinks as he rolled to his side and swung his legs over the edge of the bed. He frowned at his clothing. The Merithian commoner garb must have been offensive when compared to the lavish threads Maeverly had worn, or any of the Hook's garments for that matter.

"Sorry," Kylan offered. "They were all Andion could find."

Joseb grunted and patted him on the shoulder.

"And who the bloody ashes are you?" Mrs. Hywel asked.

With both cloth-shoed feet on the floor and an extra-disdainful grimace for the footwear, Joseb focused on the font of vitriol. "Jean?" Mrs. Hywel's color drained. "Jean Clienne?"

Kylan didn't move beyond breathing.

"My name is Jean Hywel now," she said cautiously. The insolent tone returned to her voice when she asked, "And you are?"

He smiled. "It has been some years, yes. Decades, I hate to admit." He bowed. "Allow me to reintroduce myself. I am Joseb Roux."

Upon hearing that, Mrs. Hywel's color faded to the point that her bonnet held more than her cheeks. Even the wintery locks escaping her headpiece were vibrant by comparison. "I see. I didn't . . . Yes. Well, Joseb, with all of the respect I have for your family, I shall ask you to respect mine and stay out of this argument."

Joseb turned his head to Scarlett, who studied the floor. "As the person asked to provide tutelage, I'm afraid I can't do that."

Red reappeared in the mother hen's face. "There is safety in her remaining home with her family. That is what matters here. These are dangerous times in Merith."

"That doesn't sound like the girl I knew." Joseb clicked his tongue. "Is it your teachings that required the disabusal? Oh, Jean . . . you convinced your own daughter she was weak?"

"Don't judge me, Joseb! I did what I had to do to keep her safe."

Scarlett's eyes slid back and forth between them. Her lips had pressed to a line.

"Safe. Deluded, but safe." Joseb delivered a shaming look with quite some skill. "Would the Tower not protect her better?"

Mrs. Hywel shook her determined face. "What if she doesn't care for the discipline of the Tower? She'll just run off like you did. I shall not capitulate, Joseb. I'd sooner tempt a varrow! She's my daughter. It's my say!"

"The say of a dead woman?" He drew himself up and folded his arms. "She knows, doesn't she?"

"What?" Mrs. Hywel asked, stepping forward and giving her bonnet another tug for good measure.

"My sister told you I left the Tower, didn't she? You were dead beforehand, though that was obviously an exaggeration."

She flushed a deep crimson.

"What portentous controversy have you two entangled yourselves in? You're no less audacious than they are." He waved a hand at the silent observers. "It must be worthwhile to risk fraudulent charges."

Mrs. Hywel's mouth started and stopped half a dozen excuses. Kylan's cheek ached from smirking at the dethroning of the queen of verbal battery. Spying his reaction, she groaned. "I won't discuss this in front of them! Their minds are corrupted enough." She thrust out her palm at Kylan.

A *whoosh* startled her. Mrs. Hywel reeled next to him.

Fire roared in the hearth behind Scarlett. "I was cold," she said with a wince.

Kylan snickered at the lie.

"You started her lessons with fire, did you?" Mrs. Hywel huffed. "Sorcery, no less! I wonder how many towns have burned from that witless mistake."

"You had ample opportunity to choose where to start her lessons," Kylan muttered.

With inhuman speed Mrs. Hywel sank a thumbnail into Kylan's ear and pinched. She dragged him toward the door.

"Ow! Ow! Ow! Ow!"

"You too!" she said to Scarlett. "Give me your key," she demanded, her face red.

Scarlett put it in her hand.

Crossing the hall, Mrs. Hywel turned the knob to their room. Once inside, she released Kylan's ear. Her flabby arm scooped Scarlett next to him before closing the door on them. The lock clicked. "You stay there and pray Rorry arrives before Lord Gwirion gets back!"

* * *

Cord rested his head against Scute's neck and observed Rorry sitting with Carolle near the cluster of spruces Andion had used. "You take care of Carolle now. I'll be back, so don't go gettin' fat and lazy on me, pal." He stepped aside and let Scute return to Nightingale.

He would be back. He had a vow to fulfill and Marlone's curse to break.

Andion yipped from the trees. Spitting and swatting the needles, he fought his way out. "Andion found the trunk! Heard Brute across the hall."

"Well done, you," Carolle said. She ran a hand over Rorry's shoulder and gave her shiny queue a tug. "This is where we part, Freckles."

"You should join us," Rorry said. "Did Teague not want you to see Cord safely to Racine?"

Carolle ran her hand through Rorry's hair and blinked a few times. "I'm out of balance, *bach*. The monks of my order strive to live on the verge of death—not throwing ourselves into danger, but living without regrets or desires that may lead to a sense of unfinished business in the Glades. I have to fix me first."

Rorry hugged her tight. "Be safe, and do not laugh. They will hear you coming." The woman did just that. Rorry rubbed her ear as she pulled away with a smile. "Find me, when you get to the continent."

"Ugh," Carolle groaned. "Racine. All that air kissing and scraping in those heavy dresses." A twinkle entered her eye. "If I'm honest, I did enjoy it, some." She held her thumb an inch from her fingertip. "Now off with you! Go find those other two trouble-makers. *Pob lwc*, Rorry te Gwirion."

Placing his hand on Rorry's back, Cord said, "I'll be right behind you."

"Hold tight," Andion said up to Rorry.

With a firm grip on Andion's hand and a fistful of his tunic,

Rorry looked back at Cord as she hunkered under the branches. They began to sink into the shadows.

Cord gave the best reassuring smile he could muster until her crown disappeared. "Carolle, I didn't wanna say anything in front of Rorry . . ."

Her brown eyes widened. "Maeverly? She wasn't just unconscious, was she? Is she dead?"

"No, *he* is fine," Cord growled. Carolle grinned in relief, then laughed. "Just . . . I couldn't save him and Bevin. I'm sorry."

She squinted. "How? What occurred?"

"Bevin was standing next to the vardo when it exploded. If he hadn't been there, I'd be dead."

Her smile never left the edge of her lips. "Was he decapitated? Was there silver in his wounds?"

"No. Why?"

A black mound careened over Carolle. She spun just as the wolfkin landed on her. They crashed into Cord.

Knobby roots jabbed into Cord's ribs when he hit the ground. Rolling over, he nocked an arrow. Ferix's red blade already singed the hair on the beast's chest.

Carolle groaned under his weight, then yelled, "Sodding mongrel!" Her hand covered a deep scratch on her arm. Shoving him off, she slid out from beneath the wriggling slave's corpse, branded with a wave. South Thornton?

A tan-pelted wolfkin loped toward them from the same direction. Cord tensed Veen's bowstring and set his aim. He released just as a plank crushed the beast's head, sparking small bolts of lightning as it struck.

Stepping into view, Bevin kicked the body. Cord's jaw dropped as Bevin pondered the arrow in his club.

The half-ogre thudded to Carolle and hoisted her in his arms. Through the bloodstained holes in Bevin's shirt, his skin was whole. Bevin whimpered at the blood on her arm.

"I'm all right," Carolle said. "If it scars, I'll put Stille's bog orchid there. Seems fitting, really."

When she saw Cord's face, Carolle brayed a laugh and squeezed the half-ogre's cheek. "Poor Bevin. I was just telling Cord that you weren't dead. You should've seen how guilty he looked."

Bevin's thin lips parted, baring his snaggleteeth in a smile.

"You know," Carolle said, "our boy here probably hasn't heard the expression 'easy as killing an ogre.' How many times have you been buried?"

Bevin grunted as he put her down. Sucking the air deep into his nostrils, the half-ogre circled them and readied his club.

A whimper announced Andion's return. He settled onto his knees and crawled out of the spruce needles.

Bevin raised his club over the trees.

"Stop!" Carolle yelled.

The pik squealed and flattened on the ground. "Andion thought you were dead!"

Confused, Bevin slowly lowered the plank.

Cord helped Andion to his feet. "Is Rorry safe?"

"Rorry is there." A yawn overtook Andion.

"Then we're off to piss in Beez's strawberries," Carolle said, earning an approving grunt from Bevin. She extended her hand to Cord. "Safe travels, handsome."

He shook and said, "Carolle, Kylan said Veen drew some symbols with his blood—"

"I won't lie to you, Cord," she interrupted. "Stille didn't share them. Made me swear never to use them if I ever came across them." She slapped Cord on the arm. "Trust in Joseb. He's fought Dregs before."

"Teague's friend?"

She smiled. "Maeverly."

Now Teague's stories made a little more sense. Maybe he hadn't been exaggerating.

Bevin grunted impatiently before realizing they were exchanging farewells. He waved to Cord, then grunted at Carolle again.

After tightening his belt over the scabbard, Cord gripped his bow and arrows in his left hand and pressed the hilt of Kylan's sword against his side with his forearm. Then he took Andion's hand.

When they stepped into the prickly needles, his sandals began to sink into the icy darkness. He recited a silent prayer and held his breath as Andion brought him down.

Carolle tossed her hair behind her as she walked Bevin toward Scute and Nightingale.

"Be safe," Cord whispered.

The shadow stole his senses. If not for the blasting wind, Cord wouldn't have known his eyes were open. The freezing blackness sucked his foot in one direction and grappled along his back in another as he fell upward. All the while, Andion squeezed his hand and wove their path.

Their fall slowed before each turn, serving as Cord's only warning of a sudden jerk. They drifted sideways, then the path abruptly twisted twice. A blinding light rushed at them.

* * *

With her ear pressed to the door, Scarlett thumbed a hole in her sleeve and listened to her mum's diatribe. Every now and then, Joseb's cogent argument crossed the hall. Most of it was mangled by the solid oak.

She still felt stunned to have learned Joseb and her mum were indeed acquaintances. "Why did Mum pretend to die in Racine?"

Kylan didn't hear the question over his pillaging of their possessions.

She moved to the window in the northern wall while he searched for inspiration in the ammunition, the basilisk hide, and Andion's "thiefed" treasures. Scarlett jostled the pane open to fight the stale air in their corner room, furnished nearly identically to her mum's. A gush of sea air rewarded her effort.

Up the hill in the Northern District, the ancient dwarven halls took her breath away. Downhill, barely within view through the homes and warehouses of the Southern District, the stark granite Great Barrier guarded Llandir's port. Lucky nobles. Their stolen vista from the retreats would clear the Barrier to the Gallaic Channel.

Threats from across the hall littered the tranquility. Scarlett scurried back to the door, hoping Lord Gwirion hadn't returned. She flapped her lips with a puff of air when her mum insisted upon her weakness, yet again. Joseb's refutation warmed her.

If her mum had faked her death before Joseb had left the tower, had she completed her training? Had she even received the mantle of a full mage? How much of what her mum had told her about magic was a lie?

Scarlett retrieved her poultice bag and dumped its contents on the vanity. She slid *Essential Focus* inside. It fit snugly, as though the bag had been made for it. After sliding Julian's dagger atop the tome, she closed the bag.

Kylan flung himself onto the simple bed and grumbled. This new side of him, the side that didn't propitiate her mum to avoid discipline, the same side that sent his tongue dancing over his teeth as he planned to defy her, felt oddly sensible. His tongue polished his canine, much the way it did when he discarded strategy in a game of Mice and Traps and secured a win with blind luck. It paused. His lips curled.

She sighed, knowing he was working out which phrasing would sell the less desirable aspects of his plan to her. Before he could speak, she put her hand up to stall him and went to the serving tray on which a pitcher of water and two agate cups rested. She righted the cups and tapped each with her ring. A small amount of clear liquid gushed out of the gem, releasing the scent of sugared strawberries.

Kylan received his. With a suspicious eyebrow, he thanked her.

"To furthering our education," she said. "In more ways than one."

"Cheers to that!" He clacked the brims together.

Previous experience told her to take it all in one quick gulp. The mist he spewed over her suggested she share that wisdom next time.

Chapter 53: Father Knows Best

Light broke through a tall crack between the doors of the cherrywood-scented wardrobe, easing Rorry's eyes and helping her focus on the empty hooks overhead. She joined her hands over her stomach as it settled from tumbling through the chilly dark.

"You're gullible," a woman's voice said. "We have to hope they don't jettison a few out of boredom. It has happened."

Easing the door ajar, Rorry murmured, "No." The same apricot bonnet she had given her tutor years ago bobbed in and out of view. Andion had made a mistake! Was it possible he'd taken them all the way back to Brewing? No. He said he couldn't travel that great of a distance. Had Mrs. Hywel donned that old gift to feign nobility and to hunt them down?

"There are no options here, Jean," a bald man said. "It's the fastest way back to the continent, and time is not our ally."

Rorry knew his face somehow. Regardless, Andion must take

them back! If they were found by Mrs. Hywel, they would be stuck!

She ran a hand along the interior of the wardrobe, pressing against the darkness. She had to stop Andion and return before Carolle left. Hair hit her fingers just before Cord's head crashed into her, tossing her out to the floor with him on top.

Wobbling in the wardrobe at first, Andion collapsed onto the pile.

Mrs. Hywel's mouth worked like a fish's. Scarlett's mother gawked at Andion and Cord and Rorry, and repeated. Kylan would enjoy hearing about this if she ever saw him again.

Cord rolled aside and placed his hand on Andion's forehead. "He's just sleeping." Helping Rorry to her feet, he said, "Pardon our interruption."

"Pardon?" Mrs. Hywel managed. "Where in the Hells have you been? And why are you popping out of closets? What are you wearing?"

Cord recoiled at the barrage, even though the disapproval was directed at Rorry.

Her tutor rounded on the bald man. "This is your influence! You convinced my daughter she's a bloody Sepholina and dressed this one like a strumpet? I know your ways."

"Joseb?" Rorry gasped. Why was he barefaced and bald?

"Hmph," Mrs. Hywel said. "You children, you're not ready for the world." Her hand searched in her pocket and came out with a key.

"Where are Scarlett and Kylan?" Cord asked Joseb coolly. He moved Andion to the bed.

"Across the hall, lad," Joseb answered.

Rorry's shoulders relaxed. Andion had done well. Well enough. Their reunion only had one obstacle left. Rorry raised her chin, ready to remove the obstacle. "If we are ill-prepared, the blame falls on our tutelage. Cord, this is Mrs. Hywel, Scarlett's mother and my *former* tutor." The emphasis on former, earned Rorry a threatening glare usually reserved for Kylan. "Why should I return? My father has already declassed one daughter into slavery. This would be enough justification for him to do the same to me."

"He did no such thing!" the mage said, baffled.

"I have always trusted you, Mrs. Hywel. Please do not change that now. I have heard the tale. Alis did not die as we were meant to believe. She fell in love with a slave and incurred my father's wrath. Would you wish the same for me?"

With an abrupt tug on her bonnet, Mrs. Hywel said, "Now you listen to me! I don't know what you did to fear your father, but Darren te Gwirion is one of the most honorable men I've known." Rorry rolled her eyes. Releasing a grunt, Mrs. Hywel threw her hands up. "I have failed you; three children, believing whatever gossip you want with ample proof to the contrary."

"Have you given them reason to believe the lies, Jean?" Joseb asked. He knew her, casually even.

"You stay out of this, Joseb! My family and my charges are none of your concern."

"*No longer* my concern, you mean?"

"I would like to hear why you believe my father is falsely accused," Rorry said. "You were in Brewing at the time of my sister's shaming. Correct me, if you can." If there was one challenge Jean Hywel could not resist, it was correction.

The older version of Scarlett's owl-like eyes weighed Rorry. "All right. Let's air these skeletons so you may see your foolishness and come home. Alis did fall in love with a slave named Gadiel. Your father did everything within his power to stand between them. That's the truth of the rumors." She took a deep breath. "But your sister was determined. If your father wasn't going to allow the relationship, she would force his hand. In the dead of night, Alis snuck into the slave house, found the tools, and branded herself."

Rorry resisted the urge to put her hand to her cheek.

"Your poor father, he grieved for days while your mother nursed your sister's burn and kept her out of sight." Mrs. Hywel gave the wall a tiny smile. "Gadiel still loved Alis, even with the scars. He snuck in to see to her whenever your father wasn't around.

"After a few days, Darren blessed the relationship, so long as they promised to wed and to celebrate with her family. Once the celebration ended, we found them safe passage to the continent where they could live freely." She regarded Rorry warmly. "He loved your sister as much as he loves you, Rorry. And he would've come around on his own if Alis had given him time."

If her father had not been unreasonable, he might have listened to Rorry and upheld justice. She might not have been ruined; yet she'd run away like an ungrateful child. Her behavior, her animosity . . . Rorry swooned. Joseb brought a chair from the vanity and guided her onto it. She put her face in her hands.

Cord rubbed her back.

Mrs. Hywel resumed her lecture. "The rumors that spurred this misadventure were started to cover the truth and to protect your father's reputation. Certain opponents may seek an advantage if given the chance."

"Where is Alis now?" Rorry asked.

Mrs. Hywel pursed her lips. "I don't know. The last I saw of them, they were sailing to Racine. From there?" She shrugged. "He was from the desert regions, you see? And that is no place for you to follow. We're going back to Brewing in the morning."

"No." Rorry rose. "I misunderstood, and perhaps I misjudged my father. But I will not relinquish my pursuit. Secrecy is the cause for folly here, not our 'misadventure.' Both sides share in the blame."

Mrs. Hywel's mouth opened in disbelief. She must have thought her victory secured.

"And before you chide, you should ask yourself what exactly you taught us."

"I beg your pardon!"

"You taught us of a better life beyond the Barrier, and now rebuke our pursuit of it."

A glimmer of understanding registered before Mrs. Hywel shook her head. "You're safer at home, Rorry. That's the end of it!"

"No." Rorry chilled herself by the tone that came out. "People have died for this! You will not strip our successes and their sacrifices. I am of age now, as is Scarlett. Our paths are our own."

"This is absurd." Mrs. Hywel pointed at Cord. "Is that where this pretty face is heading?" Swinging her anger from his meek stance back to Rorry, she said, "I should be at home defending Brewing from the wolves, not running across Merith collecting you lot."

"Now that's not fair, Jean!" Joseb said. "Tell them what truly brings you here, and what has brought you here for the past—well, I suspect it started with Alis."

Mrs. Hywel propped herself against a refreshment cart and turned up a chalice on the serving tray. A dark liquid poured out of the pitcher in her hand, spreading the fragrance of spiced wine. Someone actually believed her tattered bonnet's ruse and served her alcohol as though she were a noble?

"Your tutor," Joseb said to her back, "Mrs. Jean Hywel, is a criminal." His aim was meant to get a rise out of her but only managed to get a subdued head shake. "She has been freeing slaves, sending them off overseas, and using the Starlight Tunnels to do so. Tell them, Jean. This is your operation, though I suspect my sister has a hand in it."

They waited in silence, watching the faded bonnet.

Mrs. Hywel finished her drink in one take. "It's true," she said. "I would be here regardless. I've been sending Merithians off to the continent for years." She placed the chalice on the tray and poured another drink. "And would deny you lot that privilege. Maybe I do have myself to blame for this. Serendipity brought you all back to me. I see now it may have been to say farewell."

When she glanced at Rorry, Mrs. Hywel's face looked wizened and forlorn. "Kylan can decide his fate, but you and my daughter must convince us you want to leave of your own will. Know the burden you lay on your parents' hearts."

Rorry had not expected to gain respect for her tutor out of this argument. Why had she hidden this from them? "I know Scarlett keeps her secrets, but she would never have kept this quiet in all of our planning." That is, unless she wanted to get caught.

"She didn't know." Mrs. Hywel grinned and let out a small laugh. "Scarlett is so easily distracted and never seems to question why new books are suddenly hidden around the house before Hansweighn." Rorry squinted in disagreement but remained silent. Mrs. Hywel shuffled her shawl. "Her father knew, of course, and Barrey. Your parents provide the means."

Rorry pinched her fingers, embarrassed again for her false

assumptions against her father. "You will thank them for me? And give them my love?"

The doorknob turned.

Mrs. Hywel wiped her eyes as His Grace, Lord Darren te Gwirion, entered the room. Weary-eyed and scragglier than Rorry had ever seen him, there stood the one person she had convinced herself to run from. "Jean, they have not arrived at the Gilded Lavender. We are going . . ."

He trailed off when he noticed the others and halted when he saw Rorry. She took in his crumpled doublet, striped in pale green, which he believed brought out the color of his eyes but only accentuated his small belly. He looked over her leathers.

"Father, I am so sorry," she said, crying before she finished speaking.

Tears welled in his red eyes. He stretched his arms out for her and pulled her tight against him, sheltering her in his arms and the scent of bath powder. "My baby girl." The pipe in his coat pocket pressed into her cheek as she laid her head on his chest. He kissed her crown. "There is blood in your hair. Are you injured?"

She shook her head.

His Grace took her head in his hands and wiped her tears away with his thumbs. "I thought I would never see you again. I do not know what I did to make you hate me so, but I am sorry."

"Nothing," she moaned, burying her face into the striped green silk.

"Did you run for Kylan?" he asked. "We would have visited. I arranged for a very nice life for him here. He did not need to worry for anything." He straightened and cleared his throat. "Are you going to introduce me to your friends, daughter?"

Sniffling, she nodded. "Of course. Joseb Roux is a mercenary of the Hook, who has graciously been safeguarding our travels."

"Well met," her father said.

Joseb curtsied, then cringed, which set Mrs. Hywel's eyes rolling.

She began to introduce Cord when someone in the hall said, "I ordered the slave girl to bring us some ale, Your Grace." She recognized that baritone voice.

Her father smiled at the stalwart man with a scar running up his cheek to his nose, a scar Kylan had carved there. Grary ran his eyes over her and smirked.

Rorry stopped breathing. Ice coursed through her veins.

"Look who has been helping me search for you, Rorry," her father said. "He came to see you before he set out and insisted on helping us find you."

Grary raised his arms to hug her as he approached.

After shoving her father into Cord, Rorry stepped forward and slung her leg behind Grary's. With a solid thrust of both palms against his chest, she toppled him back. Mrs. Hywel gasped as he hit the floor.

Rorry leaped onto Grary's chest and buried her knees in his shoulders. He heaved against her weight with each inhale. His glare threatened her even now. Grary's thick hands reached for her but stilled when he felt her throwing knife against the ball of his throat.

"Rorry te Gwirion, get off him!" her father shouted.

She opened her mouth, but she was not sure what to say. Nothing would have been worth breaking the stare that put fear in Grary's eyes.

"Your Grace," she heard Cord say. "I'm sorry, but you can't interfere. This is her fight."

"My daughter does not fight!"

"No, you don't, Rorry," Grary said innocently. "What's gotten into you?"

She nicked his skin. "Do you not enjoy being pinned down, Grary? I know I did not." Her words killed every other sound in the room. No one moved except Grary. "Since you did that to me, forced yourself upon me, I have changed. I have stolen. I have fought. I killed a High Guard and three wolfkin, one an alpha. They are much bigger than you. So you tell me why, after blackmailing me to marry you—after threatening to tell my father what you did, as though it was what I wanted—I should not kill you as well."

A panicked sweat gathered on his brow. "Your Grace," he pleaded. "I haven't done—"

"You took everything!" Rorry yelled.

Grary's eyes jerked back to her after glancing her father's way.

Certain his fear went to his bones, she said, "You are lucky. The monk who taught me how to bring you down also taught me not to kill to make a point." She pressed the blade in a little harder and sat back. "I do not enjoy cleaning blood from my hands, so I suggest you do not speak of me or my family again. Our association has ended."

Someone gently grabbed her arm to help her up. She was surprised to see it was her father. There was sorrow in his eyes, then fury when they swept to the blacksmith's apprentice. "Do not believe your sentence will be so light."

Grary scrambled for the door. He made it two steps before falling flat on the rug. His arms slapped to his sides. He screamed but no sound escaped his mouth.

"Thank you, Jean," His Grace said.

Mrs. Hywel glanced at Joseb but said, "You're welcome."

Joseb cleared his throat.

Rorry's father pulled her into a tight hug and put his chin on her head. It trembled for a moment. "I have been a fool. I believed you had reached the age where you needed to push me away and spent my attention elsewhere when you needed me most. I am sorry, Rorry. I did not protect you. I should have—"

She shushed him.

They stood there until Mrs. Hywel said, "I'll get the other two."

"Wait, Jean," her father said. "I have another burden to ask of you, dear friend." He released Rorry and ran his hand over her cheek. "Please ensure my daughter reaches the continent safely. Get her on a trusted roster; whatever the price to secure hers and Kylan's safety, I will pay it."

Rorry put her hand on his. "Father?"

"If you believe your mother would forgive me for dragging our daughter across a war-torn country in order to wait for the invasion to reach Brewing, you have misjudged her also."

Joseb snorted a laugh.

Mrs. Hywel curtsied and said, "Of course, Your Grace." The older woman wiped her eyes on her sleeve. "Scarlett shall join them as well, if you'll allow it." When he nodded, she turned away from them and pretended to study Andion as she worked her frizz back under the bonnet.

"It was you," Rorry said. "Mrs. Hywel, you were the one Andion was waiting for in the Starlight Tunnels."

Mrs. Hywel's eyes darted as she thought it over. "I haven't seen a pik since Racine. Strange that one would know about that."

"His parents came from the continent," Cord said, which baffled her even more.

Rorry was relieved to see the Ghost Augur crossbow on the vanity. "Mrs. Hywel, I do hope you will thank Master Clienne for, unwittingly, allowing us to use his weapons for our escape."

Cord slid the scabbard free of his belt and placed it on Rorry's waiting palm. Rorry ran her finger down the silver script before her father lifted the sword from her.

"I think it might be best if they find their way back without mention at all, dear." Mrs. Hywel leaned in for a closer view of Andion and the wardrobe.

"Forgive me," Rorry said, "but I must ask. Do you know the meaning of the writing on the weapons?"

The large woman wheezed a few laughs. "You'd have to be an Augur to read that. Fools, the lot of them."

"Shall we free Kylan and Scarlett?" Joseb asked Mrs. Hywel.

Her eyes still watered, but she agreed and led the way to the room across the hall.

His Grace said, "Go share the good news. I will keep an eye on Grary." His voice sent chills through Rorry, though she did not wish to dwell on why.

With a quick glance at Andion, she left.

Across the hall, Mrs. Hywel turned the key and pushed the oaken door open to Kylan and Scarlett's corner chamber. Decorated in a nearly identical manner to Mrs. Hywel's room, its walls were lined with furniture, mismatched in style and woods. Intricate knots bound a trail of linens stretching from the bedpost to the window.

"Curse that Kylan Nock!" Mrs. Hywel bellowed.

Rorry was apt to agree with her this time. They were so close! He should have held out just a little longer.

Mrs. Hywel hauled the linens up and paused when the material changed. Kylan's britches added the last extension.

Joseb leaned out the window. "That would've still been a ten-foot drop."

"Well, he won't be hard to find," Mrs. Hywel said with a huff. "Am I so dreadful that you lot would run nude through a city to get away from me?"

Joseb and Cord could not contain their laughter after the first snicker. The sorcerer held his hand out to Cord. "I assume I owe you my life, Cord, and can never thank you properly; but I shall try."

Cord shook firmly. "Thank Kylan, sorcerer."

Mrs. Hywel took notice of the tension. Rorry should have been there to smooth Cord's discovery. Burn that Julian!

About to rejoin her father, Rorry noticed her satchel among the clutter. Placing it next to the bottles on the vanity, she opened the bag. Then she caressed the swaddled perfume and breathed deeply. Rorry ran her hand back inside to search for the diamonds her father had given her. She could never part with them now. She released the gems from her fingertips, put the perfume back on top, and closed the satchel before slinging the strap over her shoulder.

An explosion rumbled outside. Rorry moved to the window and parted the curtains. Clouds of dust billowed above the buildings. One of the towers at the distant gate slowly fell back before crushing the homes behind it. Screams spread as people ran through the streets.

Rorry's father dashed into the room. The kerchief in his hand wiped a dark red smear from Master Clienne's katana. "What was that?" he asked.

Cord locked eyes with Rorry. "The Dregs are here."

Chapter 54: Eyes in the Sky

A peculiar sensation swept through Scarlett, a pleasant one swelling warmly behind her bosom, an unlikely refuge for pride. Her concealment spell had fooled at least one watchman and had enabled them to pass the throng of panting women mobbing the inn's exits. Even in a sorcerer's version of the spell, the potency foretold strength within her. Her mum's lies be burned; she would get into the Tower.

Bountiful hedges, honeysuckle-woven lattices, and a trellis dripping with golden Vahllana's Trumpet blossoms now hid them from the busy Northern District avenue. The privacy of the vacant garden had allowed her to drop the illusion and explore without bumping into Kylan. Scarlett had never imagined the difficulty of walking without seeing her feet or the person dragging her by the hand.

At a pool from ages past, Kylan leaned between the blushing hydrangeas guarding a marble rail. In the midst of the crystalline waters, marble giants had once held hands and encircled a geyser. Now broken, the circle left only the humans, a man and a woman. These survivors of the Purge defied their censoring foliage and precisely draped cloth, permitting a sensual appreciation for the human form. The other races of Cyr lay crumbled in the celadon depths. Their features, a horn here and the curl of a beard there, filtered bubbles, though none of the piles would count as a crooked man.

"That is a pretty big leaf," Kylan mumbled. His tunic barely hid his loose shorts underneath. He'd scandalized the few Llandirites who had seen him in the market, until he'd made them an offer too good to refuse. Did he realize how silly he looked in his smallclothes with a bundle of radishes looped through his belt?

A belfry's bird sang the time. Four chimes rang from the unseen aerie to the south, likely an academe.

The sweet scent of the trumpets made Scarlett wish she had *Ivy or Silkshade*. But that curiosity needed to wait. Others demanded her attention. "'A crooked man passing gas will open a new world to you'?" she asked. "That's what he said verbatim? You didn't clean the wording?"

"Have you ever known me to clean the wording?" Leaving his distraction, Kylan plucked a honeysuckle bloom. Picking it apart for the stamen, he said, "I'm telling you, Ferix had to be referring to something in the dwarven ruins. Most of their cities were underground. There must be a hidden road to the continent."

Ferix's involvement tempted her to forgo solving the puzzle altogether. "I realize that, but the Northern District is enormous. How do you propose we find it before Mum finds us?"

"You're talking to someone who traded a basilisk skin for a bunch of radishes—while in his smallclothes! This is an adventure, Scarlett!"

"It doesn't sound like an appealing one," she said, dulling his enthusiasm. "By trading that skin, you've put all of our hope in that satyr. How can you put your faith in him?"

Thunder rumbled through the ground. She only had time to see the worry in Kylan's eyes before a watchman ran down the avenue behind the hedges shouting, "Get inside! Bar your doors! We're under attack!"

As people panicked, armored footsteps clanked in unison. A battalion of soldiers marched along the street. "To the gate!" a man ordered.

Scarlett stepped closer to Kylan when another shout directed more soldiers to the bridge over the Seles River leading to the Southern District. "Protect the Almighty!"

"The Almighty?" Kylan asked. He braved a peek to the avenue. "The Chancellor's here?"

A breeze sent Scarlett's hand reaching for her absent shawl. She put the hand on Kylan's warm back and leaned in to share the view. Baskets lay abandoned in the street. Rustling banners and flags whipped about above the empty bartering stalls.

"They said they were heading to the gate," he said. His finger skimmed the air, tracing something in his memory.

She put her shoulders back. "I'm not heading toward the cause of this alarm, Kylan. We need to find Rorry and Cord or solve the riddle. Or go back to the inn. Mum's harangue won't maim us."

"We'll keep searching," he said and bounded uphill before she could argue. "They will be here."

Racing through the trimmed lawns and gardens separating the ancient manors, she had to cry out for Kylan three times to get him to slow down. She sucked the air deep and snagged his sleeve next to more marble statues feigning frolics through the topiaries and beds of violet wine cups. The display seemed extra frivolous at the moment. Gluttonous luxury filled the Northern District.

Curtains fell into place as Scarlett surveyed the purple-tinted homes. "We're being watched."

Kylan grumbled, "I can't deny we're giving them a spectacle to discuss over tea." He rushed ahead, streaking by on his long legs before the flustered crones and jealous dotards at the windows.

She followed him out of the garden, running higher toward the ruins. Occasionally, Kylan stalled for her sake and scanned the streets. When the street hit a steep incline, she caught up to him again.

"This is impossible," he said. "Llandir is two Brewings smashed together. I'd swear the other inn was near here. He must have thought we'd have a chance to figure this out."

"As opposed to sending us on a fool's errand?" she asked under her breath. Louder, she asked, "Did he know you would be sent to the

Gilded Lavender? You are common."

The twinkle of excitement in his eye dwindled.

Scarlett couldn't abide crushing his hope. "If you truly believe there's a tunnel beneath the sea, then we'll find it. We should go to the oldest buildings." She nearly stopped speaking when she realized that meant the top of the retreats carved into the mountainside.

"Steady!" a man shouted from downhill.

They crept to the corner of a hedge to spy. The road dipped past three elegant estates and straight into the jostling Northern Gate. More than thirty Judges huddled behind tower shields in the road, waiting for a breach. A short distance behind them, several watchmen spun, either searching for enemies or considering an escape. Their short swords convulsed at each shake of the gate.

A black wolfkin topped the town wall. Wasting no time, the beast leaped at the soldiers below. Someone launched a spear from a side street and brought the corpse down upon the Judges. They let it fall and stepped forward again as the body convulsed.

The gate doors stopped reverberating. The watchmen gathered closer together. Instead of issuing assurances, the armored Judges held their rank.

In a crescendo, the gate lapsed. Stone chipped and scattered. Dust filled the air and swarmed the soldiers as splinters rained over them. One of the giant lifewood doors fell in, crushing a few Judges too slow to evade it.

The road collapsed beneath the watchmen. They screamed as claws tore at their legs and pulled them down into the ground. Slicked with blood, an enormous wolfkin led his pack out of the hole in the road.

Using the distraction to their advantage, wolfkin precipitated the demise of the front line, tearing through their victims with a trajectory leading toward Kylan and Scarlett.

Above the wolfkin, a brunette hovered. Her lustrous jade-green dress concealed little. The neckline of the tightly bound scales started at her navel. Her wafting slit skirt ended well above her knee. "Are those dragon scales?" Scarlett asked.

The Dreg raised a brown hunter's cap with a white feather to her head.

"Oh no," Kylan moaned. "That's Teague's cap! That's Beez!"

The vessel's pinched nose turned as two wolfkin slapped the cobblestones in a mad dash uphill, straight for Scarlett.

Kylan grabbed her arm and dragged her into an uphill run. They burst through quaint fences and trampled prized flower beds while keeping the wolfkin out of sight. The battle raged on in the screams of grown men.

Breaking through hedges, they found a street. Three buildings converged to block any direction but back downhill. "Can you hide us?" Kylan asked.

Scarlett gave a noncommittal whine but set about the attempt. Meekness darted like quicksilver through her grasp. Ignoring her heartbeat, she closed her eyes and took a deep breath to slow her thoughts. She snagged it.

Just as she began casting, Kylan asked, "Will they smell us even if they can't see us?"

Fear inundated the spell. They were visible when she finished. Kylan guffawed. Scarlett turned. Her face loomed in the sky, as large as a small cloud. She leaped about to be rid of the spell and saw herself panicking. It tracked her every flail.

Kylan scooped her up and slung her over his shoulder. He rushed downhill, back toward the wolfkin.

"What are you doing?" she shouted, clinging to the strap of her poultice bag.

"Don't struggle!" he said. "If this is wrong, at least I'll die with a smile on my face."

* * *

Close behind Rorry, Cord swam through panicked commoners and the heaped two-story homes pressing in on the narrow streets of Llandir's Southern District. Scarlett's mother had sorted their group out in short order, surprising Lord Gwirion by assuming control.

The noble never questioned her commands and now ran behind them with Andion in his arms, leaving the others free to attack if necessary. Cord had no trouble keeping an eye on them. Even in their panic, the crowds parted for the noble and stood in awe once they saw a pik in his arms. If it wouldn't have made them targets, Cord would've suggested they lead the way instead of Mrs. Hywel.

Two more eruptions had echoed since they'd begun searching the docks for Scarlett and Kylan. Each time, Mrs. Hywel gave her bonnet a tug and waddled faster, swaying Kylan's scabbard with her gait.

Cord checked on Joseb behind him and spotted a familiar face. He balked, almost causing Joseb to run into him. Mrs. Hywel shouted back, but Cord could only stare at Marlone's grin in the crowd. When the dimples vanished, Marlone flipped the hood of his gray cloak up. In a blink, he blended into the crowd.

"No!" Cord yelled. He broke from the others and chased after him.

Rorry called for him as he got to the spot where Marlone had stood. Scanning the crowd, he didn't see the gray cloak running back up the street. Dashing to his right, he stepped around a corner in time to see Marlone slip out of sight at the base of a wide staircase cut into the hillside between two buildings.

The others caught up to Cord at the top of the stairs. "Did you see them?" Mrs. Hywel asked.

"It was Marlone," he said to Rorry. Her sympathetic frown didn't match her tone as she started a response intent on urging him away. He didn't have time for it.

As he chased after Marlone, commoners screamed and fled up

the stairs away from whatever occupied the tan-bricked square below. Slinging Kylan's britches over his shoulder, Joseb skipped steps and descended at Cord's side. A watchman's corpse crunched against an elm at the base of the stairs, bringing them all to a stop.

"Wait!" Mrs. Hywel ordered. She unsheathed the sword and moved to spy through the leaves of the elm into the square. Her form impressed Cord until she gaped and let her arm relax.

Preparing for the worst, Cord drew Veen's bow and leaped down by the watchman's body.

To his right, the scene in the square relaxed Cord's form too. Led by alphas, two scores of wolfkin snipped at a herd of townsfolk, corralling them up the massive staircase to the alabaster academe of Llandir. At the top, an immovable blockade of armored High Guard stood shoulder to shoulder. The heads of their war hammers glowed white.

The humans screamed for sanctuary, pleading to the soldiers' youthful faces pretending not to see them. Their shields and hammers denied entry to all. Three men were struck down when they shoved against the warriors. As a mother neared the top with her infant clutched to her breasts, the High Guard parted.

A young man stepped into the gap, barring her way. His prominent nose and red plate mail identified him to all. Cord stumbled forward a few steps, adrift between reverence and cold accusation when he realized the Chancellor carried a glass staff shaped into a clover bloom at the top. It was just as Mortin had described.

The Chancellor looked over the crowd kneeling and clamoring for protection. He clinched the stem, igniting a white beacon inside, and raised it overhead. Blinking away his enthrallment, Cord reset his arrow. The commoners screamed, then instantly fell silent.

Wolfkin stepped back as bodies tumbled down the stairs to the bricks of the square.

Two Dregs rose into the air out of the throng of wolves. The one closest to Cord wore a heap of tattered black robes. It hovered for a moment, then turned its ragged hood toward him. A pocked leather mask, as gnarled with age as the Dreg's gray-skinned arms, concealed the lower half of his face. Inhuman eyes of solid black considered Cord for what felt like an eternity before they swept back to the Tribunal.

The other Dreg, in a healthy young man with jewelry encrusted forearms and britches of green scale, waited for the gray man's lead.

Lowering the clover end of his staff at them, the Chancellor yelled. "*Karnath unkarelle!*" Light burst from the clover in blinding arcs, burning away the flesh of the advancing wolfkin and the corpses on the stairs. The random arcs sliced cleanly without spilling blood.

Both Dregs launched through the air at the Chancellor. The eldest Dreg's cape trailed its tatters behind him. A woman wrapped in the same green scale flung herself at the Tribunal from the academe's bell tower.

Prince Rhyn righted his staff and drove the end of it into the stone at his feet.

"Hypocrite!" Cord shouted over the commotion. "You killed them!" Within a blink, Cord released the arrow aimed at his deity. A dome of light too bright to look upon encased the Tribunal. It vanished.

The High Guard, the Chancellor, half of the academe's doors, everything touched by the dome had disappeared, including the Dregs and Cord's arrow. The Dreg wearing the woman hadn't entered the dome fast enough. Wolfkin nuzzled the legs of the vessel on the steps before sniffing out the magic users behind them.

Cord roared as he released another arrow. The first wolfkin toppled. Only when pale skin appeared beneath its shedding fur did he search for Marlone again. Was he one of the wolves swarming them now? Had Marlone led him down here to see that?

Rorry's bolt struck one in the heart. Another pink-skinned man writhed.

"Save it for the Verdict Ring in Trône d'Argent!" Mrs. Hywel shouted. "They stand a better chance at delivering justice than you!"

Cord nocked another arrow. He released, striking a sand-colored beast between the eyes. As long as he avoided the darker ones, he might not hurt Marlone. He slid another arrow on his string and shot it.

Mrs. Hywel snatched his arm. "Run!" she ordered and shoved

Cord back up the stairs.

They all chased after Lord Gwirion.

Joseb gestured with his hands. The spell briefly burned the coat on a wolfkin's chest. Witnessing the worry in Rorry's eyes, the sorcerer grabbed her arm to keep her running upstairs. "It's just an abeyance. It shall pass once I feel like myself again."

"That's why sorcery is not an acceptable path for my daughter!" Mrs. Hywel panted. A few steps up, she spun and tugged free a pouch from behind her belt. Tossing it at the wolfkin, she said, "*Este gral.*" The pouch burst. Whirling into a dusty mass, the contents settled on two of the howlers, sealing them in glass. They shattered beneath their relentless brethren, stumbling over the obstacles on the stairs.

Steadying her crossbow, Rorry took aim. Cord gripped her wrist and towed her farther up the stairs. They wouldn't survive if they stood against this mass. Mrs. Hywel ran after. Their hunters were faster.

By the time they reached the top, Mrs. Hywel had fallen behind, within range of being taken down by one of the monsters' leaps. Cord had an arrow ready to guard her when the plump mage spun again. She raised her arms and splayed her fingers. Erupting bolts of lightning cascaded down the stairway. Several beasts stopped at the edge of the square. The prancing lights punched through the less fortunate as the spell continued to surge, even after she caught up to them.

"Speaking of hypocrisy," Joseb quipped, "were you not frugal enough with your little pouches?"

Her rude gesture told him where to go. "That spell doesn't last long. We can discuss the sanity of an amalgamation after we find my daughter, sorcerer."

"It's just lovely to see you acknowledge sorcery's practicality, Jean."

Farther down the street, flames engulfed the crammed row of homes. Smoke filled the air. The blaze swarmed quickly, sowing chaos.

Lord Gwirion's calls directed them toward the crowded bridge to the Northern District.

Glass shattered, causing Cord to swing his aim from covering

Lord Gwirion. Joseb had rammed his elbow through the window of a cordwainer's shop. The sorcerer pinched a pair of large boots with heels and tucked them under his arm.

"Petty crime, Joseb?" Mrs. Hywel shouted as they ran. "This is meant to embolden my faith in you as a mentor for my daughter?"

"You understand this," Joseb stated.

Rorry and her father stopped to stare at the sky.

Mrs. Hywel continued past Cord. "It's the only reason I'm letting you do it! If I had my wits about me, I'd—"

Mrs. Hywel clutched her shawl as her mouth fell open. In the sky, Scarlett's face hung in the clouds. Her wide eyes bounced, frustrated and terrified. A flash of orange appeared behind her head.

"Ah-ha!" Lord Gwirion shouted. "Ivy's Poisons has an orange door. They are in the retreats. Come quickly now!"

Chapter 55: A Stone Clever

Out of the corner of her eye, Scarlett saw her head bobbing in the sky. She'd tried everything to dispel the sight; well, everything she could while outrunning a crazed horror. She thrust herself up the street's incline faster each time Kylan checked behind him. His radishes wagged in a bundle tied at his belt. Curse that satyr!

The other wolves had been so preoccupied with the army's reinforcements that they hadn't paid the trouserless boy any attention as he had run by, never mind the girl slung over his shoulder. Perhaps the soldiers' blood covered the scent of her abilities to all but the exception wearing them down. Part of her wished Kylan was still carrying her. Her lungs burned.

Either Llandir was laid out very poorly, or Kylan had a knack for finding the ends of roads. Scarlett bent to catch her breath as he concluded the inevitable. Then she kept his pace and doubled back, regaining sight of the shaggy brown howler. The wolfkin barked a message back toward the battle before loping after them up a side alley.

"This feels wrong," Kylan said.

Scarlett didn't have the breath to ask what was supposed to feel right about it.

The beast closed in, a few hundred feet away now. Her legs wobbled.

Kylan's eyes weighed her. He fell behind and gave her a push. She whimpered but strode up the hill. He said, "Call Spectre and keep going!"

Of course! Why hadn't she thought of her steed? The hem of her dress was up to her thigh before she realized Kylan's boots weren't slapping the road behind her.

He had poised himself to face the cursed one, squatting into the stance her uncle had taught him. The wolfkin raced toward its prey.

Scarlett's emotions entangled with her exhaustion. She wouldn't leave him! Her mind listed the novice spells in *Essential Focus* as she released her dress. Her left hand opened her bag and removed Julian's golden dagger.

Within striking distance, the wolfkin pounced. Kylan slumped his right shoulder and attempted to roll the attack, but he'd misjudged the wolf's agility. An effortless swipe of its paw knocked Kylan to the cobblestones.

Red circles grew on Kylan's sleeve and chest.

Drool streamed over the cursed one's black lips. On all fours, the beast settled its weight on its haunches and prepared to strike.

Scarlett wanted to scream. Opening herself, her mind swam through her wants, overwhelming her decision with fear. Like a twister, the core of her ability struck her. It swirled through her, filling her insides with warmth and her mind with power before spiraling out of her reach. The sensation startled her and left a warm enigma throbbing in her right palm.

A silky oval of clear skin no larger than a butterbean confined a yellow light within. Its jellylike innards condensed with her squeeze and darkened to orange. The heat intensified. Pulsating faster, the thin membrane threatened to burst. Scarlett flung it away. It ruptured in the air, emitting a blaring screech and broad flares of golden light.

Its beams punched through the wolf's head, waist, and leg; but they also penetrated the ground at Scarlett's feet, the blade of the dagger, a sapling next to her, and every window across the street. Chips of glass showered over her and Kylan as a headless, mangled body fell where the beast had stood. Screams and murmurs poured out of the buildings.

Kylan rose slowly and surveyed the damage her errant spell had caused to the dwarven constructs. "Well, that was something," he said.

Scarlett stepped back from the chasm at her toes. "Something I will never do again," she said, as though she'd meant to do it in the first place. Bumps formed on her skin at the very notion.

With the golden handle of the now bladeless dagger stowed in her bag, she ran her fingers through her hair and gave a good jostle to work out any glass.

Composed again, Scarlett avoided looking at her oversized nose in the clouds. She was certainly leaving her mark on Llandir.

From the hill's vantage, she saw smoke consuming the Southern District. One of the tendrils started at the Ale and Pumpkin. Her mum would never forgive her for this. And she would see Scarlett's spell in the sky. The skin on her bum burned just thinking about it. Scarlett blew air through her lips.

Kylan rounded the bottomless hole her spell had created and got her moving. He clutched his wounded arm as they dashed farther uphill into the bowels of this strange retreat for the privileged.

They hustled under a banner that read: *Welcome to the Gilded Lavender, Home of Llandir's Hot Springs!*

The ancient buildings purpled the higher they climbed. Veins in the ore deepened to plum. Every post, balcony, and window had a dyed ribbon or some other affronting nonsense tied to it. Gold cushions covered the benches left exposed to the elements. How did people live like this? What a waste of dye!

The road leveled at the crest and rounded to a finish in a garden of tidy foliage and life-sized Trinity game boards full of opposing tiles: onyx orbs, jade trefoils, and red jasper dragon tails. Above them, curtains fell into place along the private balconies as she and Kylan explored.

He snickered at her face next to the sun before his expression soured. "What is that ungodly stench?"

They wouldn't empty chamber pots into the street at a place like this. No, she knew that scent somehow. The rotten egg odor brought her mind back to the cabinet in her uncle's armory, to a yellow substance in her mum's joint balm. Through her sleeve, Scarlett answered, "Sulfur."

Admiring a long pool, Scarlett's eyes traced the water up the back of a curved golden sculpture leaning against the Gilded Lavender. The water trickled out of an orb-shaped waterspout in the courtyard above. She drew closer and moved to its side. The sculpture's two golden legs were planted in the ground, creating archways.

With the waterspout as a head, it could resemble a hunched person. Wind fluttered the flags on the balconies and knocked a cloud of steam between the sculpture's legs. Scarlett gasped. "You lucky bastard." She charged toward the mist.

Beneath the crooked man, sulfurous vapors whisked upward through a grate surrounded by lilac slabs. The slabs led to stairs curving downward. Scarlett and Kylan spiraled into the burrowed hole. She reveled in the hot, humid air, all the while salivating over the possibilities of this "new world" Ferix had promised. Was it a dwarven city? If so, they'd be the first humans to see it since the elves had disappeared.

The tunnel bored into the mountainside and dumped them into a vacant cavern. To Scarlett's left, forgotten oil lamps burned dimly between cushions arranged for lounging. Steaming springs fed five pools in the cavern. Towels had been folded into triangles and stacked high on tables next to each. Scarlett stepped onto the woven mats creating a pathway and examined the painted folding screens spanning the right wall.

Something rustled behind them. Kylan jerked the panel aside.

"Please, please do not kill me!" a stocky man yelled, clutching a towel around his waist.

Grinning, Kylan said, "Sure. Go on. Take shelter."

As the man bowed and nearly lost his towel, Scarlett spied the top of a door beyond the last steaming pool. She swept under the bars of light from the grates above to see where it led.

When Kylan caught up to her, he whispered in her ear, "And we should find Rorry and Cord. We can all search for the answer, now that we know where to look."

Scarlett nodded but opened the door anyway. From the landing inside the room, her eyes devoured every detail as the darkness lessened its hold. A simple brass railing descended three steps into the rock-walled room, no larger than their chamber at the inn. Littered with barrels and upended crates, the storage room didn't align with any of her imagined scenarios. She sighed. None of it interested her besides a jar.

"We should go," Kylan said. "I'd hate for us to keep this stench to ourselves. Burn Ferix. He's probably laughing his tail off right now."

A high-pitched squeal sounded behind them. At the exit to the stairs, the stocky man went limp under a wolfkin's bite. Its teeth squeezed blood from his chest. Golden eyes locked on to them, but the beast let his bite take hold to spread the curse. The man jerked violently as the liquid drained, thick and oozing.

Kylan's unnecessary assistance carried Scarlett into the storage room. She sped down the steps, scooped up the jar, and tried to concentrate on passion. Julian wasn't going to work anymore.

He slammed the door, killing the light. "The spell must still be following you!"

"Please be silent," she said evenly. Scarlett put the jar down and stomped an empty crate. The moist wood didn't break easily. Working a board free, she set it aflame.

The door lurched in, then banged shut as Kylan threw his weight against it. He lodged the heel of his boot into the railing for extra support. "There's a way to bar the door!"

Two iron ells were sunk into opposite sides of the frame. "Why would they need that in a storage room?"

"Scarlett!" Kylan shouted.

She scampered to find something to slip into the narrow space. In a manic search, she cast aside everything she could lift with one arm. The frenzy paid off. Three stacked cauldrons towered over their spits in the corner. When she bent to collect the spits, she noticed something peculiar. On the dusty floor, a U-shaped outline presented itself in the torchlight.

"He was here; Ferix was," she said excitedly.

Kylan grunted and squirmed. "Hurry!"

Through the crack behind him, a golden eye narrowed on her. Disappearing again, their attacker pounded against Kylan's resistance.

The metal rods were too heavy for her to carry more than one. She let two clatter back down and lifted the other over the rail. Kylan got it into the first slot. Lowering the other end, she forced it between him and the pounding. It clinked into place.

In half steps, Kylan moved away, cautiously watching their innovation with each test of the wolfkin's strength. "Thank the gods for oak," he said.

Hurrying back to the evidence, she lowered her smoking torch, little more than a couple of flames now.

Kylan didn't budge from the landing. "Can you tell how he got out?"

"Through the door. I'm trying to figure out how he got in." Shoving a barrel aside, she tracked the satyr's marks. Where the floor met the wall, half of a hoofprint protruded from solid stone. "This is it! There must be a secret entrance, like to my uncle's armory."

Visibly torn between joining her search for a latch and guarding the door, Kylan took one step down. "Do you see how it opens?"

She scooted a few crates out of the way and, between the wolfkin's slams, rapped the wall. The wooden ceiling offered no solutions, though she did lower her crude torch.

Kylan said, "It might be like the stumps. Put your hand on it."

"Ferix wasn't a magus. If he were, the Hook wouldn't have been able to hold him," she explained.

The thudding stopped. Sniffs whispered from the cavern. A howl ruptured the silence, propelling Kylan to her side. "He's calling for help!"

Scarlett pinched her bottom lip. "If the dwarves built this doorway," she thought aloud, "they wouldn't have used magic. The talent was rarer in them than in humans. None of this wood is old enough to have existed at that time, only the stone. Perhaps the trigger is just hidden."

The wolfkin battered the oak again. Scratching preceded more calls. Two hunters howled now.

Kylan rummaged through the clutter. "Even if we find it, how will we save Cord and Rorry?" Growling in frustration, he kicked the wall concealing their exit. Something clacked and began to grind. A sliver of shadow appeared by the ceiling as a section of the wall scraped the stone on a slow descent into the floor. "Did that really work?"

The wolfkin continued their bombardment, warping the iron ells. Scarlett whined and shook her hand in the air. The slab sank at an excruciating rate.

Kylan retrieved one of the spits and stood between her and the landing.

A yelp interrupted the howls, then came a gurgle. Chortles barked and ended incomplete.

The wall had sunk half a foot now. She listened for something beyond the agonizing grind.

The spit rattled against the ells again. Kylan swept her toward the wall, as though he planned to stuff her through the minuscule gap. A shining arc cut through the door, chimed against the spit, and split it in half. Both pieces clanged to the landing.

Scarlett didn't trust her abilities but readied to throw her torch.

The door opened. A gore-covered katana breeched the entry. Her mum held it. Clasping at the air repeatedly, she beckoned Scarlett. The katana slid atop a barrel as Scarlett handed Kylan the torch.

Scarlett buried her face in her mum's woolen shawl, ignoring everything beyond the solace as she rambled apologies.

"A bit drafty in this town for that kind of display, wouldn't you say?" Joseb asked Kylan. "Fancy a pair of trousers?"

Scarlett beamed at her mentor, until she remembered she had abandoned him while he'd fought with her mum on her behalf. He twitched his nose at her and smiled before throwing Kylan his britches. The sorcerer looked quite handsome, despite his outfit befitting a Merithian farmer.

"We need to find Rorry," Scarlett said to her mum.

"I am here," Rorry said from behind Joseb. She and Cord entered. Kylan swooped Rorry off her feet, spinning her around. She giggled, still wearing Carolle's leathers, now bloodied. What had happened with Julian?

There was no joy in Cord's eyes. His chiseled jaw tensed relentlessly. He put the arrow in his hand back in his quiver, rather than acknowledging Kylan.

Scarlett curtsied as Lord Gwirion came down the stairs after them. Andion lay cradled in his arms.

Lord Gwirion responded to Kylan's bow with a simple, "Son." Then he examined the descending portal. Having fallen as low as the top of Scarlett's head, it held her mum's interest as well. His Grace passed Andion over to Cord.

Frowning at the pik, Kylan asked, "What happened?"

Cord repositioned Andion. "I think he lied about the dangers of taking humans through shadows."

That sparked Scarlett's curiosity. "That's how you got into Llandir?"

Kylan whistled soundlessly. "That's a bit daring for you," he said, impressed. Cord coldly shrugged it off. "Thanks for bringing Rorry back."

"Who said I needed him to?" Rorry asked and backhanded Kylan's chest. He winced and sucked in air through his teeth, causing her to cover her mouth daintily.

Staring at Kylan's chest, Cord said matter-of-factly, "You're injured."

"It can keep," Kylan replied, raising both hands, "at least until we're on the other side of this trial of patience."

"Where does it lead?" Lord Gwirion asked.

"And how did you ever find it?" Joseb added.

"It should take us under the Gallaic Channel to the continent," Kylan said. Quieter, he admitted, "Ferix told me about it."

"Who?" her mum asked.

"A satyr," Joseb said.

Her mum blinked several times as the answer settled in.

Lord Gwirion shot Rorry a worried look. "This is not a dragon's favor, is it?"

"No, Your Grace," Kylan said. "He told me out of gratitude, not in exchange. I set him free first." Cord sneered at him. "There was no point in him dying with the rest of us, if it came to that."

Her mum shook her head. "This is the leadership you followed across the country?" she asked Scarlett. "'Dying with the rest of us'?"

Less oblivious to her mum's manipulations than her friends believed, Scarlett forgave it. Her mum wasn't privy to all of the revelations, or even the incitements, of their journey, nor did she need to be.

"You did the right thing," Joseb said. "If the Hook needs to correct it, it shall be on us later. And call me Joseb, now." He held out a hand. "We haven't been accurately introduced."

Without a second thought, Kylan shook. "I know. Of course, there will be questions later. And, yes, they may get uncomfortable."

Lord Gwirion cleared his throat.

"Saucy," her mum reprimanded. "You've got your work cut out with that one, Joseb."

The sorcerer grunted a laugh and sat on the steps. He unbuckled a pair of leather boots with shorter heels than she would have expected for him.

"Can you run in those?" Kylan asked, thrusting a leg into his trousers. "We saw a Dreg. Beez, I think. He may come after us."

"I was born in heels," the sorcerer said. Slipping his ankle in, he tugged the boot up to just below his knee. "They're a bit snug, but they'll do for now."

"We saw Dregs too," Rorry said. "And the Chancellor."

Cord turned his back to them. Kylan raised his eyebrow for Scarlett.

Scarlett reached through the silence to the tool she had given up on earlier. Her ring clinked against the glass. Caressing the jar against her chest, Scarlett explored. What did it matter if he was so much older than she? No one else needed to know what fodder she used to feed her emotions, especially that one. The glass shone green.

She held the jar out to her mum, who pressed it back. "You are all the light I'll need," her mum said, smiling as proudly as Joseb at the conjured green flame. Tears gathered in the deep lines around her eyes. Her blanched hair poked out of the faded bonnet. When had age taken her this far?

"In lieu of castigation," Joseb said, "Jean has agreed to surrender you to my supervision until you reach the Tower. I believe this seals that pact?"

Her mum's hands rubbed Scarlett's cheeks and kept her mouth closed. "I've left an inn full of people seeking salvation. My charges need protection. They wouldn't be there if it weren't for me. I promise I shall fell anyone in my path, pea."

"We both will," Lord Gwirion said, rubbing Rorry's shoulder.

"No!" Rorry said. "Absolutely not! You saw what the city is like. Neither of you are going back out there."

"Brewing needs me," he said. "My place is at your mother's side. I will not leave her all alone to face this, not by my choice."

Something had changed indeed. Rorry shook her head as she buried her face into her father's doublet and appeared genuinely pained.

To Kylan, Lord Gwirion said, "I will inform Wil and Kit that you are well." He tousled Kylan's hair like he had since he was a little boy. "If I can find them, I will collect Ellick and Seamus on my way home. We could use your brothers right now." He grinned. "I never thought I would say that."

Kylan laughed.

Crushing Rorry against him, Lord Gwirion whispered, "I love you, Rorry. Find Alis. Tell her that we love her and that we think of her every day." He stroked her hair and swayed with her. "Do not worry for us. Jean and I know the shortcuts and secrets of Llandir like the backs of our hands. We will be in the wilds shortly."

Scarlett clung to her mum. "Don't worry about that spell following you around," she told Scarlett. "I took care of it. He should have started your lessons there. Undoing magic is just as important as casting it. Find the erudite mentor you deserve in the Tower, pea. They'll never deny someone as strong as you." Her mouth twitched as though she wanted to say more. But her wave brought Kylan and Rorry to them as Lord Gwirion shook Joseb's hand.

The portal clicked behind the huddle, revealing a tunnel as dark as pitch. Instantly, the grinding returned, shrinking the opening. Holding out Spectre's coin, Scarlett said, "Take this. Give Papa my love. And please tell Uncle Barrey we are sorry for taking his weapons."

The statement prompted Rorry to hand the crossbow to her father.

Her mum laughed. "So that's where Spectre went."

"Is that a beast coin of Yacille?" Joseb asked. He admonished her mum with a glare. "Stolen from the Tower?"

"You hush!" her mum said. Joseb adopted a broad smile when her mum turned back to her. "It's a long walk from Brewing to Llandir, thank you very much. Luckily, Darren found me before I had made it too far. Still, I shall have to rest for a week before my hip forgives me." She kept her eyes on Scarlett as she took the token, smiling through her frustration. "Don't fret about Barrey, pea. He never wanted this life for you. One year, he had me half convinced he was going to take the lot of you out of Merith himself."

Scarlett said nothing, burning her mum's image into her mind, even her ghastly nose. Her chest ached from the effort of holding her breath steady. She had to appear strong for her mum's sake. Her lips betrayed her first. It was a nice sentiment at least.

One by one, the others stepped into the darkness. Her mum removed her shawl and bundled the warmth around Scarlett's shoulders. "Go on, now. I love you and am so proud, pea." She kissed Scarlett's cheek.

Lord Gwirion kissed his fingertips and waved to Rorry. "Brewing is proud of each of you. Know that you are always welcome home. Same for you, Cord."

The darkness shied away from the green light as Scarlett took her place next to Rorry. She turned to watch her mother's face as the cleaver rose, cutting her off. Twice, she tried to step back into the room to return home, but her legs didn't move. Her mum had put Scarlett's safety and wishes first. Bless her.

When the wall resealed, Kylan rubbed Scarlett's shoulders. An attempt to thank them for waiting came out in a strange whimper. Rorry held her close as they braved the satyr's passage and descended into the darkness.

After walking in the green light for a while, Joseb asked, "Why do you have radishes?"

Chapter 56: Snake Eyes in Your Future

Lagging behind the circle of green light, Cord listened as the others discussed the night's events and traveled down the steep passage toward whatever trap the satyr had planned. After confessing he had lost his temper while arguing with Bevin, the sorcerer asked questions about alphas and Carolle's plan, none of which they could answer. Rorry suggested ways Kylan could've retained Ferix as a prisoner but let the argument go when Kylan asked where they'd be if he had. Certainly not wandering through a disused cavern under the sea. All the while, Andion slept in Cord's arms.

The temptation to cheer up Scarlett by nudging her with Andion's foot disappeared again. He didn't mind sharing the misery right then.

Rorry had worked things out with her father, to the extent that she didn't have to run. Neither did Scarlett, who had received the blessing of her domineering mother to go. Cord suspected Lord Gwirion had even worked out some deal to keep the watchmen off Kylan's back if he was caught with his hand down some nobleman's pants.

Yet Cord had been forsaken. His deity, who had received his prayers before every meal, was just a man. No, the *murderer* of Kenton. Each time he remembered defending the Chancellor, it shamed him. How long before his friends began their teasing and smirks? They must have thought he was so simple for believing in a spoiled prince who used his people to fuel his magic.

Was that what Marlone had wanted him to see? Cord's whole body felt feverish. So he kept his mouth shut and held the other orphan against him.

Bevin's resurrection and Julian's demise brought a smile to Scarlett's face. A part of Cord was thankful for that as he pondered the green flame in her hands.

"We chased after Marlone but found the Chancellor and the High Guard," Rorry said. "Lady Katrin was correct."

Kylan gave Cord a sidelong glance. Cord warned him off the topic with a glower that promised a fight. The sickness festered inside of Cord. If Kylan gloated, that sickness might send them all to their knees. Instead, Kylan gave him a sympathetic nod.

Cord's harsh tone echoed when he asked, "And what about you, 'Maeverly'? You lied to us too."

"It was dishonest," the sorcerer answered, "to you and to me."

As Joseb explained, Cord only half heard the excuses, still absorbed in what he'd witnessed outside Llandir's academe. He had been a fool. A simple fool. Poor Headmaster Angsly. He hoped he hadn't seen the truth of the Chancellor's Light before he'd died.

Joseb slowed, bringing Cord back into the conversation. "In your shoes, most would agree to save the magus," the sorcerer said to Kylan. "Although I'm afraid my efficacy is greatly reduced at the moment, heels notwithstanding."

"Oh!" Kylan said. "I tucked this away to protect it." He sat next to a ring of dingy mushrooms and removed his boot. After digging around inside it, he plucked free a vial of slimy flesh.

Swiping it from his hand, Rorry scolded, "Kylan Nock! You have been running around with basilisk venom in your boot?" Only rewarded with a shrug, she sighed through her nose and slipped the vial into her satchel.

Kylan pulled out a thin stick.

Joseb's mouth fell open before he smiled. "You . . ." He cleared his throat and caressed the stick. "You have no idea what this means to me. I dared not dream I'd see it again. Years—*years* of searching. I thought I'd cost myself . . ." He cleared his throat again. "You have my thanks. I'd say you've saved me twice."

"You're welcome," Kylan said. "Scarlett mentioned it was somehow a key to your power."

"Indeed, it is." A freshly lacquered red nail pointed to the rosewood-handled dagger in Andion's belt. "May I?" he asked Cord. Rorry retrieved the weapon and gave it over. "That's the reason I had to uphold that specious charade." Joseb burnished the blade on his sleeve and moved closer to the jar. Using the metal as a mirror, he went about drawing over his face.

Kylan giggled first, followed by Rorry. Cord refused the silly infection, even when Scarlett succumbed behind her hand.

Joseb scoffed and said, "I had you all fooled, and you know it. And before any of you feel compelled to ask, I invite women to my bedchamber." That elicited more laughter. Outlining his eye, Joseb grinned broadly. "Juveniles."

"The Hook got their answer, Joseb," Rorry said. "What now?"

"Pray the Dregs haven't obviated our task by slaying the innocents. Once we're in Trône d'Argent, Remy shall handle it. We've all seen enough to take it to the Verdict Ring in Racine or even to the Luminary of the Bonded Nations, depending on whom our secretive benefactor actually is."

He outlined his eye to a point and began coloring his eyelids. "The Bonded Nations should never have let this continue for so long, but coin speaks the loudest in the rest of Cyr. For all the rumors of oppression, none of them included riches to be had. They used the lack of evidence as a convenient excuse not to get involved. They share the opprobrium in that regard."

Scarlett released her bottom lip and said, "That doesn't explain why the Dregs are interested in Merith. One Dreg surely could have gotten to the Chancellor, if they were after him."

The sorcerer stopped his preening and looked at Cord with sympathy. "That clover staff the prince wields is unknown to me but likely their target. Given the source of its power, I'd wager my life on it." He resumed coloring his face with determination and a rumble in his voice. "The Tribunal must have known the Dregs were coming. That's why they harvested the lives of so many villages to fuel it. Powered to such a degree, who knows where its limits fall? Teleportation, immortality, and that trick with the light slicing through everything it touched. But why not just absorb the souls of the Dregs and the cursed ones, I wonder?" He shook his head. "I may have answered my own question."

"Right," Kylan said. "Veen mentioned magic is fading elsewhere on Cyr, but Merith isn't affected. If the Dregs want magic, that could be why they came, couldn't it?"

Rorry laughed. "Merith has no magic."

Joseb grunted softly and put the stick to his lips. "That's what most assumed, myself included. Yet since arriving, I've witnessed a staff with more power than any artifact in the Towers' galleries, a satyr, and a young lady stronger in the arts than any I have met." He winked at Scarlett. "That golem would suggest there's another." He pointed to Cord. "And an unknown talent." Then his finger lowered to Andion. "And a race's lost aptitude.

"Merith has been weeding out magic for centuries, but Shallyghal still permeates. I see now that it's more like searching for water in a desert. You just have to know where to look. More curiosities are surely hidden about."

Scarlett thumbed the blue ring that had started Cord's familiarity with magic and the cruelty the Tribunal had placed around it. His jaw ached.

Gazing into the dagger's reflection, Joseb said, "That's a bit slapdash, but it shall have to do." More jarring than a branded man, the painted sorcerer handed the dagger back to Rorry and continued his lecture as they walked. "Merith's leadership violates a lot of axioms: slavery, tyrants owning their subjects, and the like. You'd have to sail to the Yaltec Sea to find those antiquated beliefs upheld. It's remarkable how they've deceived everyone for so long."

"Yeah," Cord said. "There's a lot of lying going on around here. Remarkable." His friends seemed more affronted than the sorcerer. "What? None of this matters if we die. How long before Beez's hounds sniff us out?"

Their silence prompted him to act. He dropped Veen's bow and forced Andion into Rorry's arms.

"Hey!" Kylan yelled. When he bent to pick up the bow, Cord seized his head.

"Wait!" Joseb yelled. "Don't weaken yourself!"

Beyond the trance, Cord heard the words but didn't care. His anger fought the delving, reducing the healing chill to a steady trickle. Once the light in Kylan's wounds had extinguished, Cord released him. They both fell to the stone.

Cord remained seated for a moment. He ground his teeth together to stifle a yawn.

Vexed, Rorry said, "Explain."

He stood to answer. "Kylan oughta protect Andion while I keep Veen's bow ready." She huffed. "All right! Maybe I don't trust Joseb to do it. Is that what you want to hear?"

"You can," Joseb said.

"And we do," Rorry assured him. "Cord, if you believed us so weak that we could not carry Andion, Scarlett and I can use a bow."

"Bah," Kylan said, taking the pik from Rorry. "I like him like this. He's far more tolerable. No biting, less squeaking."

Waving off the awkwardness, Joseb asked, "How far do you suppose we have to go?"

Scarlett frowned at Cord before tailing the man's clacking heels with the light source in her hands. "Llandir is on the peninsula closest to Racine. Maybe twenty miles?"

With this much uncertainty and the blighted satyr at the root of it, they ought to have understood why he should be armed. If he had anything of himself left, he was still a soldier.

The tunnel leveled when the walls drifted out of range of the lantern's light. The sensation reminded Cord of his dream. Gathering closer, they marched on.

Something blue shone in the distance. Cord nocked his arrow, ready for the satyr's trap.

As they neared the opening to another cave, Joseb insisted on entering first. The sorcerer crept inside. He turned about, lost in thought, and waved the others forward.

Like in Cord's dream, colorful crystals grew out of stone pillars around the small cavern. However, these crystals matched the light they cast on the walls, and there was no exit. They were trapped!

Cord ran his hand over the seamless stone that hadn't appeared in his dream. "This shouldn't be here."

"What?" Rorry asked.

"I dreamed of this." They waited for an explanation. "Visions come to me after I mend others. That's how I knew about the stumps. But the crystals are different, and this wall . . . there should be a passage."

They didn't seem to know what to make of that.

Joseb was about to say something when Kylan kicked the wall where Cord pointed, prompting the sorcerer to ask, "What exactly do you hope to accomplish?"

Kylan shrugged. "It worked before."

Scarlett hummed. "You said the crystals are different? How so?"

Rorry waved a hand over a set of gem spikes, as blue as a robin's egg.

"The colors are wrong," Cord answered, tapping an orange crystal with the bow. "In my dream, the light they cast was different from the crystals."

Rorry jerked her hand back. "Wait!" she said, leaning closer over the blues. "Something moved. Cord, do that again." As he moved the bow closer to the orange cluster, its shadow penetrated the light behind the blues. Rorry swept her hand behind the glowing gems. Her shadow didn't interrupt the light.

Scarlett studied the other clusters and pointed to the red spikes. "There!"

Rorry's shadow flickered on the wall.

"I've seen something similar to this," the sorcerer said, "on the Isle of Agramead." He gripped the blue cluster and tried to turn them. The top of the pillar rotated. With a heave, Joseb lifted it. Rorry helped him. Iron stuck out of the bottom of the stone base, toothed like an arm-length key.

Scarlett and Cord lifted the reds. Gently, they settled the blue crystals into their mismatched aura and spun them. The base clicked. Within the wall, something rolled.

A small explosion echoed down the passage they had taken. "That wasn't us," Joseb said. "Hurry!"

Kylan laid Andion aside and grabbed his own cluster as they lugged the heavy crystals to their auras.

After doing the same with six more, they exchanged glances when nothing happened. The exit remained sealed. But the colors matched their position in his dream. He was sure of it!

Barks sent Cord's pulse racing. He growled, "Why isn't it working?"

"Perhaps they must be turned in a certain order?" Joseb asked.

"If you wished to stay in my foyer," a voice rasped, "why did you knock?"

Scarlett gasped. Cord spun and aimed his arrow.

Where the wall had been seconds before, a snakelike green man filled the opening, balancing on his coiled tail. The creature clacked his curved talons on the scales of his torso. Green scales covered all of him except for his human-shaped face, where white scales formed an oval from his chin to his crown.

Kylan picked up Andion and stepped away from him.

In the middle of the snake's black eyes, fiery yellow slits thinned on the pair. "I smelled your payment." His forked tongue darted as he spoke. "You took your time in delivering it. Luckily for you, time does not see me. Come." He slithered back down the opened tunnel and waved with his long scale-plated hands for them to follow.

The sorcerer led the way. Cord refused to let the others pass him.

They clung together as they entered the small chamber that had been empty in Cord's dream. Now bowls, candlesticks, and cutlery—anything one might want in gold—lay mounded on laden shelves and bulged from recesses. Three braziers hung from rafters, providing the light reflecting from every nook and cranny.

Winding himself on a pallet of fringed rugs, the snake braved a fanged smile at Cord's arrow. "It will break." Cord briefly debated a retort about how strong his eyes must be but let it pass and eased the tension on the string. "The radishes go there." A claw pointed to a set of balances on a table at the end of the room. White sand weighed down one dish, causing the other to dangle high above it.

Kylan removed the bundle of red roots from his belt and placed them on the scale's empty dish. It settled lower than the sand.

"Ah," the snake moaned. "You brought enough for questions. Lovely. Your fortune I can sift, if you wish it."

"Who are you?" Joseb asked.

Amused, the snake eyed him. "Is that the answer you seek? Many have found their demise in pursuit of the treasures I can give, though none planned to ask about me."

Joseb nodded.

"Then bring me a radish."

The sorcerer mulled it over and silently consulted Scarlett, who shrugged.

Cord looked for the exit and found it sealed, once again. "Forget that. How do we get to the continent?"

In an exaggerated gesture, the slits of the creature's eyes slid toward the radishes. Kylan plucked one from the dish. The plate lifted, still well below its sand-filled twin. He chucked it to Cord.

Outstretching a hand longer than Cord's forearm, the snake lazily waited. When Cord dropped the payment onto the sheen of his palm, his fingers sprung, stabbing the radish with their talons. Moans filled the room as the creature kissed the root and caressed his face with it. He took a nibble, then devoured it. Swaying, his body paled from green to fully white. Lost in ecstasy, he answered, "You ask me to open the door for you."

"That was helpful," Kylan muttered.

A howl echoed out of the tunnels behind them. "They are close!" Rorry said. "Will you open the door?"

The snake lay over his tail and, without looking at them, offered his palm again. Kylan threw Rorry a radish, which she laid on the greening palm.

After rubbing the radish on his lips, the snake paused. His black eyes reopened. The yellow of his pupils had turned red. "I see you clearly now, creatures. The assassin sent you my way. Yes, very important to you," he said to Kylan. "Is he off to pluck the strings some more?"

"Open the door!" Cord yelled. "We're being hunted!"

The snake grinned at him, amused at his discomfort. The radish disappeared behind his spiky teeth. After moaning, he said to Scarlett, "You know your spark. But have you explored the flame? Why does it burn so hot?" She took a step closer to Joseb, placing him before the red slits. Choking laughs put Joseb's shoulders back. "Boasting of confidence does not make one confident, sorcerer. You know your triggers but run from yourself."

Barks and yips echoed closer now. "Open the way out!" Cord commanded.

The reds of the creature's black orbs whipped to him, then to Rorry. "When power lands in your hands, will you trap it or trust it to come back to you? Yes, trust . . . it does not fill your heart."

"Open it!" Cord yelled. He drew the arrow and held it a few feet from the eye wandering over him.

Again, the snake ignored him, entranced in what he saw around them. "And chaos," he said to Kylan. "The ring marks you so. How selfish it can be. Which will break first, your leash or your spirit?"

The scales on his face aligned in a frown when he finally looked down Cord's arrow. "Can you murder? Are you capable of the greater good? Your grandfather would disapprove."

Cord blinked at the snake. Grandfather?

"Oh yes. I knew him," he hissed. "Are you sure you want me to open that door, *Tek'aran?* I could tell you more."

What did this monster know of that title? "Enough!" Cord shouted. "Only evil calls me that, you son of a bitch." He released the arrow. It clinked against the snake's eye, sparking like flint.

He cackled. "I tell you and you do not hear," the snake said. "My mother . . . Your 'god' murdered her. Not a princely thing to do. That vile child has stolen life from his own kind for centuries, *Tek'aran*. Are you sure you are capable of spotting evil?"

The creature croaked before Cord tasted the bitterness. As the snake writhed, his scales sloughed in patches. He hissed and flushed back to green. Then his tail jerked upward, curled around a rafter, and lifted him away from Cord.

"You!" he coughed. "*Tek'fera'aran!* You have brought them here! Does the satyr wish me undone?" The wall jolted open. "Go! A sea of radishes to be rid of you! Rush to your suffering and never return!"

Cord didn't take his eyes off the horror until he snatched a radish from the air. The balance evened behind Kylan.

"You have our thanks," Kylan said.

Rorry gripped Cord's wrist and pulled him into the passage. They were no farther than three feet inside when it resealed with a crash.

"What was he?" Scarlett asked.

"Later," Joseb said, taking the lead again. "Make haste!"

Chapter 57: Dare to Dream

Cord's sandals slapped ahead, chasing the edge of the green light down the tunnel. The stinging wound he'd taken from Kylan, the embarrassment of his hubris, the fear of facing a new life abroad, nothing could be felt beyond the anger the snake had stoked. Joseb called for him to slow. But Cord knew what lay ahead, a door to sanctuary.

He plowed into the darkness. A sticky thread snagged his chin, jerking him back with a painful snare.

Joseb's hand blazed, shriveling the wafts of spider silk. He shoved Cord behind him.

Picking off the remnants of the web from his face, Cord spit. He'd been lucky. The green light glistened down a barrier of webbing clogging the entire tunnel a few feet ahead.

"I was afraid of this," the sorcerer said. "We've disturbed their web; they may know we're here. Be on your guard—and for the gods' sake, watch the ceiling."

Joseb brushed back his sleeves, thrust his palms out, and blasted the webbing with a stream of flames. Heat devoured the snares, releasing a wind carrying the sickly sweet scent of decay. The sorcerer put a heel down over the drifting white tendrils and set a rhythm to his flares, providing shocks of visibility beyond the ring of green light.

The room with the giant door in Cord's dream had been slathered in white. Enough layers of gossamer encased the crystal column in the center to darken it.

The nest stuck to Joseb's feet. He lowered his aim and created a puddle of flames. It swam away from them, cleaning a random path and fanning out to clear more. As the flames roamed, the light remained steady. "The Tower can't teach you that spell either. You have to travel to find the real treasures."

Again, variations to Cord's dream presented themselves. Dark openings led off from the chamber in several directions, most higher than a man could reach.

Heeding Joseb's warning, Cord raised the tip of his arrow toward the ceiling. Large holes interrupted the webbing above them, not more than twenty feet high. A cocoon, larger than two horses, dangled amid a trio of man-sized ones in the corner. Nothing moved.

Cord stepped lightly onto the cleared path and made his way toward the crystal pillar.

Rorry put her hand to the clean floor. "This is malachite and azurite." Lines of gold angled through the stone for a pattern still too concealed for Cord to make out fully. "What is this chamber?"

"If I had my guess," Joseb answered, "we're near more dwarven ruins. Possibly a city!"

Two hound-sized spiders lay dead in the center of the chamber. Eight hairy black legs curled over the bellies of their carcasses. "Cistern spiders," Joseb said. Something had bored a hole into the head of each. "Babies. I'd wager this is Ferix's work. Their poison is more potent when they're small." Raising his gaze again, he said, "Keep an eye out for the mother or for any more of the brood."

Everyone jumped when the fiery puddle dissolved, reducing the light to Scarlett's jar. Joseb created more flares, removing some of the webbing from the column. Slowly it began to shine on the white cavern well enough for them to resume their exploration.

Cord crept along the cleared path and studied the walls as he moved to where the door had been. The spider silk covering an unexpected passage bulged from a breeze as he passed. He flinched and aimed. Nothing emerged.

After another flare from Joseb, Cord found what he sought. Nudging an arrow through to the stone, he scraped the webbing off a sunken handprint.

A rattling sound echoed through the chamber. A spider, as long as Scute and just as tall, fell from the ceiling across the room. Craggy spikes covered its shiny black back like a mound of stalagmites. It raised its two skinny front legs and scurried toward Cord.

Joseb extended the reach of his flames and scalded the side of the monster.

It flinched away from the heat, causing Cord's arrow to miss a beady eye. His arrow broke against its rocky hide.

"Aim for the underside of its abdomen—the back part," Joseb yelled.

Balancing on its side, the spider spewed a wave of white gunk from its end. The goo splashed into Joseb and Rorry, sealing them against the floor.

Cord took aim again. The arrow missed but sank into a leg and drew the beast's attention. He sprinted away from the others. Avoiding the webbing on the floor, he lured it away and loosed another shot.

The spider dodged but kept Cord straight ahead as it charged.

Kylan helped Rorry to her feet, while Scarlett worked to free Joseb from the bulk of the mess.

His plan to draw it off the others worked, but he'd cornered himself. Reaching down to his quiver, his fingers counted three arrows. With one of them fitted, he pulled the bowstring to his cheek. The agile creature skittered from side to side, making it impossible to target a specific weak spot. Cord aimed for its middle and released.

The spider hissed and leaped forward. Hairy legs jabbed at Cord. The tips of the front legs chipped away rock where they struck the wall. With Cord's back to the sealed door, the screeching spider lunged and gored the stone with its fangs as Cord rolled under the beast's belly.

He realized his mistake too late; two legs curled into him, stabbing a firm grip into his left leg. Crying out, he released Veen's bow.

Seizing his last two arrows, one in each hand, he prayed. Infuriated by the habit, he thrust the arrows into its underbelly, ripped them out, and stabbed again. Lost in memories of nights praying before the Idol, his defense of the Chancellor to Teague, to Kylan, to Rorry, to the ladies of Granville . . . he thrust harder. Liquid oozed from the spider's wounds, coating his forearms.

After he shouted at what his vow to avenge Kenton had become, water and blood gushed from the spider's skin.

The massive creature ripped free of its hold on Cord's leg and sidled. It crackled as it fell aside and curled to match the other remains.

Cord scooted away from it. Pustules and gaping sores had destroyed it more than his piercing had. Disgusted by the sight, he grunted. He endured the pain in his leg and hobbled toward the others. Sleep tried to seduce him.

Rorry ran to him and braced him with her shoulder as he tipped to collapse. Near the others, he sat on the floor and nodded his thanks when Rorry retrieved Veen's bow.

Kylan cradled Andion in his arms. "That was repulsive."

"Though effective," Joseb said.

"But repulsive," Kylan repeated. Cord followed Kylan's eyes down to the blood running over his calf. "And as much as we all appreciate your shorts, maybe it's time to put on some britches? For your own protection."

Flames ran over Scarlett's hand as she burned back the webbing on Joseb's boots. "Good, good," he said. "You're a very quick study."

"So, which passage do we take?" Kylan asked.

"None," Cord answered and pointed at the handprint.

Joseb got his heels under him and started burning away the webs obscuring the door.

Scarlett's lips twisted as she eyed the blood and gunk on Cord's tunic. "I would have helped, but I was afraid I would burn you."

Laughing, Cord said, "Then thanks for not helping."

A screech erupted from the tunnel they had come through. The wolves must've had as much patience for the snake man as Cord had. He got up with Rorry's help and joined Joseb at the door. Pointing to the three handprints, Cord said to Scarlett and Joseb, "I think this'll take all three of us." Grooves marked the stone where the light had run in Cord's dream, but there was no color to it now.

"Together," Cord said, holding his hand before the impression in the wall. They put their palms against the stone in unison. Their faith in Cord made him question these mysterious dreams. They hadn't led him astray yet.

Each handprint glowed with a white light. As the markings brightened, the wall colored the impressions under their hands. Purple ran up the lines from beneath Joseb's touch and outlined the doorway. Cord's shifted to blue, filling in the shape of a squat man with two raised axes.

Then the orange from Scarlett filled in a zigzag pattern around the inscribed dwarf and two lines of strange characters. "This is Feragarth," she translated. "Those who seek peace are welcome here."

A purple line divided the doorway at its middle. It split, drawing back from their hands without sound, not even so much as a grinding pebble. Dust and webbing showered over them.

As they brushed themselves off, Cord smiled at the familiar sight beyond. Stars twinkled on a flat ceiling that stretched out of sight into the natural cavern. More malachite and azurite covered the supporting beams between panels of the cosmos. White crystal columns lit the streets of the town fifty feet below, coloring the dusty mismatched buildings as well as daylight.

Working together, they shoved the doors closed behind them. The magic faded, resealing the wall to solid stone. "That may not keep them out long," Joseb said. He started their single-file descent down a narrow path of stairs, the only entry to the dwarven ruins of Feragarth.

"How crowded does the world have to be for people to want to live underground?" Kylan asked.

"To have heard the dwarves tell it," Joseb answered, "they were made of the stone. The divisions you see in the ceiling were left intentionally by the elves. Supposedly, dwarves were uncomfortable beneath the open sky and needed the reminder they were indoors."

Squares, diamonds, and hard angles ran along the patterns in the street and along the buildings. Few of the dwellings shared their shape. Fewer still had windows, all framed to resemble cut gemstones. The colorful panes of glass must've only been used for decoration.

The five humans marred a dense layer of dust with each step into the forgotten town. The road broadened, pushing the buildings back to leave room for a circle of purple, silver, and gold tiles. Each tile retained its luster, free from dust and tarnish. They formed the image of a silver-bearded dwarf dressed more in gems than cloth. With his arms spread wide, the dwarf wore a friendly smile.

"Helfarn's Plaza," Scarlett read from the script circling the mosaic.

At the edge of the circle, slivers of purple agate decorated the leaded backs of four dustless benches. They called to Cord. He tried to keep his mind off his exhaustion.

"Helfarn," Joseb said, "the god of the stone. One of them anyway. After seeing this, I'd suspect he was more the god of the gemstones than anything."

Staring down the road, Kylan moaned, "Oh no." Over the gorge ahead, a bridge had collapsed, leaving an expanse of open air between Helfarn's Plaza and the next section of town.

"That's strange," Joseb said. "Dwarven masonry is supposed to be as immortal as the elves. The rest of it has maintained its integrity; why not the bridge?"

"They probably destroyed it to quarantine the disease," Scarlett thought aloud.

"If Feragarth was one of the first to fall," Joseb said, "that could account for why I've never heard of it."

After laying Andion on one of the benches, Kylan went to

investigate. Cord hobbled a few steps behind him. Brushing a finger over the parapet of the failed bridge, Kylan unearthed a brilliant blue ore, then wiped his hand on his britches. On the far side, a jasper aqueduct emptied into a pool overflowing into the gorge.

Kylan kicked a rock into the void. An echo never rang to tell of its impact. "I take that to mean we're trapped?"

The burning in Cord's leg sent him to the bench next to Andion's. Rorry sat by him and gingerly pulled his injured leg to her lap. He leaned back to search the moonless, Glades-less night sky. How long would they be safe here?

"Does anyone see another way out?" Kylan asked.

Shaking her head, Rorry asked, "Someone has been tending to Helfarn's image. If the dwarves are all dead, then who?"

Returning to them, Kylan snorted. "Maybe they didn't all die from their plague. If any of our history is true," he grumbled. "And, if not, I'd like an apology from the bastards who got it wrong."

Joseb opened one of the dwelling's doors, a square of slate with three roses etched into its facing. He crouched at the short doorway to examine the interior of the ruin. Scarlett peered around his shoulder.

"What do we do now?" Kylan asked the explorers. "Ferix couldn't have come this way. We need to find a way out, not hunt for treasure or something to read."

Scarlett stuck her tongue out at him as Joseb's mouth worked soundlessly to form an excuse.

"We're staying here," Cord said firmly. "Teague was right. We'll never outrun them. We have to face Beez."

"Face him?" Kylan asked. "Us?"

"Yes," Cord answered. "My dream brought us here for a reason. Now let me see if I can find out why."

Kylan's incredulous eyebrow rose. "I'll believe that when you can tell me why you're having these visions."

"Let Cord rest," Joseb said. "We should take a quick peek around and see what might be useful."

Kylan surrendered by throwing his hands up and stalked over to Helfarn's mosaic. Bouncing on his heels, he kept glancing at the entrance. "This feels . . . this is wrong. But by all means, nap."

Cord cut off a prayer, closed his eyes, and opened himself to the dream.

* * *

Ruins no longer, Feragarth glistened around Cord as he spun, taking in the rainbow of ores around him. It bordered on gaudy but encouraged the child inside of him to explore.

Cord dashed across the now whole blue bridge. About ten feet below the ledge of Helfarn's Plaza, landings bordered the cliff. He hadn't ventured close enough to the gorge to notice them. Fishing poles and baskets were strewn about on the yellow bricks. But the bridge didn't cross water. This wasn't going to help them. Letting his questions go, he moved on.

After running under the red jasper aqueduct, he entered a new plaza with a mosaic for a different old god. Pale green stone had been laid to create the armor of a beautiful lady wearing a crown of antlers. He wished he could read the Old Tongue running down the blade of the sword in her hand. Cord looked up and stopped breathing.

Four slender women in soft pink robes knelt around a fountain containing a life-sized green porcelain tree. Whether tar-black or pale, their hair fell braided to their waists. Each wore a matching headdress of silver branches with golden leaves. Their eyes remained closed.

He didn't know them, but the points on their ears told him of them. Elves. "Ashes," he breathed.

From a dense cloud covering the top of the fountain's branches, water dripped and cascaded down grooves in the porcelain bark before ambling over roots to gush into a basin feeding eight shallow recesses in the floor, one on either side of each elf. The water babbled over acorns lining the bottom of the trenches and trickled on into the buildings behind them.

The elves kept their hands submerged. Cord stepped closer, then flinched when one of the women moved. She pinched an acorn in her fingers, placed it in her mouth, and returned her hand to the water.

Cord swallowed. "Excuse me," he forced himself to say. They didn't budge, too entranced by their meditation. Or maybe they didn't hear him at all.

Palatial white towers were visible above the buildings in the next plaza, beyond a regal pink alabaster bridge. Tempted to continue, Cord couldn't bring himself to leave. His gut told him to wait.

"I beg your pardon, ladies," he tried again. "We need help!" They didn't acknowledge him. He rubbed the back of his neck and decided to check the next section of town. As he turned, something moved at the edge of his sight.

A slender elven woman in a blue robe stood before the next bridge. Her white-blonde hair was braided the same as the others. She stared him in the eye. "You are healed now," she said, her voice melodic and familiar. "You need to wake." The other elves vanished.

"Wait! We need help!"

"There is no time."

"Can you tell me how to defeat the Dregs?"

"Have faith in what is true to you. Fight your fear and remember you have allies beyond those in Feragarth, *mer'aran*."

"*Mer'aran?*" Cord asked.

Her robe melted into silver armor, dropping a chain-mail skirt to her knees. A crown appeared. At the front, silver twisted into a single spike.

"Cord, you must wake," she yelled. "It is time to fight!"

* * *

A cold blast brought Cord to his feet. The world twirled as his vision caught up. Just rising over the buildings across the chasm, the cloud above the porcelain tree faded as he blinked. Or had he imagined it?

He flinched when Rorry touched his leg, which was no longer injured. It had healed far quicker than normal. The elf had said he was healed. Had she healed him? Joseb said elves only had one power. That was why he thought Cord might be one. His mouth slackened as he considered the possibility. *Mer'aran?*

Rorry squinted at him but then rose and pointed her chin to where the others stared.

At the base of the narrow stairs to the entrance of Feragarth, a wise pair of eyes met Cord's. The man was taller than Andion, about chest-high, and much broader. His wintry beard sprawled as it willed. He wore tattered piecemeal scraps, held to him by a few pieces of twine and a rope belt. Unblinking, the squat man waited without expression on his severe brow.

"Did you dream about this?" Kylan asked.

"Not if that's a dwarf," Cord whispered. "Is that a dwarf?"

Joseb hummed a yes. "Though he doesn't seem to be nearly as intrigued by us. He outright ignored our greetings."

The dwarf raised his nose and turned toward the stairs. "Tell me he's not sniffing," Kylan said. "Dwarves have a keen sense of smell, right? Keen enough not to need the enhancement of a certain curse?"

The stout man began to disrobe, dropping his scraps to the floor. Uncomfortable with the display, Cord turned to Rorry, who watched with as much interest as Kylan. Cord grabbed Veen's bow.

Scarlett gasped.

Shreds of skin flew from the dwarf. A heaving torso of fur swelled through the remaining skin as the beast gurgled. Only slightly larger than his original size, the dwarven cursed one kept his proportions, stubby and broad at the shoulders with a narrow waist set low to the ground. His tail was little more than a nub.

"Bugger me," Joseb muttered.

Kylan's hand grabbed Andion's dagger and two throwing knives hidden in the pik's tunic.

Sniffing, the squat beast looked back at them. He didn't growl or drool. Instead, he gave three succinct barks. The sound was returned.

"There!" Scarlett said. On the cavern wall, higher than the buildings, another stocky wolfkin clutched the rock face. Digging its claws into the stone, it rolled along and dropped out of sight. Two more did the same on the opposite side of town. Each released the cavern wall and disappeared into the streets below. Soon after, they fell in line with the first howler facing the stairs.

Grunts sounded behind them. Six more thickset beasts scaled the edge of the gorge by the broken bridge. Cord reached to his empty quiver. They ignored the youngsters and the sorcerer's casting hands as they rushed to their pack.

Before Cord could ask what in the blue blazes was happening, thunder rattled the cavern. A boom at the entrance cracked the wall back into a door. Pebbles and boulders sprayed out above the stairs.

A lankier wolfkin appeared. Then a dozen cursed humans assembled. They filed down the narrow stairs, challenging the dwarves' line with their own at the bottom. The invading pack snarled their warnings and advanced as reinforcements arrived, trickling down the steps.

The first three who had descended tested their luck and swiped at the dwarven wolves. Claws snatched their arms and jerked them forward to the stocky wolfkin. The ferocity of the attack didn't stop until human parts were flung back upon their brethren.

"Well," Kylan said, "this will be interesting."

Chapter 58: Buffer

Cord tapped his finger rapidly on Veen's bow. Despite the uncertainty of the dwarves' intent, he wished he could aid them against their common enemy. There was no guarantee they would let them leave if they were victorious, of course.

A phalanx of human cursed ones poured through the opening and down the stairs. They fattened their line a short distance from the squatty wolfkin. Those who didn't fit on the stairs drooled from the cliff's edge, excitedly yipping when they spied the plaza's offering. As the numbers increased, the gap of peace between the lines shrank.

"If we're no threat to the dwarves," Joseb said, "we should aid them and be prepared if their protection is ruptured. When the Dreg shows, let it try to possess me. My ward shall weaken it."

Cord nodded. Maybe he owed Joseb an apology. If he proved himself and got them to Racine, he'd receive it.

"You believe they are protecting us?" Rorry asked.

"Either that or they're guarding their territory," Joseb answered.

Kylan handed Rorry the knives he had retrieved from Andion and held the rosewood-handled dagger at the ready. "The one time in my life I try to be responsible, you all ignore me. Now we have to rely on vicious, furry triangles to save us."

Straining, Joseb pressed his palms together. He groaned and spread his fingers. Three silver shafts grew between his hands. "Shite," he wheezed, shaking his head at what he had created. He offered them to Cord.

Cord smiled when he realized they were arrows with black fletching, slick and strange, not the usual plumage. Lightweight and straight enough, each should fly true. A different color appeared within a tiny divot on each arrowhead.

"Select targets on the stairs," Joseb said, "and use them sparingly. I can't make more today." He guided Scarlett by the arm to stand next to him and told Kylan and Rorry, "You two, watch our backs. Do nothing unless we're in danger."

"No magic sword then?" Kylan asked.

"Not today, no." Joseb sighed. "Scarlett, I'm afraid it's time for some practical application of your lessons. That fear in your belly, I want you to acknowledge it. Grab it. You need to turn it around into excitement, as we discussed before."

The gap closed between the packs into an outright brawl. Scarlett's wide eyes swept to the guttural noises.

Joseb tapped her on the nose. "You can do this. Let's practice, shall we?"

She nodded, then pulled his attention back to her with a tug on his arm. Taking his collar in her hands, she flared it up against his neck and grinned.

The slick fletching tickled Cord's cheek as he selected a target for the arrow with a yellow divot. For what the invaders brought in numbers, the dwarves had in determination and sheer brutality. Their formation held, despite the wave of wolfkin crashing upon them. They rose as they balanced on the remains of the fallen.

It wasn't long before Cord selected a champion among their defenders. A white *V* marked the fur on his back. Swiped across the face by a brown paw and struck by a gray shoulder, the champion held his ground. With a swift flick of his wrist, he removed the brown's paw, splattering red. The brown's whimper sounded briefly before another dwarf sank his teeth into its neck. The champion's other paw probed the gray's back and gave a quick jerk. Cord heard the beast's spine snap. The gray became shaking fodder for the pile.

A wall of flame roared over the top of the stairwell. "Good," Joseb said, patting Scarlett on the back. It only slowed the reinforcements, however; something flung a flailing victim through the fire before others leaped through, issuing whines as the blaze took its toll.

Even claws honed on the stone didn't entirely safeguard the dwarves. Blue shimmered beneath slick spots on all of the defenders' coats. The dwarf next to Cord's champion cupped its matted side. One of the invading wolfkin braved the fire above. It studied the fray and settled his posture to leap upon the weakest link in the chain.

Cord released.

Nailed against the stairs, his target panted yellow breath. The puffs clung to the air, forming a small cloud around him. Rushing past, another invader inhaled the spell. Its body collapsed in instant death. The fetid gas drifted and lingered, frightening the invaders back and granting a reprieve to the line.

Choosing the blue arrow, Cord prepared.

"Now we bolster ourselves," Joseb said. He closed his eyes and waved a hand. Three of the dwarves faded from sight, including the champion. Uneasy with the disappearance, the other dwarves tapped the air where their comrades had been. A series of barks settled their nerves and refocused their attention.

The barrier of flames dwindled, tempting a new wave of foes from the seemingly endless supply. The first two down the stairs slowed at the thinning yellow air and retched but kept coming. To the side, a foolish wolf dropped the fifty feet from the entry level. Limping on an injured leg, it wasn't in pain long before Joseb set fire to its throat.

Selecting the first in a line of three who leaped through the fire, Cord released the arrow with the blue divot. Upon impact with the beast's chest, the enchantment encased the wolf in a layer of ice. Icicles spiked away from the point of impact, skewering the wolfkin behind. A sheet of ice blanketed the stairs, capturing the feet of several invaders. The invisible defenders didn't let the advantage pass.

Joseb and Scarlett continued to supply stratagems while Cord nocked the last arrow. "Cord, what color is that one?" Joseb asked.

"Purple."

Furrowing his brow, Joseb asked, "Purple? Huh. I had hoped it would be green—or red. Red would have been nice."

"What does this one do?"

A bark was interrupted, turning their attention back to the battle. The injured dwarf now shook. His corpse fell backward. Cord focused his aim beyond the murderer being ripped asunder by unseen claws.

"I don't know," Joseb said. "Just be ready to use it."

A hulking brown mass breached the flames without noticing its singed coat. It strode over the bodies of the unfortunate Merithians on the stairs. Matching Julian's size and arrogance, it was definitely an alpha.

"Oh bollocks," Joseb said. He raised a cupped hand. Fifteen-foot spears of stone broke through the fire and fenced off the stairs behind the alpha. "Cord."

Cord released, hoping this alpha was slower than Julian had been.

It wasn't. The brown caught the arrow and snarled. A purple gas whirled from the shaft, surrounded it, and vanished. Where the alpha had stood, a mouse scampered to climb the step behind it. It was scooped up and disappeared into the throat of an invisible dwarf.

"Transfiguration?" Joseb said, beaming. "Well that's bloody marvelous, that is! Do you think that's my purple?" he asked Scarlett.

The fence of spears shattered, flinging rock as far as the plaza. Shrill whines suggested an invisible dwarf had fallen. "Find me the *tek'aran!*" a woman's voice said, echoing throughout the cavern.

Three beings moved into view over the fresh pack of invaders. The heads and shoulders of two alpha wolves, a brown and a gray, flanked a hovering Dreg. "Mivvy?" Cord asked.

Her scant clothing drifted with her every move. The shirt was little more than an apron of green scales. Under Teague's cap, her eyes found them. She tossed the snake man's head aside.

"Beez," Kylan said.

Chapter 59: Faith

The pandemonium was deafening. More howling short-limbed wolfkin rolled along Feragarth's chamber and dropped from the ancient dwellings, taking the place of their fallen pack members. "Do not harm the humans!" Mivvy's voice resonated through the cavern. "The *tek'aran* will be mine!"

Cord looked to Joseb.

"Now let me give everything with panache," Joseb said, stepping up onto the bench where Andion slept. He tensed his hands, jutting his red nails upward. The ground mimicked the gesture beneath two of the wolfkin making their way past a dwarf. The stone gripped the beasts. Joseb squeezed and let the spell dissipate. "Remember the plan! We have to enervate the Dreg before we can defeat it. This new host is especially powerful."

"That is undeniable," Mivvy's body said. Beez demonstrated the deadly combination of his darkness and Mivvy's raw talent with a snap of her fingers. A foggy sphere encased Joseb and Andion, slicing the long bench in two. As the seat fell, it dumped Andion at Joseb's feet.

With a smirk, Joseb wiggled his fingers. Nothing happened. The whites of his eyes expanded. "I can't cast," he said and pounded against the barrier. The whisking mist trapped them.

Cord pummeled the shell. He might as well have been striking marble.

Beez grinned, snapping again. Water spouted between Joseb's heels, filling the interior. "That's two. Four to go."

Joseb picked Andion up out of the bubbling fountain. He climbed the angled seat, leaving a foot of space between his head and the top of the sphere.

"If we take down Beez, will the spell break?" Cord asked.

Joseb shrugged.

"It would be a good place to start," Kylan said. Then he groaned, "Oh no." Glancing back over his left shoulder, Kylan searched the ruins behind them. "I think I have to go."

"What?" Rorry asked.

"Where is Teague?" Beez demanded. Mivvy's eyes filled with rage as she looked them over. "That one!" she growled and pointed at Kylan. "Lirus, feast." The brown alpha leaped down the stairs and hurdled the battle line.

"Yeah, that's definitely Beez," Kylan said. He raced toward the houses and yelled, "Help them!"

Rorry began to give chase until Cord pulled her back. Scarlett whimpered but stayed.

As the alpha chased after Kylan, Rorry seized the opportunity and flung one of the throwing knives. It stuck below the beast's haunches without slowing it. Kylan cleared the stunted entrance to a building at the edge of the chasm just before the alpha smashed against the unyielding entryway. Its mass held it back. It wouldn't keep a regular wolfkin at bay.

Mivvy's body sauntered down the stairs, stepping around the gore. Beez wore a mischievous grin, pondering them. A dwarven wolfkin lunged for the Dreg. Vines of green light erupted from the ground, tangling the beast. They contracted and juiced the dwarf against the floor.

The gray alpha lunged ahead and parted the wolfkin, friend and foe alike, with shredding swipes to clear Beez's path.

More leaped for the Dreg. Beez clicked Mivvy's tongue and raised her open hands while spinning in a circle. The ground quaked as tiles and rock swelled together. "Back to the stone, they go." Beez laughed. A golem, taller than the buildings, combined its fists and smashed the end of the warring line.

"Scarlett," Rorry said. "Now would be a good time for something clever."

Reaching to his empty quiver again, Cord cursed. He looked to Joseb for guidance. Water had risen up to the sorcerer's knees.

"Run!" Joseb yelled.

* * *

Hunched under the low ceiling, Kylan pressed himself against the far wall of the dwarven antechamber, empty aside from a stone table. The brown alpha stretched for him, its claws falling a few feet short. Unfortunately, the stairway to the next level fell well within its reach, just to the right of the entry.

Thankful his jittery pulse had returned to normal once he had run, Kylan scoffed at his defense: the rosewood-handled dagger. Little more than a cheese knife, though Andion's blade was longer than his dad's carving knife.

The alpha's claws screeched against the stone in their frenzy. Abruptly, the sound died. Its furry paw relaxed and shrank as its bones popped. Gold eyes shifted to green as it released its mass to fit inside.

Bolting from the wall, Kylan dodged the changing man's flailed arm. He ducked into the stairwell and leaped the steps in two bounds. The upstairs, nearly as barren as the antechamber, had ceilings high enough for him to stand. A wall of rusted bars caged the left side of the room. "Two steps off Merith and I'm already in jail," Kylan joked and opened himself to options.

The charging pulse returned, guiding him to the side of the room where two tall windows depicted a dwarf with a mallet in orange-and-green glass. The windows didn't appear to open, but bars didn't protect them either. They overlooked the gorge, offering nothing but a view of darkness. "Shit. Shit. Shit." It was a madcap scheme, but his gut urged him on. "All right, fine."

Kylan tucked the dagger into his belt, squashed a momentary doubt, and mumbled a wish for luck. He backed away from the window and the sound of his nude hunter's footsteps padding up the stairs.

A clean-shaven brunet stranger walked in with a smug smirk. He was shorter than Kylan. Thank the gods for that.

"My compliments to your tailor," Kylan quipped.

The alpha sneered. "You won't win."

"Nah, we'll both die."

Gold ruptured the green of his irises. Kylan raced forward. He clutched the man's neck and threw his weight against him, sailing them through the stained glass. Tumbling, Kylan closed his eyes, preparing for the long fall to the bottom of the gorge.

They struck the ground much sooner than expected. Kylan crushed into the alpha. The ability to breathe was knocked from him for what felt like an eternity. He lay there for a moment before deciding to draw breath and managed to roll off his hunter.

On his knees, he pulled the dagger and prepared to defend himself. His lungs sucked air in to their capacity.

The man didn't move. Golden eyes stared through Kylan. A jagged piece of glass had punctured most of the alpha's throat. Trailing blood turned the dust around the corpse into a crawling sludge.

Squatting, Kylan examined how fortune had favored him. A ledge spanned the brim of the plaza, roughly ten feet below the visible edge of the abyss. Yellow bricks revealed their sheen where he had rolled. Near the cavern wall, steps led up to the main level.

Kylan rolled his shoulders and cracked his back. "Well, that'll do, I guess."

The cavern shook with crunching booms from the plaza. Stirring, the wind in his blood guided him toward them. "Shit."

* * *

Rorry hustled after Cord through the back door of the dwarven home. As another dwelling exploded under the golem's fists, the cavern shook. She struggled to stay on her feet. Where were these supposed legendary weapons of the dwarves? She saw no magma-forged, god-shattering blades of death, just rocks, rocks, and more rocks. They were as useless as . . .

"Wait!" Rorry grabbed Cord's wrist. "I have a plan." She waved behind her for Scarlett to come closer, but no one was there. "Scarlett?"

"Keep running!" Cord said. "I'll find her."

"No! We need to end this." Rorry sifted through the contents of her satchel. Upon finding the vial she had taken from Kylan, she cast the bag aside. The basilisk's gland bobbed in its thick secretions.

Dropping his quiver next to her satchel, Cord considered the vial in her hand.

She retracted the venom from his grasp. "No. You hide near me; Beez will sense you or smell you. I will distract him—her—him. Then you can sneak up and lock him in a trance. A few drops of this might trap him inside the body."

"Rorry, no. We can't just kill Mivvy because Beez is inside of her."

She rolled her eyes before the naïveté of his words translated into innocence. "That is a lovely notion," she said. "Yet our current situation—"

"Fine," Cord said, reaching for the vial again.

Rorry swatted his hand away. "Tell me how you would save her."

His hemming did not encourage her. "At least let me try! Beez wants me; he'll get close enough for me to use the basilisk spit if I can't free her. You hide!"

"No," Rorry said. "Beez does not know you are the *tek'aran*. I will draw him to me. You take him by surprise and heal the magus. But,

Cord, if you cannot save her, I will end this."

"I won't use you as bait!"

"Does bait volunteer? And where do you expect me to hide? In one of these homes? That is not safe!" Where was Scarlett?

The muscles worked in Cord's jaw.

She put her chin up. "I thought we were a team in this? We defeated Julian. This time we will take down Beez—without Carolle's help." His reluctance ebbed when another building crumbled in thunder. "We can do this. I trust you, Cord."

* * *

Tucked into the corner of a back room in one of the empty dwarven ruins, Scarlett flipped through the pages of *Essential Focus* to calm her nerves. Rorry and Cord had disappeared as soon as they had entered the alleys. She had selected the nearest house they might have ducked into but had chosen poorly. Now her stomach knotted as she tried to scent the air around her. She should have run after Kylan. At least she wouldn't be alone.

A rumble jostled the cavern. Howls from the plaza filled the small room when it ceased. Her ears searched for any muttering of her friends' voices.

Picturing Joseb's face as they'd run away, deserting him, she gripped her dress in her fists. There wouldn't be much time left for him and Andion. Instead of facing Beez, she hid and tried to find answers on the pages she'd already memorized.

But how could they take on a Dreg? Cord had no arrows and would only be harming the vessel if they struck. What would Rorry do? What could Rorry do? Fling a knife? Expel a tantrum?

No, Scarlett had the best—perhaps the only—chance of saving them. She had to make her choice. Death in an ancient storage room or death defending her friends? Or no death at all. Her mum believed in her strength.

She closed the book and set her mum's shawl against her neck. Remembering Joseb's words, she gripped the fear within her and redirected it into a challenge. Armed with her creativity, she would slay the Dreg, or die trying. The excitement was intoxicating as it grew. Except for the fluke when her core had hit her in Llandir, she had never felt so powerful, and yet unsteady. As her desire shifted, her dress wafted out of sight. Invisible, she rose.

Maintaining a chokehold on her fear, she studied the hallway. A door to her right offered her an exit. It slid open easily to reveal the cavern wall a few feet away. Poking her head out, she ignored the howls and used only her eyes to survey it. Scarlett traipsed the empty alley to the edge near the gorge and peered around the corner of the last building. Stairs led down to the chasm before her. Ignoring her curiosity, she moved toward Helfarn's Plaza.

A blond-pelted wolfkin ran into sight before her. She didn't gasp, clinging to her warming fear. A darker one joined him. Neither smelled her. *Thank you very much, Kylan.*

Recalling Ferix's suggestions, Scarlett decided to experiment. Focusing on the memory of the day her mum had first helped her dye her hair, she recalled quenching her thirst on that hot summer day. Tasting the lemonade, Scarlett aimed the novice spell down the alley and into a junction beyond the wolves. The wolfkin caught the lemony scent instantly and scampered away from her to investigate. Two more joined them at the focal point of the spell and swiped at the air in confusion.

Rorry walked backward to the broken bridge in the distance. She stretched her arms out to her side and shouted something Scarlett couldn't make out. Was she offering herself? Distracting Beez for a moment would be all she could achieve and would surely be fatal.

They had risked too much to let it end here. Her shawl, Teague, Veen . . . Anger roiled through Scarlett when she remembered her mum admitting to her lies, convincing Scarlett her talent was miniscule, wittingly crushing her dreams of following in her footsteps and joining the Tower. Had these creatures gone through her mum?

She glared at the wolves in the alley. Instantaneously, the blond wolfkin disappeared into blackness shrouded in a roaring fire. The others jerked away from it. Easily, she set the second cursed one crackling.

With the other two roasting and emitting floating cinders, Scarlett sauntered in Rorry's direction. Selecting another wolfkin target from the neighboring alley as she passed, she basked in the warmth coating her bones.

Scarlett's ire turned to Julian. Her reaction to the way he had sneered at her talents but had fawned over Rorry helped her take out a new target, who had been running at Rorry from the alley.

As her mind turned to the accretion of comparisons and losses to Rorry over the years, another tremor from the golem challenged her balance. At the edge of the plaza, Scarlett brazenly stepped out to spy.

Beez scrutinized Rorry as he lazily gutted a dwarven wolfkin with three arcs of light. A brilliant green aura surrounded the magus Beez wore before she lifted into the air. The Dreg hovered, slowly drifting in Rorry's direction with a knowing look. Rorry climbed onto the bridge.

Behind Beez, several wolfkin followed while the gray alpha rolled under the dwarves. The golem had wandered to the far side of the cavern to smash more homes that the wolves had fled into. Frugality of power didn't exist within Feragarth, and it thrilled Scarlett.

She took a deep breath and planted another scented trap behind Beez, drawing the wolves away from their master. Gathered together, the six barely managed whimpers before a blaze consumed them.

Yes, fire was easy. Scarlett stood up straight and walked briskly to Rorry's side. She suppressed her sympathy for the magus Beez wore and kept her ire roiling for the Dreg within. If he had hurt her mum . . . She wasn't in a forgiving mood.

* * *

Cord hated this plan, but Rorry was right. This was their best chance without Joseb. Still, he couldn't believe he was hiding between two buildings while Rorry offered herself to Beez with her back to a pit. To her credit, she'd enthralled the Dreg.

A glance away gave Cord his timing. Joseb held Andion against the top of the sphere while barely keeping his head above water. Beyond them, human wolfkin now fought other human wolfkin alongside the dwarves. Thankfully, the golem didn't care what it smashed, giving the dwarves an advantage in setting up their foes. Chaos reigned in these ruins.

"So young and malleable," Beez moaned, almost within striking distance.

All Cord had to do was incapacitate the Dreg. Once Beez was down, he could figure out how to save Mivvy, and this nightmare would end. Mivvy hovered twenty feet away now. Cord sprang at her back and squeezed Veen's bow as he focused on his hatred. Nausea wafted through him.

Mivvy's outstretched hand flung Cord back. His shoulders smacked against the ground. Vines of light ensnared his limbs. Whatever supposed defense the bow would've offered, whatever Teague had enchanted it with, didn't matter now. It landed several feet away.

"I sensed you this time," Beez said. "Your power has grown, *Tek'aran*. Alas, it is still too pathetic to reach me. The Ancients are not to be trifled with." Beez discarded his interest in Rorry and grinned at Cord's squirming. Raising Mivvy's arms, he asked, "You thought you could hide here? Flawless! This place was flawless when I saw it last. Centuries ago . . . centuries before your parents, *Tek'aran!*"

Rorry charged as Beez lowered beside him. Glowing vines gripped her arms, binding them to her torso without Beez ever looking back. They sucked her to the floor, where she wriggled. "She is a pretty thing. Hours of fun. Fun to play! Fun to break! Would you like me to wear you when I do? I reward loyalty." Mivvy's finger ran up Cord's thigh. Rorry shouted words more natural from Carolle's mouth but stopped to listen to something. "You are a handsome prize and will bring handsome rewards. Yes, a good pet."

"I'll destroy you," Cord growled, "even if I have to cut the head off every person you taint!"

Beez laughed. "You could not make me cough! Are you going to heal me to death? Yes, I know what you can do, *Tek'aran*." With Mivvy's hand gripping the top of Cord's thigh, Beez leaned down. "Tell me. Who would you like me to wear when I break you?"

Something mottled the air around Mivvy's head. Hissing, the Dreg rose. Beez sneered at Rorry. Scarlett appeared out of thin air and slumped forward to the floor. "Clever, clever," Beez said. "I know how to shield myself from your kind. But, my . . . you are strong."

Cord groaned, struggling against his restraints. "No! Leave her alone!" Thorns punctured his skin.

"Learn your place, pet," Beez said.

Ripping his flesh, Cord stretched for Mivvy's ankle, but she lifted out of his reach.

"Stay away from her!" Rorry yelled as Beez lowered next to Scarlett.

Lifting Scarlett's head, Beez put Mivvy's mouth on hers.

"No!" Cord yelled. The thorns sliced farther up his arm. Suddenly, his restraints disappeared.

Mivvy's body collapsed.

Cord sprang to his feet and sprinted straight for Scarlett. Her body rose to her knees. Without pause, he pounced and crashed into her. Her eyes opened as they slid. Cord seized her forehead.

The chill of his power surged. Scarlett jerked back against the ground, unable to move. But he didn't know how to save her.

When he looked to Joseb for advice, Cord saw the sphere had faded. The sorcerer coughed on the ground with an arm draped over Andion.

Cord directed his attention to Scarlett and lost himself in his search for something, anything, that would break the bond between Beez and Scarlett.

Beez cackled through the trance, though Scarlett's lips hadn't moved. "You cannot kill a wraith, boy!" Beez yelled in Cord's mind.

Rorry ran forward.

"I can fix this," Cord yelled. "I'll save her!"

She moaned, "Cord . . ."

"I can do this!" He refused to give up on Scarlett. There had to be a way to stop Beez without making that sacrifice! Holding the trance this long already made him yawn.

Beez laughed. "I will wear . . . you out . . . *Tek'aran*. When we get . . . back . . . you will know pain." The light of the trance dwindled. Scarlett's hand dug her nails into his arm. "You cannot hold me!" she said aloud.

"I won't let you have her!" he yelled.

Settling to her knees, Rorry held the basilisk venom in one hand and put the edge of her throwing knife to Scarlett's throat with the other. "Free her, or I will," Rorry said.

He couldn't look at her. He wouldn't fail them.

What was it Joseb had told Scarlett, turn her fear into excitement? He'd try anything to save her. After all, he didn't care what a murdering coward claimed of him. The Chancellor—no, Rhyn, just Rhyn—could call him Abandoned; it meant nothing. This was his gift to wield. If he couldn't kill Beez, maybe he could force him out of her.

Cord slapped his hand over Scarlett's heart and opened himself to the light of his own power. His vision sharpened, finer than tissue and bone. Her body was mapped out in his mind as she writhed against the stone. He breathed a laugh when he noticed something strange, a darkness hiding from the blue light filling her body. It crawled like a bug, racing from nook to cranny over organs in a muddled attempt at escape.

"I found you," Cord whispered.

"You see what . . . I want you to see," Beez wheezed and cackled through the trance.

"No," Cord said. "I can kill you." When he plunged harder into the chill, something Cord hadn't seen before filled Scarlett's chest, a brilliant light branching out through her body. A sliver of it decayed to blackness where it connected to the scuttling darkness.

Training the healing surge on that branch of light, Cord smiled at Beez's shock. The bug leaped at him through the connection but twitched when the bond with his host began to glow again.

"No!" Scarlett screamed. "Kill—"

Fighting the edge of his ability, Cord refused to let go. He could do this! "I am the *tek'aran!*" A crash of frigid power curled Scarlett from the floor as he guided it into the darkness inside her.

Beez screamed. The parasite crumbled. An ashen cloud flew from Scarlett's mouth and nostrils. Cord held the power within them until all of the blackness left her.

Rorry grabbed Scarlett's arm and hauled her back from the cloud condensing next to her. It formed a sleek, shadowy man on the dusty road. His featureless face tore apart when he shrieked, jarring Cord back into his fear. The Dreg collapsed, crumbling into a mound of ash.

Cord sagged on his knees. Rorry rocked Scarlett against her chest and smiled at him through her tears.

The victory barely registered before the gray alpha landed before him. Its forearm struck Cord's chest, slinging him toward the chasm. Stunned, Cord watched the ground disappear from beneath him.

Chapter 60: Allies

The golem froze in midstep, allowing the wolfkin Kylan had lured under its foot to scramble free. Reclaiming his attention, the wind directed him toward the gorge. He stabbed the dagger into the human wolf's back and sliced it out. Then he ran right into the hirsute torso of a black alpha sniffing the air.

Kylan stepped back as the alpha loomed over him.

It caught a wolfkin leaping at Kylan's back. The catch's whimpering death was swift, spraying Kylan's back with warmth. "Thanks?"

"Cord!" Rorry screamed in the distance.

The alpha bolted toward Helfarn's Plaza.

Kylan started to follow when the wind left his chest. The charge funneled into his right wrist and down to the ring on his forefinger. Pain shot up his arm when the ring glowed red. It receded, tingling down from his elbow. For an instant, the red light filled in the feathers on his ring. When it disappeared, so did the duck tail feather.

The wind filled his sails again. Shaking his arm, he darted for Helfarn's Plaza and checked each alley for his friends along the way.

Ahead, a cursed dwarf fought a cursed human. Beyond them, human wolfkin fought human wolfkin alongside the dwarves now. Kylan couldn't tell who was an ally. Chaos—he felt far too safe to be sane.

Water had spread out over the mosaic from where Joseb knelt in a puddle. Andion slept next to him. Joseb waved off Kylan's attention, directing him toward the bridge where the black alpha was tangled in glowing green vines. Thorns appeared along the spell. Kylan dashed before the growling beast.

Beez snarled at the alpha.

Kylan was about to lunge for the Dreg when Rorry shouted, "Beez is gone!" On the other side of the magus, Rorry laid Scarlett on the road. "Watch her!" Rorry ran to the edge of the gorge.

Scarlett's chest rose and fell. Relief washed through him. She lived.

Kylan put away the dagger and swallowed. The wind told him he was exactly where he was supposed to be. He put his hands up. "Mivvy? Is that right?"

Draped in her arms, the woman didn't answer him. He wasn't sure she'd heard him over her fear.

"Mivvy, this one saved my life." Behind him, the alpha stopped struggling against the slicing vines. "I know how strange it sounds, but we should let him go."

She hugged her knees and shook her head. A wolfkin appeared from the alley next to her. Magic vines hogtied it faster than Kylan could blink. Thorns rippled along the bindings. They grew, sending panicked yips through the cavern. She pulled her fingers into a fist to tighten the vines around the struggling beast. Then she splayed them out, misting the air with red.

Kylan shuddered and backed up to the alpha. What had Beez taught her?

A lump of stone, engorged by magic, grew into a pile by her side. Appendages broke free as the smaller golem stepped forward. Another mound formed as Mivvy rose.

"We need help over here!" Rorry shouted from the cliff. Her queue disappeared as she jumped over the edge.

"Go!" Joseb yelled. He raked his hands skyward. Bright streaks of golden light arced across the ceiling over the pit. "Go now!"

* * *

Cord's whole body throbbed. He ached from his left knee up through his shoulder to his neck. Slowly, he scooted away from the gorge, smudging the filth-covered yellow bricks on the ledge where the fishing rods had been in his dream. He didn't know how he had landed there. Something had caught him, something soft like a down pillow. Whatever it was, it had slung him back hard into the bricks.

A growl churned. It sounded distant, but Cord knew it was meant for him. A short way down the landing, the gray alpha struggled against a pair of dwarven wolves. Raising its hackles, it stared Cord down. He had killed its master; now it sought retribution.

Magic evaded Cord's reach. He winced. He was too tired. The support for the bridge sealed off the ledge behind him. Defenseless, he scooted back against it.

Three more dwarven wolfkin climbed over the chasm ledge, not realizing the danger awaiting them. A mighty blow flung one back into the blackness. The alpha attempted to claw the second, only to have it cling to its arm with nails just as sharp as the alpha's. The yelping dwarves assisted their pack members and rolled the alpha, snipping and swiping for dominance.

A streak of orange caught Cord's eye from above. Rorry's queue hung before her shoulder. She smiled in relief. He managed to stand with his weight on his right leg and tried to get a grip on the smooth wall. She reached down for him. Her eyes widened when she saw the battle on the ledge. "Help is coming!" She turned away to yell something behind her.

Distracted, Cord didn't see the body of the dwarf launched at him. He flattened beneath the weight of her corpse. Working against the ache in his shoulder, Cord freed himself in time to see his last defender hurled into the nothingness, snarling as it fell.

Rorry slid down the cliff, landing between Cord and the alpha. The alpha raced forward until brilliant arcs of light lit the chasm from above. Rorry flung her throwing knife. It stabbed into the alpha's leg and was just as ineffective as she must have known it would be. Fidgeting with something in her hands, Rorry cursed.

The alpha leaped for her and struck.

"No!" Cord screamed.

Strips of leather trailed in the wake of its claws. Rorry staggered back and fell. The bottle of basilisk venom rolled from her hand into the wall.

Cord stepped forward. The pain in his knee brought him down. He crawled through the dust to her, glaring at the grin on the gray alpha's maw.

A black alpha landed beside Rorry. Its growl promised the end had come.

But when Cord glanced up, it warned the gray alpha back. Clipping the gray's left leg with a claw, the black alpha sank its teeth into its opponent's right shoulder. It drove the gray away from them.

A cricket's wish. Cord didn't dither; if there was a hope of saving Rorry, he'd take it! He dragged his body to her, squeezed her hand, and kissed her fingers. She didn't stir. Her wan lips slackened. Blood ran freely from her side to the puddle forming on the tile.

Whatever awaited them in the Glades, she could find him there. Keeping his eyes elevated out of respect, he leaned over with her head in his hands and funneled all of the power he could pull. Unable to see if she jolted, he shivered and watched the battle.

The alphas collided. Soul-shaking barks echoed back from the abyss. Wetness splotched the black's pelt when they broke apart. Standing guard over them again, the black spared a quick glance at Cord. Then it crouched, unwavering.

The gray pounced, knocking the black alpha back a few steps. Their defender scraped its claws over the gray's chest.

Dodging the black's next strike, the gray stepped back blindly.

Kylan ran along the ledge above them. He leaped and with all his weight jabbed Andion's dagger into the gray alpha's shoulder. When Kylan fell to the side, the black swung both arms, knocking the gray back into the gorge. It clawed at the air as it disappeared into the darkness. Kylan knelt to watch it fall.

Rorry moaned.

Cord sighed his relief through his chattering teeth. His lungs jerked in short breaths. Pain crept through the trance, like ice stabbing his innards. He wanted to look at her, to see she was well.

Tossing the broken rosewood handle over the ledge, Kylan eyed the alpha sniffing him. He raised a hand to someone above and said something Cord didn't hear.

Scarlett appeared. Taking in the scene below her, she cried out.

Mivvy and Joseb joined her. Andion was slung against Joseb's shoulder. They were safe, rougher from the wear, but safe. Grim-faced at the sight below, Joseb passed Andion to Mivvy. Without hesitation, he slid down the cliff side. Cord heard his heels click and tried to laugh.

Cord's hand drifted over Rorry's face. Her breath warmed his frozen fingers; he released the mending and fell flat. Blood warmed his side as he went numb. Struggling to blink, he tried to see her face, just a few moments more. There wasn't a freckle he'd forget.

As he drifted away, an arm lifted her. A familiar voice spoke. Marlone had Rorry now.

She was safe. They were all safe.

Chapter 61: An Elf in the Garden

Soft hums strung together a lullaby, easing Cord awake. His body ached. "Nemma?" He opened his eyes and found himself lying on the grass in an unkempt garden protected by the tall winter trees of the Mint Coast, without any lifewood. The pain only let him rise to his elbows. He was dreaming again.

Near his feet, the white-blonde elf from his dream in Feragarth knelt in her soft blue robe. She smiled warmly and said, "Not quite."

An unusual sight filled the overgrown garden. More than thirty chest-sized flowers hung from vines draped through the woods and running across the grass, spreading a sunset of hues. A peach-colored bloom curled its petal around the elf's slim finger and swayed with her hums.

As she smelled the flower, her robe melted into her strange armor. Silver plate covered one shoulder and her chest. A matching belt circled her waist. It dripped a chain-mail skirt and sprouted white-blonde hair at her back, curving like a horse tail. Her hair swept itself back into a single braid, revealing the points of her ears. Silver crowned her head and coiled into a spike at the front.

She throttled the stem of the peach flower, which never halted its dance. A dagger formed in her hand. *"Lethlan methanlon,"* she breathed and slid the dagger through the thick green stalk. The blossom turned ashen as she settled it on the forest floor.

In robes once more, she rose. "I am glad you are well, *mer'aran.*" For a moment, she just watched him and smiled expectantly. "Yes, it means 'my child.'" Too many questions fought to be asked as Cord looked into his mother's eyes. "I do hope the aid I sent did not frighten you. Calling on favors is a detestable act, especially when put upon the poor dwarves, let alone the cursed ones."

"That was you?" Cord asked. "Did you send Marlone?"

Settling down at his side, she brought the scent of gardenias with her. "You saved his will all on your own."

"Am I an elf?" Cord felt strange asking the question, oddly hopeful.

"Not fully," she answered. Her slim fingers entwined with his. "I wish your father could see you, but humans are limited to what is in front of them."

"My father is human? Are you still on Merith? Where can I find you?"

"No!" she said. The armor returned, covering her hand in leather and silver. "Avoid Shallyghal." When he agreed, her robe returned. "Someday, we will meet, when the Ancients have returned to the Cloud."

"Tell me you're safe."

Leaning in to kiss his cheek, she said, "They could never find us." She released his hand, rose, and walked away toward the entrance of a cave behind him. The armor returned.

"Wait," he said. "Please. I have more questions. Please, Mom! Don't go!"

Without looking back, she said, "The valiant need my help. In your dreams, we shall speak again, mer'aran. Know that we love you very much and wake, Cord. Your friends will be overjoyed to find you well."

* * *

A wave of warmth washed over Cord, the same sensation as when the mending trance receded. Surrounded by his dream, he searched behind him for his mother. Solid rock sealed the cave she had entered. Of course she wasn't there. And yet, the stalk had browned where she had cut the flower.

His friends moved about the garden in awe. Relieved to see them alive and well, he decided to watch for a moment before drawing their attention.

An indigo petal curled around Rorry's touch. She giggled as it swayed. Through the shreds in her leathers, her skin was perfect. Aside from Joseb's feet, there wasn't a blue glimmer to identify a single wound.

At a loss for words, Joseb shrugged at the bloom dancing for Rorry.

"There are rumors of them," Scarlett said. The sorcerer tilted his head for her to explain. "I read about them in your book, the one Julian burned. *Ivy or Silkshade: Where Magic Meets Botany.*"

"Burned?" he asked with a grimace. "Remind me not to return to the Tower of Rosamond. Actually, it's probably best if I avoid Virtud Luz altogether."

Mivvy stood apart from the others, lost behind her eyes. What had become of Granville?

Kylan nudged Andion and pointed at her. Drawing a circle in the air, he tried to tell Andion something the pik didn't comprehend. Then Kylan clapped slowly. When Scarlett clapped too, Andion nodded.

After the pik explained the dancing ritual to Mivvy, Joseb and Rorry joined in. This time, Andion ended his dance celebrating the lives of the dead with a handstand on Kylan's head. They both grinned as Mivvy mustered a smile before she gathered her green-scaled skirt, covered her cleavage, and retreated back to her thoughts.

They all needed rest and new clothes. Cord's stomach growled. And food.

Kylan lowered Andion without a surly comment. Maybe he *had* died.

But where was Marlone? Attempting to stand up, Cord fought the makeshift tourniquet of torn sleeves. He untwisted the bandages and took a full breath. Careening on their vines, the flowers turned as he stood. His friends followed their bright faces.

Rorry rushed to his side. Her hands fought his from untying the bloody scraps. She stopped her fussing when he revealed the solid skin beneath the stiff wrappings. Not even a scar remained. Cord threw the bandages aside and held out his arms.

She laid her head on his bare chest. Lifting her chin with his finger, he said, "See? I told you I wasn't going anywhere."

Rorry pulled his lips to hers.

"Put on a shirt, man," Kylan said. "We can see how cold it is."

Rorry laughed. She bent to gather the quiver and Veen's bow.

Kylan crushed him in a hug, staggering Cord back.

"Where's Marlone?"

Kylan let go and answered, "For a while, we talked about how horrible of a liar you are. Then I mentioned that you'd found your friend, Leila, in Granville." Mivvy's expression didn't change when Kylan mentioned her town. "He said he would get her and . . . Tommin?—someone, if he had to?"

"Tomlin."

"Sure," Kylan said. "He said they'd find you in Trône d'Argent."

Scarlett took her turn to hug him.

"Marlone only stuck around long enough to wink at Scarlett before he left," Kylan said. "You saw that, right, Scarlett? That he winked? You were looking at the naked man's face?"

She released Cord and slapped Kylan's arm.

Worried at first, Cord decided to be patient. Marlone had proven himself formidable. Ashes, he was an alpha! Cord would never hear the end of that. "Good," he said. If she was all right, he'd find Leila. "Mivvy, please don't think me cruel, but I gotta ask—"

"I don't know," she said apologetically. "I told Joseb already. Beez didn't know where Teague is. But he made me relive every minute I saw of him in Granville. Obsessed . . . filthy . . ."

Joseb raised his finger, but Cord shook his head. "No," Cord said. "Do you know if Leila is all right?"

Mivvy thought as she spoke. "The last I remember, Beatrice was dragging her to the Temple of the Twins. I believe most of the town escaped into the tunnels."

Out of habit, Cord started a prayer. He paused, unsure who to address it to. What god would the human child of an elf worship? Which god had blessed him with the ability to save Marlone from the curse's control? Did a deity even care they had survived to the continent? He knew someone who cared; and he prayed for Headmaster Angsly to watch over Marlone and Leila.

Taking what must've been painful steps forward in his tiny boots, Joseb pretended to be unaffected and asked, "Any idea why your friend wasn't enslaved to the Dregs like the other wolfkin?"

"I healed him before he died," Cord answered. "That freed him from the curse's control."

Joseb hummed as he considered it. "One could posit that as a possibility, certainly. Yet you didn't heal the dwarves, did you?"

"My mother may have." They all stared at him. "*Tek'aran*, I think it means—"

"Elf child," Mivvy said. "I heard Beez say it to the snake." Her face blanched at that memory.

They all resumed their staring until Scarlett asked, "Don't they have pointy ears?"

"Joseb was right," Cord said. "I'm also human." As he relayed what had happened in his dreams, Rorry wrapped her arm around his waist and started the procession out of the watchful garden in the Racinian woods.

The sorcerer seemed more worried by the news than satisfied at having guessed the origin of Cord's ability. "When we reach the capital, we shall have a lot to report and even more to research. But let's keep this *tek'aran* business between the seven of us, shall we?"

Cord gave him an appreciative nod.

"So . . ." Kylan started with a smirk, "Rorry said when you defeated Beez—and saved Scarlett, thank you for that—you yelled, 'I am the *tek'aran!*' Does that mean you actually yelled, 'I am the elf child'? That's embarrassing, isn't it? Not much of a title."

"Shut up, Kylan." Cord chuckled. "How'd y'all get out of the ruins?"

"When the gray alpha fell," Rorry said, "Beez's wolfkin dispersed and ran back to Merith. The dwarves collected their dead and scaled down into the chasm without a word."

She exchanged a glance with Kylan, who shook his head in response.

"What?" Cord asked.

"Three other tunnels," Kylan griped, "before we found the right one." He jumped ahead and walked backward while he spoke. "Very convenient that you woke after I carried—"

Joseb pointedly cleared his throat.

"Sorry, *we* carried you all the way back up. Andion had the decency to wake up after a few hours. I don't think we'd ever have found our way out without him."

The pik didn't acknowledge the praise, planting his feet firmly with each step around the ferns.

"And you, Andion?" Cord asked. "You're all right?"

"I am. But I don't know what to do now." Each "I" was emphasized by a quick glance at Kylan, who gave his approval.

Kylan offered a hand up to his shoulders, which the pik gladly accepted. "We'll find out together. You're hardly alone, brat."

No. They weren't alone. Not anymore.

* * *

S carlett twisted the ring on Kylan's finger one more time.

"I'm telling you," he said. "There were seven feathers and now there are six."

Joseb and Cord descended the fern-clad hill behind them. "The Troyes Mountains aren't far to the north," Joseb said. "We're no more than a few days from Trône d'Argent."

"There's a clearing in the woods about a half mile from here," Cord added. "It might be a village."

Sticking close to her mentor's side as he set their path, Scarlett probed the darker thoughts their escape had bored. The faces behind her expressed the same concerns no one wanted to voice. Bodies lay in their wake, kith and kin. No one knew if Lord Gwirion and her mum had made it out of Llandir, much less if Brewing still stood. They walked for some time like that, silently counting woes and chipping away at their victory.

As they waded through a slick stream, Rorry released Cord and took Mivvy's arm to assist with her decency.

"Are you well?" Cord asked the tall magus.

She nodded but immediately blinked away tears. On the other side of the stream, Mivvy wiped her cheek. "They attacked as Teague said they would. Nella tried to protect me from Beez." She strained to smile at Cord. "You avenged her. Thank you."

Joseb averted his eyes. As kindly as he treated Mivvy, he hadn't been able to look at her for long.

Scarlett quietly asked him, "What's wrong?"

For her ears alone, he said, "It bothers me. The Dregs wore jade dragon scales. I'm afraid it may have been a friend of mine."

So they were dragon scales. Scarlett glanced back at the garments Mivvy clasped to herself. "One didn't. Rorry said the elderly Dreg who charged at the Chancellor wore black robes."

Nodding, Joseb asked, "Yes, if he was a Dreg. I'm not sure. They concern themselves with vanity, while he hid beneath a mask. Above it, his eyes . . . they were solid black."

Her mouth refused to ask if that particular entity was possibly—though surely not, but possibly—a demon. Whatever it was, it had disappeared with the Tribunal, but had also left Dregs in Llandir.

Scarlett lifted her shawl to her nose and breathed in the scent of her mum's vanilla lotion. "Joseb, would you mind attempting that vision spell again?"

Reassuring her with a smile, he said, "As soon as I have a mirror, dear. We all have someone to search for, don't we?" Pursing his cranberry lips, he tilted his head. "I haven't had any luck with it. However, we're in Racine now. My sister could probably manage. And why wouldn't she want to locate her accomplice?"

"Maeverly?" Scarlett asked. "Did she complete her studies at the Tower?"

"No, not Maeverly . . . gods. My little sister, on the other hand, is a properly mantled mage. She's a proper everything as far as the public is concerned." In all seriousness, he said, "The Tower can't teach you spells like that, you know?"

Scarlett playfully groaned. "I know, Joseb."

He laughed. "I beat a dead horse for a reason. I'd hate for someone with your mind to squander it in such a restrictive place. None of those priggish tossers in the Tower would dream of luring the wolves with scent and torching the bloody bastards in an inferno."

She ran her hand over the ferns and smiled for herself. "I didn't know you saw that."

"It's a teacher's privilege to take notice when his pupils shine, Scarlett. With your talents, the challenge shall be remembering what mediocrity looks like." Flatly, he added, "The Tower can show you that. They adore the basics."

He put his hand on her shoulder to regain her attention. "Bah, it shall serve as a safe enough place for you to learn until I return with my band. Then say one word, and you're free. I may just send Bevin in to carry you out himself."

That singular offer, the option to change her mind, meant more to her than he could have known. "If Kylan doesn't kidnap me first," she said. "On the other hand, should I find myself at home in the Tower, I'll be thrilled to see what we can discover together, what with the Tower's resources and our looser interpretation of the rules of magic."

His grin broadened. "Oh dear. I am a bad influence."

* * *

Kylan could get used to this crisp Racinian air. The summer morning felt like autumn. Without breaking a sweat, he had carried Andion on his shoulders until they came upon a farm in the clearing Cord had mentioned.

Between fenced-in fields, a two-story stone cottage released a thin trail of smoke from its chimney. No fortifications and no guards protected the Racinian home, simply a meadow overgrown with wildflowers. They marched toward it, determined to know their exact location and to barter for food.

By one of the fields, a scrawny kid a few years younger than Kylan whined as he struggled to line up a gate door with its hinges. Spiky green plants danced in the breeze behind him. When the kid saw them, he started and released the gate with a crash. "Mum!" he yelled and bolted for the house.

Studying the plants over the fence, Joseb said, "Menji farmers."

"Menji?" Cord asked.

"A plant used for . . . recreation," Joseb answered, "usually." The sorcerer put his hand up. "Wait here. Let me see if I can work a different kind of magic."

"Is that safe?" Cord asked, barely beating Rorry to the question.

"Trust me. I've dealt with their kind for ages." He pouted at the judgment on Cord's face. "This is Racine, not Virtud Luz. It's perfectly legal here."

As the others watched the sorcerer climb the hollow steps to the porch surrounded by desiccated flower beds, Kylan noticed Scarlett reaching over the fence. With a quick snap and a grin for him, she deposited her harvest in her poultice bag.

Before Joseb knocked, the door flung open. "I don't read the cards until dusk!" a woman's voice scolded. "Come back then."

Joseb caught the closing door and leaned forward. His words were too quiet to hear but were delivered with an assertive stare.

Stepping brusquely out onto the porch, the farmer's wife all but shoved Joseb back. Kylan felt conflicted seeing such an unimpressive creature in a dress dyed with blue slashes about her sleeves and skirt, even if the frock had frayed at the hem and was splotched with stains.

Rorry and Mivvy tried to cover their skin as she stared with all the warmth of a midnight stroll in a winter spit. Andion ducked behind Kylan's leg.

"Come on, Andion," Kylan said, pushing the pik to stand beside him. "We don't hide anymore."

Her harpy eyes picked them over but softened as they devoured Cord's body, briefly pondering his shorts and sandals before wandering up him once more. Kylan could tell Cord tried not to appear revolted, but he should have tried harder not to stare at the mole on her jowl, which was as large as a button with three long whiskers.

"Twenty crowns," she said. "Silver. Not the ol' copper kind."

Joseb sighed. "Bread is more expensive than when I left a few weeks ago."

She rolled her shoulders in an ignorant dismissal.

"Do you at least have gooseberry wine?" Begrudgingly, she nodded. "Very well. Shall we go inside?"

"No!" she said, barring his way with a meaty arm. "Wait here." Shifting out of sight, she yelled, "Claude, get Papa!" The door slammed behind her.

When Joseb rejoined them on the ground, Kylan said, "Let's go. She doesn't deserve your coin or our company. *Her* treating us like riffraff?"

"We're paying for her food," Joseb said, "not her conversation. Besides, if you run from adversity, you shall never stop."

"We will pay you back," Rorry said.

He brushed off the notion. "Compliments of the Hook. This isn't the welcome I wanted to provide, but the pickings are slim. In any event, they do seem to know a thing or two about eating. Let's hope that transfers to their culinary skills."

"I'm sorry," Cord said to the sorcerer. "I was wrong. I've been wrong about a lot of things." Joseb squinted, probably as unsure as Kylan as to why Cord was telling him this. "I've treated you like a . . . well . . ."

Kylan was going to say "spoiled brat," but Rorry said, "A cock." She didn't even blush. Impressed, Kylan patted her on the back.

"Right," Cord agreed. "The truth is Scarlett wouldn't be here without your instruction on using fear. You meant it for her, but I think it worked for me too. There's a lot I don't understand about all of this. But if you're willing, I'd be honored to be trained by you."

Was he already trying to secure an invitation to join Joseb's return for his band?

Joseb clapped Cord's shoulder. "They say a man never truly knows himself until he's known the road. Hells, I've been down hundreds and I'm still learning—perhaps, even how to create a golem?" They laughed at his persistence, though Mivvy didn't seem to hear it over her thoughts. "If you deny the Tower for my tutelage, then I'm the one who's honored." The revulsion on Cord's face said the Tower hadn't given Joseb any competition.

A fitting partner for his wife, the master of the house rounded the corner, toting a long, rickety table with his son. Kylan was able to determine exactly where the food went in their family. The farmer released his end of the table unannounced and eyed them as if they were skunks in the clean linens.

Claude dragged the table a few feet more before stopping. He sped out of view when his father waved Joseb over with a roll of parchment and a quill.

The others waited while Joseb read the agreement. Rorry ventured closer to see it for herself.

Kylan elbowed Cord and whispered, "Why do I get the feeling you want to undo everything we just did?" Scarlett listened in. "You're going to try to find your mother, aren't you?"

"What can I say?" Cord asked. "Kenton was wealthy. We had two village idiots." They grinned. "Nah. I thought about it, but I'll wait to see what Marlone wants. If he needs me to help him find a cure, I'll do as I was told. If not, well, just let me tell Rorry."

"Hah!" Kylan laughed. "You think we'd kick that hornets' nest?

Just be sure to invite us. Between the Tower and finding Alis—and common sense and love of life—the fates may not allow us to join you, but the offer may be vital to your survival when telling Rorry."

"You're always welcome in my company. I'm one of you, right?"

"That's the rumor, elf child."

Claude placed four chairs at the table before rolling a barrel to the head of it. When two more barrels and the dishes were set, the farmer yelled, "Get!" The kid ran inside and didn't look back.

Joseb plopped down on the barrel at the head of the table to sign the agreement. He said something to Rorry, letting her read it, before handing it over.

"Pleasure doing business with you, mercenary," the round man said. Combing a hand through his greasy hair, he pretended not to see the others as he passed through them on his way indoors.

Andion sat cross-legged atop a barrel. Kylan took the other, letting Cord and the ladies have the chairs. Around the table, they waited in a silence of possibilities, some on pensive grins and others in lowered gazes.

Out of the blue, Scarlett said, "We should do our Hansweighn toasts!" She ignored the disgusted sneer she'd conjured on Kylan's face, turned his chipped wooden cup upright, and picked up a knife.

"Must we?" Kylan grumbled. "I found great pleasure in believing I had done that for the last time."

"What am I supposed to do?" Joseb asked.

"Do not drink until we have all toasted," Scarlett said. "We'll use spirits, so take it all in one gulp." She gave Kylan a small glower. "You say something you are thankful for."

"Thankful to the Chancellor for," Kylan put in.

Scarlett shushed him and chimed the knife against the gold band on her finger. A gush of fluid poured out of the gemstone. "And something you wish to achieve in the next year," she finished. When everyone had one tap of the bubbly strawberry drink, she said, "I will start." She raised her cup. "To Jean Hywel and making her proud."

Joseb stood. "To new friends and saving Teague Fuch's arse once again."

"To my father and finding Alis," Rorry said.

"My parents and . . . living here," Andion said without certainty. Scarlett had to keep him from drinking after he spoke, spilling a bit on his tunic.

Through tears, Mivvy said, "Nella Tallow and reclaiming Granville."

"Cheers to that," Cord said, earning him a cautionary glance from Rorry.

Accepting his turn had come, Kylan laughed uncomfortably and rubbed the rim of his cup. What should he say? Toast Veen and no longer having to steal secret glimpses of men amid distraction? Buying a boat, maybe? They were all watching him. Finally, he said, "To Stille van Veen and getting my feet wet."

Rorry blushed and rolled her eyes. Scarlett grinned. They understood what he meant.

Their faces turned to trap Cord, who laughed and said, "My friends, a bunch of perverts, witches, and thieves, who saved my life." Rorry slapped his arm. "Admit it; I'm not as backward a wooder as y'all thought." There were a few uncertain hums and grunts. "And to putting up with Marlone and Leila again."

They drank. Cord choked and Andion coughed, while Kylan accepted the burn searing his throat with ease this time.

"What was that?" Cord asked.

Kylan patted him on the back. "Now, elf child, you're an elf man."

As they discussed their trek to Trône d'Argent, Joseb changed his mind twice between going to the Hook and visiting his sister first. In the end, he decided on his employer, claiming it'd be best to get their preparations in the works immediately.

Silence returned as the Racinians brought out the food. Kylan wasn't sure if twenty crowns was as high a price as he had interpreted. The dishes kept coming. Chops, potatoes, chicken, grapes, and even pastries shoved for space on his plate. Andion helped himself to the cheese before Joseb had finished pouring the gooseberry wine he'd requested. Kylan even felt he should say thanks before the farmer's wife insisted there was no need for them to dally when they finished.

It wasn't as good as Bevin's cooking, but Kylan kept that opinion to himself.

Between chewing, the conversation turned to Racinian fashion and a quick lesson on the language the noble ladies spoke using their silk fans. Judging by how pale he'd become, Cord feared that more than the wolves. Naturally, it captivated Rorry.

"You won't find me quaffing about the High Houses," Kylan said around a grape in his mouth, "discussing my latest hunts while wearing a gilded codpiece." The others laughed, except Cord, who was confused again. Kylan leaned over to his ear. "You'll know it when you see it, often on the man with the most to prove."

Looking them all over, Joseb said, "I must say I'm thoroughly impressed, by all of you, but you three magi in particular. Your abilities are more tremendous than I had estimated." Well-deserved pride sparked in Scarlett's eyes from behind her cup.

"One might even say volatile," Kylan mumbled, then swallowed.

Admonishing him with a look, Rorry said, "Candid as always, Kylan."

"Yes," Joseb agreed. "I'm going to enjoy dropping you into the heart of Trône d'Argent. A minute of hobnobbing and their fans shall be all a'twitter."

* * *

Stuffed to the gills, Rorry walked next to Cord as the wayward group left the ravaged table to the hosts whom she had seen peeking through the windows. With a lazy pace and renewed hope, they traveled the country road toward the next village, Annersby.

The more time Rorry spent around Mivvy, the more she reminded her of Scarlett. If Scarlett's goal had been swapped with Rorry's, Rorry would have believed Mivvy to be her friend's long-lost older sister. Alas, things were not going to be that simple.

She did hope Alis, a woman who had branded herself for love, possessed more reason now that she was closer to Mivvy's age. At the moment, Mivvy did not. Her fear and meekness had diminished during their meal. Now she denied interest in anything beyond returning to Granville.

"Mivvy," Rorry said, "I feel it would be amiss if someone did not say it. You will be a vessel again if you return."

"No," the woman said. "The Ancients have moved on from Granville."

"They didn't occupy the city?" Cord asked.

"Croathe was their goal," she answered, "but not their only one. Beez's sister called their invasion a harvesting, though they never said exactly what they were looking for." Rorry felt ill at the possibilities. "Whatever it was, they didn't find it there."

To Joseb, Cord said, "Teague promised Lady Katrin to send aid for Granville. The Hook needs to uphold that promise."

Joseb agreed. "I suspect our mysterious benefactor is already working on that."

Assuming Beez's posture, Mivvy let her garments fall naturally and seized Joseb's sleeve. "If you promise to take me with you when you search for Teague, I'll teach you how to summon my friends."

As happy as a farmer's cat at milking time, the sorcerer promised and immediately peppered her with questions. Scarlett moved closer to eavesdrop.

Rorry could almost see the threads of fate weaving. She prayed it was in their favor.

Relaxing, she removed her hands from concealing the gashes in the leather over her midriff. Other, more intriguing, questions lingered for her as she caught a glimpse of Cord's chest out of the corner of her eye. After all, she had already kissed him in front of the others. Rorry took his wrist and wrapped his arm around her.

She slowed them to trail behind the group and said, "I want you to make me a vow."

"Like the way I vowed to the Chancellor to seek vengeance against him?" He posed it as a joke, but his laugh was empty. "I'm not good with vows."

She squeezed his forearm with her hand and stowed her frivolous thoughts. "On the contrary, you fight tooth and nail to keep them." With his pinky finger interlocked with hers, she said, "I vow to you, Cord Sullivan, that no matter what occurs between us, I will always be honest with you."

His grin was bashful, but he said, "I vow to you, Rorry te Gwirion, to always be honest with you, most especially when you're behaving like a pampered, spoiled—"

He howled when Rorry twisted his nipple. Everyone turned. "Sorry," she said to them.

"No, my fault," he groaned, covering his chest with his hands. "I should've seen that coming."

Satisfied, she giggled.

After ambling along the road for a while, the air grew heavy with her regrets again. "My misjudgment of my father is more shameful than your faith, Cord. Whether devout to a man or devout to a god, you never acted against your heart.

"Here and now, I have my father's blessing. I should feel inspired to find Alis and witlessly enthusiastic to pursue the adventure Kylan and I had planned. Yet all I feel is concern for my parents and Brewing."

He kissed her temple and said, "His Grace forgave you for not trusting him. In time, you'll forgive yourself. If you don't wanna celebrate now, you'll still be free of Merith later when you learn your parents are fine."

"In some ways." She released a long breath and raised the flap on her satchel. "I do want to keep the good memories from Merith. Before, I believed I had to cut myself off from my past entirely. But I could not manage that." She removed the diamond earrings from her bag and put them on. "Perfume is a silly thing for what we just went through."

"Downright deadly when running from wolfkin," Cord teased. "But I enjoy it."

"Be that as it may," she laughed, "my mother gave it to me. I could not bear to leave Brewing without something of her. Fortunately, I also have the diamonds from my father, which I can no longer barter. Wherever the road takes me, I will be reminded of them." Her fingertips dipped back into her bag and brushed the soft vellum scroll. "Given the uncertainty I harbored for you at the time, I am glad I stole this now. When Kenton burned, part of me feared you would lose everything." She put the aged scroll in his hand.

Unfurled, it stopped him cold. Figures drawn in black ink illustrated battle stances down the length of it. She waited for an explanation. "I saw you admiring it in your headmaster's chamber."

His brown eyes blinked rapidly. "Headmaster Angsly drew this when we were just beginning our training. It hung on the back of our door for years. After Marlone and I left, he must've tacked it over his desk." He rolled the scroll and kissed it. "Thank you."

After taking his hand, she offered the safety of her satchel to the vellum once more. Unable to take her eyes off him, she grinned until he blushed.

"What?" he asked.

"I do trust you."

Chapter 62: A Racinian Welcome

"Quit looking at my ears," Cord said to Kylan. It was the third time he'd told him since they'd left the menji farm.

Rorry and Scarlett giggled.

"Ah," Joseb said. "Here we are. Annersby."

Hardly able to believe it, Cord stared wide-eyed at the tree-lined road ahead. They had walked right into Annersby. At each junction, white fountains spouted water from sculpted animals, flowers, mermaids, and seemingly whatever had entered the artist's mind. Flowers hung in baskets from street lanterns and filled the beds of every garden ahead. This charming little town existed without walls. But where were the people?

Something rapped hard on the road behind them. Two expressionless standard-bearers blocked their retreat. Their uniforms, striped ice blue and white, matched the banners dangling from their staves, which were topped with silver dragons. On the standard, white embroidery depicted a dragon in flight, carrying a stag by the antlers in its claws.

Beneath the ruffled edges of their coats were what Cord suspected were codpieces on the fronts of their tight pants. Yet no one smirked besides him.

"Blasted butterflies," Joseb moaned. "Here comes our benefactor."

Properly armored men appeared from behind the trees on either side of the road, all wielding halberds. Impressions of dragons embellished the pristine steel chests of their full-plate armor. Dark brown horns protruded from the soldier's forehead nearest Cord; they curled upward halfway to the tip of the white plume on his helm. A slit—a mirokar! The otherwise human guard glared back, sending Cord's eyes to his friends.

The color drained from Rorry's face. Andion dropped from Kylan's shoulders and crouched behind him. One by one, his friends turned away from the standard-bearers and knelt. Only Cord and Mivvy remained standing.

"Kneel," Kylan whispered.

"Why?"

A pair of soldiers clasped Cord's shoulders and forced him low. If not for Rorry's nod, he would've struggled.

Two more had the gumption to do the same to Mivvy. A golem swelled from the road, sending the halberds into action.

"Easy," Joseb called. "We're all friends here."

The golem slumped when the soldiers backed away from Mivvy. She knelt, though a second golem joined the first to flank her.

The banner posts struck the ground twice in unison, beckoning six crossbowmen from a side road. They took aim at the group without wincing at the heft of their massive weapons. The shafts, thick as logs, were fitted with a crank far more burdensome than the one on the Ghost Augur's crossbow.

Behind them, four white horses lugged a white carriage dripping with more silver than Cord had seen in his life. On the carriage door, the dragon crest glimmered as the sunlight crossed it. Two female soldiers inspected the Merithians from the driver's bench.

A fancy man in pointy-toed shoes jumped from the back of the carriage and placed a cushioned step beneath the door. After rolling out a white rug, he bowed his head, which was adorned with a flat cap. Lace dangled from his collar as he almost kissed his shins. Perhaps Joseb was actually more Racinian than Patevian.

The guards descended from the bench and eyed the group again before opening the carriage door.

More blue fabric rustled within. A puffy, brightly dyed dress, filthy with pearls, shuffled out. Silver streaked the bodice of the middle-aged woman's dress to match the crown woven into her brunette hair. She didn't have the face of a ridiculous woman, despite her outfit; a smile of success looked at home on her lips.

Her large green eyes promptly sized them up. "Do be at ease," she said, flaring open a white fan. The guards released Cord from his forced decorum but didn't step back. Drawing up, the crossbowmen rested the ends of their weapons on the ground. "We welcome you to Racine."

Following Joseb's lead, the Merithians rose. The woman turned her smile to Joseb and slapped her fan closed against her wrist without changing her expression. "Friends," Joseb said. "Please allow me to introduce my little sister, Her Majesty Queen Ameera of Racine."

Rorry gasped. They all stared at the sorcerer with a mix of accusation and wonder. For all of his spells and tricks, no one had suspected this.

Light brown hair bounded past Joseb. Cord yelled, "Andion, no!" As the crossbowmen hefted their arms, Andion tumbled into a roll, ending beneath Queen Ameera's dress.

She squawked. With the guards' help, the queen danced around, hefting her skirts to examine her lace-trimmed boots. Andion was gone. Queen Ameera's eyes demanded an explanation from her brother.

Kylan snickered.

Epilogue

"Jean?" the icy woman's voice inside her head asked. "Is that truly your name? I suppose it is plain enough, for a Racinian." Jean's lips frowned in the stately mirror. Blood stained the stenciled paint on the wall next to it where an unfortunate noble hadn't survived Llandir's fall, a common sight around the Gilded Lavender. The Dregs had spared little time in establishing their new hive.

Her hand ripped the apricot bonnet from her head and flung it aside as Jean saw herself sigh. Retreating into silence, Jean tried to ignore the ichor of the monster roaming through her body. "Monster? That is what you think of me?" Flashes of slaughter and pain assaulted Jean's mind. "Think nice thoughts, or next time I will show you children. I can even use your daughter's face, if you prefer."

Lust entered her expression when a copper-skinned Cercaffian man with maroon lips stepped into the reflection. His eyes lowered in obedience. The Dreg had insisted that he change into a ridiculous garment, hardly larger than a scarf over his groin. "Oh, but I sense you like it," the voice said. "I can increase your pleasure or take it away, just as I can the pain."

A knock sent the pet to answer it. The Dreg ogled his bare cheeks as he walked and cracked the door ajar. In his thick, silky accent, he said, "The satyr has arrived, my master."

"Send him in," Jean's body said. "You can tear my clothes off later." Her cheeks didn't flush, though they bloody well should have! "And, pet, there had better be appropriate furnishings in this room tonight. Culling the prime from the fodder takes time. I expect to be comfortable."

He went down on his knee before exiting behind the taller man.

It was indeed a satyr! Interwoven black and red leather strips covered his beastly legs. Jean's eyes jerked away from his black vest before she had finished examining it. "Vesper," he groaned.

"What is it, Ferix? I am training a new cow." Jean's anger swelled within her as she stretched for a grasp on her power. It dangled just out of her reach. Each time she missed, laughter filled her mind. "What would you do if you had it?" the voice asked. "Kill yourself?"

The satyr waited for an answer.

"Repeat yourself, assassin. The day has been long."

"Do you have a man named Teague?" he asked. "In their jealousy, your brother's flock claims ignorance. Now they're bowing before Beez's urn and won't acknowledge me."

Vesper waved over a Dessrini girl, no older than Scarlett, covered in red tribal tattoos. She left the lineup of healthy nude bodies watching them from behind the room's carnage-splattered luxuries. "I have obtained him," she said to Ferix. "Was my brother not successful against the *tek'aran*?" The satyr didn't respond. "Well, no matter. If there is one, there may be more. When Beez is restored, and has finished his ravaging, we will continue our search."

Vesper's Dessrini pet presented a leather collar with a golden token in her youthful hands. The medallion lacked the usual caress Jean felt around magic, tainting the power with foulness, like a displeasing odor you could barely smell and couldn't trace. "Which would you like, my master?"

Scanning the line of men and women, she settled on a broad-shouldered shell of a woman with a stern face and taut breasts. "We have an assembly today; I had better wear Selesta." Upon hearing her name, the vessel sprinted to kneel before Jean's chair.

The satyr scanned the line. Then he did so again with his eyes lingering lower. "Really, Vesper, even for me this is vulgar."

"You want something from me, assassin," the Dreg reminded him. The leather collar locked around Jean's neck. Its medallion sucked against her throat, sticking to her skin. "That will keep you docile," Vesper thought.

As Jean's wrists were bound, her mouth said, "This one's thighs rub together when she walks; it annoys me. Feed her nothing but greens. And tell Roscar he can take his time breaking her. She is not my first choice, but her strength intrigues me."

The Dessrini girl bowed.

Vesper lowered Jean's mouth to touch the stern woman's. Air moved between them. A spark released Jean from Vesper's hold.

With control of her body restored, Jean stood and stretched for her anger to lash out with flames. Pain jolted her throat. Her knees buckled. She shrieked as she fell to the carpet. Panting, she saw a dead noblewoman looking through her from across the floor.

"Pathetic," Vesper's new husky voice said. Addressing Ferix, she sighed. "If you want to plunder him, he had better be clean before Beez wakes. And be gentle with my gift. His flesh is not yours to tear."

"You ask the impossible." The satyr shook his head. "Regardless, I merely wish to speak with him."

Vesper looked him in the eye, her smirk growing. "Does this have to do with your disappearance, Ferix?"

"I have my own interests," he answered. "And know yours."

She raised a finger to his lips, her face holding a threat.

"The Exalted trusts me," Ferix said. "I wouldn't tempt his fury."

Vesper favored him with a frosty glare but lowered her hand to her side.

A gong clamored from the hallway. "Take her to be trained with the others!" Vesper shouted. She hurried out of the room while her pets tied a shimmering white dress around her.

Forcing Jean to her feet, the Dessrini girl said, "Don't cause trouble for yourself, cow. Swallow what they give you and keep your skin." She fastened a lead to Jean's collar and towed her past the satyr.

Jean decided to ask the question she dared not think while Vesper was inside her. Getting choked in the effort, she asked, "Are you the satyr Kylan freed?"

His dark eyes followed her but gave nothing away.

Tugged into the hallway, Jean let the question go. He couldn't be the only satyr in the world, if they still existed. It was wishful thinking that she could find someone in all of this madness who might help her.

She was about to try a new tactic and appeal to the stone-eyed tribal girl, when Ferix called from the doorway to Vesper's chamber. "Wait." He came to them and said, "Follow me." They moved behind the satyr's walk down the plush carpets in the hall and out to the shining ores of the grand lobby.

Nearly as large as a coliseum, the lobby's every plum-colored surface had been decorated by the dwarves with their angular patterns. Vesper and over twenty others gathered in a silent circle, listening to nothing in the middle of the room hewn into the mountainside. They began chanting in a harsh, unfamiliar tongue.

Through their legs, Jean made out bodies heaped on the floor. A ribcage gleamed through shredded silk in the pile of gore. She fought the urge to sick up.

The girl gripped a handful of Jean's hair and pulled her gaze down. "That's not for you to see!" she hissed, nearly missing the first step down toward the entrance to the building.

Seeing the daylight ahead, Jean wanted to make a run for it. But where would she go? The city was theirs. She prayed Darren had made it out alive. Lizbeth would never forgive her if Brewing lost its councilmember because she'd parted ways with him to try to save the people at the Ale and Pumpkin.

The satyr stopped them on a broad landing. He squinted at an alcove where several aged urns topped pillars. Two shaggy brown wolfkin guarded them. They were so still Jean wasn't sure they were alive until their golden irises whipped to her. Below the urns, servants groveled on the floor. Seven young men in loincloths prayed to one. Another Dessrini cried, "Choose me, master! I wish to be your favorite!"

Ferix took Jean's arm, assisting her down another staircase on the opposite side of the landing. More bloody handprints covered golden mirrors as they descended into a corridor, once ornate, now battered and desecrated. Thick with the stench of fright, the hallway was filled with human whimpers and screams from behind closed doors.

Ferix opened a door on their right. Three families clung to each other and cried out. "Wrong room. That's always awkward," he said and moved on.

Cracking the next door in line, he tensed. Then he flung it open.

Jean hesitated outside.

The purpose of the room was evident. Naked occupants lay on mounds of pink pillows, waiting inside the lantern-lit chamber. All wore collars, though none had the magic-inhibiting medallions. Chains connected them to their respective posts. A blonde beauty bawled and clung to a cushion, her only option for decency beyond the curtains outside of her reach. Though they had filled the positions, the Dregs wouldn't have had time to set this up.

The Dessrini shoved Jean inside and spat on her.

Ferix stepped between them. "I can deliver Vesper's message, vessel," he said. "Leave her to me."

The girl sneered as she thrust her face inches from his. "And if you lie, I get punished, goat."

The satyr backhanded her, knocking her onto a whimpering young man, who never opened his eyes to see what had fallen on him. "Know your place, shell! I outrank your master. One word to the Exalted and her secrets destroy her. How will you fare then?"

Sniffling, the girl held her cheek as she rose. She bowed to him and left, pulling the door closed behind her.

The satyr's face relaxed. "I loathe zealots. Take a seat if you like."

Jean opted to stand, thankful for her clothes that she never would have believed were a luxury prior to today.

"Did they really make it into Llandir?"

Unsure how much she should give away, Jean simply answered, "Yes."

He chuckled to himself with a wild smirk. "You're whom? Scarlett's mother? Yes, she has your face." Jean felt her muscles relax. Maybe there was still hope to get out of this. He shook his head, as though he'd heard her thoughts. "I cannot help you."

She began to shake as her hope dwindled.

His hands squeezed her shoulders. Startling her, he yelled, "At least not yet."

Trotting to the far end of the room, Ferix snapped to awaken one of the prisoners with silver hair. Jean followed at a distance. "I can tell you're not sleeping," Ferix said. "I see now why Beez is so obsessed."

The chained man's foxlike face grimaced at the satyr.

She recognized him. "Teague Fuchs?" Jean asked.

Teague's hands covered himself.

Ferix squinted back at her and stretched his lips into a wry grin. She suddenly felt she'd given the assassin a weapon.

Teague's mind worked to place her. It had been years since they had parted. Nature certainly had been kinder to him. "Jean? Jean Clienne?"

Ferix nodded in annoyance. "Mother of Scarlett. I could get her out of this. All you have to do is give them to me."

Teague cast Jean an apologetic wince and said, "I've no clue to what you're referring. I do, however, find it amusing you're allowed to walk freely amongst the Dregs and their ilk, so I do."

"You're ignorant, mercenary. If you don't tell me where you have hidden them, we're all doomed."

Lying back on his pillows, Teague stared at the wall. "You couldn't help her any more than you could help me, if you had them. Try again, fairy trickster."

"Teague, what's this about?" Jean asked.

"He wishes us all to die," Ferix answered. "To protect some meager plan he'll hatch from this post?" Ferix rattled Teague's chain.

Teague considered her again. "Have you seen Scarlett?"

"They're fine!" the satyr growled. "My rings! Now."

Jean nodded to Teague. "They were safe the last I saw. He gave them a way to the continent."

The assassin shot her a glare that put frost on her bones.

When he looked down at Teague, those piercing blue eyes that she'd fawned over as a girl were amused. "I swallowed them," Teague said.

Ferix drew a deep breath. "I've used that trick before. Let that whet your appetite when next they appear."

The door burst open. "What am I to make of this, Ferix?" Vesper asked.

Jean stepped back, trying to clutch her lead in her bound hands.

"Are you forcing my new vessel to watch your deeds? I was not aware she required punishment."

The satyr dismissed her with a wave, which made Jean's hair stand on end as the Dreg swept past.

"My brother's urn just disintegrated. Some blamed a *tek'aran*. In his fury, the Exalted desiccated their vessels and ended the assembly. What do you know?"

Ferix betrayed Jean with a glance.

"Roscar," Vesper called.

An ogre brute ducked into the room. He had more scars than a stray had fleas and cold, dead eyes. A black mask that ended in a point at his chin hid his face. Jerking Jean's leash, he hauled her mercilessly behind his rotten-onion stench. She wanted to resist but feared what punishment he would dole.

"Don't eat the meat!" Teague yelled after her.

Jean trained her ears to the conversation as they moved into the corridor but only managed to hear Vesper say, "Suffice it to say, Teague is available for trade. What do you know?"

The ogre pressed Jean into a lavish chamber full of familiar captives, surrounding her in her failure. The magi from the Ale and Pumpkin didn't see her, unable to break their terror for the ogre's golden eyes.

Jean screamed and stepped away from him.

He moved to stand over her.

Her heart thundered. She closed her eyes and prayed Darren had gotten out. He'd tell Barrey and Dale. They'd come for her. A voice in her head told her they couldn't save her even if they did.

No matter what, Scarlett was safe. Ameera would protect her baby.

THANK YOU FOR READING!

If you have enjoyed *Opprobrium*, please write a review and share with others.

About the Author

Wade Lewellyn-Hughes is an author, screenwriter, and general creative based in Montana. Aiming to bring a vivid world and robust characters to life, he values diversity and differences in this world and the one he's writing.

Sign up for updates on upcoming books and find out more here: http://wadelewellyn.com

Acknowledgments

This book would not be what it is without the support of those around me. With a hefty dose of patience, my beta readers helped me whittle it into the tale it wanted to be. Bryce braved being honest. Domonique mentored me. Nicole cleaned the bones of it. Mindy's enthusiasm added sparkle. Roxanne leered at it. Shawn likely put it in a spreadsheet. I don't know why, either. Jamie made Brandi read it. Finally, Meghan liked it.

And now, there's a book, and more importantly a beginning.

Yet it took far more than those few. The impossible list of deserving names would bore us all to tears. In short, from my parents down to the delivery drivers who didn't judge my plentiful orders, you have my thanks.

Other Books in the Lamentation's End Series:

www.ingramcontent.com/pod-product-compliance
Lightning Source LLC
Chambersburg PA
CBHW030838030726
47495CB00005B/1283